Berkley books by Tom Wicker

ON PRESS
UNTO THIS HOUR

UNTO THIS HOUR

TOM WICKER

BERKLEY BOOKS, NEW YORK

UNTO THIS HOUR

A Berkley Book/published by arrangement with
The Viking Press

PRINTING HISTORY
Viking Press edition/February 1984
Berkley edition/February 1985

ISBN: 0-425-07583-4

A BERKLEY BOOK ® TM 757,375
Berkley Books are published by The Berkley Publishing Group,
200 Madison Avenue, New York, New York 10016.
The name "BERKLEY" and the stylized "B" with design
are trademarks belonging to Berkley Publishing Corporation.
PRINTED IN THE UNITED STATES OF AMERICA

For Cameron and Bruce,
Grey and Sarah,
Christopher,
Lisa and Kayce.

                    . . . I see
The imminent death of twenty thousand men
That from a fantasy and trick of fame
Go to their graves like beds, fight for a plot
Whereon the numbers cannot try the cause,
Which is not tomb enough and continent
To hide the slain. . . .

Hamlet, IV, iv

Author's Note

>∞∞∞∞∞∞∞∞∞∞∞∞<

The repulse of the Confederate Army at Malvern Hill on July 1, 1862, ended what became known as the Seven Days' Battles. General R. E. Lee, exercising his first major command, had hoped to destroy the Federal Army of the Potomac; he failed, but the Seven Days put an effective end to Major General George B. McClellan's efforts to capture Richmond in a campaign up "the Peninsula" between the James and the York rivers.

A second Federal force, the Army of Virginia under Major General John Pope, had been organized that summer in northern and central Virginia. On July 13, in order to counter Pope, Lee sent an independent force under Lieutenant General Thomas J. Jackson to Gordonsville.

Jackson collided with elements of Pope's command near Culpeper on August 9, in a battle called Slaughter's Mountain or Cedar Mountain. The Confederates won the day but so narrowly that Jackson returned to Gordonsville on August 11. Pope followed across the Rappahannock to the Rapidan River.

Meanwhile, over McClellan's vigorous protests, the Army of the Potomac had been recalled from the Peninsula. When some of its elements began moving out, Lee assumed they would join Pope's force and move on Richmond from the north. Lee determined to guard the Confederate capital with only a small force, unite the rest of his army—under Lieutenant General James Longstreet—with Jackson's command, and attack Pope before he could be joined by McClellan.

Lee's reunited army moved across the Rapidan on August 20. Pope retreated behind the Rappahannock, and five days of inconclusive fighting and maneuvering failed to drive his army from that line. But on August 22, in a raid on Catlett's Station, General J. E. B. Stuart's Confederate cavalry had captured documents disclosing that before the end of August Pope would be reinforced by Peninsula veterans, from his base strength of about 70,000 to over 100,000 men.

Lee then commanded about 55,000 troops in the two wings—Jackson's and Longstreet's—of what he had dubbed the Army of Northern Virginia. On August 25, he took a calculated gamble, in a final effort to smash Pope before the two Federal armies could be joined in one overwhelming force. He divided his command, sending Jackson on a secret march around Pope's right flank while Longstreet demonstrated along the Rappahannock.

This novel is about the campaign that followed. It was waged between armies* that maneuvered and fought in an inadequately mapped countryside through which ran no paved roads, in a time when the railroad and the telegraph were just coming into military use, when electric light was unimagined and horses were about as valuable as humans. Rifled barrels had made weapons more lethal than ever but battle tactics took no account of that and medicine remained primitive.

Men and women, I assume, and the truths of human nature were much the same as always.

—*Tom Wicker*
January 4, 1983

---

* These armies were organized in regiments known by numbers and states—the Thirteenth Georgia, the Sixth Wisconsin. Two or more regiments made up a brigade, usually known by the name of its general, and two or more brigades formed a division, also known by its commander's name. Two or more divisions formed a corps.

CONTENTS

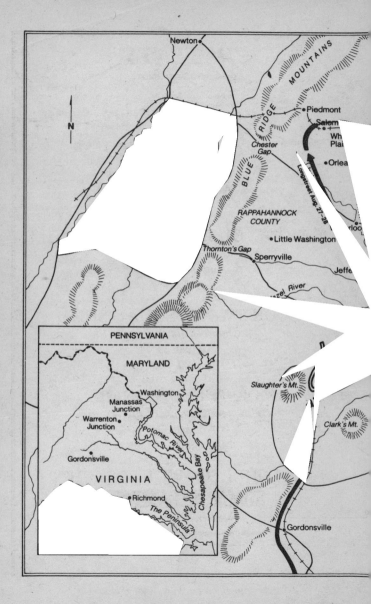

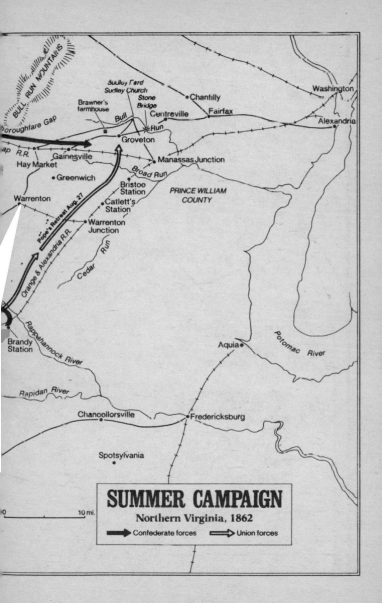

BULL RUN MOUNTAINS

Thoroughfare Gap

Sudley Ford
Sudley Church
Stone
Bridge

Brawner's
farmhouse

Bull

Run

• Chantilly

Washington

Centreville

Fairfax

Alexandria

Groveton

ap R.R.

Gainesville

• Manassas Junction

Hay Market

• Greenwich

Broad Run

Bristoe
Station

PRINCE WILLIAM
COUNTY

Catlett's
Station

Warrenton

Pope's Retreat Aug. 27

Warrenton
Junction

Orange & Alexandria R.R.

Cedar Run

Rappahannock River

Aquia•

Potomac River

Brandy
Station

Rapidan River

Chancellorsville

•Fredericksburg

Spotsylvania

0   10 mi.

SUMMER CAMPAIGN
Northern Virginia, 1862

➡ Confederate forces   ⇨ Union forces

Brawner's Farm

~~~~~~~~~~~~~~~~~~~~~~~~~~~~~~~~~~~~~~

Meeting a wounded soldier hobbling along, I asked
him if he knew where I would find [General Jackson];
leaning on his gun and looking up at me with a twinkle
in his eye he said . . . "Do you hear that 'ar firing?
Well, that's just where you will always find old Jack."

—W. W. Blackford
War Years with Jeb Stuart
Charles Scribner's Sons, 1945

August 28, 1862

THE ROAD WAS blue with them. From far up the slope, where the horseman rode, their close-packed column seemed to move as sinuously as a snake. The gray mist raised by their pounding boots hung above them like a shroud. Dust powdered the bell-crowned black hats they wore and streaked their sweating faces. Dust dulled the gleam of the musket barrels slanting across their shoulders and filtered the rays of the sun sinking red as blood behind them.

That summer, old men told one another they could not remember a time so hot. But the rains had been heavy, and the fields and pastures of Virginia were yellow with goldenrod; Queen Anne's lace lay like froth along the roadsides and fence rows. So the horseman, peering down the slope at the dusty marchers, might have seemed to them afloat on a heaving sea of yellow and white, atop the green depths of broomsedge that rose to his horse's belly. But none of the marching men noticed him.

From one of the ranks on the road, as the Sixth Wisconsin marched over a knoll and toward the shade of woods ahead, Private Hugh Williams did glance at the thin fringe of flankers pushing through the broomsedge on the slope. Spose to be Rebs about.

But Private Williams—lost in the monotony of the march, his free arm and his legs in their long western stride swinging as rhythmically as scythes in his father's wheatfields—had his doubts. He was beginning to think, in fact, that Gibbon's Brigade might never see bloodshed and death, that perhaps God in His infinite wisdom had willed that worthier men should punish the wielders of the lash.

Neither Hugh Williams nor any of those marching with him gave a second glance to Brawner's farmhouse, standing starkly above the open pasture rising gradually to their left. They had

3

marched past many such houses, gaunt and unpainted in the relentless Virginia sun. Recently they had done little but march, march and countermarch and march some more, up and down the rutted southern roads, through the bleak crossroads hamlets, past worked-out fields and the hostile faces of women in drooping bonnets and men who looked as if they'd been left out in the sun to dry like cornshucks. Niggers with their mouths hanging open.

They could have Virginia, Private Williams thought, and welcome to it. God Himself seemed to have turned His back on the land of the slavers.

Major Reverdy Dowd, who was temporarily second in command of the Sixth Wisconsin, had no use for Virginia, either; too damned hot and dusty, and the land was rocky and poor by Wisconsin standards. Swinging easily with the level stride of Rosie, his sturdy old mare, Major Dowd turned to look back along the ranks of the Sixth, and caught a glimpse of the horseman on the hillside above. Skulking Reb farmers everywhere, picking up anything the army dropped, probably doing a little spying on the side.

But Dowd was more concerned by the aimless marching, wearing down a brigade that deserved a chance to pull trigger; so he had eyes only for the impressive blue line moving over the knoll behind him. Beyond it, the rest of Gibbon's Brigade, Doubleday's behind it, and Patrick's—bringing up the rear of King's Division—stretched westward for miles along the narrow road.

When these boys finally see some action, Dowd thought, hell won't have it, fine as they're trained, and tired of all this hoofing.

The horseman trotted parallel to their line of march, across the face of the gentle slope rising to their left. Abruptly, he pulled his horse about and trotted the other way, to the west, never taking his eyes from the troops going by four abreast, beneath their gray shroud, in the thick heat of the dying day. Hunched oddly on a small sorrel, as if perhaps his stirrups were too short, he was gray himself, ghostly in the dust; sometimes he held half a lemon to a mouth that seemed little more than a slit in his long brown beard.

Just up the slope above, where Brawner's roof stood stolid as a tombstone against the hot blue sky, a dozen or so men sat their horses or stood about in an old orchard. Flies from the horses' dung and from the apples rotting on the ground swarmed about them. Some stood in their stirrups, gazing at the blue mass moving on the pike. Most were watching the dark figure of the horseman as he trotted across the face of the slope below. When he wheeled about, they could see the forage cap pulled low, like the visor of a battle helmet, and the beard rust-brown on his chest.

Fargo Hart, a bronzed young man wearing the bars of a captain on a jacket that betrayed hard usage, sat relaxed on a black horse, his right leg crooked around the pommel of his saddle. As he gazed with brown, pensive eyes at the horseman and the troops on the road, he suddenly—as if remembering—murmured:

"The spirit that goeth downward . . ."

In the stillness of the afternoon, the words just reached an older man, looking more nearly ready for sleep than for action, who slouched nearby on a horse as bony as he.

"What's that, Cap'n?"

Unsettled, Hart brushed away flies, weighing words to explain himself—as much *to* himself as to the other man.

"He could lie still, Colonel. But he won't."

That was not quite what he had been groping for. Of course the horseman would strike; but military tactics had little to do with Hart's sudden sense of inevitability. *The spirit of the beast*, he thought.

Colonel David Channing shook his head, perhaps in reproof, his long, gray-streaked beard flowing across his ill-fitting jacket. He, too, knew the horseman would strike —even though the blue troops were going past unaware, even though the hillside position was hidden, secure, and even though smoke as black as mourning signaled above Manassas Junction the destruction already visited on the invaders. But Channing was not a man to waste time pondering the nature of things. He said only what experience had taught him:

"Ol Jack's got'is reasons, son."

Behind Brawner's deserted house and barn and apple orchard, a thick belt of pine and scrub oak climbed gradually toward a higher ridge that local residents rather grandly called Sudley Mountain. In these woods, well screened by them from the turnpike more than half a mile away, thousands of soldiers lay like pine straw on the indifferent earth. Mostly lean, ill-kempt men, heavily bearded, tanned to the color of smoked bacon, they lay at ease in the drowsy, cricket-loud heat of the summer day. Many were barefoot, but for once all were well-fed.

Most of that day, from behind Brawner's orchard more than two miles northeast to Bull Run, they had lain about between the trees and the long rows of stacked muskets, laughing, talking, sleeping, playing cards, gibing one another in the heavy-handed, sometimes cruel way of all soldiers since the first armies. From the orchard where many of their field officers had gathered in the steady sunshine beating down from the vitreous sky, the woods behind sounded like a great, humming beehive.

The horseman had pulled to a halt, raised himself in his stirrups, and stared back along the blue snake writhing into the distance. Then he wheeled his mount away from the road, touched his spurs to its flanks and the lemon to his mouth. He pounded up the slope, broomsedge and goldenrod parting before the sorrel's passage, spraying up again behind him. A natural pacer, Fargo Hart noticed.

A young man with a beardless face flushed with excitement pulled a skittish gray to a halt beside him.

"Here he comes!" Captain Thad Selby clapped Hart heavily on the back. "Be some action now!"

Seeming not to move, Hart caused his horse to edge away. The horseman, his elbows flapping like dark wings, crested the hill and rode toward the orchard. A corpulent young major with a black scab running from his forehead down his nose to his chin declaimed suddenly to no one:

"The fire of God . . ." His rumbling voice seemed to catch the rhythm of the oncoming hoofbeats. ". . . is fallen from heaven!"

The officers were no longer watching the blue snake on the road. All were mounted by then, their horses edging toward each other, toward the spot where, in a moment, the sorrel was drawn to a jolting stop in its own spray of dust. The horseman raised his hand perfunctorily to his pulled-down forage cap, then sat slumped in his saddle, the rust-brown beard covering his cheeks and chin and flowing to his chest. From beneath the cap's battered visor, pale blue eyes stared out like muzzle flashes.

"Gentlemen . . ."

Ol Jack spoke so softly that only their attention riveted on him enabled them to hear. Fargo Hart sensed the horseman barely able to restrain a warrior's energy. And in spite of himself, Hart too felt a shiver on his spine, the drum of blood in his temples.

"Gentlemen . . . bring out your men."

All but a few of the listening officers instantly spun their horses and galloped toward the woods behind Brawner's house. The soldiers lying nearest the treeline, who had been watching the officers milling about the orchard all day, saw them coming and passed the word. In the way of armies, it moved as if on a hot wind, alerting each of the troops at ease under the pines, amid the scrub oak and the long skeletal rows of stacked muskets. From the woods, where men in their thousands had waited through the day, a hoarse roar rose toward the redly sinking sun.

BOOK ONE

~~~~~~~~~~

Ol Jack
Can't Lie Still

~~~~~~~~~~~~~~~~~~~~~~~~~

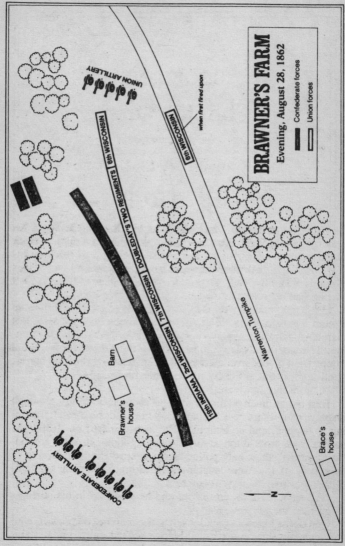

BRAWNER'S FARM

Evening, August 28, 1862

Confederate forces
Union forces

UNION ARTILLERY

6th WISCONSIN

when first fired upon

DOUBLEDAY'S TWO REGIMENTS

7th WISCONSIN

2nd WISCONSIN

19th INDIANA

Barn

Brawner's house

Warrenton Turnpike

CONFEDERATE ARTILLERY

Brace's house

N

Chapter One

August 26, 1862

BY THE SILVER turnip watch that was his only memento of his father, Captain Fargo Hart saw that it was just past eight o'clock in the morning. He grunted in surprise, feeling dust thick on his dry lips. Only eight! and the sun in his eyes already a vicious blaze in a sky as harsh as granite. It seemed incredible to Hart that he had been on the road no more than two hours.

His horse, picking its way through stragglers, had come up behind a reasonably solid group of marching men—more or less marching, anyway, and making good time in the breezeless morning. The rear files were compact but the muskets of the butternut troops were braced over their shoulders carelessly, the long barrels at all angles, like a rickety picket fence on its side.

"Comin through there!"

Hart put as much command into his shout as he could, although displays of military rank embarrassed him. But he expected nothing to happen, and nothing did. The men marched on, filling the narrow road from ditch to ditch, swaying along in their ground-eating stride, their hats pulled down against the sun shining in their eyes. A few were laughing and talking; in the rear file, two of the four marchers were barefoot.

"All right!" Hart's voice rose and he stood up in his stirrups. "You men there! Move aside!"

One of the barefoot men looked at the marcher on his left, who was conspicuous in a red-and-black-checked shirt; sweat stains had spread from its armholes in great half-moons until they almost

9

met between his shoulder blades. Above the steady stumping of hundreds of feet up ahead, the clink and rattle of swinging canteens and bayonets, the murmur of talk and laughter, Hart heard the barefoot man's twanging voice:

"You say sump'm, Lott?"

The marcher in the checked shirt half-turned and spat behind the barefoot man, a long brown stain lancing through the rising dust to the surface of the road.

"Naw." Lott shook his head and his musket barrel swayed from side to side. He looked up at a tall private marching on his other side. "Hey, Sowbelly. Ol Gilly been marchin so long he's hearin ghosties."

"Dawg if I aint." The barefoot man named Gilly took off his hat and fanned himself with it. His shock of tow hair hung wetly about his ears and Hart saw that he was little more than a boy. "I could of swore somebody uz tellin me to move over."

"Why'd I wanchuh to move over? I *like* smellin yuh."

The men around them broke into laughter but the barefoot boy was game. His voice twanged louder:

"Yeh . . . so's you can't smell y'ownself!"

This brought more laughter, from check-shirted Lott, too. But Fargo Hart, whose neatly trimmed mustache betrayed a concern for standards, had been through such rituals too often. He was in a hurry, he had been riding most of the night, and enough was enough.

"Goddammit, open up there! Sonsabitches lemme through or I'll make you wish you had! Move it over now!"

Lott suddenly leaped into the ditch to his left, pushing and pulling the tall man and another private with him. Gilly leaped the other way.

"Sakes alive!" Lott's shout carried up the ranks of marching men. "Must be Gin'al Lee! Move over, boys . . . let the gin'al thew!"

As if by magic the marching men squeezed toward either side of the road, leaving a narrow path up its center. Hart clucked to Mercury; the horse, his black coat grayed with dust, stepped a little faster into the opening.

"Why, that ain't Gin'al Lee!" Tow-headed Gilly stared up at Hart in slack-mouthed amazement.

"It's Joe Johnston!"

"Look at that Frenchy mushtash. Must be ol Bory!"

"Come out fum unner-at hat! We know yuh, Jeff Davis!"

Grinning and embarrassed, despite his ill-humor, Hart made his way through the parting ranks, the shouts and catcalls of the troops following him all the way, until he had cleared the marching company and could trot on ahead, toward the Bull Run Mountains rising greenly to the east. At the rate he was going, he feared he would never catch up to Ol Jack.

Sometime after midnight, he had set out from General Stuart's camp on the Rappahannock with instructions to deliver to General Jackson some information a scouting party had picked up describing alternative routes over the Bull Run Mountains, if Thoroughfare Gap should be blocked. Stuart had told him he would find Jackson bivouacked about fifteen miles to the north, at Salem. Until he heard that, Hart had not even known that Jackson's troops had been pulled out of Lee's line south of the Rappahannock.

He had had no idea where Jackson could be going except that after Ol Jack's lightning movements in the Valley that spring, Hart—like everyone else—believed that anything was possible. But Fargo Hart was a native Virginian and despite several years as a student in Europe, he knew his home state. As he and Mercury made their way through a dark night, he conjectured that if Jackson was at Salem but needed instructions on routes over the Bull Run Mountains, he was bound to be marching around Pope, into the rear of the great Federal army stretched from Waterloo Bridge to Catlett's Station—maybe farther. Though he held war and soldiering in cool regard, Hart could not help being thrilled at the notion of such an exploit.

He was willing to bet, too, that Jackson's objective was the Orange & Alexandria Railroad, slanting down through Virginia from the Potomac. Had to be. Cut the O & A and you might as well cut Pope's jugular, for along that lifeline passed the food and forage and ammunition and reinforcements without which his army could not long survive in hostile territory.

But in the darkness, over unfamiliar roads and with no guide, Hart had not reached Salem until 5 a.m. There he had learned that the last of Ol Jack's troops—getting the early start the general always demanded—had marched out of the village an hour earlier, followed by his ammunition train and a small herd of gaunt beef cattle, the only commissary the quartermasters had been permitted to bring along.

Pausing at a friendly doorstep for cornbread and ham—the salt lingering taste of which, in the heat and the dust, he now regretted—Hart pushed on after the marching army, marveling at how unchallenged Jackson's route seemed to be, though miles in the Federal rear. But it was not long before he learned a hard truth. For a horse and rider to pass a column of marching men coming toward them might be easy enough, since the marchers could hardly pretend they did not see anyone approaching; but to get past an overtaken column on a narrow road was something else entirely.

To men on foot, a man on horseback was not a popular sight anyway, and one coming up behind them was a proper object for frustration, then derision. So all morning, Hart had shouted himself hoarse—his tonsils felt as if they were coated with dust, like the rest of him—trying to move from Ol Jack's rear to the head of the column, through troops who delighted in delaying him as long as possible. He had not even passed one division—Taliaferro's, once led by Jackson himself—and there were two more on the road ahead.

Mercury trotted around a sharp curve, and Hart cursed aloud at the sight of another company blocking his way. Save for the absence of the man in the checked shirt, it could have been the company he had just got through—men barefoot, ill-clad in ragged butternut, blankets rolled and slung across one shoulder, with wide-brimmed, sweat-stained hats, moving rapidly along at route step with their musket barrels pointing over their shoulders in all directions. A dust cloud hung over the marchers as if vapor from their sweating bodies were rising toward the sun.

Fargo Hart had been in the army little more than a year, and at that only because a sense of obligation more powerful than the rationality which normally guided his affairs would not let him remain sensibly in Europe while his state was invaded and his contemporaries were dying. But he knew enough of military tactics to recognize that Taliaferro's men—veterans of Ol Jack's Valley campaign—did not march like most others he had seen in the Confederate ranks.

The men received frequent exhortations from their yelling officers, but they made little effort to keep closed up on the companies or the regiments just ahead. Instead, they moved along rapidly, but at paces and intervals that seemed to suit them individually—as if each man, having been set a destination, was allowed to get there as quickly and efficiently as he could. Hart had seen stragglers fall out to nurse sore feet or rest in the shade, promising their sergeants or officers to catch up when they could; but he had seen none of the alternating halts and quicksteps that locked other troops into a sort of faceless unity in which the weak were expected to equal the strong. Yet, Hart calculated, these Valley veterans were moving along at a pace close to three miles an hour. No general could ask more of his men than that—except that Ol Jack could and did when the mood was on him.

Damn it, Hart thought; he would not beg and threaten another company into clearing the way for him. On the left, the land was mostly cleared of trees, though overgrown with underbrush; and at a touch of the reins, Mercury leaped gracefully over a shallow ditch and into the field beyond, then trotted ahead. For a moment, Hart could exult at least in his horse's strength and beauty.

"Hey, boys!" someone shouted on the road behind him. "Le's jine the cav'ry!"

"Can't jine'em, man . . . can't even ketch'em!"

The old joke could turn some cavalrymen apoplectic, but Hart admired the jocularity with which the marching men bore their hardships—even at his expense. Trotting on past the jeering company, he sat straighter in his saddle, squaring his shoulders, not just to impress his onlookers but to stretch muscles growing taut from his long ride.

He had no particular pride of service; in fact, Hart had no military background at all—"and very little future," he had once unwisely quipped at Stuart's mess table.

That had caused Major Burkeley Allen to eye him across the table with suspicion. Under the large tent fly that sheltered Stuart's sizable mess—frequently enhanced by guests of all varieties—gaiety was the general rule and the worst form was to speak of death, however grim its presence just over the nearest hill.

"Surely now, you don't mean that?" A minister in private life, but in the field a hard-fighting, self-styled "soldier of the Lord," the Reverend Major—huge and bearded—always spoke in a booming pulpit voice.

"Oh, not *that*." Hart hastened to put himself in better grace. "Just mean, this war's over, I'll be out of this army fast as I can go."

"Be over this summer." Coke Mowbray, a lieutenant of engineers hardly two years out of West Point, was the staff optimist. "Pope'll be changin'is base as quick's McClellan did. Wait 'n see."

The Reverend Major was not to be diverted from the pursuit of heresy. "Fightin for God and country. What better life you want than that, Cap'n?"

Hart enjoyed upsetting Major Allen's solemnity. He touched his half-empty tin cup of milk. "Glass of claret evry now'n then. Seen little enough of *that* in this army."

The major's mouth, almost hidden by lush black whiskers, pursed in disapproval and Hart braced himself for a temperance lecture.

"What's that?" A shout down the table from Colonel Snowden, at Stuart's left, stopped conversation completely. "Say you don't like the army, Hart?"

That had been on a brilliant day at Hanover Court House, a week or so after the fighting around Richmond; the long table under the tent fly was strewn with the remains of roast chicken and summer vegetables pressed on Stuart's mess by a grateful neighborhood. At the head of the table, the general and his senior aides had been regaling each other with stories of a Yank advance from Fredericksburg the day before, which they claimed had run for it at the first sight of Stuart's cavalry moving out to meet them.

Hart calmly took a bite of cornbread, but in the sudden silence he carefully considered how best to answer Colonel Snowden. Stuart, who liked to think of his staff as a sort of happy family, a "band of brothers," was surely listening. A friendly, casual man who loved song and show and who was only three years older than Fargo Hart, the general would tolerate almost anything save cowardice or a sullen face and a gloomy manner. Hart had no wish to incur his suspicion; whatever he thought of the war, he preferred his present role in it to any other.

"Why, Colonel, nothin's wrong with the army. Just on the whole, I'd as soon be in Paris."

As he expected, this brought a shout of laughter from the head of the table, hence from the rest of the officers around Hart, even a snort from the Reverend Major Allen.

"Oh, them mam-zells!" Colonel Snowden banged his cup on the table and raised it in toast to Hart, who—on little evidence other than his years in Europe—was considered by the staff to be a ladykiller. Nevertheless, the captain had resolved that day to be in the future more circumspect in expressing his attitudes toward the war that Jeb Stuart and most of his aides waged with such enthusiasm.

Now, Hart was approaching a rail fence at the end of the field and felt Mercury gathering himself for the jump. The big black soared over, and Hart moved easily with him. Around Stuart's mess, it was commonly said in Fargo Hart's favor that no one could match him on a horse, or in his knowledge of horses. And his three mounts—his body servant Robaire rode one and led another—were the envy of the headquarters group.

Hart's impeccable horsemanship—in addition to the silver watch, his mother insisted—was the legacy of his father, who had died of a miasmatic fever before Fargo was six years old. Maxwell Hart's legacy to the boy's mother had been somewhat more substantial: a house and a parcel of decent land in the Northern Neck, which she had promptly sold, investing part of the proceeds for a meagerly financed but eminently proper life where she belonged, in the best circles of her native Richmond. She then banked the rest for what had been her young husband's fondest wish—a European education for his son.

Fargo Hart was not sure if the sense of obligation that had brought him home to the Confederate uniform was primarily to the dead father or to the living mother or to the society that had shaped them both, and in which he had assumed until the war that he would always have his assured place. But the obligation itself was not to be questioned, even though he now feared there would not "always" be such a society.

Hart did not think much about who would *win* the war, considered as a contest. He tended with the confidence of youth to assume that his own side would at least not lose, since it seemed to him improbable that Yankee clodhoppers could defeat men like Stuart and Ol Jack and the hard-fighting butternut soldiers who had been mocking him on the road.

Nor did he think of himself as fighting the Yankees to save his "way of life," since he did not regard the Yanks as the real threat to it. Rather, he believed the only way to have preserved something like the life his forebears had known would have been to avoid the war altogether. Fargo Hart had been an indifferent history student, but he had learned that war was change, a great fire breathing beast of change brutally reshaping or destroying all in its path. Win or lose, the world of his father could not survive war.

That world had given Hart such certainty of his own worth and place that he could scarcely conceive of another in which he would not be equally at advantage. But in a deeper sense than the merely personal, Hart despised change itself, other than the immemorial cycles of nature—the seasons coming round, the generations giving way, the surging of tides, the wax and wane of the moon. Except for these reassuring evidences of constant renewal, change seemed to Fargo Hart forced and unnatural, the uprooting of things, and war its most powerful proponent.

Hart wanted life to be as he once had thought he had a right to assume it was—an enormous pigeonhole desk, like that of the portly Richmond banker who hoarded Elizabeth Sligoe Hart's meager wealth. He wanted everyone to be able to find, and be sure of, a fixed and accepted place. In any system lacking such constancy, he believed, reason could barely exist and never flourish; and without reason at its core, no society could confer the identity Hart valued, nor preserve it in the civility he cherished.

But he knew that with every marching column, every whining ball, every exploding shell, war—change—destroyed part of the pigeonhole desk. Thus, to Fargo Hart, no matter how the *contest* came out, the essential war was lost the moment it began. He did not, of course, consider that reason enough to stay out of it. He was too much a part of his world even to have thought of doing so. In coming home from Europe to take up arms, he had done what his father would have done—what he never doubted it was his place to do.

Mercury's quick passage over field and fence had given him a lift that proved short-lived. The road east from Salem ran through cultivated country; at least it had been cultivated before the war. He soon found that at the border of every field there was a fence to be crossed, or a ditch lined with thick growth to be jumped. An occasional branch or briar patch or thicket added to the difficulty. Hart had too much concern for Mercury to leap him so often, particularly on a day of such heat; so he had to pull down too many fence rails and put them back, else return to the road too often, to make much better progress than he could among the troops.

Eventually, he stuck to the road, shouting and shouldering his way through the catcalling companies, past Taliaferro's Division into Hill's, he and Mercury dragging with heat and thirst and caked with road dust, Hart occasionally blaspheming the sun that rose like the glowing end of a gigantic cigar toward the noon sky. They trotted over the track of the Manassas Gap Railroad, which crossed the single street of the dusty village of White Plains, and Mercury gamely breasted the steep slope of the road just beyond. The Bull Run range, green against the eastern horizon, could be plainly seen from the crest they soon reached.

The downward slope of the road on the other side was far less steep than the ascent, so Hart allowed himself a treat—the last can of peaches he had plundered from Catlett's Station during Stuart's raid on Pope's supply depot there, four nights earlier. That had been behind Pope's lines, too; the Federal commander, Hart thought with boyish satisfaction, would soon be getting tired of having his coattails twitched.

As he opened the can with his jackknife while the reins lay slack on Mercury's neck, Hart reflected glumly that he would give a whole case of canned peaches for a little of the rain—just enough to settle the dust—that had soaked them that night at Catlett's. Then, the torrent had been a disaster, foiling Stuart's prime objective of firing the O & A bridge over Cedar Run. But a little rain now might redeem a day that had started badly and was going worse.

This cooling thought unfortunately invited others less attractive. Sometimes Fargo Hart sensed dark places in himself, where he feared to look; and as the war progressed—*in* him as well as around him—a deepening shadow lay on his understanding of things. His part in the raid on Catlett's Station, he supposed, was unexceptional, an infinitesimal episode of war; but that was why it troubled him.

The dust settled back on his lips as quickly as a slice of peach erased it; his bruised bicep began to ache, as if memory throbbed in his flesh; and he muttered into the oblivious backs of the company marching ahead:

"Damn fool engineer . . . I told'im to stop . . . I *told'* im . . ."

When Stuart had given the order to attack, four days earlier, the comfortable evening clatter of Pope's supply depot had been abruptly obliterated by the piercing screams of two thousand Confederate cavalrymen and the drumbeat rumble of their horses lunging forward.

The night was hot and dark, the more so because of the thick clouds that presaged the rainstorm to come; but the tent city Pope's men had erected at Catlett's had been lit up like a circus, by lamps and by cooking fires neatly ranked down the company streets. The unsuspecting quartermasters, functionaries, blacksmiths, and other rear-echelon specialists were just sitting down to supper, the splendid aromas of which had piqued the spirits of the hungry Confederates quietly forming in the encircling darkness.

"Sound the charge, Freed."

Stuart's voice was quiet but edged with excitement; and Chief

Bugler Freed's first note set off the shrill Rebel yell from thousands of throats. Chaos erupted immediately on all sides of Fargo Hart as he went clattering into the suddenly teeming tent streets with Rosser's Fifth Virginia Cavalry.

Perfect, Hart thought; total surprise. He caught a glimpse of an officer running with a napkin around his neck, a cook in his apron falling with arms flailing, a tent collapsing on an apparently frozen group at mess.

Then a vicious rattle of small-arms fire began to punctuate the blood-curdling southern yells. Startled Yanks, kicking over chairs and tables, firing back where they could, mostly running for cover, added shouts of anger and confusion to the cacophony. As surprised as they had been, they could offer no more real resistance than a hill of ants kicked over by a careless boot.

"Vengeance! Vengeance saith the Lord!"

At Hart's right flank, the Reverend Major Allen's pulpit boom rose above the melee, and the crash of his revolver struck an echoing blow against Hart's eardrum. Rosser's objective was the rail depot building, where the camp's supposed defenders, a detachment of Pennsylvania Bucktails—so captured pickets had disclosed—were bivouacked. To get there, Rosser's troopers, Hart and Allen near the lead, had to ride through the whole camp.

In the headlong dash from secret darkness into the riotous firelit terror under their hooves, in the grotesque explosion of noise and confusion and the fierce screams of his companions, wanton exhilaration seized Fargo Hart and bore him high. Unaccountably, against all reason, he felt the moment of battle, of brute conflict, death and survival, as if it were the rush of wine in his veins, or the rich carnality of entering a woman. As Mercury galloped toward the dark bulk of the depot beyond the flaring light of tents going up in flame, Hart heard himself screaming, too, his heart pounding, the double-barreled Le Mat revolver he had brought with him from France ready in his hand.

The Bucktails had been alerted, but in his first glimpse of them Hart saw that they, too, had been surprised at supper and had had time only to form a ragged line on the loading dock. As Rosser's horsemen charged them from the leaping fires of the tent city, a Bucktail officer bellowed an order from within the depot, and a blaze of musketry from the loading dock swept the oncoming Confederates with a whistling hail of Minié balls.

Directly in front of Fargo Hart a cavalryman rolled from his horse, and as a ball whined past Hart's cheek only Mercury's nimble feet saved them from crashing over the tumbling body. The Reverend Major's horse took a Minié in the eye and went down headlong, his legs still galloping, throwing the major out ahead. Hart had one glimpse of the burly minister, arms outflung, plowing face down along the ground as if he would burrow head-on into it; then Mercury was past and leaping. With the other leading riders, Hart and his horse sailed the three feet up onto the loading dock, catching the Bucktails in the frantic interval of reloading after their first volley.

The huge horses and the screaming riders leaping wild-eyed from the night, the crash of pistols in the Bucktails' faces, the monstrous drumming of iron hooves on the wooden dock, saber blades flashing in the garish light of burning tents—all these, following hard on the first shock of the raid, quickly shattered the Bucktails as a fighting unit. Hart saw a Yank in an undershirt, perhaps surprised while changing his clothes, his eyes wide and incredulous, his hands up and out as if to catch a baseball, reel back from the tremendous impact of Mercury's chest and fall under another horse's slashing hooves. Then the big black cleared the collapsing Bucktail line. Hart ducked low as they charged into the depot itself, where the Yanks had become a milling, disorganized mass, and rifles and pistols cracked and echoed under the low ceiling.

Hart's throat was raw from yelling. To his right, a Bucktail with a red drooping mustache leveled a musket at him; in the dim hellish light of the depot interior, its barrel seemed as long and as round and as deadly as a twelve-pound Napoleon. Hart put the muzzle of the Le Mat as near the red mustache as he could reach and discharged the .40-caliber upper barrel. In the ungodly uproar, he felt the weapon kick rather than hearing its report; the mustache split apart, a neat round hole appearing in its center, until a brilliant gush of blood from the nose above disguised it. The Napoleon disappeared.

Other horsemen were clattering and yelling all around, and some of the Bucktails were throwing down their arms and huddling together against the flailing hooves and flashes of fire.

"Surrender!" Hart sensed rather than heard himself shouting. "Down those guns!"

A massive Yank sergeant swung the butt of a rifle at him instead. Ducking instinctively but into the blow, Hart took it on his bicep. He seized the barrel—cold, he noted, with the precision of a sharpened brain that seemed to be recording every detail of the chaos about him—and wrenched the weapon away. Mercury pranced sideward toward the sergeant; and Hart, freeing his boot from the stirrup, put it in the man's face and kicked him into a huddle of Yanks on the floor.

"Praise the Lord . . . praise God Almighty!"

Miraculously, the Reverend Major Allen had appeared in the midst of the melee, his face and front smeared black as if with tar, except for a nose and forehead down to red meat and white bone. The preacher fired his revolver into the back of a Yank who had run a bayonet through the chest of one of Rosser's troopers. The Yank dropped shrieking to the floor that was becoming smeared with blood; the trooper fell on top of him, an amazed round grin of death fixed on his upturned bearded face. The shrieking stopped and the Reverend Major stared down at them. A Yank behind him swung a rifle to club the minister's massive bent head; but Hart smashed his pistol, both heavy barrels and the trigger guard, across the man's face. The rifle fell from his hands and he sank to his knees, covering his face with hands—Hart saw in the eerie light— curiously white and womanish.

"Bastards!" He felt himself yelling with his raw throat. "Surrender, you goddam bastards!"

From his lordly seat on Mercury's broad back, looking down on the heaped bodies and the strewn weapons and the scarlet slippery floor, with the clatter of hooves and the triumphant shouts of Rosser's troopers echoing under the low ceiling, it seemed to Hart that he could do anything, meet any challenge, whip any man. And he wanted to. He looked eagerly for any last foolhardy Yank resistance.

"The Lord's work!" The Reverend Major Allen boomed somewhere nearby. ". . . Thy will be done!"

Just then, as the echo of the last shot faded from the interior of the depot and the shouting began to die away, Hart heard a train. He instantly recognized the sounds—a hiss of steam, then a rapid huff-puff-puff as the wheels slipped a little on the rails, than a slower, steadier huffing and a clank of iron couplings.

Hart's brain, sorting out impulses and impressions with a speed that matched his sense of physical power, told him at once that a train, waiting at the depot when the attack broke on the unsuspecting camp, had got up steam and was pulling out. Just as quickly he realized that if the crew made it to Weaversville Station, next up the line toward Washington, they might raise Pope's whole army against Stuart's raiders, and prevent his return across the

Rappahannock to the distant shelter of Lee's lines.

Hart wheeled Mercury, and the quick-footed black picked his way across the littered depot floor—scattered not only with men and weapons but with the remains of the supper the Yanks had not quite had time to eat. Hart ducked through the wide door opening on to the trackside platform and saw cars rolling past, moving east, gathering speed. Two or three cars ahead, steam and smoke spurted from a locomotive, and sparks rose from its tall, balloon-shaped stack into skies already lit by the blazing tent city.

Hart touched his spurs to Mercury's sensitive flanks. As if his hooves were as winged as his namesake's heels, the horse leaped along the wooden platform, covered it in two thundering bounds, soared into the air, and landed ten feet beyond the steps, galloping hard after the locomotive. Hart knew the footing along the track would be dangerous for a horse, but he had little time to think of that as Mercury charged beside the moving cars, passing one quickly, the next a little more slowly as the train gained speed, then pulling beside the tender.

"Hold up there! Engineer! Stop that train!"

From the locomotive just ahead, a man's face and shoulders suddenly emerged, ten feet in front of Mercury's flattened ears. The face was only a blur until the locomotive passed into the light of some fiercely burning wagons, their canvas tops blazing like a row of giant torches by the track. In their lurid glow, Hart saw clearly the engineer's contorted face—heavy eyebrows under a billed cap, a bulbous nose, a straggle of chin whiskers and lips drawn back over gapped teeth. A shrill defiant blast of the locomotive whistle drowned for a moment the sound of Mercury's hooves and the huff of steam, the clacking wheels on the rails and the shooting, sporadic now, from the tent city behind them.

Then Hart saw the engineer's mouth forming words and hurling them back along the track:

"Got to hell, Reb!"

The form and face disappeared inside the locomotive. *Hell, is it?* Anger burst in Hart like a phosphorous shell. His spurs touched Mercury again. In seconds, the great black horse had drawn up beside the locomotive. Its side panel was garish with ornate script: *Vulcan.* Through the window Hart could see the engineer's dark form on the other side. He did not think to shout again; afterward, he realized he had not thought at all.

He shifted with his thumb the movable hammer of the Le Mat, sighted swiftly, and fired its buckshot load at point-blank range into the engineer's left side. He saw the man's body jerk upright. *Hell, is it? Hell for you!* But before he could shove the Le Mat into its holster and leap for the iron bars by which he could pull himself aboard *Vulcan* and shut off steam, Mercury suddenly shied and slowed.

As the tender and first car rolled past him, still gaining speed, Hart saw in the fading light of the burning wagons, now far behind, that they had charged within yards of the bridge over Cedar Run. He pulled the horse to a halt at the stone abutment, judging swiftly that the creek at that point was too wide even for Mercury to leap and that by the time they had forded it, the locomotive would be out of reach.

Hart stayed by the bridge, gently patting Mercury's quivering neck as the train passed. The exultant shouts and the flickering firelight seemed far behind. Soon, the last car went by in darkness, even its rear lamps extinguished. And as the dark shape of the train disappeared beyond the stream, the warrior's exhilaration flowed out of him like the rain that began to fall from the blackly swollen heavens, slowly at first and then in a torrent.

He sat there a long time, alone and shivering on Mercury's patient back, under the cold beating of the rain, thinking of pilotless *Vulcan* moving on ever faster into the night, into the unknown out there to the north and east, maybe speeding on unchecked, faster and faster, until it plunged hissing and steaming into the Potomac. Even after he could no longer see the train, the clicking of the wheels and the huff of the locomotive came back to him across the darkness and the trickling of the creek below.

The rain and the sounds accused him. He had killed a man whose face he had seen, who was not a dim and featureless shape in the smoke of war but an identifiable person brave enough to defy him. For the first time in Fargo Hart's experience, war's impersonality could not acquit the pulling of the trigger; and he wondered if the wild surge of battle at last had made him a part of the war and nothing more—at one with the beast that would destroy all he knew, against whose ravages nothing could stand.

After awhile, Hart dismounted and led Mercury back along the track toward the depot. And from miles away, across an even greater distance within himself, he thought he heard again the defiant, mocking whistle of *Vulcan*. Walking along in the rain, he could not be certain whether a live hand had pulled the cord or whether the sound was only remembered in his soul.

• • •

General W. F. Hoke Arnall of Hill's Light Division, sitting his bay horse Rambler on the rising ground beside the road through Thoroughfare Gap, was worried about his immortal soul; therefore, he was determined to avoid thinking about Amy, his wife, and to quell his un-Christian sentiments toward his corps commander, Major General T. J. Jackson. But General Arnall was losing on both counts.

The state of his soul had been no small matter to him at least since his days as an Old Army cavalry lieutenant in the southwest, where his life had been saved by what he firmly believed was the intervention of Providence. An arrow, which would otherwise have pierced his left side and probably his lung, lodged instead in the thick pages of a Bible just that day arrived by mule train from his mother back in Duplin County, North Carolina. On a routine patrol, Lieutenant Arnall had taken it from his saddlebag and was carrying it under one arm, not with the intent of reading it but with the premeditated idea of impressing his captain, a God-fearing soul whose black-haired daughter, Amy, the lieutenant aimed to marry.

The arrow in the Bible not only had made the wedding possible a year or two later. It had impressed Hoke Arnall even more than it did his captain. He had become a student of the Word and a devout believer, who let no dawn or sunset pass without falling to his knees in devotion to his Maker and—so he believed—greatest benefactor. Arnall's faith was simple and direct; he gave credit to Providence for all good things, and believed they would come only to those who accepted entirely the will of God, kept His commandments, and prayed for His blessing.

"Beats all, don't it?"

Sam Stowe sat his horse a pace or two away, fanning himself with the planter's straw hat he claimed encouraged his troops. If the Yanks couldn't hit him while he wore such conspicuous headgear, he insisted, the troops would believe Yanks couldn't hit anything. Which was mighty near the truth anyway.

"What beats all?" Arnall was glad to be reprieved from thoughts of his soul.

"Gettin through this gap to the east scot-free."

Arnall nodded and squinted at the dust cloud over the marching men. Twice lucky. He had traversed Thoroughfare Gap safely once before, coming down from the Valley with General Joe Johnston's army a year earlier to reinforce Beauregard behind Bull Run, for the first big battle of the war. Anyway, it had seemed big at the time to Hoke Arnall, an untested regimental commander.

Then, however, Arnall and his regiment had rollicked along on the wooden cars of the Manassas Gap Railroad—whose tracks, now rusting with disuse, lay just across the road, beyond the dusty marchers of the brigade Arnall had since been promoted to command. Hoke Arnall knew military history and he liked to say around companionable camp fires that he had been with Joe Johnston when he took the first major military force—if you could call 10,000 men a major force—in any country into battle by rail.

With his planter's hat Colonel Stowe indicated the steep gorge, not a hundred yards across, through which the road, the tracks, and a tumbling stream passed.

"Enough ammunition, my boys'd hold this place a week by themselves."

The two officers were gray as the road, Stowe's long blond beard looking not unlike a floor mop. He was one of Arnall's regimental commanders and the nearest to a friend among them, since Arnall prided himself not on being liked but on being respected. The general fanned himself with his own felt hat, thankful for the relative coolness of the Gap, which was wooded for most of its passage through the low chain of the Bull Run Mountains.

"Pope must be blind, Sam. Else Jackson's got'is usual luck."

"I had luck like that, I'd be commandin this division."

Stowe deferred to Arnall less than any of the general's officers. Stowe owned thousands of acres in South Carolina and more Africans than he needed to work them, and had never worn a uniform before the shelling of Fort Sumter. He did not share Arnall's wary professional judgment of Jackson. Stowe was a fighting amateur, a good instinctive soldier, just the kind of man, Arnall knew, who judged generals like fighting cocks—by success, no matter how attained. A plausible standard, except that luck and inspiration and fighting blood could run out, while sound professionalism would never let a soldier down.

Take Joe Johnston the summer before. When he had dashed by rail from the Valley through this very Gap to Beauregard's aid, he not only brought up the cars in ample time and number for the movement to Manassas. Each brigade commander had been carefully informed of where they were going and why, so that each knew what was expected; and the regimental commanders had been instructed in turn by the brigadiers—save, of course, those of Brigadier General Jackson, not then famous, a mere brigade commander under Johnston but already well-known in the southern Army as too secretive to tell a blind man if it was day or night.

Now here they were with that same tight-mouthed Jackson—crack-brained, too, some said—commanding what amounted to a corps, and not a man in it (except some of the engineers plotting the route) had any clear idea where they were going or what they would do when they got there.

Well, Taliaferro had warned him. Arnall had ridden over to renew an Old Army acquaintance, on the early August day when Hill's Light Division had joined Jackson at Gordonsville. Taliaferro had succeeded to the command of Jackson's former division; chuckling, as if it were some kind of joke, he'd told Arnall that Jackson's marching orders usually were a little vague.

"He mought say, 'March to the cross road. Officer there'll tell you which fork to take.' Then maybe he'll say, 'Go on to the next fork. A courier'll give you a sealed order point'n out the road.'" Taliaferro laughed again. "Stonewall reads his Bible. He don't often let the left hand knoweth what the right hand doth."

That was not funny to Hoke Arnall. At the moment, he knew little more than that his brigade was headed more or less east, after marching north all the day before, which meant they were behind Pope, or ought to be unless the Federal general had moved quickly to counter them—in which case surely they wouldn't be traipsing through a defensible position like Thoroughfare Gap as if on a Sunday school outing.

But behind Pope for what? Oh, Jackson could mess up the Yank supply line for awhile, but when you got right down to it, his circling movement meant that Lee's army was now divided, with a superior enemy force between its two wings. Arnall shared the army's general disdain for Pope's uncivil proclamations, but he had noticed that the loud-mouthed Federal general had handled his troops well enough, in frustrating Lee along the Rappahannock, to suggest that he would know how to use his larger force to crush each half of Lee's army in detail. Concentrating force, not dividing it, was the soundest principle of war.

"Damn stragglers bleedin us white." The last company of Stowe's own regiment was going by, the men seeming to droop in the heat.

"Yeah. Reckon Jackson ever thinks a man gets tired or hungry?"

"Not to mention sleepy." Stowe clapped the planter's straw on his head and touched it in what, from him, passed for a salute. "See you when we git ther, Gin'al."

Arnall glumly watched his favorite regimental commander canter away, then turned again to watch his brigade passing. Straggling had thinned the ranks noticeably, which was why Arnall fretted about the blistering pace of the march. Killing in the heat; men dropping like apples off the trees. Powell Hill didn't believe in wearing out troops on the road so they'd come on the battlefield too tuckered to fight. Arnall agreed, and had trained his men to fight, not to fall out from sunstroke and fatigue. He aimed, with the harsh discipline which he valued second only to the Bible, to achieve battlefield effectiveness, not speed records on the march. Hill had already had an altercation with the commanding general on the marching question, but hadn't it been A. P. Hill's hard-hitting brigades that saved an ill-managed battle for Jackson at Slaughter's Mountain?

General Arnall's concern was not humanitarian; he respected his troops, as he expected them to respect him, but he would have considered it unofficerlike to have been *fond* of them. Troops were instruments of war, and needed to be kept in good condition, like sidearms—particularly the troops of Hoke Arnall, who carried with him always the secret fear that he might—someday, somehow—miss out. Not on something decisive: more than a year of war had persuaded his military mind that its outcome would be cumulative, not the product of some Napoleonic stroke. He was afraid he would miss an opportunity he could seize for his own, that would make him, finally, what he aimed to be. He was not quite sure what he *did* aim to be, with the single-minded purpose that Amy had sometimes protested as too devouring; and he knew war too well to define his aim, even in his own mind, with such words as *hero* or *glory* or *conqueror*. But it was obvious that achieving his purpose, whatever it was, would require opportunity, and would require Hoke Arnall to recognize it when it came.

The young general saw no clash between such ambition and his strong religious beliefs. Opportunity, if it came, could fall from nowhere but the hand of Providence; success, if he achieved it, would owe less to his efforts than to the will of God—provided he was ready for the moment, both in the military sense and in the favor of his Maker.

That hot morning in Thoroughfare Gap, the latter point was worrying General Arnall more persistently than the worn state of his brigade. He knew his men could fight like tigers on an hour's rest and a chunk of bacon. But he found it hard to follow the curt and mysterious Jackson (everybody in the army knew that when reliable old baldheaded Dick Ewell got his first taste of Jackson in the Valley he had pronounced him "crazy as a March hare") without un-Christian resentment and unsoldierly questioning; *that* was hardly what the Lord expected of His military servants. And the letter from Amy that had caught up to him two days earlier at Jefferson had caused him even more disturbing thoughts.

Ever since, even on this exhausting march, he had been unable to get her out of his mind, seeing at one moment her long black hair falling about her white shoulders, remembering at another her heavy bosom . . . for the hundredth time, he shook the sinful vision from his treacherous imagination.

What would Amy think of him if she knew how often he actually thought of her naked and enfolding, as she had been at Sycamore on that last morning of his leave, of which she had so tartly reminded him? What if the warning in her letter turned out to be true, that he had got her in the family way again? What was he going to say when he wrote her? What could he say?

He had been thoughtless, careless . . . *yes sinful* . . . everything she had charged in her letter. And yet how could he or anyone have resisted, with such a woman in his bed, after so many months of rough camp life in the company of nothing but men and horses and death? And nothing better to look forward to. But he felt himself mortified by his betraying flesh; he sensed Amy's righteous contempt; and he feared that God would turn His face from none so finally as from those who surrendered to the sin of lust.

Arnall squared his shoulders and sat straighter on Rambler, trying to rouse himself from such gloomy speculations. One of the troubles with war and the army was that a man had too much time, on the march and in a lonely tent at night, to brood, to think things best left unthought. Suddenly, Arnall craved action, to be consumed in action; and for that purpose, he had to admit to himself, a man could hardly do better than to follow Ol Jack. If he only knew where they were going.

Dixon's Rifles—a North Carolina regiment that had been allowed to keep the name under which Colonel Arthur Dixon had organized it, rather than being redesignated by number and state— were moving past General Arnall now. Every man in the ranks had a rifled musket, which was unusual for a whole regiment in that army. Each prided himself on being able to put ten out of ten

.58-caliber balls in a one-and-a-half-inch circle at 220 yards. Not that there was time or much need for such marksmanship in battle, but it was good drill and good discipline and good for morale. Hoke Arnall believed that victory would be woven from such strands of detail—provided, of course, that the Lord willed it, which depended on whether those who planned and prayed for victory were worthy of His blessing.

On the road below, barrel-chested Private Lige Flournoy nudged Private Josh C. Beasly with the butt of his musket. Most of the brigade knew General Arnall as "Ironass" but Lige had given him another name since the day the Light Division had crossed the Rapidan, Arnall's Brigade leading. When the first Yank prisoners had been hauled in, two were identified as deserters from the brigade who had been caught, tried, convicted, and sentenced to death the winter before, but who had then escaped and gone over to the Yanks.

Jackson ordered the two shot immediately. Then Arnall had their bodies hung from a tree limb high above the road by which the brigade would march. Lige Flournoy realized upon passing beneath one man's bare dangling feet—a pair of fine Yankee boots having been snatched from the corpse by some opportunist—that he had shared a hut with him in winter quarters at Manassas. Pretty good boy, seem like at the time, Lige told Josh Beasly.

"At damn Hangman up yonder lookin y'ovuh, Meat," he said to Beasly now, jerking his head toward the general sitting his horse by the roadside. Lige called all his company mates "Meat."

Private Foxy Bradshaw, marching on the other side of Flournoy, laughed through a nose curved like a pistol grip. Hoke Arnall heard the hyena-like squeal and was reassured by the high spirits among his men.

"Look like he got Josh's ramrod up'is ass."

Foxy Bradshaw enjoyed fanning Beasly's undisguised hatred of General Arnall, just as he might have ruffled up the feathers of a spirited rooster before loosing him in the cockpit. Foxy went for men's sore spots and irritations the way crabs went for the crotch. That helped him conceal—though never quite forget—the nagging fear that ate at his innards all the time, every day he had spent in the army, a fear he did not dare to reveal to his rough companions. Foxy would have deserted long ago except that the only standing he had ever had was that he sometimes could make them laugh at other men's weaknesses; but he knew they would disdain his own.

"Stuffed-up sonomabitch."

Josh sent a long parabola of tobacco juice through the dust, just past Foxy's shoulder blades, toward the general on his horse. A lean, scar-faced Carolina mountain man, Josh Beasly fought hard, never complained of it, and vowed to take plenty of Yanks with him before he went under. Between fights, he regarded himself as free, white, and twenty-one, and devil take the man who fetched him an indignity.

Josh had been brooding about Hoke Arnall since, as a result of the general's rigid discipline, he had been tried for drunkenness and "bucked" without water for eight hours—during which his knees were drawn up, a fence rail was passed under them, and his arms were tied under the rail to his ankles.

Josh had regarded that as an easy sentence, even in the hot Virginia sun. But to him getting drunk was an inalienable right; and he could not understand why he should be punished at all for something as natural as breathing or pissing. So he figured Ironass had it in for him—no other possibility. Hence, Josh Beasly aimed to get even, as he had been raised to believe a man had to do.

"Damn Hangman sittin ther like a tin sojer," Lige said.

Though the terror of the company in battle, Lige was otherwise easygoing, especially in comparison to Josh. To Lige desertion and execution meant nothing but one more way to go in an army in which everybody, sooner or later, would be killed. As near as Lige could tell, they were all merely meat; so he rarely even bothered to learn others' names. But he had been genuinely shocked by the stringing up of dead men. Not even war could justify a lack of respect for the dead, he thought, in a world in which there was so little for the living.

None of the three privates nor General Arnall on his horse noticed Fargo Hart, erect on dust-coated Mercury, trotting forward past Dixon's Rifles, between the road and the railroad track. Private Larkin Folsom did see him, upright as a knight on as fine a horse as Folsom had ever seen.

Not much of a horseman himself, Folsom—Hoke Arnall's headquarters orderly—was glad the general had halted to watch his brigade go by. The youth had thrown himself down under a tree, glad of the shade and of a chance to get off his old mare's hot, broad back.

He wished he had his fiddle, which was back somewhere with

the baggage train on the other side of the Rappahannock. He also wished he had the Bible his mother had given him; she would be scandalized to know he had left that with the baggage train, too. Not that Folsom had much interest in the Bible, save for some of the poetic passages; he only wanted his verses, written on scraps of paper that he had tucked in its pages for safekeeping.

Folsom particularly wanted to rework a sonnet he had written at Gordonsville and entitled "For Flossie Blooms the Rose." Best thing he'd written, but as he recalled the final lines, the meter might have wandered a little bit off the track.

Larkin Folsom did not know a woman named Flossie, let alone one for whom roses bloomed. He scarcely knew any women other than his mother—who could hardly be the object of romantic speculation or even imagination—and one or two giggly neighborhood creatures of his own age back in Chowan County. These latter had only caused him to wonder how they could conceivably grow into the visions of beauty and purity his reading had led him to believe the fair sex inevitably presented at maturity.

Lately, the orderly had been deeply troubled by his exalted idea of womanhood. Because he believed in it wholeheartedly, though he was not yet nineteen years old, he feared he had disqualified himself forever from the company of this morally and spiritually superior femininity. The disgusting truth was that Larkin Folsom had fallen victim to vice—a plunge the more disquieting because of the abjurations to nobility and godliness with which his mother had raised him, then prayerfully packed him off to the Light Division.

How could he conceivably fail his mother? But he had, within the month—awaking one night from a blissful dream to the horrid realization that it had been evoked by his own hand between his own thighs. But as those in pain succumb first to the relief, then to the wicked sublimity of opium, so Larkin Folsom had found succor in the sin of Onan.

Soon he could not keep his hands off himself. Prayer, whatever its other powers, proved no match for the flesh; neither did mental appeals to his mother's reinforcing maxims of the godly life and the pure heart.

"Hey, boy." A rough voice, almost in his ear, startled him. "Wotchuh got'n yuh hand?"

As if he had touched something red hot, Folsom jerked his hand out of his lap; without realizing it he had been feeling himself through his pants. Squatting at his shoulder, Corporal Amos Gilmore guffawed, making as evil and suggestive a sound as the orderly could imagine—far worse than the loud farts his coarser classmates at Chapel Hill had prided themselves on loosing.

"Nothin, Mister Gilmer."

Corporal Gilmore laughed again, poking a rough finger into Folsom's ribs. "I *bet* it's nothin!"

Corporal Gilmore had been pulled out of ranks by General Arnall and was used officially as a messenger, usually in battle, but mostly in a roving and informal assignment as the general's personal scout and forager. Gilmore was a big man, powerful, with broad shoulders and legs that caused the trooper's trousers he affected to stretch like skin when he sat a horse. Folsom knew that when Gilmore had been in ranks, he had taken on all challengers with his fists until no more would come forward. After that, Arnall had found a special assignment for him.

"Know what to do with that thing?" Gilmore leered at him and winked ostentatiously.

"Uh . . . with . . . uh . . . what thing?" But Folsom had a terrible feeling that he knew.

"At nubbin you been pullin on down ther."

Folsom wished the earth would open and take him. He wished his mother were there to shoo this ape away. He thought of the life ahead, the long years of mortal shame he would have to bear.

"I . . . ah . . . I don't . . ."

"Course you don't." Gilmore winked at him again. Then, his voice confidential: "Just teasin, boy. Aint no reason you to be flustered." His eyes, bloodshot and narrow, bored into Folsom's but the smile on his wide mouth seemed warm. "Tell you what. You got'ny problems, you tell ol Amos bout'em. I kin maybe hep you out."

Folsom could not imagine how. "I'm . . . I don't have any problems, Mister Gilmer."

Gilmore poked his ribs again, this time gently. "Ev'ry man got problems, boy."

He stood up, towering to what seemed an impossible height over Larkin Folsom, who gazed up at him in fear and mystification, neither of which was appeased by the unmistakable huge bulge in the crotch of Corporal Gilmore's tight cavalryman's pants.

Three and a half miles to the east, the leading regiments of Forno's Brigade, Ewell's Division, were entering a sun-smitten hamlet. They had been preceded only by General Jackson and his staff, with a screen of Munford's cavalry out front.

At the intersection of Hay Market Road and the one coming down from Thoroughfare Gap, along which Jackson's troops had been trudging under their tell-tale cloud of dust, a man quietly sat his horse and watched Forno's Brigade passing. He wore a long, dingy linen duster, a hat with a wide, stiff brim and a tall peak, and smoked a thin cigar. His hat and the duster were not so dirty as the marchers' nondescript uniforms, suggesting that he had been traveling alone rather than in the column.

That fact, together with the stranger's mere presence along the line of march, meant to Captain Eben Holmes, a lanky company commander, that this must be a native gawking at Confederate troops unexpectedly appearing in what for months had been Federal territory. The stranger might know, therefore, not only where the deuce they were, but where a thirsty soldier could forage up a glass of milk or a decent bite to eat.

Captain Holmes stepped up to the man's horse and gave him a more or less military salute. Forno's Louisianians—until recently known as Hays's Brigade—did not much hold with military niceties.

"This here village, sir . . . you tell me what it is?"

The man drew on his cigar. "Hay Market." He moved his head to the right. "Gainesville down the road a piece."

Hay Market meant nothing to Captain Holmes and was only a house or two and some rickety outbuildings, as far as he could see. But he had studied maps of northern Virginia enough to know that Gainesville was on the pike running between Warrenton and Washington. Washington! Maybe Ol Jack's a-takin us ther. But first things first.

"Reck'n anybody these parts'd give a man a glass-a milk?"

"They got it, reck'n they would."

Damn Virginians a close-lip crowd. Then Holmes realized the man did not sound like most Virginians. "Live hereabouts?"

The man in the long, flapping duster took his cigar out of his mouth and looked at it as if it might give him the answer.

"Fraid not."

"Hot country, huh?"

But Captain Holmes was turning this unexpected information over in his mind. Be jus like some goddam Yank spy, sittin ther cool's a cucumber, countin Ol Jack's men goin by.

He put an edge to his voice. "Maybe I better see some papers, Mistuh."

The man put the cigar in his mouth and looked at Captain

Holmes with unexcited eyes. He reached inside the duster and pulled a folded paper from some hidden pocket. Holmes watched narrowly; it did not occur to him that the stranger could as easily have told him he *did* live thereabouts, thus avoiding suspicion. Holmes was congratulating himself, instead, on his alertness.

He unfolded the paper and read it, first impatiently, then with surprise. It requested that anyone concerned should give Mister Andrew Peterson, Esq., of Atlanta, Georgia, safe conduct within Confederate lines and extend him insofar as possible all necessary food, transportation, courtesy, etc., etc., by hand of Jefferson Davis, President, C.S.A., done this seventeenth day of May, 1862, at Richmond, Va. A prominent seal impressed Captain Holmes almost as much as the signature.

He handed the paper back to Peterson with a flourish and gave him a somewhat snappier salute than before.

"Yes-SUH! Atchuh service!"

Peterson returned the paper to his pocket, looking at the passing troops rather than at the excited young man. From another pocket, he took one of his thin cigars and held it out. "Have a smoke, Cap'n."

"Yessuh!" Captain Holmes took the cigar gratefully. "Don't mind if I do." Saluting again, he hurried off after his company, long vanished in the dust.

Peterson watched in amusement tinged with sadness until the captain disappeared. Amazing what a boys' war it was! Including a lot of so-called generals, hardly old enough to vote. Which was at once the war's irony and its tragedy—the lark they made of it, some of these high-spirited boys, cavaliering around for glory and the Cause; and the slaughter of innocents and innocence it would inevitably become—already *was*, after Shiloh and the Peninsula. If that officious youngster hoping to catch a spy survived the summer, he'd be lucky.

And if he survived the war. . . Peterson shook his head. How lucky the ultimate survivors would be depended on the kind of a world left them. And what could war yield but a nation of blood and iron—flourishing as war did on material and mechanics and money, rapaciously devouring humanity along the way—a nation in which the merely personal would be irrelevant?

But for the moment, despite these forebodings, Peterson was relaxed, almost comfortable, even in the brutal sun and choking dust. It was a relief to be with southerners again, no doubt about it, since the paper he'd shown the young captain was genuine, good as a passport. But in a hollow heel of his boot, Peterson had *another* paper, worded more or less like the first, but this one signed "A. Lincoln." A forgery, of course, and the seal—though Peterson had expended much art upon it—would stand no more than a cursory examination.

Just the kind of examination, he reflected, that the young captain had given the real seal under Jeff Davis's name; just the kind that in recent weeks numerous Federal officers had expended on the forged Lincoln paper—a quick, impressed glance, a sudden haste to get into good graces with a stranger presumed to have high connections.

The forged pass had worked well enough, that summer, behind Pope's lines, so that Peterson and Joe Nathan had come away with a treasure in their growing collection of glass plates, in the record they had been able to make of an occupying army readying itself for battle, in the nightmare scenes of battle's aftermath they had recorded after Slaughter's Mountain and along the Rappahannock. They had captured the human image of history.

A useful summer, but a long, hard, dangerous summer. Then, the night before, while sharing a meal with some of General Sigel's staff officers—good German sausages had been obtained from somewhere, obviously not from the war-ravaged country around Warrenton—Peterson had listened to casual camp-fire conversation about a strong Reb column spotted that day moving up the Rappahannock, past Sulphur Springs, on the Federal right flank. The German officers were convinced that the column was going west to the Valley.

"Vere else?" A fat major peered around the camp fire confidently. "Even Rebs not such fools dey go de udder vay." He chuckled hugely.

A man with muttonchops along his jaw nodded his head vigorously. "Dey do dot, ve hold'em dis vay one hand . . ." He made a hard pushing gesture to the west. "Chop'em up dis vay de udder." He clubbed an enormous fist through the air to the east.

"Yah, yah." The fat major licked sausage from his fingers. "Dem Rebs for de Valley. Back vay to Vashington."

As soon as he decently could, Peterson made a rapid exit and got ready to move the next morning. He had no trouble at all; he just saddled up his horse at daybreak in Warrenton, leaving Joe Nathan to follow with the Whatsit Wagon and the equipment, and in his duster rode peacefully east long the pike, unchallenged and unhindered by any marching men of Pope's.

Peterson's instinct told him the Germans were wrong. A bold stroke into the Federal rear was just the sort of thing the outmanned Confederates might do, substituting dash and surprise for power. Near Buckland Mills his hunch got its first hint of confirmation: off to the left, a dust cloud rose above the road from Thoroughfare Gap. Peterson turned his horse into a country track from Buckland to Hay Market.

Now he sat watching the butternuts go by, feeling safe again with a legal pass, marveling at the ease with which he had passed from Pope's territory to what suddenly was Jackson's, a little excited despite himself by these developments. Whatever Jackson aimed to do, Peterson could see, he was in a fair way to do it: in Pope's rear with a considerable force, probably unknown as yet to the confident Federal commander.

Peterson thought briefly of seeking Jackson out, telling the general what he knew of the Federal situation—which, he reckoned, was a good deal more than Jackson could possibly know. But Andrew Peterson, though a Georgian among southerners again, had little partisan sense and even less patriotic sentiment. And he could aid the one side or the other only by the betrayal of his real loyalty.

"Close it up back ther!" an officer shouted on the road. "Move it on, men...close it up!"

Peterson spurred his horse and followed the passing brigade, not knowing it was Forno's. A lonely figure in the dust, he rode along with a kerchief pulled over his mouth and nostrils, feeling himself as isolated as he appeared, a stranger in a linen wrap, moving with interchangeable identities among alien armies, claiming no regiment as his own, giving and receiving no orders, holding or yielding no ground.

He had not always been so alone, and he thought briefly of the wife he had loved beyond all things, even his work. But he had long since ceased to dwell on that, could hardly imagine anymore how such a thing could have been. Nothing now could displace the work he had set himself to do.

Alone among these hosts, he reckoned, he cared nothing for victory, did not even believe there could be such a thing. It mattered only to him that Joe Nathan and the Whatsit Wagon should catch up, so that he could get on with his work, make the record, sear it forever on collodion-coated glass.

Determination twisted his mouth under the red kerchief grayed with dust. For he had a cause of his own: the Whatsit Wagon and its equipment, the incorruptible lens, a truth as harsh as justice. And to their demanding service, he would give his only loyalty.

From his house fronting the Warrenton Pike, Durward P. Brace could easily see the dust cloud rising over Gainesville, a mile to the west. Nothing unusual about dust on the roads, all'em confoun Yanks around.

But the way Brace made it out, *this* dust was rising over the Gap road. Aint heard tell no Yanks up thataway.

Since the big battle just down the pike the summer before, around the Henry House, Brace had thought of himself as well-versed in war, although with the mouths he had to feed he could see no chance to get off to the army where a Virginia man belonged. Not that any Virginia boys—Brace did not think much beyond Virginia or, for that matter, Prince William County—were around anymore to join.

Sho would be a relief to git off with 'em, though. Get shut of all em mouths I got to feed.

Some kind of racket erupted inside the house—angry female voices, what might of been somebody's face being slapped, a wail of pain and outrage. Brace sighed, settling himself on the lower step of the rickety stoop he kept meaning to have Henry steady up. Seem like a man can't get no peace no matter what.

The commotion came nearer and Missy came out on the stoop above him, holding twelve-year-old Wash firmly by the arm. The boy was barefoot and dirty all over. He always was. Under the grime, one cheek was red from the slap.

"Got to do sump'm bout this boy, Paw."

Missy was tall for sixteen. As Brace looked over his shoulder and up at her, she stood with one arm holding a faded robe around herself, the other hand clutching Wash above the elbow. Her black hair, piled and wet, was on top of her small head, and little streams of moisture ran down her forehead and temples, glittering like her angry blue eyes.

"You lie!" Wash bellowed. "I ain't done nuthin!"

"Peepin at me inna bath, Paw. Second time I caught 'im, too."

"What I wanna peep at her for?" Wash glared from Missy to Brace. "Ugly ol crow!"

Brace sighed again. Ugly was one thing Missy was not. Having often peeped at her himself, Brace was sure of that.

"I ain't gone have it, Paw. Hangin round like a owl with'em

eyes a-hissen. Can't even git'n bed he ain't creepin up on me."

"Lyin ol bitch!" Wash twisted to get free but Missy was strong; she clamped down hard on his skinny arm. "I ain't been peepin at'er, Paw, she's . . ."

"Wash'is mouth out with soap." Boys'll be boys, but callin is sister a bitch won't do.

"It aint nuthin he *said*, Paw, it's what he *done*."

"Wash it out good. Learn'im some manners."

Missy rolled her eyes heavenward and dragged Wash, yelling, inside the house. Vaguely, past Missy's thin shoulders, Brace caught a glimpse of Kate's fat anxious face in the gloom of the house. Can't get no confoun peace atall.

He turned away and watched the dust cloud, listening to Wash's outraged shouts until they suddenly blubbered into silence. Henry came around the corner of the old clapboard house, marching with his stomping tread that shook the walls anytime Kate let'im in the house. Henry walked right up to the stoop like he owned it. Cept even a snickety coon like Henry knows better'n speak to a white man till he's spoke to.

Brace sat on awhile without looking up, just to let Henry know what was right and fitten. Then he spat and wiped his mouth on his sleeve.

"You got nuthin to do but stand ther?"

"Mare startin-a limp on'er off foreleg."

"I *tole* you to check the shoe."

"Aint the shoe."

Brace looked up then, knowing from the tone of Henry's voice that it wasn't the shoe. Henry's face, as always, was grim. "One nigguh that *nevuh* smile," Brace liked to say at the store in Gainesville. "Leastways, not that I evuh seen."

"Must be a toucha thrush then. Aint I said a thousand times I want at confoun stall kept clean?"

Brace knew this was a mere gesture of authority, since Henry kept the mare's stall cleaner than Kate's kitchen. And Henry knew more about horses than anybody. Got to give'im that.

"Somethin ail the *leg*." If he had been a white man, Henry's voice might have sounded contemptuous. "Look like the big knee to me. Feel all hot."

That sounded bad. Alarmed, Brace accepted defeat with what dignity he could.

"Big knee, huh? S'what I thought all along."

"Better take'er to Centreville. See Daddy Ben."

Brace sighed. Daddy Ben would charge a pretty penny. God-dam free nigguh runnin a smithy'n doctorin horses like a white man.

"Soon's I see my way clear, then."

Henry marched off and Brace spat after him. Brace's mare was his only prized possession, save Missy. But in a way, the mare— Brace had bought her for a song from a drunken liveryman in Warrenton—gave him more distinction than a pretty daughter. When you got right down to it, the daughter was another mouth to feed, but a good horse set a man apart. Like ownin darkies. So, dear as money was, Brace was willing to pay Daddy Ben if as sound a judge as Henry said it was necessary.

Brace looked at the dust cloud, turning darker as the afternoon waned. He had been expecting another fight since the summer before, and dust from the direction of Thoroughfare Gap seemed a kind of signal. Cept all'em Virginia boys spose to be down round Richmond.

But he was sure there'd be a fight before the summer was out. Maybe I ought to git while the gittin's good, he thought. Ol Brawner up the road skedaddle more 'n a year ago. Wilmer McLean, too, way they shot up'is place last summer.

On the other hand—Brace looked up at his weather-beaten house, sagging uneasily on its old stone foundations, one upper window glassless and patched with greased paper. Maybe this time they'd burn it down, or blow it away with'em big guns way they done the Henry house last summer.

Brace almost hoped they would. *Then,* by God they'd pay off. They'd have to make the confoun war worth some real cash money for a man.

Missy came out on the stoop again. Standing above him, she gazed at the dust cloud off toward Gainesville.

"Aint seen none goin thataways before."

"Umph." Brace thought hopefully about his house burning down in the coming battle. If they'd just burn his house, it wouldn't be like the other time, after last summer, when he'd gone clear to Richmond and come back with no more than a worthless piece of government paper to show for a ruined cornfield and six hogs he could *prove* was tooken.

"I could run down ther aways, Paw. See whut's goin on."

"Dawg if you will." Brace peered up at her sternly. Having dealt with Wash, she had put on her usual long loose skirt and washed-out blouse; her long black hair hung in a braid down her back. "Got no truck with em sojer boys."

"Shoot." Missy, barefoot, ran past him down the steps and around the corner of the house.

Seem like Missy never move, she don't run. Light on'er feet as a mockinbird. Brace was proud of his long-legged daughter and aimed to marry her above herself. Iffen the confoun war gits over fore she turns ol maid.

"Gone be fightin again, aint they?" Kate's mournful voice, from the doorway above, told him she had seen the dust cloud, too.

"Mebbe. Mebbe not."

"Gone be worse'n las time. Just feel my bones gone be worse'n las summer."

"Yeh," Wash squealed behind her. "Gone be dead Yanks alla way to Stone Bridge!"

"Hesh at talk!"

No use scarin Kate any more, Brace thought, hearing them retreat from his sharp tone. He thought of Missy skipping around the corner of the house. Times I see in'er face how she take after Kate. Way Kate used to be, flittin round here like a junebug.

Brace stood up heavily, a big man once, looking smaller from the stoop of his shoulders. His teeth were yellowing in his lined face; but his eyes were still sharp and clear, and the hard line of his jaw showed through his stubbled brown whiskers.

Kate hogfat now. Scairt outen'er head by the confoun war.

Brace sighed and went on around the house toward the barn to take a look at the mare's off foreleg before finally consenting to pay out hard cash to the likes of Daddy Ben.

He saw Sajie walking across the back yard toward the small, shed-roofed house where she and Henry lived—fuckin up a storm, Brace was convinced. Sajie carried a small white bundle on her head. Ass on at bitch like a Richmond whore.

Brace's face brightened momentarily as it occurred to him: maybe em goddam guns'll blow Henry away witha house.

From behind the grapevine Missy watched Brace enter the barn. She ran out behind him, circled behind the house, and trotted toward the pike. Then she saw Henry pulling on the well-rope, watching her with his unblinking eyes. Sometimes Henry gave her the shivers. But it was Henry kept the place going, with Paw down in the dumps most of the time. Lately drunk too much.

Missy pointed at the dust cloud. "Goin to see. Donchuh tell now!"

Henry's face did not change. It seldom did. "Paw gone tan you."

"Oh Paw fiddlesticks!"

Henry watched her trot down the pike toward Gainesville, light on her feet as a biddy. Serve'er right, some sojer cart'er off, playin round where she got no bidness.

He took the bucket of water and carried it across the littered yard to his house. Sajie met him at the door and took the bucket. She peered past him at the dust cloud; it was beginning to spread out, as if whoever had raised it had tramped on from beneath.

"Missis say gone be fightin agin."

Henry snorted. "All she evuh say."

He sat on his own front step, unaware that except for his black skin he looked much as Brace had on the flimsy stoop of the main house. He could hear Sajie moving around inside, getting up supper. He did not look at the dust cloud, since he knew it was only something out of the white folks's war.

Henry did not believe the war had much to do with him. Blue troops having white skins like the Virginians he thought all southerners were, he saw little difference between them. Co'se nigguhs spose to be free up nawth.

Henry had heard that, and Henry wanted to be free—so desperately that he sometimes lay awake at night thinking about it, so longingly that he feared the idea must be a dream that could never come true. But in more hopeful moments, Henry had his own idea of freedom and it did not include living beholden to white skins. Up nawth'r nare place else. Henry had no illusions about white skins.

In that uneasy area between the armies, he knew he could easily have walked away from Brace's rundown farm, anytime he wanted to, and followed along the pike until he came up on some blue troops. They'd take him along. White skins always glad of black hands.

But Henry had two reasons, one instinctive and one practical, for sitting stolidly on his doorstep instead of walking off along the pike. One was that, even though desperate for freedom, he thought of it as something in which he could be his own man. He had no intention of exchanging Brace's easy, slovenly world for what his instinct told him would be less open but no less certain—

perhaps more demanding — dominance by some other white. Or whites. Nigguhs got no say where white skins run things. And where did they not?

Better to stay put, Henry reasoned, and see which set of whites survived their war, and how the cat would jump after that. Both could not survive. There would be no point that Henry could imagine in fighting a war if the winners let the losers survive.

The other reason he did not follow the blue troops was much more certain in Henry's mind. If he ran off and took Sajie with him, the blue troops might take her for themselves. If he ran off and left Sajie here, Brace would take her to the hayloft before the sun came up again. Or Sajie would kill Brace when he tried, which meant they'd hang Sajie.

After awhile, Henry walked out to Brace's fence and looked along the pike to see if Missy was coming back. But the road lay empty and quiet in the lengthening shadows. He stood there a long time, one foot on the lower rail, until at last she came running into view. Henry was relieved in spite of himself. Chile caint hep it, she ol Brace's girl.

Missy saw him and waved, not missing a stride. "Henry! Guess what?"

He waited until she pulled breathless to a halt in front of him. Her eyes shone in her thin flushed face and the long black pigtail had flipped forward over her shoulder.

"They's our'n, Henry! Virginia boys!"

Not mine, Henry thought. But he knew then for sure that there would be another fight.

"Fines thing I evuh seen . . . miles 'n miles of 'em!"

"Git on in fore yuh Paw ketches yuh," Henry said.

By about 4:30 p.m., as he returned to his horse from his fifth trip to the woods, Colonel Channing thought that at last his innards ought to be just about cleaned out.

"Should of known better'n eat em dadburn roasen ears."

He swung his leg up wearily and eased his raw bottom into the saddle, his ill-fitting jacket tight across his thick chest. Channing had a red, weather-beaten face, competent hands, the look of a farmer rather than a soldier. He wore a black hat with a broad brim turned down all around, so that he seemed to peer out at the world as if from under an umbrella; but subordinates on Jackson's staff had learned that Channing's sleepy-looking eyes missed little. Just at that moment, they did not miss young Thad Selby trying to hide a grin.

"You, Selby! Git on up-at road'n see if Munford's scouted up anything."

It was an unnecessary order and Channing knew it; Munford would instantly have sent back any word worth having. And the Selby boy had done nothing a half dozen other officers hadn't done that day, as word of Channing's plight spread among Jackson's staff.

Still . . . Channing was vaguely aggrieved that on this day of all days, the hardest march the demanding Jackson had ever led, he'd had to come down with a case of shits. Selby had just happened to grin at the wrong time. Besides, what was the good of being a colonel and the senior staff officer if a man couldn't work off a little steam on a goddam greenhorn captain?

But Selby had scarcely disappeared around a bend up ahead when he came galloping back. Boy's a good rider, Channing thought. Likes to gallop a little on that black horse, though. Little too well got up. In fact, Selby made the rest of the staff, not to mention Jackson himself, look like a crowd of foragers. But when he'd been around a little longer, the fine new uniform'd be as dirty as anybody else's and he'd save the sword for dress parade.

"Sir!" Selby was shouting before he skidded his horse to an unnecessarily dusty halt. "Gin'al Jackson . . . he says tell you Munford's up on Bristoe a half mile ahead'n stakin it out. Says halt Forno when he gets here, let the troops get some rest while the rest-a the column closes up."

Bristoe, by God! On the O & A! Crazy damn Jackson's done it again.

Channing did rapid sums in his head. Salem through the Gap to Gainesville, then on to Bristoe. Not a goddam mile less than twenty-four and in the hottest sun he'd seen since Mexico. Men could hardly make a better march in a single day—and Jackson's boys had done it right on top of another parched and blistering twenty-five miles the day before, with nothing in between but an hour or two of sleep. And nare bite to eat cept apples'n roasen ears.

"Cap'n," Channing said, "you never went to the Point."

"Nossir." Selby's voice was stark with apology.

"You did, maybe you'd know you just rode a horse alongside

one-a the goddamdest marches any army ever made." And behind
one-a the goddamdest generals, too.

"Know it anyway, sir. Proud to be here, sir."

"You get to be an ol man, Cap'n—*if* you get to be an ol man—
tell your grandchildren you marched around Pope with Ol Jack."

"With you, too, sir!"

Touch of the suck-up in the boy. But even that could not spoil
the colonel's pleasure in the moment. Fifty miles in two days.
The O & A! Pope's jugular. There had been nothing like it in the
war—maybe in any war.

He looked around. Work to be done still. An open field, grown
over in broomsedge, lay to the left of the road; another farm going
to seed while war rolled over the country. But Channing had
learned not to let waste and destruction worry him too much.
Nothing he could do about it, and a small price to pay for Virginia's
rights, anyway.

"All right, son. Git on back-er'n find Gin'al Ewell. He'll be
ridin with Forno, I spect. Guide Ewell to that field over ther'n
tell'im to fall'is men out for rest. Keep'em quiet'n closed up'n
ready to march, he gits word from Gin'al Jackson."

Trouble was, Channing knew, the three divisions were spread
out along maybe ten miles of narrow road. When Ewell's van
stopped here, Taliaferro's tail-end company would just about be
making Hay Market. But there was a lot of space in between units,
and each one was strung out longer than it would be in close order.
Channing gave Selby further instructions for Ewell to send couriers
back to the other division commanders with orders for them to
press on until their regiments closed on those ahead.

"But no cookin fires'n stay ready to move up, minute they git
word. Keep plenny-a pickets'n flankers out."

Selby galloped off, though a slower pace would have done.
Channing sighed, feeling hollow and still a little rumbly inside,
and nudged his horse into a trot, the reins loose in his big-knuckled
farmer's hands. He was not really a professional soldier, despite
a West Point education and the campaign in Mexico. He'd spent
most of his life farming in the Valley, but since the outbreak of
war he had taken to the field again, as old General Trimble put
it, "like a mule eatin briars."

Channing's rise to senior position on Jackson's staff was nevertheless a matter of wonder in the army, not least to Channing
himself. When he'd first found himself assigned to the secretive

Jackson with his iron discipline and indifference to men's physical limitations, Channing had hardly bothered to hide his opinion that the general was a lunatic. As for Channing himself, he was profane as a teamster, indifferent to religion, and jovially indiscreet—as unlike Jackson as a man could be.

But the two shared a zeal for action, and that proved in the Valley Campaign to be the only common ground they needed. Kernstown and Winchester had earned Channing's appreciation of even a crazy general who could win battles; and he thought he'd clinched his place in Jackson's confidence with his handling of a vexatious delay in the retreat up the Valley from Winchester. An immense tangle of troops and wagons at a road crossing was holding up the whole army; Channing, coming upon the scene, immediately and instinctively unleashed his blistering barnyard vocabulary.

As his voice rang across the countryside, a hand touched his shoulder. Turning, he saw Jackson hunched on his sorrel, a flush rising above his brown beard to his pale, fierce eyes.

"Channing . . . I'm afraid you're a wicked fellow."

Channing, then a major, knew a rebuke when he heard one, even when it came in a mild voice he had to strain to hear. But David Channing was not a man to back off.

"Gin'al, you want mules to move, aint no use prayin over'em."

He turned back to the road tangle, bellowing blasphemies at the top of his voice. Suddenly, within moments, the jam broke, the crossing began to clear. Other officers shouted their orders; teamsters' whips cracked. Stalled troops began to march.

"Ummm," Jackson said. "Good . . . good." He spurred away, ungainly on the sorrel, his elbows out like wings, the old forage cap pulled low on his forehead.

But even now, months and many battles later, Channing feared that the delicate subject of religion, never discussed between them, might yet bring trouble. He had tried to respect the general's strange scruples—put aside only at the demand of necessity—against fighting and marching on Sunday; but he sometimes had the ominous feeling that Jackson was only waiting for the right moment to preach him a sermon or have him burned at the stake.

A minister who had come out from Winchester one Sunday to hold services for the army had engaged Jackson at the mess table in a rambling conversation about religion and the war. Channing, bored to distraction, had seldom seen the general more animated.

"Let us all unite more earnestly," he told the minister, "in imploring God's aid in fighting our battles for us."

Channing would have settled for another brigade or two. But Jackson's voice rose with excitement.

"If God be for us, who can be against us? That He will still be with us, and give us victory after victory, until our independence shall be established, and that He will make our nation that people whose God is the Lord, is my earnest prayer. Whilst we attach so much importance to being free from temporal bondage, we must attach far more to being free from the bondage of sin."

Talk of bondage sounded too abolitionist for Channing. And freedom from sin was not the colonel's idea of a war aim. But if that was what made Ol Jack jump, he was willing to live and let live. He only hoped the general was, too.

As Channing rounded the turn in the road, he saw several horses—among them Little Sorrel—standing in the shade of a sycamore tree in the yard of a rickety farmhouse. He hoped that meant the general was snatching a little sleep. As the day had worn on, he'd turned jumpy and snappish, a sure sign that fatigue and concern were wearing him down. Channing had long since realized—certainly at White Oak Swamp—that Jackson needed lots of sleep, although he refused to admit it or act on the need. And for six days, since they'd moved up to the Rappahannock chasing Pope, Jackson's wing of the army had been constantly marching and skirmishing, with little enough sleep for anyone, including its commander.

And me, Channing thought, swinging down from his horse in the farmyard. Not that anybody gives a hoot in hell. But even a staff officer could be tired. Even one of Jackson's staff officers.

Major Douglas Worsham, the surgeon of the Stonewall Brigade who often rode with its former commander, came out on the porch, stepping softly as if he feared his spurs might jingle. He spoke in a whisper as Channing climbed the creaking steps. "Gin'al's sleep-in."

"Good for him." Channing was damned if he'd tiptoe around for anybody, even Ol Jack. "Better try it yourself."

Inside the house, in a wide hallway that ran its length, several other officers were stretched out on the floor. From the rear stoop, a frightened child's face peered into the hallway, then vanished. Channing knew the story without asking—the father off somewhere in the army, maybe even back along the road to Gainesville, the mother and children taking refuge from this sudden frightening descent of the war on their quiet existence. Could be happening in his own household near Winchester, if the Yanks were stirring themselves in the Valley these days. Bastards.

He stepped over the exhausted, sleeping bodies of colleagues and opened the door to a room on the left. A woman sat there alone, in a corner chair, her hands busy with darning needles. She looked at him without interest, her eyes as dull as the homespun dress that even in the stifling afternoon heat covered her from neck to floor. She was not old; the hair pulled severely back across her forehead was dark and might once have been lustrous. But beneath it, the face was worn and sagging, and the corners of her mouth turned downwards, whether in sorrow or anger or disappointment, or all three, Channing was too wise a man to guess.

"Servant, ma'am."

He closed the door slowly, conscious of the dull eyes steadily on his. Channing had seen the woman before, had known her most of his life—the worked-out, used-up brood mares of the small-farm South. Well, all that would change when they'd licked the Yanks; they'd no longer have to pay life's-blood tribute to goddam northern money changers.

He opened the door to the room on the other side of the hall. General Jackson sat in a wooden chair tilted back against the plank outer wall of the house. He was sound asleep, his mouth a little open, a thin-lipped slash in his flowing brown beard, his old cap in his lap, his large hands, not unlike Channing's own, folded across his chest. If Yank newspaper writers had a look at him now, Channing thought, they'd never believe this was the great Stonewall himself.

Channing closed the door quietly. One good hour of that, he knew from experience, and Jackson'd be rarin to git up'n go for Yanks. The colonel went down the hall to the front porch. Major Worsham was asleep there, propped against the wall in a meager patch of shade from a chinaberry tree. The horses snuffed and shuffled quietly under the trees; back up the road, the dust cloud hung over the troops coming on from Gainesville.

Save for that dust and the military equipment on the horses, a man would never know he was in the middle of a war. Not even the breath of a breeze stirred the torpid summer heat. The sun beat down like perdition. Channing had not heard so much as a rifle shot all day, although with the dust hanging over them like a signal flag, he'd been half expecting Yanks to jump out of the woods any minute. Goddam Pope probably writin another proclamation stead of fightin'is war.

Beyond the bend in the road, the faint echo of voices and the rattle of equipment suddenly brought the war back; Forno had reached the designated resting place. Channing sighed gratefully. He had the good soldier's ability to seize the moment. He was worn out from the long march, his rumbling bowels, and the preceding days of strain and danger. There was fighting just ahead, no doubt about it. But for a still summer evening hour, nothing was likely to happen; he could lie down with easy eyes.

Channing shucked his heavy boots, unbuttoned his tight jacket, opened the front door, and lay down in the hall, where anybody coming in would have to step over him. He tipped his hat down over his face and was asleep in thirty seconds. Five minutes later, Fargo Hart shook him awake.

Channing moved the hat that covered his face and squinted up at the dusty officer squatting beside him. The colonel's eyes, seeming shrouded with sleep, at once took in everything—cavalry insignia, captain's bars, heavy coating of dust, neat mustache, steady confident eyes, nothing urgent in them.

"Tell Stuart he needs some sleep, too, Cap'n." He pulled the hat back over his face.

"Stuart? He anywhere around?"

Channing's voice was muffled by the hat. "Aint you from Stuart, son?"

"Well . . . uh, yes, but . . . I thought he was back around Waterloo somewhere."

Channing gestured vaguely over his shoulder. "Ride over that-aways a mile or so'n you mought be in time for supper with'im."

Stuart was running a cavalry screen between Jackson's right flank and any forces Pope might hurry up to meet them. The young cavalry general had come riding up at Gainesville, grinning and yelling like a hunter after coon, having led the main body of his horsemen over a route paralleling, but just inside, the roads Jackson had followed during his two-day march.

"If that don't beat all. He's here first and it was me spose to find you."

Channing took the hat off his face. "Why so?"

Hart, looking embarrassed, pulled a paper from his pocket and handed it to the colonel. Like a Christmas present in June, he thought, as Channing looked over Stuart's note.

"Shit, son, we went thew the Gap this morning. Not a Yank in sight."

"I know." Miserably, Hart explained that he had pushed all

night and day and had just now managed to come up with General Jackson. As he expanded a bit on the difficulties of the road and of overtaking marching troops, a horse clattered into the yard outside.

"Goddam Main Street around here."

Channing sat up and Hart stood. Captain Selby, his fine uniform as dust-covered as Hart, came hurrying up the steps with a considerated rattle of boots and spurs. He gave Channing an exaggerated salute but the colonel only stared at him.

"Sir! You know Gin'al Jackson's orders for the Bristoe turnoff?"

"I ought to, Selby. I passed 'em on myself."

The road from Hay Market into Gainesville did not cross the Warrenton Pike and lead directly on to Bristoe. The troops had to turn right, march west on the pike maybe a quarter of a mile, then make a sharp left on the Bristoe road. Jackson had ordered Forno's Brigade to leave a guide at the left turn to make sure that the following troops did not miss it. As each brigade came up to the turn, it was supposed to leave a guide for the next.

"Well, Gin'al Arnall didn't leave a guide. Pender marched on down the pike aways fore Hill got'im back on the Bristoe road."

Hart thought the young captain seemed delighted with his report, but Channing almost groaned aloud. The colonel was tempted for a moment to tell Selby just to keep his sophomoric mouth shut. But Stuart's captain was standing there taking it all in and anyway, a story like that would be all over the army by nightfall. Arnall was not a popular man, and everybody knew how Jackson regarded his marching orders—as ranking only slightly beneath Holy Writ.

"Well, goddammit to hell." Channing struggled to his feet, a bony and awkward figure who reminded Fargo Hart of a weary mule being backed into the traces. "Looks like Ironass's in the shit."

Channing went down the hall, buttoning his jacket across his thick chest, and opened the door on the right. Hart, curious, and not knowing if he himself ought to report to Jackson, followed at a discreet distance. Past the door standing ajar he saw Channing touch the general's shoulder.

In the chair tilted against the wall, Jackson's whole body seemed to tense and the big hands folded on his chest might have gripped each other more tightly; but only his eyelids actually moved.

Beneath them, his pale eyes burned as if he had not been asleep at all.

"Sir . . . Gin'al Arnall failed to put a picket at the turnoff and the followin brigade took the wrong road."

"Put 'im under arrest and prefer charges."

The quiet voice crackled like lightning in the arid hot stillness. The lids dropped back over the incandescent eyes and Ol Jack slept again, the thick mat of whiskers around his mouth stirring slightly with his breath.

Channing crossed the room and closed the door noiselessly behind him.

"I was you . . ." He gave Hart back the note he'd carried from Stuart. "I b'lieve I'd just forget to give'im this right now."

Chapter Two

August 26–27

CAPTAIN MICAH G. DURYEA lit a candle on the corner of his camp desk, wishing he had Garrison, his big Newfoundland, at his feet. A man needed a dog, Duryea thought, and he murmured aloud: "Somebody's going to pay, Garrison. A lot of somebodies."

Neither the words nor the candle did much to dispel the gloom and silence of what had been a front bedroom of the old country house in which Major General John Pope's army headquarters had been set up, near Warrenton Junction on the O & A. The damned Reb slavers that once had lived in the rambling, rather ramshackle structure had moved out lock, stock, and barrel, leaving nothing but bare walls and floors and a scatter of trash. Served a crowd of child-selling barbarians right, in Captain Duryea's Christian opinion. *Fiat justitia!*

But the creepy old place did nothing for his nerves, and made him wish all the more for Garrison there at his feet. Colonel Russell had given him special permission to bring Garrison into the field, because Colonel Russell knew better—Duryea thought without embarrassment—than to refuse such small favors to men as valuable as he was. But during the Rebel raid on the supply depot at Catlett's Station on August 22, Duryea had been away on a mission, leaving Garrison in the care of a staff lieutenant, and some cowardly Reb had shot the dog in the eye. For which, Duryea had quietly resolved, a lot of Rebs would certainly answer.

The artillery that had been booming in the distance all afternoon finally had muttered into silence. Duryea did not know who had been firing, or at what; but he assumed it must have been some of Sigel's Germans. Sigel was a Prussian, trained as an artillery-man; he was known throughout the army for banging away with his guns whenever he could, whether or not artillery happened to be the appropriate weapon—and sometimes with little more than the empty distance for a target.

Still, the unexplained firing had done nothing for Duryea's nerves either. Since the raid on Catlett's Station, when the Rebs had caught the baggage train from Pope's headquarters on an overnight halt, he and Pope's other staff officers had been apprehensive about another cavalry raid. But then Duryea was always nervous when he was deskbound and surrounded by the bustling headquarters apparatus that inevitably grew up around a commanding general when he stayed in one place for a day or two.

He had been confined to headquarters for too long, Duryea thought, as the artillery firing died away. Jumpy as a cat.

Duryea was thin, ascetic, scholarly; he combed his dark hair straight back, wore neither beard nor mustache on his chiseled face, and in civilian clothes might have been taken for a minister or teacher. But Duryea was comfortable only when in the field; he was confident only when alone, unhampered, doing what he did best, what no one else could do for him.

He longed to be at it that moment. The night before, a signal officer from General Banks, reporting personally to Pope, had been assigned to share Duryea's tent, although Duryea hated proximity. The close presence of others made him irritable, and when he decently could, he spread his blankets well away from his noisy staff companions.

But the unwelcome visitor had brought news. Gossiping in the dark, he had repeated to Duryea what he had come to report to Pope—that from a signal station near Waterloo Bridge a large enemy force had been seen moving on the Federal right by way of Amissville and up the Rappahannock, beyond Carter's Mountain.

"Thirty-six regiments of infantry, Duryea. Some cavalry and four six-gun batteries. At *least* four."

"Going where?" A force that large was no mere raiding party.

"Your guess as good as mine." The visitor's voice was trailing off into sleep. "But they warn't out for exercise."

That had not been soporific news; and all that day, as Duryea had worked to improve Pope's inadequate maps with information from patrols and engineer observations, the ominous Reb column had been on his mind. It was Duryea's business to know such things as where that column might be going. Pope's maps were important, of course, but that marching column could be fatal.

So the real root of Duryea's nervousness was those thirty-six regiments, moving as clearly in his mind as if he were perched on a hillside with a glass, seeing their actual passage. Beneath Duryea's donnish haircut, his eyes were opaque, inscrutable; beneath his neatly fitted uniform, he was wiry and tough as the dogs that, in another life, a world away in Vermont, he once had bred and trained for hunting. When he came back from his long and solitary forays, his reports on enemy forces and positions, on terrain and possibilities, were so informed and useful that Colonel Russell, Pope's chief of staff, usually sent him right out again. It was bad luck that the map job had caught him just when the Rebs apparently were making some move he needed to see for himself—the only person Micah Duryea trusted.

"Oh, Duryea. I was hoping to find you."

Startled, the captain looked up from his maps at a figure standing in the dark doorway. No lights had been lit in the broad upper hall.

"Who's that?"

The figure came forward into the dim circle of candlelight. "Cass Fielding. I looked in your tent."

"Working a little late." Duryea put down his pen reluctantly. He had little use for Lieutenant Fielding, whose thin voice he should have recognized; it grated on Duryea's nerves.

"Did you see Crook's parade?"

"Been at this desk all day."

"Some sight."

Fielding invited himself to sit on an upended packing crate that was serving as a stool for another camp desk. He leaned back, clasping an upraised knee with two fat hands; his face, with its sharp nose and chin trying to meet over his mouth, was just beyond the circle of light, but Duryea caught an occasional glint from his spectacles.

"I mean I never saw troops drill like that Thirty-sixth Ohio marched today."

"Um." Duryea wanted to finish the map he was updating and call it a night, then go find out if there was news of that Reb column marching in his mind.

"Precise. Like a machine, Duryea. I'm going to feel better with a guard like that around here."

"I guess so." Though in Duryea's opinion, precision drill was what any headquarters guard did best. That was how it got such a plum job. What would make *him* feel better would be a proven fighting unit.

"I...uh...was wondering. You hear about that Reb column they spotted yesterday?"

Other than for the grating voice, Duryea disliked Fielding for what he considered the lieutenant's unwarranted nosiness. Nothing more than a headquarters clerk, a quill pusher. Duryea had noticed, too, that Fielding never got farther from the headquarters camp fire than he could help. But he was always poking around where he had no business, asking questions that shouldn't have concerned him, making people nervous. Fielding was like one of those old women in small towns who want to know everything about everybody, for no real purpose but to be knowing. Duryea had no intention of telling him anything—particularly not military information he might not otherwise know.

"What column was that?" Maybe Colonel Russell would let him go and find out where those Rebs were headed.

Fielding described the Rebel force the visiting officer had told Duryea about. In the lieutenant's telling, it had grown to forty-six regiments and a whole division of cavalry.

"Don't know a thing about it." Maybe he could get started tonight.

"Well...ah...just trying to figure out...you know, where they might be going. You got the maps, haven't you?"

Before Duryea could lie, they heard a stentorian voice from the lower hall:

"Fielding? Fielding, goddammit!"

Colonel Russell's voice always made Duryea think of an alligator's roar. He had never heard an alligator roar but he was sure the sound would be about as awesome.

The lieutenant bounded off the packing crate. "Gotta go." He trotted across the room. "Coming, sir...coming!"

Though he sounded—to Duryea's satisfaction—frightened by the roaring colonel, Cass Fielding was only annoyed to be interrupted, just when he had the gullible Duryea ready to hand over the maps. Fielding had long ago learned that Colonel Russell's bark was worse than his bite, even if the colonel had dared to get rough with *him*. But the lieutenant was always careful to show proper deference, even fear, if that seemed useful. Fielding knew the value of being underestimated by pompous West Point knuckleheads. Or professors like Duryea.

Colonel Delancy F. Russell, General Pope's aide and confidante, was waiting for him at the foot of the steps, a sheet of paper in his hand.

"At the double, Fielding. Copy this into the dispatch book and get it off."

He thrust the paper at the lieutenant, glaring unnecessarily over the mustache that drooped like a pair of horses' tails around a mouth that barely concealed prominent, yellowing, and constantly aching teeth.

Fielding went to his own camp desk in what once had been, he supposed, the formal sitting room of the abandoned house. Except for having been interrupted in his "research," the lieutenant did not mind the sudden summons to work. He had no stomach for the shooting war; and for his place on Pope's staff instead of somewhere in the line, he could thank a father from Illinois who was important enough not to be ignored by a President from Illinois. But Fielding had discovered in himself a sharp brain for the paper-and-map war waged from army headquarters, and to which as a copy clerk he had just enough access to whet his appetite for more.

The letter was headed "7:00 p.m." and was from Pope to Major General Fitz-John Porter, who was still on the way overland from the Peninsula army, via Fredericksburg. After instructions for Porter to hurry his movement to the vicinity of Warrenton Junction, Pope outlined the disposition of his other troops—Buford's cavalry screening Waterloo Bridge, McDowell's Corps in the Warrenton–Waterloo–Sulphur Springs triangle, Reynolds in Warrenton itself and Sigel nearby, Banks at Fayetteville, Reno at Warrenton Junction. Heintzelman's Corps was there, too—10,500 of McClellan's Peninsula veterans who had joined Pope just that day, only an hour or so earlier.

But the really interesting part to Fielding was Pope's description of the Rebel forces he believed he faced. As Pope saw it, Lee had moved his main body to the Rebel left, up the Rappahannock, the van well past Waterloo, until Lee's front faced roughly east rather than north. That put him in position to send wagons into the Valley to the west and provision himself from there.

But also, Pope wrote, Lee had pushed "a strong column still farther to his left toward Manassas Gap Railway in the direction of Salem." That was the column Fielding wanted to know about. But even Pope apparently had no knowledge, the sharp-eyed Fielding deduced at once, of where that "strong column" might have gone from Salem. Supposing it got that far.

One other sentence gave Fielding something to chew on:

Franklin, I hope, with his corps will by day after tomorrow
night, occupy the point where the Manassas Gap Railroad
intersects the turnpike from Warrenton to Washington City.

That was at Gainesville. Did that sentence suggest that Pope
thought the commander of the mysterious Reb column might be
crazy enough to come that way, where Pope could fall on him
with his whole army?

The back of Fielding's neck tingled. The sentence might mean
that before long the Rebs would have the whole Union Army
coming down on 'em like a fox on a henhouse.

Not unnaturally, Mrs. Dabney Williams was excited. Seventeen
crow's-flight miles—many more by Virginia's crooked dirt roads—
northwest of John Pope's barnlike headquarters at Warrenton Junction, she was serving a lavish dinner to the commanding general
of the Army of Northern Virginia.

Verna Williams's country house near the hamlet of Orleans
was a long way in more than distance from Pope's echoing quarters. War had little touched her foothill region, under the Blue
Ridge misty on the western horizon, although Sigel's Germans
had recently been a few miles away at Sperryville, and Banks at
Little Washington. Not far from the Williams house, Stonewall
Jackson's troops had gone swinging along in the noon sun, just
the day before.

But Verna Williams's parlors were furnished in style, her floors
were polished until they would reflect a face, her silver and crystal
gleamed in the candlelight, and her table linens were snowy as
her daughter's powdered arms and bosom. The Williams house
was an island of comfortable living in a sea of war; except for
the faraway rumble of cannon from the direction of Waterloo, no
shot had been fired in anger within hearing distance of its red-
brick walls or its ordered gardens, the special joy in the pastoral
life of Verna Williams.

She well knew, of course, that the man in the gray uniform at
her right was the savior of Richmond and the Confederacy. But
that flustered her less than his personal grandeur. She could think
of no other word. As the servants came and went with ham,
chicken, spoonbread, and fresh vegetables from the truck garden,

she thought she had never seen a man of more self-possession or finer looks—though, like the officers with him, his uniform, hair, and beard showed lingering dust from the day's march. General Lee, she thought, might be a great soldier; he was unquestionably Virginia's first gentleman and a man of exquisite courtesy; but he appeared to her more than those things—cold, quiet, grand, and far distant, somehow, from the convivial table where he happened to be physically seated.

At the moment, the general appeared absorbed in the chatter of Verna's Cousin Alice, seated on his right. Cousin Alice could talk the ears off a donkey. She could spin out Richmond chat and family blather for hours on end, but Verna suspected that General Lee could listen politely—even converse, when it became necessary—with some detached part of his consciousness, while continuing to ponder his own concerns in private.

She turned to General Longstreet on her left. "And have you been in our beautiful Rappahannock County before, General?"

Longstreet was intent on his plate, which had been filled a second time. An entirely different breed of cat, in Verna Williams's opinion. She watched him chewing stolidly on a piece of ham. Not a Virginian, obviously.

Longstreet was rather short and heavyset, with massive shoulders, a high forehead, and eyes too narrow in his face to be attractive. Unlike Lee's, his beard was unkempt, growing down to the second button of his uniform coat. He seemed a strong man, dependable. It was wonderful, she thought, to have such men protecting southern tradition. With motherly instinct, Verna noted that a button was missing from his coat.

But Longstreet remained silent, chewing on his ham. In a somewhat louder voice, Verna repeated her question. The general immediately put down his fork and answered pleasantly: no nearer than Manassas the summer before. In faint embarrassment Verna realized the man must be a little deaf. All those terrible guns booming in his ears.

". . . and so," Colonel Tatum was saying at the other end of the table, "we have to allow for the fact that a brigade of four regiments with six hundred men each, you give'em proper spacin, they'll take up a thousand yards of road, mighty near."

"Think of that."

Dabney Williams had no more idea of the extent of a thousand yards of road than of the distance to the moon. But he felt at last a part of the war. Imagine these great generals in his house! He hadn't even known the legendary Jackson was in command of the troops moving by the day before, until he'd been told so right here at his own table. Now Lee and Longstreet were eating his victuals. Nothing more notable had happened to Dabney Williams in the fifty-seven years he had lived in that house his father had built.

Major Jesse Thomas sat back in his chair to Dabney's left. "Not that we can put many six-hundred-man regiments on the road."

Dabney did not know that he had heard an implied rebuke from an officer of Longstreet's fighting force to the rear-echelon impracticalities of a headquarters Brahmin.

"Lucky they average three hundred."

Colonel Tatum, one of Lee's closest aides, spoke with the authority of a man who had spent many an hour poring over morning reports. Apparently he had not caught the rebuke either; Tatum was not one, Thomas decided, to pick up nuances and implications. He seemed like a man of requisitions and receipts. If it was not on paper, Tatum probably would deplore, maybe even ignore it.

But here in civilian comfort, the portly colonel also talked too much, in the opinion of Major Thomas, who would have been in the line rather than on Longstreet's or anyone's staff had he not suffered a hand and wrist cleanly severed by solid shot at Blackburn's Ford the summer before, while he was waving his sword in the air to rally his company of raw troops. Of course, their host was harmless enough, but just the sort to blab everything he'd heard to the first acquaintance he saw—which was a good way to let the cat out of the bag for Pope's spies.

"Did y'all hear what Stuart did?" Captain Franklin asked. He was seated between Tatum and the Williams daughter, Miss Letty.

"Well, after they captured ol Pope's dress uniform at Catlett's Station, they dressed up a nigguh boy in it, sat'im on a mule, and paraded'im right through Warrenton!"

Major Thomas was carefully rationing his glances at the powdered bosom that swelled above Miss Letty's pink bodice. Too long in the field! he rebuked himself halfheartedly.

"Headquarters in the saddle!" Captain Franklin drove home his punchline as laughter erupted around the table.

Pope would never live that down, Major Thomas thought. Assuming his first command in the east, the Federal general not only had bragged in a proclamation to his troops about the achievements of the western armies; he was reported to have headed the proclamation: "Headquarters in the Saddle." Who could resist the conclusion that he had his headquarters where his hindquarters ought to be?

But Major Thomas was less interested in Pope's bluster and Stuart's childish jokes than in Tatum's loose talk. The major had not himself known, until the colonel had blabbed it a few minutes before, that Pope's dispatch book, as well as his dress uniform, had been snatched during Stuart's raid on Catlett's Station. He doubted that even Longstreet had known what Lee had learned from the Federal general's correspondence; but Tatum had spilled that, too.

"I'd-a like to seen that nigguh." Dabney Williams sat back happily as the laughter died away. "Wearin Pope's uniform, I mean."

Major Thomas had listened with a mixture of fascination and disapproval as Tatum expansively described the captured letters to the pop-eyed Williams. The letters disclosed, so Tatum said, that Pope had been ordered to hold the line of the Rappahannock until McClellan's Peninsula army, some of it marching overland from Aquia Creek, some coming down from Alexandria by the O & A, could reinforce Pope's Army of Virginia. In fact, when the dispatches were written—before August 22—some of McClellan's veterans already were near enough to Pope, Tatum had confided, "to see is camp smoke, mighty near."

". . . ought to cut up that *wicked* man's uniform for bandages," Miss Letty was saying patriotically to Captain Franklin.

So by the time Lee had read the documents on the 24th, Major Thomas calculated, some of those reinforcements from McClellan probably had reached Pope. Which meant that Lee might already have failed in what must have been his central purpose in moving the army from Richmond to Gordonsville and concentrating it against Pope's so-called Army of Virginia. Obviously Lee had intended to fight Pope singly, before he and McClellan could join hands in a force Lee could not hope to match.

"And what do you think, Major . . ." Dabney Williams's soft voice pulled him back to the table. "Of the fightin qualities of all these Yankee people trampin round our state?"

Major Thomas appeared to ponder the question, but he was really thinking: no wonder the Old Man sent Jackson around Pope's rear, just a day after reading those captured dispatches. He was obviously trying to flank Pope off the Rappahannock and pull him away from the reinforcing columns marching from Aquia. That would be like Lee. Hoping to the last for some chance to whip Pope alone, before McClellan—who'd proven on the Peninsula to be as slow as grass growing—could get up the heft of his forces.

"They fight like the devil, sir." He nodded emphatically at Dabney Williams. "Even Pope, far's I can see."

"Alexander." At the other end of the table, Verna Williams had raised her voice only slightly but a nigger in a tailcoat rushed to her chair. These Virginians make the monkeys jump, Thomas thought.

"Too hot in here, Alexander. Open the French doors, please."

The breeze Alexander admitted flickered the candles; it was fresh and cool, like the mountains westward in the darkness. The major thought for a moment of the blazing heat of the day just ended. No relief likely tomorrow. But he could not enjoy the breeze for wanting to be on the road again. Heat and dust be damned. Maybe generals could be as calm as mules in the traces, but as for Jesse Thomas—the stump of his arm was itching, the way it always did before a fight.

"I de*clay*uh," Miss Letty said, "that ol Pope must be the *meanest* Yankee they could find. Threatnin to burn down folks' houses'n shoot innocent people!"

And it would be a hell of a fight, Thomas thought, watching her bosom swell. If Tatum was right that Pope in his dispatches had put his own strength at 45,000 men, not counting any additions from McClellan, Lee was not much better than even to start with. Thomas knew—though he was not about to tell Dabney Williams—that Longstreet had brought no more than 30,000 men from Richmond to Gordonsville.

"... unheard of in civilized warfare," Colonel Tatum boomed.

After six days of operations along the Rappahannock, Longstreet now had maybe a thousand fewer effectives bivouacked in the fields around Orleans or with Dick Anderson's rear guard at Waterloo. Jackson, having also suffered losses at Slaughter's Mountain and in the Rappahannock fighting, could not be leading more than 20,000 troops up ahead.

"I was graduated with Pope at West Point." General Longstreet put down his fork decisively, the way he did everything. His strong voice easily stilled all the others at the table. "Handsome, dashin fellow. Sat'is horse beautifully. I b'lieve he stood at the head for ridin, but didn't apply himself to his books very much." He chuckled hoarsely. "Bout as much as I did. I reckon he maybe even knew his lessons a little better."

"What class was that, sir?" Captain Franklin's voice trembled with respect.

"Forty-two. Quite a class, Gin'al." Longstreet spoke now to Lee, who nodded gravely. "Harvey Hill. McLaws. Dick Anderson. Earl Van Dorn. On our side. Over there . . ." Longstreet jerked his head over his thick shoulder. "Rosecrans. George Sykes. As well as Pope. Oh—Abner Doubleday, too."

"Gin'al Lee, you could command quite an army out of that class alone." Tatum looked to the younger officers at the table for approval of this banality. They nodded vigorously.

Not a real winner in that whole crowd, Thomas thought, except Longstreet himself. Maybe Harvey Hill, except he was too damn prickly. Anderson was bad to drink.

General Lee looked sternly about the table and spoke quietly but with finality. "Pope must be suppressed."

Thomas had heard the Old Man was outraged at Pope's orders to his army, particularly one decreeing death for any person within Federal lines who communicated in any way with Confederate forces—an order under which indignant southerners liked to say that a Virginia mother could be shot for writing a letter to her soldier son.

"Don't worry, sir!" Lieutenant Buchan of Longstreet's staff leaned forward to look reverently down the table at the commanding general. "When your army gets through with Pope, he'll be on the other side of the Potomac raisin dust!"

Not likely, Thomas thought, despite the approving laughter in which even the taciturn Longstreet and the dignified Lee momentarily joined. Not if McClellan gets up with Pope before we do. And those documents Tatum had prattled about had apparently shown Fitz-John Porter among those on the way from Aquia Creek to Pope's left flank. Porter's Corps they all knew from Boatswain's Swamp on the Peninsula. Hard fighters. Which meant there was damn little time left to hit Pope alone. Crush him.

Miss Letty was thrilled by Lieutenant Buchan's outburst. She nevertheless thought it marked him as not much more than a schoolboy playing at war. The major at the end of the table, his sleeve neatly pinned up to conceal his missing hand, was something else. His probing dark eyes, the clipped mustache flecked with gray, his soldier's bluff speech, had attracted her at once. Happily, she had worn a dress that he obviously found attractive.

Miss Letty leaned forward, perhaps farther than necessary, to begin a conversation with him. But Cousin Alice, with that bland indifference that marked so many ladies either too high-born or too hopelessly out of the marriage race, or both, to weigh the effect of words—or perhaps only in the intoxication of her journey with General Lee through the family-tree jungles of Virginia—Cousin Alice just then mentioned the unmentionable:

"And is it true, my dear General, that that rascally Louie Marshall—your own nephew—is on this awful Pope's staff?"

The old nanny goat knew very well it was true, Miss Letty thought, since it was the talk of every Virginia living room. She determined to ask her mother to send Cousin Alice packing to Letty's aunt in Lynchburg. The next day.

General Lee nodded sadly. "I could forgive the boy's fighting against us . . . but not his joining Pope."

In the awkward following silence, Major Thomas decided that the commanding general was downright unnatural. Longstreet was phlegmatic as a Dutchman, but Lee! Lee could make decisions risking the most appalling dangers, then go about his business with no more hint of strain or worry than if he had merely sent out for a barber. And for sheer guts, Major Thomas doubted if he or anyone had ever seen the beat of Robert E. Lee.

Here was the Old Man, with his army divided in the face of an enemy who could operate on interior lines and with a force about as large as his own—and maybe tens of thousands of men stronger by now—with no guarantee that Jackson was not at that moment being cut to pieces somewhere on the other side of the Bull Run Mountains, or that he and Longstreet could ever be brought together again. And Lee sat there as if he were still maybe the superintendent at West Point, making polite talk with a rude old crone about his scamp of a nephew.

"Majuh, I b'lieve the cat must of got yoah tongue." Miss Letty, perhaps trying to dissociate herself from cousin Alice's tactlessness, leaned toward him enchantingly.

"Why, no, ma'am." The major allowed himself for the beat of his pulse to take full advantage of the view. "I reckon I'm just not much of a hand for talk." Their eyes locked and he imagined he saw in hers a glint of interest that stirred him powerfully.

Colonel Tatum, who knew Lee far better than Thomas did—well enough to know that no one knew the general well—was under no illusion that the Old Man was undisturbed. Certain little signs—the overly attentive courtesy, the elaborate civility of the small talk, the carefully modulated voice—indicated iron self-control, not repose.

"Oh, I spect you could tell some stories that'd scare me to *death*, Major Thomas."

"Ma'am, I'd surely never do that."

Nor was Tatum himself as garrulous as Jesse Thomas thought. Tatum had been talking, in fact, not for Dabney Williams but for the specific benefit of Major Thomas himself, who had influence—if anyone did—with stubborn James Longstreet.

Tatum knew the undercurrents and sensibilities of the army as well as anyone, better than most. He knew Longstreet was not among Stonewall Jackson's admirers. Ol Pete, as his troops called him, remembered too well Jackson's delay on June 26 and his failure at White Oak Swamp, when others talked about his brilliance in the Valley. And Longstreet was as conscious of his own reputation as anyone else; he did not appreciate Jackson's greater—and he thought undeserved—fame.

None of this shocked Tatum; at 54 he was a veteran of life and of army politics. But he did not want Longstreet to be in any doubt about the gravity of the moment. He did not want Longstreet in a mood to let Jackson sink or swim, over there to the east, wherever he was. If Lee was too careful of his subordinates' touchy sensibilities to make such things clear, Everett Tatum would do it for him without a qualm. Major Thomas was the best instrument at hand, and Tatum wanted him primed.

Alexander put a slice of pie in front of Colonel Tatum. Rhubarb, the colonel could tell by the aroma and the color.

"Mistuh Williams, I'm just liable to move right in here, you folks eat like this all the time."

"Well, not evry day, I reckon." Dabney Williams's hospitality was an obvious matter of pride. "But we'd be right happy to have you, long's you want to stay."

"Ah, me . . . this terrible war."

But Colonel Tatum's mind was not really on Dabney Williams or even the succulent rhubarb. He was thinking, instead, of what he knew also preoccupied General Lee, behind that calculatedly unfurrowed brow. Would they find Pope dug in at Thoroughfare Gap, between Jackson's advanced corps and Longstreet's relief column?

If so, nothing could save Ol Jack and his troops but that Providence in which he and Lee might put their trust, but which in Ev

Tatum's view concerned itself no more for the outcome of battles than for the turn of a card.

At the other end of the table, Verna Williams was feeling all right again, now that the breeze was moving in the room. She felt vaguely unpatriotic at having grown so faint at her own table, in such company, for such a reason. Praise be, no one had seemed to notice, since it was the odor that finally had just about turned her stomach; and since that was the one thing she could not conceivably have mentioned, even if—after all these great men had endured—it was understandable that the highest generals of the Confederacy and their aides smelled bad.

Not just horse-bad, either. Most men smelled like horses most of the time. The sad truth was that these generals under their hastily brushed uniforms needed a good bath—and as for that hoteyed major in animated conversation with her daughter, if it weren't for his poor mangled arm Verna would have had Dabney turn him out of the house for staring like a ruffian at innocent Letty's bust.

The first train escaped. Puffing into Bristoe just after Munford's cavalry had swarmed over the place at sundown, the engine *Secretary* came rattling around a curve at high speed, scattered the ties Stonewall Jackson's butternut troops had hastily piled on the rails, and sped on for Manassas with only a few bullet holes to testify to its daring. That meant the Federals soon would know an enemy force was in their rear.

Jackson was displeased. He brought up his engineer officers; and just past the depot, where an embankment plunged down steeply on the north side of the track, they found a siding switch. Shooting away the lock they opened it halfway, to derail following trains. There was not long to wait, as captured Yanks had readily volunteered that several more trains were coming, on their way back to Alexandria from Pope's line of operations.

Darkness had fallen by the time the next one rounded the curve, its headlight beam probing ahead like a plump, cautious finger. The engineer, obviously unwarned, came on at undiminished speed. As the big locomotive lunged past the small station building, Fargo Hart had a quick flashing memory of the contorted face of the engineer of *Vulcan*, glaring back at him in the light of burning wagons at Catlett's, four nights earlier.

As the locomotive and the first few cars cleared the station,

Forno's infantry poured a thunderous volley into them. *Useless useless* Hart thought; but around him on a knoll to the rear of the troops, his milling colleagues of Stuart's and Jackson's staff raised a cheer. Stuart himself was dancing with excitement. As their high-pitched yells rang out above the crash of musketry and the iron clanking of wheels and couplings and the pounding steam of the locomotive, its front wheel truck, just ahead of the huge drivers, hit the opened switch.

The great black engine lurched to its left. For a moment, its snout seemed to bore like a gigantic auger into the earth and cinders of the embankment, throwing lengths of rail and ties into the night, like matchsticks scattered by a careless hand. Then the cab and the front of the tender rose majestically from the track, as if they were the hips and rump of a monster plunging to its knees. With a wild scream of twisting metal, a hellish white blast of escaping steam, the locomotive toppled on its side, down the embankment, still chewing forward into the ground. The tender and the following car plunged down on top of the black mass of metal, the leaping flames from the broken firebox.

The second car, its couplings twisted loose at either end, shot out into the air and sailed as serenely above the wreckage below as if it were a horse taking a fence. Just beyond the long, smashed barrel of the locomotive, the flying car landed nose first and splintered itself against the unyielding earth. Objects that might have been bodies hurtled from the wreckage.

Another car, and then another, still a fourth toppled over the embankment, piling up wreckage until the top of the steaming heap of shattered cars rose level with what seconds before had been the roadbed of the O & A; and as the following cars crashed into the jagged rising mountain of wood and iron, the wreck itself finally put a screeching stop to the onrushing cars.

Some, near the front, were telescoped into those ahead. Farther back, they slanted across the track, half on and half off, in zigzag precision, like a flight of steps toppled on its side. As the train at last lay smashed and motionless and the popping of Forno's muskets faded into the night, an appalling, echoing silence fell on Bristoe Station. A dying hiss of steam from the buried locomotive, the agonized rhythmic squawk of a lone wheel turning slowly atop an overturned car, sounded the train's death rattle. And as even these sounds faded into the night, Hart heard the soft voice of Ol Jack, somewhere behind him, unnaturally raised:

"Good . . . good . . ."

"Capital!" Stuart shouted. "Better'n a circus!"

Then the cries and groans, the occasional shrieks of the wounded began to leak like dripping blood from the cars in which they had been returning to the hospitals in Alexandria. Forno's men got as many out as they could. From the wreckage beneath the embankment, of course, there was no escape. Probably anyone in there, Hart told himself, would be dead anyway. Still—as he helped organize the rescue work along the track—he could not help but shudder when flame began to lick up through the wreckage from the locomotive firebox at the bottom. And just then the whistle of another train, coming fast, sounded beyond the curve.

Forno's officers shouted orders; the butternut troops began to stream down the embankment, back to their stacked rifles. An engineer officer ran for the rear of the train carrying a long heavy splinter from one of the wrecked burden cars. He swung it vigorously against each of the two red lamps burning on the last car, miraculously still erect on the track, just before the headlamp beam of the oncoming train began illuminating the curve.

"Get the rest of the wounded out of there!" Hart shouted.

But no one heeded. Stuart was with Jackson fifty yards away and out of hearing, the two of them casting ominous shadows from the flames beginning to burn brightly up through the wreckage below the embankment. Apparently the station building hid those flames from the engineer of the approaching train because there was no sound of screeching brakes or vented steam.

Hart spurred Mercury toward the station, with wild thoughts of somehow stopping the imminent crash, the crushing of the wounded men in the cars already lying crazily across the tracks. But as quickly as the thought flickered in his brain, he knew it was as useless as Forno's musket fire. He pulled up Mercury as the engine thundered toward the station building, sparks flying from underneath its lean black silhouette.

Then the headlamp's beam fell on the tangled wreckage blocking the track. The engineer hit his brakes and his whistle simultaneously. Hart's eardrums were blasted with the sharp hysterical scream of metal locking, wheels gripping rails, steam escaping through the whistle's tightened throat. Too late.

The long pointed ram of the speeding locomotive ploughed under the rear car of the wrecked train and threw it up in the air like a jackstraw. It came down on its side across the roof of the locomotive cab, just as the ram ploughed at only slightly diminished speed under the next car, upending it so that the barrel of the locomotive chewed on through it like a gargantuan drill, and smashed into still a third car.

These massive blows had been transmitted to the cars ahead, each adding its own weight against that of the next, so that at the front end of the first wrecked train, the cumulative impact shot two more cars off the embankment and onto the spreading pile of burning wreckage. The next, which had been slanting across the track, tipped on its side and skidded like a sled into the darkness beyond the leaping flames.

The second locomotive, its own cars buckling and flipping behind it like a deck of dropped cards, destroyed the four rear cars of the first train and telescoped three into two ahead of that, before it came to rest in a mammoth tangle of splintered wood and grotesque metal shapes. The car that had been tossed on top of it balanced on its precarious perch, wobbling a little from side to side, like a huge, incongruous seesaw.

All around Fargo Hart exultant Rebel yells were going up again. Men leaped and whooped and waved their hats in the rising fire-light, and Forno's troops popped their puny muskets at the sky. Hart could not hear, amid the celebration, the cries—if any—of broken and crunched men in the wrecked trains. But he knew the men were there and again he began organizing troops to find them in the wreckage and pull them out. But he had hardly begun the grisly work when someone shouted:

"Bastards gettin' away . . . there they go!"

In the flickering firelight, Hart saw a man running back along the track in the direction from which the trains had come. Just then, another man scrambled from the second train's caboose, which was still upright, and also ran back along the track. A few Reb muskets cracked but too late; both fugitives disappeared past the wall of darkness at the edge of the firelight.

Scarcely thinking what he was doing, Hart turned Mercury's head and galloped after the two men. For a moment, he welcomed escape from the tangled wreckage, the licking fires, the groans and screams that at any moment would have begun to assault his ears and being. Then he realized that he was risking his tired horse's limbs and life, galloping along a railroad bed in the dark-ness; and besides, what would he do if he caught up to the two fleeing trainmen and they fought back?

The last thing Hart wanted was to cause more bloodshed, more destruction. So he pulled Mercury gradually to a halt; and as the hoofbeats slowed into silence, he heard for the first time another train coming on. The glow of its headlamp began to reflect from the curving track ahead.

Hart's first instinct was to wave the train down and warn its engineer about the fiery fate waiting at Bristoe. In the next instant, he knew that that was only the sane and civilized thing to do, only a humane impulse; it was not war. It might even be treason, in the inverse world of Ol Jack—although treason to what value, Hart could not say.

Indifferent to these considerations, the train came on, the light from its headlamp expanding toward him along the track. Then he realized the locomotive was slowing, exhaling its giant breath at longer intervals, its brakes beginning to squeal, iron on iron. The two fugitives, or others from the first train, must have managed to signal the engineer. Hart felt a vast relief—whether because there would be no new pileup of wreckage or because he had been spared the moral choice between stopping the train and doing his soldier's duty, he could not be certain.

He sat motionless on Mercury's stolid back as the blurry light, slowing all the while, crept on toward him along the track he now could see. Just as he sensed that the glow had begun to illuminate him, just before the headlamp itself could appear around the curve, the train stopped with a last iron shudder of wheels on the track.

For a long moment, an eternity, with the unseen locomotive breathing hard in the darkness up ahead, Hart, unmoving in the dim light, felt himself apart, alone, as if he had been picked out by some unknown authority and made to sit there exposed against the darkness all around. And he knew, when the engine with a great pant of its steaming breath began to push backwards, withdrawing the cruel edge of light, letting him slip back into the common invisibility, that he would not so easily escape judgment. He *had* been picked out; he had set himself apart. And therefore he would have to answer for the warrior spirit that surged in him, too; he would have to answer, if only *to* himself—who, alone among men and whatever gods might be, had no capacity for mercy to the accused.

Slowly the locomotive picked up speed, moving backwards and away; and as if to celebrate its survival, a long blast of its whistle shrieked across the scrub woods that screened it from view. Hart could not help wondering if *Vulcan* was escaping again, defiant and mocking and just beyond his reach.

•   •   •

The telegram from Manassas reached the headquarters of General Pope at Warrenton Junction just after 8:20 p.m. In Pope's ground-floor room in the abandoned house Colonel Russell was stretched out on the commanding general's camp cot, his hands behind his head and his legs spread to keep his boots off Pope's blankets. He was thinking, as he had been off and on all day, about that damned Reb column.

Pope himself had gone down to the telegraph key at the railroad station but the colonel knew the general's thoughts, too, had been on those troops moving . . . where?

Whatever their goal, of course, Lee's main body was likely to follow; and reports had been coming in all day that the whole Reb army was sidling to its left, up the Rappahannock. But if Pope only knew where the detached column was finally heading, he could destroy it before Lee could rejoin it with his other troops. Or maybe Washington could send out a force to fall on the Reb column, while Pope went for Lee.

Russell damned, not for the first time, Pope's lack of adequate cavalry. No eyes, he thought, no damned *eyes*. Even John Buford, the cavalry commander and one of the best, couldn't do the job with inexperienced troopers and worn-out horses.

Russell swung his legs to the floor. Grunting—his lower back, after so many days in the saddle, hurt as badly as his teeth—he pushed himself to his feet and picked up McDowell's report from Pope's table. McDowell might be a little schoolmarmish but he had judgment. Pope and Russell had been suspicious at first of the loyalty of a man who had once commanded the whole eastern army in the field; but they had learned to rely on Irvin McDowell, who had reported that day:

> What is the enemy's purpose is not easy to discover. Some have thought he means to march around our right through Rectortown to Washington. Others think he intends going down the Shenandoah, either through Thornton's or Chester Gap. Either of these operations seems to me too hazardous for him to undertake with us in his rear and flank. Others, that it was his object to throw his trains around into the valley, to draw his supplies from that direction and have his front looking to the east rather than to the north.

That last *had* to be the answer, as Pope had written Porter. Especially since the pesky Reb cavalry had grabbed Pope's dispatch book at Catlett's Station. Lee would certainly have concluded from those dispatches that, with McClellan's troops coming from the Peninsula, Pope would be too strong any day now to be attacked with good hope of success. Still . . . Lee hadn't hesitated to pitch into McClellan's whole army on the Peninsula and had come near destroying him. In the Old Army, Bobby Lee had been considered primarily a staff man; but that summer in Virginia he'd shown himself a fighter.

Russell drew a thick gold watch from his pocket. Eight twenty-three. Just then there was a clatter of hooves in the yard, then the sound of boots on the porch of the echoing empty house. The front door slammed. John Pope's unmistakable brisk stride—more of a stomp—came down the hall.

The portly general flung open the heavy double doors of the old dining room as if bounding on stage for a theatrical. He stared at Russell over the stump of a cigar protruding from his beard. His eyes were excited, his face a little flushed.

"You seen a ghost?"

Russell had been with Pope a long time. He knew such a moment required him to provide a foil for Pope's dramatic instincts.

"Russell . . ." The deep voice paused dramatically. "Everything has failed."

"What's failed, General?"

Pope waved his arm in a wide sweep toward Washington. A piece of paper fluttered in his fingers.

"All those promises. All those reinforcements. Hah!"

As if flinging down a gauntlet, Pope thrust the paper at him. Russell seized the telegram from the plump hand.

Manassas Junction
August 26, 1862

Major Genl. Pope:

Engine Secretary fired on at Bristoe. Smashed barrier and reached here. Conductor believes secesh cavalry to attack Manassas

No signature. Cut the damn wires, Russell thought. Suddenly his teeth ached viciously. He looked up from the unfinished telegram into Pope's hot, red-rimmed eyes.

"That Reb column was headed through Thoroughfare for the

O & A, Russell. Bound to be their cavalry already there."

"But maybe it's just a raid like on Catlett's. Maybe..."

"Heintzelman's sending a regiment by the cars to see. But I tell you, Russell..." Pope flung his dusty hat on a table and dropped into a chair. "I *know*. That column we been trying to track... now we know where it is."

Russell sat back down on the general's cot. A Reb force of thirty-six regiments, maybe more, in their rear! They'd have to fall back on Fredericksburg.

"And I'll tell you what else I know, Russell." Pope paused to let silence heighten the moment. The colonel knew he was not expected to break the spell. "If Franklin had been at Gainesville, even at Centreville, the way we had every right to expect... we were *assured*... he'd have intercepted those Rebs coming down from Thoroughfare. They'd never have got to the O & A. But Franklin isn't there, Russell. He *can't* be, if they're at Bristoe. We were fools ever to expect it."

Russell did not remind Pope that only an hour before he had written Fitz-John Porter that he expected Franklin at Gainesville, *the day after tomorrow*. The colonel was well aware that neither he nor the general had expected anything like a sudden descent by Lee on their rear; but he was just as well aware that John Pope would not be pleased to face that fact.

"So everything's failed," Pope said again, almost as if in satisfaction. "All those reinforcements they promised me aren't there, Russell. They weren't meant to be. If they had been..." He flicked his hand contemptuously at the telegram in the colonel's hand. "*This* couldn't have happened."

"You mean you think they deliberately held back..."

Pope raised his hand dramatically, to halt the inquiry—but not the thought, for a shrewd old army man like Russell could hardly avoid the general's implication. Suddenly, his aching teeth, his tense back, seemed to redouble their assault on his nerves. What reason, Pope was asking implicitly, would George B. McClellan have to hasten forward reinforcements for a rival general, to help that rival cope with the same Lee who had driven McClellan from the Peninsula? And who would the President be forced to turn to, to save Washington, if John Pope's Army of Virginia should be isolated, caught, and crushed by Lee?

"General, if you're right, and I reckon you may be, the safest thing for us is to slip down the Rappahannock toward Fredericksburg. Join up with Porter and the others there from the Peninsula."

"Hah! Maybe the safest. But look at your map, Russell, look at your map. That'd leave Washington wide open for Lee to march in."

Or for McClellan to save, Russell thought. "But, General, the Peninsula army's . . ."

"How do *we* know where McClellan is? All *we* know is Franklin . . . Sumner . . . Cox . . . Sturgis . . ." Pope enumerated them on his fingers. "They aren't where *we* were told they'd be, helping *us*. Even Porter . . . where's Porter for sure? I tell you, Russell, we're on our own. We don't even have a telegraph wire up the O & A to Washington anymore."

Russell stared at the incomplete telegram in his hand, forgetting for once his insistent teeth. On our own, he thought. Against Bobby Lee. A big Reb force in our rear. No reinforcements we can count on. The railroad cut, the wires down.

Delancy Russell was neither imaginative nor cowardly. But for the first time in the war he felt a small, chill touch of personal fear; and for the first time in an ambitious career, as he looked across the room at John Pope—angry and bristling in his camp chair—he did not wish to be in his superior's place.

And if *I'm* thinking *that*, Russell thought, what's *he* thinking? He realized, then, that as well as he had thought he knew Pope, he had no real sense of the inner man; he had no idea what Pope was *thinking*. But he did know what the general was going to say, even before Pope cocked his handsome head defiantly and glared at the ceiling.

"So we'll *fight*'em, Lancy. If we're on our own . . . we'll fight, by God!"

In what had once been the Spartan yard offices of the Orange & Alexandria Railroad, Colonel Herman Haupt sat in an undecorated room at a littered but businesslike table overlooking the switching yards in Alexandria, just across the Potomac from Washington. Everything seemed unnaturally quiet after a typically frantic day. In the yellow light of oil lamps he shuffled reports, telegrams, requisitions, orders—each of which could tell him something, however insignificant—trying to make enough sense of all the bits and pieces before him to form a decent idea of John Pope's situation out there in the darkness and silence of Virginia.

Colonel Haupt was bone tired. He had been called back to Washington less than two weeks earlier for his second tour of duty as Superintendent of Military Railroads. Since then Haupt had slept little and been constantly in action, not under fire (he sometimes regretted) but as constantly engaged with men and machines (he was never quite sure which was most satisfying to manage properly) as if he had been in the forefront of battle itself. So the colonel felt himself near exhaustion, when the message clicking in from Manassas Junction purged the fatigue rudely from his bones.

J. H. Devereaux:

> No. 6 train, engine Secretary, was fired into at Bristoe by a party of cavalry—some say 500 strong. They had piled ties on the track, but engine threw them off. Secretary is completely riddled by bullets. Conductor says he thinks the enemy are coming this way.
>
> McCrickett, Dispatcher

When Devereaux, the yard superintendent, handed this telegram to Haupt, the colonel thought instantly: *on Pope's lifeline.* Then, with a kind of grim satisfaction of which he was not proud: *I warned him. I tried to tell him.*

"Not a wheel moving," the Assistant Secretary of War, Peter Watson, had wired Haupt in explanation of the colonel's recall to take over the railroads. Watson had had enough of Pope's arrogant attempt to manage the railroads through the Quartermaster Department, which did not know a track switch from a car coupling.

Haupt's first move after his return, therefore, had been to visit Pope on the Rappahannock to work out a command agreement with the general. He'd found Pope seated under a tree that overlooked the Rappahannock valley and some of the country beyond—green with summer but brooding, too, under the shadows of war.

The general had an open and genial manner, and did not seem at all the blustery braggart Haupt had been led to expect. Pope's face was pleasant, with a broad forehead and a long brown beard. He spoke in a strong, carrying voice, and his constant cigar seemed almost a part of his features. To Haupt, the only discordant note was a certain look of well-fed sleekness about Pope's form and countenance. The man seemed too comfortable for a general in the field, Haupt thought.

Pope, too, it developed, had had enough of Quartermaster bungling and readily agreed to yield Haupt all the authority he needed to keep the Army of Virginia's supply trains running on the O & A. As they talked, numerous messengers came and went, most reporting orally. Haupt listened with his precise engineer's mind and thought he detected a pattern: Reb wagons, most of the reports stated, were moving up the river, north by west, toward Pope's right flank.

Haupt had asked Pope how far up the river his scouts were posted, and the general, puffing his cigar, showed him on a map spread across his legs.

"Is that far enough, sir? What's to prevent the enemy from going as far as Thoroughfare Gap and getting behind you?"

Pope smiled at him with his cigar still clenched in his teeth.

"No danger, Colonel. No danger."

Well, I tried to tell him. Now, days later, God alone knew what was happening out there on the rolling plains around Manassas, so close that a regiment could march it in one hard day—yet, for all Herman Haupt or anyone in Washington knew of events, as far away as the moon. Had he been a cursing man, he would have sworn at the darkness that shrouded Virginia, the vast silence that enveloped the armies moving somewhere on its dusty face.

But Haupt was not a man to waste time in vain reflection. Quickly, he forwarded the message from McCrickett, the reliable station manager at Manassas Junction, directly to the War Department Telegraph Office, which would rush it to Henry W. Halleck, General in Chief of all Federal armies.

To Halleck, Haupt added on his own:

> The engine Secretary was being followed by four other trains, which are in great danger, as there is no communication. The wire is cut between Manassas and Warrenton. We have transportation for 1,200 men. This number might be sent to Manassas to protect the road while we repair it. I suppose the bridge at Bristoe will be destroyed.
>
> H. Haupt

That the Manassas–Warrenton Junction wire was cut was merely supposition but Haupt did not hesitate to make it, since he had a high regard for the Rebs' tactics. Nor did he shy from suggesting to the general in chief that 1,200 men might be sent to Manassas. Herman Haupt was used to taking responsibility, giving orders, and seeing that they were carried out.

Perhaps from his West Point education, more probably from the vast projects he had conceived and supervised as a widely sought railroad construction engineer, Haupt had an air of quiet authority. A thin, straight mouth, piercing eyes, and dark eyebrows that slanted in and down in an ominous V toward a sharp nose gave him a look of barely controlled anger. In fact, he was of even disposition; but men sensed that Herman Haupt was not to be trifled with, or lightly frustrated; and they soon learned that he usually knew what he was talking about.

Now, after getting off his message to Halleck, Haupt peppered his operators along the line of the O & A with requests for information. He sent Devereaux to round up the latest reports on the power and cars available at Alexandria. By 8:50 p.m., he could wire Halleck again—but not with welcome news:

Major-General Halleck:

In addition to the transportation for 1,200 men, some other trains are coming and are this side of Manassas. We may have in a few hours transportation for 3,000 or 4,000 men. They can be advanced as far as possible and then marched forward.

I am just informed that the four trains following the Secretary are captured, and that the Rebels are approaching Manassas with artillery. These may be exaggerations, but the operator and agent are leaving and prompt action is required. It is unfortunate that a portion of our force did not march. I await instructions.

H. Haupt

And just ten minutes later:

General Halleck:

Operator at Manassas just says: 'I am off now sure.' I directed the agent to run the two engines at Manassas forward, wait until the last moment, and then escape on the engine if real necessity existed. Operator had just commenced message to headquarters of General Pope when wire was cut. It is clear now that the railroad can be relied upon only for supplies. No more troops can be forwarded. By marching they will protect communication: in cars they are helpless. Our capacity by this raid will be much reduced.

H. Haupt

He hovered anxiously over the instrument, fuming at the usual slowness of the general in chief, until at 9:25 "Old Brains" as Halleck was irreverently called—answered:

Colonel H. Haupt:

General Smith, General Slocum, General Sturgis, or any other general officers you can find will immediately send all the men you can transport to Bristoe Bridge or Manassas Junction. Show this order.

H. W. Halleck
General in Chief

Not Sturgis, Haupt thought. Anybody but Sturgis.

The mere name symbolized to Herman Haupt the petty jealousies and arrogant personalities that plagued the army. Four nights before, one of Haupt's trains had been fired upon by a Rebel raiding party at Catlett's Station, well in Pope's rear. A mounted Reb had ridden beside the locomotive *Vulcan*, fired his pistol and hit the engineer, one D. D. Morgan.

But Morgan had opened the throttle and the train had pulled away before the Reb could leap from the horse into *Vulcan* and take over. Morgan did not know what might have happened to several trains running behind him, some carrying wounded from the Rappahannock, or if the Rebs had fired the Cedar Run bridge after he crossed it.

"Lousy shots." Morgan defiantly held up the arm in its bloody bandage. "Nuthin but a little Reb buckshot. Sides, I poured whiskey on'er."

And taken a little internally, too, Haupt saw. He would ordinarily have disapproved of one of his trainmen imbibing alcohol; but he was too good a leader to rebuke a man who had saved his train and deserved his toddy.

Haupt surmised that the Rebs at Catlett's Station had been cavalry raiders, striking quickly and running for cover. But what had happened to the trains coming behind Morgan and *Vulcan*? Had the Rebs bottled up or wrecked them? Hours passed with no word. The superintendent became more and more worried.

Finally, Jed Turner, conductor of one of the missing trains, strode angrily into the yard office, lantern in hand. All the missing trains, he reported, had run safely past the Rebs, who had been prevented by a heavy rainstorm from firing the Cedar Run bridge near Catlett's. But just four miles outside the Alexandria yards all the trains had been stopped by General Samuel Sturgis of McClellan's army.

"The devil you say!" Devereaux banged his fist on Haupt's desk. "What's he think he's doing?"

Turner shook his head. "Four mile I walked in here'n the dark'n I aint figgered that out yet."

Haupt had immediately made his way by handcar to the halted trains and found Sturgis's nearby headquarters. Though it was then not long before dawn, the general received Haupt from the comfort of an armchair just outside his tent.

"Glad you came, Haupt. I just sent a guard to your office, arrest you for disobedience my orders to transport my command." He swept an arm imperiously to the west.

"Well, I wish you could, General. Maybe I could get a little sleep if you did."

Sturgis eyed him a bit blearily. He was slurring his words and Haupt thought that the general might have been taking a dram or two of D. D. Morgan's favorite medication. "Sugges'in I *can't* arrest you, Colonel?"

"I'm suggesting you'd be taking on more responsibility than you probably want. Some of those trains are loaded with wounded. The surgeons have been waiting hours in Alexandria. And this holdup of yours means serious delay in reloading cars with troops and supplies going out to General Pope."

"Pope!" Sturgis fell back in his chair as if he had been shown a snake. "I don't care for John Pope a pinch of owl dung!"

Haupt had argued that Sturgis had no authority to take over the trains, but he could make little impression on the belligerent general.

"Don't care for old Pope a pinch of owl dung," he insisted, savoring the phrase. "Not a pinch, Haupt!"

Only when Haupt obtained an order directly from Halleck for Sturgis to release the trains had the ridiculous impasse been broken. And from it, Haupt had taken a bitter impression that, every day since, he thought he had seen confirmed.

Around him near Alexandria, 70,000 or more of McClellan's troops, returned from defeat and stalemate on the Peninsula, were in camp not more than a day's march from Pope's presumed field of operations. But McClellan and his generals were in no hurry to send forward help to their rival Pope and the Army of Virginia. One of their tactics was to wait on railroad transportation that was mostly needed for moving supplies and wounded, when troops could have been marched to Centreville or Manassas in a day.

Sturgis alone had been the cause of a day's delay in moving 10,000 men out to Pope. No wonder Assistant Secretary Watson once had cautioned Haupt in a laconic dispatch: "Be as patient as possible with the generals. Some of them will trouble you more than they will the enemy."

But now someone would have to act. Brooding over the information he was receiving and passing on to Halleck, Haupt knew they were not dealing this time with some rain-spoiled cavalry raid like the one on Catlett's Station. Out there in the Virginia darkness, along the lifeline O & A, the Rebs had captured or cut off four trains and were moving on Manassas with artillery. A strong force was in Pope's rear; McClellan's army would have to respond. And armed with the order just received from Halleck, Herman Haupt aimed this time to brook no interference from any gold-braided popinjay.

"Devereaux, put some trains together. As many as you can. I'm going to find troops."

"I'll get the trains but you won't get the troops." Devereaux was an able railroad man but a pessimist about the army. "All the generals'll be at Willard's bar. Or worse."

"I'll find somebody."

And Haupt meant to. But his recent experience with Sturgis grimly underlined Devereaux's warning as the colonel set out, this time on horseback, for the army camps scattered around Alexandria.

The lantern he carried was of little help in the unbroken darkness; and to his orderly engineer's mind, the various bivouacs seemed to have been flung down in the countryside without reason or scheme. It was near midnight, after much tedious riding and numerous fruitless requests for directions, before Haupt at last found a picket who pointed out the faint yellow glow from Franklin's Sixth Corps headquarters tent.

When he entered, Haupt could hardly believe his luck; he found—not Sturgis, thank heaven—Brigadier General Winfield Scott Hancock, the corps' senior officer, present. Hancock, a tall young man who looked like a fighter, was relaxed and open-collared, chatting with another brigadier. Haupt wasted no words.

"General Hancock... the Rebs are across the railroad near Manassas. Troops must go out at once."

He handed the youthful general the order from Halleck, confident of a quick response. Hancock had made a reputation on the Peninsula, and the mere fact that he was there with troops, not carousing in some Washington sinkhole, suggested that he was ready for action. Briefly, Haupt told him what he knew of the night's developments.

"Whatever these Rebs're doing at Manassas, General, the main thing now is to hold the rail bridge over Bull Run. If they've burned Pope's stores, we can't bring'em back. But if they destroy that bridge, it could be a death blow to Pope. Because we can't replace whatever he's lost until we rebuild it."

"My brigade's near the track," the unknown brigadier said. "I can have'em ready to board in an hour."

Hancock nodded decisively. "So ordered, Taylor. Get moving as soon as you can and report back as much information as you can."

Taylor snapped to attention. "What about an attack, General? If there's a good chance."

"Only if there's a real opportunity. Hold that bridge at all costs and don't go looking for trouble."

Haupt thought General Taylor's face fell a little. That vaguely troubled him as he followed Taylor out of the headquarters tent; but he was elated at Hancock's fast action. No quibbling, no squabbling.

By camp-fire light, Haupt watched General Taylor mount a fine bay with white stockings up to the knees on its front legs.

"Trains'll be ready one hour from now, on the main track south of Alexandria yards, General. Put fifty men to the car and a guard force on the front end. Tell'em to keep their eyes open for an ambush."

Taylor looked down at Haupt impassively. "We'll be ready, Colonel." The horse pranced, as if eager to get at the job, and Taylor quickly steadied him. "If we get lucky, maybe we'll even bring you back some of those Rebs that cut your wire."

Arriving at Manassas with Stuart, whose headquarters group he had rejoined rather sheepishly, Fargo Hart looked about as best he could in the abysmal darkness of an August midnight, broken only by the light of pine-knot torches. The black shapes of warehouses stretched away from the tracks in neat lines. On the sidings, long trains of cars stood in what seemed to be endless ranks. They had captured, Hart saw even in the fitful light of the torches, a vast Federal storehouse beside which that at Catlett's Station had been small potatoes.

Just before 9 p.m., the Twenty-first Georgia and the Twenty-first North Carolina, under General Trimble, had set out up the tracks of the O & A for Manassas Junction, four miles northeast of Bristoe. Stuart's horsemen swept around the infantry on a road parallel to the rail line. About midnight, under this combined assault, the junction was taken after little more resistance than had been seen at Bristoe.

"Brothers," rumbled the Reverend Major Allen to no one in particular, "the hand of Providence has blessed this night's work."

Hart doubted that Providence had even noticed. As meticulously as if he were returning from a day's ride over his ancestral tobacco fields, he first saw to Mercury's needs. Then he spread his blankets on the railway station loading platform, on which many of Stuart's officers already had dropped heavily into sleep and where the Reverend Major Allen was rolling his bulk into a buffalo robe. Hart stared for a moment at his ponderous maneuver, then stretched himself at full length on the hard and uneven platform planks.

So the Reverend Major got that robe. Some Reverend.

But Hart was tired after nearly forty-eight hours without sleep, and depressed by the spectacle of the trains smashed and burning; he did not want to think about the Reverend Major.

He lay back in his blankets and silence fell over Manassas Junction, the warehouses, the trains, the sleeping soldiers who had slumped to the ground almost before the firing had ceased. It was a silence so deep and unbroken, except for the natural night noises of insects and the wind whining in the dangling telegraph wires, that Fargo Hart could almost believe there was no war, that he was alone under the immense sky, in a secret place of solitude and peace, where he need never lift his hand against another man or feel death a menacing companion on the march. But as he clasped his hands behind his head and gazed up at the reflected glow of the burning wreckage they had left at Bristoe, Hart knew the quiet was momentary. Those redly lit skies would alert every Yankee brigade within miles.

Below the loading platform, a pair of infantrymen passed complaining on their way to relieve the pickets Trimble had set up.

"Know what this place smell like?" one asked.

"Can't smell a thang cept hawshit."

"Smell like prosperity round here, Jimbo. Dam'fit don't."

Their voices chattered away in the night. *Yes prosperity.* Food and saddles and blankets, shot, shell and rifles packed in grease. Prosperity for Ol Jack, prosperity as real as the red sky of destruction over Bristoe. Buildings burning, woods aflame from shellfire, bridges fired or blown to make rivers impassable, the tools to wreak such havoc—all were as much a part of warfare as death and pain. Denying those trains to Pope, destroying them, doubtless had been as useful to the Confederacy as, say, killing or capturing a Yank brigade. Maybe a division.

But how narrow the gap—Hart thought—between barbarism and the destruction and carnage that civilization accepted as a necessity!

Colonel Snowden, lying beside Stuart farther along the platform, arose and pissed noisily over the edge.

"Look at that sky," the colonel murmured, apparently to no one. "Purty as a picture."

He buttoned his trousers, farting in two breezy blasts, and returned to his blankets, muttering like a far-off grumble of artillery.

In the silence of General Hoke Arnall's tall old house in Duplin County, North Carolina, Amy Arnall slipped out of bed and went to look at her son, Luke. Amy often rose at night to make sure Luke was all right; it seemed to her that it would be all too easy for a little boy to smother himself, or choke, and make so little noise that no one would wake. She would have removed Luke's bed into her own room, except that the General thought such pampering was nonsense. He wouldn't have his son spoiled by a fretting mother, he'd insisted.

Everything seemed all right as Amy went to Luke's bedside. His breathing sounded normal. But she thought the sheets were pulled up too far over his head. Carefully, she turned them down around his shoulders; and there, brilliant eyes icelike in its triangular head, the snake lay black and evil by her son's sleeping body. A tongue darted at her like a tiny spear...

Amy sat straight up in bed, wide awake, terrified, the shock of the dream drenching her almost immediately in perspiration. Still shaken, she jumped out of bed and threw back the single sheet she slept under in the summer. Nothing. She hurried to Luke's room, wondering how, after such a dream, she could bring herself to look under his covers; but he'd already kicked them off and lay peacefully sleeping.

The snake dream was the end of sleep, which for the last few days had been fitful anyway. Dawn found Amy wide-eyed and tense, and the first faint glow was as welcome to her as a neighbor's voice would have been, or the sound of the General's laughter. She was not ordinarily a nervous woman, though she loathed even the thought of snakes. As the wife of a professional soldier—she had married the General when he was only a lieutenant—she was more accustomed than many her age to solitude, common as it was now that war had swept off husbands and sons and fathers and cousins.

Nor was Amy alone in the tall old house that looked out over the fields of Duplin County. The General's father, Judge L. Q. Arnall, was asleep across the hall, as was his namesake and grandson, little Luke. And in the yard, there were forty-two Africans—soon to be forty-three when Chessie's baby came. Chessie'll have to stop workin' soon, condition she's in.

Amy tossed her head on the pillow. Worryin bout Chessie first off, she told herself in exasperation, when for all I know she'n the rest of 'em might be right this minute gettin ready . . . but that's crazy. They'd never . . .

Still, Easter the cook *had* been strangely quiet these last few days—not her usual loud self. And Pettigrew, the driver . . . if anybody in the yard had anything in mind like what had happened at Lakeview, Pettigrew was the one who'd know how to manage it . . .

"Stop it."

Amy heard her own voice hollow and faint in the high-ceilinged old room where once she had slept dreamlessly, resisting daybreak with its new round of trials and responsibilities. In those days—so recent yet so long ago—even Pettigrew's bleak disdain had seemed merely an affectation, an insolent reminder of his responsibility and station, and her inability to manage without him. But since Lakeview, everything seemed changed.

Amy crept from beneath the sheet, glad the night was over but reluctant to face the day. Not good light yet but already she knew it would be another hot one. She went across the room in her nightgown, bare feet silent on the polished floor that Judge Arnall's father had laid down himself, when Jefferson—the Judge never failed to say—was still in the White House.

Approaching the window cautiously and from the side, mainly because she was conscious of her nakedness under her nightgown, but also just in case, Amy peered anxiously into the morning light, to the east, where before long the glaring August sun would rise into a bone-hard sky. Dew lay thick and glistening on grass browning with summer. The old trees that shaded the house looked limp and weary, as if borne down by the burdens of heat and years. Amy decided, with the grim humor that sometimes annoyed the General, that she felt much the same.

Amy loved the view from her window at Sycamore—or once had thought she did. In the spring, the breeze stirring her curtains would be laden with the scents of violets, crabapple, roses; and the dogwood and Flowering Judas and spirea, the one big snowball bush at the corner of the house, mixed their whites and reds and yellows as if in an exotic quilting pattern. In the fall, the dogwood and the oaks turned brilliantly from green to gold and scarlet, later to the sere browns of the coming winter; and even in North Carolina Amy could expect once or even twice a year to rise to a pure and undisturbed blanket of white across the lawns and the drive and the fields beyond, to drifts of snow running like ermine trim along the branches of the gaunt trees and the top rails of the worm fence enclosing the Judge's house and lawns.

But this summer . . . Amy flinched at the window, crossing her arms over the heavy breasts that embarrassed her, gripping her shoulders as if chilled, even in August. Since Miss Tippy's death at Lakeview four days earlier, especially since the whole horrible story began to come out in bits and pieces, nothing had seemed right. Since the first word that Miss Tippy had not, after all, just died in her sleep the way 75-year-old ladies could be expected to do, Amy could not look out her window, or move about the quiet halls of the house, without dark consciousness of what, for most of her life, she had willed herself to ignore—that over every southern landscape, no matter how beautiful, and every southern hearth, no matter how gracious, hung a pall of sadness and shame and fear, not less real for being concealed under layers of sophistry and custom and defiance.

That summer, after what had happened to Miss Tippy, Amy had had to concede to herself that the African slaves in their numbers and demands cast shadows on life at its core—as if these dusky creatures, their deceptive smiles and chatter masking their inscrutable secret enduring reserve, were mirrors reflecting the dark sides of their masters and mistresses, the sides that could countenance involuntary servitude and barter humanity for no real reason of necessity but from simple inability either to admit wrong or to imagine how to right whatever wrong might be sensed, even if not admitted.

Amy hated slavery. She knew now that she had always hated it, though she had been reared, unprotesting, in its habits and attitudes. She hated slavery for its wastefulness, for the sloth and indifference it could induce in master and servant alike, imprisoned as they were in a mutual dependency neither knew how to change or could imagine life without.

She hated slavery for its burdens, for the endless unceasing tasks of birthing and rearing and feeding and clothing and housing and nursing and disciplining a dependent people, when a single good laborer could have been hired for less than the upkeep of an African and his wife and his sickly mother and his unproductive children.

She hated the institution, as the Judge called it, for the duty it laid on every southern woman—each of whom Amy believed to be a secret abolitionist—to be kind and loving in the never-ending care of people to whom it would have been easy to be cruel, because nothing but self-interest and self-respect prevented the cruelty inherent in power.

But Amy hated slavery most of all for the corruption it fostered—the black faces with the unmistakable, indelible markings of the old Judge in their features. Or there would be a man with his fingers, even a grandchild with his way of moving—or perhaps it was the Judge's *father's* blood still running in their veins. She hated what slavery had made of southern men, even of the General's own forebears, turning them into careless patriarchs surrounded by wives and concubines and the children of both, all in the same house and yard.

She hated, too, the hypocrisy of a society that would banish one woman for the least hint of impropriety or scandal, while easily tolerating the most debauched behavior in another, so long as the latter was black and aproned and a slave. Amy hated slavery for the lust it encouraged and the lust it exposed—the most wanton corruption, she thought, of all.

In the growing light over the yard, she could see Penny coming from the cabins—ranged like a village behind the Judge's house—

across to the kitchen, with characteristically flaunted hips. Not fifteen years old and before another year was out, Amy guessed, she'd be midwifing the shameless little monkey.

She turned away from the window, disturbed at the thought; at least the Judge was too old and drunken and Luke was too little to be drawn in the night to the depraved promise of those swaying hips. And the General, even when he wasn't off in Virginia doing a soldier's duty, was not like that; the General was as horrified as she at the casual immorality in the village behind the house, let alone the abhorrent thought of a white man seeking his pleasure there (although even the General, the most honorable man she knew, yielded to the common hypocrisy in his stone-faced refusal to notice or in any way concede that the blood of his own forebears was visible in his own yard).

As if to remind her that the General, too, had his weakness, as he called it, Amy felt suddenly the faint, throat-filling nausea she had suffered every morning for a week—no, six days, she carefully counted. And her monthlies overdue. Might's well give up hope. She knew the signs too well; any woman would. For a moment she was furious at the General; but at least his weakness had nothing to do with the likes of Penny or Chessie. At least the General knew the difference between a slut and a decent woman.

Amy climbed back into her bed, under the sheet she had embroidered herself in a pattern of entwined roses. Bess would be in soon with warm water for bathing and the usual glass of milk. For a moment, she wondered what the General was doing, right that minute—up and about, if she knew him, and turning out his men for the drill he said was a soldier's saving. At least he would be drilling them if there was no battle, although she knew from his letters that in Jackson's army battle was a daily possibility. Amy tried not to let herself think about battle, which even as a soldier's wife she could scarcely imagine.

Instead, she thought of the General as he had been on his recent leave, filling the house with his presence, his strength, the force that had seemed to grow in him unbounded since he had received his star. After all those years he had spent in the West—with promotion, he had told her, seeming as far away as the actual stars in the heavens—he was proud of his command, of his troops, of himself. As she was proud of him, and the name he was making.

She stretched luxuriously in the feather bed, her fears of the night suddenly distant and unreal in the morning light beginning to fill the room. Just the time of day the General was at his most passionate, waking tousled and sleepy-eyed, reaching for her with his big, strong hands.

That last morning of his leave was when it had happened; Amy was sure of that. And for a moment, there in the soft bed still redolent of his big body, his long legs, it was as if he were over her again, enfolding her, his avid mouth hot on hers, his huge maleness insistent; when she had felt his seed flooding warmly that morning, she *knew;* could not fail to know, feeling the hot lost idiot surge of her own body draining his, her own weakness rising to his . . .

Amy put her hands over her face, to hide its flush and the dismay she thought must be written upon it at such unbidden memories. As if she were Chessie or Penny. No wonder the General . . . if he sensed in her what she was all too dreadfully sure might be there, beneath the cool demeanor she believed out of her whole life and training that it would be worse than dishonorable to betray . . . no wonder he was so weak in that way. Men being as they were about women, only women could maintain proper standards. White women.

Amy Singleton Arnall could not easily accept that perhaps she had not always done so. To concede that would have done too much violence to her rigorous sense, not just of propriety and morality, but of womanhood itself; it would have brought her too near the animal level on which she believed Penny and Chessie existed. Anger flashed in her again at the mere idea; she would, in the future, simply put down whatever weakness she might feel, even if it brought conflict with the General. She would resist him, conquer weakness, as a decent woman must.

Nausea rose in Amy's throat again until she thought she would have to run for the chamber pot; but it would pass quickly, as her morning sickness always had, first with poor stillborn little Hoke— as they had planned to call him—later with Luke. But her anger was not so fleeting. How *could* the General have been so . . . inconsiderate? So insistent. He *knew* she had been told not to risk another pregnancy, even if she had wanted more children. He knew that, and yet . . .

But Amy was a willful woman; she would not let herself think about weakness again. She sat up in bed, the sour taste of nausea in her throat, coldly angry at the General, her plight, at fate, life, the war, the Judge's house and its responsibilities, and because the one thing no woman could do was to walk out on it all.

A woman couldn't go off to war, die gloriously, or live for a cause. A woman had to stay home and deliver babies, manage things, even—she thought with a sudden flashing return of the night's unease—even if she was essentially alone in the middle of an African village, miles from any other white person strong enough to protect her, or from any help at all. And Amy knew Pettigrew, not she, really ran Sycamore and managed its people. What if he should turn on her?

The door opened a crack. Amy sat up straighter.

"I'm awake, Bess."

Bess put her shoulder against the door and it swung back almost to the wall. She was a tall mulatto, powerfully built, with strong hands and features that looked as if they had been chiseled from oak; as far as Amy could tell, there was nothing of the Judge or the Arnall family in her face or her movements. Amy could not have abided that, to be waited on by a woman who might have been the General's half-sister, or his aunt, or some other unspeakable relation. As it was, Bess was strong-minded, sometimes a bit sullen, but usually reliable, a willing worker. Amy was careful to humor her for best results.

But Bess was not bringing the usual pitcher of water and glass of milk. Instead, she struggled through the doorway carrying a mattress of rough ticking; it drooped over her bare stalwart arms like a drunken dancing partner. Bess peered above it at Amy with a look of determination.

"I done made up my mind, Mistis. Y'ought not to stay in a room by y'self, times like dese'n no man about."

Amy was astonished, then terrified. Bess must have heard something. She *knew* something. "What is it? Bess . . . what's goin on?"

Bess dropped the mattress under the window; it settled to the floor with an expiring *whump*.

"Em nigguhs." Vast contempt brimmed in her deep voice. "All at talk inna yard."

"What talk?" But Amy knew. Fear stroked coldly across her heart.

Bess went across the room to the door. "I be right back, Mistis."

The door stood ajar behind her. Amy stared at it in dread. What were they saying in the yard? Did they know what had happened at Lakeview? Who would have smothered an old lady in her bed, a woman the whole county knew was the soul of goodness? Never even raised her voice, let alone her hand, to the laziest African in her yard, and spoiled them all like so many children.

Bess came back, carrying sheets. "Ain't talk about nuthin else since it happen, em nigguhs aint." She dropped the sheets on the mattress.

"Do they . . . does anyone know . . . ?"

Amy could not bring herself to ask; but Bess understood and made a disdainful face.

"Em nigguhs aint know nuthin cept when to eat'n lie down. Jes talk-talk-talk's all dey do."

"It's so hard to believe . . ." Amy was reassured that the yard knew no more than she. If Bess was telling the truth. ". . . that any of her people would hurt Miss Tippy."

"I get some milk."

Bess's voice was toneless, her face impassive, as she left the bedroom again. Amy looked at the mattress under the window, the sheets dropped carelessly across it. She realized, rather uncertainly, that she did not want Bess sleeping in the room with her, probably snoring and invading what little privacy she had. But Amy did not know how to tell Bess that; she did not want to offend Bess, who took offense easily. Besides, if Bess thought . . . but it was hard to know what Bess really thought. Or Pettigrew. Or any of them.

Bess returned with the milk and warm water, putting the glass on the bedside table and taking the pitcher to the little dressing room next door. Amy watched her moving silently across the polished floor and the throw rugs they had hooked, working side by side.

"Jes talk." Bess brought a robe from the dressing room and laid it out at the foot of the bed. "But talk put notions some folkses heads."

Amy stared at her in cold terror, exerting all her will power to control herself in front of a servant, as she had been trained always to do—even to keep her hands under the sheet, rather than to clutch her throat in fear.

"What notions?" Her voice was little more than a whisper.

"Donchew worry none, Mistis. I be here, keep you safe."

Bess's strong hands straightened the robe. Amy watched them involuntarily, seeing just such hands—ruthless, implacable— bringing the pillow down over Miss Tippy's peaceful sleeping face and the gray hair that had stood up on her old head like dingy tufts of cotton. Except Amy had also heard that someone had smothered her with a folded quilt.

"I gotta soul t'be saved, Mistis, I gone guard you wid it."

"Thank . . . thank you, Bess."

But as Amy turned back the sheet, her eyes fell on the glass of milk. Easy to put something in it. Maybe some kind of ground-up root or berry they'd know about. They could do something like that anytime.

She forced herself to rise to face this horrid new knowledge, as well as another demanding day. She knew it was too late to tell Bess, without total rebuff, to take the mattress from the room. But as Amy's bare feet touched the floor, distrust touched her heart; those powerful hands could as easily kill her as protect her, in the darkness and solitude of night.

Amy's knees nearly buckled at the thought, made plausible by a lifetime of belief that the people in the yard cloaked truth in deception as blithely as they laughed or sang. And it was only that same lifetime, with its ingrained habits of superiority and the obligations of behavior they enforced, that enabled her to stand upright and take the robe from Bess's lifted hands.

Chapter Three

August 27

WHEN THE SUN came up yellow and murderous in the cloudless sky above Manassas Junction, Ol Jack's troops could hardly believe their luck. Warehouses, stretching in orderly ranks for hundreds of yards away from the tracks, were stuffed with every conceivable luxury of food and clothing, and equipment. Loaded cars stood like sheep to be shorn on the sidings and up the right-of-way of the Manassas Gap Railroad, which intersected the O & A at Manassas Junction—more than two miles of cars in all, according to Quartermaster Lieutenant J. M. Fullenwiler of Arnall's Brigade, Hill's Division, whose passion for exactitude led him to pace off the distance.

Before the dew was dry on what little grass had been left alive by months of tramping Federal feet and ironbound Federal wheels, the smell of bacon and coffee was rising above Manassas like a cloud from paradise. For miles back along the line of march to Bristoe and beyond, hungry butternut troops sniffed those glorious odors and quickened their step.

To the end of their lives, the men who were with Ol Jack at Manassas Junction on August 27, 1862, never forgot the treasures that had fallen into their calloused hands, or the day on which they found them. Warehouses and cars alike were overflowing with supplies of every description, for here Colonel Herman Haupt, with the diligence of a squirrel preparing for winter, had pushed forward the stores that would be needed when McClellan's army joined Pope's in the great juggernaut meant to grind overland to Richmond.

When General Jackson arrived at the head of his main force shortly after sunup, he took a quick look at the rich haul before him and gave two orders. One set out Trimble's and some of Taliaferro's men as guards around the warehouses and loaded cars. The other was for all whiskey and spirits, save what could properly be designated as medical supplies and carried off in ambulances, to be destroyed.

The first of these orders was as a mote upon a mighty river. Stuart's cavalrymen were already stuffing their saddlebags before Trimble's men were posted. Hill's hungry troops, arriving before 10 a.m., pushed aside the guards as if they were not there. The Stonewall Brigade, among the last to arrive, had to be shepherded past the warehouses virtually at gunpoint, and at that with little success. From all units, stragglers swarmed around the goods like bees around a hive.

Privates Lott McGrath and Gillum Stone, blithely ignoring orders and guards alike, suspended a camp kettle over a fire and set about boiling a captured ham, while Private James F. Sowell made a huge pot of good presweetened Yankee coffee at the side of the same fire. Then Wagonload Weems, another private taking informal leave from whatever the Stonewall Brigade was supposed to be doing, arrived with a fifty-pound sack of beans.

"Git at goddam hunk of hog outen-a way." Wagonload was recognized as the company's premier forager; around its cookfires he automatically took charge. "Kin haul ham along raw. Jes cut a slice offen it to season these-yer."

Within minutes, Private Alonzo Rule arrived with a bag of potatoes and inquired, "Who the shit needs beans?" Weems having gone in search of other delicacies, Rule lifted the bean kettle off the fire and hung another one, shiny new from a warehouse nearby, and began emptying potatoes into it.

This affronted Wagonload Weems when he returned with a sack of flour slung over his shoulder.

"Gilly, goddammit, light off another far. I aim to eat beans'n fart 'Yankee Doodle.'"

But Gilly was helping Lott McGrath strip open a box of bagged dried vegetables. "I reck'n I must be in heaven, Lott." He ran his hands lovingly over the bags. "Nobody but angels eatin soup like these gone make."

"Hey, Sowbelly." Lott winked at Private Sowell. "Gilly aint et like this since'is mama's tit."

The main attraction for officers and men alike was the abundance of food Colonel Haupt had sent out for the Yanks—although Fargo Hart, like most of Stuart's officers, had exchanged his worn saddle for a new Federal issue of the excellent McClellan model. Captured documents listed 2,000 barrels of flour, 2,000 barrels of salt pork, 1,000 barrels of corned beef, 50,000 pounds of bacon. Uncounted bags of mixed sugar and coffee—in the Federal Army style—bulged the walls of one warehouse. Sutler's stores, of a variety unimaginable in the South, were stocked with everything from canned oysters to French mustard, Rhine wine, and champagne. Men who had had little to eat for two days, and not much for months on end, simply could not be held back from such riches.

But Jackson's second order was more successful. His officers, who did not want drunken troops on their hands, figured that *they* could salvage enough spirits for their own needs. The warehouse of liquor supplies was duly located, and under Colonel Channing's morose direction the barrels were carried out one by one, smashed with an axe, and their contents drained into the dry Virginia earth.

"Hurts worser'n earache." The colonel gazed thirstily at the rivulets of whiskey running off into the sand. "But I reckon they aint no choice."

Captain Thad Selby nodded vigorously. "Gin'al Jackson says whiskey's the ruination of good men." Selby's father thought so, too; and it would not have occurred to the captain to question either one.

"How would Jackson know? I doubt he ever tasted a drop in'is life." Channing was calculating his chances of getting away with a barrel for the staff, but he knew he could not keep that much hidden from the inquisitive general.

"Don't you believe it." Major Worsham, Jackson's favorite surgeon, stood nearby, glumly watching the destruction. "He knows, all right."

"Ol Jack? With all that God-fearin a-hissen?"

"Up'n the Valley. One night when we were runnin from Shields'n Fremont?"

"I aint likely to forgit."

"He was tuckered down to a frazzle'n so was I, so I mixed a couple of toddies and took'em in and told'im a stimulant was just what he needed. Even so, he takes maybe one sip, considers it a little, puts down the glass'n says to me, 'Major, do you know why I abstain from intoxicatin drinks?'

"Like you, I figure it's religion but I don't want to get into *that*. So he says, and I'm givin you his exact words, he says, 'Why, sir, because I like the taste of them, and when I discovered that to be the case I made up my mind to do without them altogether.'"

"Sounds like'im. Sounds just like'im." Channing sighed and gestured to a corporal standing by. "Bust in anoth'un, Fogarty. A sad day for the Irish."

Selby clutched his arm. "Colonel! Look at those men!"

He pointed toward three privates kneeling in front of the warehouse. One was trying to scoop whiskey into his cup from a trickle falling over a small rock outcropping; the others were trying to drink from the trickle itself.

"You men!" Selby's voice trembled with outrage. "Stop that! Get up from there!"

None of the three men so much as looked up from their frantic efforts. Selby started to stomp down from the porch but Channing closed a big farmer's hand around the lieutenant's bicep.

"Orders is just to pour the whiskey out, son. We're doin it." He nodded at the kneeling men. "All they can drink that way won't hurt'em—or Jackson neither."

He did not add what he really thought: that no men had ever more dearly earned a dram, let alone what they could sop up off the ground, after marching better than fifty miles in two days through enemy-held country in an August sun—all on top of a week of chasing Pope's tail on the Rappahannock.

Channing might not have been so tolerant of Sergeant Owen L. Cade had the colonel known that while foraging for molasses the sergeant had discovered a barrel of rum in one of the more remote warehouses. Cady sent someone to spread the word through Company D, Thirteenth Georgia, a regiment that had been detailed to forage for Lawton's Brigade, which was on rear guard duty with the rest of Ewell's Division. Company D quickly gathered at the barrel. The men, unfortunately, had already filled their canteens with molasses and their cups with sugar; but Cady quickly solved this problem with the discovery of a funnel no doubt used ordinarily to fill Federal officers' flasks.

"Awright, boys." He waved them into line. "One atta time. Grice, you draw."

Cady was the only man in Company D who knew Grice's name. The rest, for convenience, referred to him as the New Man, since he had been one of them for little more than a month, since the fighting around Richmond. Those who might have heard Cady call him Grice were not sure if that was a first or a last name.

The New Man bent over the bung, into which Cady already had driven a faucet with one stroke of a mallet. Cady drained the funnel in one pull, handed it to the next man, then swaggered along the line.

"No seconds till evry mother's son's had'is swig... Jonesy, keep sharp watch onna door ther! Your turn'll come."

That Cady uz alway in charge. The New Man drew another funnel-full, obediently waiting until the sergeant would give him his own turn. Handles men like Ol Jack hisself. Iffen Ol Jack ever drunken any booze.

At that moment, in sharp contrast, Private Alf Gurganous of Overholt's Battery, Jackson's old division, was an unhappy man. All morning, a Federal battery somewhere in the woods toward Bull Run had been throwing shells into Manassas Junction rather aimlessly, most falling short, few doing any damage. But the long-range fire had grown harassing enough that Overholt's Battery had been ordered out to silence it.

So Private Gurganous—riding into action in the No. 1 seat behind Matthew, on the left of the caisson ammunition chest—not only had been pulled away from a sumptuous foraged breakfast of boiled beef, beans, sugared coffee, and fresh-baked bread from the Union bakery, where Federal prisoners had been ordered to keep baking. He had also been deprived of the chance to inspect a pair of three-inch bronze rifled guns that had been found on a flat car in an ordnance train. Alf Gurganous remembered guns like that from the Peninsula, where the Confederates had learned to recognize them by the peculiar whistle of their shells.

A dedicated artilleryman, Alf did not know whether he most resented his unfinished meal or the lost chance to look over two really fine pieces, the like of which no butternut gunner had ever fired. The only compensation, and that a poor one, was seeing Ol Jack himself, riding hard by the caisson with the cavalry general, Stuart. Alf had seldom had a better look, though the old forage cap was pulled so low on Jackson's forehead that there was not much to be seen of his face but the flowing beard. Sets a horse peculiar, Alf thought.

He watched the two generals and several staff officers ride on ahead, dust rising from their horses' hooves. Then Cap'n Over-holt—Cap'n Overhaul, the irreverent gunners sometimes called

him, because he had them constantly working on the pieces and
the caissons, all the equipment, to keep it in top condition—led
the battery into an old earthen redoubt, on which grass and weeds
were beginning to grow. Gurganous and the other cannoneers
unlimbered, lined up their pieces behind the collapsing embra-
sures, and waited the order to load.

A hundred yards or more ahead, Alf could see, beyond a flimsy
gray curtain of dust, Ol Jack and his staff men sitting motionless
in a lane that led on across a flat meadow. Suddenly, as he peered
across this open plain, Alf was astonished to see blue infantry
swinging out of the woods that bordered Bull Run and forming a
battle line on either side of the lane. So *that's* what Ol Jack's
been a-studyin.

"Look ther!" Jeff Jernigan, the No. 2 man, pointed behind Alf.
A long butternut column was coming up behind them and to their
left, screened by the earthwork and the rise of ground on which
it had been built. "Aint that some of Hill's Division?"

"Look like it. Ol Jack must aim to hit'em Yanks over ther."

Alf turned quickly back to the bluecoats, coming on by columns
of companies spread across the lane. A sight of em. A whole
brigade, as near as he could make out. Paradin along fancy.

Just then Jackson wheeled his horse and the staff group trotted
back along the lane, left it and came across the broomsedge to a
position just to the right of Overholt's Battery. Hill's column,
meanwhile, had moved on to the left, reaching for the flank of
the oncoming Federals.

"Goddam Yanks is crazy." Jeff Jernigan shook his shaggy head.
"Fixin to git blowed to hell."

Jeff was resplendent in a new black hat, foraged from one of
the warehouses. Alf envied it but what he really wanted, if he got
another crack at the plunder, was a new pair of drawers to replace
the ones he'd been wearing since they left Richmond in July.

"Stiffer'n a preacher's collar," he'd complained to Jernigan.
"Even goddam lice can't hardly stand em drawers." He wished it
was true.

Captain Overholt quickly passed the order to load with spherical
case. Jernigan took the round from the five-man and placed it in
the tube. Alf rammed it home. But the Yanks were coming straight
on, quickstepping now, some kind of high muckety-mucks officer
out front on a bay horse. Alf thought he had never seen a wider-
open target—an open field of fire and a battle line coming on
with no artillery cover save the lone battery rumbling uselessly

beyond the trees. Range less than a thousand and closing fast.

Ol Jack took off his forage cap. His long hair tumbled about his ears. He waved the cap above his head and Overholt swung around to face his troops.

"Fire!"

Matthew, Mark, Luke, and John roared as one. The four case-shot shells exploded right over the first rank and spewed thirty-two musket balls each into the oncoming bluecoats. The mounted officer went off his horse in a blue crumple; the horse reared, knee-high white stocking on its forelegs flashing in the brilliant sun. Then the horse galloped away, empty stirrups flapping. A quarter of the men in the leading company had gone down, and a few on the right flank of the following company, which caught the edge of the spread of shot coming in at a slight angle.

"Jeee-hosophat!"

Jernigan's awed voice broke the echoing stillness. General Stuart, his horse prancing, swung his hat above his head and sang out something gleeful. But stepping over the carpet of blue that suddenly lay in the dust, the Yanks held their lines and marched on, as if toward a reviewing stand.

"Crazy aint the word." Alf swiftly sponged out Matthew's smoking tube. "Them sons're *dumb*."

But Jernigan paid him no mind. "My God, Alf . . . look at Ol Jack!"

Alf caught his breath. The general was riding slowly forward, alone, toward the marching Yanks still six or seven hundred yards away. Over his head he was waving a white handkerchief. For a moment Alf thought the whole world had turned upside down and Ol Jack was surrendering. Then he realized it was the other way around—the general was inviting the Yank brigade to surrender. Overholt's Battery alone was enough to cut them to pieces, and they seemed not even to have seen Hill's men forming on their right.

Ol Jack rode on, little plops of dust rising about the sorrel's feet, the handkerchief waving above the general's pulled-down cap. If this aint the beatenest, Alf thought.

A Yank in the leading company stepped out to the side, went down on one knee, sighted his musket carefully—Christ! Alf thought. Ol Jack's a goner!—and fired. Alf saw the puff of smoke from the long barrel before he heard the crack of the shot, hollow across the dusty plain.

A Minié ball cut the air—*wheeat!*—and Alf fancied he saw it flutter the handkerchief; but the dust puff was off to his left, and short. Jackson pulled rein, turned the sorrel, and trotted back toward the battery, no faster than he had gone out. But he stuffed the handkerchief in his jacket.

"That'll learn'im." Jernigan thumped a fist into his palm. "Shoot Yanks first'n take pity later."

Alf wondered if Stonewall Jackson had ever before offered mercy to anyone, let alone Yanks. Anyway, Jeff's right—bet he never will again.

Just then, the general raised his cap a second time. And again the four guns behind the earthwork poured a withering blast of case shot into the blue ranks, which went down like broomsedge under the mow.

"Good work!" Stuart yelled. "Give'em hot pepper!"

But the quickstepping Yankees closed ranks and came on.

"Can't be just Yanks, Alf. Made outten iron maybe."

Alf was only half-heartedly sponging out for the next round. Not iron, he thought. Brave men out there, no matter what color coats they wearin.

Captain Overholt ordered a change to round shot. At the waving of the forage cap, the four pieces again fired in unison, at less than five hundred yards. This time, as more blue bodies were swept to the ground, the survivors broke—first, in the remnants of the leading company, where men simply turned in their tracks and ran for the rear; then, in the following ranks as the weight of the running men hit them and their panic spread like fire. In twenty seconds, the orderly ranks turned into a tumbling blue river of running men, throwing aside their weapons, losing their hats, fleeing for their lives.

"Cease fire!"

Alf was relieved to hear Jackson's shrill voice. Then he caught his breath again as over the rise from the left Hill's butternut brigades came charging in a long whooping battle line that overlapped the running Yanks in front and rear.

Jernigan let out a whoop. "Turkey shoot, Alf!"

But Hill and his men apparently had no heart for the slaughter. They dashed shouting for the road, only a few muskets popping as here and there some Yanks made a show of resistance. Within minutes, many were surrounded and surrendering in the road. Those who evaded Hill's advance and ran on toward Bull Run, so far as Alf Gurganous could see, were not immediately pursued.

"If that don't beat the devil, Alf. What'n hell em Yanks think they-uz doin?"

"*Think?* Pore souls don't think no more'n ususnes do. Just do what they told, same over ther's over here."

Which also meant, Alf thought rather bitterly, as Overholt's Battery harnessed up to return to the waiting loot, that if a man was in the ranks on either side, all he knew about the war was what he could see with his own eyes. Damn little, 'n clear as powdersmoke.

Early that afternoon, Fargo Hart encountered the Reverend Major Allen astride a new horse, his skinned face streaked with a scab that ran from his forehead down his nose to his chin like an Indian's war paint. Across the horse's rump, the Reverend had strung one pillow case full of mixed coffee and sugar, tied for balance against another full of beans and dried vegetables. His neatly folded buffalo robe was tied on above the bouncing sacks. Hart's own saddlebags were bulging with two bottle of champagne and two more of Rhine wine.

"Well, Preacher! Look like you can stock the mess for quite awhile."

"The Lord be praised, Brother Hart. You see His hand in *this* day's work, don't you?" Even an infidel like you, his tone suggested.

"Like the Good Book says." Hart already had sampled the champagne from a bottle cracked by Coke Mowbray and incautiously offered around. "He *will* provide."

"That it does, Brother, and that He will." The Reverend Major eyed Hart's saddlebags. "Look like the hand of Providence laid itself on you, too."

Hart dared not disclose his booty, since the major was a renowned evangel of temperance. "Just a little grain for the horses, Preacher, and a clean shirt for the next time you hold services."

"Blessed be the name of the Lord!"

The Reverend Major spurred his horse and trotted away, the fat sacks bouncing behind his saddle. Like a Dutch girl's breasts, Hart thought, remembering suddenly with the help of Mowbray's champagne the buxom daughter of his Amsterdam landlady. My God, he thought, the night we got the old lady drunk on schnapps. She had passed out by the fire with a final stentorian belch, and they had borrowed her feather bolster and spread it on the floor. Suddenly, Hart wanted nothing so much—not food, not wine or a good night's sleep—as that ample Dutch girl he had known long ago, with hips like an angel's haunches and breasts resembling Preacher Allen's full pillow cases, enfolding him happily while her mother snored a few feet away.

"Oh, yes," Hart sang out to the troops milling about. "Someday, boys, this stinkin war gone be over!"

Scarcely a man looked up from his plunder; but an amused voice spoke nearby. "Some grain you got there, Cap'n. Some shirt."

A civilian, wearing a wide-brimmed hat and a long linen duster over a decently cut coat, far gone with wear, and a rough shirt open at the neck, sat his horse just behind Hart. He was smoking a long, thin cigar.

The captain put a finger to his lips, looking around with exaggerated caution. He knew the champagne, after so long a drought, had affected him slowly, but he didn't care. It was good to be cheerful again; and he gloried in the way the dusty scarecrows around him had mostly stopped being soldiers in long regimented lines and had become boys again, greedy and uncaring as babies at the suckle.

"Little warmth for the inner man. Not the Reverend Major's kind."

"Spoils of war." The stranger drew on his cigar. "Unfortunately, I don't think us civilians are entitled . . ." He gestured around him. "To the fun. Not to mention loot."

"Hell, no. To the *victor* belong the spoils."

"Cap'n, you happen to see a Whatsit Wagon round here?"

"A who?"

Hart suddenly wondered what a civilian was doing in the middle of Ol Jack's army. Not that anything couldn't happen, anybody turn up, on a day like this, full of champagne and hope.

"Photographer's equipment wagon. What the troops call'em. I thought maybe one of the Yank newspapers might have stored dark-room supplies round here."

"Photog'fer?" At the insistence of his mother, Hart had sat— stiff in a new uniform, his head in a vise—for a *carte de visite* at a Richmond studio that used papier-mâché Greek columns for a background. But it had never occurred to him that photographers might be taking pictures of the war.

"I'd of swallowed my scruples, I reckon, I'd of found some glass plates. Or pyrogallic acid. Hard to get in the field. Silver nitrate, too."

"Just how'n hell . . ." Hart feared the champagne had hit him harder than he knew; the man in the duster seemed to be talking Greek. "You get out here'n the middle one army that's God knows how far'n the rear of th'other?"

The photographer produced his credentials. "Andrew Peterson, Cap'n. Here by permission of the highest authority."

Hart studied the document, then pushed his hat back on his head. "Must have some kind of influence, gettin that signature on there."

Peterson puffed on the cigar, his pleasant blue eyes squinting against the smoke. "I made a portrait of 'is wife. I got through with it, even *she* looked good."

Peterson would not have tried this sally on most southern officers, given their childish pleasure in rank and protocol and their born-and-bred deference to women; but something about this rakish young man and his irreverent repartee with the praise-God windbag major had made the risk worth taking. Sure enough, the captain laughed out loud, and handed the paper back to Peterson.

"Bet you couldn't do it for *him*."

Peterson put his passport safely away. "Some things, Cap'n, beyond the powers of the lens."

Neither of them noticed anything peculiar—if they even saw him—about General Hoke Arnall, who sat not far away in a wooden chair tipped against the wall of the railway station. But had Fargo Hart been in the general's confidence—had he known what the general was painfully trying to say in a letter he was writing to his wife, Amy—he would have had little sympathy for Arnall's discomfiture. He might even have been faintly contemptuous.

Having found himself occasionally in the beds of some of the most fashionable women of Paris and Rome—some titled, wealthy, married, and welcome in any drawing room—Hart had made a relatively simple discovery that would have shocked most American men of his generation and background. Europe had taught Hart that women who were neither whores nor African slaves could be sensual and lustful. Once this was clear to him, Hart accepted it happily; that women should be as human as men he found far more natural than the preenings of the creatures he had returned to America to find passing themselves off as vessels of purity, offended—or frightened?—at the notion of a bodily need or function.

General Arnall, on the other hand, was more nearly a man of his time in matters of sex and in his regard for the higher nature of women, all of which he found inextricably entwined with his faith in God.

"Dear One" (he had begun nearly an hour before):

> Of all the temptations paraded before Our Father's humble creatures in order to test their faith in His word and ways, base passion, so distressing to you and so lacking in consideration of your physical and spiritual well-being, seems the one your poor and repentant husband has been least able to conquer in himself. And if the consequences you fear, from the delay you report . . .

General Arnall's letter there broke off in confusion that reflected his own swirling thoughts. It was not just that he did not know what to say to Amy, or that he found it painful to concede himself in the wrong, or even that the insistent sounds of battle had been noticeably creeping up the track toward Manassas.

As the sun had moved slowly westward, the battle sounds had risen in volume. Clouds of white smoke drifted in the hot sky. Ewell's Division, posted as rear guard on the banks of Kettle Run, beyond Bristoe, was coming under pressure from Pope—alerted at last to the danger in his rear. Arnall's professional ear and battle instinct told him that Ewell had some time since abandoned Kettle Run and withdrawn his line through Bristoe and along the track toward Manassas Junction.

But the truth was that, distressed as Hoke Arnall was by his sinful behavior with Amy, concerned as he was by Pope's pressure on Ewell, he could scarcely think of anything but Jackson's intolerable insolence in putting him in arrest the night before. With the army behind enemy lines! He had put aside his first instinct, which was to call the madman out; but he nevertheless burned with anger and resentment.

As if failing to post one picket at a turn-off was a heinous crime, or even much of a misdemeanor. As if any harm had been done, save maybe a quarter-hour delay on a day's march. Besides which, Arnall had not *failed* to post the picket; Jackson's order simply had never reached him. For which, Arnall thought, somebody's fool head would roll if he found out that that somebody had received the message from Archer's Brigade up ahead, then failed to pass it along to brigade headquarters.

At least the crazed Jackson had not removed Arnall from command; so the arrest, as long as the campaign lasted, was only technical. With *his* fighting record, he thought, to have a career ruined or even smirched because... but of course he would not let that happen. Under no circumstances. Powell Hill—with his own reasons for questioning Jackson's erratic ways—would certainly back him up. Jackson's follies would never stand up under formal inquiry; Arnall was so sure of it that he forgot the letter to Amy and began to compose in his head his formal response to the idiotic charge.

He soon broke off, however, to watch with distaste the wholesale plunder going on around him. Jackson with his draconian marching orders had nevertheless turned the troops loose like so many rats around a cheese. Stuffing themselves, running around like idiots in fancy underwear and frilled shirts, some of them drunk despite orders. How did Jackson expect his officers to keep up *real* discipline, the kind that made men in action obey orders without question? Up to me, Arnall thought, I'd have some of these rascals in irons—bucked anyway. Like that one there.

He shook his head, watching a skinny private prancing across the tracks in a woman's hat and veil, who called out to others in shrill falsetto: "Now you boys jus *stop* all at goddam cussin, they's ladies present!"

Sam Stowe lounged up beside the station and leaned with his elbow against the porch on which Arnall was sitting. Stowe tipped back his planter's hat.

"You reck'n Pope's really got women with'im? Where'd that stuff come from?"

"Sutler's stores, probly." Arnall shared his brother officers' contempt for the Yankee general who had boasted to the Army of Virginia: "I have come to you from the West where we have always seen the backs of our enemies." But he did not believe that even Pope would actually stock up clothing for camp followers. Hooker, maybe, if what they said about him in the Old Army was true.

"These men're gettin out of hand, Sam."

"Let'em play a little."

To Arnall's irritation, Stowe was grinning at the antics of the man in the woman's hat, who was now dancing clumsily with a private Arnall suspected of inebriation. Then Stowe looked up at Arnall with the grin fading from his face.

"Won't be havin much fun fore long, will they?"

Arnall flipped his hand toward the sound of Ewell's guns. "Sound to me like Ewell's fallen back on Broad Run this side of Bristoe. Pope's closin in on us."

"Pope." Stowe made a sour face. "We could lick Pope sideways on Sunday. *If* the army was all together. Hear anything from Longstreet?"

Arnall shook his head. It had been a bad day, he thought, when the Old Man ordered Hill's Division to join Jackson. Under Longstreet, a man knew where he stood and didn't have to put up with a lot of lunatic notions and a general who kept secrets mainly from his own officers.

"Thing is . . ." Stowe pounded his fist lightly on the porch. "Longstreet's got to get thew Thoroughfare Gap. Now Pope knows *we're* here, even he's got to have the horse sense to seal that gap up tighter'n lockjaw."

"Better men than John Pope might not seal Ol Pete, Sam."

"Well, I'd feel a lot better knowin he was thew that Gap."

Stowe ran his hand through his blond beard; dust drifted from it like dandruff. Toward Broad Run a slight rise in the volume of artillery fire caught Arnall's experienced ear. Ewell was likely starting to pull his infantry back across the railroad bridge, under cover of his guns.

"Hoke, you mind if I go see Gin'al Jackson?"

Arnall stiffened in his chair. "What for?"

"Maybe he knows if Longstreet's thew the Gap."

"I'd see'im in hell with'is back broke fore I'd ask'im for the sweat off'is brow."

Stowe took off the planter hat and rubbed his forearm across his dirty face, smearing it wetly. "Hoke, don't getchuh back up. We got a war to fight. That fool arrest order's just Ol Jack's way. Won't mean nothin in the long run."

"Means plenny to me. Long run or short."

Stowe sighed and put his hat back on. "I reck'n I'll go on over'n ask'im anyway." His voice was casual but Arnall did not even have to think about it to know that he was hearing in those casual words the echoes of thousands of acres and hundreds of slaves and a family that went back into the centuries—beside all of which, in Sam Stowe's sense of things, military rank was happenstance.

"Then I want it distinctly understood..." Hoke Arnall had his own sense of things, not less real to him than the planter's. "You go on your own, Stowe. Not officially. Not as from me or in the chain of command."

Stowe touched the brim of his hat. "You ever get at ramrod outen your rear end, you'll find life a sight easier."

Walking away to find Jackson, he half regretted the remark. Not that it wasn't true. But Arnall was as touchy as a virgin about the flanks. Stowe genuinely admired and had learned much from the man as a fighting officer; and though Arnall was a remote and difficult man, their friendship had been growing—not least, Stowe knew, because he was not intimidated by the General's stern manner, his insistence on discipline and the prerogatives of rank.

Stowe had observed of his drivers and overseers in the old days that the tougher they were on the hands, the more they feared they might lose control of them, or lose their jobs, or not bring in a sufficient crop—the more they feared *something*. In any case, Arnall had shown some willingness to relax and talk with a man he could not scare off; and Stowe hoped he had not jeopardized the intimacy, scant as it was.

Efforts had been made to preserve the sutlers' stores for Jackson's and Stuart's officers, but they proved futile. The men were too hungry, the temptations too great, discipline—never certain in most of the army—too lax. In the afternoon, even Jackson gave in and called off Trimble's and Taliaferro's guards, since there was no possibility, anyway, of carrying off any but the most vital medical supplies, plus restocked shot chests on the caissons and limbers. The troops were told to take four days' rations and fill their shot pouches, but to leave alone the huge blue mounds of coats and trousers. Shoes, socks, drawers were fair game. Everything else would be burned, and the remaining ammunition destroyed.

Sometime in late afternoon, Josh Beasly and Lige Flournoy broke into a railroad car standing so remotely on a siding that it had been passed over by more official foragers. Foxy Bradshaw, his beakish nose quivering like a bird dog's on the scent, the undertow of fear deep in his belly momentarily lost in avarice, followed them into the car. The three privates were bitter, because Hill's expedition that morning had cost them an early chance at the booty. Now the best was gone.

"Shit." Josh held up a box of cotton bandages. "Medical stuff. Our stinkin luck."

"Wait a minute, Meat." Lige looked around, stroking his bristly jaw. "Them aint jus any ol banages. Surgeons use em thangs sop up blood, they cutchuh goddam arm off. This-yer's surgeon's stuff."

"Yeah. You had your arm cut off lately, Fox?"

"Like to *fell* off, time I lug em tater sacks back to the comp'ny." The three had just slipped away from such onerous duty.

"Point is . . ." Lige's patience was exaggerated. "Ain't never been no Yank sawbones didn't have sperrits to pour down em suckers' thoats, time he git ready to hack."

Josh's face lit up. He clapped Bradshaw on the back. "Smell out em goddam sperrits, Fox! Use-at nose for sump'm sides sniffin Ironass's shit."

The three privates rummaged through the car. In a few minutes, with a whoop, Lige summoned them to a wooden crate he had pried open with his bayonet. It held twelve bottles of brandy. There were two more crates beneath the one Lige had opened.

None of the three knew what brandy was, as distinguished from corn liquor or cider. But they had no difficulty identifying the flat brown bottles as what they had been looking for. Josh plucked one out of the crate and tucked it inside his waistband, then grabbed two more and handed one each to his companions.

"Yanks aint half-bad after all." Foxy's yellowing teeth looked like an ear of corn beneath his hooked nose.

"Hey in ther! Whatchew men doin?"

A captain none of them knew was peering at them as they cavorted about the dim twilight of the car. He leaped swiftly inside.

"Medical splies, suh." Lige, the smoothest operator among them, moved confidently forward. "Mess-a stuff here to ease the pain."

"By God right." The officer looked around and rubbed his hands. He wore quartermaster insignia. "Nuf here fill two amblances."

"We-uz jus goin to call somebody to come git it." Lige moved past the officer, toward the open door, and jerked his head to the others. Foxy hurried to the door, too, but Josh paused to pick up several towels from a stack of them.

"Reckon em docs can spare these-yer, Cap'n?"

"Sure. Take'em." The captain moved farther into the car.

"What's in at open crate ther?" Behind him Foxy and Lige jumped to the ground.

Josh looked calmly at the remaining nine brown bottles. "Dang if I know."

The captain stepped past him and took one of the bottles from the crate. "Brandy." His voice quivered with reverence. Then he straightened and turned back to Josh. "How come they's only nine bottles in a case-a twelve?"

Josh was walking toward the door of the car. "Beats-a shit outta me, Cap'n. Somebody must of drunk em."

"You men bring at goddam brandy back-yer." The captain's voice suddenly rang with authority. "Tha's govment propitty."

Josh turned and stared at him. "What brandy is at, Cap'n?"

He was a big man and his eyes, the captain suddenly saw, looked a little like a catamount's, glowing and slightly yellow around the edges of the iris. The car was far out at the end of the siding; it was quiet inside, and dim away from the open door. The big man stared at him yellowly; the captain wished suddenly that he had unbuttoned the flap of his holster. His Adam's apple bobbed as he swallowed convulsively.

Josh Beasly, who had faced many a man with his fists or his knife before the war had given him a license to kill with a musket, noticed that small familiar movement in the captain's throat. Josh smiled, a strange, narrow smile; he extended a large hand and pushed the captain gently aside. Then he took another brown bottle from the crate.

"Show this-un to the boys, Cap'n. Maybe they seen some like it round somewheres."

He turned and followed Foxy and Lige out of the car, the brown bottles clinking as he shoved the second one into his waistband beside the first. Behind him, the captain's hand went to his holster; but by the time he got the flap loose and seized the cold pistol grip, the big man with the yellow eyes was out of the car and gone, and it seemed to the captain that he might's well leave well enough alone. No skin off his ass nohow.

Colonel Sam Stowe found Jackson inspecting the ambulances being loaded with medical supplies. Not hesitating, because he never questioned his own rights or welcome—had never even understood that there *could be* a question about them—Stowe approached and gave the general a salute only slightly more military than the one he had offered Hoke Arnall. Jackson returned it, his pale eyes clear and direct under the dusty brim of his forage cap. He was sucking on half a lemon.

"Gin'al . . . some of us a little uneasy . . ." Stowe nodded his head in its straw hat toward the guns roaring across Broad Run. "Just wanted to ask you on m'own account if Longstreet's got thew Thoroughfare Gap yet."

As he asked, he remembered Jackson's passion for secrecy. *Even if he knows, he'll never tell me.*

Jackson sucked on the lemon, his unblinking pale eyes fixed on Stowe's. Then he peered closely at the lemon, as if in its pulp and seeds he might augur the right answer. What might, on another man's face, have been a smile stirred behind his heavy brown beard.

"Go back to your command, Colonel. Say 'Longstreet is through. And with the help of God, we're goin to whip in the next battle.'"

"Thank you, Gin'al."

Stowe saluted again and turned away. It was not true. He knew that from the false heartiness in Jackson's usually calm voice—knew he was only being turned away with a message to shore up the morale of the troops. Curiously, Stowe did not mind; even more curiously, he was cheered himself. Because in the glowing light of Ol Jack's eyes, Sam Stowe had found renewed inspiration.

Stowe had seen enough war to be skeptical of mere glory, but not enough to cool his patriot's fire or to tarnish his cavalier's sense of great deeds to be done. His heritage and his acres had made him liable to high expectations. War and a cause had stimulated them, and become indispensable to their satisfaction. So in no more time than it had taken the general to speak, Stowe's worry had vanished. A fight was coming, by God, and Ol Jack meant to whip! Great deeds were to be done and Sam Stowe cared only that he should be a part of them.

Pressing along the O & A tracks in search of General Hooker, Duryea saw the evidence of battle at every hand—abandoned muskets, canteens, blanket rolls; a shoe with a foot still in it, the underbrush by the track broken and bent as if with a great rake. Wounded men glared up with incredulous eyes or called to him for water. The stench of burnt powder, scorched flesh, of blood and death lay along the tracks as tangibly as the dust that rose from his horse's hooves.

With Pope's staff, Duryea had forded Kettle Run below the charred ruins of the railroad bridge, near where Hooker and the Rebs had first collided in midafternoon. Hooker had been forcing his way northeast along the railroad ever since. Stragglers and walking wounded, limping back from the front, said Ewell's Division had spread a battle line a mile wide, on both sides of the tracks, and was making Hooker pay for every yard.

Duryea could see that, easily enough. In the hot glare of the sinking sun, he passed an abandoned and shelled-out house, where Hooker's surgeons had set up a hospital. Duryea counted upwards of a hundred wounded men lying about the house, their groans and cries for water audible even against the sounds of battle just up ahead. Litter bearers brought in a constant stream of broken and bleeding bodies from the fields by the railroad.

In those same fields, as he pressed on to the sound of continuing battle, Duryea—with his sharp, observer's eyes—counted nearly eighty Union and Reb dead, the latter lying crumpled as they had fallen, most of the Union men stretched out and neatly covered with blankets.

Ewell, Duryea thought. Ewell's Division had been prominent in the fight at Slaughter's Mountain three weeks earlier. If Ewell was out as rear guard for the Reb force that had struck Bristoe and Manassas Junction in the night, that force had to be Jackson's whole corps. Stonewall himself.

But a corps? Even Banks's signal officer, gossiping in Duryea's tent two nights earlier, had not suggested that the column moving on Pope's right flank was anything as big as a corps. Yet the battle smoke up ahead provided all the evidence needed. Stonewall Jackson had moved into Pope's rear and onto his lifeline before anyone knew he was there.

Duryea cursed himself again for the day spent at the map table, instead of in the field looking for that moving column. Of course, Russell or Pope should have sent him out, but that was no real excuse. He should have followed his instinct. That, Duryea told himself grimly, was an oft-learned lesson he had ignored for the last time.

Duryea had been sent to find Hooker and inform him that Pope had arrived at Bristoe, after riding up the tracks from Warrenton Junction. At least, Pope's move had taken the staff out of that gloomy old slaver's house. Headquarters in the saddle again. And Duryea sensed himself basically on his own again, which always cheered him up.

Hooker, on the big white horse known throughout the army, was not hard to find as he rode close in the rear of his battle line, slowly advancing along the tracks toward Manassas. When Duryea saluted, the sun was almost down; Hooker was peering over Broad Run. The rail bridge over it had been burned to its abutments and the tracks twisted crazily down, like metal vines, into the slow, muddy water.

"General Hooker . . . sir . . . General Pope directs me to say he's arrived at Bristoe. Would like to know, sir, the situation in your front."

Hooker gave a perfunctory return salute. Just then the Reb batteries, which had been silent for a few minutes, opened with a roar from a slight rise beyond Broad Run. Hooker did not look around or flinch, but waited calmly for the scream and crash of the shells to subside. Duryea forced himself to sit still on his nervous horse.

"Driven 'em to there." Hooker pointed to the batteries. "Four brigades of Ewell, maybe six thousand muskets." Duryea, knowing generals, knocked that down to five thousand, maybe forty-five hundred. "Dug in and fighting like sonsabitches."

The remark offended Duryea. Hooker had a reputation for profanity and of course the battlefield was no place for sensitivity. Still, a general of division should have a sense of the proprieties. In the gathering dusk, Duryea eyed Joe Hooker's florid face under the fair hair and the pushed-back slouch hat. A handsome man all right; everyone said that. But that red face was not just sunburned; it seemed to confirm Hooker's reputation for high living.

"Tell General Pope . . ." Hooker again waited unmoving through a Reb barrage, some shells of which kicked up gray earth not ten yards away, showering them with a fine rain of Virginia dirt that made Duryea's gelding shy and prance. "Tell'im I'm down to about three rounds per man reserve." He looked at Duryea belligerently. "What comes of hustling us out here 'thout the trains. So I can't attack beyond here . . ." He gestured at Broad Run. "But Ewell don't know I'm down to piss and vinegar for ammunition. So I'll just hold on here and *look* like I'm going to attack. Lessen he attacks me."

"Yessir." Duryea saluted and started to turn away, as the Reb pieces roared again. This time, no shells came near as the gunners registered more closely on Hooker's battle line.

"He does that . . ." Hooker tapped Duryea's knee with a gloved finger. "He'll go through me like a dose of salts."

Moving at a canter back to Bristoe in the late-day gloom, Duryea's distaste for Hooker's vulgarity was outweighed only by his concern for the position. He had heard enough headquarters talk to know that Pope was hastily pulling back from the Rappahannock line, mobilizing his whole army to crush the Reb force that had bobbed up in his rear. The general had been quick— quicker than he, Duryea, acknowledged to himself—to conclude that Bristoe and Manassas had suffered no mere cavalry raids, like Catlett's before them.

"Cap'n . . . sir . . . hep . . ."

A bearded man in butternut was sprawled under a poplar tree growing ten yards from the road, on the side away from the tracks. Duryea did not remember seeing him when he had passed that way, moving up to Hooker's front. The man's face, under the straggling beard, was contorted in pain; he was nearly doubled up, his hands clutched into his stomach as he lay on his side.

"Water . . . Cap'n sir . . ."

Duryea could barely see the man's musket lying behind him. The sun had disappeared, a red ball dropping suddenly out of sight beyond the rim of the earth, and the afterglow was soft and cool.

"You one of Ewell's men?"

The man groaned and nodded. "Dyin', Cap'n. Water . . . plizz."

Duryea realized that the stretcher-bearers had long since passed and would not likely be back. He dismounted and approached the man, watching carefully for any attempt to grab the musket. He had his canteen in his left hand.

"You gut-shot? Water's no good if you are."

The man peered at him blankly, moaning something inaudible. His eyes were red-rimmed, his jaw clenched. Duryea squatted and reached for the hands tightly locked over the man's midsection. The man recoiled backward, straightened, and pointed a pistol in Duryea's face.

"Dead man, Cap'n, you move a goddam muscle."

He rolled up on his knees, the pistol steady in his hand, the red-flecked eyes bright and alert. "Thow the cantee ovuh ther onna ground."

Duryea did as he was told, watching the man pick up the

musket, then stand up—a tall, cadaverous-looking fellow, probably not a real Reb at all, since he did not have the usual blanket
roll over his shoulder. *Should have noticed that right off.* Some
rear-area skulker, preying like a carrion bird on the leavings of
both armies.

The tall man fished up the canteen with the butt of his musket
through the carrying strap. The pistol barrel never wavered from
its aim between Duryea's eyes. Snaggled teeth showed between
thin lips in what appeared to be a grin.

"Jes squat ther now, Cap'n, while I find me a horse somewhere
round here."

He backed away three steps toward the road, well out of Duryea's reach, then walked rapidly toward Duryea's waiting horse,
the pistol still pointed back at him in the twilight. Duryea stood
up, turning.

"Hold still ther!"

The tall man turned back to face him, thrusting the pistol out
at arm's length. *Can't hit me in this light.* Duryea felt the knife
he had pulled from his boot easy and balanced in his hand. He
took a step forward.

"Blow yuh damn head off, now!"

Panicking, Duryea took another step forward. The pistol crashed,
a finger of flame stabbed toward Duryea, and he felt his hat
snatched from his head as if the finger had swiped across the
crown. *Close.*

But before the tall man could cock and fire again, Duryea came
at him out of the shadowy light, the full weight of his wiry body
plunging into the marauder's bony midriff.

"Whoo-oof!"

The man collapsed, his breath gushing foully past Duryea's
shoulder, the rifle, the pistol, and the canteen clattering to the
ground. He went down on his back, the back of his head slamming
into the hard earth. With one tigerish movement, Duryea was
astride him; with another, he cut the man's throat; with a third,
he stood up, out of the way of the upgush of black blood spouting
into the falling night.

*Stinking dog killer. Damned coward, plundering the dead.
Wonder you had the guts to pick on a living man.*

Duryea gazed with unmitigated contempt at the surprised gog-
gle eyes, the snaggle teeth, the subsiding blood. Then he picked
up his canteen and hung it from his saddle. He fetched his hat,
poking a finger through the hole in the crown. Then he kicked

the tall man's jerking body into the roadside ditch.

That's one for you, Garrison.

But Duryea had to take Hooker's message to Pope; and he put the dead skulker out of his mind before he mounted his horse, and rode toward Bristoe in the dusk.

The same dusk was coming down around Sycamore plantation and L. Q. Arnall's tall white house in Duplin County, North Carolina, as the old judge sat on the porch, apparently listening with grave interest to Sheriff Maxton's report on Miss Tippy's murder, four days earlier.

"... not so much's a smell of 'im round here." The sheriff's voice was lugubrious. "Was, them dogs'd flush 'im in two seconds."

Judge Arnall nodded, his lips pursed, his expression serious. Amy Arnall, sitting nearby in a rocker that creaked on its back swing—a familiar and reassuring sound in the gathering darkness—knew the old man probably grasped little if anything of what he was being told. He had been drinking steadily since before noon, as he did every day, and had for years; how he even remained awake until evening—which he also did every day—was a mystery to Amy.

Sheriff Maxton sighed heavily. "Right down disappointed not to find Jason, Judge. I bout made sure that coon'd be hit out here someplace."

The very notion terrified Amy all over again, even though she knew that the hounds leashed at the steps already had swarmed through the barns and outhouses and cabins. How drowsy and lazy the lean, panting beasts looked in the fast-falling dark! But nothing terrified the Africans more than the hounds that helped patrol the southern roads and could follow a fugitive, they believed, through swampwater.

"Bein'is woman's here, I mean. She sure got'erself a bad nig guh, that Jason."

"You're sure it *was* Jason."

Amy was more nearly making a statement than asking a question. Since waking that morning, she had thought of little but Miss Tippy's mysterious death. Then the sheriff and his men had appeared in the afternoon with their terrifying news of Jason's complicity. She had had to force herself, after that, to sit quietly on the porch, or at the supper table, picking at the sewing basket now neglected in her lap, calming little Luke—who, understanding nothing, still *felt* the excitement of the visit, and the tough-looking men, and the suddenly stone-faced Africans. But all the while Amy had wanted to scream, or run, or hide under the bed.

Of course, she couldn't give way like that. The Judge was nothing but a drunken old man, despite his ability to maintain a deceptive front of dignity, like a starched shirt over a chest ravaged by consumption. Amy was in charge if anyone was, and would have to act if anyone did.

"Ain't a doubt in this world he done it, Miz Arnall."

The sheriff, a stout man who frequently mopped his wide brow with a red handkerchief, pronounced it "Arnawl" instead of the "Arnel" preferred by the General—a subtle method, Amy suspected, of cutting the high and mighty down to size. She had become so used to the common mispronunciation that it no longer irritated her.

"Found the purse'n money hid up under Jason's bed. And the nigguh boy that stood watch for'im while he...uh...done it ...broke down'n tole us all about it."

The sheriff chuckled, not quite humorously. "At boy seen my dawgs'n heard some talk bout hangin, he aint held back *nothin*."

That seemed conclusive enough. But Jason a murderer!

"I know Jason," she said. "I remember when he asked the General for Easter to be his broad wife." The General had still been a captain then, still under the old flag, in those days that now seemed from another age.

"Cose we'll git'im yet."

In spite of herself, Amy was fascinated, as a bird must be at the stalk of a cat, by what Jason had done. As the dusk turned toward night, she could not help but think that even Sycamore, beneath its beauty and seeming tranquillity, was a world of darkness more profound than the mere absence of daylight.

The sheriff heaved himself to his feet—a man who must have been a considerable burden even for the huge horse he rode.

"No runaway nigguh got outen Duplin County since I been sheriff."

Amy wondered briefly why he wasn't in the army, why he could be home while the General was risking his life in Virginia. Why couldn't it be the General here now, when she needed him?

"I sure aint aimin to let'em start now. Be sure-a that, Jedge."

He held out his hand and Judge Arnall rose with perfect courtesy to take it, walking the sheriff to the steps with a murmured flow of thanks and banalities. Amy marveled at this display but she really wanted to cry out for the sheriff not to go, not to take his dogs and his men, not to leave her alone there in the night, and in that other, more fearful darkness. Not after Miss Tippy. Not after Jason . . . oh, she knew him all right—a short, powerfully built African, very dark, with a massive head and intense eyes, who had been often at Sycamore visiting Easter. Not as much humor about him as most Africans showed, at least to whites. Once Amy had come upon Jason in the kitchen, waiting for Easter to finish up. He had been respectful but Amy could remember something silent, watchful, about him, as if he were taking a sort of measurement of the household and its mistress. Or maybe she only thought she remembered that, in the lurid glow of his later crime.

She knew from the General that Jason had run away once, been caught in Kentucky, and returned to Miss Tippy's husband at Lakeview, years before he'd come courting Easter at Sycamore. By then, Miss Tippy's husband was dead in agony, of a mad dog's bite, and the Africans at Lakeview were being pampered and spoiled and petted by the old woman. Miss Tippy was utterly dependent on them and was known to believe that if she treated them with extra kindness and generosity she would never have to doubt their love and loyalty. And to think that Jason . . .

Suddenly, Maxton turned and came heavily back across the porch to where she sat in her creaking rocker. He swept off his straw hat with one hand and with the other mopped the red handkerchief across his brow. She looked up at him, glad that the growing darkness hid what she thought must be the plain terror in her face and eyes.

"Be back real frequent, Miz Arnall. Case he come see 'is woman."

The coarse voice was low and reassuring, businesslike. She realized that he had known all along that the Judge was helpless— probably everyone in Duplin County did—and that whatever had to be done, she would have to do it.

"Not that any harm'd come to you or the Judge anyhow. Jason got no call for that. But you see hide ner hair of 'im round here, I'd be right down glad you'd send for me soon's you could, ma'am."

"Of course."

Amy forced herself to try to speak naturally; but her voice sounded in her own ears squeaky and trembling, not unlike the creak of the rocker. Behind them, Judge Arnall moved with stately pace back to his chair and sat down with a sigh. Even drunk, he would never have left his son's wife alone on the porch with a man who, whatever his official status, was neither a gentleman nor a familiar in the house. The Judge was never too addled to remember the rules of behavior.

"You trust that Easter?" the sheriff asked.

Amy had already put the question to herself, answering only with a conclusion she seldom had to face—that she did not really know any of them; or much *about* them, either.

"As much as you can trust any of'em, I guess." Then she added, as if it mattered, "She's our *cook.*"

"My way of thinkin'..." Maxton mopped his brow again, the red handkerchief a blur in the night. "I wouldn't turn my back on none of'em."

"What'll happen if...when you catch Jason?"

"He'll hang."

The words themselves hung in the still summer air, like corpses, and Amy had a sudden horrid vision of bulging eyes—whether Miss Tippy's or Jason's she banished the image too quickly to know.

"Reck'n Easter mought try'n run off to'im?"

Would God she would, Amy thought. "The General's people don't run away," she said—pleased, this time, at the forceful tone of her voice. "They know they have a good home here."

"Yessum." The sheriff cleared his throat with a sound like a distant wagon train. "Bout's good as Jason had at Lakeview. How come you folks let a bad nigguh like at marry one-a your people?"

Even in fear, Amy Singleton Arnall had no intention of being interrogated like a criminal. She rose stiffly, indicating the steps with subtle movements of her arm and head.

"The General has always wanted his people content, Sheriff Maxton. I shall certainly inform you of anything that...ah...that happens."

"Much oblige." He turned away, clapping the straw hat back on his big, sweating head. "Evnin, Jedge."

Amy listened for him clumping down the steps out of the light, rousing the dogs. In the darkness, voices muttered, rose, fell; someone laughed, like a terrier barking, and fell abruptly silent. Horses clattered away, indistinct moving shapes somehow terrifying in their vagueness; one of the hounds yelped despairingly, as Amy wished she could do. Then the night, thick with heat and silence, closed around Sycamore.

No moon, no stars glistened in the ominous heavens; the darkness seemed absolute, impenetrable, and she was glad when gray-haired Willis, carrying a candle, came to lead the Judge up to bed. The empty-eyed old man insisted, of course, on first seeing Amy to her sewing room, where servants had lit other candles. Then he padded off obediently, with Willis's thin hand on his elbow.

Amy tried to sew but she could only listen to the brooding silence. She was not overly afraid, for surely the sheriff's hounds would have found Jason if he had been anywhere nearby. But the thought of his crime consumed her with horror. Nor could she rid herself of the sight of Easter's tearstained sable face, as the cook went to her knees before her mistress, screaming and swearing that she knew nothing of her husband's whereabouts or what he'd done. Had it not been for Pettigrew, who had seemed to have a calming effect on her, Easter would have gone into real hysterics.

Odd, Amy thought, that she had never sensed in the cook, usually such a jolly woman, a capacity for the kind of soul-searing grief she had shown that day; odd, too, that the distant and aloof Pettigrew, the grandest figure in the yard, had been able to deal with her so gently, yet strongly.

But the real reason Amy could not concentrate on her sewing basket, or anything useful, was her persistent sense of herself as alone, the white center of a dark universe . . . No, there was little Luke. At the thought of him, she jumped up, spilling the basket, and started for the stairs. Bess seemed suddenly to materialize from the shadows near the door to the hall, startling Amy, who realized the tall mulatto woman had been standing there while she tried to sew. Watching over her? Or just watching?

"I bring a candle, Mistis."

"No . . . no, I'll take my own."

Amy caught up a light from a table by the door. She would be no more dependent on Bess or on any of them than she had to be. From now on.

As she went up the curving staircase the Judge's father had designed and watched his slaves build, she moved in a small patch of light cast by the candles; but the darkness into which she was climbing seemed thicker, deeper than she had ever known it, persistently reminding her that she was all but alone among these alien souls as inscrutable, finally, as the mules turning the Sycamore millstones in their endless circles. So gay, so charming, in so many ways so childlike—but finally *threatening,* in the deliberate reserve with which they guarded their inner world, their secret selves.

Take Pettigrew. The General relied on him utterly, and had for years, since long before the war. Neither the General nor his father—in better days—believed in white overseers. Thieves at best, the General was convinced, and unable to get the work out of the hands that a good black driver could. The General said Pettigrew—born and bred at Sycamore, under training to take over as driver even before he'd got his man's growth—knew more than any outsider could about farming the Arnall land, managing the smithy, the mill, the livestock, and the various craftsmen—carpenter, cooper, stonemason—who made the place thrive.

"Pettigrew knows the *people,*" the General had often told her. "He doesn't have to whip work out of 'em."

Amy did not doubt it; she doubted nothing the General told her. And if *he* trusted Pettigrew, then surely Pettigrew could countenance nothing so wicked as what had been done at Lakeview.

Still . . . even though she was the instrument by which master and driver communicated—writing Pettigrew's reports at his dictation, reading him the General's replies—she really knew no more of the driver than his opaque, ageless face told her. In fact, in any other of the General's people, Pettigrew's disdainful manner, the contempt she sensed behind his indifference to her, might have brought swift punishment.

But at Sycamore, when the General was away, Pettigrew ruled virtually as judge and jury and meted out punishment as he saw fit. "No molasses this month for Rachel and none for Callie," she had written the General at Pettigrew's direction, only a few days earlier, "on account of weighting down cotton sacks with rocks."

Amy had never complained of Pettigrew to her husband because, cold-bloodedly, she had chosen to accept his managerial excellence and ignore, as best she could, his high-handed manner. Besides, she did not want to undermine his authority with the rest of the people, as she surely would by punishing or denouncing him.

But that afternoon, for almost the first time, Pettigrew's icy reserve had nearly cracked. Plainly, he had not liked the appearance of the sheriff and the search of the yard and outbuildings.

"Some nigguh hidin dis place, I gone know fo him take two

brefs." His voice came as close to registering anger, or any emotion, as Amy had ever heard it. "Ain't need no dawgs yolpin round scarin folks."

But was that merely the indignation of a driver securely in control of the people, outraged at the suggestion that the sheriff's hounds might find something or someone he did not know about? Or the agitation of a culprit who had something or someone to hide?

God forgive me for being suspicious, Amy thought. But what had Pettigrew ever done to win *her* confidence, however well he managed the General's property?

She moved in the yellow patch of the candlelight up into the darkness of the second floor. But at the top of the stairs, a candle down the hall near Luke's room helped dispel her sense of aloneness, of enfolding and smothering darkness.

"Bess." Again, she managed to infuse her voice with crisp authority. Or she thought she did. "Come right up and move Luke into my room, please."

With none of the grumbling she often indulged in, Bess rapidly moved the boy, then his little bed, into the big room overlooking the lawns and fields to the east. Through it all, exhausted no doubt by the excitement of the afternoon, Luke slept peacefully. His mere presence made Amy feel better. He was a miniature of the General, a little man. A little *white* man. And though it was really her role to protect *him,* Amy believed that Luke in her room was somehow an essential guardian. He stood for something. She was almost relaxed as Bess began to undress her.

"Bess . . . do you believe Jason did it?" She knew the yard would have had the whole story ten minutes after the sheriff arrived with his dreaded hounds, if not before.

"Aint know nuffin bout dat, Mistis."

Bess slipped a robe deftly around Amy's shoulders, over her petticoats. Amy never allowed servants to undress her completely or to see her naked in her bath.

"Will he come for Easter?"

"Long gone, Mistis. I speck Jason long gone."

"If he comes here . . ." Taking her candle, Amy moved toward her dressing room, then stopped and looked back at Bess, tall and still in the yellow light. "The dogs'll get him. The dogs'll get him and he'll hang."

"Jason long gone, Mistis." But Bess's voice was so toneless, Amy could not tell whether or not she believed her own words.

She went into the dressing room and to a little table in the locked drawer of which she tried to keep a few things private even from the African women who swarmed through the house—even, for that matter, from the General. A Bible lay on the tabletop and in the candlelight she opened it to Revelations, where with its pink ribbon the key to the desk drawer lay hidden. She unlocked the drawer and contemplated her treasures—a diary to which she only occasionally confided her thoughts, some particularly affecting letters from the General, Luke's first little shoes and locks of hair from each of his three years, a pot of rouge she would have died rather than confess to owning, a small bottle of laudanum. At the back of the drawer was the heavy pistol the General, on his last leave, had left for her protection.

Amy looked down at the open drawer for a long time.

"Lord save us," she said at last, to the surrounding darkness.

Then she took the pistol from the drawer, its cold presence heavy and assertive in her hand. She knew it was loaded, as the General had left it. He had taught her how to cock and fire it, too, though she wondered if her hand would be steady enough for her to hit anything if she ever had to.

Maybe not. But Amy Singleton Arnall did not intend to be murdered in her bed like Miss Tippy. Nor would she sit by and have harm come to her son or, for that matter, to the General's wretched husk of a father. She put the pistol in the pocket of her robe, its dead weight less reassuring than ominous.

"You ready, Mistis?" Bess called from the bedroom.

"Not yet, Bess."

Not ready for bed, anyway, Amy thought, beginning to remove her underclothes. But she would carry the pistol with her from now on, for she meant to be ready when Jason came.

General Pope received the news of Hooker's ammunition shortage with no emotion, although Colonel Russell turned a dark night darker with profanity. Duryea, disapproving of such language, nevertheless gathered between oaths that there would be no ammunition up from the main body of Pope's troops before morning. Duryea regarded Russell as a number-two type anyway, and was more impressed with Pope's calm than depressed by the colonel's language.

He watched the two of them go off to sit on a wagon tongue overlooking Kettle Run, on the south bank of which the headquarters camp had been pitched. Bristoe itself, never much more than a railroad crossing, had become a graveyard of train wreckage, although Pope's engineers had offered some hope that one locomotive might yet be hauled away and repaired. Not more than a half-dozen burden cars, out of what Duryea had been told were two whole trains of them, would ever roll again.

To the northeast—Duryea supposed over Manassas Junction— the sky was turning red with the glow of Reb fires. The noise of battle along Broad Run had fallen to the occasional crump of big guns muttering pompously at each other.

Duryea had a cup of coffee and a plate of beans and bacon by the camp fire. Rations were scarce. And Jackson on the O & A between them and fresh supplies. Duryea eyed the glowing sky over Manassas bitterly. A lot of rations were going up. A lot of forage for the animals. He felt the loss almost as keenly as that of his dog Garrison. Damned slave-whipping dog killers.

"Rebs must be having fun over there."

Duryea sighed. That voice, he thought, wanting to throw hot coffee into the darkness beside him. He could barely make out Fielding's slight form; but the glint of the firelight on the man's spectacles placed him about six feet away. Too far for the coffee.

"But he better be getting out of there, he knows what's good for'im."

Duryea surmised that Fielding was talking about Jackson. It gave him pleasure not to tell Fielding that Hooker was so low on ammunition that Jackson was in no more danger than Duryea's mother, at home in Vermont. Or maybe I should tell'im. Shake up his sleep a little, to know there's only three cartridges per man 'tween him and old Stonewall.

"I tell you . . ." the aggravating voice screeched on. "I saw today why Mister John Pope's a general and I aint."

Though not loud, the voice was piercing enough to still other conversations around the big fire near which most of Pope's staff was lounging. Somebody in that crowd's bound to tell Pope what that suck-up's saying, Duryea thought. Which, of course, Fielding knew as well as he knew Pope's reputation for vanity.

"I mean did *anybody* expect Jackson to do what he did? A regiment of cavalry maybe, but a whole *corps?* Fifteen miles in our rear."

Duryea had to admit to himself that he hadn't—although he *had* smelled a rat; he just hadn't gone out and found out where the smell was coming from. He cursed himself again.

"So the general's as surprised as anybody else, but I bet none of you sons *ever* seen anybody pick up the pieces quicker'n he did this morning."

"Run me right into the ground."

A general murmur of assent followed this disembodied voice.

"So old Stonewall's over there tonight burning up the whole world, looks like." Fielding's voice, Duryea thought, was enough to turn a man secesh. "But what *he* don't know is General Pope's slammed the door on'im. Got McDowell and Sigel up to Gainesville today. Reno in Greenwich, plus one of the Peninsula divisions that came in last evening with Heintzelman."

"That's Kearny."

"Kearny. Right. And Hooker up front here with Porter coming up behind us. Banks guarding the trains down the railroad line. I tell you, boys, moving an army around like that in one day, that takes some doing."

"Dang right it does."

"Cut old Jackson off, sure's shooting."

"Six divisions in *his* rear now."

"Now that's the point." Fielding's voice rose enthusiastically and Duryea shrank further from the sound. "Way the General's got'em lined up now, no way on God's earth Jackson ever can link back up with the rest of the Rebs. Pope's got us right square in between'em and getting ready to take Jackson right off the map, he hangs round over there burning up stores."

There's the rub, Duryea thought. Suppose Jackson didn't hang around for Pope to cut him up. Suppose he attacks Hooker, out there with three rounds per man? But Duryea reluctantly agreed with Fielding's main point—Pope had made the right moves that day, and Jackson would have no way of knowing Hooker was down to his last few shots. And if Pope *could* take a whole Reb corps out of the war—let alone the great Stonewall himself— then the fire sending up that red glow to the heavens above Manassas would be a small price to pay. Pope's name would go into the history books with the biggest victory of the war.

A hand touched Duryea's shoulder. He looked up to see Colonel Russell beckoning him away from the fire. Duryea rose swiftly and followed the colonel to the field headquarters tent—a big Sibley, the only one left after Stuart's raid on Catlett's Station. When Duryea ducked inside, Russell was already bending over a camp table spread with maps. Two candles cast flickering light over them.

"Way the general figures it . . ." Russell put a large forefinger on Manassas Junction. "Jackson's got cavalry and he'll know by now that McDowell and Sigel are at Gainesville with enough troops to whip'is tail. So he can't backtrack that way to hook up with Lee."

"Not likely."

Duryea had stared at these maps so often that the Virginia countryside—the crooked, narrow roads, the dusty little hamlets, the meandering creeks the natives called "runs," the low hills they called mountains, and the two railroad lines that joined at Manassas to give the region its dominant military feature—was graven on his mind, as if it were the view of the White River Valley out the rear windows of his Vermont home place.

"He could make tracks for Centreville." Russell's finger sketched a quick line across Bull Run at Blackburn's Ford. "But if he does, he takes himself farther away from Lee all the time and closer to Washington, and if he does that he's bound to know we'll swallow'im up like a cat on a titmouse."

That, too, made sense to Duryea, especially since McClellan's troops should by now be reaching Alexandria in force. Centreville, for Jackson, would be as near into the cannon's mouth as Gainesville, maybe with the certain end a little delayed.

"So what's he likely to do, Duryea?" The tone was rhetorical and Duryea knew the colonel too well to suppose that he really wanted an answer from a mere captain. "I'll tell you what he's likely to do. You got to remember, I was only one class behind Jackson at the Point."

From many a night around the headquarters camp fire, Duryea knew it all too well—hence what was coming next.

"And if you'd of told me the cadet I knew back then'd be the secesh general everybody's so afraid of today, I'd of said you were touched in the head."

"Never know how things'll turn out, Colonel."

"Not that Old Jack wasn't smart, and a worker. But there wasn't any *dash* to'im. Just a farm boy, sort of."

Russell brooded over this judgment—as if, Duryea thought, having known Jackson and misjudged him conferred on Russell some of the Reb general's reputed genius. Outside, Fielding's grating voice rose insistently, although Duryea could no longer make out his words.

"But anyway," Russell said at last, "knowing Jackson *now* and figuring what he's already done, General Pope thinks—and I believe he's right—we think he'll *attack*."

Again, Russell stabbed the map with his finger. "Either he'll come out tomorrow and hit Hooker along Broad Run with every musket he's got. Or else he'll move around our right, south of the O & A, and try to wreck some more trains back here." His fingers moved to the line of track between Warrenton Junction and Catlett's Station. "Get in our rear *again*. That's'is game, Duryea."

The captain pondered the map—mostly for time, as he did not really need to see it. His instinct told him something was wrong with Russell's reasoning, and Duryea had made up his mind that he was not going to neglect his instinct again. What else could he trust? On the other hand, he was not sure whether Russell really wanted a response, even yet; colonels and generals didn't usually. Duryea was, for a moment, uncertain what to do.

"What . . . uh . . ." Russell cleared his throat. "You know the ground in these parts better'n anyone. You think the general's got it figured right?"

So he and Pope were not absolutely sure of their conclusions after all. Duryea decided they really did want his opinion. At least, Russell did.

"Suppose he does go for Hooker in the morning, Colonel. He'll . . ."

"He'll put'is tail in a crack. Pope's ordered Porter to move up along the track at one o'clock tonight and be here by dawn to support the line on Broad Run."

"And you could move Kearny and Reno in from Greenwich on his flank." Russell nodded enthusiastically, chins wobbling in the candlelight. "But why should Jackson do that, Colonel? If he knows, like you think he does, that we've got McDowell and Sigel at Gainesville already. Wouldn't he be getting our whole army between him and Lee?"

"Exactly." Russell looked smug. "But I tell you, Jackson's cagey. He'll think we won't expect him to do it."

"I don't quite see that."

It made Duryea nervous to take such a conflicting stance, and he did not fail to see Russell's eyebrows pull together a little at his words. But Duryea felt he had crossed the Rubicon and might as well press on.

"As for moving around our right to hit us in the rear again . . ." Duryea shook his head. "He'd be risking running into whatever troops McClellan's got coming overland from Aquia—or whatever Jackson *thinks* McClellan's got coming, which is probably more than the fact. Besides, he's cut the O & A once. What's he need to do it again for?"

"You civilians." Russell's voice dripped contempt. "In war, you have to *study* the other side. Now you study Jackson in the Valley last spring . . . the very fact he tried this flank march of his right into the bear trap Pope's setting for'im . . . Duryea, Jackson'll do what ordinarily you'd *least expect* him to do. He always does. He'll hit us on the right. In the morning."

So Pope's mind *was* made up, which of course meant that Russell's was, too. And Micah G. Duryea's neck was out far enough. Still, if they'd sought his opinion . . . then somebody somewhere had some doubt. And Duryea's instinct was strong.

"Colonel . . . I . . . ah, respectfully, sir . . . I just don't think Jackson'll do it."

"Dammit, Duryea, give me one good reason he won't."

Duryea knew that Russell wanted a *tangible* reason—fortifications here, an impassable river there, troops moving in this vicinity or no supplies available in that. He had no such reason, hence no chance to change Russell's mind, but Duryea followed his instinct anyway—feeling not unlike a man tiptoeing over quicksand.

"Sir, by your own reasoning, he might just as easy hit us at Gainesville. If he always does what you'd least expect."

Russell stared at him in the candlelight, his broad face, over the horse's-tail mustaches, dark with disapproval. His mouth worked as if he were sucking on a candy, and Duryea remembered that the man was in constant pain from rotten teeth. Nobody could think straight when his teeth hurt.

"Even Jackson, Duryea . . ." Russell paused for emphasis. "Even Tom Jackson aint likely to commit suicide. We got an order for you to take to McDowell." He pulled a folded paper from his pocket and handed it to the captain. "Pope wants you to see to it McDowell gets that personally and understands what Pope wants'im to do. Because listen, Duryea . . . Pope means business. He aims to concentrate the better part of fifty thousand men on Manassas tomorrow morning and bag the whole crowd of 'em. Can't be more'n twenty, twenty-five thousand over there. And he don't aim for anybody to mess it up. Read that and look here."

Quickly, Russell explained Pope's plans, tapping his fingers as confidently on the map as if he were moving rooks and pawns through a chess problem. McDowell and Sigel—McDowell in command of both corps—were ordered to march "at the earliest dawn of day" on Manassas Junction, keeping their right flank on the Manassas Gap Railroad tracks, extending their left "well to the east," toward Bull Run.

"We're also bringing Kearny up from Greenwich to Bristoe, starting at Dawn. So we'll have Hooker and Porter moving in on Manassas along the O & A, with Kearny in support from Bristoe. And we'll have McDowell and Sigel coming down the Gap line to the Junction. With luck those two jaws'll close and we'll bag the whole crowd, Duryea."

Trying to memorize the order in case he lost the written version, Duryea quickly spotted the key sentence:

> If you will march promptly and rapidly at the earliest dawn of day upon Manassas Junction, we shall bag the whole crowd.

Pope and Russell obviously liked the last phrase but to Duryea's mind it was too positive, represented too simple a view of too complex a situation. Duryea's insinct told him the plan was wrong, the order was wrong, everything suddenly was going wrong. He stared at the map, ready to speak out, but he knew he had nothing convincing to say, unless he could tell Russell *what* was wrong.

And that, Duryea had to admit, he did not yet know. But he would have time on the seven-mile ride to Gainesville to figure it out. He looked forward to the darkness and solitude of the ride, away from the nerve-jangling complexities and involvements of headquarters—away from Fielding's voice and Russell's overbearing manner. Out there in the night maybe things would come clear to him. They usually did.

"Now put on some speed, Duryea. Show McDowell just what I showed you on the map. He'll have to hustle, he gets five divisions moving by daylight."

The colonel followed Duryea out of the tent. Beyond the Bristoe the red glow from Manassas had spread across the eastern sky. Duryea could hear the measured tramp of a sentinel, the restless clatter of the headquarters guard horses somewhere in the darkness. There was a burst of laughter from the camp fire, and as it died away a familiar resonant voice resumed some military yarn. John Pope had joined his staff. Which would mean, Duryea knew, a sleepless night for most of them.

"Duryea." Russell touched his elbow. "You got a better notion, now's the last chance to tell me."

So Russell, too, knew the order to McDowell was wrong— at least feared it might be. Duryea looked at the red glow over Manassas. Not five miles away, he thought. Nearer than McDowell. And all they needed to know was in one man's head over there beyond Broad Run.

But Russell and Pope couldn't divine that. Duryea couldn't either. And unless he could make an educated guess . . .

"Colonel . . . I better get on to McDowell."

A quarter mile from Manassas Junction, on the road to Blackburn's Ford, Private Ambrose Riggin placed his knapsack against the bottom of an overturned wagon. Then he eased himself down against the knapsack, which—for once—was jammed with good things: a can of sardines, a hunk of Yankee cheese, two bars of soap, a jar of hard candy and another of pickles, and a fine linen handkerchief knotted around a good half pound of coffee.

A good haul, Private Riggin reflected. And the best of it was the clean underwear, clean socks, and heavy new Yank shoes with which he had outfitted himself. He was doubly lucky, moreover, since most of Ewell's Division, fighting as rear guard, had gotten little more than maybe a couple of potatoes after the rest of the army had plundered the Yank stores.

But General Lawton had foreseen that and had detached the Thirteenth Georgia to salvage what it could for the whole brigade. Ambrose Riggin of Company B, like Sergeant Cade and Private Grice of Company D, had not missed his opportunity. He felt so much like a new man that, as he waited with Lawton's Brigade to move out with the rest of Ewell's Division, he decided to write home. The night was good and dark by then—Taliaferro's Division was already marching away from the Junction on some other road—but Private Riggin could see well enough in the light from the fires rising over the warehouses and the cars. The leaping flames also had destroyed whatever cool the evening might have brought, and his new drawers were already damp with sweat.

He gazed at the fire with awe. Never seen the beat of it. Man don't get to see no fer like at more'n oncet a lifetime. Kindly sicknin, though, burnin all'em stores folks at home could live off for months.

By the reddish light, he read over Maggie's last letter. Maggie wrote a good hand for a woman; at the sight of it, something stirred in him proudly. A good day's work when Ambrose Riggin stood up to the preacher with Margaret Ann Hopewell, and not just cause he'd got two good mules outten her daddy for dowry.

Maggie'd been a better wife than even he expected. Like the hand she wrote and the way she put down her feelings there at the end:

Of the thousand aching hearts all around and God only knows how many yet to bleed Dear I pray always that you may be spared but the best day I pass I fear for you and feel that if you are taken from me life will be a heavy burden.

I can't feel that you are to be killed tho you are greatly exposed but the Lord is able to preserve you, that he may be a wall around + about you I never cease to pray. Dear above everything else it is a consolation to me to feel, that if you fell, it will be in the arms of Jesus, where there will be no wars or trials after death. And you must ever know that I shall endevor always to serve my Maker right + lead our little ones to Christ while young.

Yours + etc.
M. A. Riggin

Ambrose had foraged up a stub of pencil and some forms blank on one side from a desk he had rifled in one of the warehouses. He had also found a silver-framed likeness of a woman, some Yank's wife, probly, with a high head of hair. He was a little ashamed that he had taken that, too. But maybe someday he'd have a likeness of Maggie to put in the frame and for all he knew that Yank was already in heaven or hell, as the case might be.

Ambrose tongued the pencil point and began to write.

Dear Mag how are you wee are fine but awful hot got some yankey boots today were oblige to burn all the stores wee captured for wee are in the rear of the whole yankey army but on the march soon for old Jack can't lie still.

Weal have a big fight up here before long but I hope theyd put it off untwill the weather turns cooler so many of the wounded die this hot weather + there is all ways 10 times as many wounded as gets killed.

Not far away, as Company D also waited for the Thirteenth Georgia to move out, Sergeant Cade inquired of the New Man:

"Seen 'ny dead Yanks yit?"

"I uz on burl deetail back to Slaughter Mountain." Grice was anxious, as always, for Cady's approval.

"Then you know."

"Know whut?"

"Whut us-uns gone look like gits kilt today'r tomarr."

"Like deaders, I reck'n." Death was not a popular subject with the New Man, though a major topic in Company D.

"Yankee deaders." Cady happily built suspense from his superior knowledge. "You seen how they swole up'n turn purple?"

"Uh-huh." Grice had noticed nothing about Yank deaders except that they were dead. But he would agree to anything Cady said. Grice followed Cady about like a friendly, mangy dog.

"Reason is," Cady said, "Yanks is vittled so good. Practic'ly stuffed, you mought say. Lie out'na sun dead, all at food inside'm spoils. Puff'em like toad frogs. Ever seen one-a us-uns kilt'n swole up like at? Hungry's we usely is?"

"Shoot, no."

"Will soon." Caddy nodded wisely. "This army got so dang much Yank food'n its gut now, man git kilt gone swole up like a Yank. Ol Jack might not even stop to burr'im."

Farther out from the Junction where the firelight barely relieved the dark night, Larkin Folsom slept under a tree, the victim of fatigue, a full stomach, and two long drinks of warm Rhine wine permitted him by Corporal Gilmore. The corporal had pilfered the bottle practically from under the eyes of General Arnall and shared it with Folsom over a splendid supper of Yank beefsteak, fresh-baked bread, and canned stewed tomatoes. That was after the abstemious general, replenished with the same fare minus the wine, had ridden off to Powell Hill's headquarters back near the burning warehouses. Corporal Gilmore and Folsom were of the opinion that Arnall had no idea where they were supposed to march to that night.

Since their encounter at Thoroughfare Gap the day before, Folsom had begun to wonder why he had ever been scared of the corporal. He was big and rough and dirty-talking all right, but there was a kindhearted side to him. Like sharing the wine— Folsom's first. And when the General had stomped around in a bad mood that day because of being in arrest, the corporal had helped Folsom with all the chores Arnall kept thinking up for him. Folsom's knapsack, moreover, was stuffed with good things to eat and a pair of clean drawers Gilmore had rustled up. Folsom did not want to put them on until he had found a creek to wash in.

He slept on his side, his head on his blanket roll. He was dreaming, as he often did, that he was safe in the old crib at home in Chowan County. His mother had given him his bath and dried him with warm, soft cloths; then she had powdered him all over, her gentle hands touching him, patting him. His body throbbed with the good feeling of his mother's hands. Now they were soft on the bottom of his feet, and her touch felt so good Folsom writhed at the gentle stroking of those hands, and rolled over on his back.

Then he was awake, or thought he was, but his mother was still touching him, between his legs now. But the red sky glowing above him couldn't be Chowan County. Never felt so good, his whole body feeling warm, melting, soft, like his mother's touch. Eyes closing again, feeling so good all over.

A half mile away a burning warehouse collapsed with an enormous hissing roar. Startled, Larkin Folsom sat straight up.

"Easy, now." Corporal Gilmore's hoarse whisper was close to his ear, so close Folsom could feel the corporal's warm breath on his neck. "Go back to sleep, boy." His hand pressed gently on Folsom's shoulder.

Folsom started to lie back down, seeking his dream again. As he did so, he realized Corporal Gilmore's other hand was between his legs, holding his thing. Folsom opened his mouth to cry out but the big hand on his shoulder closed quickly over his mouth and bore his head powerfully back down to his blanket roll.

A mile or two northwest Lott McGrath—still in his checked shirt but clomping along in clean socks and new Federal brogues, the first crooked shoes he had ever worn—was expressing his displeasure at being ordered on a night march.

"Aint's if we aint already marched our ass off to git *to* Manassas." He poked Private Sowell's arm. "Why'n hell we got to march *away* fore we even had time to git to know the place?"

"You want to stay, go back'n stay. Yanks gone gitchuh, they'll gitchuh, back ther or up ahead, don't make no diffrunce to them wher they do it."

"No Yanks behind us that I can tell. How come Ol Jack marchin us off on our lonesome?"

"He aint," Sowell said. "He come with us hisself. Don't that make you feel no better?"

"He carry this-yer piece for me, it mought."

They tramped along in silence. Then Sowell inquired solicitously. "How's'em boots?"

"Rather had a pair of straights. They gonna cut'em diffrunt for each foot, look like they got to fit'em right on you."

"S'why I aint tooken'um." Sowell's voice dripped with satisfaction. "Didn't I tell you? Better stick with what a man's use to."

"Yeah, well," Lott said. "Crooked or straight, these-yer beats barefoot."

The Stonewall Brigade, bringing up the rear of Taliaferro's Division as usual, marched on in the moonless night, the lurid glare over Manassas falling behind them. The tramp of hundreds of feet echoed back from the rolling slopes through which they seemed to be passing, although the night was too dark for them to see much.

"Hey, Sowbelly. You know the beatines thing I seen in this war yet?"

"I reckon I'm gone know pretty soon, whether I care or not."

"Last summer right round here somewhere. Usunses come down on the cars from the Valley under Joe Johnston and had a big fight with Yanks comin crost Bull Run. That-uz fore you jined up."

"I-uz here." Private Gillum Stone was marching in his accustomed place at Lott's right.

"Not so's em Yanks ever knowed it. But they's this old cockeyed boy in the compny then, Tobe somethin'is name was . . ."

"Only man I ever seed could look at'is own nose," Gilly said.

"Yeah, well. That's the one. We-uz comin'on the double up the road — mought of been thisun rightcherc—'n Ol Jack's poundin longside yellin 'Close up, men! Close up!' way he alluz does. Tobe turns to me, Tobe sez, 'Lott, in two hours I'm-a be a dead man. Send this home to my woman.' Then he hands me'is ol silver watch on a chain."

"Had a vision, did'e?" Private Sowell knew that many a soldier had foretold his own death. Like most veterans, he was intensely interested in such phenomena.

"Must of. So we goes up this hill where the Yanks comin. Seem like to me back then it-uz a pretty big fight. Might not seem like much now but that-uz a year ago."

"Hottest day I ever knowed," Gilly said.

"But after a while, kind of a letup come along'n I'm lettin my bar'l cool'n I look to one side'n there's ol Tobe peerin at me with at cockeye of hissen. 'Why, Tobe,' I sez, 'you aint kilt after all.'"

"Shit you say!" Private Sowell's voice was severe with shock and disapproval. "You *tryin* to put the bad mouth on'im?"

"Maybe I done it. Cause the words aint no sooner outten my mouth, this solid shot come whislin along'n took Tobe sideways inna hip. Tore off a leg'n spread'is bowels all over me, shit'n all."

"Serve you right." Private Sowell registered final judgment. "As good as kilt that pore son yourself."

"Sperrit flown fore'is body hit the ground. I sent'is watch home the next day."

"Not if I know you," Gilly said.

"Never heard nare word from the widda, though."

Wee had to shoot 3 men in front of the hole army for desertion this I think the 2d time they was caught this time leading the enemy round into the rear of our army. The shooting is bad punishment that I regret to witness but am compelled to see it Capten says in war it is a just punishment. It is a sight that I hope I never have to witness again all stout able bodied young men such is militery law.

Private Riggin, chewing his pencil stub, could not bring himself to tell Maggie that he had been one of the firing squad, although his conscience was easy that he had not shot any of the deserters. He read back over his letter, wondering why he'd told his wife about the executions. Mought upset her some.

But before he could decide whether to tear off that part of the letter, the order came for Lawton's Brigade to fall in. Ewell's Division was ready to move, although nobody in Ambrose Riggin's company had any idea where they were going.

"Nobody does," his company commander told anybody that asked. "Ceptin maybe Ol Jack and I aint right down sure bout him."

Duryea rode the seven miles of country road between Bristoe and Gainesville—as he surmised, exactly the same road by which Jackson's men had marched to the O & A the day before—in pitch darkness, arriving before midnight. But it proved harder than he had expected to locate Irvin McDowell's headquarters.

That general was then commanding two corps—his own, consisting of King's and Ricketts's divisions, augmented by Reynold's Pennsylvania Reserves, the first reinforcing unit that had arrived from McClellan; and Sigel's Germans, with divisions commanded by Schenck and Schurz, together with an independent brigade under Milroy.

This great force, more than 30,000 men, was spread in all directions over miles of countryside around Gainesville—a veritable overnight city sprung from the dusty earth like Virginia broomsedge. Its camp fires dotted the night, the silence of which was broken by the low hum of men talking, laughing, snoring, moving about—of horses' hooves on the lanes and fields, the occasional rumble of a wagon and the harsh squawk of ungreased metal. The smell of the army hung no less tangibly in the August air—a smell of frying meat and steaming coffee and resinous fires, of unwashed men and human offal, of horses and their droppings, littering the roads by the ton.

Duryea rode west on the Warrenton Pike, inquiring everywhere he could for McDowell's headquarters; but no one seemed to know. Finally, when he thought he was bound to have gone too far from Gainesville, he dismounted and led his horse into what looked like a regimental headquarters area. Officers lounged by a blazing fire, some on the ground, one in a camp chair. On the rim of the firelight other men moved about, and a lantern gleamed from a Sibley tent. Pretty good life here, Duryea thought.

"Any of you gentlemen point me to General McDowell's headquarters?"

"Sure to be in the rear. If we only knowed which way the rear is."

The men around the fire laughed uproariously at this voice from out of the darkness beyond their circle.

"I'm carrying a dispatch from General Pope."

That silenced the laughter, although it was more than Duryea had wanted to disclose. The man in the camp chair rose and came across the ring of firelight. Duryea saw the eagles on his shoulder straps and saluted smartly.

"Captain Duryea, sir, Pope's staff."

The colonel's return salute was perfunctory. "Colonel Bullock, Sixth Wisconsin. Gibbon's Brigade. Reckon we'll be moving thataway?" He jerked his head toward the red sky to the east; it had grown even brighter since Duryea, who had been riding west, had looked back.

"Couldn't say, sir." Duryea disapproved of the question as unmilitary, though he knew Bullock was only being convivial and could hardly have expected an answer.

"Cuppa coffee?" A major had come up beside Bullock and Duryea saluted him, too, even if western troops like these were known for their informality.

"Good of you." Duryea followed the major to the fire and accepted a steaming tin cup almost too hot to hold.

"That stuff'll make bullets bounce off your belly." The major held out his hand. "Reverdy Dowd, Captain. Come far?"

"Bristoe. Most likely I've come too far to find McDowell herebouts."

"Most likely." Dowd waved his hand toward Gainesville. "Leastways you'll find our division HQ—General King—bout half a mile that way. King usually stays near McDowell's coattails."

More western informality. Duryea tried to remember what King's Division or Gibbon's Brigade might have done to distinguish themselves.

Dowd shoved a broad-brimmed hat back on his head. "Pope's at Bristoe, is he? What's all that business over there?" He nodded at the glowing eastern sky.

Duryea sipped scalding coffee while considering whether to answer. He concluded that it would be silly to treat a fire like that as some kind of military secret. And these men would soon be looking at the ruins, if Pope was right about Jackson. A big if.

"Stores at Manassas. Rebs're burnin' 'em."

Dowd shook his head glumly. "Had to be that, I figured. Don't cheer me up much."

Colonel Bullock spoke from behind Duryea. "Some fire for a cavalry raid."

Might's well let 'em know the worst. Duryea thought. Before they find out the hard way. "That's not cavalry, Colonel. That's Jackson over there. Three divisions anyway. Hooker run straight up on 'em today."

Bullock's face, in the firelight, tightened in shock. "Three divisions in our rear? How the hell can that be?"

"Well...uh..." Duryea decided he'd said enough. "What I hear, anyway."

"No wonder you're hunting up McDowell." Bullock looked at

the red sky and swore fervently, offending Duryea. "What'n hell we sitting round here for?"

"Tell you what." Dowd seated his hat firmly on his forehead. "I'll ride along, help you find'im."

"Much obliged." Duryea tossed the rest of his fierce coffee into the fire, part of which went out with a hiss.

But even with Dowd as a guide, it took more than a half hour to locate McDowell's headquarters in the intensely dark night. The two officers trotted along the pike, getting confusing suggestions at every camp fire, but eventually Dowd proved right. McDowell's tent was on a rise of ground above King's headquarters. Duryea was taken immediately to McDowell himself.

Reverdy Dowd dismounted and joined a ring of staff officers around a camp fire much like the one he had just left; he was handed a cup of coffee that he immediately realized was as different from the Sixth Wisconsin's muddy brew as a corps was from a regiment. These generals knew how to live.

"Who you brung in, Maje?"

Dowd, though not yet blooded in battle, was a veteran of field life. He had a little information, which meant that if he played his cards right he might be able to get a little more. He decided to put no more than one card on the table at a time.

"Messenger from Pope."

There was a small stir around the fire and Dowd sipped coffee smugly. "Good java," he said.

"Pope, huh? Still got'is headquarters in'is saddle?"

Dowd joined in the general laugh, and looked over his shoulder at the red eastern sky. A smallish man sat on the ground a few feet behind him and to his right, his hands clasped about his knees.

"Where's'is saddle at right now, Maje?"

Dowd tossed out another card. "Bristoe."

A dark shape came into the firelight and turned into a fat lieutenant colonel of engineers. He poured himself coffee. "O & A must be cut, I reckon."

Dowd loosened a third card in his hand. "Figures."

"Could hear fighting over round there this afternoon."

"Hooker." Dowd played that one quickly, a throwaway.

"Hooker's up?"

The small man sitting behind Dowd unclasped his knee and sat a little straighter. But no one paid him any attention, or noticed that he wore no insignia on his uniform coat.

Dowd was perilously near the end of his information but he

still held his ace. "That was Hooker fighting Jackson you heard all afternoon."

"Jackson!"

The word muttered and whistled around the fireside. Dowd was immensely pleased, although he had gone down to his ace with nothing to show for it. The fat lieutenant colonel, who had eased himself puffing and mumbling to the ground, blew on his coffee. From across the fire, a quiet but sharp voice silenced the others.

"Did Hooker round 'em up?"

"Who?"

"Jackson's raiding party."

"That raiding party . . ." Dowd decided to come out with it, as nonchalantly as he could. "Is Jackson's whole corps. Three divisions at least."

Silence fell on the camp fire, as if a hand had been clasped over every mouth. Then the sharp voice: "That fire's them burning our supply dump at Manassas?"

"Figures, don't it?"

"Then we got'em!"

The small man without insignia had risen and drifted back into the darkness beyond the firelight, still within earshot of the conversation. He was not trying to hide or avoid observation. Even in daylight, for more than a week, since General Halleck in Washington had ordered newspaper correspondents away from the Army of Virginia, Charlie Keach had been moving virtually unchallenged among the various units of Pope's army. For two days he had been practically a part of McDowell's headquarters staff, and no one had seemed to notice that he was a stranger or that neither he nor his horse was in regulation dress. This did not improve Keach's opinion of McDowell's escort troops but it didn't surprise him, either.

Keach was an enterprising reporter, quick and resourceful, and the Army of Virginia was maneuvering in the field in the near presence of an enemy it feared and respected. Its officers had better things to do than to try to sniff out correspondents defying Halleck's order. Keach, in fact, had taken his cue from none other than Major General John Pope, with whom he'd been talking the day Halleck's directive clicked over the wires.

Keach had discovered in his first dealings with Pope that the general would not discourage publicity—although, Keach wrote Hale, his Washington bureau chief: "He will have facts his own way."

Keach had quickly gained Pope's favor with a certain flattering tone in his dispatches—a small price to pay for the news Pope fed him. So Keach was dismayed when Pope read Halleck's order aloud.

"Can I see that?" Keach held out his hand, thinking Pope might be playing some heavy-handed joke.

"Oh, no." Pope folded the telegram and placed it with other papers on his camp desk.

"Why not?"

"Keach..." Pope puffed on his cigar, staring past the correspondent at the green valley of the Rappahannock. "This ain't an official interview, is it?"

"If you say not."

Pope nodded and took the cigar out of his mouth. "Then if I were you, I wouldn't leave until I *received* the order."

So Keach hadn't. But he'd stayed away from Pope, so as not to embarrass the general. That night, however, as he listened to the strange major and McDowell's staff chatting, he decided he needed Pope's own version of the surprising news the major had brought. Soon's he could, he thought, he'd find his horse and head for Bristoe.

"I tell you," the sharp voice was saying, "that means we got Jackson cornered."

"How's that?" The fat engineer sounded bewildered.

"Cause if Hooker's up, that's Heintzelman's Corps and Heintzelman must have brought Kearny, too. And we got five divisions on this side of 'em. We'll smash old Stonewall tween us in the morning."

Five divisions plus Hooker and Kearny. Dowd raked in the pot for which he had been playing. March to Richmond, damn near, with that size of an army. So the man with the sharp voice was making sense. Jackson was lying there like a dog bone, with a pair of hungry jaws ready to close on'im.

"You count them damn worthless German cabbage heads?" The fat engineer spat into the fire.

"Yeah," somebody else said. "Even if they was worth a hoot'n hell, they's out to the west somewheres. Guarding some gap or something."

In his nearby tent, General McDowell looked down at his map and put his finger on Thoroughfare Gap. He looked up at Duryea quizzically. The question he had just asked echoed in the yellow light of a lantern hanging from a tentpole overhead; a candle sputtered and smoked on the map table.

"I couldn't say, General. Colonel Russell didn't discuss that with me."

But in that moment, Duryea knew what was wrong with Pope's order. He knew why his instinct had told him it was a mistake, why Russell—his instinct probably bothering him, too—had pressed him for his views. It was as if the map had been picked up from the table and held an inch from his face, so that what he had not seen when Russell showed him the plan, what he had not grasped on the long night ride from Bristoe, suddenly flared like a candle in his eyes. It was the worst moment Duryea had had since the news of his dog's death.

The fact was plain. If McDowell and Sigel marched on Manassas as ordered, "at the earliest dawn of day," they would leave Thoroughfare Gap wide open and unguarded for Longstreet's Corps, the other wing of Lee's Rebel army, to pour through on the way to rejoin Jackson. And then it would be a question of who would bag whom.

"Well . . ." The word was almost a sigh, as McDowell straightened up from the map. He was plump, deliberate, schoolmasterish; in the heavy undershirt and suspenders in which he had received Duryea he looked a little ludicrous, his round face owlish and distressed. "General Pope must surely have planned for that. I'll give the orders immediately."

Duryea did not believe Pope and Russell had "planned for" anything about Thoroughfare Gap. Russell had not even mentioned it. Duryea wanted to cry out, protest, snatch back the order he had brought from Pope. But he knew that even to say a word would shock the general and certainly would do no good. Irvin McDowell was a soldier who followed orders.

"I'll . . . ah . . . I'll take back your response to General Pope, sir."

Army and corps headquarters had been too rapidly on the move, and no telegraph line had been laid between Bristoe and Gainesville—negligible hamlets, both of them, just the day before. So even if Pope saw the problem and changed his mind it would be too late to stop McDowell's movement.

"Tell General Pope . . ." McDowell's voice was heavy with responsibility, and unspoken doubt. "Tell'im I'll march . . ." He glanced at the order again. ". . . At earliest dawn."

Chapter Four

$\text{\textbf{\textreferencemark}}$

August 28—
Morning and Afternoon

SHORTLY AFTER MIDNIGHT an explosion shot a flash of orange across the reflected firelight above Manassas Junction. Fargo Hart stirred in his blankets and sat up. He lightly shook Andrew Peterson, who slept a few feet away. The photographer awoke instantly.

Enormous stocks of powder, shot, and shell had been accumulated by the Federals at Manassas; after Jackson's men had carried off what they could in cartridge boxes, limber chests, and the few wagons available, enough to stock an army remained to be destroyed. Hart guessed that the first magazine had just gone up.

He had brought Peterson as a guest to Stuart's bivouac, which had been set up near Ball's Ford on Bull Run. As the explosions continued, the two men strolled up a nearby hillside and sat down to watch the fireworks. Neither realized that atop the same hill, but a mile to the west, Jackson and his brigade had earned their nicknames thirteen months before.

Hart produced one of his filched bottles of champagne. "Drink to the engineers." He set to work on the cork.

"If that stuff's warm, it'll go off like a geyser."

"Peterson . . ." Hart pressed on the side of the cork with both thumbs, the bottle clenched between his knees. "What I don't already know about champagne, I seriously doubt you or any man this side of the water can tell me."

"How long were you over there?"

"Five years. Champagne always puts me in mind of a certain French lady I knew name Janelle. She didn't drink anything but."

"Five years studyin history?"

"You could spend that much time on the Romans alone. Or the Greeks. Still not know all there is to know. You a married man, Peterson?"

The cork popped out of the bottle with a satisfying report. Champagne rose from the neck in a white spray; but before as much as a spoonful had escaped, Hart had his mouth over the opening. For a moment, he remained bent forward, a blissful expression on his face, the champagne fizzing against his palate.

"Not any more," Peterson said.

Janelle's doddering, titled husband had been happy to have a young stud around to keep his child bride satisfied, and had openly hoped she would deliver an heir as a consequence, though there was no chance it would be of his own thin blue blood. Janelle and the old count or marquis or whatever he was, in their easy acceptance of things, had been a little too much for Fargo Hart—though his experience in Europe had been more sophisticated than imagined by those who teased him at Stuart's mess.

Hart took the bottle out of his mouth, wiped the opening with his sleeve, and handed the champagne to Peterson.

"Neither of us with a woman to go home to. Might's well drink."

"Maybe we're better off."

"Not if it was Janelle." Small crimson mouth that could do things Hart had never even dreamed about.

Above Manassas, white phosphorus flares hung blindingly.

"Some show," Peterson said. "Better'n a battle."

"Hell of a lot better. Nobody gettin killed."

Another huge explosion caused the earth under them to tremble. Shells traced bright arcs into the air and flared like gigantic matches. Peterson drank from the bottle.

"Mmmmm. Even warm, that's good. Hart, you ever think about the energy bein wasted on this war?"

Hart retrieved the bottle. "Whose energy?"

"All that over there." Peterson gestured at the fireworks over Manassas. "What it takes to fight this war. Say six horses pullin a Napoleon. Horsepower. Nine men servin the piece. Manpower. Twelve-pounder shell, gunners tell me it actually weighs thirteen with a powder charge. That's explosive power. All just for one shot that might do nothin but kick up dirt somewhere."

"Not to mention somebody's brainpower decidin where to put the piece and what to aim it at."

"So you multiply all that energy out to the whole Federal army. Then add this one. Plus Longstreet. Bragg out west and all the other armies. Harness it up. Hart, you know what you could do with that much power?"

Hart handed him the bottle. "Shoot yourself out of that Napoleon right over the Atlantic Ocean into a featherbed in Amsterdam."

More explosions rocked the ground and filled the sky over Manassas with fireballs and glowing tracers. Peterson drank while the explosions muttered into silence.

"You could move the Blue Ridge Mountains and plant corn where they used to sit. Dam up the Mississippi and water the country from Pennsylvania to Santa Fe. But we aint doin any of that, Hart. All that energy's bein wasted. Like over there tonight. All that burnin and blowin up. For what? Just sheer waste and destruction. Oh, I know Jackson'd say he's denyin it to the enemy. But that kind of logic assumes logic in war to begin with. The *real* logic is that one tenth the energy he's blowin off in the sky, you could feed a thousand families God knows how long."

"Crazy goddam war."

Hart took the bottle of champagne, as shells crumped and burst in the eastern sky and ammunition dumps went up in nearly rhythmic explosions. Even though Peterson's talk interested him—not the kind of thing he usually heard at Stuart's mess table—he was cautious about opening himself to a virtual stranger.

"Worst of it is, you can't expect to spend off a country's energy in a year or two—I mean whole generations of energy—and not pay a price. This country'll pay that price, Hart. Bound to be steep."

"Which country?" Damn bottle about empty. Good things never last.

"Come on, Cap'n. You aint a damn fool like most. You know history, you know can't be but one country."

Hart, who knew much about the written history of the world but not much about the portion of it called America, was vaguely shocked.

"Then what'n hell's this war about?"

"What kind of country it's goin to be."

Brumpp! went a small magazine. Hart assumed that Peterson meant whether African slavery would be abolished, a question he did not like to discuss and about which he had not let himself think very much. He suspected that if he did, the historian in him would be able to find no justification for the idea or the institution. But abolition also meant displacement, upheaval, the disruption of a rational order—hence, to Hart's deepest nature, had always seemed the greater evil. Besides, Fargo Hart had been reared to regard Africans as people who washed his shirts and shined his boots, and rearing always outweighs history.

He wondered briefly what had become of loyal Robaire—as Hart called him and Hart's mother spelled his name—somewhere back there with the trains and the rest of the army. Mrs. Hart had sent him along with her son less to look after him than because to her it was intolerable that he should be without a body servant when other well-bred officers had them.

"Spawn a country from war . . ." Peterson took the champagne bottle from his hand. "From waste and destruction, seems likely to me you'll get a country with all that in the blood."

Hart looked at him sharply, in the flare of exploding shells. Not talking about slavery after all. "Goin to make everything different," he said. "This war. Win or lose."

"*Nobody* wins." Peterson tossed the empty bottle down the hill. It made a tiny clatter against the distant booms and crashes of the exploding dumps.

Hart was surprised to hear his own deepest thoughts in another's words. He had thought of himself as isolated, heretical, a secret onlooker, skeptical among believing hosts. Sometimes he had cursed the fate, the education, the chance, whatever, that had made him different and conscious of it, questioning, unable to accept assurances or claims—yet bound by some dark root of instinct to the warriors around him, even to Ol Jack himself.

"Yet men die by the thousands," Peterson said, "with no end in sight."

"The killin's not the worst of it."

"It is to the ones that die."

"But for some people," Hart said, "the worst thing is if you come not to *mind* the killin. If you just get to be a part of it."

Peterson sat silently for a while, then took two thin cigars from his pocket and gave one to Hart.

"*Nobody* wins," he said again.

The match Peterson produced from a waterproof pouch made the tiniest of flares against the waning flash and crump of munitions over Manassas; but as he lit both cigars their eyes met, and in the match's glow Hart saw that Peterson, too, was a heretic, as isolated as he from the commonality of the war.

Odd to find an officer, Peterson was thinking, who did not seem to consider the war necessary to his manhood. Especially a staff officer. They were often the worst, in fancy uniforms, spouting Napoleonic couplets about flank movements, enfilading fire, strategic maneuver—yet they were the ones who had to do the least fighting, dashing around giving orders from the backs of horses that would carry them quickly out of the consequences of the orders they gave.

"Where's your Whatsit Wagon?"

"Comin on behind. Somewhere."

"Had it here, you could make a picture of that." Hart pointed at the sky just then brilliantly lit with exploding star candles.

"Couldn't stop it."

"The war?"

"I mean my camera aint fast enough to arrest the movement. I'd just get a blur."

Peterson realized immediately that this could mean nothing to Hart, who knew no more of photography than of alchemy. Almost no one did, or cared. Those who had known Andrew Peterson as a respectable lawyer, for instance, had looked upon him as more than a little crazy when in the 1850s, he had started to spend time and money—every penny begrudged by his wife—on Archer's collodion process for glass-plate photography. But the very smell of the dark-room chemicals had fascinated him —even the silver nitrate that ate holes in his coatsleeves and blackened his fingers; and he never tired of the miracles emerging on his negatives in their coating of pyrogallic acid, or the unblinking reality he saw fixed in them forever.

So he persisted, spending more and more of his time with his plates and potions and lenses; and acquaintances thought him positively daft when in 1858 he abandoned the law and converted his Peachtree Street offices to a portrait studio. Ol Peterson a little tetched by what happen to his wife, they said.

Their views had hardly changed, even when the craze for photographic *cartes de visite* had brought a beginning prosperity to Peterson's studio, the American Pantheon. For why would a professional man turn himself to the commercial trickery of light and shadow?

"When my wagon gets up, I'll show you how the camera works, Hart. If you want."

They sat in silence a while longer, until the last of the explosions echoed into the night over Manassas and the fiery streaks had faded into the duller glow of dying fires. And as darkness reclaimed the skies, Peterson thought regretfully that at least in its grandeur the spectacle might have been equal to the waste and destruction, the energy gone crazy, that had caused it. He would have given much for equipment capable of capturing the scene on his plates, as Hart had suggested—the fire and the smoke and the flashlit movement, lurid and chaotic as a Turner oil.

"Arrest the movement," Hart said. "If a camera could do that, it could stop the war."

Peterson chuckled. "Not exactly. But every time I take the cap off my lens, there's a moment of time that's caught and fixed. With luck, you could say forever."

He did not think of himself as an artist. He had little interest in abstract conceptions of beauty, such as the flowers and garlands he did not even know were then being painstakingly arranged for the camera by Adolphe Braun; the staged allegories of Rejlander and Robinson would have repelled him had he had the opportunity to study them; and while he sought earnestly in his portraiture to bring out the most powerful qualities of his subjects, his method was too direct and uncalculated to have gained him comparison with Nadar or Carjat or even Brady's experts.

Peterson thought of himself as a photographer of history. He had found his purpose in the war and, recognizing it instantly, had thrown all the profits from the sale of his Pantheon into making war's record—a true record, uncolored by the persistent romanticism and vainglory and religiosity of those who fought it. Peterson followed Pope or Ol Jack or any other general only to register the grim sights of the field, to freeze on the sensitive plates behind his opened lens the moments in which death and havoc wrought the truth of war—and shaped the future, he feared, into a monster as grim and devouring as war itself.

"Doesn't take a camera to fix a moment forever," Hart said. "Happens sometimes in your head."

"But your head'll play tricks on you. The camera never does, not if you let it alone to do its work."

Hart flipped away the cigar he had hardly smoked and began to talk, surprising Peterson with the sudden flow of his speech. He had seemed a taciturn young man, even a little haughty. Now his words seemed to come readily and without thought or prearrangement, as if the explosions over Manassas might have jarred them loose. He talked for a long time before he paused. Then:

"That's what I mean by a moment being fixed in your head. I can still see the way that engineer looked back at me, his face twisted up, tellin me to go to hell."

Hart had fallen silent momentarily because he had suddenly begun to *hear* himself talking, and was astonished to find himself doing so, on such a subject, to the virtual stranger beside him on the hill. Damn champagne, he thought.

But in the renewed stillness—no explosions now from the ruins of Manassas, nothing but night sounds and the steady clop-clopping of a trotting horse on a nearby road—he sensed that Peterson had been listening and was waiting for him to go on. It occurred to him then—a revelation in his short life—that having someone who would listen might have *caused* him to talk—was, in fact, the only good reason to talk, and rare enough to be taken advantage of.

So he went on, talking steadily and even a little more rapidly, just as the train had gathered speed pulling out of Catlett's Station, until he came to a stopping point, as Mercury had come that night to the impassable gulf over Cedar Run. And when that much of the story had been told, he could only marvel at the ease of the telling.

"Maybe the last thing that engineer ever did was pull that whistle cord, just to spit'n my eye. I wouldn't blame'im if he did. Because when I rode up beside that locomotive and drew down on'im—Peterson, that was *personal*. Not just war. That was between that engineer and me, just the two of us."

"He wasn't shootin back?"

"He was just gettin the hell outta there's fast he could."

"Won't do to stop and *think* about killin," Peterson said. "Not in a war."

"Remember when you were a boy and the others started runnin or chasin a dog? Even if you didn't want to, you'd go along."

"So you wouldn't be left alone."

"Only boys chasin a dog, pretty soon they get tired or the dog outruns'em. In a fight, though, a man goes along, he gets to be part of it. Then it's part of *him*. In that depot, in the middle of all that blood, the killin just took *hold* of me."

All one breath, Peterson thought, falling back on the ancient wisdom that had helped him through the worst time of his life. *Yea, they have all one breath, so that a man hath no preeminence above a beast; for all is vanity.*

"'All go unto one place,'" he said out loud.

Hart seemed not to hear. "Something down deep . . . it just *rode* me that night . . . the way I rode Merc after that train."

"'All are of the dust, and all turn to dust again.'"

"And I didn't think more than a second about stoppin that train from spreadin the alarm. That wasn't it. It was just that engineer and me . . . the killer in me."

"'Who knoweth the spirit of man that goeth upward?'" Peterson said. "'And the spirit of the beast that goeth downward to the earth?'"

The quiet words echoed at last in some locked, forgotten room of Hart's childhood. He remembered, fleetingly, a parched old man with trembling hands and flaring eyes who had preached far different, more ominous words in a voice that hissed like hellfire from the pulpit of St. Paul's Episcopal Church on Grace Street in Richmond.

"Didn't take you for a Bible man."

"I'm not. Not anymore."

From Manassas they heard a sudden burst of what might have been musketry, as if a last box of cartridges had been set off, and the fusillade seemed to set Hart's words flowing again.

"So the rain came and I led Merc back along the track to where the boys'd set the Yankee camp afire. But it rained so hard the fires went out like somebody pinchin candles. I came down off the tracks between some burnt-out wagons and found a big tent didn't look like it'd been touched. Pretty neat tent, maybe a colonel's. There was this buffalo robe on the camp bed, thick and warm-looking. I wanted that robe in the worst way. Only there's this dog lyin on top of it. A really big dog, a Newfoundland, I think."

"Must of been at least a colonel, he had his dog in the field with'im."

"Minute I reached for that robe, this dog rose up and showed me'is teeth. Like he'd tear me to pieces. I ducked back out and got my saber off the saddle and tried to poke the blade under the robe to pull it out from under'im. Peterson, that dog took the blade right in'is teeth and hunched down there growlin at me. Eyes burnin like fuses. I saw I'd have to jam the saber right down'is throat, I wanted that robe."

"But you couldn't do it." Peterson stood up and stretched stiff muscles.

Hart stood up, too. "So you tell me: how could I try to kill a man runnin for his life, then ten minutes later back off from killin a *dog* guardin something I really wanted?"

Peterson flipped away the cigar stub, its glowing end tracing a miniature of the arcing shells over Manassas.

"That's why I quoted you Ecclesiastes. If I believe anything, I guess it's that everything's right here." He clenched his fist against his chest. "The spirit of man, the spirit of the beast."

"Side by side in the same person?"

They walked in silence, stumbling a little in the darkness, toward Stuart's bivouac. Exactly, Peterson thought. Like two people in one body. How else could he explain what she'd done? Except that there was another person in the woman he'd married that somehow he'd never seen, had not been able to see, because loving the woman he *did* see had stopped him from looking for any other.

But that was not to be spoken of, or thought about, except when it came flooding back.

"I judge that every man's a universe, Cap'n. The worst things he's capable of. Or the best."

"That'd make it a lie. The idea of the righteous and the wicked. All that talk about heaven'n hell."

"Not a lie. But heaven and hell are in us, too, if they exist."

"Ain't all this a little convenient, Peterson? Can't we just tell ourselves, in that case, we didn't know if what we did was good or bad, it was just *in* us?"

Too painful, Peterson thought, to believe anything but that it *was* just in her to do what she did. As natural and unpremeditated as the way she used to laugh. He could not bear to think that she'd *deliberately* left him.

"Thing is," he said, "you can *try* to live in 'the spirit that goeth upward.'" Even if sometimes you have to run away from it to the earth. The way she must have had to.

Hart laughed briefly, the sound harsh in the night. "Not easy in a war." He stopped and looked up at the western heavens, where the dimming firelight from Manassas no longer reached. "War gets you right down to the nub of things. Down where we're all killers . . . every mother's son of us."

"Maybe. But everyone of us could have spared that dog, too."

Hart walked on in the darkness. "Cept the Reverend Major Allen," he said over his shoulder. "Aint but one way he could of got that nice buffalo robe he's sleeping under these nights."

By the time Durward P. Bracc had his great idea, a dirty gray dawn was breaking. But in the dark and fetid cellar of his house,

rank with the odor of rotten potatoes and damp earth, Brace had
no idea what time it was; he only knew that the great battle he
thought had been fought around Manassas Junction had died away
an hour or so earlier. By that time, even Kate had stopped her
terrified whining and sobbing and had fallen lumpishly into a sleep
of exhaustion. Missy and Wash, with the confidence of youth,
had long since been sound asleep, unperturbed by the rumble of
battle or anything else, although in the airless heat of the cellar
both tumbled restlessly on their shuck pallets.

But Brace had been well aware, as he listened to the explosions
booming across the nighttime fields of Prince William County,
that Henry was as wide awake as he. Henry said nothing; Brace
could not hear his breathing or make out his solid shape in the
cellar darkness, but he knew Henry was awake. Henry's wakefulness was as much a presence in Brace's cellar as what Brace
feared was the cause of it—Sajie, sound asleep beside Henry on
the blanket he had brought for them from their cabin.

When they had first heard the explosions after midnight, Kate
had started whimpering and groveling like a whipped puppy. Wearily, Brace had roused his children from the attic and ordered them
to the cellar, much to Wash's delight.

"They fightin?" Missy asked, yawning.

"Aint huntin rabbits." Brace had no idea that armies did not
usually fight at night. The explosion of the dumps and magazines
at Manassas sounded to him, as to Kate, like full-scale warfare.

Missy ran ahead with a candle to fix Maw a pallet in the cellar.
She was only a little less excited than Wash by this break in the
routine of their nights and days.

"Gone see Jesus," Kate muttered, between sobs. "Gone see
my Jesus soon."

"Now, now." Brace, his galluses hanging about his lean hips,
almost wished it might be so. "Be safe inna cellar."

"Safe inna arms-a Jesus. Onlies place I be safe."

Kate was all Brace could handle, with her bulk and her weak
knees, as he wrestled her down the narrow cellar stairs. Wash had
run for Henry and Sajie, on his father's reluctant instructions.
Sleeping in the same room with Africans, even in a cellar in
wartime, offended Brace's sense of fitness; but on the other hand,
Henry and Sajie were too valuable to let run off or be blown up.

Brace had always been a little afraid of Henry, though careful
to order him about contemptuously enough to conceal his nagging
fear. He told himself that he only resented Henry's insolence, as

any white man would. But Brace was well aware that Henry was as big as the side of a barn, with arms like a mule's hind legs. Probly could thow down a mule, Henry, he took a mind to.

Not, of course, that Henry or any other darky would dare hit a white man or cause him any trouble at all. Unless maybe one got drunk. But as far as Brace could see, Henry never touched a drop. Cept a man can't trust nare of'em, one day the next.

Brace had inherited Henry and Sajie along with a pretty good house and the worn-out farm from Kate's skinflint father. At the time, Brace had considered himself lucky to have done so, although his principal sentiment had been sheer pleasure that the old man could no longer work like a field hand, while regaling passing neighbors with tales of his worthless, white-trash son-in-law. Ol bastard act like he got some kinda high blood.

Lately, Brace had begun to fear that the farm would work him to death, with so many mouths to feed. Still, a roof over their heads, a good mare, some stock, and two darkies in the yard was a sight more than some had. But that night Brace sensed trouble, more immediate in some ways than the two armies roaming all around his house. Henry lying awake and resentful in the dark was more real to Durward Brace than any of Pope's brigades or the return of the Virginia boys Missy claimed to have seen.

Wash had come bouncing back from Henry's cabin and down the cellar steps, excited and chattering about the battle noises off toward Manassas. "They keep at it till sunup, Paw, le's go see! Kin we go see, Paw?"

But Brace was watching Henry stump down the steps with his powerful stride. In the poor light of the single guttering candle, Henry's face seemed without expression, as always. Sajie moved behind him like a tall shadow.

"Y'all kin have at corner over ther." Trying to sound commanding, Brace nodded carelessly at the corner farthest from Kate and Missy. But for one heartbeat of time, Henry stood unmoving at the foot of the steps, looking at Brace, his eyes in the candlelight wide and stary.

She told'im. Brace knew it for sure. Bitch tole'im.

Then Henry led Sajie across the cellar to the corner. No one else seemed to have noticed; Brace tried to tell himself he'd only imagined the moment.

"Paw... *please* le's go see inna mornin, le's..."

"Snuff out at candle'n git to sleep."

But Brace was paying no real attention to Wash. Jus my confound luck, mean nigguh like Henry, stead of a decent darky knowin'is place. Keepin'is mouth shut.

As the night wore on and the explosions continued, finally beginning to wane, then grumbling into uneasy silence, Brace lying sleepless was in no doubt that Henry was not that kind of darky. If he had not known that before, he would have learned it from his sense of Henry sleepless, too, watching in the darkness, waiting, unmoving on the blanket by Sajie.

Put nuthin past at stiffneck buck. He thought somebody sniffin round Sajie with'is dick out, he'd as soon go for'is thoat as spit onna ground. Even a white man.

Right then. Brace had his idea—actually, it was more of a revelation, since he knew he was going to have to do *something,* and then suddenly knew exactly what he was going to do, without any questions or review, without any real thought at all. *Yeah,* Brace said to himself. *Cose.* That was all; and what he was going to do immediately seemed as natural as what he'd already done with Sajie.

Brace had been down in the woods the morning before, along Dawkins Branch, tramping around in a black mood. Alone like that, away from Kate's bleating and moaning and the eternal squabbling of Wash and Missy, Brace could usually figure things out. But in the heavy heat of the day, with his head throbbing from too much whiskey the previous night and the brooding feeling that another big fight was about to bust out all around him, Brace could not think straight at all. He tried to nap under an oak but flies pestered him and the long summer's sun had made even shaded ground too hot for comfort. So he roused himself and started for home, half wishing to come out of the woods and see the whole thing gone, blown down by some errant shell, Kate and the young-uns—maybe not Missy—gone with it, so that he would be free again, could start over, maybe out beyond the Blue Ridge, with no mouths but his own to feed, long gone from the hot, rocky, scratched-out earth the old skinflint had bequeathed Kate.

Instead of a devastated house, he saw Sajie. Having paid little attention to where he was, he had emerged into the fallow field, usually planted to roasen ears, behind Henry's rickety cabin. He thought at first, as he plodded dispiritedly across the lumpy earth, that Sajie was washing clothes—peculiar, since it was not Monday. Then he stopped dead still, amazed and breathless in the brutal sun beating on his head, sweat trickling on his brow and along his sides, under his faded shirt. Sajie, out of sight of the

main house and the barn, was stripped to the waist. She was bent
over a wash kettle, soaping her oaken-colored skin.

Since Kate's rapid deterioration into fat and misery, so that
mounting her would have been like topping one of the sows in
the muddy pen behind the barn, Brace had been well aware of
Sajie's lithe, strong body and the hips swaying under her usual
layers of cheap skirts and petticoats. For that matter, Brace—
having enjoyed no woman save a four-bit Richmond slut in more
than three years—had even taken to watching his daughter with
a lascivious eye, telling himself the harm was in the doing, not
the looking. But Brace had no more intention of messing with
Sajie than with Missy, not because he had any compunctions but
because he was too afraid of Henry.

So he had never touched Sajie, though he often had had to
restrain himself, and never missed a chance to watch her great
jiggling dugs that made him want sometimes to tear the clothes
off her and get down to business. Nigguh women wanted rough
handling, anyway. But Henry was never far from her side.

Never, at least, until that moment. Brace stood stock still in
the midday sun, staring across the open field at the woman a
stone's throw distant. She was bent over the washpot, her broad
haunches rising toward him like a promising new world. Henry
was nowhere around; Brace did not know how he knew that—he
had been two hours in the woods—but he was certain nevertheless
that this was a moment between him and Sajie.

The woman straightened and in the brilliant sunshine Brace
could see the muscles rippling under the tight skin of her back.
Slow, languorously, as if she were dancing, she began soaping
her long glistening arms. Brace was transfixed, as if the sun had
struck him motionless. His mouth was dry; blood raced giddily
in his veins, thumped violently in his heart. He could scarcely
breathe. He had no thoughts, nothing but an elemental awareness
of the woman and the heat and the silence and the smell of the
broken, baked earth under his feet.

Brace had made no sound; remembering later, he was sure of
that. But in the slow and sensuous dance of Sajie's movements,
she had turned finally toward him, as tantalizingly as if timing
herself to music he could not hear. Then she saw him and
without reaction or expression became as still as he, in the hot
silence, the primordial sun.

How long they stared at each other across the stubbled patches
of broomsedge Brace had no idea. Sajie was only partially turned
toward him, looking across her shoulder; he could see the

high still curve of her breast past the shield of her arm. Then it seemed he was moving toward her, fearfully, lightly, as a hunter moves up on a deer, not startling it with sudden gestures or speed.

Sajie stood quietly, looking at him over her shoulder, her skin glistening with water, splotched here and there with white soap-foam. When he was near enough to read her eyes, they were dark, low-lidded, sleepy; her heavy lips were parted slightly. Brace was noticing everything about her, with a kind of sharp-honed clarity, as the events of a dream sometimes seem to impress themselves more profoundly on a sleeper's brain than anything conscious could do.

He was close enough to smell the strong soap when he sensed he should go no closer—the lidded eyes lighting a little, the heavy mouth closing. He stopped, but his pumping blood was too strong, too commanding; the fierce sun had him too hotly in its spell. The earth under his feet seemed throbbing with promise. Brace could no more have stopped himself from reaching for her breast than he could have turned and walked off.

As his hand passed across her bicep, Sajie's eyes flashed and he thought *she* would turn and run; but still she did not move and then he held it in his hand, heavy and yielding as fruit on his palm, the nipple hard as the stem of an apple between his fingers. For a moment, no more perhaps than two or three pumps of blood to his heart, they stood unmoving, he not breathing, the sun coming down heavier than silence, hotter than fire, her flesh soft in his calloused hand. Then the touch and the nearness and the heat inflamed him and he flung his other arm around her waist, pulling her naked back against him, ramming himself against her haunches . . .

"Paw," Wash said, "it's gittin light. Kin we . . ."

"Hesh yuh goddam mouth!"

The piping voice, startling Brace from his reverie, infuriated him, just as had Sajie—wiry as a bird dog and slippery with soap—when she twisted out of his grip and sprang free, big breasts with their black nipples flashing in the sun, taunting him, mocking the lost, the squandered promise of that elemental moment unique in Durward Brace's hardscrabble life.

"You wanted it! You did!"

He heard himself squealing at her in a voice like a woman's, and saw in the hot eyes what he took to be defiance. That was too much, from a black slut; he was a white man, he had his rights, and he stepped toward her, his hands clenching into fists, as she twisted her dress up over her shoulders, hiding those mocking heavy paps she'd teased him with.

"Milk your own cow, white man!"

Brace watched her running then, toward the old cabin, around its corner—light on her feet as Missy. Strange he'd never noticed that before. He stood there in the sun, shocked, angry, fearful, finally despondent. But he did not follow her. He knew she would have run to Henry.

Light flooded down the steps as Wash threw back the creaking cellar doors. Brace put his hand over his eyes and twisted his legs to conceal his hard-on, in case Missy was looking. But Missy seemed still asleep, and after awhile his blood went down and he could stand up without bother. Except that Henry was up, too, and staring at him across the dirt floor. Oh, she'd told'im all right. Evrything, cept that she'd wanted it too, could of run anytime, had no call to let'im touch'er atall, she gone take on bout it later.

But then Brace remembered what he had decided to do and that cheered him up. Bitch find out what white dick feels like, soon's I git Henry outten-a goddam way. And it occurred to him that he might even get paid for losing his property in the confoun war.

"Henry! Git at woman inna kitchen. Night like at, I crave some decent breckfus."

He strode up the cellar steps, feeling manful, blinking in the light. Gone be another goddam hot one. But just maybe the day Durward P. Brace's chance would come.

Missy watched him go, watched Henry and Sajie follow silently. Hard to understand Paw these days. Mad all the time and swearin. Mean to Maw. Didn't useter be like at; seem like back when I-uz little, Paw's the sweet one and Maw did alla yellin.

Missy knew Maw was awake, playing possum. Postponing the day as long as she could. Missy felt much the same. One day like another; nothing to look forward to. Although just for a moment when she'd watched the Virginia boys tramping through Gainesville, she'd felt . . . something. Missy did not know enough to call it hope.

Her whole life had been bounded by the farm and the rail fences and dirt lanes of Prince William County, and an occasional heady trip to Warrenton. She knew no other life and few people other than Maw and Paw, Henry and Sajie, the unspeakable Wash. Such young men as in the past might have come calling, under

Paw's watchful eye, were off to the war. Maw and Paw kept her busy at chores; and she had no fine ladies or rich experiences to envy or dream about. She did not consciously long for a better life or hope for a Prince Charming to bring it, because she had little idea of the arid emptiness of the life she had, or the fulfillments of any other.

But in Missy, watching surreptitiously from the roadside underbrush as young men by the thousands marched past in the dust, a new and never-known excitement had stirred. They were coming from far off, too many of them to be all Prince William boys; so they were out of some other life which, for the first time, in their mere appearance, she could sense beyond the dreary horizons of *her* world. And although it was too dizzying to be consciously realized, the puzzling excitement in Missy was insistently suggesting that something else could exist for her, something other than Brace's farm. She had only to recognize the possibility.

Maw groaned and rolled over heavily. "They stop fightin?"

"Seem like. Y'all right, Maw?"

"Jesus, save my soul."

Wash squealed down the cellar steps. "Paw says y'all females git up down-er'n come on up to breckfus."

"Come on, Maw." Missy got a slender arm around Maw's blubbery shoulders and helped her sit up. "Kin smell Sajie's got coffee on."

"Don't trust at nigguh trash," Maw said suddenly, viciously. "Got eyes on Paw."

"Oh, Maw." Missy barely restrained a giggle. The idea of Sajie making eyes at Paw! Him all but dodderin and Sajie a darky to boot. "War's got you seein things."

Four hours later and nearly eight miles away, in front of a stone church on the pike running through Centreville village, General Hoke Arnall sat his horse in the sparse shade of an apparently dying tree. A fine gray powder of dust covered the tree and the run-down houses nearby. Arnall was listening with much interest to a spruce-looking young man of military bearing who was nevertheless clad in expensive civilian clothes. Sitting a fine stallion, he wore the most impressive set of riding boots Arnall had ever seen; but the effect of his finery was somewhat spoiled by his head-covering—a military cap with a long flap of linen flowing from under it and down the back of his neck to below his shoulders.

Arnall had seen nothing like it since the first summer of the war, when such desert equipment had been briefly in vogue.

". . . on the Peninsula with McClellan until a few weeks ago." The voice was brisk, assured. British, Arnall thought. A smug British look, too, about the closely clipped mustache and the red-cheeked face. "Now I need to see *you* fellows fight."

"Could of seen *that* around Richmond, most any time."

"From *your* side of the line, I mean."

"Mmmm." Arnall was preoccupied with his own and Hill's problems, not this stranger's prattle. The unfathomable Jackson had sent the Light Division off on another wild goose chase without the least instruction what they were to do when they got where they were going—if Jackson even knew where that was. Hill was furious.

"What'd you say the name was?"

"Redmund." The voice turned starchier as if Arnall should have known. "Late of Her Majesty's Embassy at Washington. Before that Captain, Fourth Hussars. Service in the Crimea. Now military correspondent . . ." He cleared his throat portentously and named a famous London publication.

"Gin'al Hill don't take to newspapers."

Which was an understatement. Ever since his dispute with Longstreet over the *Richmond Examiner*'s description of their parts in the Peninsula battles, Hill had shied away from anything to do with the public prints. The affair had come perilously close to a court-martial or a duel, or both, since neither general would back down. Which was why, Arnall believed, Hill's Division had been assigned to Jackson's Corps, to get Hill away from the implacable Longstreet.

Redmund's mustache twitched. "I take it your . . . uh . . . general is aware that his government hopes . . . I daresay prays . . . for the intervention of mine in your . . . uh . . . struggle for independence."

"Oh, I daresay."

Arnall looked past the Englishman with studied indifference. He had a soldier's aversion to politics and resented Redmund's obvious stratagem. Besides, on the crowded road through the nearly ruined village, in the hot morning sun, the troops were beginning to bunch up and break ranks, wandering around in the kind of disarray that troubled Arnall's military soul.

He had learned long ago that these fox hunters and back-woodsmen could not be disciplined into well-drilled ranks or made to stand motionless as statues in the blistering sun. Still, and conceding that they were the best fighters—so Hoke Arnall and his brother officers believed—the world had ever seen, their lack of military style and precision offended him. And what if, say, McClellan had had the gumption to run enough troops out from Washington to surprise them from the rear? Arnall shuddered at the thought.

"What England knows of this war, sir..." Redmund's chest was beginning to puff like a toad's. "It knows best from my accounts."

"Hope you told'em we run McClellan off the Peninsula with'is tail twixt'is legs."

Of course, Jackson was to blame for the infernal tangle of troops and horses in the rutted, sloping dirt stretch of the Warrenton Pike that served as Centreville's only real street. Arnall could make no sense, and he knew Hill couldn't either, of the order that had sent them there, miles away from any sensible place where they ought to be, without any known purpose. What *would* have made sense, after they'd torn up Pope's railroad and burned his dump, would have been to skedaddle west and join back up with Longstreet, pulling the army together again.

As it was, and as if it hadn't been bad enough for the Old Man to divide the army, Jackson's order to Hill meant that he had divided *his* force, too. Pretty soon, they'd be fighting brigade by brigade. Here the Light Division was, all alone at Centreville and hanging like an apple on a tree, waiting to be plucked by any Yank general with the stomach to try it. God alone—*maybe* Jackson—knew where Taliaferro's and Ewell's divisions were.

"Well, as to that," Redmund said, "you southern chaps may be hearing from McClellan again. His retreat to the James across your front was masterly, sir. Masterly!"

Arnall said nothing, intending to convey by silence a proper disdain for McClellan. He had about made up his disciplinarian's mind to let Redmund fend for himself and to start restoring some order to the lounging, laughing, skylarking troops, before they got completely out of hand. Trust troops, he thought, to know when there's confusion at the top. It would be quickly reflected in the ranks, whether in battle or in bivouac.

"And I must say, sir, I didn't notice..." Redmund was now drawn to the full height of a stiff military posture, chest out, chin up, fist on hip; even the length of linen down his neck looked starched and brittle. "...this great Jackson of yours distinguish himself in the White Oak Swamp."

Hoke Arnall was not so angry at Jackson for the humiliating arrest order under which he still labored, nor so critical of him as a commander—he conceded the man was a fighter; showing Jackson a body of blue troops was like trotting a fox in front of a pack of hounds—that he would for a moment have acquiesced in such a criticism from any outsider, let alone an insolent Limey newspaper writer. Nevertheless, Redmund finally had caught his attention and gained his grudging respect with an insight that Arnall knew to be correct—in fact, Hill knew it, Longstreet knew it, Lee knew it, anyone who had followed the Richmond fighting professionally could not help but know it. Only certain armchair generals and the Jackson-worshipping public could ignore the fact that he had failed to distinguish himself—had just failed, to put it more accurately—at perhaps the most crucial moment of the effort to lift McClellan's siege of Richmond. But Arnall only said:

"Reck'n McClellan saw all of Jackson he wanted to see."

The trouble, he thought, was that outside the army Jackson had rapidly become a legend—the invincible Stonewall. Which was why he could get away with almost anything—an almost fatally late start at Gaines's Mill, the delay at White Oak, the killing march to Bristoe that would have left his exhausted force easy prey to any commander smarter that Pope, the foolish detachment of Hill to Centreville for God only knew what reasons—even such indefensible acts as placing Arnall himself in arrest for failure to follow a minor order he'd never received. And no officer in the army was likely to forget that Jackson had had Dick Garnett court-martialed after Kernstown for the heinous crime of having saved his brigade by retreating before he received orders to do so.

"Then you've no reason, sir, nor has General Jackson, to fear anything I'll report. Mine, sir, is the quest for the true history of this war of yours."

No more than Hill did Hoke Arnall regard truth as something likely to be found in newspapers—especially British newspapers. But at least Redmund, whatever his posturings, was not taken with the bothersome Stonewall legend, a fact that spoke well for his military judgment. And he had professional credentials as a military man, which was more than could be said for most of the American upstarts and nitwits who held themselves out as "war correspondents" without—in Arnall's experience—having any notion whatever of the difference between war and dress parade. Most of 'em probably spies.

"Tell you what." Arnall spoke casually, still looking a little past Redmund's aggressively upthrust head. "If you were ridin along with my staff, like maybe an observer, I'd have no call to object."

"I see . . . an observer."

The starchy voice was a little warmer. The Britisher didn't have to have anything spelled out for him, Arnall was glad to see. "Can't answer for Hill. Let alone Jackson."

"My dear sir . . ." Redmund's teeth, a little the worse for service in the Crimea and elsewhere, suddenly showed in a wolfish grin he turned off as quickly as it had appeared. "I shall take care of myself . . . if . . . uh . . . occasion arises."

Arnall touched his hat brim, satisfied that Redmund understood: if challenged by higher authority, he was on his own. And if he just happened to pick up the scent of Jackson's disorganization and recklessness and foolhardy notions of secrecy and discipline . . . well, it wouldn't be from Hoke Arnall. And anyway, maybe a little criticism, after all the glory, would be good for that unaccountable man. Bring him into line a little.

Arnall spurred toward the stone church just up the sloping road. Around it, the depredations of war had left the landscape as bare as the surface of the moon. Numerous panes of glass had been broken from its three tall windows on either side; and atop its plain roof a tiny chimney stood like a sentinel against the bleak hills that had so often been marched over by both armies. On their crest, Arnall could see the lines of fortifications first erected by Joe Johnston the summer before, when few thought the war would last longer than another battle or two.

Arnall wanted to suggest to Hill that they move the men into a more secure position, maybe the old earthworks, while awaiting further word from Jackson. Anything was preferable to all this milling around in the village, lounging about like boys on a lark. The looting and indiscipline at Manassas had been unavoidable but a bad precedent, nevertheless. Today was inexcusable.

He was riding past Dixon's Rifles—undisciplined in the best of circumstances—when he saw several men not just lying by the roadside but actually inside some Centreville householder's fenced yard, apparently sleeping under an apple tree. It was one of the few houses of the village that was set back from the rutted road and around which there was still some vestige of lawn and shrubbery not trampled under by the feet and hooves of war. Obviously a house of some substance.

Lee's orders strictly prohibited such intrusion on private property. And in this case, a young woman stood by the fence, offering dippers of water to troops in the road. Not right that three louts like that should be anywhere near a lady on such a mission of generosity.

As Arnall debated with himself whether to make an example of the trio—and where were their officers?—one of the apparently sleeping men pulled a brown bottle from his waistband and held it to his mouth. Now that, Arnall thought, is just too much.

At his command, Rambler took the low picket fence easily, into the shaded yard. From the corner of his eye, Arnall saw the young woman, startled, back away from the fence, her eyes wide.

"Here . . . you there!"

Arnall dismounted before the horse had come to a full stop. He stood over yellowish bleary eyes, as if he had been often consoling himself with the bottle he still held in one hand. Arnall drew back his foot in its heavy boot and kicked the bottle twenty yards away, into a flower bed.

"On your feet, soldier!"

The big man rolled over and pushed himself slowly to his feet. His two companions rose more quickly and all faced the angry general more or less at attention. One of them had a huge hooked nose and seemed to be trying not to grin.

"What's your unit?"

"Comp'ny B." The third man, bigger even than the first, had a calm voice and a barrel chest. "Dixon's Rifles."

"Get back in ranks, you and you. Send your sergeant here."

Arnall stared steadily into the yellow-tinted eyes of the man who had been drinking. Back-country type the army could never break. Still . . . examples had to be made.

"Where'd you get that liquor?"

"What likker was at?" The man's eyes were sleepy, drunken.

"In that bottle." Arnall jerked his head toward the flower bed.

"What bottle?"

"Sir! What bottle, *sir!*"

"What I said . . . sir."

Arnall looked over his shoulder and saw the young woman staring at him with interest, her bucket of water forgotten. Beyond her a lean sergeant was coming on the double. He gave the general a snappy salute and eyed the private warily.

"One-a your men, Sergeant?"

"Yessir." Reluctantly, the sergeant supplied the man's name.

"You always let your men intrude on private property?"

"Not if I kin he'p it, sir."

"Where'd he get'is liquor?"

"What likker, Gin'al?"

"Buck this man." Arnall stared again into the yellow eyes, startled despite himself by their sudden intensity. The man was not drunk after all. "Eight hours. Next time we go into camp." He looked at the sergeant. "Don't think I'll forget either. I'll want a report in writing, Sergeant . . ."

"Barlow, sir."

"Barlow. You better look sharp yourself, want to keep those stripes."

Arnall mounted and swung Rambler through the gate, back to the road. He took off his hat and bowed to the young woman. She had dark hair like Amy, but was thin as a rail by comparison. Abruptly, overpoweringly, he thought of Amy that last morning of his leave; Amy's lush body made this girl look like a skeleton.

"Sorry, ma'am. They won't disturb you again."

She smiled and curtsied, and Arnall rode on, vaguely disturbed, even though he had resolutely shut Amy out of his mind. Not that Private Beasly didn't deserve bucking and Sergeant Barlow the reprimand. But something about the yellow glare of Beasly's eyes . . .

Behind the house so poorly protected by the picket fence was a whitewashed kitchen with a red-brick chimney. Inside, Sally Sutherland Crowell was completely unaware of the small drama that had just been played out in the front yard. A few minutes earlier, she had to retreat to the cool kitchen of her brother's house—her childhood home. All morning, she and Anna Sutherland, her sister-in-law, had stood by the fence offering cool water to the butternut troops who had miraculously, as if sprung from the parched Virginia earth, appeared that morning along the pitted pike on both dusty sides of which most of the houses of Centreville were ranged. The troops' tramping feet had coated Roger Sutherland's and the other houses of the village with a new layer of dust, but no one minded—Virginia troops were too welcome, after the long months in which Centreville had been within Yankee lines.

Many of the soldiers lay down by the roadside to sleep; others milled aimlessly about; no one, not even their officers, seemed to know what to do next or why they were there. But Anna and Sally could not keep the buckets of water coming fast enough; and before long Sally's palms were raw and stinging from the well rope.

But it was not for that reason that Sally had run off to the kitchen to rest. Nor was it likely that the hot morning or the excitement of the southern boys' unexpected arrival had caused the flush of dizziness and nausea that had driven her away from the bucket and the dipper and the troops at the fence. Sally was not sure of anything, anymore—not since the battle three weeks before, after which her trouble had begun.

She was a small woman, small-boned, small-faced, slight as a child, with long blonde hair she wore in braids, and shadowed blue eyes. She moved almost furtively; something seemed haunted about her thin features and the quick way she reacted to sounds and movements others scarcely noticed. Those who had known her as a rather placid child in Centreville attributed her nervous manner, as a young woman returning, to the sad fact that at twenty, Sally had been a widow for a year, since the armies had first collided, just down the pike beyond the Stone Bridge.

"Y'all right, Miss Sally?" Old Phoebe, the cook, rose ponderously from a corner where she had been napping and stumped across the room.

Sally had seated herself at the round oaken table in the center of the kitchen, where in the old happy days she had taken more meals than in the formal dining room in the house. Even when Phoebe stirred up the fire on the hearth, the kitchen was somehow darker, breezier than anywhere else; and it smelled—or used to—of good, trustworthy things: fresh bread and spices and ham and molasses. The white scrubbed floor, the old iron pots and pans, the cream-colored stoneware, were familiar and comforting. *They* had not changed, any more than Phoebe, ageless and untouched as the heavy skillets she handled like toys.

"Just a little hot is all."

Sally's words, in her thin voice, always trailed a bit at the end of sentences, as if she had lost track of them. She did not mention—she wondered if she only imagined—that even in the August heat her right foot was cold as ice, numb with deathlike chill.

"Men grown got no bidness runnin round dis heat. Wanna glassa milk, honey?"

"Yes, please."

Sally did not really want milk or anything else but she also did not want to explain why, and she knew Phoebe would demand to know. Sally only wanted to figure out what had disturbed her that morning. Obviously something to do with her trouble—the nausea, the nightmares, the icy foot, the unnameable fear that could grip her so unexpectedly. Today it certainly had been nothing anyone had said. Those poor thirsty boys had been as polite as members of a dancing class—except the three rough-looking ones in the yard, and even they had said nothing objectionable.

It was not a familiar face that had caused her trouble, either; she had seen none. But suddenly, seized by fear and nausea, she had to get away, although she and Anna together had had all they could do to meet the soldiers' need for water. And then, sitting in the kitchen, she had realized her right foot was like ice again.

Maybe someone who looked a *little* like Lawrence—not enough for her to consciously realize it. But actually, she could scarcely remember Lawrence's face. So little time they'd had. Gone now a bit longer than they'd been together. And why should a reminder of someone so beloved make her fearful, much less nauseous?

Phoebe set a cup of milk in front of her and Sally clasped it in her frail hands, grateful in spite of her foot for its coolness. She wanted to press it to her forehead but Phoebe was watching and she dutifully took a sip instead.

"Slip of a thing." Disapproval dripped from Phoebe's words, drew the massive planes of her face into something like severity. "Least wind blow you way."

Sometimes recently, since she'd had to leave Lawrence's house in Culpeper County—her own since he'd been gone—Sally had wished the wind or something *would* take her away. Even now, almost three weeks after that terrible day of the battle, she could not think clearly about what had happened. The armies had come and all around the old house under Slaughter's Mountain death and terror had fallen like bloody rain. She could never go back to Lawrence's house, after that day—even if it was still there, spared by some whim or oversight of the indifferent armies.

Anna rushed into the kitchen, her face lit with excitement. "A gin'ral . . . just ran those soldiers out of the front yard."

Anna was more excitable than Sally, a chatterbox—kind-hearted, Sally thought, but rarely interested in listening. Sometimes Sally wished she could talk, really talk, to her brother's lively wife. Recently, she had wished she could talk to anyone, although she had no idea what it was she wished to say.

"He was like a god!" Anna threw herself into the opposite chair. "Can I have some milk, too, Phoeb? Sally . . . you never saw anything like the way he'n his horse took the fence. And his voice . . . I declare . . ." She broke off quickly, a faintly stricken look on her face, as if she had just recalled that Sally's Lawrence would never again cut a romantic figure on horseback "Feelin better, Sally?"

"Fine . . . jus fine."

But Sally was scarcely listening. For as Anna had talked of the splendid general on horseback, Sally had remembered that just before running from the fence she had given a drink of water to a mounted officer wearing chaplain's insignia. And for some reason, remembering that, she saw again the one thing she would never forget from the day of the battle, that she awoke often in the hot and murmurous nights to see again—the arms and legs and fingers and feet piled like garbage in the corner of the parlor, under and around and on top of Lawrence's mother's harpsichord, which the surgeons had not troubled to move. Sally could not think why the chaplain had reminded her of that.

Hoke Arnall had quickly found Hill and his staff on the outskirts of Centreville, in an open field beside the Warrenton Pike. Hill, thin and frail-looking, his long auburn beard halfway down his chest, was wearing—despite the heat—the red flannel shirt he favored when he thought battle imminent. He stared in concentration at a map he had folded and rested against his horse's neck.

"Pretty pickle," a staff officer murmured to Arnall.

"What's happenin?"

"Orders just in from Jackson to dig in this side-a Bull Run'n hold the fords. He thinks Pope's tryin to slip away east maybe to Alexandria."

"With'is whole army?"

The aide shrugged. "Trouble is, one of Hill's scout teams just come in with a captured courier. Carryin a message says Pope's concentratin on Manassas."

Arnall grimaced. Hill was in a pickle, all right. The captured order, if valid, made the direction to hold the fords useless, since no one would be trying to cross Bull Run. But if the document was a trick, or out of date, and Hill failed to dig in at Bull Run and stop Pope's crossing, Jackson would have him cashiered. Ignoring one of Ol Jack's orders, no matter how crazy, was sticking your head down the cannon's mouth, as both Hill and Arnall had reason to know.

Arnall moved Rambler through the knot of mounted officers to Hill's side. The general looked up; above the flowing beard, his deep-set eyes were haunted with decision.

"Freeman told me, sir. Tough problem."

Hill nodded and handed the map to a junior officer standing by. His movements were nervous, jerky, as if his small body was feverish. But when he spoke, his words were resolute, his voice firm. Nobody accused Powell Hill of lacking courage, in battle or out. Arnall remembered him in the hottest hour at Slaughter's Mountain, coat off and sword bared, rallying fleeing troops of the Stonewall Brigade.

"Pope's not retreatin. He aims to fight." Hill squared his shoulders and touched Hoke Arnall's arm. "So I deem it best to push on'n rejoin Gin'al Jackson at Groveton."

Until then, Arnall had had no clear idea where the rest of Jackson's force might be. But he knew from the campaign of the summer before that Groveton was a crossroads hamlet on the pike west of Bull Run, near the old battlefield where Jackson had won his fame, maybe four or five miles from Centreville. If Jackson had lingered at Groveton with his other divisions, there was no doubt that he, too, aimed to fight.

"Then we better get goin," Arnall said. He felt his blood pumping; if there was going to be a fight, there was going to be opportunity, too, even for an officer in arrest.

Through the woods on a gradual slope overlooking the pike between Gainesville and Bull Run ran an abandoned railroad right-of-way. Where it passed behind the abandoned house and orchard of a farmer named Brawner, the engineers had thrown up an embankment to keep the single track they had planned on an even grade. But not far along the line's shallow arc to the northeast, for the same reason, they had had to gouge a deep cut in the rolling earth. Along alternating banks and cuts, occasionally at grade level, the old right-of-way eventually reached Bull Run, which the track was to have crossed on a trestle, on its way to Alexandria and Washington. But that had been years before, in another world, long before the war; now the embankments and the cuts were overgrown and crumbling. No trestle had been built, no tracks ever laid; but Stonewall Jackson, who had ridden many times over the ground after the summer fighting of 1861, had known the old line ran like a scar through the woods.

That afternoon, on either side of the abandoned right-of-way and for more than two miles along it, from Brawner's all the way to Bull Run, the troops of Taliaferro's and Ewell's divisions lay at their ease, their muskets stacked and ready. General Jackson, his staff and numerous field officers had by then settled themselves in Brawner's fly-swarming orchard. A blistering sun glared down and the long-untended apple trees offered little shade. But the bellies of officers and men alike were full from the day of plunder at Manassas, cool well and branch water was available, and a dying plume of smoke against the cloudless sky offered an encouraging reminder of the destruction of Pope's stores.

Some of the officers slept in what shade they could find; others sat about talking and fanning off flies. None approached their commanding general, who slouched against an apple tree sucking a lemon (of which a trove had been found at Manassas for his mess chest).

"Mood he's in, damn thing probly tastes sweet." Colonel Channing leaned against Brawner's unpainted barn, in the meager shade it cast.

"Like one-a them dumps we blowed last night. Drop a spark on'im, star shells'd start goin off."

"Yeah." A knot of lesser staff officers lounged about Channing, some sitting or lying on the ground. "Probly broodin on all that ammunition he couldn't haul off."

"That ain't it." Channing shook his head. "Give'im one word of Longstreet comin threw the Gap, he'll be lookin for a goddam tiger to take on barehand."

"Longstreet'll be through." Captain Thad Selby spoke with the supreme confidence of the inexperienced. "No Yanks gonna stop Ol Pete."

"Is at a fack?" Colonel Channing peered around in mock surprise, blowing a fly off his nose with an extended underlip. "Any you other boys heard tell no Yanks kin stop Longstreet?"

Fargo Hart joined in the comfortable mutter of laughter that passed around the group, discomfiting Selby—whom Hart recognized as the young officer who had seemed such a caricature of military zeal when he reported General Arnall's failure to post a road guide on the march through Gainesville. Romantic young gladiators gave Hart a worse headache than the champagne of the night before.

The laughter momentarily disturbed the slumber of the Reverend Major Allen, who lay mountainously on his back with his hat over his face. He raised his head, the hat falling away to disclose the black scab bisecting his features, and looked at them with bleary, puzzled eyes. Flies immediately swarmed over the scab; the Reverend Major, muttering something unecclesiastical, brushed them away and slumped back, reminding Fargo Hart of a beached whale he once had seen on the Breton coast.

"Just sposin Longstreet *don't* come anytime soon." Major Worsham, the surgeon of the Stonewall Brigade and a close friend of Jackson's since before the war, lay on the ground with his hands behind his head; he was clean-shaven except for long black mustaches drooping under an outsize nose. He did not sound much worried by the prospect he had raised. "How we fixed for hangin on, Dave?"

Colonel Channing looked at the steely sky as if for guidance, then lowered his head and laid a brown stain of tobacco juice precisely in the angle where the lowest clapboard of Brawner's barn touched the earth. "Rode the line an hour ago, most of the way toward Sudley Springs. That ol railroad makes bout as good a position to defend as a man could hope for. High ground behind it just made for guns. Move Hill in on the left, Pope couldn't thow us outta here, he had Napoleon to show'im how."

"Cose," said Archie Rogers, one of Jackson's staff engineers, "Pope got to *find* us fore we tear'im up."

This produced another laugh in which Captain Hart did not join, since the remark seemed to him as asinine as Captain Selby's. All very well to low-rate Pope, but the Yanks were bound to have a hell of a lot of troops in the vicinity. Even Jackson could lose a battle if he was outnumbered enough. Hart had a sense, anyway, that the fun was about over; he could almost feel a blue ring drawing closer about the small army hidden in Brawner's woods and along the old rail line.

He could tell from the sporadic rumble of light artillery that Stuart's cavalry units already were fighting scattered actions along the inner circumference of that blue ring. Flung out in all directions, most frequently to the south and west, these detachments evidently were encountering Yank scouting and advance parties coming up from the old Rappahannock line to close in on the marauders in their rear. And though none of the bursts of shelling had lasted long enough to suggest a serious encounter, each one seemed a little nearer than the last.

Hart felt rather guilty that he was not riding with one of those detachments, instead of drowsing in the hot sun above the empty pike, fighting nothing but flies. But he knew the ultimate action, when it came, was likely to be here, on Ol Jack's chosen ground— about which he was not so sanguine as Channing seemed to be.

Earlier that day, Stuart had sent Hart and the Reverend Major Allen to Jackson's headquarters with orders to carry out any necessary liaison between infantry and cavalry. They had had to spend a hot hour looking for the commanding general's camp. Hart, having developed something of an eye for ground himself—or so he thought—had come to the conclusion that Jackson's right flank was in the air, at the point where the old rail line reached the pike. Hart thought an attack there, driving northeast from the pike along the right-of-way, would roll up Jackson's line like a parchment scroll.

And Channing's caveat was substantial—for Hill was *not* on the left flank of the line, or anywhere else on it. Maybe Channing or Jackson knew where Hill was but no one else seemed to. All of which was no doubt another reason why Ol Jack, snappish as a barnyard dog, was lying all alone under the apple tree, sucking his lemon and shooing off flies like the rest of them.

"Ol Pope'll find us, all right." With his huge farmer's hands, Colonel Channing took off his broad-brimmed black hat and combed back a shock of hair as streaked with gray as his beard. "Onliest question is, he gone do it fore Longstreet jines up?"

"Iffen worse come to worse," Rogers said, "can't we light out west thew Aldie Gap?"

"Sure we can." Channing clapped the hat back on his shaggy head. "Over his dead body." He nodded toward Jackson under the apple tree.

Captain Hart looked that way just as the general raised his left arm straight up, as if reaching for one of Brawner's scrawny apples. At first, Hart thought he was waving or signaling to someone or trying to catch a fly on the wing. But long seconds passed, then a minute, and Jackson's arm remained stiff and motionless above his reclining body.

"What's he doin *that* for?"

Major Worsham lifted his head long enough to take in the raised arm, then slumped back.

"Oh, he took a slight wound in that hand on Henry Hill last year. Had to wear a sling for awhile. When he got rid of that, he said the hand still hurt'im sometimes but if he held it up at way, blood ran back into'is body and made the hand feel better. Got to be a habit."

"You think it really helps, Major?"

"Doubt it. But Jackson's pe*cu*liar. Makes'im feel better, it's as good a medicine as any."

"He don't eat pepper." Channing shook his head rather sadly. "Says it makes'is left leg weak."

Hart was still staring, bemused, at the general's raised, rigid arm when someone touched his shoulder. He looked up into the beaming face of Kirk Connelly, a boyhood friend who, two summers before, had spent a carefree month with him in the best Paris bistros, salons, and boîtes.

"If it aint ol Hardhat hisself!" Connelly grabbed Hart's hand and pulled him to his feet. "How you gettin on with no ladies to swoon over you?"

"If *you're* here, ladies got to be somewhere nearby."

They wrung each other's hands, exchanging genial insults, as young men do who know no other way to express affection. They had not seen each other since a last bleary morning in Hart's old rooms on the rue Bonaparte.

"How could *you* be a captain, Hardhart? Bein of such low character? An me still a lootenant."

"Courage and ferocity. Also you probly don't know I'm Gin'al Lee's illegitimate son."

Connelly looked around nervously but no one was paying attention to their reunion. "Same ol tongue on you. They's hotheads in this army'd call you out for that." He linked his arm in Hart's and they strolled away from the group around Channing. "Sides, the Ol Man couldn't of been the one. Nothin but icewater'n *his* veins."

As they talked and laughed, recalling better days, speaking irreverently of the war, their superiors, the Yanks, each other, the sun shone for a moment warmly rather than brutally. Brawner's farm seemed suddenly a cheerful place, despite the deserted buildings and weed-grown yard, the murmur of the troops massed in the nearby woods, the stacks of muskets like gaunt sentinels, the smoke staining the sky over Manassas.

"Should of been with me last night, Kirk. Put down a little Yank champagne I just happened to find at Manassas."

"Damn! Time I took a look around, best thing I laid hands on was some clean drawers. I'd-a traded'em for champagne, though."

"You always would of. How'd you come to lose out?"

"On Ewell's staff. Case you didn't know, Ewell spent the day fightin off Hooker so's you could load yourself up."

"Much oblige. Hear tell Ewell's right feisty."

"More of a gamecock, I'd say. Him over there."

Connelly led Hart toward a short, erect officer resplendent in something close to a dress uniform, who sat on a tree stump using an upended powder barrel for a desk. His hat lay on the ground beside his boots and the sun beat directly on his bald head, already burned to a rich saddle-leather brown, over which flies crawled unopposed.

"Gin'al Ewell . . . beg pardon, sir . . . like to introduce my ol friend, Cap'n Hart. Stuart's staff."

"Stuart?" The bald little man looked up at Hart with popping eyes and what seemed intense interest. The flies rose from his skull and settled back again. Under the general's beaklike nose, an enormous brush of chin whiskers concealed his scrawny neck. "Cavalry, is it? By Gad, sir, cavalry's just what I need."

"Why, Gin'al . . ." Hart pointed vaguely east, having no idea where Stuart was. "I think . . ."

"Oh, you'll do for cavalry, sir, you'll do. Take your troops here . . ." The pop eyes flicked to Connelly, came back to focus brilliantly on Hart. "Reconnoiter west on the pike. First house you come to, sir, scouts tell me . . ." He leaned toward them, his shrill voice dropping dramatically. "Confidential report. That house, sir, is *afloat* in buttermilk."

"Buttermilk?"

"Buttermilk! For God's sake, get me some!"

"Yes, *SIR!*" Hart saluted more enthusiastically than he had for months.

General Ewell returned the gesture solemnly, his pop eyes flashing. "Trust a cavalryman for foragin."

"See what I told you?" Connelly punched Hart's arm, as they went for their horses. "Reg'lar damn gamecock, ain't he?"

They rode at an easy gait through the broomsedge, down the gentle slope to the pike, and headed west.

"At little baldhead fool you." Connelly chuckled ruefully. "First time he gave me an order, I was so flustered I had a courier detail show up at *his* headquarters rather'n old Trimble's, where he wanted'em. So he asks me what's goin on'n I'm more flustered than ever. 'Gin'al,' I says, 'I sposed . . .' But I never got'ny further. 'You sposed,' he yells. 'You say you sposed! What right has a lieutenant to spose anything, sir? Do as I tell you, sir, and don't spose!'"

"That's the army for you." Hart nudged Mercury to a trot. "On the whole, I'd sooner be in Paris."

The dirt road shimmered emptily before them. No sound but that of crickets and the *clop-clop* of hooves broke the silence. Hart wondered where the birds had gone. The sun, nearing high noon, glared from a brazen sky. Small clouds of dust rose behind them. Except for the absence of the birds, Hart thought, it was hard to believe that armies were on the alert hereabouts—men in their thousands eager to fall on one another like beasts in the jungle. He watched a rabbit dart in front of them, its cottontail flashing against the gray surface of the pike.

Connelly spurred his horse and charged, the sudden heavier beating of hooves startling Hart and confusing the rabbit. Instead of bounding on across the road and into the safety of the brooms-edge, the animal swerved straight down the pike, Connelly's roan mare right behind. The lieutenant drew a long-barreled pistol from a holster on his saddle and, leaning almost over the bounding rabbit, aimed down at it.

"No!" Hart tried to shout just loudly enough to be heard over the roan's hoofbeats. "No shootin, Kirk!"

Even as he called, the rabbit took a quick leap to its right and disappeared into the broomsedge. Connelly pulled up, grinning.

"Just practicin. Could of got'im with one shot, easy as shootin Yanks." He sheathed the pistol and pulled his horse back into a trot beside Mercury.

"Mighty bloodthirsty, I see."

Connelly patted the holstered pistol. "Me'n Thunder here, we love a good fight."

A good fight was just what they were likely to get before the sun moved much farther west, Hart thought; not like shootin rabbits, either.

"Now what I'd love'd be a clean bed, another bottla that Yank champagne'n a mam'zelle pickin graybacks outta my hair."

"Who wouldn't? But come on, Hardhart . . . Paris was great, but aint this war really the most fun you ever had'n your life?"

"Fun?" The question did not so much astonish Hart as perplex him. Kirk Connelly was not the first to put it to him, but Hart had not yet devised a satisfactory answer.

"Damn right, fun. I mean, you get right down to it . . ." Connelly made a sweeping gesture. "You ever been so *free* in your life? Livin in the open, movin around all the time, no need to earn a livin or read law or look after some goddam farm." He made a face. "No persnickety women makin a man dress up, go to tea parties, watch'is language. No strings on yuh, Hardhart, *that's* the ticket. Cept goin where the army goes, and who'd wanta be anywhere else? Best men we'll ever know for friends'n a good cause to fight for . . ." He patted his holster again. "An Thunder in my hand."

That was it, Hart thought, the heart of the matter, Kirk's real "freedom." They trotted on in the noon sun, the dust of the empty pike. No one was set so free as the warrior: *no strings attached.* Who need pay so little heed to the ordinary restraints of civilization—persnickety women and their requirements? Because no one else had thunder in his hand, a license to kill, the ultimate exquisite power of mortal combat—vanquish or die, kill or go down. No wonder men in war became friends as close as brothers. They were warriors together, bonded in a fiery freedom.

But Connelly was wrong on one point, Hart thought. A good cause had nothing to do with the freedom he found so pleasing. Warriors were the same no matter the cause; and in war, who could tell the good from the bad anyway?

"Trouble is, Kirk, Yanks aint rabbits."

"Hell, no . . . can't run half as fast."

A hundred yards farther on, they rounded a curve, past a small point of woods, and saw an unpainted farmhouse rising behind a rail fence; the gate was swinging carelessly open. A barn and a Negro cabin stood on the edge of a rather forlorn-looking cornfield. Far beyond the field, a treeline rose against the sky.

"Tastin buttermilk already, Hardhart." But Connelly had scarcely spoken before he flung up his arm in warning; both men reined in.

"Horses under the tree."

Hart took field glasses from his saddle bags and trained them on the farmyard. Two saddled mounts were hitched to a tree between the house and the fence.

"Yanks." He handed the glasses to Connelly. "See their gear?"

"Yanks all right. Le's take 'em."

Hart, in the wake of his reflections on warriors, had no great hankering for a fight. But he knew the Yank riders might have information useful to Jackson; besides, he really did want buttermilk. *That* was a cause of some value.

"We'll go in fast, Kirk. You jump the fence, if that nag of yours'll make it. I'll cut 'em off from the horses. No shootin less we have to."

"My, my. You *are* cav'ry." Connelly drew his huge pistol, winked at Hart, and spurred the roan.

Hart charged down the pike after him, pulling the Le Mat from its holster. He watched Connelly take the fence. Damn fool yellin like a banshee. He pulled Mercury sharply through the open gate, just as two men in blue uniforms came running down the rickety front steps of the farmhouse. Hart hauled Mercury to a stop between them and the tethered horses, leveling the double-barreled Le Mat above Mercury's alert head.

"Hold up there! Or you're dead men!"

One of the Yanks—a lanky youth whose cap had fallen off in his leap down the steps—jerked his arms high over his head and froze in place. The other, a stocky corporal, made a dash for the corner of the house, his spurs jingling. Hart swung the Le Mat after him.

"Halt!"

Before the fleeing man could get around the corner, Connelly—having galloped completely around the house—appeared from behind it, huge pistol in hand. As if a great claw had seized him from behind, the stocky corporal stopped in his tracks. Slowly he lifted his hands over his head.

"Goin nowhere, Gin'al Pope." Connelly gestured with the pistol for the corporal to back up against the house. "Or maybe you're McClellan hisself?"

The corporal put his shoulder blades against the clapboard, then spoke as casually as if greeting a friend. "Goddam stinking Rebs."

"Didn't smell us soon enough." Connelly grinned at him amiably.

"Over there with Gin'al McClellan." Hart pointed the Le Mat again at the hatless boy, who edged along the wall, his eyes fixed on the pistol barrel, until he bumped against the corporal.

"Goddam sonsabitches." The corporal turned his head watchfully from one to the other of his captors.

Hart swung down from the saddle and put the Le Mat back in the holster at his belt. "Keep an eye on'em and I'll get the buttermilk."

Connelly laughed. "If these sons aint drank it all."

Hart started up the shaky steps and stopped abruptly. A girl stood in the doorway, white-faced against the dim interior of the house. Around her long, nondescript skirt another face peered grinning and snaggletoothed.

"Mornin, ma'am." Hart smiled and took off his hat. "We'll take care of your ... ah ... guests for you." He gestured toward the captured Yanks, and the girl leaned past the door frame to see them; quickly, as if the sight offended her, she looked back at

Hart. Her long black hair fell in a single pigtail to her waist.

The face by her skirt pushed past; a skinny, dirty boy leaped from the steps to the ground and ran toward Connelly, who was still astride his roan.

"Kill'em! Dirty Yanks!"

"Wash! Hesh-at foolery!" The girl's voice had a sharp edge of authority, but still she hardly took her eyes from Hart.

"Shoot'em *dead!*" Wash yelled. "Nothin but dirty Yanks!"

"Piss-ant." The corporal did not even bother to look at the shouting boy. His young companion seemed to be shrinking back into the unpainted wall of the house, his eyes tightly closed.

"Watch your tongue there!" Hart did not intend to let a Yankee use language like that in front of a southern girl—even a farm girl with a piney-woods voice. He went up the steps, feeling them tremble beneath his heavy boots. "Hope they did no harm, ma'am."

The girl retreated into the gloom of the house. "No . . . no harm. Jus some ham."

"Ainchuh gone shoot em Yankee shits?" Wash evidently was not concerned for the girl's ears or sensibility. Hart hastily followed her into the house. After the brilliant sunlight outside, he could hardly see her shadowy form in the sudden dimness.

"Why, sure." Connelly's voice carried clearly across the yard. "But we got to torture'em first."

The floorboards of a long hallway creaked under Hart's feet. "They ate your ham?"

The girl nodded, still retreating. The hall ran like a runway between doors opening into two rooms on either side. The walls were of chinked boards, unplastered, unpainted. A poor place, sheltering a hard life.

"What about the buttermilk?"

She took another step backward.

"I won't hurt you, ma'am. One of Gin'al Stuart's staff officers. We heard tell you might have buttermilk you could spare."

The girl turned and ran down the hall, light on her bare feet as the rabbit that Connelly had chased. And about as scared, Hart thought. He had not meant to frighten her and wasn't sure how he had. Probly their unexpected appearance, with Yanks already there. Or maybe . . .

Putting his hat back on, he followed the girl quickly to a narrow back porch and into blinding sunlight; across one side of the porch several shirts drooped from a clothesline. At the other end a rough table had been set with plates and cups for two, a platter of ham and cornbread, and a moist-looking crock covered with a cloth.

"Ah, yes." Hart smiled at the girl, who stood by the table. "That famous buttermilk."

"They made us. Said they'd burn the house down, we didn feed'em."

"They would of, too. You'n the boy alone?"

"Maw's in bed. Em sojers nearbout scairt her to death. Paw'n Henry's took the mare to Centreville."

"But you're sure they didn't . . . uh . . . hurt you?" That Yank corporal, Hart thought, looked villainous enough to grab for more than ham and buttermilk. Though the girl was a skinny creature.

She shook her head emphatically. "Y'all kin have the ham. Buttermilk, too." She poured a cup and held it out, moving quickly as a butterfly.

"Why, ma'am, that's kindly of you." The buttermilk was cool, rich; Hart had had none for weeks. Then he turned quickly, at the sound of a creaking floorboard in the hall. A Negro woman with an expressionless face came out on the porch; Hart looked at her with casual lack of interest, the way he regarded most Africans.

"Mistis say she aint know whut's hapnin. Say not to leave her lone."

"Alone?" The girl's voice took on again the sharp edge of authority. "You with'er, ainchuch?"

"Ain't no use tellin *her* she all right. She bout outten'er mind."

The girl moved her head angrily, her blue eyes snapping. They made, Hart thought, a nice contrast with the dark hair in the swinging pigtail. But he was more interested in the buttermilk and ham and the two captured Yanks; bound to be more where those two came from. Maybe headin after'em right now.

"Go on back up-er, Sajie, 'n tell'er it's all right, Virginia boys run'em off. Tell'er not to take on so."

Sajie disappeared into the creaking hall. The girl began wrapping the ham slices in a checkered cloth she took from a cupboard against the wall. Hart sipped buttermilk, watching her supple hands. She handed him the package.

"Want the buttermilk jug?"

"Why, thank you, ma'am." Hart stuck the wrapped ham under his arm. "We brought a coupla extra canteens. If we could just fill 'em . . ."

She moved swiftly and silently to the task. Wash came running around the corner, his dirty face alight with ferocity.

"Missy! Man sez'em two Yanks might git shot fer spies!"

Missy paid him no mind but poured more buttermilk.

"At your brother, ma'am?"

She nodded.

"Kind of warlike for a young'un, aint he?"

Missy plugged the neck of the last canteen. "Mean's a snake." She looked over her shoulder at Wash, who had swung himself up by the porch rail and was leaning over it, staring avidly at Hart. "He-uz older, take onna whole Yankee army, I reck'n."

Hart, awkward with the ham under his arm, slung the canteens over his shoulder and winked at Wash. "Don't rush it, bub. Plenty of Yanks left time you get your growth." He started to turn away, then remembered regulations. "How much we owe you, ma'am?"

"Nuthin. Run off'em Yanks is pay enough." She seemed to be getting over her fear, Hart was glad to see. "Paw'd be right glad to thank you, he'uz here."

"Wa'nt but two of'em," Wash said, sneering. "Din't even shoot'em, neither."

Snotnose brat needed a good tanning. Hart saluted the girl with the long black hair, ignoring Wash, and went back along the hall, the boards creaking under his boots, and out to Mercury standing patiently in the front yard.

"Hey, cav'ry!" Connelly was still holding his pistol on the two Yanks. "We gone walk these beauties back or let'em ride?"

Hart glanced once, appraisingly, at the mounts tethered to the tree. "Horses aint worth the trouble. Let'em walk."

"Maybe not good enough for cav'ry. But us staff heroes might could use'em for remounts."

Hart shrugged. He put the cloth-bound ham in his saddlebag and gathered up the reins of the captured horses. "Saddles worth a mite, too." He led the horses beside Connelly's roan, opened one of the buttermilk canteens, and handed it up. "Next best thing to champagne."

Still keeping his pistol aimed at the captives, Connelly took a deep draught.

"Bastards," the corporal said. "Thieving assholes."

Connelly handed the canteen back to Hart, nudged his horse near the two Yanks, and kicked the corporal hard in the ribs, sending him sprawling into the swept dirt of the yard.

"Nuffa that mouth, McClellan." With his pistol, Connelly pointed first at the corporal, then at the road. "Git your ass up'n start walkin."

"Shit-faced Reb." But the corporal struggled up and started for the gate. The hatless youth, tears streaking his face, followed him quickly.

"Old friend..." Hart pulled himself up on Mercury's back, still holding the reins of the captured horses. "You gettin downright mean." They followed the Yanks at a walk.

"Havin a little fun. Sides, I promise that sassy kid I'd touch'em up a little."

As if summoned, Wash bolted down the steps and across the yard. He grabbed Hart's stirrup. "Take me widyuh, huh? Lemme jine up, Mistuh, lemme..."

Hart shook his stirrup loose. "Told you not to rush it, bub."

"Wash! Stop at!"

Hart looked back as Mercury took him through the open gate to the pike, the led horses following. The girl with the pigtail ran across the yard in her bare feet and seized Wash by the arm. Hart noticed then that she was graceful, and the legs outlined under the long, thin skirt were well-shaped.

"Well, lookather," Connelly said. "Smackdab middle of a war'n Ol Hardhart still found hisself a filly."

Hart grunted. "Leave me the buttermilk, *you* can have'er. *And* the snotnose. Hey, Yanks! Move it on up there!"

Just over three miles to the southeast, Major General John Pope dismounted and climbed on the station platform at Manassas Junction. As far as he and the officers with him could see, nothing but desolation greeted them—burden cars burned to the wheel trucks, the smoking ruins of row upon row of warehouses, rails twisted like black lace, roadbed torn up and ties flung aside, as if rooted out by mammoth pigs. What had been a rich storehouse of everything Pope's army needed—particularly food, forage, ammunition, medical supplies—had been rendered overnight a wasteland.

Charlie Keach, with his sharp reporter's eye, mentally recorded what he saw—not only the destruction of buildings and cars but the plain strewn with barrels, cans, boxes, pots and pans, sabers, muskets, saddles, and all sorts of military equipment, meat, salt, canned vegetables, blankets, shoes, hats, not to mention the discarded rags and tatters of the Rebel marauders. A scene, Keach thought, that would challenge his ability as a writer, for few who had not seen it would be able to conceive of such wanton destruction. Off toward the earthen walls of an old Reb fort rising from the plain, a small mountain of bacon hunks—apparently all that Jackson's men could not carry off with them—burned greasily, sending a forlorn strand of black smoke into the burnished sky and the smell of fried meat over the surrounding wreckage.

Colonel Russell was not concerned with what he saw, or even with the loss of the army's stores. Grievous as this blow was, he had been prepared for it and he had more immediate worries; for one thing, his rotten teeth had never hurt him worse.

"Fielding!" The colonel's stentorian voice rang over the vast, desolate wreck of the Junction and what had been the army's supply depot.

"Yes, sir!" Lieutenant Fielding spoke so quickly, from so nearby, that Russell, in the echoes of his bellow, felt momentarily foolish.

"Goddammit, Fielding, I need you I don't wanna have to shout like a hog-caller."

"Yessir. Sorry, sir."

"Find Surgeon Brown. Bring him here right off. On the double!"

His aching teeth had turned Russell's head and most of his body into a raw-nerved mass of pain. For most of the morning, he had tried holding his mouth full of whiskey. But that did little good—less, he had discovered, than going ahead and swallowing the stuff.

But the real trouble with the colonel was that he sensed everything suddenly going wrong. Plainly, they were not going to bag Jackson's whole crowd after all—not at Manassas anyway. First, Porter's column had not appeared along the track from Warrenton Junction at dawn, as Pope had ordered. By 10:30, Porter *had* appeared at Bristoe—complaining that the night had been too dark for marching! Somebody was going to hear about *that* when the campaign was over—Russell guessed in the form of court-martial charges.

Then the goddam German fat-ass, Sigel, had turned out to be late, too, not because of the dark night but because the pompous old fart had refused to send off his 200 wagons to the army reserve under Banks, as Pope also had ordered. But, of course, Sigel's political connections, reaching right up to Lincoln himself, would protect him from deserved retribution.

Even McDowell had failed—remarkably for such a professional—to follow orders in one particular. Instead of sending his whole force to Manassas as commanded by Pope in the order Duryea had carried to Gainesville, McDowell had sent Ricketts's

Division and some cavalry to guard Thoroughfare Gap. Just took it on himself, and did it, as if one division could stop the whole other half of Lee's army, supposing they actually were coming through the Gap.

But McDowell's initiative might, Russell had to concede, turn out a good thing. Because the truth was—and it hurt Russell damn near as bad as his godforsaken teeth to admit it—he and Pope, especially Pope, had been wrong about Tom Jackson. He hadn't come out at dawn to attack Hooker along Broad Run—missed a chance, too, since Porter hadn't shown up for support. Best they could figure out, Jackson hadn't moved around to their right, either, to make another attack on the O & A.

Russell looked at Pope as he gazed impassively over the destruction of his depot—maybe of all his hopes. Nothing was moving anywhere but Federal troops. There was no sign of Jackson, no suggestion where he'd gone. The smoke from the smoldering bacon seemed to point derisively nowhere. But Pope had to find Jackson now and destroy him. Nothing less could salvage Pope's own reputation. Not after what the Rebs had done to him at Manassas.

Surgeon Brown came up briskly and saluted. "You sent for me, sir?"

Russell eyed him malevolently, thanking his stars he was only chief of staff, not in Pope's shoes. "That whiskey cure aint working. What else you got this side of amputating my head?"

John Pope had little time to brood, even had he been given to it. He and his other staff officers, not so distracted as the unfortunate Russell, had no time to lose in recrimination. They had to piece together what information they could from captured Rebs, skulkers, stragglers, neighboring farmers. Most of what they were told they already knew, or found worthless—either deliberately misleading stuff planted by secesh sources, or as full of error as casual observation always is. But everything had to be considered.

Cass Fielding, acting as a sort of collating clerk for all the reports, reliable or otherwise, soon saw that at least one piece of information was being repeated several times over. This seemed of sufficient importance to an ambitious young staff officer that the normally cautious Fielding, knowing Russell to be off his feet, decided to take it directly to the commanding general.

"Sir!" His salute was bristling. Pope, staring at him with hot, red-rimmed eyes, touched his hat brim impatiently and puffed blue smoke around the stump of his cigar. Suddenly Fielding devoutly hoped the general would think his information significant.

"Sir, they's three reports here—one from a captured Reb, one from a scout, and one from a sutler coming out from Washington. All of 'em say A. P. Hill's Division was in Centreville this morning. Up till near noon, anyway."

A portly major, overhearing, snapped his fingers loudly. Fielding noticed that Pope jumped a little at the sound.

"That fits with this, General," the major said. "We just got in another scout says Reb cavalry hit the O & A again this morning at Burke's Station . . ." Pope took the cigar out of his mouth, threw it away, and stood up before the major had finished. "That's *beyond* Centreville, General, toward Washington. Looks like they're headed that way."

Later in the hot afternoon—under the cloudless sky that stretched like a pane of glass over northern Virginia—Major Jesse Thomas of General James Longstreet's staff, riding with a brigade detached from Jones's Division, approached Thoroughfare Gap. Longstreet's main body of five divisions, with General Lee accompanying, had been following Jackson's route of two days before. This force had reached the slopes leading to the western entrance to Thoroughfare Gap, and bivouacked there.

The detached brigade of Jones had been sent forward to secure and hold the mountain pass, which scouts had reported to be unoccupied by the Federals, for a crossing the next morning. But Major Thomas, going along to report back what he could to Longstreet, and sweating profusely in the heat and dust of the narrow road, was not thinking just then of the Gap, or of what might lie beyond it.

Instead, he was remembering Miss Letty Williams—that sweet voice, that snowy bosom—and still trying to comprehend the incredible thing that had happened. At Dabney Williams's table, he had scarcely let himself believe that the beautiful Miss Letty was really interested in him, though it was hard to put any other interpretation on her intense glances and breathless way of listening to his every word, however dull—as Major Thomas believed most of his words inevitably must be to a woman. Nor, try as he might, had he been able to have even one private word with her or a moment to press her hand in leave-taking.

The brigade van, with which Thomas was riding, was about to enter the Gap, a narrow and threatening place with steep wooded rises on either side. A skirmish line was going forward cautiously; behind him the tramping feet of the rest of the brigade broke the afternoon stillness. But he scarcely heard the marching rhythm. He put the stump of his arm inside his butternut jacket and felt the soft handkerchief he had pinned there, just over his heart, and for a moment he held the end of his mutilated arm against the delicate linen, taking a kind of comfort from it, as a child does from a favored old bit of rag or a familiar soft toy.

Just then he saw a strange thing. One of the skirmishers, fifty yards ahead, threw up his arms and his musket whirled up above his head. A sharp cra-a-ck! echoed from high up in the Gap. As if air had gone out of a balloon, the skirmisher's lank figure collapsed spinning, facing to the rear as it hit the ground. The musket tumbled on top of the body. The other skirmishers began to trot forward, bent over and zigzagging, and suddenly the quiet of the day was torn by the ugly crackle of musketry and the sinister *wheat wheat!* of Minié balls.

Brigade officers began yelling orders. Major Thomas, forgetting Miss Letty's handkerchief and how he had come by it, spurred near the acting brigade commander, a sharp-faced, combative Mississippian thin as a whippet and willing to argue with the sun. Thomas detested him.

"Undefended, huh?" The musketry had risen steadily in volume. "At least a regiment in there, sounds like." Now the skirmishers were coming back on the double. "Think you can handle it, Colonel? Or want me to get help from Longstreet?"

"Kin handle it." The colonel spat tobacco juice past the nose of Thomas's horse, spooking him more than the gunfire. "Few goddam pickets is all."

"Don't take many to hold a keyhole like at."

"Kin handle it, Major." Behind them a Georgia regiment was moving swiftly into a battle line that would stretch solidly across the narrow Gap.

Thomas thought of Jackson's Corps somewhere beyond the mountain barrier in front of them. Like Longstreet, he did not think much of Jackson. He had been all right in the Valley but second-rate in the main battles before Richmond. But this belligerent axe blade of a colonel probably didn't understand that forcing a passage here wasn't just routine; it was vital. Jackson's survival, hence that of the army, depended on it. Longstreet should decide how and with what troops and when to lunge through the Gap. It was his responsibility, not that of an acting brigade commander hungry for his star.

"Colonel, I was you, I'd hold up till Gin'al Longstreet gets a look. We got no idea what's the other side-a the Gap—Pope's whole damn army maybe."

The colonel spat again, just missing Thomas's boot. "Then tell'im I'm attackin in one hour, I don't get word to hold off."

Thomas spun his horse and galloped back along the road. The Georgians' forming battle line made way for him, despite a few catcalls about officers heading for the rear. The musketry was slacking off as the skirmishers fell back. But some Yank sharpshooter must have caught sight of the galloping horse, for a dying Minié threw up a plop of dust just beyond and to Thomas's left.

That caught the major's eye, as had the last pirouette of the skirmisher; and for the first time ever, including the moment when he had lost his wrist and hand to a roundshot the summer before, it occurred to Jesse Thomas that he could be killed—that the blind and malevolent chances of war might any day, any hour, deprive him of everything promised by the soft folds of the handkerchief next to his pounding heart.

Gainesville lay four crow's-flight miles behind Major Thomas— just a little too far for the bored men of the Sixth Wisconsin, Gibbon's Brigade, to hear the firing that had driven back Longstreet's skirmishers. They probably would have thought little of it anyway, since all that day they and their brother regiments had been hearing the rumble of horse artillery—as the more experienced officers identified it—first in one direction, then another.

Brigadier General John Gibbon, as disgruntled as most of his troops at what seemed to them the pointless marching to which they and the rest of King's Division had been subjected, was staring in angry disbelief at a courier who had just come in from General McDowell.

"*Centreville?*"

"Yessir. Orders just in from Gen'ral Pope. Whole army's concentrating on Centreville."

That morning, at 3 a.m., with dawn just beginning to brush its gray stroke on the eastern sky, King's Division had started for

Manassas Junction from its camp near Warrenton. But the division had spent much of the day standing still. Bringing up the rear of McDowell's Corps, with thousands of men trying to file onto the narrow road ahead of them, and with more than the usual stupidities and misunderstandings, King's leading brigade—Hatch's—had just passed Gainesville at mid-afternoon and turned off the pike toward Manassas.

"Ev'ry bit of four miles in twelve hours," Reverdy Dowd grumbled to Colonel Bob Bullock. "Wonder weeds don't grow up round this army's ankles."

Now the Sixth Wisconsin, with the rest of Gibbon's Brigade, was milling about in Gainesville on the Warrenton Pike, just west of the railroad crossing and the turnoff to Manassas. Behind it, Doubleday's and Patrick's brigades were halted, too, in equal ignorance of what was happening up ahead. But Hatch's Brigade had already made the turn-off and was trooping southeast toward Manassas when the division received Pope's order to march by the direct route along the pike, through the old battlefield of the summer before, and on to Centreville.

So the three trailing brigades had to wait—strung out along more than three miles of the pike—in the hot, late-day sun, while Hatch's men countermarched back to Gainesville, then filed right on the Warrenton Pike. Their route would take them past Groveton, a mere crossroads hamlet not even designated on some maps, to the Stone Bridge over Bull Run, scene of the dreadful pileup of men and wagons during the Federal rout in July of '61. The other three brigades would follow Hatch eventually—if, of course, they didn't all get still later orders from McDowell, who'd have got them from Pope, who'd get *his* from God maybe, or at least Old Abe in the White House.

But all that was typical of Major General John Pope's Army of Virginia, as its officers and men knew it that blistering summer of 1862. And as far as Gibbon or any of his officers could figure out, the new orders seemed to mean that the enemy they supposed they were seeking—said to be Stonewall Jackson's whole corps, maybe as many as 50,000 Rebs who marched like lightning and fought like thunder—must be at Centreville or thereabouts. Troops in the ranks, of course, had no information at all. They just marched or waited.

"I had a dollar for ever time I got up inna dark and waited all day, I'd be a rich man." Red-haired Private Tom Johnson of the

Sixth Wisconsin was regarded as just that by his company mates, about half of whom he had taught to play stud poker.

"You wanna bet two bits to four we wind up back inna same camp we started out this morning?" Private Cappy Swartz took a swig from his canteen, then spat warm water disgustedly into the dust.

Private Johnson considered this tender seriously. He was known as a man who would bet on the day it would next rain or the number of hairs in a cat's whiskers. This time he shook his head.

"I figure we gone stand right here till bivouac time."

Private Hugh Williams thoroughly disapproved of Johnson. He was as tired of aimless marching as any of the men of the Sixth; but unlike most, Private Williams longed deeply and sincerely for the regiment to get into action against the Rebs, not so much because he disapproved of secession or abhorred slavery or treasured the Union—although all those things were true of him—but because he was curious about himself. He wanted to test his faith in God. All very well to go to church and say your prayers and accept the Lord Jesus Christ as your Savior. But how would you measure up against the severest tests, which he imagined battle must provide?

Private Williams also had a strange and secret sense that the time was at hand. The lurid night skies over Manassas had signaled the unmistakable nearness of Rebs. The angry mutter of artillery had excited him as never before. The regiment had been moving all day, albeit less than a mile an hour, in the right direction. Surely the Sixth Wisconsin was at last marching into the crucible, where Hugh Williams would be put to the only challenge that mattered.

So he was irritated by Tom Johnson's irreverence, as much as by the inexplicable halt. "I'll take that bet," he told Swartz, rather more loudly than necessary.

"Lord God." Johnson pretended to stagger back in amazement. "Never knowed you to be a bettin' man, Preacher."

Private Williams was not secretive about his religious beliefs and did, indeed, contemplate the ministry if he survived the war—more particularly, if his faith survived its test. But he felt his irritation rising.

"And I'll bet *another* two bits we see some action before sundown."

"I'll take *that*." Private Fritz Schiml spoke quickly, as if to fend off other takers. He was the leading company grumbler, who loudly proclaimed his conviction that the Sixth Wisconsin was a victim of political conspiracy to deprive it of opportunity for distinction, on the one hand, or easy duty, on the other.

"Pick any card." Private Johnson held out his deck, fanned in his hand, to the Swede, a private who spoke little English. "Two bits says it'll be under a ten."

The Swede pulled out the ace of diamonds.

"You lose," Johnson said. "Ace counts as a one in this game."

When the brigade finally marched, the sun was sinking toward the mountain ridges to the west and the troops' shadows spilled out long ahead of them. And as they tramped past the Manassas turnoff, straight on along the road that ran past Groveton, it took all Hugh Williams's faith to stop him from swearing; so they were again being marched away from battle—from the Lord's crucible. Maybe the grumbling Schiml was right; maybe somebody had it in for them. Or maybe it was the Lord's own will.

But Private Williams marched on faithfully, legs and arms swinging rhythmically, his disappointment turning to stoic resignation, then to a veteran's bored suspension of concentration. On they marched, in their blue ranks, choking on their own dust and that of Hatch's Brigade up ahead, past neglected cornfields and orchards, between the slopes of broomsedge and goldenrod and Queen Anne's lace, past weathered houses—from the steps of one of which, hard by the road, a dirty little boy shrieked curses at them until a big stone-faced nigger came out and hauled him bodily inside. War or no war, Private Williams thought, he'd be glad when they got shut of Virginia.

Private Lott McGrath of the Fifth Virginia, Stonewall Brigade, lay on his back in the woods behind Brawner's deserted farmhouse. His hands were beneath his head and a long straw of broomsedge bobbed from his teeth. His red-and-black-checked shirt easily distinguished him from the butternuts all around.

"I'm-a tryin-a tell you sons . . ." The broomsedge waggled as he talked. "Y'all kin relax. Aint gone be no fight today."

Private Sowell, sitting cross-legged on the ground nearby while sharpening his bayonet with a pocket steel, spat a stream of tobacco juice near McGrath's new crooked shoes.

"Who said they was?"

"Yeah." Private Gillum Stone was waiting his turn for the steel. "Aint nobody noticed you talkin lately with Ol Jack."

"Jus go on, keep at it." Private McGrath spoke without rancor. "No skin off my ass, y'all wanna missa chancet for a nice long nap inna shade like I aim to git me."

Private Stone was more impressed than he wanted to admit. "You really seen a sign, Lott?"

"Plain's I see what Sowbelly ther calls'is face. Night Ol Jack put Jube Early crosst the river'n like not to got'im back. Member the way it rain that night, Gilly?"

"Like to wash us all away."

"Yeah, well, I'm wetter'n a drowneded cat'n can't sleep for cussin. Rollin'n turnin like crazy when I seen some son comin off picket, I reck'n. Swinging a lannern, makin a kinda rainbow-like inna rain. Inna middla that durn rainbow I seen it clear's I see you this minute. Standin out like fire inna rain."

McGrath lifted his long arm and with a dirty forefinger wrote a two and a nine in the air.

"Two-nine. That-ar rainbow says. I knowed right that second when the next big fight gone be'n slep like a log ever since."

"Shit." Sowell whipped his bayonet on the steel.

"Augus twenny-nine's tomarr." Gilly looked apprehensive.

"Shore-god aint today. I ast the cap'n just to make certain." McGrath turned his head and winked elaborately at Gilly. "Not that ol Sowbelly'd know one day from another nohow."

Despite the swarming flies, Fargo Hart lay sound asleep not far away in the shade of Brawner's barn, hat tipped over his eyes, his belly full of buttermilk. Kirk Connelly had ridden away on some errand for Ewell—both full of buttermilk, too. Andrew Peterson, who had spent most of the day getting his Whatsit Wagon and his African handyman, Joe Nathan, set up safely behind the old railway line, had ridden to Brawner's and given Hart the welcome news that Hill and the Light Division were at last filing into position on the left of the line, extending it to Sudley Springs. So Hart slept easily.

He came awake instantly alert, as a year of war had taught him, at a slight rise in the sounds of voices and horses moving about. Most of the officers in Brawner's orchard had moved out to where they could see down the slope to the pike. Hart stood up, rubbing his eyes, and saw blue troops marching far below. Leading Mercury, who had been quietly cropping nearby, he found Captain Thad Selby standing in his stirrups for a better view.

"What's goin on, Cap'n?"

Selby pointed down the hill. "Gin'al Jackson doin'is own scoutin."

Hart saw then the lone horseman moving through the broomsedge, across the face of the slope, ominous in his deliberate movements, his unhurried pauses, the care with which he turned his horse and headed in the other direction. His head, under the old forage cap, never turned from the blue passing troops.

Hart swung into the saddle and moved at a walk to Colonel Channing's side. The staff chief sat still as stone on his mount, his heavy chest straining the buttons of his ill-fitting jacket. Hart lifted his right leg around the pommel of his new McClellan saddle and pushed his hat back on his head, careless of the buzzing flies. Even low on the horizon as it was, the sun was heavy, burning on his face and neck. On the pike below, the Yank troops moved solidly past, thousands of them, no doubt more following, a long blue snake that stretched sinuously beyond the western horizon. And from the hillside, the horseman peered down at them still, gauging them, the hour, the chance.

Hart felt unfamiliarly at bay. All day, he had sensed the blue ring drawing tighter around him, around them all. Now it was visible, there on the dusty pike—endless, threatening. The power and inexorability of the opposing forces, the avenging troops come to crush them, had never seemed to Hart so overwhelmingly at hand. Of course in his wooded stronghold Jackson probably could remain hidden and secure until Longstreet came, if he ever did; the blue horde appeared to have no hint of the butternut presence in the woods above.

But Hart new Ol Jack would not be content with burning Pope's supplies, momentarily cutting his lifeline. The warrior would strike; that was his nature—relentless as the tides, imponderable as truth, grim as the blue mass plodding onward.

"The spirit that goeth downward . . ." Hart heard himself mutter.

"What's that, Cap'n?" Flies rose from Colonel Channing's lips and beard as he spoke.

"He could lie still, Colonel. But he won't."

Channing shook his head and waved away the thought, or perhaps only the flies.

"Ol Jack's got'is reasons, son."

Maybe. Hart was not so sure. But he knew they would go down the hill with him anyway. They would descend to the earth, even into the fire, at Ol Jack's command—inexplicably, unprotesting, warriors all.

Chapter Five

August 28—Evening

CHAPLAIN E.P. HORNBY of the Twenty-fourth New York, Hatch's Brigade, was riding back along the Warrenton Pike in the mile-long interval between the last company of Hatch's men and the leading regiment of Gibbon's Brigade, which was coming on behind.

He was a big and imposing figure, and he sat his horse as if he knew it. Chaplain Hornby did not lack confidence; just the night before, as he had passed a closed tent, he had heard the click of chips and a voice asking:

"All right—who'll go it?"

Chaplain Hornby had not hesitated to push aside the tent flap, step into the smoky interior, and drop his New Testament on the chip-and-card-strewn table, saying calmly:

"The Lord and I'll go it, boys."

Now the chaplain was riding back along the pike to find a clerical colleague—unfortunately a Baptist—the chaplain of the Nineteenth Indiana, with whom he had held gingerly discussions about joint services. It had seemed a good, Union idea, New York and Indiana worshiping together, not to mention Hatch's and Gibbon's brigades, easterners and westerners between whom little love ordinarily was lost.

But Chaplain Hornby had changed his mind. A devout, well-educated Methodist, he was not going to share a pulpit—even a makeshift pulpit in the field—with some arm-waving, total-immersion, Baptist Bible-thumper. And his conclusion was final.

But as he rode to deliver it, not unaware of the stalwart figure he would shortly present to Gibbon's oncoming farm boys, Chaplain Hornby was not thinking so much of ecclesiastical confrontation as he was of Sally Sutherland Crowell. He had thought of little else since Slaughter's Mountain, during which day of carnage and terror he had chanced to find her—rescue her, he liked to think—and almost been captured doing it. Indeed, he'd often thanked a Heavenly Father who in His divine wisdom certainly must have had His reasons for permitting the chaplain to be on a visit to his brother, a surgeon with the Ninety-seventh New York, just as the armies battled near Slaughter's Mountain.

That chance visit had made Chaplain Hornby one of the only men in his regiment who had actually seen battle, a fact to which he had frequently found opportunity to make modest reference ever since. He rode on, thinking of Sally Crowell's soft hands, straightening himself in the saddle against the critical gaze of Gibbon's western bumpkins.

Fargo Hart, sitting Mercury calmly in the fly-swarming orchard above, watched his brother officers racing at Jackson's command for the woods and the troops hidden there. Martial orders rang across the hillside. The first excited shouts of the troops died away in the clatter and rumble of an army forming itself for action.

From the woods, a column of men moving by the flank stepped into the open. From where Hart sat, the ranks seemed as perfectly dressed as if the men were on parade. Muskets gleamed in the last rays of the sun. Officers' voices crackled in the air like lightning. Above the line of troops uncoiling from Brawner's woods red battle flags stirred limply in the still air. Even the troops' nondescript clothing suddenly seemed crisp and smart as uniforms.

It might have been a scene from any war, all wars, Hart thought—the panoply, the color, the intricate and orderly formations with which men since the dawn of civilization had glorified and thus cloaked the organization of their warrior instincts. Even he—for in spite of himself, Hart felt something like a small boy's excitement as he recognized the Stonewall Brigade filing out of the woods in its long lines, angling to his left, at that distance its men looking jaunty and even fit after their long day's rest, forming the battle line that gave them their identity. But Hart feared and resented his own excitement.

A rider crashed from the woods, bent low over the neck of a

lathered horse. Hart recognized one of Stuart's headquarters couriers. Introspection fled at the sight.

"Le's go, Merc!" He spurred to intercept and the courier reined in. A long bloody scratch had opened across the nose and one cheek of his sweat-streaked face—a souvenir of the thick Virginia woods behind Brawner's farm.

"Gin'al Jackson, Cap'n!"

Hart whirled Mercury, pointed, and galloped with the courier to where the general sat his little sorrel quietly beside Richard Ewell, who had mounted a huge horse. Both looked around as Hart and the courier clattered up. Far down the gentle slope, Hart again glimpsed the blue snake gliding undisturbed over the knoll. The courier saluted and started reporting before the general could touch the brim of his cap in return.

"Gin'al Jackson, sir . . . Gin'al Stuart sends you'is com'plints, sir, 'n says tell you he's in position, sir, right back-er on your right'n rear."

The courier pointed. Beyond the ridge line, off toward Hay Market and Thoroughfare Gap, where they'd passed only two days before—seems more like two weeks, Hart thought—a cloud of dust rose toward the setting sun.

Hart could barely hear Jackson's muttered thanks to Stuart. The courier saluted again, whirled his horse in a spume of dust, and galloped off toward the dust cloud on the horizon. Hart watched Jackson pull the forage cap from his head and rub his coatsleeve across his high forehead, leaving dirty smears in the sweat trickling from the thick dark hair combed back over his rather large head. Then the general put the cap firmly on his head and pulled it low over his brow. His face was expressionless, save for his fierce, pale eyes. He touched the sleeve of the pop-eyed general at his side.

"Ewell . . ." General Ewell, too, obviously had to strain to hear the soft voice. "Advance."

"Yes-*SIR!*"

Ewell's piping voice rose above the clatter and rumble of the forming troops as he saluted and spurred away. Ewell was a renowned horseman, and Hart watched appreciatively as he took Brawner's rickety fence on the fly, then pounded on toward the woods from which the Stonewall Brigade was still marching in even, unhurried ranks.

Jackson, moving as deliberately on his small pacer as he had when surveying the blue marchers on the pike, rode out of the orchard and away from the center of the field below Brawner's house. Hart and Mercury followed at a respectful distance, until the general drew rein on a slight rise of ground that would give him a good view over the field.

Hart tried to watch as clinically as a history student taking notes. Yet the butternut columns wheeling from the woods under their red battle flags, the horses galloping, the tension thick as the gray shroud hanging over the long blue line on the pike—even as he was repelled by these evidences of the duty or courage or foolhardiness that drove men clear-eyed toward their deaths, he was gripped again by the excitement of the moment; he had to resist the urge to send Mercury flying down the slope like a knight's charger.

A battery of artillery rumbled from the woods, its horses at the gallop, guns and caissons bouncing on the rough terrain. Another battery raced behind it; Fargo Hart counted eight pieces as the horses with their mounted drivers swung the guns into a rough line facing southeast. The gunners began to unlimber, the drivers quickly moved the horses to the rear.

Before Hart expected it, a puff of smoke rose from two of the pieces at once—then two more. Professional work. A harsh wind whipped across the hillside, and the boom of the cannon came rolling like thunder. Ol Jack sat immobile on his sorrel, but—as at Bristoe—Fargo Hart heard him mutter in a voice hoarser and stronger than before: "Good . . . good!"

Down on the road, Major Reverdy Dowd, who had just ridden out of the shade of the woods, wondered in the sudden sunlight if he was hearing things, or if perhaps a giant cloud of insects had swarmed rustling and sighing over the heads of the Sixth Wisconsin. Chaplain Hornby, riding toward Dowd, saw ahead and to his right a puff of smoke, like an incredibly fast-blooming flower. Another such flower bloomed beside it, and another.

Then, both men heard the booming of the guns—close and personal as at Slaughter's Mountain, Chaplain Hornby thought, and the same inhuman whine overheard. Just to the right of the blue mass of Gibbon's leading regiment, as it strode four abreast toward him, Hornby saw another burst of smoke from an exploding shell.

Reverdy Dowd thought: Sixth Wisconsin under fire. At last! Panic surged in his heart. For what may have been no more than a second, but which seemed to him an hour, he had no idea what to do.

The inhuman whine swelled suddenly into a monstrous scream. Chaplain Hornby's horse reared high. Hornby clung with his legs, sawed frantically at the reins, while the universe in which he and the horse were playing their tiny game exploded. He was still hanging on when the horse went over backward.

The old mare under Reverdy Dowd was steady as a rock, and as more shells whistled obscenely overhead and burst—two, three of them, another—like slaps across his eardrums, he heard Colonel Bob Bullock's confident shout, a reassuring chord of sanity:

"Talion, *halt!* Front! Load at will . . . load, men!"

More shells burst short of the column in sudden turmoil on the road. Iron ramrods jingled against musket barrels in the sudden chaos of cannon, shells, voices shouting, hooves pounding. Hugh Williams, ramming home a Minié ball and returning his rammer to its rings, thanked the Lord for the precision of his movements. Under fire! and I'm calm as old Nellie pulling the plough.

Another shell burst, nearer this time, the concussion nearly deafening him. Someone began pushing him from behind and he half-turned, shouting angrily. Tom Johnson, the red-haired cardsharp, tumbled to his knees, clutching at Hugh Williams's coat. Oddly enough, the red hair was gone. Hugh looked down at Johnson's brains, and saw blood boiling up through them. Then Johnson pitched face forward in the road.

"Lie down, men!" Colonel Bullock shouted, in the same parade-ground roar with which he had so often damned them to hell for clubfooted drill. "Lie down!"

Even with Johnson dead at his feet, God's terrible will that closely in evidence, Hugh Williams knew from Bullock's hoarse, familiar voice—as much as from his own fingers fitting a cap—that he was all right, under control. He sprawled with the rest of the regiment under the slight protection of the bank at the side of the road. He tried not to think of Tom Johnson's brains. The shells were bursting regularly overhead and Cappy Swartz, lying next to Williams, raised his face from the dirt, looked around and asked of no one:

"But where *are* they? Where they coming from?"

"Up the hill." Hugh Williams raised his own head an inch or two; but he could see nothing beyond the bank but the white nodding wildflowers and what looked like the smoke of a huge fire drifting against the sun-reddened sky.

"But I didn't *see* anything . . . I can't figger . . ."

"Clear the road there!" someone shouted from down the line of march. "Clear the goddam road . . . get the hell over there!"

Major Dowd, prodding Rosie along the sprawled ranks of the Sixth Wisconsin, heard a familiar voice shouting:

"Gainst the bank, boys! Close against the bank! Guns're coming!"

He realized it was his own voice. He was all right, then, he was under fire with the regiment and doing his job. And if he kept on doing his job, he'd keep on being all right.

He watched a battery of twelve-pounders rumbling down the road, trace chains jingling, the horses straining forward. Battery B, according to the gold letter on the guidon. Campbell's Battery, and a fine goddam looking outfit, particularly right now. Never saw a better.

Just after passing through the woods that straddled the road, the battery pulled up, scattering dirt and sand, and an officer on horseback waved away the men lying at roadside. Gunners leaped from limbers and caissons and tore away the rails of the fence atop the bank. Then, heaving and struggling, gunners at the wheels, the horses pulled the six pieces one by one up the low bank and into the field beyond. The caissons with their ammunition chests quickly followed, their handlers grunting and swearing.

"Steady, boys, and stay down!" Colonel Bob was shouting somewhere nearby. Dowd saw the colonel through drifting smoke, sitting straight up on Duke, the dark bay he treated like a close relative. He might have been leading the regiment down Pennsylvania Avenue itself.

Out in the field, the battery was lining up and unlimbering on a rise of ground about a hundred yards from the road; before the last piece was readied, the first was booming back at the Rebel cannon, and for the first time Reverdy Dowd felt the intense relief it brings a soldier to hear his own guns giving shot and shell to the enemy.

But it seemed to Private Fritz Schiml, hugging the bank a few files farther along from Hugh Williams, that this was a strange situation indeed. It made no sense that they were being fired on, since they had done nothing to warrant such treatment—just marching along. So somebody, as he'd suspected, had it in for them. Still, the whole thing seemed so unbelievable that he forced himself to peep over the bank for some kind of evidence that this was reality, that he had not gone momentarily mad. He saw a gun carriage leap backward, smoke erupting from the long gleaming barrel; gunners quickly ran the piece back into position.

In the second of staring he allowed himself, Private Schiml saw little else but the smoke drifting over the whole field, so thickly that it seemed to him that the shells apparently bursting above and near him were coming out of a netherworld of flame and darkness, through which the red rays of the sun cast exotic searching beams.

Schiml, putting his head back down, was amazed. He had not dreamed that there would be so much smoke in battle. He had expected to see grand spectacles of armies maneuvering, not this murky, flash-filled confusion before him. He was a rational man and prided himself on that; but as he pushed his forehead against the coolness of the earth, tried to thrust his whole body deeper into its protection, he was not quite sure whether this was a battle or a nightmare from which he would yet be waked.

Farther back along the road, on the other side of the woods, two of the Sixth Wisconsin's brother regiments had formed a battle line and were preparing to roll over what Brigadier General John Gibbon, supposing Jackson's main force to be at Centreville, had no reason to doubt were the horse batteries of some Rebel cavalry detachment—the kind of guns he'd been hearing off and on all day.

So when the shelling started, Gibbon—without even consulting General Rufus King, the division commander, who was a mile or so ahead—ordered out his two rear regiments, the Nineteenth Indiana and the Second Wisconsin, to chase off the horse batteries on the hillside. Gibbon had a reputation for driving his boys hard and looking after them well. He had personally outfitted them with their distinctive black hats; and for troops never before under fire, his well-drilled midwesterners moved quickly.

Stripping away the fence along the road, they quickstepped into the pasture in battle line and strode up the slope, yellow with goldenrod, toward Brawner's house. The Nineteenth Indiana was on the left and the Second Wisconsin brushed its right along the edge of the woods that had shaded the troops ahead of them on the road. Skirmishers formed a long arc in front of both regiments.

The Reb gunners quickly turned their attention to the advancing Yank regiments. Almost at once, from obliquely left, a shell ripped through the Nineteenth's close-packed ranks. Men screamed and fell. Several broke and ran until an officer on horseback, rounding them up like a sheep-herder, crowded them back into line with the flat of his sword. More shells whistled in. Some were set to explode in the air, scattering jagged bits of metal like lethal hailstones. Others were solid balls of iron that ripped men apart as if they were paper dolls in the hands of children.

Private Jamie Hatton of the Second Wisconsin felt a hard hot blow just below his knee, spun around, and fell on his back. Someone jumped over him. Jamie was relieved to be unhurt except for the hard fall. Then he raised his head and saw his leg was shot away clean at the calf. Blood spurted from the stump like rusty water from the old pump at school in Waukesha County. But that bothered Jamie less than the screams coming as regularly as his own pumping blood, filling his head with their devilish screech. Who could be screaming? he wondered.

Private Philip Keefe, the man who had jumped over Jamie Hatton, marched on across the pasture, his jaw set, trying not to hear Hatton's rhythmic screams, tramping down hard on his right foot to shake off the bits of Hatton's flesh and blobs of blood that clung to his uniform trousers. He was too horrified by this mess on his normally neat clothing to be afraid, and he was about to stop and flick it away with his handkerchief or maybe his black hat, when he stopped, instead, in astonishment.

Over the brow of a rise maybe two hundred yards ahead, in an alignment that to Keefe looked like that of toy soldiers on a shelf, red flags fluttering above them as they came, rose a long brown battle line that filled the horizon with butternut troops coming toward him. Moving at the quickstep, their muskets thrusting at the Second Wisconsin like iron teeth, the advancing Rebs— when three strides over the brow of the hill, and as if by signal— raised a shriek that rang down Keefe's spine like raking fingernails, as if a thousand devils had screamed at once. The sound rose even above the roar of cannon, and echoed back from the slope above. And no sooner had it died away once than it rose again.

Lord God Amighty. Phil Keefe had never seen Rebs before, much less heard their fuss. His concern for the bloody mess on his leg disappeared. He could hear commands ringing out from the Reb officers—cutting harshly through the high-pitched screaming—almost as clearly as he could hear his own captain shouting:

"Close it up, Keefe, goddammit! Git back in line there!"

Afraid, suddenly, not so much of battle or of the oncoming

Rebs as of being separated from his comrades in the face of the screaming line ahead, Keefe ran to catch up. The two lines seemed to him to close toward each other with astonishing speed, skirmishers falling back swiftly, through the drifting smoke of the artillery fire and the last red rays of the sun. But just as he jumped back into the line of the Second Wisconsin, feeling better to be in place, the butternut ranks ahead came to a halt. Keefe did not need to hear the Reb officers shouting to know what was coming next.

Mother. Watch out for me now, Mother. Pray for me now. Lord God Amighty.

A sheet of fire seemed to leap out from the Reb line, now no more than a hundred yards away, and to flash from one end of it to the other. A single crash, louder, sharper than the cannon's roar, rolled down the hill. Something angry snarled past Keefe's right ear. Obeying commands he scarcely heard, did not need to hear, he went down on one knee and raised his loaded musket to his shoulder, sighting along the shining barrel into the smoke and flame ahead.

From a good vantage point in Brawner's orchard, Theodore Alford St. John Redmund had watched the brown battle line move over the crest of the hill and down the slope. He had heard its barbaric screaming and its first deafening volley, all with growing disbelief. As he watched, and the Federals began to return fire, everything on the field soon was clouded in smoke. The musketry became continuous, the shots, even the volleys of companies, merging into a roar broken by the more isolated booming of cannon, the occasional rising scream of the Confederate troops.

Teddy Redmund had ridden in from Centreville with Hill's dusty column. In the woods along the old railroad right-of-way he had encountered another civilian—a photographer, of all useless things. Redmund had no interest in mechanical toys and couldn't understand what grown men saw in the camera. But for an American, the photographer Peterson seemed relatively civilized—certainly civil. They had ridden together to Brawner's, arriving just as a group of officers broke up and began galloping for the woods.

Peterson in his long duster, Redmund in his kepi and havelock, attracted more attention than they realized, even amid all the commotion. Perhaps for that reason an officious young captain in a handsome new uniform—Redmund envied it until he saw that it was not well-tailored—had ridden up to demand their credentials. But when Peterson showed him some sort of paper, the captain stiffened, saluted, and became almost obsequious. Redmund had been proffering his own impressive documents, when the captain suddenly stood in his stirrups and stared up the slope toward the woods. A long column of troops was winding into the open ground.

"The Stonewall!" The words had been all but lost in the martial clamor on the hillside, but Redmund noticed a look of near-reverence on the captain's face.

"Damn'fit aint." Peterson took a half-smoked cigar from his mouth and flung it away—a gesture, Redmund thought, that belied the calmness of his voice. "What's left of it anyway."

Redmund had watched the column with growing wonder, until he could no longer control his impatience. "I say! What's this Jackson think he's doing, sir? What *is* all this?"

Peterson touched his horse's flank and moved toward the brigade spilling from the woods. He waved at Redmund and called to the young captain: "Looks like you got another gin'ral there."

Since Redmund considered himself a professional military officer—if not quite a general—he had failed to perceive the irony in what he saw only as the usual offensive American jocularity. He was not, in any case, a man to perceive irony about himself.

Besides, he had been graduated from Sandhurst, held a captaincy, seen active service in the Crimea, before his father finally had pulled the strings necessary to get his third son a diplomatic post. And it had been this military background that had caused the London newspaper to ask him to take leave of that post, in the pigsty that was Washington, to write professionally about this ridiculously unprofessional war.

Redmund had come to regret his descent into odious journalism—scarcely a calling for an officer and a gentleman, even though of course his articles appeared under a pseudonym, "Sertorius." He nevertheless worked hard, in the field when he could get there, in the offices and Congressional halls, hotel lobbies and barrooms of Washington when he could not. He had ridden to Centreville on the pretext of inspecting the fortifications there, but he actually had hoped to find Pope; and when he had stumbled onto Confederates instead, he had immediately seized the opportunity to see the war from the other side.

Redmund's principal problem as a journalist was in trying to take the American armies seriously enough to justify the military style of his dispatches. Oh they were lethal, all right, killing one another with the wanton joy of the rabbit- and squirrel-hunters that they were back home. But in every other respect, Redmund thought, these bumpkin armies deserved what he had recently written of them, after what the Federals vaingloriously referred to as "the battle of Slaughter's Mountain"—that "the two mobs blundered into each other like drunks on a dark night, reeling about in confusion."

Redmund had not seen that battle, unfortunately, but his assiduous questioning had gleaned good accounts of it from the wounded coming into Washington, officers on leave, confidants in the military telegraph office, and the columns of the Washington and New York newspapers. And the incredible scene he was witnessing now, from Brawner's orchard, not only confirmed those reports but what he had seen for himself during the truly epic chaos of the fighting around Richmond. This Jackson creature was no more than a military clod who had made a reputation of sorts in the Valley against the dregs of the Federal army and because the idiots in Washington, knowing even less of military matters than he, had lost what little nerve they had.

The same Jackson had been a conspicuous failure at Richmond when faced with McClellan, who appeared to Teddy Redmund to be the nearest thing to a real general the whole benighted continent could produce for either side. Redmund had interviewed McClellan and knew he had served as an American observer in the Crimea—thus had seen at least the rudiments of professional warfare.

Redmund had to admit, however, that Jackson's troops had made a workmanlike advance down Brawner's hillside—save, of course, for the dreadful screaming, no doubt a legacy of the redskin savages against whom Americans had learned what little of war they knew. But the black-hatted Federal line, though nearly overwhelmed by numbers, had stood the first blast of musketry without flinching and now the black hats seemed to be firing back steadily. Some of these Americans had the makings of soldiers, if they could only be properly handled by officers who knew what they were doing. But that was the rub of it.

"Idiocy!" Redmund yelled at the natty captain.

The captain evidently did not understand him through the infernal roar from the slope below; he took off a quite presentable hat, swung it over his head in jubilation, stood in his stirrups, and shrieked something incomprehensible into the din of battle. His beardless face was slight, transported, and he clapped the hat back on his head, drew a long, rather handsome sword and dashed down the hill like a dragoon. For a moment, Redmund thought he was charging into the battle, which he would have considered not much more foolish than anything else going on.

But with much skidding and rearing the young captain pulled his gray mount to a dusty halt near a scrubby horse on which a deplorable-looking officer slouched, with an old cap pulled down over his beak giving the last unmilitary touch to his demeanor.

Could this be the famous Stonewall? And why was he holding his arm straight up in the air?

If this odd creature *was* Jackson, maybe he was not only incompetent but as crazy as some claimed. Here he was, isolated in enemy country with the mere rump of an army, not more than a fraction of what the imbecile Federals could pull together against him if they only had the wit to do it, with the rest of what passed for the southern army too far away to reach him if the boastful ass of a Federal commander could put together any kind of concentration at all.

So what did Jackson do, out of whatever obscure impulses passed for his military knowledge? He gave away a reasonably secure position where his worn-out ragtag troops could lie low and rest, a day anyway, maybe two, to attack a Federal force he didn't have to attack, that wasn't even aware of his presence, that offered no decisive or even important opportunity, in a battle so ineptly managed so far that the two sides, in the thick smoke that covered their lines, were doing no more than stupidly pouring fire into one another at cricket-pitch range.

"Madness," Redmund muttered to himself. "Not war!"

Captain Thad Selby did not regard Ol Jack as either incompetent or crazy. He would have called out the British correspondent for such opinions, and shot him on the spot. It never would have occurred to Captain Selby, either, to wonder why the general had ordered the late afternoon attack. If it had been done at all, Selby knew without question, it had been necessary. That Jackson would manage it magnificently was equally unquestionable.

Selby had scarcely slid his horse to a halt near the general, who sat quietly watching the battle—what emotions, Selby wondered, must be raging in the lofty brow hidden by the low-pulled cap! How he must have longed to strike a blow personally!—before Jackson looked around, saw Selby, and with an abrupt waving motion called him to his side.

The young captain, who had joined the staff after the Richmond

fighting and who had been away on a liaison mission the day of
Slaughter's Mountain, had never before been quite so personally
summoned by his hero. At that moment, he desired in the fullness
of his heart nothing more than to be of service to him. And as if
his desire had been transmitted by his spurs to the horse beneath
him, the animal fairly leaped toward the general's modest sorrel.
Even before Selby could pull up again, a long arm was pointing
straight down the slope, toward the battle hidden in smoke, its
ceaseless roar making the air around them seem to tremble against
Selby's ears.

Private Alf Gurganous of Overholt's Battery knew they were
getting the worst of the shellfire before the orders came to shift
aim from the two Federal regiments in the field back to the Yank
battery near the pike. He knew it from the hail of shells coming
in and bursting all around their own pieces. Bastard Yanks had
the range right on. Served their bloody pieces like sonsabitches
too. Shells going off around Matthew like popcorn. Two horses
down and Wall-Eye Coggins, the fuse-cutter, hit bad in the shoulder with a hunk of iron the size of a lemon.

Fifteen yards to Gurganous's left around Mark, the second piece
of the section, Alf knew things were worse. A shell had burst just
over the trail, the gunner was down with the No. 3 and No. 4
men, and one of the platoon corporals was having to do the sighting. Loading and ramming his own piece with shells for the Yank
battery, Alf couldn't see what was happening to Luke and John,
the other guns over in the second section, or in Garber's Battery
farther on. But they were more in the open and bound to be taking
a beating.

He pulled the sponge on the end of the ramrod staff from
Matthew's heated brass maw. Jeff Jernigan, the best No. 2 man
in Overholt's whole battery, tore the paper bag off the sabot and
pushed the shell into the tube. Alf flipped the rammer staff in his
powerful hands, bringing the rammer end to the mouth of the tube,
and shoved home the load, putting his weight behind it. He and
Jernigan stepped clear. The No. 4 man moved back and pulled
the lanyard. Matthew leaped backward, flame and smoke gushing
from the tube, the roar of the exploding powder charge barely
distinguishable in the din of battle.

They were a good crew. Alf was proud to be a part of it,
knowing they always got the most out of the piece. A good battery
all around. But two more shells burst nearby and an iron fist whined
past his ear and chipped the metal rim of Matthew's off wheel.

Alf knew they'd soon be limbering up, because the six-pounder battery had never been seen that could stand off twelve-pound Napoleons served like sonsabitches.

Lott McGrath had gone screaming down the hillside with the rest of the Stonewall Brigade, yelling perhaps even louder than most of his comrades. Lott was in a rage. As he worked his musket expertly, he sent a scream with each bullet into the smoke. "God-dam yuh goddam ass!" he shrieked every time he pulled the trigger. He was not sure at whom he was cursing.

It was bad enough that the orders to fall in and move out had caused Sowell, rumbling with laughter, to flick him in the ribs with his newly sharpened bayonet, bad enough to see the re-proachful look of betrayed trust in Gilly's eyes. But what really burned him, what—if the truth had been known even to Lott McGrath—struck cold fear into his belly, fear he concealed even from himself by the rage with which he cursed and fired, was the knowledge deep in his soul that they were all flying directly in the teeth of fate.

"Goddam yuh goddam ass!"

They had no *business* that day in any kind of fight. The sign had been too powerful. Lott McGrath had seen it clear as a rainbow in the lantern's light. No reasonable man, after seeing a sign so clear, could possibly doubt it. *29.*

That was the sign, that was the day, *that* was when they were supposed to fight. Now, here, on the wrong day, against the sign, they were on the devil's ground; and the devil alone knew what would come of it.

Ever since the firing began, Durward Brace had been trying to get his family into the cellar again; but only Kate would stay put. The Yanks had been tramping past an hour or more before the fighting began, and Brace had watched them sullenly, torn between fear that they'd steal him blind, like the two that had come that morning had intended, and hope that this time maybe they really would blow away his confoun house and Henry and every damn thing else that held him back. Still . . . he had his obligations as head of the family.

"Wash!" Sweat poured down Brace's lined, sunburned face and neck. "Where's at boy now?"

Henry came around the corner of the old clapboard house, holding Wash firmly by the arm. The boy was barefoot and dirty, as usual.

"Tryin-a run off wid'em sojer boys."

"You lie!" Wash tried to twist free but he could more easily have broken chain than Henry's grip. "I-uz only gittin ready to chunk some rocks at'em."

"Then you-uz gitting ready to git kilt." Brace wiped his forehead with a dirty sleeve. "Git'im inna cellar, Henry. Tie'im down ther, you got to. Wher's Sajie at?"

"Wid de mistis."

"Then gitchuh ass on back up here'n guard this house. Damn Virginia boys aready clean me outten buttermilk'n half a goddam ham. Now they's goddam Yanks everwher a man looks."

Virginia boys, too. So many of both that Brace and Henry had had to give up trying to get the mare to Centreville that morning, even by the back roads and narrow tracks Brace knew like the wrinkles and creases of Kate's fat face. He was convinced that either side would take the mare away from him, once they spotted her; so when they had returned to find that Yanks had been to the house, the ham and buttermilk gone with the Virginia boys, and a fight starting just up the road, Brace had sent Henry to hide the mare in the woods by Dawkins Branch.

Shit, Brace thought. This war's shit for a man with mouths to feed.

He watched Henry drag Wash around the house toward the steps leading down into the small, dank cellar. Missy came running out the front door and stared down the road at the dust of the Yanks, and the smoke beginning to rise toward Sudley Mountain.

"Better git on in at cellar'n hep look after Maw."

"Maw's aright. Paw, I could run over inna woods'n find out wha's goin on. Nobody'd see me. I could . . ."

"Git on down at cellar like I tole you, fore Maw gets inna fit."

"Shoot." Missy ran past him around the corner of the house. What she'd really hoped to see was the young captain again, the one with the dark eyes and clipped mustache and manners like an angel, who had saved her from the grabby Yank with the dirty mouth. She'd been thinking about the captain all day—way he smile at me'n tooken off 'is hat, I like to fell down faint.

Missy had not been anywhere near so frightened that morning as Fargo Hart had thought. The foul-mouthed Yank had left bruises on her thighs and bottom but she'd been edging closer to the butcher knife all the time. If the captain and his friend had not arrived when they did, she thought, they'd of found a Yank pretty bad cut up.

But they had come in time, so she had not needed the knife. After that, she hadn't been afraid of the captain at all—far from it. Just couldn't take her eyes off his face and his curly hair and his lithe body. Missy had never seen a man so . . . beautiful; most of the men she knew looked more or less like Paw. She'd hardly been able to speak for staring at the captain, for hoping he'd see something in her to look at, too.

She stopped at the cellar doors, hating to go down in the darkness and the bad smell. Wash. Like as not trying to git'n my pallet'n feel of me. Maw whinin all night. At that moment, Missy wished with all her heart that the captain would come back on his big black horse, sweep her up like a rag doll, and take her far away.

The mere thought told her she could not bear the cellar again, or Maw, let alone Wash. She ran on in the dusk toward the barn, not thinking at all beyond the hiding place she knew in the hayloft.

In the front yard, Brace imagined he could feel the earth trembling under his feet, as it had during the worst of the fighting the summer before. The booming of the guns came deeper and faster, as if more and more were joining in the shooting, across the woods and fields, the low rolling hills between his house and Brawner's.

Ol Brawner smart to skedaddle when he did, Brace thought. Like Wilmer McLean.

Henry came back around the corner of the house and Brace pointed to the front steps. "Keep a sharp eye now." He spoke brusquely as usual, though he was still unable to look Henry in the eye. "Set right er on'em steps'n don't let a soul in, Yanks least of all. You hear?"

Henry sat down silently, as solid and immovable as if Brace had rolled a boulder in front of his door. Brace stopped at the corner and looked back.

"Any'em shells get to goin off nearby, you come on down."

In the failing light, he saw Henry's head incline an inch or so. Brace trudged on. All right by me some shell come right square down on'is thick skull. Git him *and* the house in one shot.

But as he threw back the cellar doors, he knew there'd be no such luck for Durward P. Brace. So, he thought as he went down the steps and turned to close the doors after him, tomorrow he'd take Henry and they'd go off to join the war, by God, the both of us.

"Cept the onliest one comin back aint gone be no thoat-cuttin nigguh," he muttered into the silence of the cellar.

From the guttering candlelight, Kate's fat terrible face floated up at him like some bad, whiskey dream.

"Y'all right now, Maw. He all right down-yer."

"Pray to my Jesus," Kate mumbled.

Sajie, sitting beside Kate on the dirt floor, watched Brace go across the cellar and stretch himself out on his own blankets. In Sajie's eyes, Brace was such a sorry specimen of white man—or any other color—that she had been, if anything, more amazed than he by the hot moment in the sunlit field the day before. She had told Henry nothing about it, of course—would not have dreamed of such a thing, not because he would have killed Brace two minutes after she spoke, but because, in the time between, Henry most probably would have killed her first. Iffen I tolt'im true.

Sajie had been studying for two days on what had made her hold still for Brace as long as she had. She knew—the knowledge was just a part of her, like bones and hair—that in her world, however remote she and Henry might be from other Africans, nothing was more severely frowned upon than married women trifling with men, black or white. Sajie had never done it before, or even thought of it—not that she'd let ol Brace do anything but squeeze her bare titty. But even that would be too much, if Henry found out.

And that—Sajie sensed, but had no ability to articulate, even to herself—was at the bottom of it. In Henry's house, in their life together, his word and will were law and her submission to them total. But that day in the field behind the house, with the sun baking down like Creation, when she had turned and seen Brace staring slackjawed—then, for the first time since she'd been a girl in the fields, since long before the Mistis's daddy had bought her for Henry, Sajie had sensed her power as a woman.

Henry took her often and at will, as his right, leaving her no sense that she could, or needed to, attract him or anyone. But that morning in the earth-smelling field, she'd known at once that *she* could do what she wanted with Brace, have him or not, bend him as she wished, break him as easily. And it was that unaccustomed sense of sexual power that had caused her to draw him on, looking at him low-lidded and wet-mouthed—that had held her still while he touched her, until in the cruelty common to all power she had chosen to crush him.

But sensing all that, without being able to give it form in her head or words in her mouth, was of little help to Sajie—in fact, eased not at all the fear and anger and shame that for two days she had felt at having betrayed not just Henry but herself, as a wife of whom a certain standard of behavior was expected—not least by Sajie herself.

Be's a wicked thing, she had told herself a hundred times. A wicked thing I done. Good Lawd fuhgive.

And the wickedest part was that she'd loved it—not the touch of Brace's hand but that moment, that power, that long-forgotten sense of herself. Even wild ol foxface Brace, no-count's lie be. Lookin like he struck by lightnin.

"Good Lawd fuhgive." Sajie's murmur was lost in the far-off thunder of guns, in Kate's sobbing pleas to Jesus, in Wash's piping squall across the cellar's dimness:

"Paw! Damn ol Missy done run off."

Under the sheltering roadside bank, Reverdy Dowd felt that he was getting the hang of things, and not just because the shellfire on the Sixth Wisconsin had ceased. He had not yet learned that long-range shelling even on massed troops seldom did much damage because the powder charge inside the shells was usually too light to cause real fragmentation. Veterans knew that half the time, maybe more, the fuses didn't go off and the things flew by like screeching birds, doing no more harm.

What pleased Dowd was that he could hear a terrific fight going on beyond the woods, and even his inexperienced ear was able to tell that the lines were holding where they were. Nobody was being driven. Dowd, moreover, had passed—at least he had got by—what he had always believed would be his big test. He had looked on blood gushing out of wounds and flesh torn away; he had seen the open oozing head of what had been Tom Johnson and had not yet flinched or run away or—worst of all possibilities—thrown up in front of the men. He had been doing his job, mostly steadying down the ranks, and he had a peculiar, happy feeling that he was going to be all right, maybe even as good an officer in battle as he knew he was in camp and on the march.

From Rosie's broad accommodating back, Dowd watched Captain J. D. Black pounding along the road. Old Blackie, the ladies' man, Gibbon's errand boy. Dowd had no use for staff, less than ever now that he felt himself a battle officer. But he saluted civilly enough when Blackie pulled his winded horse to a halt, shouting:

"Where's Colonel Bob?"

Dowd pointed out Bullock and Duke thirty yards down the road, barely visible in the stinking smoke.

"You boys're going in!"

Blackie's words were almost inaudible, but Dowd read his lips, partially from expectation. He spurred after the staff officer as he rode up to Colonel Bob and saluted.

"Sir! Gen'ral Gibbon says take your reg'ment in this side of the woods and move out front of the battery far's you can go. Rebs're out there somewhere."

"Who'll be on my left?" Bullock's ordinary voice somehow cut through the uproar.

"Sec'n Wisconsin, the other side of the woods. What part's not shot to hell!"

Fifty yards farther along the road, unnoticed by anyone in the Sixth Wisconsin, Chaplain E. P. Hornby lay sprawled under his dead horse. Much of Chaplain Hornby's coat sleeve and a scoop of his right bicep the size of a sausage cake had been torn away by an iron fragment of exploding shell. His leg was broken. Bleeding heavily, he was only semiconscious, in a dreamlike state in which he was drifting through an earlier day of battle, his first, when he had stumbled upon Sally Sutherland Crowell's house while looking for the brother he feared had been killed or wounded.

More than two weeks later, in the shock of his own wounds, in the blue-edged murk of his fading consciousness, the chaplain saw Sally's white face in the gloom of the charnel house the surgeons had made of her once-elegant sitting room; he saw the lifeless stare of her green eyes, the harpsichord, the bloody mound of arms and legs and feet as carelessly cast aside as burnt matches.

At the time, the young chaplain, unused himself to the excrescences of the battlefield, had been horrified to find this creature gentle as a doe caught up in the hell of war, with the battle raging around her. Of course, she had been grateful to him for her rescue, but certainly not improperly so. Sally Sutherland Crowell would have been incapable of acting improperly, as E. P. Hornby would have been incapable of taking advantage of her fright and helplessness, all alone as she was in that nightmare house.

The blue edges of his senses were moving together. Just before they closed over him, he tried to call her name aloud, but made no sound at all.

Somewhere in the blinding smoke of the field, Captain Thad Selby was desperately seeking the whereabouts of General William B. Taliaferro, commanding Jackson's old division.

Selby seized a passing major's arm and bellowed in his ear, "Gin'al Tollivuh?" The major looked at him with mad, glaring eyes, pulled his arm free, and rode on.

Bullets whirred about Selby. Riding high on Jefferson D., the black horse that had been his father's parting gift, he felt himself suddenly the target of a thousand marksmen. And down there near the battle line, the smoke could not obscure the carpet of wounded and dead weighting down the broomsedge, or the litter of battle— muskets, caps, ramrods, canteens—scattered everywhere.

Feeling Jeff shy from something, Selby had to guide the horse around the whole torso of a man lying in his path like a plaster bust toppled by vandals. He suddenly wanted to turn and race away to the level ground, where death was not directly beneath the hoof. The impulse was so powerful that he reined Jeff momentarily away from the line. But immediately Thad imagined the general watching from above. So he had to find Taliaferro.

His resolution calmed him. He thought it even transmitted itself to Jeff, as they turned back to the battle. But it shocked Selby to know that he had been afraid, even briefly. Fear was a possibility his life had not allowed him to consider. He thought at once of Rachel's father. Great God! Mr. Clayton would seize any excuse, the least moment of unworthiness, to declare Thad Selby not fit for his daughter's hand. And if that happened, Thad's own father would never forgive him, might even disown him. Fear was not an alternative open to Thad Selby.

A rifleman wandered out of the line, blood gushing from a hole in his chest. He dropped his musket, seized Selby's leg, and looked up at the captain with pleading eyes, trying to speak. Selby leaned down and shouted, "Gin'al Tollivuh! Got to find'im!"

"Please . . . God . . ."

At least, that was what the man seemed to be trying to say as Selby yanked his leg away and rode on, blood smeared on his boot. A bullet plucked rudely at his sleeve, but he saw with panicky relief that it had only taken out a swatch of cloth. A mounted officer coming toward him went off his horse with his arms flung up as if to heaven. The horse raced past Selby with flaring nostrils and red eyes. Just then, through a rift in the smoke, the young captain caught sight of the Yank line, its rifles flashing in the gathering dark. Shooting at *him*. But before renewed fear could turn Jeff D.'s imperious head toward safety, Selby also saw Taliaferro.

The general was slumped on his horse, another officer hovering at his side. Selby rode quickly to them, miraculously in control of himself again. As he pulled up, he saw the left sleeve of the general's uniform soaked with blood; blood streamed from the fingers of his dangling left hand. Selby forced himself to salute.

"Gin'al Jackson's complints, Gin'al. He wants..."

Taliaferro slowly turned to look at him. On the side of his neck that had been hidden from Selby, a long red gash reached diagonally from his collar to beneath his ear. The other officer, a major, leaned across the general's horse and screamed, "Speak up, man!"

"Gin'al Jackson!" Selby leaned as close as he dared to Taliaferro's ear. "He wants a reg'ment shifted right to take th'enemy in flank!"

Taliaferro's eyes suddenly glared hotly. As if forgetting his wounds, he pulled his body erect. He seemed to be trying to speak. "...shit you think..." Selby just caught the major's words through what seemed to him a new volume of musketry. Were the Yanks moving in more troops? "...we been tryin-a do?"

As suddenly as he had straightened, Taliaferro slumped again. Selby stared for a moment over the general's shoulders into the angry eyes of the major.

"Gin'al needs a surgeon!" Selby yelled.

The major shook his head. "Won't leave! Can't get'im to leave the troops."

Selby shrugged, saluted—even if Taliaferro was too slumped to notice—and whirled away, all too thankful to be heading back up the hill, away from the carnage around him, the general's soaked, ominous sleeve. But he was proud, too. He had been in battle, found Taliaferro. And Ol Jack would be needing Thad Selby again.

On the road, Captain Black was pounding importantly away from the Sixth Wisconsin, returning to General Gibbon. Reverdy Dowd watched him go. As if the whole damn war depends on him, Dowd thought. The Second Wisconsin shot to hell, though... if Blackie knew what he was talking about, there must be all hell out there in the smoke. Still, if Dowd's ear told him right, the Second had to be at least holding on. He watched Colonel Bob rise in his stirrups—a big, white-maned man who'd fought in Mexico and resigned from the army to make a fortune as a railroad lawyer.

"Sixth Wisconsin!"

Colonel Bob riveted the whole regiment, huddled under the bank, with a parade-ground roar that could blast an owl out of a tree at musket range. "Soldiers! For flag and country! For-*warrrd* . . . guide cen-*terrr!*"

Now we're for it, Dowd thought, watching the men of the Sixth stiffening in line. Save five, two of them dead from the shellburst that had opened Tom Johnson's head, three wounded and reclining against the roadside bank. First blood to the Rebs. But the bastards hadn't seen the last of the Sixth Wisconsin, by God!

"March!"

The colonel's voice boomed like one of the Napoleons. The men scrambled forward over the bank, lifting away the rails of the fence above, where the gunners hadn't already knocked them down. Dowd spurred Rosie more sharply than usual, and as if in indignation the old mare took the bank as cleanly as a hunter and pranced into the field. The men were re-forming like veterans beyond the downed fence.

"Follow me!" Colonel Bob was pointing with his sword as Duke stepped niftily out ahead. The line moved into the smoke, Dowd riding to the left of the regiment, wondering again at the noise, the stinking pall of smoke. A solid shot screamed well over his head.

"Close it up!" Dowd shouted. "Give it back to'em soon! Close it up . . . keep going there!" Through the smoke the colors could be seen briefly, and something choked in Dowd's throat at the sight. "Follow the colors, boys," he screamed. "Follow the flag!" He had to hold Rosie in against his own excited spurring.

They passed Battery B to their right, the gunners not even looking up from their hot work. Another shell burst, couple of men down. Goddam shells short of the battery, dropping on us. Jesus, another one down. Just ahead and to his left Dowd saw a solid shot plough into the earth, throwing up a spume of dirt and dust. Bastards sighting in. Another ball hit right behind the first. It did not plough in but bounced like a piece of rubber, straight towards Reverdy Dowd.

Watching death fly at him, he sat, unable to move, frozen forever, except that he watched no more than one pulse-beat of time before he fell forward against Rosie's neck and the foul swooshing breath of the thing passed behind him, snagging something, tearing, Rosie stumbling to the right, then going on steadily. Dowd, still draped on the old mare's neck, looked over his shoulder. The cantle of his saddle had been torn away.

The smoke drifted off for a moment, and some in the front rank of the Sixth suddenly saw the Rebs kneeling and firing. Million of 'em, Hugh Williams thought. No wonder the general had thrown in the Sixth. Best regiment he's got.

But miraculously, the Rebs weren't shooting at them yet, except for the gunners doing their dirty work with solid shot and canister. The infantry fire was still concentrated on the other side of the woods.

Smoke closed in again and Hugh marched into it as if blind, his eyes smarting, his ears splitting from the noise. Somewhere up ahead, Colonel Bob's mighty voice commanded a wheeling turn half left, and Hugh Williams exulted in the precision with which he and the rest of the regiment carried out the maneuver under fire.

Private Fritz Schiml, too, had seen the Rebel line through the momentary rift in the smoke. The sight appalled him. He knew instantly what he had begun to suspect while lying under the roadside bank—that he had made a terrible mistake. He had gone along with the crowd, joined the company, marched the roads, because that was what was being done and because he was no different from anyone else. But at the sight of the Reb line he realized at last and with devastating clarity where the tide had carried him—to this place where men were shooting to kill, at people they did not even know. At *him*, any second now.

Private Schiml heard Colonel Bob's bull-roared order for the left wheel. Without thought or hesitation, he executed instead a smart about-face, right out of the rear rank of marching men, and started at the double back toward the road and the bank under which he had lain in safety. He was not conscious of fear. Fear had nothing to do with his departure. He simply had no intention of walking straight into a line of strangers who were trying to kill him. To do so would be absurd, mad. And Fritz Schiml knew he was not crazy.

"Schiml! Back in line there!"

Private Schiml trotted on toward the road. It did not enter his mind that he was disobeying orders, deserting. He was obeying the higher command of reason.

Someone grabbed his collar from behind, jerked him sharply to a halt, choking him.

"Goddam coward! Back in that line . . . back!"

Lieutenant Gregson, the one with the ridiculous deerhorn mustache, twisted Schiml's body around and glared down into his eyes with maniacal fury. Still Schiml remained calm as he struggled against the bigger, stronger man. The lieutenant obviously did not understand the situation. But if he could just get back to the road and the shelter of the bank, there would be time to explain that no sane man should take part in such madness.

The lieutenant jammed the muzzle of a pistol under Fritz Schiml's chin and forced his head back until Schiml was staring at the horrid blue smoke swirling above his head.

". . . blow your goddam head off!"

Private Schiml—his neck wrenched, the pistol biting up like an auger under his tongue, the lieutenant's mad screams in his ear, the glaring eyes above the long twirled mustache seared on his brain—Private Schiml collapsed at last into terror. This lunatic would kill him, too, with a twitch of his finger. Everyone wanted to kill him. No reason. Madness everywhere. No reason. Madness.

Something warm ran down Private Schiml's leg. He wanted to scream but the pistol jammed his jaws. He gagged instead. The lieutenant threw him bodily toward the insane booms and shrieks piercing the infernal smoke. The sudden absence of the pistol under his chin was like freedom; but before Fritz Schiml could turn and run toward the road, something heavy seared his back. The lieutenant flailed at him with the flat of his sword. Private Schiml, blubbering, terrified, his trouser leg clammy with urine, stumbled toward the unseen line in the smoke ahead. He still carried the heavy musket he was too well-trained to have dropped. As he staggered and fell and staggered up again, blundering on, Lieutenant Gregson's sword whipped across his back like the lash of a crazed god.

Reverdy Dowd, sure after the ricocheting shell had missed him that death had no designs on him that day, was amazed to find his nervous system keyed to its highest pitch and his mental machinery running at utmost speed. What he saw and felt passed through his brain as clearly, in as good order, as troops at drill. If anything, battle seemed to be heightening his perceptions, and he saw right away that Colonel Bob's tactics were masterful. Coming in on the right of the field, the Sixth Wisconsin was overlapping the Reb line, and the half-left wheeling move would give the boys a field of fire obliquely into the Reb flank. And just as he felt Rosie dipping down into a slight swale of ground, Colonel Bob commanded a halt to take advantage of this bit of cover.

When the colonel's command to fire finally came, just after the halt, pleasure surged through Private Hugh Williams. Though he was aiming only into the smoke, at nothing definite, certainly at no particular Reb, the kick of his musket against his shoulder was invigorating.

First volley, praise God! Sixth Wisconsin in action!

But he was a soldier trained by hard taskmasters and even on such an occasion he stared for no more than a split second after the fancied flight of his Minié ball whistling toward the Rebs.

Then he dropped the stock of his U.S. Model 1861 rifled musket to the ground, trigger guard facing the enemy. The practiced fingers of his left hand pulled a cartridge from the box attached to his belt and lifted it to his mouth. With his teeth, he tore the paper from the powder end of the cartridge. A slight taste of the bitter stuff clung to his lips as he emptied the charge down the barrel of the musket. It was not quite five feet tall, putting the muzzle just below his shoulder height. He thumbed the blunt-pointed .58-caliber Minié ball after the charge, pulled the ramrod from the rings attached under the barrel, pushed the rod's cup-shaped end down the barrel, and seated the ball firmly on the powder charge. He slipped the ramrod back into the rings, lifted the nine-pound piece, half-cocked the hammer with his right thumb while with his left hand he picked a copper cap with a fulminate charge from the capbox also attached to his belt. He pressed the cap over the nipple under the hammer, pulled the hammer back to full cock, aimed quickly into the smoke again, closed his finger on the trigger, and felt again the satisfying kick against his shoulder.

Hugh Williams and the men of the Sixth Wisconsin had been endlessly drilled to get off three shots a minute. All that drill soon paid off. The black-hatted troops, from a point in the smoke and confusion where it had not been expected, began pouring a killing fire into the Rebel left flank and front. And doing what for so long they had been drilled to do calmed and reassured the inexperienced men of the Sixth; in the strange world of battle, the familiar routine of loading and firing was a discipline that steadied them.

"Give it to'em, boys!" Reverdy Dowd, whooping, ranged up and down the line on reliable Rosie. "Go it, Sixth! Go it! Give it to'em!" Then through a rift in the smoke, as he gazed incredulously, he saw the brown ranks up ahead begin to break.

"God Amighty!" he screamed. "God Amighty, boys, the Rebs're running!"

They were only pulling back slowly, firing as they went, veterans giving ground reluctantly, but Dowd had never felt such excitement, such exhilaration. He thought his heart might burst, and he waved his black hat in the air and screamed again, wordlessly, exultantly.

Although Lott McGrath's throat had gone too dry to emit sound, he was still yelling curses at the Yanks, who now were only powder flashes in the fast-falling night. Kneeling between old Sowbelly and Gilly, as in so many fights—every one the good old Stonewall had fought for Ol Jack—but still apprehensive that things were out of kilter, all wrong this time, Lott loaded and fired, loaded again, the barrel of his musket long grown hot in his hands.

He raised the piece to his shoulder, sighted on a flash, and screamed: "Goddam yuh goddam ass!"

He squeezed the trigger and felt the hard kick against his shoulder, a split second before the Minié ball entered his head at the hairline, just above the left side of his left eye, turning his consciousness instantly to darkness and leaving a ragged black hole that gaped, as he went over backward, at the uncaring heavens above the devil's ground.

A blood-colored edge of sun hung above the ridge. Fargo Hart, having no duties, sat Mercury quietly, gentling him against the din. He nodded knowingly as Overholt and Garber limbered up their batteries and moved farther up the hill to put a rise of ground between themselves and the blasting Yank guns that had overmatched them. Those black hats were giving as good as they got.

When the left began to fall back, Hart rode that way in search of something useful to do. But before he could volunteer, General Trimble—old enough to be home in a wheelchair but a raging lion in battle—was shouting in a voice that must have echoed over Bull Run two miles away: "For-*warrrd* . . . guide cen-*terrr* . . . *harch!*" His brigade of veterans moved smartly down the hill in battle line, going in to shore up Lawton's Brigade on the hard-pressed left of the line.

Suddenly, pop-eyed General Ewell, sitting his huge horse as

if he were part of it, galloped down the hillside, too, and disappeared into the smoke that shrouded the brigade of his division. Hart saw Kirk Connelly, riding beside but a little behind the general. The whole army knew that someday Ewell would pay the price for his reckless forays into the thick of battle. But everybody knew, too, that you could sooner stop a catamount from hunting.

Hart watched the battle, going forward by then in virtual darkness, with no such excitement as earlier had seized him; gradually it had lost its force as the stalemated struggle wore on without involving him. He was not concerned that the left had given ground, knowing it was too late in the day for either side to gain decisive advantage. He understood no better than Teddy Redmund why the battle was being fought, why men were dying at that time and place—except that Ol Jack was a warrior, and the business of warriors was to fight. That was reason enough for the brigades to be slaughtering each other on the hillside.

Stuart had sent Fargo Hart to Jackson with messages the night after Malvern Hill, at the peak of the Peninsula fighting a weary six weeks before. Passing the night in the general's camp, Hart had been amazed to find Jackson, early the next morning, personally directing the clearing of the dead from the field, as well as the pieces of scattered human flesh, legs, arms, dead horses, abandoned caps, muskets, scraps of clothing, and canteens that littered the ground.

When the grisly task was done and the field was swept as clean as a housewife's floor, someone had ventured to ask why so thorough a job had been required, under the general's personal supervision at that, so soon after the battle of the day before.

"Why, sir, I'm goin to attack here presently," Ol Jack had said in his soft voice, looking puzzled at the question. "It won't do to march the troops over their own dead."

Warriors who ordered battles, Hart supposed, could have no other attitude. Dead men, strewn flesh were detriments to morale, impediments to the next battle. And in the warrior instinct battles had the only justification they needed.

Someone rode up beside him and in the near-darkness Hart recognized the photographer Peterson in his long white duster.

"Never see anything . . ." Peterson had to shout to be heard. ". . . Nearer hell on earth than that." He pointed down the hillside to Trimble's line plunging into the smoke and flash.

Maybe it *is* hell, Hart thought. All the hell we need, anyway.

But he only shouted back: "Ol Jack bit off more'n he can chew this time!"

Incredible, he thought, how long it had been going on, the two lines so close, neither giving enough ground to make a difference. Just then he caught sight of Thad Selby coming across the field at a gallop, his black horse lathered and blowing. Even on brief acquaintance, Hart could tell that Selby was a believer. Selby would kill any horse, gallop him into the cannon's mouth, because Selby believed—in the cause, in Ol Jack, in what he was told—Hart was not sure exactly in what. It didn't even matter. Thad Selby had *faith*. He was not torn by unanswerable questions; he did not demand justifications no one could give. Selby might even have been enviable, except that Fargo Hart was too proud to envy anyone, and knew just enough to despise ignorance.

The beardless captain pulled his panting horse to a halt. He did not look so dapper as he had earlier in the day. Sweat streaked his face, and his new gray uniform was wilted and shapeless. The fine black horse—a man with such taste in horseflesh, Hart conceded, was not hopeless—drooped, his coat shivering, his eyes white and staring.

"Got to find Gin'al Early . . . Gin'al Jackson sendin him in on the left!" Selby waved a crumpled piece of paper in his left hand.

"Bout time." But Hart made no effort to be heard.

In fact, as he had observed, Trimble's Brigade already had straightened the line. And as Trimble took his fresh troops in, Lawton's men, too, had regained their footing and advanced again. These Yanks in the black hats were standing up, though. The hillside fighting was as ferocious as anything Hart had seen on the Peninsula, maybe worse for the lack of cover and maneuver and the way the two lines just stood there in the smoke and gloom, blazing away, neither side giving ground. If Jackson wanted anything better out of this particular fight than getting as many of his own killed as they killed Yanks, he'd *better* get Early or somebody in there quick.

Peterson pointed along the old railway line through the woods now lost in the darkness. "Back in the woods bout a quarter mile. I left Early a half hour ago behind the railroad cut with Forno in'is rear. Both of 'em rarin to go."

Selby nodded, stuffing the paper in his pocket. Suddenly he drove a clenched fist into the open palm of his expensive glove.

"Gotta *drive*'em! Gin'al Jackson says we gotta drive'em!"

He spurred his lagging mount in the direction Peterson had

indicated. The photographer and Hart watched him gallop away. Peterson shook his head and shouted:

"Win the war all by himself!"

Major Dowd was on the left flank of the Sixth Wisconsin, near the woods, when he saw the Rebs coming again. Colonel Bob had ordered him over to see what kind of gap lay between them and the Second Wisconsin, on the other side of the woods. A message from Gibbon had informed them that the Seventh Wisconsin had gone in to shore up the Second, which had taken such hard licks in the first minutes of battle.

Dowd had no way of knowing that the new wave of Rebs charging down on the Sixth—still giving itself some protection in the slight depression of ground Colonel Bob had found for it—was Trimble's fresh brigade. But he saw that this new crowd was presenting no exposed flank. The Rebs were coming straight in. And to his dismay, Dowd had discovered that the gap on the left of the Sixth was wider than he had thought. A thousand men could have been formed in battle line in the woods between the Sixth and the right flank of the Second and Seventh beyond the woods. If the Rebs got into those woods—into the gap—they could roll up either wing of the Federal line.

It was dark by then. Dowd could see the oncoming battle line only as a vague shape, lit sporadically by powder flashes and shell bursts, preceded by the fiendish Rebel yelling.

Rosie trotted him steadily back into the lines of the Sixth, which was momentarily holding fire so that over the right of the line the thunder of battle had diminished. But beyond the woods, on the left, muskets crashed unceasingly, and the Napoleons in the rear of the Sixth boomed off round after round.

The dark tide of Rebs rolled down on them. They were a hundred yards way, maybe less, when Colonel Bob shouted the order to fire. The line of the Sixth Wisconsin erupted into flame. The detonation of nearly 500 muskets, discharging as one, might have signaled the end of the world. In the single moment of unearthly illumination it caused in their front, Dowd saw a mounted Reb officer swept from his horse as if by a mighty wind . . . gaps opening in the charging wall of men like teeth knocked from a giant's mouth . . . a color bearer running madly ahead, as if the battle flag streaming above him could by itself repel the lead and fire into which the Rebs were advancing. Then the color bearer pitched forward and down, and another Reb picked up the colors and came on.

In the next minute the Sixth Wisconsin, on its knees in the dip of ground, poured in the swiftest musket fire Dowd could imagine. The regiment—no longer untried, blooded now by its numerous maimed and killed—presented so blazing a front that no more than forty seconds after that first lethal volley the Rebels moving at the double-quick had been forced to a halt fifty yards away from the muzzles of the Sixth. But Dowd could tell even then that these were veterans, fighters—bound to be Jackson's men. The blast of fire had halted but not broken them. Within seconds, they were giving back musketry as fierce as they took.

For all his recent training and a lifetime of military reading, Dowd had never dreamed of such a fight—two stand-up lines of infantry, facing each other point-blank, giving no ground, raking each other with unceasing fire, the dark of the night relieved only by the hellish flash of powder, as if an indifferent hand suddenly had flicked away the earth above the devil's pit. Reverdy Dowd thought he had seen nothing so terrible—or so beautiful. But he was filled with pride for the men of the Sixth, these boys he'd taught their letters, then helped to train as soldiers. And suddenly he realized that no other hour of his thirty-six years had been so filled with shock and excitement and emotion. He had never lived so fully as on that field, in the midst of death. And it was his old life in the schoolhouse that now seemed unreal, even childish.

Hugh Williams's rifle barrel had grown so hot in his hands that he was afraid to pour another powder charge into it. He flung away the rifle and seized one that had been dropped next to him by Cappy Swartz, who had been shot through his bearded cheek, the ball emerging through a ghastly rent torn from inside out in the other. Hugh loaded Cappy's piece and fired again, scarcely missing a beat from the rhythm of his movements.

"Aim low, men!"

He heard Colonel Bob's shout, but Hugh was not really aiming at anything. He was concentrating on getting off his shots as fast as possible. He gave no thought at all to what the bullets he was sending into the smoke might be doing to the Rebs. He had hated fighting all his life and unlike most of his friends took no pleasure in hunting; but to bring home a squirrel or a turkey for the pot was sometimes necessary. So it was here, on his first battlefield. Hugh Williams thought no more of war than of killing a squirrel, as a man had to do. The Sixth Wisconsin hadn't started this war but it had to be finished and he aimed to do his part, a man's part, the Lord's work, whatever it took.

At the moment, he had the impression that the Sixth's fire was slackening, that the massed Rebs up ahead were getting an edge on them, moving in, about to smother their line. But Hugh had neither time nor sight to confirm this impression. Nor was he afraid. He realized danger was all about. It whispered obscenely in his ear, had once even clipped the hat from his head, so that his instinct was to burrow into the earth like a groundhog.

But he was among his friends, men in his company that he had known all his life, who would never let him down. In the powder flashes he could sometimes see the colors that identified them all. He had a debt to this company; he had to stand by Cappy Swartz, all of them. Colonel Bob's and Major Dowd's voices told him he was in good hands. And he knew without having to tell himself that as long as he believed it he was also and always in the hands of a Heavenly Father whose merciful care and protection could go with him across the field, and stay with those who had fallen; and who, if He willed it otherwise, would do so for His own purposes, unfathomable to man.

Reverdy Dowd, too, had the creepy impression that despite its strong stand, the Sixth Wisconsin was sooner or later going to be outgunned. Then, peering through the dark night with eyes that smarted from smoke and strain, he saw something strange in the light of a shell burst far to the left. He waited for another. In its eerie flash he saw that troops were moving in the woods between the Sixth and the other regiments of Gibbon's Brigade on the Sixth's left.

Dowd spurred Rosie hard. The old mare tossed her head in annoyance and moved off with dignity toward Colonel Bob Bullock, riding up and down in the flicker of the powder flashes. Before Dowd could reach him, a crashing volley echoed from the woods—at least a regiment firing, his newly trained ear told him. And the muzzle flashes were pointed at the Rebs.

The major took off his black hat, shouting, "They're ours! Our boys up on the left!"

He was still waving his hat when he got to Colonel Bob's side. "Coming up on the left, sir . . . support on the left!"

By then, the firing from the woods was steady and massive. More than a regiment, Dowd thought.

"Bout time," Colonel Bob shouted. "I thought..."

Dowd distinctly heard the sound of the bullet that struck the colonel—a thud like that of a heavy Bible being closed at the end of a sermon. Bullock's voice broke off in a deep grunt, as if he had been punched in the stomach. Duke reared high. The colonel reined him in, then bent over and clasped his thigh with both hands.

"I'm shot, Rev! I'm hit!"

Dowd saw that the bullet had gone through the colonel's thigh, emerged, and raked a nasty bleeding gash along Duke's flossy black flank. Blood gushed from the colonel's leg.

"I must leave the field!" Colonel Bob's shout seemed to Dowd astonishingly controlled. "You'll have to take over."

"But...but...Bob, I never..."

"I'm *shot!*" Bullock suddenly screamed at him. "I'm *shot*, Christ sake!" He wheeled Duke away and trotted toward the rear, their blood mingling on the horse's flank.

God, Dowd thought. God in heaven. What now? Some of the boys would have seen Colonel Bob leaving the field. The word would spread quickly. They'd be unsettled, as he was.

But in the brief moment of his hesitation it came to him that when reinforcements were fresh on the field, it could hardly be wrong to go forward. The thought had no sooner struck him than Dowd instinctively lifted his black hat, swung it over his head, turned in his saddle, and shouted at the Sixth Wisconsin:

"Follow me, Black Hats! Follow me!"

Lott McGrath's body lay sprawled on its back, its arms extended over its head like a man leaping. On either side of him and in the Federal line not far down the slope other bodies lay equally still. But the wounded were far more numerous than the dead—men hit in the arms, legs, shoulders, most terribly in the stomach, sometimes even in the neck and head, but whose torn bodies somehow sustained life.

Most lay where they had fallen, shocked and unbelieving; others limped out of the line, making their way to the rear as best they could. Some brought off their muskets. Some crawled, forgetting weapons and everything but the will to get away, live, find help. Others collapsed after a few steps. A few officers of rank were slung in blankets and carried by troops designated from each company as infirmary aides. The walking wounded, the crawling, and those carrying the officers were looking for the field surgery areas, supposedly marked by flags.

In the last smoke-filtered light of one of these—the Stonewall Brigade surgery, established in a clearing under the trees behind Brawner's house—Major Douglas B. Worsham was paying no attention to the battle, or to the groans and cries of the wounded lying around him as thickly as hogs in a pen. He had no time for anything but the ripped bodies hoisted one after another to his operating table—a pile of Brawner's fence rails covered with three rough boards. The boards, although occasionally sloshed down with water, were slimy with blood and bits of flesh, but Major Worsham did not notice that, either. Sweat dripped from his face and drenched the long mustaches drooping below his prominent nose; sweat and blood soaked his rough shirt. The odor of human gore had long been accustomed in his nostrils.

"Done." His voice boomed across the surgery area, where two other operating tables were as busy as his own.

Orderlies quickly removed a man whose thigh wound Major Worsham had just sutured and dressed. The boy had been lucky; the Minié had gone through him like a sharp augur, not touching the bone, leaving a hole easy enough to clean and close.

Eighteen months earlier, though he had been a physician for many years—numbering Major Thomas J. Jackson of the Virginia Military Institute among his patients—Douglas Worsham had never treated a gunshot wound. Now it seemed to him that he had never treated anything else but rents in human flesh, bones shattered like kindling wood, stumps of arms and legs, intestines slashed by spiraling lead.

Before his first field operation, he had had nothing to go by but a single copy of Chisholm's new manual that he had had to share with two other newly appointed regimental surgeons. Now he seldom even had to think what to do. One look at some violated body usually sufficed, and he would set about his work with the reflexive skill of an infantryman loading his piece or a cavalryman saddling his mount.

At the moment, even in the failing light, he needed no close inspection of the man newly laid on his table to see that the wounded arm was going to have to come off just above the elbow. A Minié had splintered the bone and spread the shards through the flesh as if bone and flesh had been ground together under a giant heel. Even if he had had decent light and time, without all the other wounded clamoring and groaning around him, Major

Worsham knew he could never get all those bone splinters out; no surgeon could. If he tried, infection would be certain as sunset, and death not much less so.

The wounded man was chomping on the butt of a rank cigar and gazing up at Major Worsham with sunken, reckless eyes. His shirt had been cut away and his chest, abruptly white below the leathery tan of his neck and face, looked scrawny, defenseless as a child's.

"Rid of that stogie." The major took it from the man's clenched teeth and threw it away, finding the soggy stump more distasteful than a severed finger. "Swallow that thing'd be worsen what the Yanks done to you."

The man grinned. His teeth were yellow and sharp, wolflike in his hatchet face. "Yanks ain't shit."

"Neither's that arm any more." Major Worsham reached for the funnel and sponge. "Got to come off, son."

The grin was fixed, unwavering; above the wolflike teeth, the sunken eyes were hot and wild as the pine-pitch flares the orderlies had lit against the darkness.

"Don't at rate a man a drink, Doc?"

"If you don't tell Ol Jack."

The major nodded to his operating aide, a skinny boy who had lost an eye in bayonet drill. The boy held a bottle of whiskey while the man on the table took a long gulping drink from it and the major poured chloroform liberally on the sponge in the funnel. Thank God, since the reorganization of the medical services earlier that year they usually had chloroform. He did not like to think about the amputations he had performed without anesthetic.

The one-eyed boy took the whiskey bottle away and the wounded man grinned up at Worsham, almost cheerfully.

"Dang near worth it, Doc."

Major Worsham put down the chloroform bottle. The man watched the movement with his feverish eyes.

"Shit, Doc, let'er rip. One wing's good nuf to whup Yanks."

The major leaned over him with the funnel. The man's grin disappeared as if wiped off his face, and his eyes closed. Worsham put the open end of the funnel over the mouth and nose; then, above the tin rim, the hot eyes flared again. The one-eyed boy took over, holding the funnel loosely; the major had taught him to let some air mix with the patient's intake of chloroform.

Major Worsham, eager to begin, lined up his instruments. He was a good surgeon, sure-fingered and nerveless, as good with his instruments as these stringy, rawhide boys with their muskets, or Ol Jack choosing his ground. And after all those drab years of pills and poultices and old ladies' complaints, nothing so excited Douglas Worsham as the chance to use his skills for something worthwhile, to do a job for Ol Jack's boys. Send them back to kill more goddam money-grubbing abolition bastards.

Wringing sweat from his mustaches, the surgeon watched the fire slacken in the cycs above the funnel rim. He believed he could save this man. He believed it was worth doing. Might come a time even this-un'd have to go out again, killin Yanks for Ol Jack. Even with one wing.

Major Reverdy Dowd was just about then running into trouble. When he had led the Sixth Wisconsin forward, the Rebel line in front of him already was under severe pressure from the advent of the two fresh Federal regiments in the woods at the center of the field. Dowd's instinctive order to the Sixth brought his troops rushing and firing and cheering up the slight slope toward the point where Lawton's and Trimble's brigades were more or less linked. That section of the Reb line went reeling backward—but not for long and not for more than about thirty yards.

Pushed that far, the Thirteenth Georgia found itself partially behind a segment of Brawner's worm fence, pushed down in its earlier advance. Out on the flank, Sergeant Owen L. Cade of Company D, taking over after all company officers had gone down, directed his men to pile the sprawled rails, rotten and gray from years of exposure, into a makeshift barricade. Behind it, Cady's company held fast, returned fire for fire, and felt the line—first the rest of the Thirteenth Georgia, then all of Lawton's Brigade—stiffen on the anchor its stand had provided.

The New Man marveled again at Sergeant Cade. Feeling almost comfortable behind the rails and with Cady in charge, the New Man took time out to unbutton and pee where he lay.

"Grice!" Cady bellowed at him from what seemed no more than a foot away. "Git to far'n at piece, goddammit!"

The New Man was too startled to stuff himself in or button his pants. He seized his musket and fumbled for a charge. Dang Cady's eye uz onna sparrer.

• • •

Much farther to the right of the Georgia boys a sudden cheer went up from Lawton's Brigade, and those near enough could hear a stentorian southern voice bawling:

"Three cheers, boys . . . here's Gin'al Ewell!"

But some of the Yank troops who'd come up in the woods might have heard the same shout. As if to answer the cheers that rose from the Reb line, they delivered what seemed like several concerted volleys of musket fire toward the cheering Rebs.

General Richard Stoddard Ewell had thrown his diminutive figure from the big horse that had carried him into the battle. He was helping with drawn sword to rally one of Lawton's regiments against the new Yank threat in the center when a Minié ball, fired from not much more than fifty yards away, struck him in the center of the right knee, shattering it as if it had been a gourd.

Ewell was whirled about until he faced nearly backward, then went down like a steer felled by a mallet, the sword still in his hand, his hat falling away, his bald head pointing at the Yanks and his popping eyes glaring angrily at the indifferent sky.

Six yards away Lieutenant Kirk Connelly, hit in the same volley, lay face down in the broomsedge, the back of his head torn out by a Minié ball that had entered the roof of his mouth as he, too, cheered on Lawton's troops. The huge pistol he had been aiming was still gripped in his outflung right hand.

From both lines in Brawner's field the wounded came limping and crawling in a steady hemorrhage. And even as the Sixth Wisconsin made its short advance on the right, Gibbon's other units on the left, the Nineteenth Indiana and the confused mass that had once been the proud Second and Seventh Wisconsin regiments, were being forced to give ground. They gave it as grudgingly as had Trimble's Reb veterans at the other end of the line, so that the whole battlefront, running nearly a half mile from its one terminus below Brawner's house to its other extreme at the right flank of the Sixth Wisconsin, had been revolved ever so slightly and slowly, as if on a pivot.

Even in the darkness this relative movement was clear to Major Dowd as he looked to his left along the line lit—by the blaze of muskets and the explosion of shells—as if by a continuous flash of lightning. Without hesitation, in no doubt as to the ability of his newly blooded boys to maneuver in darkness and on the field— hadn't he and Bob Bullock drilled them until their socks wore out?—and with the confidence that had surged in him as soon as the Sixth swarmed at his orders from the protection swale into the open field, Dowd ordered his men to walk backwards, firing as they went. He halted them only when they were once again partially sheltered in the swale. The Union line, Dowd observed with satisfaction, was then solid and straight across the whole front. The Rebs might've bent it but they hadn't broken through.

Six miles to the east, on the road from Manassas Junction to Centreville via Blackburn's Ford, only the lurid glow from the guns could be seen, and the occasional fiery arc of a shell across the sky. But these were all too clearly visible from the heights rising toward Centreville, and across the mostly cleared fields that lay on the rolling plains on either side of Bull Run.

Charlie Keach was sure that John Pope had been as surprised as anyone when the battle had erupted *behind* them, just as dark was coming down. All the general's orders, as near as Keach had been able to learn from assiduous eavesdropping and a quick exchange with Pope himself, had been designed to concentrate the Army of Virginia at Centreville, where Jackson was thought to be digging in behind the old entrenchments.

Late in the day Pope had started in that direction himself. As his headquarters group had trotted along the rising ground between Bull Run and Centreville, the first grumble of artillery had reached them—but from the wrong direction, so that Keach had thought for a moment that he was hearing thunder from one of those sudden Virginia storms that had drenched him more than once that summer.

But soon, even to his unprofessional ear, the repeated roar of cannon, the sharper continuing crash of musketry, were unmistakable; and great clouds of white smoke rose into the darkening sky. Keach was as excited as a child with a toy. His gamble had paid off; the armies had lunged at one another at last, and he would have the story all to himself. Hale would surely forgive him now for a week of silence.

After night closed in, Keach and the headquarters group watched the reflections of the gunfire flicker across the opaque night. A little in front of them, as they faced back toward Bull Run, John Pope and Colonel Russell sat their horses and quietly watched the distant battle, sometimes summoning and dispatching a courier. Keach was debating whether to stay near Pope or strike out across the fields toward the shells flashing like evil stars, when the dark shape of a horse and rider trotted out of the darkness from the direction of the dying battle. Pulling rein before Pope and Russell, he asked for General McDowell in a voice loud enough to catch Keach's ear.

"McDowell?" the reporter heard Russell say rather sharply. "With'is troops, I spose."

Keach edged his horse—Hale had laid out the cash to mount and equip him well—nearer the front of the confused headquarters group of officers and couriers. In the darkness of the road the three men up ahead could barely be discerned even by eyes accustomed to the night; and over the tramp of hooves, the jingling of spurs and sabers, the creak of harness, and the excited chatter of men, Keach could make out only a few snatches of the talk among Pope, Russell, and the newcomer.

". . . hide ner hair of'im since midday . . ."

General Pope's horse shied and snorted, adding to the commotion, so that all Keach could understand of Russell's answer was that the colonel had said something about "that infernal affair back there."

The rider wheeled his horse and began talking rapidly in a low, intense voice. Charlie Keach edged his horse boldly ahead. He was not even thinking about being challenged in that crowd of milling shapes. At age 22, Keach still tended to see opportunity in what others might consider obstacles. That was one of the reasons Hale had picked him to go out with Pope. And Keach knew that if he could find out what was going on back there on the plains beyond Bull Run, where somebody was having a hell of a fight with somebody else, the risks he'd taken would surely pay off in a story even Hale would have to admire. Especially since no other correspondent had defied Halleck's order, even as reluctantly enforced as it had been by Pope.

So Keach persisted and got within spitting distance of the dark form that was Russell. Keach was sandwiched between two officers who ignored him as they, too, eavesdropped on their commander's consultation with the eagerness of men to whom any bit of information, amid the dust and uncertainties of war, was a gem. In the darkness, they did not even notice the reporter. People often did not notice Charlie Keach even in broad daylight; that was not a small part of his talent.

". . . Jackson's whole corps," he heard the newcomer conclude emphatically.

Keach immediately understood that if the ruckus back along the road was *Jackson's* doing, General Pope would be in deep trouble, despite all his brag. Headed east with his Army of Virginia on roads converging at Centreville, he had been barking up the wrong tree, like a coon dog with a sour nose.

But Pope himself, Keach did not fail to recognize, seemed less angered or surprised than exultant. He swept off his slouch hat, rose in his stirrups to peer westward, hulking and belligerent shape against the night sky, and spoke rapidly to Russell. But over the damnable bother of a fat major on his left, who just then began excitedly rattling off to Keach something about the real by-God fight they'd been looking for, the reporter could hear only that for somebody—Jackson, he reckoned—General Pope had roundly promised there'd be no escape, ". . . no escape, sir!"

". . . cut the Rebs to ribbons now!" The fat major gave Keach an openhanded slap between the shoulder blades that pitched him forward on his horse's neck.

"Uh . . . rumph . . . yessir!" Keach hastily agreed, instinctively taking the part of some suckass lieutenant.

"Oh, by God!" The major put his face close enough for Keach to sense his greasy mustache, and for a moment the reporter thought his game was up. "Thought old Ferguson . . . what'n hell happened to Fergie?"

"Rightchere, Maje," Ferguson said from Keach's other flank. "You damn near broke the wrong man's back."

As their horses pinched together ahead of him, Keach—frustrated as he so often was in this frustrating army, this frustrating war—was squeezed out of earshot of the commanding general and the chief of staff. Nor could Keach later get close enough to Pope to know that as the headquarters group clattered back along the country track to Blackburn's Ford, near which its camp had been set up for the night, the general had started to spray out orders faster than couriers could be rounded up to carry them.

Now that darkness had descended on the Virginia countryside, General Hoke Arnall had little expectation that he or any of Hill's Division would be called upon. He had spent most of the afternoon getting his troops into position on the extreme left of Jackson's line, where the railroad cut reached the Sudley Springs Road near Bull Run. Putting him in such a vital spot, Arnall thought, showed some respect, even if he was in arrest. But he had been so busy

that when battle sounds burst out at the other end of the line—
maybe two miles off, Arnall calculated—he had had no idea what
was happening.

Tents and camp equipment had been left far behind on the
Rappahannock. Having dispatched couriers to Hill and Jackson
asking about the engagement in the distance, General Arnall sat
down with his back against a tree to finish by firelight the letter
to Amy he had started the day before at Manassas. He was satisfied
that he had found the answer to their problem in his prayers the
night before.

As the rising sounds of musketry at the other end of the line
crackled viciously in the hot summer night, he told Amy the
conclusions to which the Lord had led him:

> In the unhoped for event that, as I most sincerely hope is
> not the case, you have not escaped to consequences of your
> loving husband's earthly weakness, then I fear we can only
> conclude that the positive and direct will of God must be
> evident in this event; and that we shall have no recourse but
> to regard ourselves as somehow the object of His concern,
> and to submit humbly and willingly to His judgment—
> which, as we know, must be "true and righteous altogether."

General Arnall had thought carefully through this matter and
felt sure that he had reached the right answer. If God's will was
everywhere apparent in the works of man—if God's will be done
on earth as it is in heaven—then there simply was no escape from
the conclusion that God had willed Amy's condition.

If, of course, Amy was in fact again in the family way. The
general had found time, on the dusty march from Centreville, to
consult his brigade surgeon. Not without profound embarrassment,
he had confided the date of his last day of leave and letting that
speak for itself, raised the question whether sufficient time had
passed for Amy to know for certain that she was with child.
Surgeon Boyd had assured him that, indeed, he had good grounds
for believing that she wasn't, since women often and for any
number of reasons suffered false symptoms.

> I am enclosing a small packet of pills obtained today from
> Surgeon Boyd, a most discreet and sympathetic gentleman,
> who informs me that if taken as directed the possibilities
> are considerable that your fears will prove unfounded. Nor,

I am assured, is there any risk attendant upon such a course.
I leave, of course, to your sound judgment and ever-present
sense of duty and propriety, not to mention your love of
God's Holy Word, the decision whether to follow Surgeon
Boyd's advice.

On this point, too, General Arnall—before throwing himself
into the business of placing his brigade properly in line—had had
ample time to consider the implications. He could see no incon-
sistency in his suggestions. If Amy were already *sure* she was
carrying his child, that would of course settle matters; but since
she was not sure, and in Surgeon Boyd's considered opinion couldn't
be, the recommended medicine could hardly be viewed as thwart-
ing God's will, since that will was as yet undetermined.

"Gin'al Arnall . . . sir?" A young lieutenant, one of Arnall's
staff, approached and saluted. The General looked up from his
letter. "Gin'al Hills sends you word, sir, the engagement up the
line, Gin'al Jackson attacked a Federal column on the Warrenton
Pike just before sunset. Taliaferro and Ewell engaged, sir. Gin'al
Hill says unlikely he'll be engaged on the left tonight but asks
you to keep pickets well advanced, sir."

"Thank you, Lieutenant. Have young Folsom there rustle you
up a bite of something."

Arnall listened carefully to the racket of battle as the lieutenant
strode away. Two divisions engaged, or parts of 'em. Odd to be
fighting on into the night. The whole business was odd. Jackson-
like. The line of the old railway had provided a nearly perfect
defensive position in which to wait for Longstreet, but Jackson's
attack surely had given it away.

He scribbled a few more paragraphs to Amy, telling her in a
general way—Arnall was careful to disclose nothing of military
value, since mail pouches could and sometimes did fall into enemy
hands—what the army had been doing and where they were:

There's just no way to figure out *what* this man might do
next. But I don't see how we can avoid a big engagement
now. I suppose he didn't want to.

He made no mention of his arrest. But as the cannonading and
musketry continued, Arnall grew uneasy at being left out of the
affair at the other end of the line. No matter how unjust against
him, no matter how trivial, and even with Hill's undoubted support, the arrest could prove a serious problem—particularly if,

after the campaign, it took time to straighten out and deprive him for awhile of his command. But in the meantime, if he could play an important part in actual combat—even a capricious and vindictive man like Ol Jack might be persuaded to forget so petty a matter as the missed order at Gainesville.

But this fight near the pike was a big one, to judge by the sounds and the report of two divisions engaged. And, of course, Jackson himself was there.

Arnall stirred uneasily in the firelight, the letter forgotten in his lap, Amy now far from his mind, the musketry continuous in the distance. He feared nothing so much as being in the wrong place at the wrong time—unless it was the wrath of God.

Private Josh Beasly, bivouacked in the woods nearby, was not even listening to the battle sounds. During the Richmond fighting he had learned that armies soon quit the field after nightfall. So he sat at ease with his back to a pine tree, cracking lice between his nails, occasionally nipping at his remaining bottle of brandy. Josh was in a black mood, made worse by the brandy and lighted by only one thing—the recollection that the bottle Ironass had kicked out of his hand that morning had been empty of all but one or two drops. That sonomabitch.

On either side of him lay Privates Bradshaw and Flournoy, Foxy turned to one side and surreptitiously jacking off, Lige on his back with his head cupped in his massive hands. Each had been tapping his own supply of brandy.

Private Beasly tucked his bottle inside the waistband of his butternut trousers. "Gone do it." His voice was a little thick. "Sure's shit."

"Dawg if you are." Lige opened one eye, squinting at him.

"Dawg if I aint. Sonomabitch is *spotted*."

Lige Flournoy sighed heavily. "Need'ny hep, Meat, ask any these sons." He gestured widely with his free arm at the men of Dixon's Rifles, dark shapes sitting or lying about in the woods. "Nare one got'ny use for at damn hangman."

"Don't need no hep." Josh cracked another grayback between his nails. "Sonomabitch bucked me the last time."

"Hey, Meat." Lige stretched a long leg past Josh and gave Foxy a light kick. "You gone pull at thing out by the roots?"

Foxy pretended ignorance and drew up one leg to conceal himself.

"Wha's . . . wha'd you say? I-uz sleepin."

Even Josh laughed, a rare thing, and took another shot of brandy.

"Go on'n play with it now, Meat. Might git shot off tomarr."

Foxy clutched his peter in agony. He knew Lige was ony funnin'im, but still . . . man mought's well be dead he lost his works. Foxy knew no pleasures other than those from the bottle and between the legs. He made up his mind to git shut of the army, first chancet come his way. And this time, he told himself, he really meant it.

"Orderly." General Arnall spoke quietly across the fire; he thought he could perceive a slackening in the sounds of battle. "Heat up some water there and try to make some decent coffee."

Larkin Folsom leaped to his feet, glad that he was rationed with real coffee from the Yank stores at Manassas. The General's body servant, who usually cooked for him, had been left far behind in the lightning march around Pope; Folsom's substitute services had not been much appreciated by Arnall.

Less than a year earlier, the orderly had been a dreamy student at Chapel Hill, reading books voraciously and writing verse in secret. After joining up, he'd disliked the rough-and-ready life of the ranks, the profanity and vulgarity. So he'd been happy when his mother, presuming on old acquaintance, persuaded General Arnall to make her son his orderly.

Now, as he worked, Folsom murmured a line of verse that had come to him that day while he and the steady old horse his mother had sent on from home in Chowan Country had swayed and dreamed along the pike from Centreville:

If all thy beauty were a summer's day . . .

"What? Speak up, Private."

"Oh . . . uh . . . nothin, sir."

Folsom liked the line. He was sure that he would find a second, and another, and more, until there would be one more completed verse to scribble on whatever paper he could find. But that was not a thing you could talk about to a general.

Then he remembered he had a new . . . he wondered if he could say "friend." The thought was upsetting; it opened certain strange avenues in his mind that Folsom did not wish to explore, since he was uncertain what he might find. But with a strange rush of excitement, he wondered if just maybe he *could* try out some of his lines on Corporal Gilmore, who had turned out to be strangely sympathetic.

• • •

Captain Thad Selby of Jackson's staff, meanwhile, after floundering through the woods, had located General Jubal A. Early of Ewell's Division, commanding his own and Farno's brigades, in reserve some distance behind the old railroad line. Early moved promptly, when Selby gave him Ol Jack's order to advance, but found the rail cut in his front so deep and entangled in underbrush that he could not cross his men through it.

Moving by his right flank through the thick woods in near-total darkness, Early groped along the edge of the railway cut. When its bottom had risen almost to grade level, Early took his brigades across it, into position to move up on Trimble's left, outflank the Federals, and roll up their line from one end to the other, as Jackson intended. But when Early moved forward, his skirmishers floundered into a slight bog unseasonally deepened by the summer's heavy rains. Swearing heatedly in the pitch blackness, Early needed fifteen minutes to get his brigades around the bog and ready to move in again.

In the meantime, Brigadier General John Gibbon, a mile away on the other side of the road, had come to believe that prudence was the better part of valor. In the fields across the road from his makeshift headquarters, his green troops and the Rebel veterans had fought it out for more than two hours, sighting each other's faces at deadly range whenever the smoke from their muskets permitted, with no shelter but a few stacks of hay, the old worm fence and the fringe of woods around Doubleday's men, who finally had come to help out in the center. Immovable as soldiers in a painting, both sides had stood in their lines, taken the other's heaviest onslaught, and returned it in full. Nothing further could be gained by anyone and the weight of numbers—Gibbon's staff believed that at least five Reb brigades were facing his four regiments and Doubleday's two—was soon bound to have effect.

So Gibbon sent his couriers flying to his regimental commanders with orders to fall back to the road and the woods south of it. Slowly, grudgingly, knowing they had nothing to be ashamed of, maintaining their lines and lighting up the night with the flashes of their muskets, Gibbon's and Doubleday's troops backed off the field. The Rebs made no effort to follow; they were fought out, too.

Hugh Williams carried his musket in one hand. With his other arm he supported Cappy Swartz, half of whose teeth and face had been blown away but whose farmer's legs were still steady. Reverdy Dowd rode off on Rosie, to whose tail Lieutenant Gregson clung as if to a lifeline. Burly Gregson, his once jaunty mustaches hanging limply about his slack mouth, could hold on to Rosie only with his left hand, since his right arm hung bloody and useless from a Minié ball between the elbow and the wrist.

Dowd halted Rosie frequently, to make sure that the men of the Sixth came off the field in good order, that in the darkness and chaos none except the dead and the most desperately wounded would be left to the Rebs. As the firing slackened enough so that more ordinary sounds could be heard, he frequently leaned from his saddle to speak to his retreating troops.

"Good boys," he would say. "Showed'em what you're made of. Know they been in a fight, don't they? Sixth showed'em something today, boys . . . I'm proud of every one of you . . ."

But as Private Fritz Schiml moved past Rosie, the major's calming voice reached him only as one more inexplicable sound. Through the long, hot hours after the raging Gregson had driven him back into the line of the Sixth Wisconsin, Private Schiml had worked his piece with the other men, moved when they did, followed orders. But since the flat of the sword had fallen on his back for the last time, as he had stumbled back into line, Fritz Schiml's eyes had been tightly closed.

He had loaded and fired, advanced and retreated, in darkness greater even than that imposed by night and smoke; and he was still walking along with his eyes squeezed shut, occasionally tripping and falling over litter, ditches, corpses, as the cannon muttered into silence and the popping of musketry gradually died away, like the last firecrackers of a village celebration. Fritz Schiml knew one thing clearly—that, having survived madness once, he was never going into battle again.

On the other side of the woods where Doubleday's men had fought, on the field where the fight had begun, Phil Keefe felt real fear when he realized he was about to be left behind. God Amighty, he thought, the Rebs'll get me now. Keefe had been told the Rebs usually rolled the dead and wounded alike into one ditch and covered them over.

"Hey!" he called desperately after the retreating line of the Second. "Hey . . . somebody lend a hand!"

Keefe had gone down sometime after dark with a ball through

his right leg below the knee. After the first terrible pain, he had lain on his back in the dark, on the warm ground, as the battle screamed and crackled over him. The pain was bad, wracking, but at least he was down under the musket fire and after a while a calm had descended on him, as if his mother's hand had touched his brow. If some officer's horse don't step on me, he reasoned, I'll be all right. Just wait it out right here.

Finally, though, he realized they were leaving him. He began to shout but no one came back. He did not know that the Rebs would make no effort to pursue, that both sides were exhausted. He thought of being rolled into a hole with dead men, and covered over. Fear shrieked in him as sharply as the awful pain in his leg.

God Amighty, I aint gonna be buried alive. Not Phil Keefe. Not by a dang sight, I aint.

He sat up, screaming only once at the pain of movement. He thought then of Jamie Hatton, prayed devoutly that at least some of his own leg remained, and slumped above his good left thigh, catching himself with both hands on the ground. Slowly, with infinite care, perspiration suddenly pouring from his violated body, he rolled over on the good leg, the wounded one dragging uselessly behind. Up on the knee of his good left leg, braced on his long arms against his plowman's shoulders, Keefe found that he could bite back his screams of pain and make slow but certain progress down the slope toward the woods across the road.

He could pull the good knee up under him, push forward on it and thrust his braced arms a foot or so ahead, then repeat the process; after awhile, he could even bear the pain. What bothered him more was the sense that, somehow, the shattered leg and the foot at the end of it were dangling too loosely, as if something vital to its function as a leg had been snapped off like a sweet-gum twig.

After the last musket shots had popped irritably, the blackness and the silence of the grave fell on the long slope below Brawner's house, over the gullies and reaches of what had been his pastures. But presently, in the hot and moonless night, a new, more terrible sound began to tremble above the blood-soaked earth—the ghostly susurration of the wounded, weeping and moaning and calling out for water, for help, opium, mother, sometimes for death and eternal relief. A vast groan of pain, it rose softly at first, wavering, broken here and there by shouts and screams, hovering as tangibly in the night as the miasmic exhalations of a deathly swamp.

Across the hillside, before long, the pinpoint lights of candles and lanterns began to flicker as men came to help the wounded and search for the missing. Among these helpers were Fargo Hart and Andrew Peterson, who walked among the fallen men to give them water and whatever relief they could.

In the darkness, fingers clutched at their ankles. Urgent whispers came up from the ground, from unseen sufferers. Messages of reassurance or anguish were mumbled through pain-clenched or bullet-smashed jaws, though Hart and Peterson knew they could not deliver them to the wives and mothers they were intended for. Some men begged for a bullet between the eyes. Some butternuts, with soldiers' resilience, promised to be up and fighting as soon as Ol Jack needed them. A soldier with a shattered knee cursed in a low, relentless monotone. One boy, trying to say his own name, gagged and gasped out his life in Peterson's arms. Around them, the never-ending groans of the wounded, Reb and Yank alike, rose and fell in a night so dark, so forsaken by the stars, that it was impossible to tell one from the other.

In the dim light of Hart's candle, he could sometimes discern in the naked eyes gazing up at him—eyes like those of rabbits caught in his boyhood traps—fright and shock that all but eclipsed pain. Even in a war, he realized, even with death all around and his own musket hot in his hands, a man never really expected it would happen to *him*—the chance missile finding *his* space, the alien iron tearing *his* flesh, the familiar universe indifferent to *his* fate. No one could ever be less than shocked to learn that the world in which he had lived harmoniously could in a careless instant strike him down and move on.

"God have mercy." Peterson seemed to be speaking to himself as he held his canteen for the sucking lips of another mangled boy.

"Mercy?" Hart rose from his knees, still sheltering the candle. "What's war got to do with mercy?"

Beyond Peterson, in the muttering darkness, he could barely make out someone else stooping to a crumpled body. A man screamed nearby, and fell silent.

"Wad-derrr," someone croaked.

"I'll find some."

Hart, scarcely believing, thought he had heard a female voice. The stooping figure arose—shadowy, indistinct—and came toward them. Then the voice again, unmistakably a girl's:

"Gotta canteen, sir?"

Hart raised the candle, and saw in its flicker a thin face, a long black pigtail, alert eyes, a head cocked like a bird ready to fly at a sound or a movement.

"The buttermilk girl." He was too stunned to take his canteen from around his neck.

The alert head moved impatiently. "Man over ther needs *water*."

Peterson stood up beside him. "They all need water. What'n the world *you* doin here, child?"

"Heppin'um best I can."

Peterson handed her his canteen. "But how'd you get here?"

"Crost the pike."

Hart saw the candlelight reflected like defiance in her eyes. "She lives down the road aways. Give us some ham'n buttermilk this mornin."

The girl turned and bent over a dark blob on the ground. The men moved after her and Hart saw that her long skirt was torn in several jagged strips.

"So war does have something to do with mercy," Peterson said. "Imagine an angel on a battlefield."

"Not a fit place even for an angel. Much less a child."

"I'm near seventeen." The girl stood up and thrust the canteen at Peterson. "Aint I heppin'um, Mistuh? Wha's wrong with at?" Sullenness hoarsened her thin voice.

"I'll let you answer, Cap'n." Peterson moved beyond the girl, stepping over the man she had given water, and disappeared in the darkness.

"Been tearin your dress. For bandages?"

"Ol piece of a skirt." Contempt for the despised garment rang in her voice.

"I'll take you home, now."

"Plen'y more needin hep."

Through the acrid gunsmoke air, he caught the gamy scent of her as she brushed past him. And as she knelt by another fallen man, anger—not at her—goaded the stubbornness in him. He had tasted that anger like rising, bitter bile since he had poured water into the parched mouth of the first wounded man he had come across in Brawner's field. Amid the human wreckage of battle, anger had swelled in him, unbidden but fierce, until he sensed himself nearly out of control, maddened by the wrath of the inexplicable: for how could reason account for carnage and death, strewn wholesale?

But carnage and death *were* the rationalities, even the commonplaces, of Ol Jack's world, in which therefore the only sanity was madness. In such a world, must not madness inevitably make him its instrument, too, Ol Jack's creature? *No,* he thought in a last desperate clutch at resistance. *Never.*

He turned away, blowing out his candle, and strode through the uplifted, reaching arms of the human litter in the broomsedge. Mercury stood quietly nearby, as he had learned to do on other fields. Hart swung into the saddle, touched the reins.

"Hummup, Merc."

The horse picked his way across the field to where the girl knelt by still another victim calling for water.

"Here . . . here's water."

She stood up and took Hart's canteen, knelt again. Then she rose, looking up at him, her white face barely visible in the darkness.

"They *need* hep . . . all of 'em."

For an instant, the anger all but crazed Fargo Hart. It was obscene that this child, even if an angel, should be witness to war's grotesque inverse sanity. Should there be no limit to Ol Jack's reach?

He leaned from his saddle and swept her up as if she had been a rag doll.

"Takin you out of here."

This time she made no protest, not even an answer, as Mercury took them across the field, picking his way in the haunted night as fastidiously as a dancing master among the flung bodies and other debris in the trampled broomsedge, the broken goldenrod.

After a while, Andrew Peterson found his horse and went wearily up the hill in search of a camp fire and coffee. He would have to get on soon to where Joe Nathan had parked the Whatsit Wagon on the ridge behind the old railway line. Joe Nathan would have him up before dawn; Joe Nathan knew he liked to be ready at first light, when his work could begin.

Peterson was tired more in spirit than in body. As he paused to light one of his long cigars, he thought briefly of riding on, moving west toward the mountains, through Aldie Gap or Thoroughfare, on to the Valley and beyond. Joe Nathan could follow with the equipment. There would be business all along the way, people wanting likenesses. But he could keep going a long time and be no farther than he was now from the ghastly harvest in Brawner's field.

A horse came snuffling up beside him. In the glow of his match Peterson saw the Englishman Redmund's scowling face against the flowing havelock he apparently wore night and day. Redmund did not bother with pleasantries or greetings.

"For what?" He had a voice, Peterson thought, like the irritable bark of an unfriendly dog. "Would you mind telling me thatsir?"

Peterson doubted that the Britisher had much concern for the death and agony of men. Damned redcoat would look at war like some kind of game. Knights and bishops and gambits. Gesturing with his cigar toward the field behind them, Peterson deliberately answered a question he knew Redmund had not asked.

"They don't even think what for. They just do what Ol Jack tells'em."

"An ass, sir! An ignorant bloody ass!"

"Maybe." Peterson drew on his cigar. "But they'll do it for'im again. Anytime. Tomorrow."

Redmund barked contemptuous British laughter into the turgid night.

"They'll have to, sir!"

He flung his head back as if looking to heaven for consolation against the unceasing mutters of pain that filled the air. But then, with angry satisfaction, he jerked his chin down and barked again:

"Because now Pope knows where to find the bloody ignorant ass! And he'll comesir! Mark my wordsir . . . Pope'll come tomorrow!"

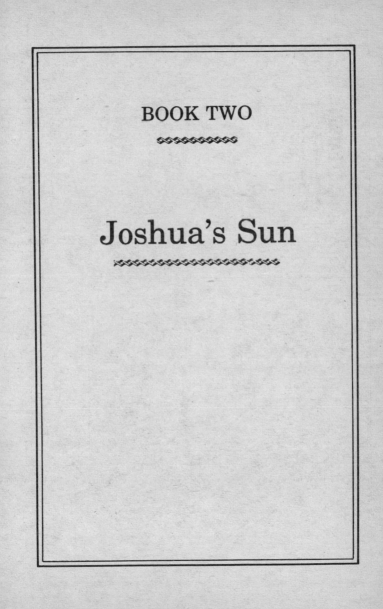

BOOK TWO

Joshua's Sun

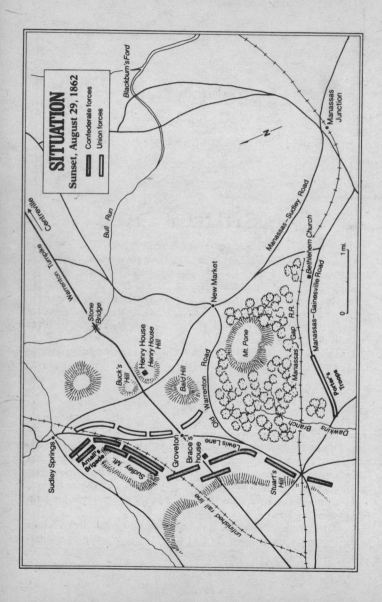

SITUATION

Sunset, August 29, 1862

Confederate forces
Union forces

Centreville

Warrenton Turnpike

Bull Run

Blackburn's Ford

Manassas Junction

N

Stone Bridge

Buck's Hill

Henry House
Henry House Hill

Bald Hill

New Market

Old Warrenton Road

Mt. Pone

Manassas–Sudley Road

Bethlehem Church

Manassas Gap R.R.

Manassas–Gainesville Road

1 mi.

0

Porter's Troops

Dawkins Branch

Sudley Springs

Arnall's Brigade

Sudley Mt.

Groveton

Brace's house

Lewis Lane

Stuart's Hill

unfinished rail line

Chapter Six

August 29—
Midnight to Dawn

NIGHT HAD BROUGHT no relief from the heat; in Washington in August, it seldom did. Even the five broad windows that looked out over Pennsylvania Avenue from the War Department Telegraph Office could catch no hint of a breeze. Insects, drawn by the yellow glow within, fluttered and whirred around the lamps. Cipher Operator James F. Grady, sweating at his desk, wished devoutly to take off his coat and roll up his sleeves, as he often could do on night duty.

He stole a quick look over his shoulder at the gaunt, quiet man who sat with his feet on a desk by the middle window, a long black coat drawn about his lank frame as if it were already fall, rather than the shank of a fetid Washington summer. If he'd only take off that coat, Grady thought, the Telegraph Office clerks could get comfortable, too. But that wasn't likely to happen—not in the brooding mood he appeared to be in.

Grady had seldom seen him sit so quietly; usually he was restless, crossing one leg over the other, or sprawling a leg over the arm of his chair, then maybe getting up, sitting down again and turning sideways to put both legs over the chair arm. Or he'd pace the office, arms behind his back, looking down at his large feet moving solidly over the floor.

But that night, since he'd put his feet up on the desk an hour earlier and settled down to read over the day's file of military telegrams, he'd scarcely moved and had said nothing at all. Of course there'd been plenty to brood about in the file—particularly the midafternoon telegram from Colonel Haupt in Alexandria. An escaped prisoner gave eyewitness testimony that Rebs had fired and destroyed the rail bridge over Bull Run, Haupt reported.

It is clear, therefore, that the Army of Virginia can receive no more supplies by rail at present, and must flank the enemy by a movement to the east, cut its way through, or be lost.

The only fresh news anybody in Washington had of Pope's Army of Virginia was coming in such telegrams from Haupt; some other messages were being relayed a day or more late via the roundabout route through General Burnside's headquarters far to the south at Falmouth.

Just an hour earlier, a message from Burnside had come through for Generals Halleck and McClellan; this one passed on the word-of-mouth information of a courier dispatched to Falmouth from Bristoe Station by General Fitz-John Porter. The news was twenty-four hours old and no doubt superceded by events, but nevertheless seemed important to Grady. Burnside quoted the courier from Bristoe:

An engagement took place near there yesterday between Hooker and a portion of Jackson's force, which resulted in the withdrawal of the enemy, leaving their killed and wounded on the field. Our loss reported from 300 to 500; enemy's about the same. Warrenton Junction and Bealeton were being evacuated by our troops, who are moving toward Gainesville and Manassas Junction.

Of course, Falmouth was as far from the action as the President or Halleck in Washington were, so Burnside had cautiously declined to vouch for this information.

Neither he nor Haupt had been able to furnish much solid information about Pope's situation—even his whereabouts. Since early on the evening of the 26th, when the Rebs had cut the wires and the railroad at Bristoe and Manassas, there had been no word directly from Pope himself. It was almost as if more than 50,000 men, with their horses and equipment, had disappeared.

But out there in the darkness beyond the Potomac, not more than maybe a day's hard march from the Long Bridge, Grady knew that armies were moving again on the blood-soaked plains of Manassas, men were dying, history was being shaped. (Grady was a romantic who cherished his own small part in the shaping.)

Yet silence hung as ominously as a thundercloud over the vast scene (clearly imagined by Grady in the manner of the battle lithographs in *Harper's Weekly*). He thought that silence must be maddening to the brooding man in the black coat, for no one ever was hungrier than he for news—even bad news.

Shortly past noon—Grady had noted in the file of carbon copies—Haupt had sent word that the Rebel forces suddenly operating around Manassas "were large and several of their best generals were in command." Scarcely had that message been deciphered than another had gone back headed "War Department, August 28, 1862, 2:40 p.m." on the standard yellow tissue paper, in the neat, tight handwriting with which all the operators had become familiar:

Colonel Haupt:

Yours received. How do you learn that the rebel forces at Manassas are large, and commanded by several of their best generals?

A. Lincoln

Right to the point. No fuss and no pretense, like the man himself. And typical of his gluttonous appetite for fact and detail. Grady was an unreserved admirer; even now, sweating like a mule as he labored over the difficult "Blonde" cipher, meticulously breaking out the gibberish of Haupt's latest telegram into eleven lines and seven columns that would enable the message to be read, he did not resent the deference that caused him in the sweltering night to keep on his heavy coat as long as the President remained wrapped in his.

Grady was used to this imposing presence at Superintendent Eckert's desk, or wandering around the office. Frequently that summer, Mr. Lincoln had worked for hours on the papers Eckert would later lock up for him in a drawer of the desk; and always when the keys were clicking and message traffic was flowing rapidly into and out of the big room overlooking Pennsylvania Avenue, he'd be up and about, reading the telegrams, chatting with the operators, his height and his reedy, ready laugh dominating the scene.

Grady had heard him say that the Telegraph Office was as much a refuge for him as a source of information. He could get a little peace and quiet there, even when it was jumping like a hen on a hot stove; but in his office a constant stream of visitors would be sending in their cards to distract him. In the Telegraph Office, with the latest news at hand, Secretary of War Stanton right next door, his own secretaries only minutes away, he could be in charge of things and yet not be swamped by the lesser duties of his office.

That summer, as the war had grown into a consuming monster, Superintendent Eckert had practically given up his desk to him, and Grady had become curious about the documents on which the President had lavished so much effort and thought. It was in the drawer now, just under the crossed ankles and the big feet in their heavy boots; and Grady wished he had the nerve to ask straight out what it was that Mr. Lincoln had worked on so long and so hard.

But he didn't, although not because he feared rebuff. As far as Grady could see, very little ruffled the President's temper or disturbed his self-possession. Most of the time, he was downright genial, even garrulous. But other times—like now, as he waited for news—he would withdraw deep within his own concerns, of such gravity as Grady could hardly imagine. At such moments, Grady would not have dreamed of intruding mere curiosity on the brooding presence that permeated the Telegraph Office like the heat of the night.

Grady only wished he could decipher more positive news. He actually resented the silence from Virginia, regarding it as a sort of insult not just to the man waiting by the window but to the clattering instruments and the wires strung like nerves across the countryside. The telegraph seemed to Grady so marvelous, so precisely suited to the needs of the war, that he took Pope's silence as a kind of rejection, a rebuff to beneficial science (although he knew well enough that, in fact, the Rebs had cut the wires beyond Bull Run).

Haupt's latest message, as Grady continued to decipher it, was more of the same conjecture and fragments he had been sending, valuable but not *solid*. Except that he could definitely confirm, from the observations of one of his own men, the destruction of the bridge over Bull Run. And a wounded soldier reported Hooker and Sigel in occupation of Manassas and the Rebs gone from that place.

Grady finished breaking the cipher into the required lines and columns. In "Blonde," the first word of the actual message was on the bottom line of column six; then the message moved up that column one word to a line, then down column three, up column five and so on. At the end of each column he had to throw out a "blind" word that had no purpose but to confuse an interceptor.

The completed message contained a startling report from a captured Reb chaplain:

> He saw General Lee today at Fairfax about 11 o'clock, who took the road toward Vienna with a large force, accompanied by artillery.

In more than a year of immersion in military telegrams, Grady had learned that information from the front—any front, any information—varied from the impressive (rare) to the misleading (commonplace) and not infrequently to the downright false. He took the report about General Lee being that close to Washington with a large grain of salt, as it seemed to him the cautious Haupt probably intended. The colonel's closing lines even raised doubts about the reported reoccupation:

> If our forces occupy Manassas, I will endeavor to pour in supplies without delay, and reconstruct Bull Run Bridge in the shortest time possible.
>
> H. Haupt

Grady made a straight copy and the required carbons in his angular, practiced hand, and took the message across the room. The other two clerks, Tinker and Bates, worked quietly at their desks. There was no sound but the whir of insects and the big clock ticking on the wall with a regularity that mocked the fallibility of men (although the cipher operator was too young and too optimistic to realize that).

Mr. Lincoln took his feet from the desk as Grady approached. His long legs swung awkwardly to the floor, rather like those of the wooden dolls Grady had seen in puppet shows. The black coat fell open and he sat up straight, his deep-set, dark gray eyes blinking in his long, thin face. His head was large, with a forehead so broad that Grady was certain the intellect it sheltered was of remarkable power. Under coarse dark hair, rather carelessly combed back, the President's other features were almost as prominent, particularly the heavy nose and full lips, the furrowed cheeks, and the wide mouth that could easily break into a smile.

Clearly, he had been napping; that surprised Grady, who had supposed that profound contemplation of great events occupied the still figure at Eckert's desk.

"From Colonel Haupt, Mister President."

He held out the telegram. Mr. Lincoln sighed and took it in his thick-fingered hand. He looked more tired than usual, Grady thought, and a bit disconsolate.

"Thank you, Mister Grady." The President put the telegram on the desk and leaned on one arm, reading it.

Over his bent shoulder, beyond the dark expanse of lawn in front of the War Department, Grady saw through the window a group of men on horseback trooping along Pennsylvania Avenue. They were only indistinct shapes under a dim street lamp, but the clink of metal, a barked military command, gave the moving forms identity. No doubt a military police unit or stray cavalry from the Washington defense forces. Grady had suddenly a sense of the sleeping city, unaware of its danger; he was only twenty-three years old, so it was perhaps understandable that he felt himself informed, an insider, and gloried in the feel of it.

A tiny breeze fluttered at the window and brought in a dank sniff of the sewage canal that oozed foul and viscous between the White House and the Potomac. He went back to his own desk. His post did give him unusual opportunities to know what was going on. So he was in no doubt that the present hour was desperate—even if that hadn't been signaled by the President's midnight vigil in the Telegraph Office. Whenever he stayed so late, something was bound to be up somewhere.

Barely two months before, Mr. Lincoln had been all but constantly on hand as a steady flow of news came in from General McClellan on the Peninsula. Coming each day across the wooded lawn from the White House next door, his tall hat adding almost comical height to his six feet four inches, he would stay for hours, sometimes all night, reading the dispatches as they were deciphered, sending back his persistent inquiries, chatting with the clerks and the operators and Eckert as if they might have been Cabinet members, telling his bantering stories, sometimes rapt in his deep silences.

Sometimes, usually in good humor, he would chide the press, whose reports all too often bordered on fantasy, and which Mr. Stanton clearly considered a nest of traitors. Grady was inclined to agree. By the time the papers got through exaggerating some minor skirmish, he had heard the President complain to Eckert, "Revolvers have grown into horse pistols."

Back then, there had been reason enough for good humor. McClellan had been kicking at the doors of Richmond, and it was possible to hope that the war might soon be over, the Rebs gutted and crushed (as, in Grady's opinion, they deserved to be), the old Union restored to its former might.

But Grady could hardly believe all that had gone wrong in so short a time. In his youth and inexperience, he had not yet admitted to himself the truth implicit in the reams of misinformation he had deciphered in the past year. He still thought Presidents and generals made decisions and carried them out as they might order breakfast from the extensive menu at Willard's, and that the results ought to arrive as surely as the morning coffee.

But the hard facts could not be blinked—McClellan's great Peninsula offensive shattered, his army in dribs and drabs from Alexandria to Aquia to Falmouth—disjointed, disheartened, lacking even a leader, with McClellan himself secluded on his steamer in a "fit of the sulks" (so Grady had heard the general's mood irately described by Secretary Stanton).

And over there somewhere in the menacing silence of northern Virginia, almost within spitting distance of the Capitol dome, Stonewall Jackson was on the loose, with Lee's whole army somewhere behind him. Before the June battles that had halted the Peninsula offensive, Grady had never heard of Lee, who in a summer's brief passing had assumed near-heroic stature. As for Jackson, everybody had known his nickname since the first battle at Bull Run; and since the Valley fighting in the spring he had seemed to be a shadow moving swiftly to cast unexpected, deadly shades.

Now the elusive Stonewall had emerged from the darkness to strike again; and nothing stood between Washington and the Rebel captain but the unknown westerner, John Pope, and his makeshift Army of Virginia—some troops whipped once by Jackson in the Valley, plus McDowell's largely untested corps, together with such units of McClellan's beaten army as might have moved out to Pope's support. Telegraph lines down, bridges burned, the railroad lifeline broken at Bull Run, supplies bound to be short, Washington at risk—Grady was too young and too optimistic and too ignorant of war to feel himself personally in danger; but he was glad he didn't have to carry the burdens of the man in the long black coat.

A hand touched his shoulder. Grady looked up, saw the dark, shadowed eyes peering down, and started to rise to his feet. But a big hand gently pressed him back into his chair. The President put a yellow sheet in front of the cipher clerk, gave his shoulder what Grady was sure was a commendatory squeeze, and turned away. In his long, deliberate stride, the long coat flapping like the rags of a scarecrow, he went back across the office to Eckert's desk, folded himself into the superintendent's squeaking swivel chair, and put his legs up again.

Turning to his work, young James Grady was as conscious of that powerful presence behind him as of his own sweating body. He ran his eye over the closely written script and saw that it did not need encipherment. From the steadily ticking clock, he noted that the time was just past midnight. He dated the telegram with the hour and the new day—August 29, 1862—and reached for his key.

Colonel Haupt:

   What news from direction of Manassas Junction? What news generally?

A. Lincoln

Colonel Haupt had no more news—none, at least, that he valued enough to send to the President. Herman Haupt was a man of facts who knew another one when he met him; and he had quickly learned that Mr. Lincoln was of the same breed, voracious for detail and suspicious of claims and generalities.

Haupt was wrestling with just such unsubstantiated generalities—the various reports and conjectures, from every source he could find, as to the strength of the force with which Stonewall Jackson had descended upon Manassas and the O & A. Most of the estimates varied from 25,000 to 60,000 men—not much help.

Weighing the Confederates' problems of supply in burned-over country behind Federal lines, Haupt doubted the Rebs numbered more than 20,000, if that many. He lingered with particular contempt over a copy of a dispatch from General McClellan to Halleck:

   Enemy, with 120,000 men, intend advancing on the forts near Arlington and Chain Bridge, with a view to attacking Washington and Baltimore.

Typical of the "Young Napoleon"—as Haupt hoped Halleck understood, too. McClellan never failed to overestimate the forces of the enemy, hence to call for reinforcements, as he did in the message to Halleck. But even assuming the Rebs *could* put 120,000 men into northern Virginia, an assumption no rational judgment of their strength could support, Haupt could have told McClellan that there was no possibility that such a host could be supplied and sustained for the kind of mad venture the general apparently believed impended. It had been hard enough, even with all the Federal advantages in resources, to maintain Pope, with no more than half that many troops, along interior lines—the O & A and the rutted wagon roads out past Fairfax and Centreville and Warrenton to the Rappahannock.

Besides, if George McClellan knew all that much about what was happening beyond Bull Run, it certainly was from no particular effort by him to get his own troops into the battle, or even to use them to find out what was happening around Manassas. Every hour that had passed since Jackson's fast-moving column had sprung out of the night to cut the O & A and Pope's supply jugular had confirmed Herman Haupt's disgusted suspicion that McClellan and his flashy entourage—like General Sturgis—did not care a pinch of owl dung for helping John Pope.

Just the day before, when it was still not certain that the Bull Run bridge had been destroyed, Haupt—willing as usual to put his neck on the line to get action—had proposed to Halleck that he load a train with subsistence for Pope's army, put 1,500 to 2,000 infantry on top of the cars, precede the train with a battery of guns on flat cars, and push as far to the front as possible. Halleck had ordered him to consult McClellan, if Haupt could reach him; "If not, go ahead as you propose."

Haupt knew only that the general was aboard his headquarters steamer somewhere on the Potomac. But Herman Haupt never needed to know much more than that. He went promptly to the wharf, commandeered a rowboat, and rowed himself downstream, searching for McClellan's steamer among the flotilla that had brought most of the general's army back from the Peninsula to the camps near Alexandria.

Some way downriver, Haupt had located McClellan and shown him the telegrams exchanged with Halleck; then he rowed the general upstream to Alexandria and took him to the offices of the O & A. With maps and the telegram file ready at hand, he had fully informed McClellan of what he knew about the situation at and beyond Bull Run.

Then Haupt explained his plan to run forward a well-armed subsistence train. McClellan listened attentively, his sharp eyes following Haupt's finger on the map. The general, like many men of short statue, held himself rigidly, as if trying to appear taller; the effect, in Haupt's small office, was that of a man sitting at attention.

"I can't approve that."

McClellan shook his head gravely, as if he might have been vetoing a proposal for an advance on Richmond. As he spoke, his naturally lowering eyebrows drew farther down, making his usual frowning demeanor even more forbidding.

"I'm afraid I don't see why not, General."

"It would be attended with risk."

Haupt was dumbfounded. "Military operations usually are," he said, feeling no need for deference; he believed without self-importance that the army needed him more than he needed it.

And no wonder Lincoln had felt it necessary to write McClellan, this frowning little man with his carefully parted hair and imposing mustache: *You must act*. The military appearance and the pouter-pigeon chest made up a facade masking—at the least—irresolution. But was that all? The proposed subsistence train offered little risk and was not even McClellan's idea.

"In this case, General, desperate as it is, surely the risk's not excessive. Train can run out nearly to Bull Run with no problems at all. Then we can dismount skirmishers to advance along the track in front. If they run into a force too strong to handle, the train can take everybody out. If not, we might get supplies within reach of Pope."

But no amount of argument could elicit McClellan's approval for the supply train, or orders for the men and battery to accompany it. Haupt had to go again to Hancock, a mere brigadier. Hancock, as cheerfully and as promptly as before, provided the necessary troops.

The armed train had not been able to supply Pope, since the bridge over Bull Run was by then destroyed. It had nevertheless brought off the last of the bridge's defenders, carried back numbers of wounded from Fairfax, restored the small bridge at Pohick, and gleaned additional intelligence—including the dubious sighting of General Lee at Fairfax.

J. J. Moore, Haupt's most reliable construction-crew chief, also had brought back valuable, if not encouraging, information about the Bull Run bridge. It was burned to its stone abutments, Moore said, and would have to be totally reconstructed.

"Not a usable timber left, Colonel."

Haupt shook his head in exasperation. "I *told* that General

Taylor. All he had to do was guard the bridge, Moore. But no—
he had to go looking for glory. So now he's dead and the bridge
is gone, eh?"

"We can build a new one. I'll have trains moving over Bull
Run in less'n a week."

"Not in time to help Pope."

But Haupt appreciated Moore's eager confidence anyway. If
McClellan only had a little of it! Men like J. J. Moore would win
this war yet—practical men, hard workers, who could invent a
short cut if they had to or build on a new idea. Men not afraid to
take a chance.

"All right, Moore. Get the crew you want together and be ready
to start in the morning. I'll authorize whatever you need and find
some troops to stand guard for you."

At least that was getting something done. Not like McClellan.
All *he* seemed to do was send telegrams—including one to Haupt,
amazingly enough, thanking him for having sent out the "recon-
naisance." Little enough *he'd* done to help when it was needed!
And it was that reluctance, not McClellan's effusive telegram,
that impressed Herman Haupt, a man wholly dedicated to the
Union cause. He was even working without pay, having refused
to accept a real commission (his colonel's rank was thus unofficial)
because of the submission to military authority that inevitably
would go with it and—in Haupt's view—just as inevitably destroy
the independence he needed to keep the tracks open and the trains
running.

Out there in Virginia, Pope's army was fighting for its life,
perhaps for the safety of Washington. And Haupt knew that just
as Lee had moved from Richmond into northern Virginia, the
Confederate Generals Braxton Bragg and Kirby Smith had lunged
north from Tennessee, threatening Louisville and Cincinnati and
possibly the separation of Kentucky, one of the border states that
had been held back, so far, from secession.

Haupt was aware, too, that in grim acknowledgment of stalemate on the Peninsula, the President had called for 300,000 volunteers—and got so little response that he had had to order state
quotas filled by a draft. Haupt read that as a warning that the
country had but a limited willingness to support a war whose costs
in blood and wealth were rising as swiftly as the prospect of victory
seemed to be receding. And in November, Congressional elections
would provide the voters opportunity to pronounce judgment on
the conduct of the war, and the man responsible.

Clearly, the President needed, above all, a victory on the bat-

tlefield to appease his critics and hold for him the political support
he needed to save the Union. But the portents from Virginia suggested that a new defeat impended, not victory; and here was the
Young Napoleon himself, hailed less than a year before as the
savior of the country, now too fretful to provide an armed guard
for a resupply train to Pope.

"Attended with risk" indeed! In disgust, Haupt thumbed through
his telegram file for the day to another of McClellan's dispatches
to Halleck:

> Neither Franklin nor Sumner's corps is now in condition to
> fight a battle. It would be a sacrifice to send them out now.

A sacrifice! What did McClellan think war was, if not a sacrifice? What kind of a general could take so narrow a view of his
country's desperation? Haupt was not politically minded, but he
thought he knew the answer: a general who was going to be a
presidential candidate.

Angrily, the colonel—who had scarcely slept since Jackson's
descent on Manassas—strode out of his office, down to the yards,
eager for something useful, something tangible to do—a *sacrifice*,
he told himself.

The night was so dark that Reverdy Dowd, though leading Rosie
by the bridle, could scarcely make out the mare's head beside his
shoulder. Even so, the darkness on the narrow road was less
impenetrable than that of the woods through which the Sixth Wisconsin had stumbled to reach it.

The woods had been Dowd's idea of what hell would be like:
a dark inferno filled with the moans and screams of suffering men.
There the wounded who could walk or crawl off the hillside and
across the Warrenton Pike had somehow collected, as if to share
their misery. They had been impossible to see in the Stygian
blackness, but they had seemed to litter the ground like stones;
and as the Sixth floundered through the woods at Dowd's angry
and puzzled direction, the troops stumbled as often over the bodies
of dead and wounded men as over fallen limbs or underbrush.

Once Dowd himself had stepped on a man's leg, setting off a
scream that startled even placid Rosie and echoed still in the
major's soul. Several times, moving through that hellish place,
trying to shut his ears and mind to its horrors, his nose to the
stench of blood and corruption, Dowd tripped and would have

gone sprawling down among the corpses, the broken bodies, the bits and pieces of men, had he not been holding fast to Rosie's bridle. He became convinced that if he did go down, he would never rise again, and the littered flesh beneath his feet would claim its kin. He clung to Rosie as if to life itself, even though the mare, too, was stumbling in the darkness and the cluttered woods.

It was better on the road, though still a nightmare. He could let Rosie pick her way along the dirt track, and the only problem was that they could not stop. If they did, the troops behind would march right into them in the darkness; most were stumbling along half-asleep, too tired to be alert even if they could have seen anything in the darkness.

Dowd half-turned and felt with his hand to make sure Lieutenant Gregson with his shattered arm was still in the saddle. He found Gregson's good hand clenched on the saddle horn. Vaguely, he perceived the shape of another man staggering along, supporting himself by a stirrup strap. Someone else, he knew, was hanging on to the old mare's tail.

"All right, boys," Dowd said to no one in particular, in not much more than a whisper. "We're getting there."

Earlier in the day, before the unexplained change of direction— away from Manassas and back on the pike toward Centreville— had been ordered, Dowd had calculated that Manassas Junction was seven miles by road southeast of Gainesville. It could not be much less than that by the route they now had taken, he figured, since they had come out of the woods onto what had to be the same narrowly winding road, at a point not more than a mile or two from Gainesville. It would be dawn before they made it.

Dowd tried to spit in disgust, but his mouth was too dry. His canteen had long been empty, its last drops poured on the parched lips of the wounded. So he swore instead. Dowd had never been in a retreat before and he did not like the feeling. Not as if the goddam Rebs had whipped them—not the Sixth Wisconsin, by God!

The boys had fought like wildcats. In the darkness he could not get any kind of decent count but the Sixth had re-formed in good order and Dowd guessed he'd lost not above fifty men. No way to tell how many dead, how many wounded. But he'd be willing to bet they'd left more Rebs on the ground than that.

Dowd wondered momentarily what had happened to Colonel Bob. Of course, Bob would know how to look after himself. Or Duke would.

The major did not concede to himself that he had made no real effort to find out where his colonel might be. In the confused aftermath of his first battle, his thoughts were jumping about like a june bug on a string. Those stirring minutes out there when he, Reverdy Dowd, had taken charge, when the men followed his lead, when he felt the Sixth in his hands like a great supple cord that he could turn and shape and knot to his desire—in those minutes, Dowd believed, *he* had become its leader. He sensed without defining the feeling that Colonel Bob had become part of the Sixth's past and of his, part of another life to which the men and Reverdy Dowd would never return, and seldom even look back.

But damn! The way the boys had fought, why the devil were they retreating to Manassas? When the order had come down from Gibbon to pull out, Dowd had been thunderstruck. Manassas! That was the other way from the Rebs, hardly the way for fighting men—veterans now—to point themselves. They knew where the Rebs were. Why not go back and whip the bastards, soon as it was light enough to sight a musket?

For the life of him Dowd could not understand Gibbon's order, although he was too good a soldier to do anything but follow it. They'd had King's whole damn division strung out along the Warrenton road, hadn't they? Had to be other divisions up ahead, too. There was no reason he could see not to hold their ground and go at it again in the morning. No doubt about it, they'd shown they could take anything the Rebs could hand out and throw it right back at them.

"Damn fool generals," Dowd muttered, and Rosie bobbed her head as if in agreement.

If there was one thing Dowd had learned in his brief military career, it was that in the army practically nobody knew what he was doing. Oh, maybe up at the top; maybe old Halleck or somebody knew. Dowd sometimes doubted even that; and the farther down the line you were, the less you could hope to know, let alone understand. By the time you got down to majors, you could put what you knew in a bird's craw with room left over for a couple of hedgeberries.

Take today. Dowd had no real idea why King's Division had set out on the road from Gainesville to Manassas—why they had been marching eastward at all, in the general direction of Washington. Save for Jackson's raid, the war had seemed to be the other way; surely by the time they could reach Manassas, Jackson would be long gone. Nor did Dowd have any notion why they had been turned back to Gainesville in midafternoon, then pointed along the pike toward Centreville. Worse, after they'd flushed Rebs and stood up to them — with a little help, Dowd thought bitterly, they'd have made'em tuck tail and run—here they were, fewer and tireder, back on the same road to Manassas they'd been pulled from in the afternoon. And no more reason given.

"*Damn* fool generals!" Dowd spoke louder this time.

Two feet to Dowd's left but invisible in the darkness, Phil Keefe heard the disembodied imprecation on generals without comprehending that he was hearing a voice, words, someone's sentiment. He was not sure that the sound was not some manifestation of his own numbed brain suddenly coming to life; or perhaps a memory out of a past he could no longer recognize. He had no realization of a living presence speaking words; he just vaguely sensed that troops were passing or had passed or might have.

Keefe was only aware of the road and the pain, and occasionally of the tepid water in the canteen that was miraculously still around his neck. The road was with him all the time. He concentrated upon it as fiercely as a starving man would have upon a chicken leg. He did not know his hands were bleeding and torn, only that it was through their sensitive palms that he could tell he was still upon the road's hard-beaten dirt surface. He fancied also that he could smell the road; it was a harsh, acid smell like that of horsepiss, but he welcomed it as he would have the odor of baking bread.

As long as he was on the road, could feel it and smell it, he was all right. As long as his hands slapped down on that cleared surface and his nostrils picked up the smell of horsepiss, he was on the road and all right. He was not crawling off into the underbrush to die, or slipping down a bank to drown in some godforsaken Rebel creek like a kitten in a croaker sack. A road had to go somewhere, so as long as he was on the road he was all right.

The pain was not so consuming as his concentration on the road. As he dragged his shattered leg behind him, sometimes it flopped the wrong way. Sometimes it bumped over things. Once somebody walking along above him had kicked his leg and gone on. At those times Keefe would scream from the pain; sometimes he screamed repeatedly, when the leg felt as if it were burning up and being thumped with a sledgehammer, all at the same time.

But Keefe was lucky; he had to concentrate on the road because as long as he was on the road, he knew he was all right. Sooner or later, in his fierce concentration on the road, the pain would go away until it came back and he would scream again.

He had no idea where he was, where he was going, what time it was. The fighting, the bullet blow against his leg, the smoke, the terrible noise—all had gone out of his head. There was only the road and the pain and the darkness.

Private Hugh Williams, stumbling along in the irregular ranks of the Sixth Wisconsin with his musket over his left shoulder and his right arm supporting Cappy Swartz, saw the man crawling at the side of the road only because Williams had unusually keen night vision. Years ago, back in Wisconsin, he had discovered that, like a cat, he could see almost as well in the dark as the light; he had no idea of God's purpose in making him such a gift but he did not doubt that it *had* a purpose—which, of course, in God's good time, He would reveal.

Though he was bone-tired and worn down with Cappy's near-deadweight, Hugh Williams was a satisfied man. He was not immune, of course, to the suffering around him; he would have helped the crawling man if he'd had another arm, or if he could have done so without abandoning his musket. When Cappy Swartz tried to mumble something through his smashed jaws, Hugh listened as carefully as if to a Sunday School lesson back home, then tried to answer with some encouraging remark—though Cappy's strangled gasps made no sense at all. Tongue probably shot off, and him the sweetest singing voice in the regiment.

Still, for all the groans of the wounded, the muttered curses of troops stumbling in the dark, the aching of his own body, Hugh was almost happy. He had passed the test. Not just standing up in battle; not just standing by his company and his friends, like Cappy. That was the least of it, no more than expected of any soldier.

But Hugh Williams had never once, not under the hottest fire or in the most awful case—like seeing Ben Otis's blood pulsing from a hole in the pit of his stomach and Ben trying to close it up with his canteen stopper, with a look on his face like he wasn't hurt so much as amazed and insulted—not even then had Hugh Williams questioned his God or blasphemed His will.

And even now, about to fall down and barely able to haul

Cappy along to wherever they were headed, Hugh knew as he
lived and breathed that the Lord's will was being done. He was
more than ever convinced, spared as he had been from so much
as a scratch or a powder burn, and confirmed more powerfully in
his faith, that Hugh Williams was a mere instrument of that limitless will, certain someday, somehow, to be called upon in God's
good time to do His work.

Far behind Hugh and Cappy and the crawling figure at the roadside, in the dark woods above Brawner's deserted house, Privates
James F. Sowell and Gillum Stone lay wrapped in their tattered
blankets. Private Stone slept with his mouth open. But Private
Sowell nudged him awake.

   "We ought to brung'im off, Gilly."

   Private Stone sat up. "Brung what?" He blinked in puzzlement,
not sure in the darkness where he was.

   "Ol Lott."

   "Lott . . . where's Lott?"

   "Snuffed, goddammit. What's wrong with you?"

   "Shit." Gilly lay back down. "Reck'n I aint used-a th'idea yet."

   "We ought to brung'im off."

   "Maybe we kin git'im inna mornin."

   "It uz the wrong day, Gilly. He tried to tell us."

   "Ol Jack must not of thought so."

   "The wrong day," Sowell said. "Put the sign on'im."

Two miles along the old railroad right-of-way, at the other end
of the butternut battle line, General Hoke Arnall was dreaming of
his wife, Amy, as she had been at Sycamore the last morning of
his leave. Except that in his dream, her cheeks were rouged like
flame and as he entered her she held up her plump breasts to him
in her hands and they, too, were red as a harlot's lips and enfolded
him voluptuously. The general moaned in his sleep.

   Beyond the dim light from Arnall's headquarters camp fire,
Larkin Folsom slept dreamlessly, spoon-style in the massive embrace of Amos Gilmore. Gilmore, awake and watchful, heard
General Arnall's ecstatic groan and mistook it for someone's battle
nightmare. The corporal knew he dared not sleep—not that he
feared what any man said, but that he knew they would take the
boy away from him if they found out. And Amos Gilmore did

not intend for anyone to take him away. He stroked his hand gently down Folsom's stomach, careful not to wake the boy from his rest.

Gilmore was puzzled. Before the war, it had been mostly on low women that he had wasted what little a Carolina man could earn hunting and trapping. To Amos Gilmore then, while fighting and drinking were fun, the necessities were the solitary huntsman's life he led and the stallion-like rutting that left tavern girls torn and weary and sent him back to the woods replenished.

Even in the army, whenever he got the chance he spent his meager pay on whores. But the chances were few and far between; and Gilmore had discovered, while hospitably sharing his blankets one night during winter camp, that he could drive himself into one kind of body about as easily as the other and get about the same satisfaction. Nobody had yet complained, either, owing somewhat to Gilmore's massive fists but more to the fact that no man wanted to admit he'd been frigged like a woman.

But this boy! Gilmore had first acted with the usual intent. But the minute he'd touched Folsom with his hand the night before at Manassas, things had changed. As soon as the boy got used to it, he'd obviously loved what Gilmore was doing, moaning his pleasure outright. Then, before the corporal realized what was happening, the boy was doing it for him, Amos Gilmore; and to his consternation, Gilmore—who'd never before been handled by any man, who'd have shot the one who tried—found himself loving it, too, and moaning the same way. He didn't understand how that could be, but it didn't matter. All that mattered was the boy.

Unlike Corporal Gilmore, Foxy Bradshaw was desperately trying to sleep. He had just taken the last drink from the brandy bottle foraged at Manassas; but since he had watered the stuff to make it last as long as possible, it was having little effect.

As always before a battle, Foxy was terrified and thinking of deserting; every time he thought of another fight he wanted to crawl off in the bushes. He knew there *had* to be a bullet over there in the Yank lines with his name on it. Stood to reason. And when that bullet found him, as sooner or later it would, Foxy *knew* it would cut off his works, just as Josh and Lige had warned him.

But Josh had sworn this would be Ironass's last day on the face of the earth. Or else Josh's. And *that* would be worth something to see, even at the risk of another fight.

If Josh really done it. And iffen he *did,* maybe they'd both take off'n kiss this horseshit war good-bye.

Thad Selby should have been lost in the deep sleep of exhaustion; instead, he woke at the least sound nearby, once at the sudden flare of General Jackson's headquarters camp fire as someone replenished it. And even when Selby slept, his dreams were vivid as lightning flashes: of men falling, screaming, dying ... General Taliaferro's redly streaming fingers, hotly flaring eyes ... Ol Jack with his long arm pointing down the hill.

Selby sat up, soaked in sweat; but the realization of where he was, the moans of the wounded still rising from Brawner's pasture, appeared a poor alternative to his infernal dreams. More and worse to come with daylight, Colonel Channing said. Everybody said.

Won't be afraid again. Just the first time. I *can't* be afraid after the first time.

He lay back, shivering. What would his father think? If something happened and he didn't measure up? Not that it *would* happen. But if Thad somehow brought down censure on Aaron Selby's name, just when he was expecting his oldest son's marriage to Rachel Clayton to provide the kind of standing that a merchant's money never could—but it just *couldn't* happen. That was all there was to it.

When Selby dropped again into troublous sleep, he dreamed almost at once that he was riding Jeff D., going like the wind, the great horse carrying him faster than he had ever gone ... faster, faster . . . almost flying ... toward a gray haze receding before him ...

Selby awoke quickly, still drenched, still shivering. *Out of control never knew Jeff D. go out of control.*

Troubling visions also filled the dreams of Private Ambrose Riggin of Company B, Thirteenth Georgia. But unlike Captain Selby, Private Riggin did not wake up sweating. He was too tired to toss and turn, having marched sixty-odd miles in three days with only one night's decent sleep, before tearing into those black-hatted Yanks who'd so doggedly held their ground in Brawner's pasture.

Ambrose Riggin had discovered something in that fight. As long as he kept loading and firing, loading and firing, thinking of nothing but loading and firing into the long kneeling line of Yanks somewhere in the smoke on the slope below, he would not see those other kneeling men—the three with their hands tied behind them, on their knees at the edge of the open graves they had been made to dig for themselves. The need to load and fire, move quick, aim low, obscured more than battle smoke ever could.

But in Private Riggin's sleep, the three men were, as usual, in the center of his vision, lit with the unblinking white glare of midsummer sun in Virginia. They were surrounded by Jackson's entire corps, three divisions, above 20,000 men drawn up in a huge, C-shaped formation to witness the consequence of desertion.

Facing the open end of the formation a squad of twelve soldiers, half of them with fully loaded muskets, the other six with powder charges only, took aim at the heads and backs of the men kneeling twenty paces away. And it was along the barrel of his musket, shining in the sunlight, that in his dreams Ambrose Riggin always saw the three men.

When awake, he knew that he had killed none of the three deserters, although his musket's kick against his shoulder had told him that it had been loaded. At the command to fire he had pulled a bit high, not enough to be observed but enough so that he, a marksman who could bring down a dove on the wing, knew he had sent his bullet harmlessly into the scrub oak beyond the killing ground. But the three men had toppled forward anyway, into their graves.

Now in his sleep, Ambrose Riggin saw them again beyond his sights, heard the crash of the volley, watched the toppling bodies, then the officer stepping smartly forward, his extended arm, the cocked pistol, just in case something more was needed. The officer's single shot into the middle grave had finished it.

The trouble was that in his dream all the deserters had the face of Ambrose Riggin, fixed forever in his own gunsight. That had not, of course, been the case at the moment of execution, or the reason he had pulled high. Rather, as he had leveled his piece at the deserters, he had suddenly *seen* them, so sharply drawn against earth and sky that he had known suddenly that Ambrose Riggin or any man of the Thirteenth Georgia, of the thousands drawn up in that huge C, might on another day have been there on his knees with his hands knotted behind him.

The view through the gunsight had powerfully cleared his understanding. He saw that men might go to their deaths bravely in battle, until one day they would not. Men might defy the worst of terrors and pain until they broke. Men might love a cause but be needed at home. What haunted the dreams of Private Riggin and placed his own face in his own gunsight was the knowledge that to be killed for deserting was to be killed for being human.

Out to the northwest, a mile or two in the direction of the Bull Run Mountains invisible in the moonless night, Colonel Channing pulled his horse to a halt at the outstretched arm of General Jackson riding beside him. Channing was sleepy and irascible; he wanted to be in his blankets and knew the general should be in his. A hard day lay ahead. But when Jackson had signaled the colonel to follow him out of camp, the disgusted Channing had had little choice but to follow.

Channing had been fuming already, because it seemed to him that the troops should long since have been on the move. He had no clearer idea than anyone else why the general had given away their position with the late afternoon attack on the innocently passing black hats. Now he could not fathom why Jackson, instead of running for the shelter of the mountains, had elected to hang on and wait for whatever Pope wanted to throw him the next day. Which surely would be plenty.

Ought to be on our way to Thoroughfare right this minute, Channing grumped to himself.

But Jackson was inscrutable and confided nothing. He had held his first and last council of war with his officers that spring in the Valley, when they had talked him out of a ten-mile night march to attack Banks. Channing knew it would never happen again; Ol Jack would keep his own counsel, and follow it, too.

Not a word was said as they rode slowly in the turbid night through woods and across fields to what Channing supposed was the Hay Market Road. They had not gone far along it, to the west, before Jackson called the halt. They sat for a moment, the horses whuffing gently, night noises of crickets and bullbats loud in their ears, Jackson as tense and alert in the saddle as if he were listening for the bay of foxhounds. Then Channing realized the general *was* listening.

Still not speaking, Jackson swung a little stiffly down from his horse and took a few steps ahead, the darkness swallowing him quickly. Channing dismounted and followed. But before he had gone ten feet, he almost stumbled over Jackson kneeling in the road.

At first, the irreligious Channing thought the general was praying, and his anger briefly rose. Dragging me out here for *that*.

Then, peering through the darkness, he realized that Jackson had his ear to the ground.

The tramp of thousands of feet on the march could be transmitted for miles through the earth. But if Jackson—hunched motionless at Channing's feet—heard or sensed anything, he made no sign. He stayed down a long time; and Channing knew then the danger they faced, their desperate need of help from Longstreet.

The toll on Jackson's corps in the last few days had been devastating. Three general officers out of commission—Winder dead at Slaughter's Mountain, Ewell's leg gone that night to the bonecrackers, Taliaferro too badly shot up to exercise command. And the men had been marching and fighting without letup since August 20. Captains were commanding regiments, and the ranks had been drastically thinned by battle and straggling.

Channing had no personal fear, but he felt a chill apprehension along his spine. In the darkness and silence of the road, the imagined wall of mountains between them and Longstreet was the more distant and formidable for its invisibility. After the clash with the black-hat Yanks, they should have taken it on the run through Aldie Gap or Thoroughfare, putting that wall between them and Pope. They could have been almost out of danger.

But as it was, Channing realized more fully than ever the peril of the little force—barely 20,000 men huddled along the old railway line on the slope of Sudley Mountain. And as Jackson crouched with his ear to the road, the colonel thought he had never seen a figure so lonely, or so understood the stark isolation of command. It had taken guts, whatever else, for the man to hold his position after disclosing it to Pope; and no one to consult but himself.

Then the general arose and the two men mounted and rode back toward camp, the men sleeping there, and those quiet forever in Brawner's field. Channing knew the sun would rise in the thunder of guns and that Jackson's army might never see it set unless Longstreet was on the march.

But the general rode in silence. Even what he might have learned from the ground, Channing thought, Ol Jack would keep a secret.

Lieutenant Cass Fielding, as instantly awake as if he had been doused with cold water, sat straight up in his blankets, his body aching from the hard ground beneath him. Ten feet away, a man sat hunched on a log, his back to Fielding, his elbows on his knees, little more than a dark shape against the low flicker of a camp fire.

There was no other light. From something like a sixth sense of time, developed from much sleeping in the open, Lieutenant Fielding knew that dawn was still perhaps an hour away. And from the alert pose and the cock of the slouch hat visible against the fire's glow, he knew the man on the log was the commanding general. And it was certainly John Pope's voice, low but carrying, that had awakened him:

"Wasn't that artillery?"

Fielding could see no one else at the camp fire. But the general often talked to himself that way and it was no surprise at all that he was awake, alert, listening to the interminable passing of the night. Fielding had never known an officer so late to bed or so early to rise as John Pope—whether from diligence or lack of confidence, Fielding could not be sure. Certainly the burden of command that lay on his shoulders alone was unenviable; and now that the Rebs had cut the wires at Manassas and torn up the O & A, Pope was more than ever on his own. And the capital of the United States might even be at stake.

Wouldn't want such responsibility, Fielding thought. He listened for whatever had caused the general to speak, but heard nothing. The night seemed silent as death, the silence as ominous as a raised fist. He watched Pope's silhouetted head turn toward the west, the jutting cigar in his jaw outlined against the fire. Fielding had no ear for war; he was as likely as not to take distant thunder for artillery fire, and if he did hear guns he could seldom tell from which direction. The uproar back along the Warrenton Pike the night before had been a noisy confusion for him; as had everyone else, he had expected a battle, if any, to be up *ahead* of them.

Now, listen as he might, he could make out no sound save a pop or two from the fire and an occasional snort or sighing breath from his headquarters colleagues sleeping all around him. These sounds seemed somehow only to deepen the essential silence of the night; and Fielding lay gratefully back in his blankets, knowing from experience that the general would have the camp up and jumping as soon as the first light touched the eastern sky.

Fielding copied out most of Pope's orders and had observed that the general liked to order troops to move "at earliest blush of

dawn" or some such flowery phrase. The lieutenant considered
that this affectation, like the French military terms the general
also employed on occasion, made unnecessary work for headquarters clerks and unnecessary confusion for the recipients of his
orders.

Fielding reflected again, however, as he lay gazing into the
inky heavens at nothing, that Pope could sure get moving when
he had to. He'd certainly wasted little enough time last night, as
the news came in that pinpointed at last the whereabouts of Jackson
and the Rebs—not that they'd necessarily stay put.

Orders had gone out by courier to Phil Kearny, who had already
reached Centreville following Pope's earlier orders, to move at 1
a.m. west along the pike to the scene of the evening battle—
described by the rider looking for McDowell as having been near
the Groveton crossroads. Kearny was to attack Jackson at dawn,
or as soon as he could. Other orders had gone to Hooker to move
from the lower fords of Bull Run through Centreville and westward
along the pike behind Kearny. Reno, for the moment, was to
remain at Centreville to back up Kearny and Hooker. Porter's
Corps was ordered to march to Centreville, too, and hold itself in
readiness there.

By the time Fielding had rolled into his blankets for the night,
he had learned, with his sharp eyes and ears, the full shape of
Pope's dispositions. The rider they had encountered on the pike—
a major on McDowell's staff, someone claimed to know—had
identified the troops that had encountered Jackson at Groveton as
King's Division of McDowell. The rider had been sent back to
find McDowell and to tell him that with King's and McDowell's
other troops, he was to hold his ground before Jackson, thus cutting
off the Rebs' escape toward Thoroughfare Gap, while Kearny and
Hooker, backed by Reno and Porter, closed in from Centreville.
The hopeless Sigel, who was reckoned to be somewhere near the
Groveton fight, was ordered to throw in his German troops against
the Rebs at dawn, too; but nobody expected much to come of that.

If these orders were carried out—Fielding was too experienced
a staff officer to take it for granted that they would be—Pope
would have old Stonewall trapped with plenty of time to finish
him off. That had been made clear to Fielding when he had copied
off a letter Pope had written—in the middle of everything else
he had been doing the night before—to General Halleck. Fielding
had learned from the letter about one surprising development:

McDowell was ordered to interpose between the forces of the enemy which had passed down to Manassas through Gainesville, and his main body moving down from White Plains through Thoroughfare Gap. This was completely accomplished. Longstreet, who had passed through the Gap, being driven back to the west side.

The letter didn't go on to say when that had happened, and Fielding had heard nothing of it before; but he supposed Pope had to know what he was talking about in a letter to the general in chief. So they had Jackson isolated from the rest of the Confederate army and Pope was rapidly concentrating maybe 40,000 men—not counting Porter and Reno in reserve—to crush him. Oh, there would be a hell of a fight the next day!

Fielding dozed for a while after the general's low voice had awakened him, still hearing nothing that sounded to him like guns. He was near exhaustion after three days spent almost entirely in the saddle—not his natural habitat. But soon after he had first awakened, the clatter of a horse coming out of the pitchy night roused him for good. He swiftly pulled on his boots, urinated against a tree, and hurried toward a small group of officers assembling around the general's camp fire and listening to the rider who had just come in. As Fielding approached, he saw Pope turn swiftly away from the messenger toward the fire, throwing up his arms in what appeared to be disappointment and disgust.

"Fielding!" Colonel Russell shouted. "The map case!"

Shrugging off the last of sleep, Fielding swiftly produced it from the general's tent. Pope and Russell spread a map on their knees and studied it by the light of a fire that even in the humid beginnings of a hot day had been hastily built up to roaring proportions with the hissing, resinous pinewood of Virginia.

Try as he might, Fielding could hear nothing of the murmured deliberations. Pope stabbed a finger decisively at the map, then began folding it. Russell stood up, looked around, and shouted for Fielding again. The lieutenant hurried into the firelight.

"Write these orders, Fielding."

Russell's voice was peremptory, with just a hint, Fielding thought, of alarm. Not unusual. But the colonel dictated lucidly enough—first, an instruction to Sigel emphasizing the necessity to attack Jackson at dawn. In the second order, Fitz-John Porter was told not to march to Centreville after all. Instead, he was to move his corps forward from either Manassas Junction or Bristoe—Pope and Russell apparently were not sure where Porter was—on the Manassas–Gainesville Road, taking King with him. The order to Porter puzzled Fielding, since King was supposed to be facing Jackson at Groveton already. There was no poetic reference to dawn, but Porter was instructed to be "expeditious."

"Take that to the general to sign, Fielding. Where's Duryea?"

"Haven't seen him, sir."

Russell stomped out of the firelight, the still-thick darkness swallowing him like swamp water. Fielding found Pope in his headquarters tent dictating to another clerk a new order to Reno, who was ordered out of reserve and told to take the pike toward Groveton, "pushing rapidly toward any enemy firing you may hear."

Pope signed that order, then looked over the one to Porter that Russell had dictated for his signature. He nodded approvingly and muttered: "Porter's got to *move*." Then he signed the order with a flourish: JNO. POPE.

By the time Fielding had sent off couriers with the two orders and returned to the camp fire, the headquarters camp was alive and bustling, men and horses breaking the silence with their movements and talk. A smell of coffee and bacon stirred Fielding's stomach, but not happily. Army bacon, he was convinced, gave him the shits. The only way he could keep his bowels tight was to subsist on bread and the apples he could sometimes forage. Nothing like an apple to bind a man's innards, he thought.

Fielding strolled to the rider who had come in with the news that had so disturbed the commanding general. A captain, he stood by the huge fire, a tin cup of coffee from Pope's own mess in one hand, a hunk of break in the other. He looked in the firelight as if he had had no sleep.

"Hard night." Fielding spoke casually and introduced himself.

"Ira Ward." The captain shook hands, then swallowed coffee cautiously. "Got the sore-ass from that old busted saddle of mine."

"Ride far?"

"Near Gainesville to here. But all day yesterday, too."

"Who you with?"

"King's staff. You headquarters here?"

"Yep. King, huh? Heard tell he's a good-un." Fielding had no idea whether King could fight his way through a field of corn.

"Run right up old Jackson's asshole last night. Gibbon's Brigade did, anyways."

"We seen it all the way toward Centreville. Gibbon whipped'im,
I reckon?" Fielding had observed that lawyers often learned more
by indirection than by straight-out questions. More flies with honey.

Captain Ward eyed him over the hunk of bread, chewing solemnly. After a while, he washed the bread down with coffee.
"Reckon it'd take more'n a brigade to whip Jackson's whole crowd.
But those black-hat boys of Gibbon's got through with'im, he
knew he'd been hit. I'll lay you that."

"Bet he did. King'll fight'im again today, huh?"

The captain swirled a last drop or two of coffee into the blaze
behind. "Pulled back to Manassas overnight." He spat after the
coffee and glared at Fielding. "Up to me, I'd of gone for'is gullet,
come dawn."

"Durn right."

No wonder Pope had been angered, Fielding thought. His whole
plan of the night before had been based on the idea that King and
the rest of McDowell's Corps, having stumbled on Jackson, would
prevent him from retreating through Thoroughfare Gap until Kearny
and Hooker could get up to join the fight, trapping the Rebs
between the two forces. The tired young captain had brought Pope
the worst news possible—that no one save maybe fat-assed Sigel
was in a position to hold Jackson at Groveton and away from his
escape route.

Which was why, Fielding realized, Porter had been ordered to
take King's Division and move toward Gainesville—to fill in the
gap left by King's night retreat to Manassas. Pope still aimed to
crush Jackson if he could get at him.

"Got to be getting on," Captain Ward said.

Fielding shook hands again and wished him well, reflecting
that if war taught any one thing it was that a general's order was
only as good as the information on which it was based. He was
glad again that he was not John Pope, fishing around in the dark
for an enemy who wouldn't hold still and trying to provide a hub
for a Federal army whose divisions were scattered around Virginia
like the spokes of a broken wagon wheel.

Colonel Russell stumbled through the darkness until he found
Duryea shaving in cold water by candlelight, near the edge of the
camp.

"Ready to ride, Cap'n?"

"Yessir."

Duryea was always ready to ride. He folded his razor and slipped it into a leather sheath. Unlike most of his colleagues, Micah Duryea shaved every day, in camp or field. He believed the smallest elements—regular habits, observance of standards, obligations met—inevitably added up to the larger requirements of self-discipline. *Vincit qui se vincit,* he liked to remember.

"General Pope wants you to find General Sigel quick as you can. Don't wait for daylight." Duryea, listening, dried his face with one of the small towels his mother had sent him and that he kept meticulously washed. "He's camped south of the pike, th'other side of Bull Run. We don't know exactly where."

"I'll find him."

"Ordinarily, you understand, I wouldn't hit a hog in the ass with that German crowd. But turns out that's the only force close enough to Jackson to pin'im down."

"Where do you think he's going?"

"Thoroughfare. He's running for Longstreet. Got to be."

"I rode out that way last night. Didn't see any sign of a retreat."

"Pope thinks Jackson was on the move out of here when he ran into King. So he'll hightail it again come daybreak. But Sigel might be able to pin'im where he is until we can move up the rest of the army and cut'im off. Here's written orders to Sigel to attack soon's it's light enough to see, with everything he's got, and hold Jackson where he is. General wants you to make it clear those are peremptory orders, Duryea. Don't give Sigel any chance to misunderstand or get around you."

Within minutes, Duryea had saddled and his horse was picking its way out of camp toward the ford. It was still so dark he could not see the animal's ears. Soon Duryea dismounted and led; he could make better time that way. Besides, he'd rather trust his own sense of direction even than his horse's.

Missy hoped the night would never end. Considering the miracle that already had happened, it did not seem so foolish a wish.

Anything seemed possible. She had never been so happy— never before had been happy at all, she had suddenly realized, not having known what happiness really was—even though her legs and back were stiff from the night air and the hours in which she'd sat on the hard ground without moving, trying not to disturb the extraordinary creature who slept with his beautiful head in her lap.

A *miracle*. When she'd seen him in the weird candlelight on the hillside, with the poor shot boys all round, he'd looked so mean and mad, like Paw ready to whop Wash, that she'd got her back up to spit and scratch.

But when he haul me up like-at'n held me up front of'im . . .

Missy sighed. Strong arms around her, the feel of him against her back, even a kind of special smell about him that overcame the remembered musty odor of blood. No doubt in her mind *then*. It seemed the closest she'd likely ever get to a dream come true.

So Missy knew she'd sit there all night and the next day and the night after that and on and on, if only he'd stay with his head just turned a little, so she could see the way the skin crinkled at the corner of his eye and how his silky hair grew almost in curls over his small ears, and the straight line of his perfect nose. And how long his lashes were, over his dark, now sleeping eyes.

She couldn't *see* any of that, of course, even leaning down to within a few inches of his face, scarcely daring to breathe for fear of waking him; the night was too dark. Maybe the darkest she'd ever seen. But she could *remember* every detail of his face from that day, when he'd come for buttermilk and caught the Yankees. And sitting there in the night, still as a mouse, she could imagine exactly how he'd look sleeping, if she *could* see him, how he was *going* to look. Iffen-at ol sun ever come up.

Not that she was in a hurry for *that*. Somewhere close by, she could hear the black horse moving occasionally, sometimes snuffling a little, or cropping at weeds and the scarce grass'in Paw's dusty yard. Come sunup, maybe even before, the horse would take him away. And she did not yet even know his name.

But Missy knew everything else that mattered. He was beautiful, anybody could see that, with his strong face and curly hair and the closely trimmed mustache. He was brave as a lion—look at how he'd caught the Yanks. Kind, too, even though he'd tried to act mean with the shot boys. So many of'em shot so bad. But Missy could tell—already she could tell every single thing about him; and somehow she knew that acting mean had been his way of not showing how bad he felt.

And he was a man, too, strong as a horse and knowing what to do. Anybody could tell that. He'd taken her up from the ground as easily as he'd pick a flower. The only reason she hadn't told him that the mean Yankee had put his hands all over her was that she feared he'd kill that Yank on the spot, when all she wanted was just to look at him a little longer and pour him buttermilk.

So Missy knew all that mattered about him, even that he was a real gentleman. Hadn't he stopped fooling around as soon as she told him to?

Missy understood what men did. She had lived all her life around animals and had watched them closely, fascinated. She'd had many a whispered talk with Sajie, who knew everything. To Missy's eternal shame, but considerable education, she'd once let Wash talk her into joining him in spying on Henry and Sajie when they were doing it. And she knew what Wash was up to lately—pinching and peeping and trying to feel up under her skirt.

Missy was not at all reluctant, therefore, to have *this* man—more like a prince or a knight, she thought—do like that with her. What men did. Nor did she mind that he wanted to, even if Sajie said they *all* did. This man could do what he wanted, touch her anyplace.

Onliest thing was last night, she thought, I'd-a-let'im touch me first off, he might of thought he could just thow me down'n do it right then'n ther.

Maybe she should have let him anyway. Maybe when the sun came up and he went away, he wouldn't come back because she hadn't. Missy doubted that, because he *was* a gentleman; she was sure of it. If he didn't come back, if the miracle came to an end, it wouldn't be because she hadn't let him but because he had to go with his old army. Or—she was stabbed to the heart at the thought—because he's married to some fine lady in high shoes.

Missy wiggled her bare toes in anguish and humiliation; one of her knees was protruding from her torn skirt. Just then she noticed the first faint graying of the sky over the barn; and whether because of that or of her slight movement, she sensed a change in the rhythm of his breathing, a barely noticeable movement of his head in her lap. He was waking up. He would leave. She would never see him again. Missy began to cry, unfamiliar tears slipping down her cheeks, without moving or hurrying her own breath, so as not to hasten his waking.

The horse snuffled again. Missy watched the lightening sky, a pink stain on the gray, feeling as if she were sinking in her misery. Then his head jerked suddenly against her thigh and he muttered something unintelligible, before lapsing into stillness again. Bad dream, she thought, the tears chilling on her cheeks. Not like mine.

Gradually dawn came on, the squatty shape of the barn emerging first, then the higher frame of the house where she had been born and had lived all her nearly seventeen years, and from which she had traveled no farther than Warrenton or Manassas Junction, to see the trains go by on the O & A. And for the first time in all those years, looking down at the dear face as wonderful in the growing light as she had remembered it in the dark, she sensed how drab her life had been, and would be, how small and dull and of no account, against the great world into which he would soon disappear, she feared forever. Probably with some pretty lady.

"Good God." His voice was muffled against her thigh. "Have I been asleep long?"

"Not long." Only a minute. Hardly even that, seem like.

"Comin light."

She felt the weight of his head leave her legs like a great loss. As he sat up, looking around, she hastily brushed the tears from her cheeks.

Bound to look like what the cat drug in, she thought, up all night in these-yer rags. But he aint apt to pay *me* no mind nohow.

"I was just sittin here against the tree, last I remember. I didn't aim to go to sleep."

"Wa'nt no buttermilk left nohow."

She was thankful for that, that she had not awakened him and destroyed the most beautiful moment of her whole life. She had come back from the house to find him sound asleep against the sycamore—sleeping so solidly that it was no trick to lift his dear head away from the tree, to slip between it and his warm, powerful body, and hold him close as the night wore on in its blackness and the feel of him entered every angle and curve of *her* body. She did not know how to say it to him, scarcely even to herself, but she knew she would never forget holding him that way, almost as if she could wrap herself around him and make herself a part of him, and him a part of her.

He ran a hand through his black curls, and Missy, marveling at the grace of the movement, thought how everything he did was *right,* the way a good horse moved, the way Paw's mare moved just right, not trained to it, but knowing in its bones how to move.

"Well . . . so you pillowed this old gray head through the night, did you?"

No one had ever joked or flirted with Missy; Wash was about as funny and charming as a fox in the henhouse and yesterday the mean Yankee had been slobbering. So she did not understand what he was saying about the gray head; in the morning light, it seemed to her that his head had an even stronger jawline, a bolder set to it, than she had spent the night remembering.

But she realized that he was smiling at her. White teeth strong and even under the black mustache. Missy sensed that she should reply in kind, although she was afraid to smile for fear he would think her uppity.

"Aint much pillow, I reckon." Too bony, she thought, despairing.

To her immense pleasure, his smile widened, as if her words or at least her tone had been right. She had never before had a lighthearted conversation with a young man.

"A soldier'd sleep many a night and never have a pillow so nice. And I don't even know your name."

For a second, Missy didn't either, so lost was she in the new pleasure of flirtation. Then she wondered whether to give him her real name, and quickly decided not to. He'd leave for sure, it was so ugly.

"They-uns call me Missy. Paw'n'em."

"That's nice. Missy. Allow me to introduce myself . . . Captain Fargo Hart, Stuart's staff, at your service."

Even sitting on the ground, he contrived to make a courtly bow with his head and shoulders. Then, abruptly, he stopped smiling and leaned toward her, peering more closely at her face in the growing light.

"You been crying, Missy?"

She was rapt in contemplation of his name—Fargo, the rhythm to it, the rich, well-bred sound of it; and since she did not know there was any other kind of heart, she supposed his last name stood for the part people were supposed to love with. *Seem like a sign.* So she hardly heard the question. But when his words finally got through her concentration, she was stricken to think how awful she must look, and intuitively put her hands over her tear-streaked face.

Hart misinterpreted this gesture. From the moment he had reclaimed his wits from sleep, from dreams of shellfire and horses rearing and men pitching over backward and blood in rivulets along the ancient traces of Brawner's plough—as soon as he realized where he was and who was with him, he had suffered the shrinking knowledge that he had acted badly with this child.

Not that any real damage had been done. But Hart *was* a kind man, as Missy had sensed, as well as a proud one. He had caused her to be upset and he disliked himself for that; he had consequently

suffered rebuff from a slip of a girl and that embarrassed him.
Having the natural tendency of people to believe that their own
actions must be the prime cause of the joys and sorrows of those
with whom they are involved, he saw her in tears and assumed
that she had been crying because he had touched her the night
before.

"Missy . . . I'm sorry." He took one of her wrists in his hand,
marveling at its thinness. "I didn't go to upset you last night."

But Missy, in fact desolate only for knowing that he would
soon leave and never know what she looked like with her face
washed and Sunday clothes on, could no longer hold back her
sobs. She blubbered like a baby, jerking away from his strong
hand and turning her face against the tree, agonizingly embarrassed
at her own childishness.

Hart watched in consternation. Missy was something new to
him, more like a woods creature than the women of his experience.
Unfortunately, he had not realized that soon enough. Life abroad,
from which war had recalled him so abruptly, had given him the
rather manorial view that farm wenches were warm, pliable, generous, only too eager for the pleasures of hay mow. This notion
was based on a single episode in Tuscany, three years earlier,
when he had been seduced by a black-eyed, laughing creature who
had shocked and enthralled him by riding him like a horse while
her swaying Italian breasts swung heavily in his face.

When he had first sensed Missy's slight but unmistakably female form against him, the tickle of her hair on his face, as
Mercury carried them steadily through the darkness, Hart had
assumed for no more reason than his Tuscan idyll that this one,
too, would be eager for the haystack and would have no pretensions
of class or virtue. He had known at once what he usually managed
to suppress—that he was starved for what her hard little body
could give him. (He had been fifteen months in America, where
as far as he could see the sexual conveniences of Europe were
nonexistent anyway; and most of that time had been with the army
in the field.) His spirit was equally starved for relief from the
constancies of war—torn flesh, brutalized men, indifferent violence—so vividly present only an hour earlier in Brawner's flaming field.

So, as naturally as he might have reached for an apple from a
tree—far more naturally than he would have kissed the hand of
some simpering featherbrain in Richmond—he had moved his
free hand to cup her breast. He was surprised to find it rounder

than her slight frame had suggested, but more surprised when she
quickly pulled his hand away and said firmly, albeit softly:

"Reckn not."

Hart knew right away that this was not a ritual move in a sexual
minuet; she was not going to be a quick, hot-eyed tumble. He
was nonplussed for a moment, then fell back quickly on what he
felt to be the natural superiority of his class and sex.

"Ah, well. Afraid I must have been carried away by the moment."

No more than a trace of mockery—and that perhaps self-
derision—colored the words. They had ridden on in silence, Mercury's hooves making little sound as he moved slowly through
the grass and underbrush just above the pike. Hart was too much
a soldier not to be alert to the possibility that Yanks could be
moving on the pike. But the night had been intensely dark, concealing them from eyes ten feet distant, and in the silence that
had fallen over the broomsedge after the scream and crash of battle
he knew he would hear troops approaching before they would hear
one horse at a walk. So only a part of him listened with care for
the tramp of boots or the jingle and clatter of cavalry, the rumble
of caissons and limbers, and the rest of his consciousness was
suddenly absorbed by this small, rigid creature sitting sidesaddle
in front of him. He did not know what to make of her.

The loose strands of hair touching his face, the stiff, alert set
of her thin body, even her wild odor intrigued him. Not an unwashed odor so much, he fancied—since he himself had not often
washed or been able to change clothes for days—as that of close
contact with animals, earth, nature. She seemed wild, free, almost
winged . . . but that was ridiculous.

Hart caught himself up for thinking nonsense about a chit in
poor-white rags. Except that to find such a child there on Ol Jack's
field trying to help mutilated and dying boys, a task from which—
Hart believed—finer ladies would have fled fluttering and screaming, then to have the same unaccountable creature quite firmly
refuse to be trifled with, despite her class . . . she was outside his
experience. Besides, that night he had wished never again even
to have to contemplate killing and destruction and his own violent
instincts, although he knew he would have to return to all of them
soon enough. Until then, she was a more than welcome diversion.

"Over ther."

Her voice had been little more than a whisper, lying on the
night like the whir of an insect.

Beyond where he knew the turnpike must run, a patch of deeper darkness rose against the black sky. Hart could not make it out to be a house, but he trusted her knowledge of her own countryside.

"Hold on."

He put the reins in her hand and edged carefully out of the saddle, letting her slip back into it as he dismounted with a creak of leather and a jingle of spurs explosively loud in the darkness and silence. He made his way to the remembered rail fence that ran along the pike opposite her house, lowered the two top rails silently, and guided Mercury over. He replaced the rails, then led the horse quickly across the pike. Running his hand along the fence on the other side, he found the gate, opened it, and took them into the farmyard where he and Kirk had captured the two Yanks. If Kirk could see him now!

Hart held up his hands and she came lightly down from the saddle, her face—a white blur in the dark—moving closely past his. So he had delivered her home and was free to go, to rejoin Stuart, prepare himself for the blood and iron of another day. But he had not wanted to leave. He had wanted a clearer sense of this girl, thinking that might help him come to a better sense of things generally, particularly himself. More likely, he had told himself, his rake's blood was still running; she was female and he had not quite given up. He let his hands linger on her arms.

"You hungry?" She was still whispering.

Hart seldom wanted to eat after a battle, particularly not meat. "Some more of that buttermilk maybe."

"Iffen Paw'n'em aint took it to the cellar."

"I'll wait here while you see."

She had disappeared, silent as a butterfly. Mercury moved between Hart and the fence, reins trailing the ground. Hart eased himself gratefully down against the trunk of the sycamore to which the sorry Yank horses had been tethered, keeping the tree between himself and the pike. A cool draught of the buttermilk, he thought, his lids heavy, and he would be on his way. Unless this woods girl showed some sign she really wanted to play. It had been a long time since he had touched a woman so closely. No wonder she had roused him, even if . . . he had not even known it when his head slumped forward and his eyes closed.

But he knew immediately upon awakening that he had passed the night with his head in her lap; and he began to wonder ignobly, as she wept with her face in her hands, whether she had somehow picked up some fancy ladylike notion that because he had done so she was "ruined."

Good God, he thought, how can I deal with that?

He was about to rise and call in Mercury for rescue, when without warning Missy turned from the tree trunk, threw herself against him as he rose to his knees, and clasped her thin arms about his neck with surprising strength.

"*Never* comin back!" Her tearful cheek was warm against his. "I know you aint!"

Startled, almost knocked over by the force of her charge against him, reflexively seeking to keep his physical balance, Fargo Hart put his arms around her, heard her breath catch in his ear as if she had been struck. He knew then that he could do anything he wanted with her. Why she had resisted, then flown like a wild thing into his arms, he would try to figure out later; but in the trembling of her body, in the passionate whisper of her breath against his skin, the moisture of her tears on his cheek, in the anguish of her single outcry, he knew she was his, ardently, completely—a sense new to him and his more sophisticated experience.

He was astonished at such a gift. In the dawning light, too, as he looked over her sharp little shoulder at the unpainted house, the rickety stoop, the scratchy yard, he sensed again the poverty and limits of her life, the elemental nature of it, the lack of adornment and artifice, and was overwhelmed suddenly with wonder that she had grown here, somehow, like a wildflower. Like Queen Anne's lace.

At that moment, behind him to the east and towards Bull Run a mile or so away, artillery opened grumpily, the first dawn sounds heralding a battle day, signaling war's iron demands. But that morning, rather than responding like a soldier to the beckoning guns, Hart was lost in an eternal wonder—not only that she should have flowered in that dust, but that despite Ol Jack's shot and cannon and the blood that seemed now to tinge the rising sun he had found her there in her warmth and openness—this incredible gift, this sudden quiet peace in the midst of war.

"I'll come back." His lips moved on her wet cheek.

"You promise?"

"Promise. I'll be back." He marveled to realize that he meant it.

"Please . . . I love you . . ."

Hart had never heard those words spoken truly. But before he could reflect on their simplicity and its meaning, or how he knew they were true, he heard at the side of the house, just around the corner out of sight, the creaking, flapping sound of cellar doors being thrown open.

As Hart rose and pulled Missy to her feet, a gaunt farmer in butternut trousers and a faded blue shirt lunged around the corner. He stopped abruptly as he saw Missy and Hart under the sycamore. A huge Negro, one suspender holding up his ragged pants, came around the corner and stopped, too, his dark face blank as iron. Behind Hart, the sharp staccato pop-popping of musketry—the unmistakable reports of skirmishers meeting pickets—crackled down the pike. The guns were booming steadily now.

"You, Missy!" The farmer tried to sound fierce but Hart detected a whining note in his voice.

"I-uz heppin-um, Paw. Overt Brawner's. Must be a thousan'um lyin shot'n needin water."

Her father stared uncertainly from Missy to Hart and back again.

"I brought your daughter home. Like she said, she was doing what she could for the wounded."

"Yeah. Uh . . . you Missy! Git on down at confoun cellar'n look after Maw. Git on now!"

Missy moved tentatively away, looking back at Hart. He smiled, thinking how she looked more than ever ready for flight, to leap and soar.

"I'll be back," he murmured. "Never you fear."

Her face lit from within, as if her senses were actually glowing in her skull. He did not know that it was not just his words, but his smile, too, that had infused her with light. Missy believed his words implicitly; but his smile told her that he wanted to come back, that he would not just keep a promise. He would seek her.

Then, like the wild thing he imagined, she was gone, moving light as a falling leaf past her father and the massive African.

"Confoun girl got no more sense'n God give a billygoat." The farmer tried to look stern and fatherly. "Messin round em sojer boys."

Hart whistled softly to Mercury, who came up immediately. "Your daughter's a fine young woman." He gathered up Merc's reins, hearing his voice perhaps sharper than was necessary. "You've no cause to be angry with her." He stared fixedly at the man; these poor whites had to be dealt with firmly and he had no intention that this one should punish Missy when he had no reason.

"Reck'n not, then. You with the Virginia boys?"

"Of course. Stuart's staff."

"Stuart! If at don't beat all." The man looked at the African triumphantly, but the black face was impassive. "I uz jus thinkin bout Stuart." Brace did not know one general from another, except that everybody had heard of Stonewall Jackson.

"What about Stuart?"

Hart did not trouble to disguise the contempt in his voice. It did not occur to him that Missy's Paw was just an older version of the fierce, rawboned boys Ol Jack had sent yelling down Brawner's hill in the bloody twilight.

"Me'n Henry here . . ." Brace jerked his head at the Negro. "Aint nobody know the country herebouts no better'n usuns. Reck'n Gin'al Stuart needs'im a coupla guides?"

Hart swung into the saddle, stiff still from sleep, and stared at Missy's Paw with distaste. There was nothing the elegant Stuart was less likely to want around headquarters than a poor-white farmer looking like a mangy hound, and his sullen darky. Still . . . Hart had learned that the road network in the vicinity was tangled and confusing. Getting Longstreet and Ol Jack back together in one army would be a hard job at best, and probably Stuart's to manage.

"Might use you. No harm to ask."

"Henry! Hustle downa woods'n saddle up at mare. You take the mule. Git crackin."

"Aint ought to ride at mare yit." Henry made no move.

"She be okay. Saddl'er up."

Henry turned and went around the house, his body heavy with disapproval. In the distance, the musketry was continuous and rising. An attack going in behind skirmishers. Hart could not tell which way the attackers were moving, out from or toward Jackson's line along the old railway.

Suddenly, he was eager to find Stuart, anxious to get back to the army, the only life he knew anymore. Already, the feel of Missy in his arms was fading, the wonder lost in the unpleasant talk with her father, the commonplace sound of gunfire over Bull Run. A hot day was coming, with hot work to do.

He recoiled suddenly from a dirty, calloused hand thrust up at him. Missy's Paw stood by Mercury's neck, grinning at Hart with yellow teeth. But Hart did not fail to notice the sharp flash of his eyes and the hard line of his jaw.

"Name's Brace, Cap'n. Durward P. Brace. Alluz wanted to shoot me a Yank."

Sally Sutherland Crowell awoke that morning to the sound of the gunfire to the west. Lying in what had been her childhood bed in what was now her brother's house in Centreville, she shuddered at the ominous rumble, now become so familiar.

But the noise of violence was no less frightening—quite the opposite—because it was so often heard, from virtually any direction. In Virginia, no escape from it seemed possible; and Sally thought fleetingly of removing to Columbia, South Carolina, where Lawrence's mother's family had offered to take her in. Surely the war could never reach as far south as Columbia.

But Sally did not want to sleep anywhere except in her own small bed, surrounded by the comforting relics of her placid childhood, until she had resolved her trouble, or at least had some idea what had brought it about. She had never been strong, but had never suffered real illness—and certainly had never known nameless fear—before the battle that had engulfed Lawrence's house three weeks earlier.

Obviously, that battle had started her trouble. As she often had in the days since, particularly with gunfire in her ears, Sally recalled how peacefully that day had begun—a clear, hot, August day with corn and wheat ripening in the fields beneath Slaughter's Mountain and along the forks of Cedar Run. But by noon the armies had closed menacingly near, on the Culpeper road, and shortly afterward the guns had started to boom.

What a fool she'd been not to leave when the servants begged her! But somehow abandoning Lawrence's house would have seemed as if she were abandoning *him;* and by the time the Yankee surgeons moved in, shells were flying recklessly, troops were massing all about, and venturing from the house had appeared more dangerous than staying in it.

At first she'd wanted to help the surgeons, because wounded boys, even Yankees, needed help; she'd have been glad for *anyone,* even some Yankee women, to have helped Lawrence when he'd gone down the year before with a bullet in his neck. But the Federal surgeons either had ordered her roughly out of the way, or had implored her not to remain in such foul surroundings, so that soon she'd retreated upstairs, with the din of battle rising outside to a terrifying pitch.

Then, as the crimson sun dipped toward the horizon, the southern boys had won the fight; or so Sally supposed, because she'd never since brought herself to read or hear a word about that grisly day. But a sort of stillness had suddenly fallen on the house, despite the battle noises outside; and she realized the Yankee surgeons were gone.

Up to that point, Sally had been mostly unafraid, even when a shell brought down the top part of the chimney on the roof, because she'd trusted in her merciful Lord God, believed that under His benign eye death could only bring joyful reunion with Lawrence in Heaven. But when she ran downstairs the first thing she saw was the mound of obscene human garbage, of arms and legs and torn human flesh, piled under and around Lawrence's mother's harpsichord.

After that moment, Sally remembered nothing of the time until neighbors found her the next day. They had nursed her for a few days back to something resembling sanity, then taken her to Culpeper and obtained for her a pass through the Federal lines in front of the Rappahannock. From there, servants had driven her to her brother's house at Centreville, where on the first night in her old room her trouble had started.

Now, in the broadening daylight, hearing the guns off toward Bull Run, Sally covered her eyes with her hands. What was happening to her? Why couldn't she resist the nauseous fear—of nothing and everything—that came without warning and departed without reason? What was the trouble with her foot? Why had the mere sight of a chaplain's insignia evoked her trouble and brought back with a sickening rush the dreadful heap beneath the harpsichord?

Sally did not know. She could not remember. She was not even sure if there was anything *to* remember. And if there was, she dreaded knowing what. She wished Lawrence were there to hold her—and at the moment she thought of him holding her, she felt her stomach turn, and fear fall on her like a shroud, and little icy needles touch her toes.

Chapter Seven

~~~~~~~~~~~~~~~~~~~~~

August 29—Forenoon

"GILMER, I'VE GOT a job for you."

"Yessir."

Amos Gilmore had earned his preferred position as General Hoke Arnall's scout, forager, and handyman by never questioning an assignment he was given, and never troubling Arnall with the details of how he had carried it out—as he always did.

"Look around beyond those woods out there." Arnall's Brigade front looked out on dense trees and underbrush. "Push ahead, as far as possible. Find out anything you can about what troops're out there, how many, how they're positioned."

"Right off, sir."

Gilmore saluted. The camp was quiet, most of the men still sleeping.

"Look sharp, Gilmer. They'll have plenty of pickets out."

"Aint worried, sir."

"And remember . . . I want information, not a dead corporal. Don't get shot by some of our boys comin back."

Gilmore grinned. "They'd be too skeert to shoot ol Amos, sir." He went off through the ranks of sleeping men, making only a slight detour to pass the boy. *See he's still gittin his rest. Ironass'll have'im up'n jumpin any minute.*

Gilmore had been astonished in the night when the boy had whispered to him some words he called "lines"—something about the beauty of a summer day. Gilmore had no idea what the lines meant but with the boy's hand touching him, he hadn't needed to

279

know; the words and the touch had given him the only sense of anything like beauty he'd ever had—except sometimes before the war, when he'd been alone in the woods with the sunlight coming through the trees.

Gilmore did not think in terms of love and romance, any more than of beauty; in his life he had only taken what he could get. But he knew he needed somehow to hold this boy close; and it had been years, back maybe to Gilmore's dimly remembered mother, dead since he was a tyke, since he had thought he needed anybody.

A brute, General Arnall thought, watching Gilmore trot over the railroad cut and disappear into the woods beyond. An animal. God knows how he does what he does.

Arnall had waked before dawn with a sense of anticipation and a feeling of satisfaction that his brigade was in an exposed position rather than in reserve or out of action. He had called the burly corporal to his side as soon as he had pulled on his boots; and if Gilmore brought back the intelligence Arnall hoped for, some Yanks were going to get a nasty surprise.

There was a sort of poetic justice in the situation; or better still, God's guiding hand. Arnall could not help thinking that, as he gulped down the hot coffee and the hunk of bacon Private Folsom provided. An officer unfairly placed in arrest for an offense he hadn't even committed, by a commander either crazy or tyrannical or both, suddenly finding himself vital to that commander's army— maybe the key to victory or defeat. Even in the latter case, Hill's Division, with Arnall's its most exposed brigade, was covering Jackson's last-chance escape route across Sudley Ford to Aldie Gap.

Well, the Lord be praised. Hoke Arnall meant to show the world, crazy Tom Jackson in particular, what he was made of. If it was providential—and of course it was—that his chance should come so soon, he believed he was ready to make the most of it. When the sun went down that day, the arrest of Hoke Arnall was going to look like the craziest move Ol Jack had ever made.

Light was streaking the eastern sky behind him, and Arnall expectantly checked the watch that had been his father's. As if on schedule, Federal guns opened somewhere near the pike. He listened as shells burst harmlessly in the woods in front of his position.

"Let it come," he murmured into the sudden commotion of his aroused camp. "Let it come."

Except, of course, for one thing. Unobtrusively, Arnall moved away from the camp fire and knelt behind a huge oak. He never made a spectacle of religion as some men did, but he knew that if God's hand had sent the day only God's favor could let Hoke Arnall realize it.

Besides, in the slowly growing morning light, with the sun signaling its presence just below the horizon, the flaws in Arnall's position were obvious to his trained eye—and worrisome enough that he made quick work of his prayers in order to be up and about.

The railroad cut running across the slope of the knoll on which Hill had posted his brigade of just over 1,500 men might ordinarily have been held against a whole army, not just the division Arnall thought was probably in his front. But he was holding the left flank of Jackson's entire line; and to anchor Arnall's own left, the farthest outpost of Jackson's force, there was nothing more than a rail fence. Running at somewhat less than a right angle to the railroad cut, it provided little cover for Arnall's troops or obstruction to the enemy.

From the fence, Arnall could look over an open field that fell away gradually to Bull Run; a stand of corn was at the far edge of the field. To the left of the cornfield and roughly in Arnall's rear, the brick building of the Sudley Methodist Episcopal Church was shaded by a grove of trees. His brigade surgery was set up there.

At least the open ground beyond the rail fence provided a decent field of fire. Arnall had posted Sam Stowe's South Carolina regiment—maybe the best in the brigade—along the fence.

"They'll come across that field, Sam. Maybe not the first attack. But don't be impatient. They'll come."

Stowe moved his planter's hat to the back of his head. "Nice of you to give us the easy job." The steadiness of his manner gave Arnall more confidence about his flank than the open field of fire.

He peered searchingly at the rest of his dispositions, seeking unspotted weak points. With two regiments on the line in the cut—Dixon's Rifles and McCrary's South Carolinians—and Sparks's Tar Heel troops in reserve over the knoll behind them, Arnall's Brigade of four regiments was deployed within an obtuse angle. Stowe's regiment faced northeast along the fence and those in the cut looked somewhat south of east, most nearly in the direction of the rumbling enemy guns.

Arnall felt reasonably secure against an attack on Stowe's tough regiment on his left, or directly against the railroad cut. And he did not lack support. Powell Hill had sent word that he was holding the brigades of Branch, Archer, and Pender in reserve, behind the front-line positions manned by Arnall, Thomas's Brigade on his right and Field's just beyond that, on Thomas's right. Arnall could tell from dust clouds that men from Stuart's cavalry also were ranging around in Hill's rear, protecting the Sudley Ford across Bull Run.

It was his right that most worried Arnall, as well as the wooded and brush-covered terrain in his front. A tongue of woodland actually entered the line from the front, leaping over the railroad cut. The woods and underbrush reduced visibility and offered cover to an advancing enemy. Worse, Thomas's Brigade, next on Arnall's right, was maybe a hundred yards distant—from Arnall's right flank to Thomas's left—and pulled back somewhat from the line of the unfinished railroad. Arnall had no idea why so excellent a commander as A. P. Hill had left such a gap in his line. And the gap was all the more threatening because at that point the railroad cut was deep and broad enough so that a substantial Yankee force might get into it and attack left or right.

Colonel Jehue Sparks rode up beside Arnall and pointed a long finger at the gap in the line. A hard-bitten North Carolina tobacco grower who had been a lieutenant in Mexico, Sparks tended—in Arnall's judgment—to get above himself with military advice.

"I was some Yank gin'al, Hoke, I'd fill that-er cut with blue-bellies, first off."

Arnall did not need to be told by Sparks or anyone that if the Yanks used the concealment of the woods and the undefended gap in the line to get into the cut between the two brigades, his regiments could be isolated and cut to pieces, Hill's line broken, and Jackson's left turned. But Hoke Arnall was a professional soldier. He had placed his brigade where it had been ordered; and though he had sent an urgent note to Hill calling attention to the gap, he believed he had no choice but to remain where he had been ordered to take position.

But rebuffing Sparks, an enthusiastic fighter, made no sense with Yanks in spittin' distance.

"They do that..." Arnall's voice gave no hint of his own apprehension. "Be your job to root'em outta there."

Even this concern, serious as it was, could not dampen Hoke Arnall's anticipation. As the light spread and the men huddled in the lines, Arnall was all over his sector, hectoring his regimental

commanders, shouting at the men, checking details he might ordinarily have left to subordinates. Time passed; the shelling increased, filling the air with smoke and noise and flying chunks
of iron but doing little damage to anything but the troops' eardrums. In the woods, skirmishers' musketry was sharp and steady.

Conscious as always of the example an officer had to set, Arnall
rode about in the open as if the bursting shells were no more than
a swarm of flies. So great was his self-control that before long he
really did pay the shellfire no attention; but the men of his brigade,
while well-protected from the Yank gunners and bothered by only
an occasional whining Minié ball, were not so oblivious to danger
as their general. Nor were they so eager as he for the attack to
develop; few of *them* felt they had anything to prove.

These were veterans of the Peninsula. They could read the
signs and sounds of battle as well as their officers; they knew they
soon would be facing a heavy attack. And they were not as understanding as Arnall—who knew that long-range artillery duels
were of little use—of the failure of Hill's artillery to respond to
the Yank guns. Soldiers under shellfire always wanted to hear
their own guns pouring it back to the enemy.

"Goddam gunners settin up ther inna hills jerkin ther dicks."
Lige Flournoy had no use for gunners and cavalrymen anyway.
"Reck'n they in the same army?"

All along the line, men were tense and anxious. Some prayed.
Some thought of wives and families and scratched off hasty notes.
Others pinned scraps of paper with their names scribbled on them
to their tattered jackets. Some resolutely stared into space or at
the ground, trying to think of nothing. A few chattered nervously.
Fear struck others dumb. Many, with the hard-won tactical instinct
of experienced troops, knew their position on Jackson's flank was
crucial. Others looked at the gap in the line or at the underbrush
in their front with as much concern as Arnall. There was no
bravado.

Arnall calculated that he had two men for every three to four
feet of front he was supposed to defend. But he knew little of
Jackson's line elsewhere. He could not be sure who or what was
beyond Hill's Division; Ewell, he supposed, unless Ol Jack had
shuffled things around in the night. Then Jackson's own division—
Taliaferro's now—on the far right.

Arnall did not know that both Ewell and Taliaferro had been
severely wounded in the battle the night before at Brawner's farm.
Alexander Lawton had taken over Ewell's Division and W. E.

Starke now commanded Taliaferro's; both, like Arnall, were brigade commanders. That they were suddenly leading divisions would have troubled him had he known it. He certainly would not have wished ill fortune to Powell Hill, but he was too ambitious not to have begrudged such sudden eminence and responsibility for men of no greater rank than himself.

Arnall slouched in his saddle, ignoring bursting shells, while he studied a hastily scribbled ammunition report provided by Lieutenant Fullenwiler, the brigade quartermaster. Fortunately, the brigade had scarcely been engaged since setting out on the march around Pope three—no, four days ago; time had flown by like a shell whistling overhead and the men's cartridge boxes had been refilled at Manassas.

"Trains parked just beyond Sudley Ford." Fullenwiler, a man of statistics and reports, was not so oblivious as Arnall to the continuing shell bursts. "We kin restock pretty easy."

And they'd have to, if it turned out to be a long day of fighting. Arnall watched Fullenwiler's shoulders jerk as another flight of shells exploded fifty yards beyond them; but the lieutenant kept taut control of his face. Not his eyes, Arnall thought, noting to himself to get a new quartermaster.

He jammed the ammunition report in his side pocket. "Take some of Spark's men and double the reserve boxes now. Garntee we gone need'em."

Before long, from the wooded ridge 500 yards to the rear and considerably higher than the railway line, Confederate guns opened with a roar—four batteries anyway, Arnall's practiced ear soon determined. A cheer went up from the troops massed in the tight angle of their flank position; and soon the shellfire bursting on them slackened noticeably as the Yank cannoneers began to duel with the Reb batteries.

By the time Corporal Gilmore came back and spoke briefly to the general, the sun stood clear and malignant in the eastern sky over the Federal artillery positions. Gilmore's information tended to confirm Arnall's instinct, and in battle he trusted his instincts more than anything except God and discipline. God-given instinct could tell you what was coming and what to do; but discipline made it possible for officers and men to do what had to be done. Thus, discipline was Hoke Arnall's credo, perfectly compatible with his profound belief in a living and watchful God; only discipline, Arnall believed, gave men the strength to put God's sometimes painful and demanding will into practice.

He spurred Rambler to where Colonel Sparks had his Tar Heels lying down under the shellfire. Arnall called Sparks to his side and leaned down confidentially.

"Colonel, we got Germans in those woods. Two brigades of 'em so far. Now here's what I aim to do . . ."

He spoke confidently, steadily for more than a minute. When he finished and rode away, Sparks hastily gathered his officers around him. The crack of musketry was closer now and Arnall could tell that his picket lines, falling back slowly, had almost reached his main line, so that before long the brigade would feel the full weight of the enemy. From the volume of shelling and musketry, he knew it would be heavy; and within his tight perimeter, the angle made by the railroad cut and the rail fence, there would be little or no room for any kind of maneuver. He would be able to watch virtually every man in action, even if on foot himself.

Reluctantly, he swung down from the saddle—it lessened his sense of command not to be on horseback—and looked around for young Folsom. The orderly was nowhere in sight and Arnall, the tension of battle rising, swore as round an oath as he permitted himself.

"Blast you, Folsom! Get up here!"

The boy came hurrying from behind a clump of underbrush, buttoning his trousers. A staff officer, grinning, watched him pass.

"Where the devil you been, Folsom?" Arnall knew, but the boy needed discipline anyway.

"Call of nature, sir!" Folsom's face was crimson. In the hot morning sun, he was already perspiring; sweat ran in trickles from under his forage cap.

"Well, when I want you here, I want you *here!*" Arnall held out the reins. "I want you where I can see you, understand?"

"Yes*sir!*" Folsom took the reins and snapped to rigid attention.

"Well, go on, man!" Arnall glared at him in disgust. "Take Rambler to the rear, but keep 'im saddled. And bring back my pistol. Snap it up, now!"

Folsom stumbled away, leading the stalwart bay he knew the general treasured; so much as a scratch on that glistening hide and Folsom had no doubt he would pay for it. The staff officer leered at him as he passed.

"Next time piss yuh pants, boy! Ironass got no time to wait."

Amid the furious noise of the cannonade and the crackling of musket fire, Josh Beasly lay on his side, at ease against the forward rise of the railroad cut, his head just below the top. Good place to fight, he thought; but that was not the main reason Josh looked forward to the day.

He had been too far off to hear Ironass's exchange with the calf-eyed orderly, but even at a distance Josh had seen the fear of the boy's face and the way he jumped like he had a bee up his bung.

"At low-down sucker." Josh muttered to himself. Foxy Bradshaw, lying facing him a yard away, read his lips.

"You really gone do it, Josh?" Foxy's face lit at the thought, though his bowels were churning with fear. Too late now to head for the shithole and never come back.

"Shut yuh goddam mouth."

Josh looked uneasily at the second line of troops waiting somewhat beneath them on the floor of the railroad cut—men of McCrary's South Carolina regiment, most of whom he did not know. Josh had no use for South Carolinians anyway. Snotty bastards.

"A good day for it." Foxy leered over his rifle barrel at an imaginary target, trying to cover fear with conversation. "Cooped up here like settin hens."

"Shut up, dammit!"

But Josh knew Foxy was right. He watched Ironass stomping around like cock-a-doodle-do. Sonomabitch wearin at fancy jacket like it don't make'im red meat for a sharpshooter.

The orderly came running with a pistol in a leather holster on a belt.

"Hey, Meat . . . Ironass gittin on his peashooter."

Lige Flournoy winked at Josh, neither of them flinching from a shell burst nearby. Foxy buried his face in the dirt, holding back a scream, trying to scrunch his peter protectively into the earth.

"Can't hit shit with at thang."

But Josh was thinking, *Not just for no goddam Yank in a tree, neither*.

Hoke Arnall carefully buckled the pistol belt around his gray tunic and settled the holster on his right hip. He was well aware of his junior officers watching him. He knew the pistol was a kind of badge—he had deliberately cultivated that idea. It was a .44-caliber Colt revolver, U.S. Army issue, that he'd had since his Indian fighting days in Texas and New Mexico. But what the other officers really noticed was the ornate leather holster he'd picked up from a Mex in the Rio Grande Valley in exchange for an army-issue canteen. Nothing regulation about that holster, decorated as it was with two silver discs, but Arnall had made a habit of buckling it on before battle. Of course, generals seldom got close enough to the enemy to use a pistol or any other weapon, but the ritual had come to be expected of him, just as some officers always buckled on a ceremonial or family heirloom sword before going into action, or Powell Hill put on his red shirt. Battle rites.

Arnall drew the revolver, half-cocked it, and spun the cylinder. All five chambers were loaded with paper cartridges and capped; the General carefully let the hammer down between the nipples, resting its head against the cylinder. The Minié balls were screeching frequently but the shellfire seemed to him to be slackening somewhat; so the attack would be coming in any minute.

He strode into the railroad cut—a tall, erect man with strapping shoulders, looking neither to right nor left. Stepping between Josh Beasly and Foxy Bradshaw, leaning into the sharp rise of the cut—about four feet deep at that point and slanting about forty-five degrees—Arnall stepped without hesitation to the crest and turned his broad back on the enemy fire.

"Men!" His roaring voice carried even above the rising crash of musketry. He pointed dramatically to his left. "This army depends on you today!"

A cheer went up along the line, most heartily from the well-protected South Carolina troops in the bottom of the cut.

"The enemy is attackin our front. Gin'al Jackson sends word . . . you *must* hold . . . at all costs!"

Even Lige ripped out a high-pitched yell at that. Ironass was one thing but Ol Jack was something else.

Arnall was striding away, along the top of the cut, so that his words barely came back to Josh Beasly through the din of the fire rising from the woods. Show-off bastard, Josh thought. Had to fight inna line some day, we'd see how much real guts he got.

". . . no firin until you get the order, men! Front line fire'n fall back. Second line up the bank . . fire'n fall back . . ."

All of which their company officers had already told them, but generals had to do something. Josh checked his piece. Tamped down and cocked back.

"Come on, Yanks!"

Josh was suddenly impatient, and not just for Yanks. He rolled over, careful of the brandy bottle stuffed into his waistband, and inched farther up the bank until he could just see the woods beyond. His sweat-stained old hat was pulled low over his eyes, and he realized that sweat was pouring from its brim, across his forehead. And the sun not yet head-high.

Nothing was moving in the woods but branches and leaves whipped about by Minié balls. Then, suddenly, the last line of butternut pickets was ducking and trotting back between the trees, bent low, as if the men were out hunting for turkey. The Yanks wouldn't be a hundred yards behind, Josh thought; he got his musket over the top and settled its stock firmly against his shoulder.

Just then Ironass came striding back along the top of the cut, peashooter in hand. Struttin like a goddam peacock. He stopped directly above Lige Flournoy, his back still to the Yankee fire, took off his hat, and waved it over his head as if signaling.

"Now, Tar Heels!" he yelled. "Give it to 'im!"

With a yell that pierced the rumble of the guns and the crack of musketry, Sparks's North Carolina regiment ran charging over the knoll, down its front slope and across the railroad cut, through the South Carolinians kneeling at its bottom and Dixon's riflemen sprawled above them. Hardly bothering to watch where they stepped, the Tar Heels, in a compact battle line and still yelling, bounded over the edge of the cut and in long, ground-eating strides made for the woods.

Goddam, Lige Flournoy thought. Can't even wait for'em to git here.

But as the Tar Heel battle line surged into the edge of the woods, Lige heard himself yelling, too.

By the middle of the nineteenth century the earth of Prince William County and the plains around Manassas had been heavily tilled for more than a hundred years. Most of the county's forests had long since fallen to the axe, and only occasional stands of timber and brush interrupted the pastures and fields that lay on the rolling hills. Scattered haphazardly on the landscape like a child's building blocks were a number of unpainted farm houses, like that of Durward P. Brace, and a few more substantial dwellings—such as the fifty-year-old Stone House at the intersection of the Warrenton Pike and the Sudley Springs Road, and Liberia, the brick mansion on the Manassas–Centreville Road that had served as headquarters first for the Confederate General Pierre G. T. Beauregard, later for Irvin McDowell, and had been visited by Jefferson Davis as well as Abraham Lincoln.

In the early morning of August 29, 1862, as Arnall's Brigade braced for the Federal assault on Jackson's left, an observer on a hill that rises just south of the Warrenton Pike, between Gainesville and Groveton and not far west of Durward Brace's house, would have had a panoramic view eastward to Centreville, eight or nine miles distant on the heights, beyond Bull Run. So unobstructed was the visibility from this hilltop that later in the battle about to unfold, General J. E. B. Stuart sited his headquarters there; and afterward it became known as Stuart's Hill.

That clear, hot summer morning, even without field glasses, an observer on the hill would have been able to see—over the winding dirt lanes, the occasional thick patches of woodland, the ploughed fields, the corn rows and pastures of the Brace, Monroe, and Cole farms—almost the whole of the battlefield of July 1861, where northern and southern armies first had clashed. A year later, virtually at such an observer's feet, a large part of John Pope's Army of Virginia would have been in plain view, before the dust of moving brigades and the black powder smoke of artillery fire began to obscure details.

As the sun rose above the ruins of Manassas Junction—visible to the southeast from Stuart's Hill—Reynolds's small division of McDowell's Corps was some distance south of the pike, fronting northwest, not far from Groveton crossroads. Reynolds's left had been exposed the night before when the Federal General King, in poor health and perhaps unnerved by the ferocity of the battle John Gibbon and Jackson had so suddenly fought, retreated with his division to Manassas. But Reynolds was tenuously in touch with Sigel's Corps on his right. In the confused marching of Pope's effort to "bag the whole crowd"—first aimed at Manassas, then at Centreville—Sigel's three divisions had camped the night before near the intersection of the pike and the Sudley Springs Road, a little more than a mile from the Stone Bridge over Bull Run. They had been within cannon shot of Brawner's farm but had made no effort to join the battle.

Following Pope's orders to attack Jackson at first light, Sigel's troops, in early morning, were deployed in a slant across the pike—Brigadier General Robert Schenck's Division south of it at Groveton crossroads and on the left of Sigel's line, nearest Reynolds's Pennsylvanians; Brigadier General Robert Milroy's Division north of the pike in Sigel's center; Brigadier General Carl Schurz's Division on Sigel's right, farther north of the pike and stretching east to the Sudley Springs Road.

Beyond the Stone Bridge and Bull Run, under a cloud of dust, the pike to Centreville and the distant hilltop village itself were crowded with Federal troops—Kearny's, Hooker's, and Reno's Peninsula veterans headed west toward the battle Sigel had opened. Once they reached the field, and King's Division followed Porter's column up from Manassas as ordered, Pope would confront Stonewall Jackson with approximately 60,000 Federal troops.

Jackson's force was less visible. Beyond the pike Sudley Mountain rose forbiddingly against the hot sky; it was wooded enough so that most of the Confederate battle line on its lower slopes, along the old railroad right-of-way, was masked from view. From the right and center of that line, however, open fields of fire sloped gently down for more than half a mile to the pike and to Young's Branch twisting lazily back and forth across it.

Jackson's extreme right, the southwest terminus of his line, was near the crossing of the right-of-way and the pike, well to the west of Brawner's farm, where the sanguinary conflict of the night before had been fought to a bitter draw. There, Jackson had placed Early's Brigade and Forno's, of Ewell's Division, both brigades still under Early's command, both fully visible from Stuart's Hill. Early had sent two regiments south of the pike near the base of the hill.

To the left of Early and Forno in Jackson's line of battle, and nearly a mile distant from them, was Taliaferro's Division, with the Stonewall Brigade in its ranks and Brigadier General William E. Starke in command. Beyond Starke's four understrength brigades—the Stonewall alone had lost nearly 200 men at Brawner's and could put no more than 400 men in the field that morning, scarcely more than most regiments—the rest of Ewell's Division, consisting of A. R. Lawton's and Isaac Trimble's brigades, under the command of Lawton, held the center. Hill's Division, more than two and a half miles away and invisible in the woods near Sudley Springs, completed the line.

In that battle line, Jackson deployed only 18,000 muskets to Pope's near 60,000. But the Confederate front was only about two miles long (not including the gap between Early's two brigades and the rest of the butternut troops). So, had every Reb been in the front line rather than some in reserve, about five muskets per running yard would have been pointed at the Federals.

All or most of Pope's men and some of Jackson's would have been visible that morning to an observer on Stuart's Hill and probably would have riveted his attention. He might therefore not

have looked over his shoulder, past Jackson's right flank and
northwest of Gainesville, or seen the dust cloud just beginning to
rise far out on the road down from Thoroughfare Gap.

With Miss Letty's handkerchief securely tucked into his jacket
against his breast, Major Jesse Thomas was almost lighthearted
as he rode beside General Longstreet; and the stump of his arm
was itching as it always did when a fight was near. The corps had
been on the road since just after dawn, and every step in the
choking dust was taking it nearer reunion with the other half of
Lee's army.

Only thing is, Thomas thought, rubbing his stump against his
side, I'd have the boys goin all out, I was in command. But there
was no hurrying Ol Pete, although they could see the smoke of
battle rising off to the left, maybe five or six miles ahead. When
Thomas had raised the question not long after sighting the smoke,
Longstreet—sitting his horse as solidly as a packsaddle—shook
his head.

"Jackson knows we're comin. He needs us to hurry, he could
send word."

And a few minutes later, in his decisive way, as if he had been
further thinking over the matter:

"Better let'em take their natural swing. No use wearin'em out
on the road."

Well, nobody knew better what he was doing than Longstreet.
Besides, General Lee, the Old Man himself, was riding up ahead
with his escort. If *he* wanted a faster pace, he could certainly order
it. Except that after the way Longstreet had carried Thoroughfare
Gap, it wasn't likely that even Lee would be telling him too much
about how to handle troops.

Thomas had been right, the evening before; not knowing what
size force Pope might have sent to plug up the Gap, Longstreet
had sent orders to the advance brigade to hold off attacking and
to feel out their situation. The twilight skirmish had raised the
dangerous possibility that Pope was holding the passage with enough
men to check Longstreet; Ol Pete said to Thomas that that was
what *he'd* do anyway, was he in Pope's saddle, so that he could
then turn on Jackson and overwhelm him at leisure.

So in the night, dark as it was, and in tangled and steep terrain,
Longstreet sent three brigades under Cadmus Wilcox scrambling
three miles north to Hopewell Gap—a higher and less usable cut

through the Bull Run range. At the same time, Hood's Texans, plainsmen though they might once have been, climbed and crawled a mere footpath over the top of the mountain through which Thoroughfare cut its gap. At sunup, Jones's detached brigade was moving through Thoroughfare against the Federal front; Hood was ready to attack one flank of what scouts had reported to be Ricketts's Division of McDowell's Corps; and Wilcox, with mustaches flowing down his cheeks like hanging vines, was in position to envelop the Yanks from the other flank.

"But them clodhoppin sons wa'nt even there," a courier from Jones later reported through Major Thomas to Longstreet. "Skedaddle sometime last night, best we could figure out."

Longstreet and the Old Man had puzzled over what that meant. Why send a division to hold an important mountain pass, then pull it out before it had fired more than a few skirmishers' shots— especially when those few had been set off by the approach of the enemy force you aimed to block? The only reasonable answer seemed to be that Pope needed Ricketts's men for the assault on Jackson even more than he needed them to block Longstreet. That rationale was what had caused Jesse Thomas's early anxiety about the unhurried pace of the march.

But the undeniable fact was that without a fight and before the dew was dry on the mountain ivy lining the two faces of Thoroughfare Gap, Ol Pete's leading brigades were through and marching to the rescue. Thomas touched Miss Letty's handkerchief with his stump. Maybe, he thought, it'll be a good luck piece for us; maybe that's what got us through the Gap.

Phil Keefe had been a half mile from Manassas Junction when daylight came. He was still crawling and the Federal wagon driver who soon spotted him—a Michigan man—was not sure at first whether he was seeing a man or some weird southern animal flushed from deep woods by the advance of the armies. But when the driver determined that the dusty, bloody apparition at the side of the road was indeed a man—a Federal soldier at that, dragging a mangled leg behind him—he immediately dismounted to help. No one else had noticed Phil Keefe for more than eight hours.

By then, Keefe was in no sense a reasoning creature, nor was his snail's progress along the littered road either a conscious matter of direction or a disciplined physical effort. The dismounted driver approached a sort of automaton, whose limbs and muscles moved not because Keefe willed them to but because some indomitable pulse of life within his mutilated body kept that hulk lurching and bucking along in spasmodic convulsions. Keefe was like a man in a late stage of dying, whose terminal shudders refused to cease; and it was these inexplicable quivers of persistent life that propelled him along the road to Manassas.

So when the driver tried to stop him, tried to get an arm around his torso, tried to get some response from him, Keefe's body kept crawling on. It was not aware of the driver, nor did whatever consciousness still flickered within it even register the Michigan man's exclamations. Keefe kept lunging along the road like an unspeakable mutation of agony, terror, and primeval urges to live and kill.

A platoon of pickets coming off duty finally helped the driver get Keefe into the wagon; but even as they carried him, gently as they could—even after he was wrapped in the driver's own blanket on the floorboards—the husk of his life continued to jerk and reach in imitation of its long crawl along the road to Manassas.

The driver quickly climbed into his saddle on the near pole mule and seized the long single rein to the near leader, with which he controlled his six-mule team.

"Yay up, you slat-sided hammerheads!"

The wagon was an empty that had followed Ricketts's Division down from Thoroughfare Gap, then got lost in the dark night. Cursing his mules lovingly, the Michigan man rattled at a trot on into Manassas, as anxious to be rid of his repulsive cargo as to get back to his outfit, wherever it was.

The bouncing of the wagon on the rough road sent such excruciating impulses from Phil Keefe's maimed leg to his nearly moribund brain that they acted upon it like a deep needle into its secret centers. By the time the Michigan man delivered him to an overworked sawbones, sleepless after two nights of duty at a field hospital General Hooker had ordered set up in the ruins of the supply depot, Keefe was not yet conscious; but the will to live sparked feebly in his being.

"Look like at leg et by a grizzly." The Michigan man was anxious, for some reason, not to be thought associated with the filthy object he had brought in. "And don't he stink!"

"You would, too, shape he's in." The sawbones peered at Keefe's wound with interest.

The Michigan man climbed back into his saddle. "Heerd 'nything 'bout Ricketts's Division?"

"Wiped out to a man." The sawbones winked. "You the only one left to take command." For all he knew, the way they were running the cases in on him, it could even have been true.

Not far from that hospital, Reverdy Dowd was falling in the Sixth Wisconsin. New orders from Pope. Seem like there were *always* new orders from Pope.

But for a change Dowd at least knew where the Sixth was going. After no more than two hours' sleep, following the nightmare march to Manassas, he had set officers to work rounding up rations for the men, then had gone dutifully in search of news of Colonel Bullock. He found none, except that some wounded had been sent in ambulances to a hospital depot near Centreville, others to the nearest point on the O & A, east of Bull Run, where trains could take them on into Alexandria. Still others were being treated in the makeshift hospitals at Bristoe and Manassas.

But no one had seen Colonel Bob—not even Captain J. D. Black, Gibbon's ubiquitous staff man, who had an ear for gossip and rumor, sometimes even fact, that reminded Dowd of a huge clothes hamper full of dirty linen into which an occasional clean shirt was thrown by mistake.

"Hell of a horse he was riding," Blackie said over coffee and hard biscuits at Gibbon's headquarters cookfire. "My guess is he got himself to Centreville but what the hell. Way things were last night he could be in Timbuctoo for all I know. General says the regiment's yourn till further notice."

Dowd was pleased but not surprised. Naturally, he wanted to find Colonel Bullock if he could, see that he was all right. But he had known in the haunted and harrowing night, and had felt all over again when he awoke among the men of the Sixth, sleeping where they had fallen in the predawn hour of their arrival at Manassas, that it was *his* regiment now. They all owed a lot to Colonel Bob—his hard camp discipline, interminable drilling, and meticulous concern for their health and morale—but Dowd sensed that he had taken over the regiment the way a man might put on a familiar old suit of clothes that fitted him better than anyone.

"Preciate the general's confidence."

Blackie sipped coffee loudly. They were sitting on the tongue of a wrecked limber. The smell of powder smoke, charred wood, burnt bacon, and horse droppings still hung over Manassas like fog.

"Got to make do with what he's got. Best we can figure so

far, we lost above seven hundred k, w, and missing last night. Second Wisconsin lost near bout three hundred by itself."

Dowd whistled. Out of five hundred that had gone in.

"But the boys gave as good as they got, Blackie. Mine did anyway."

He hardened himself to think of casualties as numbers, not men. Easy enough once you couldn't hear their groans or see their blood or the way they sprawled in death.

"So'd they all. Good training pays off, Gibbon says."

"So then why . . ." Dowd measured his words carefully. "Why not stay where we were, wait for the rest of the army to come up, and fight 'em again today?" The sound of Sigel's guns to the north made his blood race; he remembered the supple feel of the Sixth responding to his commands.

Blackie looked around elaborately, as if to spot eavesdroppers. "Old King lost his bottom. Leastways that's how I see it. But Gibbon claims *he* voted for retreat, too." He tossed the remnant of his coffee into the fire. "You believe that, you'll believe shit don't smell. These West Pointers hang together."

"But we fought 'em down to the shuck!"

"Thing was, when we come off the field and King come to talk it over with Gibbon and the other brigadiers, we got word from Ricketts that he couldn't hold Thoroughfare Gap and Longstreet'd be coming through this morning. Gibbon says the way they figured it, if they held still they'd of been facing Jackson *and* Longstreet today. Besides, the only orders King had at that time was to march to Centreville. Looked like the only way to get there was round through Manassas."

Dowd chewed over this information while Captain Black hustled off at Gibbon's shout. Bitterly, the major reflected that Blackie probably had the right of it: King had panicked. Now here they were, out of whatever was going on over there near last night's battleground. And if Blackie knew his beans, Longstreet was coming to join Jackson.

Captain Black came hustling back, looking important; but then he always did.

"Better get cracking, Rev. We're going with Porter."

Porter was out of McClellan's army. Dowd bristled immediately.

"Hell, Blackie, we're McDowell's Corps."

"But nobody's seen McDowell since late yesterday. That's why King was on his own last night."

"But what are we going to do with Porter?"

"March to Gainesville." Blackie swung into his saddle. "You want to fight so bad, that ought to suit you right down to the ground."

Sergeant Owen L. Cade of Company D, Thirteenth Georgia, was impatient with the lack of action on Lawton's front. Cady did not usually pine for action, being too wise a veteran for such foolishness. He was eagerly aware that morning, however, that he was still in command of the company, all its officers having gone down the evening before, and Captain Glover, who'd had to take over the whole regiment, being too preoccupied to recommend new company officers. When he did, Cady had a good chance to make lieutenant, which was more than any poor son of a one-mule tobacco farmer had a right to expect. But the Yanks were not cooperating. Real fight over to the left but not out front here. Em sons take one look at our line'n back off.

Cady was lying on the front slope of the railroad cut—a formidable natural defense line from which he did not much blame the Yanks for shying away. He watched with interest as a new bluebelly regiment marched out, lined up, gave a cheer, and started up the slope toward the cut. A fancy Yank officer, dressed to the teeth, led the way on a brown horse that looked like somebody'd shined'im up with tallow.

Trimble had passed the word to hold fire until the Yanks got close enough they could smell their breath. But Cady was feeling in command of more than Company D that morning and was hot to clinch his bars. He watched the pretty major on the shining horse leading the Yank brigade up the slope toward the cut. Mighty brave, aintchuh?

The major kept coming, proud as a house cat on his high-stepping horse. Behind him, his regiment didn't look half so happy to come calling. Cady believed in popping off the leaders; but when he drew a bead on the major, it was really only to keep in practice. He didn't actually plan to snuff him. But just then, the horseback major turned and waved his sword at his following troops. That was too much out of a picture book for Cady, who hated playacting.

Ah shit, he thought, and squeezed the trigger.

The piece bucked on his shoulder, the muzzle blast rang in his ears. The major went off the horse and lay still, blue against the broomsedge.

"Christamighty," the New Man said. "That open up'is collar button for'im."

Privates J. F. Sowell and Gillum Stone were a resourceful pair, hard fighters, skilled foragers, and—when they chose—adept malingerers. Since the Stonewall Brigade—"What's left of it," Sowell complained to Gilly—was on the right of the line and all the action that morning was on the left and center, they had no difficulty in drifting down through the woods and onto the trampled and littered pastures of Brawner's farm.

"They uz any webfoot'n this army I thought'd make it thew," Gilly said, "it uz ol Lott. Smart's he was'n lucky too."

"The wrong day. Put the sign on'im."

They tramped past Brawner's deserted house and barn and down the slope. A few other men moved over the field—medical details, troops looking for fallen friends, a platoon with a wagon collecting firearms. A burial detail was digging a mass grave near the orchard. To the northeast, the noise of battle had risen to a roar; smoke rose white against a glassy sky.

Sowell and Stone walked on in the hot early sunshine, through the littered broomsedge; wild flowers, purple and yellow in the fresh morning, bloomed incongruously in the debris of battle— canteens, bayonets, hats, shoes, human extremities, dead horses, cap boxes, flung muskets. Gilly kicked aside a knapsack and a redbound book bounced from it against a saddle on what was left of a horse. Sowell picked up a dead meadowlark without a visible wound and threw it away. The stench of powder smoke, spilled blood, bloating flesh spread over the hillside like a pall; but the two veterans scarcely noticed. The smell was as familiar to them as the feel of the muskets in their hands.

"Lessee." Sowell stopped. "We come down the hill right around here, didn't we?"

"More overt the right, I'd say. Oughtta be easy to find 'im, at red-check shirt a-hissen."

They walked on and Sowell pointed down the hill. "Bout right down ther they uz givin us the blazes..." His voice broke off and they stopped abruptly, staring.

"Goddlemighty," Gilly said, after awhile.

The bodies lay in straight lines, as if troops on the march had lain down to rest in the waving broomsedge. At some parts of the line less than a hundred yards apart, blue and butternut lay where

they had fallen in ranks as straight as a drillmaster could wish.
Behind each line, more bodies were scattered patchily on the slope,
mute testimony to how men may stagger or be thrown backward
when struck by flying iron or lead. In the pitiless Virginia sun,
the pattern of the bodies made the pattern of the battle as plain
upon the earth as if a general had drawn a diagram with a stick.

"You ever seen the beat-a that?"

Sowell's question needed no answer. From far to their left, a
few shells came arching overhead, strays from the Federal center.
They landed harmlessly on the ridge. Paying them no mind, Gillum
Stone braced his musket butt on the ground and stared over the
silent, sprawled remains of the evening battle.

"One line don't look no diffrunt from th'other'n, somehow."

"It aint," Sowell said. "He ought to be lyin over there aways."

They walked along Ol Jack's line of dead. Most of the wounded,
save a few too shattered to move, had been carried off. One or
two of those remaining muttered and groaned as they passed; one
cursed them, glaring with mad bulging eyes. But most of the faces
they saw were blank and stiff, the silent grimaces of death fixed
upon them like Halloween masks.

"Ol Busthead lyin ther," Gilly said. "Had'is last drink."

"Our compny all right. Hycr's Cottonmouth. Lott oughtta be
right round-yere someres."

They went on five yards, ten yards.

"Mought of passed'im," Sowell said. "You go on aways. I'll
check back."

He peered closely as scattered bodies behind that part of the
front line, covering a circle about twenty-five yards in circumference. Lightless eyes stared back at him and rictus jaws exposed,
here and there, gold or lead teeth to the sun. Sowell was shocked
to find Greasy Dick Rucker. Dint know he uz snuffed. But he
found no one in a red-checked shirt, no one with even the dead
shadow of Lott McGrath's horsey, grinning face or his thick yellow
hair.

"Sowbelly!" Gilly's voice, across the patches of dead, was
hushed but carrying. He beckoned urgently, and Sowell, picking
his way between corpses and wounded, hurried to his side.

Gilly pointed to a musket lying in the broomsedge. Clear in
the morning sun, Sowell could see on the worn butt the carved
initials LM.

"Bound to of been rightchere." Gilly pointed to a body lying
nearby, with a leg bent back under it. "Capus Warner ther. He

alluz stuck near usunses. But I aint seen Lott yet."

They searched carefully for another five minutes, gingerly turning over the face-down dead to be sure. More errant shells from the Yank battery came over, doing no harm. The sound of gunfire rolled down shatteringly from the northeast, and the sun beat fiercely on the dead. Flies swarmed on the corpses, thick as bees around a hive.

"He aint here," Gilly said at last.

Sowell nodded somberly and squinted at another flight of shells going over to his left.

"He *said* it uz the wrong day, Gilly. No wonder we aint found'im."

Gilly stared at him, awestruck. "But I *seen'* im go over deader'n Capus ther. He just natchrally *got* to be here, Sowbelly, he..."

"Aint nothin natchral bout it." Private Sowell picked up the musket marked LM. "Fightin on the wrong day."

Some distance across the hillside, near the center of what had been Jackson's line, Andrew Peterson had finished exposing a plate with his lens pointed at a stiffly sprawled body. Peterson had no way of knowing that the corpse was that of Fargo Hart's friend Kirk Connelly, or even that there ever had been such a person. But something in the flung-down form—one leg drawn up as if in climbing, the other extended full-length, the long arm stretched above the head with the pistol still clutched in the dead hand—had caught Peterson's alert eye. The body not only looked strangely as if frozen in flight—which, in a sense, it was; in its reaching posture, it also seemed to Peterson to suggest pathetically the way these eager boys clutched at life while dealing in death, descended into the dark even as they grasped for the sun.

"Aint got many mo plates," Joe Nathan said.

"This is the last one for now." Peterson hurried for the Whatsit Wagon a few feet away, carrying the exposed plate in its shield. As he moved, flies rose from the mess that had been the back of Kirk Connelly's head. "Bring the camera along."

"I gittin it."

Peterson had long since learned that Joe Nathan handled the equipment—by which he was still largely mystified—as lovingly as the photographer would have himself. Joe Nathan had once been the property of Peterson's wife; now he was a free Negro, manumitted several years before by Peterson himself after he had taken over his wife's abandoned property. Then a skinny youth, Joe Nathan had worked ever since for small wages and his keep, first as handyman at the Pantheon in Atlanta, since the war as driver and equipment handler in the field.

Joe Nathan was brave, reliable, and handy; he had rigged a folding step for the back of the Whatsit Wagon, so that Peterson could get to his chemicals as rapidly as possible. Over the bed of the wagon, following Mathew Brady's well-publicized example on almost the same battlefield a year earlier, Peterson had built a wooden enclosure lined with canvas that completely shut out sunlight when the rear door was closed. The interior was fitted out as a darkroom and provided storage for plates, chemicals, and the bulky, boxlike camera and its tripod.

The biggest problem was that in summer, especially in Virginia, the Whatsit Wagon was stiflingly hot. The sun beat relentlessly on its roof and sides, turning the inside into an oven in which not a breath of air stirred. As Peterson stepped into the wagon that morning, he began to perspire immediately; he felt like a chicken in a roasting pan.

The tinted lanterns that provided a subdued orange glow added to the heat; but Peterson could spare no time to fret, lest the collodion coating on the plate dry and the silver nitrate crystallize. With practiced hands he took the exposed plate from the shield and let pyrogallic acid flow over it, careful to waste none of the scarce stuff. Then he watched the never-failing miracle, as he considered it, of the image beginning to appear, dimly at first, then rapidly becoming brilliant. In the orange light, he found himself looking again at the body of Kirk Connelly, truly frozen this time, preserved in chemical and glass forever.

Peterson was too much of a professional to linger in admiration over his own work, and too accustomed to war to pause long in contemplation of its excrescences. Quickly he washed the plate in water—warm enough, in the heat of the Whatsit Wagon, to shave in. Next he poured a solution of potassium cyanide over the developed plate to rid it of any remaining silver salts. After giving the plate a more complete bath in the warm water, he held it near the hot lantern, moving it rapidly in the air to dry; then he varnished the plate and the job was done.

He looked at the image briefly, once again. Good. Worth keeping. Carefully he stored the plate away in the filing racks Joe Nathan guarded like treasure. Well, those plates *were* treasure;

there was truth in them. In some of them anyway.

Peterson blew out the lantern, opened the door, and sprang to the ground, ignoring the folding stair in his haste to be out of the bake-oven interior. Even in the direct sun, it was far cooler outside. Joe Nathan leaned against a rear wheel, the camera cradled in his arms like a child.

"Some fight over thataway." He nodded toward the smoke rolling whitely into the sky.

"Oh . . . sure is."

When he was working, Peterson was nearly oblivious to his surroundings; he had hardly noticed the rising crack of gunfire. So Pope did come, he thought, just like the Britisher said he would.

Shells were coming closer to Brawner's, too, though there was no evidence of infantry activity nearby. Down the slope to the pike, up it past the farmhouse and barn to the woods, the morning was hot, brilliant, still. Only a few men moved like ragpickers along the straight lines of dead, and the burial detail was still at work near the orchard. Flies swarmed everywhere.

"Let's get up under the trees'n cool off." Stray shells made Peterson uneasy. Gunfire in battle was targeted, more or less predictable; but batteries firing for practice, or to harass, could be as random as fate.

Joe Nathan loaded the camera into the wagon and secured it to the brackets prepared for it. Then he mounted the high front seat.

"Hum-up, mules!"

Peterson walked ahead, toward his horse tethered in the trees above. Now that his work for the morning was finished, he resolutely turned his back on Ol Jack's littered battlefield. Nothing he could do about it; nothing anyone could do about it. But the treasure of glass plates in the Whatsit Wagon could at least record the truth of it—the waste and destruction and senselessness, the absence of glory.

His long linen duster was draped over his saddle as he had left it. Peterson took a cigar and matches from its pocket, lit up, and sat under a tree while Joe Nathan brought the wagon into the shelter of the woods and tethered the mules—Positive and Negative, one light, one dark.

"Hot." Joe Nathan sat down facing him, about ten feet away, his back against a large oak tree. "Don't evuh seem to git dis hot'n Jawjuh."

"How many more plates you say we got left?" Peterson cocked his head ɔ the sound of another shell straying in their general direction.

"I make it maybe . . ."

But Peterson never learned Joe Nathan's count because it was lost in the suddenly rising scream of the stray, and because he had heard enough of battle to sense that this stray was coming *directly* at them. Peterson dived for the earth, trying to throw himself around and behind his tree, going as flat as he could, his arms instinctively around his head. From the corner of his eye, as he went down, he saw Joe Nathan stiffening against the tree that sheltered him, his lips pulled back stiffly over teeth startlingly white in his ebony face.

With his nose in pine straw, Peterson heard the *whock* of the ball striking a tree, like a giant's axe. The scream died abruptly and something burned his cheek; but he held still, tense against the ground, waiting for splinters or fragments to rend his body, a tree to fall on him, darkness coming down. He was not conscious of fear. In a second, he realized he was unhit, unhurt, except for the cigar ash burning the side of his face.

He hastily sat up and brushed his cheek. Hell of a way to get a scar, he thought. Then he checked the Whatsit Wagon; the mules were rearing in fright but the wagon and its cargo were safe.

"Close," he said out loud.

But Joe Nathan did not answer. He was still propped against the broad trunk of the oak, his clenched fists on his thighs, his shoulders hunched a little, as if drawn in for shelter. Above his shoulders, Peterson saw, there was nothing except a round, clean opening, like a ship's porthole, in the tree trunk. Peterson never did find Joe Nathan's head.

Duryea had reached Sigel with no difficulty and delivered Pope's orders forcefully. The German general did not remonstrate or send work back asking for reinforcements, and soon after daybreak his guns began to thunder—three batteries firing from a rise of ground near the crossroads at Groveton. But it seemed to Duryea a long time before skirmishers began creeping forward, he thought reluctantly, under cover of the guns; the skirmishers bent low to the earth and advanced slowly, as if searching for wild strawberries.

Their pace slackened when they encountered Reb resistance north of the pike. Duryea worked his way to the right toward Bull

Run, behind Sigel's front. To his eye, the blue troops crawling northward did not seem sufficiently aggressive; nor did their officers appear to be pushing them.

But Duryea was even more disturbed by his growing conviction that Pope had been wrong again. He could see no evidence that the Rebs were retreating, as the general supposed. The volume of artillery fire when their guns finally opened from the ridge, the number of skirmishers deployed to meet Sigel's leisurely attack, suggested that Jackson's men were dug in and full of fight. Duryea wanted to make certain of that before returning to Pope's headquarters.

Micah G. Duryea was a loyal soldier and a strong Union man, but he was beginning to lose confidence in John Pope's judgment. This new demonstration that the general, for all his ability to react quickly and his readiness to fight, tended to jump to unsupported conclusions reminded Duryea of the order to McDowell that had opened Thoroughfare Gap to any relief column Lee might have sent to Jackson.

On the horizon now, as he moved along the Sudley Springs road behind the slow—too slow—advance of General Carl Schurz, on Sigel's right, Duryea could see the blue rise of the Bull Run Mountains. Far over to his left, a notch in the skyline marked Thoroughfare Gap. Duryea wished he knew what, if anything, was happening there. Because if he was right and Jackson was not retreating but standing fast, then Stonewall was bound to believe that help was on the way through that notch in the hazy distance.

Teddy Redmund, conspicuous in his havelock but not in his movements, had taken post early that morning not far from a line of sixteen Confederate cannon placed on Sudley Mountain behind the left of Jackson's infantry lines. The booming guns and the shells screaming away from their muzzles were deafening, and the Federal batteries near the pike were sending back as much as they got. But Redmund was a professional soldier, despite his journalist's guise; after the first few rounds, he hardly noticed the noise or his own exposure.

In his correspondent's function, moreover, the Englishman had taught himself to ignore trivial details like noise and smoke and the deaths of men, to concentrate instead on the main lines of a battle's development. The articles of Sertorius thus conveyed little of the blood and terror of battle but had won an admiring audience among military men and drawing-room generals in his own country. They found Sertorius's descriptions of troop movements and gun positions and turning points and tactical moves clear and detailed, even when these represented events that ought to have taken place, rather than those that actually had happened.

If this approach to war reporting sometimes made Sertorius's accounts of battles clearer and more logical to readers than the fighting ever had been to the officers and men engaged in it, that was precisely what Teddy Redmund wanted—indeed, what seemed to him proper. He believed it necessary to translate the fumblings and stumblings of the American armies into something resembling the kind of patterned warfare to which he and other European students of the military arts were accustomed. How else could anyone make sense of such a loosely jointed war?

Up that morning at first light, Redmund had been surprised that the Federal force that had stood up to Jackson in the evening fight had moved out. Not a sign of it but its wounded and dead left on the field. Unsoldierly, that. He had rather thought that it would be Jackson who would have decamped, after having given Pope such clear but foolish notice of his whereabouts.

But Redmund was not shaken in his conviction that Pope now would come down on Jackson's divisions with all the force he could muster. Never get another such opportunity, Redmund reasoned.

So after the guns began to crash and growl on Jackson's left, where Hill's Division was posted, Redmund had lost little time in finding a good vantage point and breaking out his excellent English field glasses. Before long it became clear to him that the unseen blues advancing through the woods were coming in on Jackson's and Hill's extreme left—the latter apparently commanded by the rather rude young general who had nevertheless tacitly allowed him to follow Hill's Division from Centreville. Arnold, Redmund had noted down at the time. Brigadier Arnold.

That officer had a reasonably strong flank position, Redmund decided; but the ground he held was so limited and the regiments so packed into it that Redmund feared he would have trouble distinguishing their movements. And the look of the gap between Arnold and the next brigade to the right was ugly; so were the woods that rolled right up to the defense line at that point, giving good cover to an attack.

Redmund had already conceded to himself that the floundering

Jackson had at least had the sense or luck to set himself up rather nicely behind the old railway construction, with his guns elevated on the ridge behind. Not that that had taken genius, or could make up for the senseless attack of the evening before. And somebody's head should roll for the gap in the front, to the right of Brigadier Arnold.

The morning wore on. The attacking blues were taking their own good time, Redmund thought. But the sounds of their advances moved steadily, if slowly, nearer. At about half past ten, just as the volume of fire and the returning butternut skirmishers indicated that the blues were about to fall on him at last, Brigadier Arnold made a surprisingly good move. With the force of an artillery blast, the regiment that went yelling over the railroad cut ran head-on into the blue battle line coming cautiously through the trees. Bloody good counterstroke.

But even with his glasses, Redmund could not make out, through the battle smoke and the obscuring trees and underbrush, much of what happened next. He could reasonably suppose, however, that the surprise charge and the force with which the butternut regiment had gone in had caused the blues to give way.

The musketry from the woods crashed incessantly. Muzzle flashes stabbed through the smoke like sparks from a chimney. And after a few minutes, Redmund began to see wounded men straggling out of the woods, some crawling. The usual. He caught glimpses, too, of the backs of other butternuts, their line irregular, just within the woods. Pushed back, he thought. Blues rallied in the woods.

Just then Brigadier Arnold, apparently getting the same impression, moved again. A regiment that had crouched at the foot of the cut sprang up and ran for the woods, yelling barbarously. They angled to the left of the first butternut regiment, and Redmund reckoned—as he clinically observed pieces being moved on the battlefield chessboard—that the original Reb charge had caught the blues in center and on their left, forcing that part of their line back but allowing the blue right to swing around like a cracking whip on the left flank of the butternuts. Which would have been why their attack had been halted and pushed back. And why Brigadier Arnold had launched his second stroke against the right of the blues. Bloody Arnold appeared to have steady nerves.

• • •

Lying flat on the slope of the railroad cut, Josh Beasly was mad as a wet tomcat. It was not just that if Ironass kept the fight out in the woods while he strutted around behind, there'd be little chance to get a spot on the bastard. But as the second regiment went forward, one of the goddam South Carolina crackers had stepped down with a plundered Yank brogan squarely on Josh's left hand. Like to mash it flat. The hand hurt so bad he was no longer sure he could hold his barrel steady.

Josh hardly noticed, in his pain and anger, that the South Carolinians, falling in on the Tar Heel regiment's left as if they'd been one line all along, turned the tide again. But Corporal Amos Gilmore, standing not far from General Arnall out in front of the railroad cut, whooped as the Yank line, which had come surging back after the first counterattack, began to give way a second time. Gilmore thought he'd never heard hotter firing.

Corporal Gilmore stole a quick look over his brawny shoulder to make sure the boy was all right, back there with General Arnall's horse. Then he turned again to the battle in the woods—out of sight now as the Yanks gave ground—just as Hoke Arnall began to yell orders to Colonel Dixon.

Sam Stowe, his own regiment alert but unengaged along the fence, was balancing himself precariously on its top rail, unmindful in his planter's hat of the Minié balls whining over the embankment. He had watched admiringly and with not a little state pride as McCrary's South Carolina regiment bowled into the Yankee right just beyond the edge of the woods. South Carolina boys could whip a cattywhompus barehanded.

Too bad, however, the action was over there, rather than in front of his own angle of Arnall's flank position. But as Arnall said, sooner or later the Yanks were bound to try it across the cornfield. They were certainly catching the devil in those woods.

Just then, Dixon's Rifles, too, surged over the top of the railroad cut, howling like banshees, and lunged for the woods. That Arnall, Stowe thought in admiration. Perfect timing. Might chase 'em all the way to Manassas.

From his perch above, Redmund, too, noted that Brigadier Arnold had thrown this new punch at just the moment when the blues were reeling back. Equally important, he had put the third regiment in on the *right* of the original counterattack, extending a solid battle line all across his front. Redmund cursed the trees and the smoke, for once letting annoying details impede his concentration on position and maneuver.

• • •

Foxy Bradshaw was thanking his stars for those same trees, and
ducking behind every one he came to, for as long as he could.
He *knew* he was about to lose his whole works any minute now.
On either side of him the men of his company were blasting away,
but Foxy had not fired a shot since skulking out of the shelter of
the embankment. He stepped over men sprawled on the ground
as if they were mere logs in his path. But he knew all too well
that they were men like himself with peters and stones—men shot
in every part of the body, some with entrails hanging out, some
with jaws torn off, or a hole where the nose had been, or a blank
red splotch for an eye, or a gaping cavity for a crotch.

O law me Foxy thought, over and over. *O law me* I aint comin
outta these woods. Not whole I aint *o law me*.

His racing brain functioned with awful clarity, telling him to
drop in his tracks, fake a broken leg or maybe a toe, but then
reminding him that the woods might catch fire from hot lead and
powder blasts. He could not face the pain of shooting himself in
the foot or the hand. If he turned tail, Ironass would have him
shot or hung for sure.

Best thing is, go along. Duck behind trees. Far a shot ever
now'n then, git my bar'l hot. But *o law me* I'm a dead man soon.
Dead or undone.

Even in his terror, however, Foxy noticed that the Yanks were
going back fast. Somewhere ahead of him, Lige Flournoy trotted
along almost happily, dropping to one knee to fire, reloading and
trotting on, then stopping to fire again. The din of muskets going
off and the yelling of the men all around him were so loud that
Lige could hardly hear his own shots; but he could feel his piece
kick against his shoulder, comforting as a slap on the back. He
had a small chaw of tobacco, Yank issue plundered at Manassas
and just big enough to raise spit. It kept his mouth from going
dry with the yelling and the smoke.

Bullets whistled back at Lige but he was unconcerned. He had
a veteran's sense that this was just a skirmish to get things started.
Time enough to worry when the buttin'n gougin started. He dropped
to one knee, fired, and reloaded.

Just as he capped his musket, Lige saw through a rift in the
smoke a blue uniform dash from behind a tree. Lige pulled his
hammer to full cock and drew down on the running figure. But
as his finger began to tighten on the trigger, the target veered left.

A dead shot with his rifled musket, Lige still would have had time to drop him but his eye caught a flash of gold on the left shouder.

Lige rose and trotted on. He never shot at an officer, except one who was about to shoot at him.

"Alluz kill'em at's most like to kill you," he had instructed Foxy after Mechanicsville. "Kill privates, Meat, you gone kill anybody."

Just inside the southern fringe of the woods through which the Yanks were being driven, Charlie Keach crouched behind a tree, taking notes. Riding toward the scene of the night action as early as he could, he had found Schurz's troops moving and followed them closely, noting that Alexander Schimmelfennig's Brigade was on the right and that of Wladimir Krzyzanowski—in Keach's notes, KRZ—was on the left. Keach thought the Germans had gone in with spirit and determination and he was as surprised as they when the Rebs counterattacked into the woods.

He had made quick time back through the trees and underbrush, but not in panic. Keach had followed McClellan up the Peninsula and been in the thick of the action at Fair Oaks. After his newspaper colleagues first got a look at him there, Crounse of the *World* had said to Townsend of the *Herald*:

"That feller'd as lief go under fire as walk into an oyster house."

Mostly because of Keach's eagerness and his appetite for combat, Hale—his paper's Washington bureau chief—had pulled him off the Peninsula and sent him out with Pope's Army of Virginia. Hale, as usual, had chosen astutely; unlike the Peninsula, which had swarmed with correspondents assigned to McClellan, the Young Napoleon, Pope's Virginia campaign was going to be Charlie Keach's story alone. He did not aim to miss it. He watched Schurz's brigades giving ground back through the woods, noting many of the details for which Teddy Redmund had so little use—a private sitting against a persimmon tree, holding his intestines in his hands; a horse bolting for the rear, dragging a dead major with his foot hooked in the stirrup. Damn fool asked for it, going through woods on horseback.

Keach had about decided to get moving again, since the Rebs obviously were going to clear the woods, when a cheer went up behind him, just audible above the continuous musketry and the Rebs' infernal yelling. Odd how Rebs yelled and Federals cheered. That told Keach something but he was not sure what.

Just then, off to Keach's right, a regiment KRZ must have been holding in reserve dashed into the woods, between the two blue brigades that had made the first attack. Keach saw the new unit—identified by its colors as a New York outfit—stop, go down to one knee, aim; then, as if a single current of electricity had discharged every man's musket at once, the Yorkers poured a deafening volley into the smoke and confusion ahead of them.

If *they* had Rebs in their sights, Keach thought, they aint there now. Indeed, the reinforcements in the center appeared to have stiffened KRZ's and Schimmelfennig's men on either side. Over his shoulder, moreover, Keach could see two more blue regiments forming a battle line. He had no idea where they had come from but he let out an unjournalistic whoop. Damn Rebs not having everything their way *today,* by God.

Four miles east, on a hill just outside Centreville, Captain Duryea was reporting to General Pope and his staff. But before telling Colonel Russell that in his opinion Schurz's Germans were not pursuing retreating secesh troops but had stumbled against dug-in Rebs spoiling for a fight, Duryea had had a swift panoramic glimpse of the battle scene visible from the Centreville heights.

He could plainly make out, beyond the lush tree line bordering Bull Run, the white clouds rising from batteries behind both lines, the thinner smoke of small-arms fire rising above the treetops in between. Blue troops, in a steady impressive stream, were flowing westward along the pike toward the sound of guns rumbling like angry subterranean gods across the low hills of Virginia.

But what had caught Duryea's eye, even farther in the distance, was a dust cloud against the blue rise of the Bull Run Mountains. It stretched straight from the notch he knew to be Thoroughfare Gap toward where he reckoned Gainesville was. As he turned to look for Colonel Russell, Micah Duryea did not have to guess which troops *those* were, hurrying toward the battlefield Pope had chosen on the plains of Manassas.

Fargo Hart was watching the same dust cloud. Followed at a respectable distance by Brace on his mare and Henry bareback on a mule he handled as if it were a child's pony, Hart was trotting cross-country toward the Hay Market Road in search of General J. E. B. Stuart. He was uncomfortable to be in such company but, having committed himself, he felt he had no choice but to go through with his promise. A gentleman did what he said he would. Hart did not ask himself whether he was influenced by the fact that the unprepossessing Brace was Missy's father; he had put *that* firmly out of his mind.

Hart had spent too much of the morning searching for Stuart. But that tell-tale dust cloud, he reasoned, was bound to be rising above Longstreet's relief column; and he felt sure Stuart would be riding in that direction. And before long, Stuart did come trotting west along the Hay Market Road at the head of a cavalry regiment. The young general, his long beard flying like a pennant, gave Hart a cheery salute as he passed. The captain fell in stirrup-to-stirrup with Colonel Snowden, letting Brace and Henry fend for themselves.

Snowden pointed to the dust cloud out to their right.

"Just in time, Hart!"

"Looks like it."

All morning, Hart had been listening to the rising clatter of battle to the east, on the left of Jackson's line. As he had the afternoon before, he sensed in the distant sounds a circle closing, something decisive drawing nearer; and he had been bothered, as the day grew hot and humid and the dust rose from the country lanes in choking clouds, by the knowledge that he wanted to return to Missy as he had promised and hold her again in the night.

The ring of decision tightening around him, the need to break through it to Missy—Hart had never before felt his sense of self, of his place in the great pigeonhole desk, so uncertain. The duality of his attitude toward the war—his reluctance to let himself become part of it, as against his sense that his *place* was in it—had found its expression in his yearning for a child-woman whose sudden intrusion upon his consciousness was as implausible as it was irresistible.

Stuart soon called a halt. He had scouts out on both flanks and in front; he wanted another trailing on the left, in case Federal cavalry also might be moving from the pike to check that dust out toward Thoroughfare.

Hart seized the opportunity, rode forward, and saluted again. His shirt was drenched and clinging with sweat, and he felt the sun on the back of his neck like heat from a low fire.

"Gin'al . . . local farmer and his darky ridin with me. Say they want to scout for you."

"Know these parts pretty well, do they?" Stuart craned his neck for a sight of the volunteers, who were coming slowly past his halted troops.

"I'd say so, sir. Brace—that's the farmer—been livin herebouts nearly twenty years. The darky don't say much, but I take that as a good sign."

"Let's have a look at 'em."

Brace came up grinning and ducking, giving a travesty of a salute. Hart cringed, but Stuart in his hearty fashion started right in asking questions about the roads and streams; and Brace quickly showed that he knew the area intimately. He even climbed down and began sketching in the dirt a map of the tangle of woods and paths in the triangle between Groveton, Gainesville, and Manassas.

"Look like he might do, Hart. Even got a decent mare there."

Hart did not tell the general that the decent mare was limping on a foreleg. That was not the least reason he found himself caring less for Missy's unkempt father than for the strong-faced buck. Henry had warned Brace that the mare shouldn't be ridden; and Hart liked a man, black or white, who cared about horses.

"All right, Brace, reckon I can use you. Snowden! Send a trooper back with Brace and his man there. Find Gin'al Robertson and tell 'im to send out these here volunteers with any scoutin parties or other details south of the pike. Seem to know their way around down there."

Colonel Snowden looked with distaste at Brace's gaunt and tattered figure climbing back on the mare; but he led Brace and Henry back to the ranks and called out an escort. The last Hart saw of them, as he rode on just behind Stuart, they were headed back the other way.

Teddy Redmund, still patiently charting chessboard moves and counterstrokes from his post near the guns in Hill's rear, had detected from the increased volume of musket fire that the blues had been reinforced, somewhere on the far side of the woods in Brigadier Arnold's front. He would have been interested to know that the added blue troops—the two regiments Charlie Keach had welcomed so volubly—had doubled-timed from the center of the line Sigel had stretched from the turnpike at Groveton northeast to the Sudley Springs Road. These regiments, at Schurz's request, had been moved to the right to shore up Schurz's attack through the woods. If Redmund had known that, it would have given him a useful piece of information about the chessboard Sertorius would later have to describe—that Sigel was neither pressing hard nor hard-pressed in the center. The morning's fight was on Jackson's left.

But not much could be seen, except the smoke drifting above the trees and the wounded straggling back from the woods and into Brigadier Arnold's line. Business appeared brisk at a field surgery near Sudley Church.

Josh Beasly could not see much either, even within those woods gloomy with powder smoke that shut out what sunlight might ordinarily have filtered through the trees. But he could tell from the muzzle flashes and the ceaseless whine of Miniés that the Yanks up front were now too many to hold off. With a veteran's sensitivity to his flanks, he knew also that on either side of him Dixon's Rifles were giving way, making the Yanks pay for every yard but pulling back toward the railroad cut.

Josh was moving back with them, taking as much cover as he could, ignoring wet-eared officers yelling at them to hold fast. *Fuck that shit.* And he had a real reason, that day, to keep his skin whole. Off to his right, Josh saw Foxy Bradshaw jumping from tree to tree. Gutless little prick. Bet 'is barl's cold as a witch's tit. But Josh was too wise in the ways of battle to let the likes of Foxy—or even his aching, bruised hand—take his mind off his business, which was staying alive and snuffing Yanks.

Bracing his piece against a tree, he got a good line on a Yank trotting forward bent low, as if the musket in his hands weighted over him. Josh squeezed off a shot, the tree helping his bruised hand hold the piece steady, and saw the Yank straighten up abruptly, his cap flying off. Like he run up on a closeline crost 'is thoat. But Josh did not linger to see the Yank totter to the side, drop his musket, clutch his arms around a tree, and sag to his knees. Josh had seen too many such sights; they no longer thrilled him.

Sam Stowe, still holding the rail fence against nothing but shimmering emptiness, heard the musket fire coming back through the woods once more, and sent a courier running to Hoke Arnall.

"Colonel Stowe's compli'nts . . . speckfully minds you his reg'-ment's rarin to go."

Arnall was striding along the top of that cut with his pistol strapped to his side and his ear attuned—like a musician's to his instrument's pitch—to the ebb and surge of the fighting in the woods. He had made up his mind to throw in Stowe when the moment came. But he was not too lost in the battle zeal to remember the open field that lay on the army's flank. He had already sent a message to Hill to have a regiment from the division reserve ready to move behind the fence, in the unlikely event that the Yanks were adept enough to turn his flank while striking the front. But Arnall had never seen blue troops manage that well.

"Tell Colonel Stowe to hold himself ready!"

Above the din from the woods, even Arnall's battlefield voice could barely make the words audible. His throat was dry from yelling and from the acrid smoke that hung thick and grainy in the air; the sun seared the sky like a great torch, blearily red through the haze. But the General felt himself strong, confident, in charge; he knew what to do. And he felt more strongly than ever that his hour, the opportunity he had wanted, really was at hand.

Arnall called Gilmore to his side with a wave. He put his lips an inch from the corporal's ear to make sure he understood.

"Go find Colonel Thomas, next brigade on the right. Tell 'im if my force gets pushed near the edge of the woods, I'll send in another regiment 'n try to drive these people all the way out. If he sees a chance to hit 'em, that'd be the time. Got that?"

Gilmore nodded and started to turn away, saluting. But Arnall grabbed his arm.

"Say it back!"

"They push us to the edge-a the woods, you're sendin in another reg'ment. He sees a chancet, hit'em at the same time."

No way to fight a battle without men like Gilmore to get the job done. Arnall watched the strapping corporal ducking and dashing along the gap between his sector and Thomas's Brigade. Why didn't Hill close that gap?

But before Arnall could get off another warning, the firing from the woods and the numbers of his men falling back into the cover of the railway line regained his attention. Almost time to put in Stowe. He turned, spotted the planter's hat where Stowe was perched on the rail fence watching him, and signaled with his arm for the South Carolinians to wheel from the rail-fence front to the bottom of the cut.

Teddy Redmund immediately spotted the movement of Arnall's last regiment. Throwing in everything. Took bloody courage. But the correspondent was doubtful it was the right thing to do. The oncoming blues obviously were driving hard. If they shifted to their right, or if there were more blues beyond the cornfield . . . Redmund swung his glasses in that direction.

No movement. No sun glinting on metal, no hint of dust, nothing but the glazy, empty heat hanging above the ploughed field like a reflection off water. Brigadier Arnold had the odds with him, Redmund decided; at least even.

Charlie Keach, advancing behind Schurz's reinforced line at a more respectful pace than he had maintained in the earlier movement forward, just then met one of KRZ's Yorkers lurching out of the line, his left arm entirely gone, shorn off as neatly at the shoulder as if with a cleaver. Odd, Keach thought. There had been a little shellfire into the woods from either side, since the cannoneers could not be sure they weren't firing into their own men.

The sleeve of the Yorker's jacket had been sheared off with his arm and Keach could see the torn end of his shirt sleeve, the edges of which appeared to have been sucked or blasted into the red maw of the wound. Maybe a saber, Keach thought. But no cavalry in the woods either. Just then the man pitched forward on his face and lay still, without sound or shudder.

Keach carefully noted down the oddity and went on, moving from tree to tree. War, Hale had told him to begin with, was full of inexplicable horrors. Suddenly, up ahead, he could see what looked like the edge of the woods. That meant the Reb counterattack not only had been halted but the secesh had been driven for a change. That felt good.

Trample the bastards, Keach thought, ducking ahead. Run over'em.

But Hoke Arnall, his huge pistol out of the holster and reassuring in his hand, was just then sending Sam Stowe's fresh regiment of South Carolinians into the woods. At that signal, and just as the first of KRZ's blue troops became visible through the woods to the men on the Reb front line, Colonel Edward Thomas loosed two Georgia regiments, whooping and firing, on KRZ's left flank. Like a butternut avalanche, the three new Reb regiments surged down on the tired Yanks, many of whom had been loading and firing all that hot forenoon. The most exhausted Federal units had three times crossed the smoke-misted woods now carpeted with torn bodies and battle litter—and every step of the way, backward or forward, they had been under fierce fire from Arnall's riflemen.

Those battlefield veterans, needing little direction from officers mostly less experienced than they, let the fresh butternuts take the lead, then fell in step with the shock wave that swiftly sent the Yanks reeling back. Only a few walking wounded and some of those worn out by the morning's fight drifted back to the cover of the railroad cut, risking Ironass's threatening pistol.

Foxy Bradshaw, having long since had enough, dropped craftily on his face at the edge of the woods and lay sprawled in a stain of someone else's blood. He was unscathed by so much as a singed eyebrow from the sparking of the few caps he had popped, but Foxy was not going back into those woods full of death and dismemberment. He had his mind made up and his story ready. *O law me* got to git gone from this army fore I'm hogmeat.

Lige Flournoy and Josh went forward with the new butternut tide. Its first shock halted the Yanks; in less than a minute, it had them moving backward; in three it broke them and sent them running again through the vaporous woods, not in good order or taking toll as they went but—to Charlie Keach's profanely shouted disgust—running for life before the oncoming yelling Rebs. Even battle veterans can only take so much lethal pressure. Panic spreads quickly; and sometimes a repulse at what had seemed a moment of victory—the shock of suddenness—rattles troops more profoundly than fire on their flank.

The battlefield is not, after all, a chessboard, even one with human pieces—as perhaps men like Lige and Josh, even Foxy, knew better than Redmund or Keach. Battle does not merely pit men against men, or even men against the eyeless indifference of Minié and shell. The battlefield is the ultimate arena of man against himself. And it is within themselves that troops break, as Schurz's men finally did that morning in the dark and devouring woods.

But Theodore Alford St. John Redmund only wondered, as he watched what he knew from the battle din was the rout of the blues, why the Federal bumbler in command—surely it couldn't have been Pope?—had neither concentrated enough force in Brigadier Arnold's front nor turned his flank across the cornfield.

For his part, as he stood exuberantly on the lip of the cut, Hoke Arnall was congratulating himself on what he knew professionally to have been sound management of his forces, good timing and—

he was vain enough to think—considerable daring. Let Ol Jack put *that* in his pipe and smoke it! Arnall knew Hill would have high praise for him in the division report.

As if to confirm that anticipation, a courier from division galloped in with a note for Arnall, scribbled in pencil on the back of a requisition form. But the words were not what Arnall expected:

Gen'l Arnall

Gen'l Jackson does not wish to bring on bigger engagemt till Gen'l Longst arrives. Withdraw to railway line.

                                                    Hill

Larkin Folsom, coming forward with a dipper of Sudley Church well water for the general, saw him shove his revolver in his holster and stamp a booted foot in anger. Past him and over the woods, Folsom could see through the curling smoke the red unblinking eye of the sun.

Just short of noon, the boy figured, the worst of the heat still ahead, and Ironass already in a bobcat mood.

As he rode with Stuart and the regiment escorting him, Fargo Hart had watched the dust cloud moving down from Thoroughfare until there was little doubt in his mind that Longstreet was only a few minutes away.

"Or else," Colonel Snowden joked, "Lincoln's movin'is whole army in from the west."

When they turned at Hay Market into the road from Gainesville to Thoroughfare, the eager Stuart, unable to restrain himself any longer, signaled his staff officers; they galloped toward the approaching dust, leaving the regimental escort at ease in a grove of pecan trees. Hart welcomed the swift ride; it was cooling for him and gave Mercury a chance to stretch himself. He had to hold the powerful black in to keep from pulling ahead of the general and the rest of the staff.

The Reverend Major Allen, scab running blackly down his forehead and nose, leaned from his saddle toward Hart and shouted. Hart caught only a few phrases and those more by expectation than by hearing:

". . . army together . . . work of the Lord!"

Hart eyed with distaste the buffalo robe tied behind the Rev-

erend Major's saddle. If *that* represented the Lord's work, maybe
there was something to be said for the Devil. But he only smoked
a bit grimly and galloped after Stuart.

Around a turn in the road, they met General Lee himself—
appearing suddenly out of the dust, his beard and uniform and
horse laden with it, his face and eyes as calm as those of a monument, his erect figure on his great gray mount as reassuring as
a battle flag glimpsed through powder smoke. With characteristic
consideration, the Old Man was riding a hundred yards or so ahead
of Longstreet's main column, to lessen the effect of his escorts'
dust on the troops.

"Oh, by God!" Colonel Snowden could hardly contain himself,
as Stuart and Lee exchanged salutes. "*Now* we'll show Pope a
thing or two!"

Hart had seen the commanding general on numerous occasions,
but he thought Lee had never appeared so impressive—or so
welcome—as that morning on the rutted road from Thoroughfare.
Past the small escort party, he could see Longstreet and one or
two of his staff officers hurrying forward. There was no mistaking
Ol Pete, that square body solid as a caisson. As different from
Jackson as beer from champagne—no, nothing liquid or fizzy
about either general. As different as a bear from a mountain lion;
put it that way.

When Longstreet's group came up, the three generals trotted
on toward Gainesville, their staffs falling in behind, uncomplaining of their superiors' dust.

"You want to even make a guess . . ." Colonel Snowden had
to shout above the beat of hooves. "Why ol bigmouth Pope let'em
through the Gap without a fight?"

"Stupidity." Coke Mowbray never credited Yanks with anything better than that, or maybe cowardice.

"Never thought Longstreet'd come up so fast." And neither did
I, Hart thought. Ol Pete was not noted for speed.

"No, sir!" The Reverend Major's voice boomed like a twelve-
pounder. "That won't do, sir! Aint a thing but the Lord's hand in
this!"

Just short of Gainesville, Lee and Stuart left the road, dismounted and sat down in the shade of an oak tree. Longstreet,
with his aides, rode on southeast toward the road's junction with
the pike. Hart and the other staff officers watched the generals
under the tree conferring over Stuart's map. The first ranks of
Hood's Texans began to go by on the road, wreathed in dust;

when they recognized Lee and Stuart, they cheered like school-
boys.

The cheers could not be heard, of course, as far away as the right
of Jackson's line along the old railway. But there, as they listened
to the battle sounds from Hill's front in the opposite direction,
officers and men had been watching the approach of that tantalizing
dust cloud for most of the morning. Had to be Longstreet. That
was the consensus.

But was it *really?* Was there some chance Pope had managed
to bottle up Ol Pete beyond the mountains . . . that those were
Yanks swinging back down to join the fray at Groveton? Wher'd
em black-hat fellers git to, what put up at goldurn fight last
evnin?

When it was clear that, whoever the newcomers were, they
were closing in on Jackson's right, General Starke, who had succeeded the wounded Taliaferro in command of Jackson's old division, decided to settle matters. He had at hand Captain Thad
Selby, just sent by Jackson to ascertain what Starke knew of the
approaching troops. Starke, who was all but certain they had to
be Longstreet's, sent Selby to the pike to make sure.

Selby kept well up the hillside, away from the pike. That
morning he was an unsettled young man. He could not help remembering the battle of the day before—how different the ac-
tuality of death, the flame and litter of the field, had been from
the glories he had foolishly anticipated. His head still ached from
the thunder of it, echoed by the morning clash on Jackson's left
flank. Or did it ache because—he was honest enough to ask
himself—he had come so near to panicking in his first exposure
to battle? No, face it—to *danger*.

Earlier that morning as he had ridden with Jackson's staff party,
he had watched with admiration as a blue-clad major on horseback
led his troops boldly toward the butternut line. The Yank attack
at that point, on Lawton's front, had not been pressed. But the
major made a fine figure on his glistening brown horse; the regiment behind him looked threatening in its full blue ranks; and as
he turned to wave on his men with a sword from which sunlight
reflected brilliantly, Selby thought: *That's how it ought to be*.

Out of the railroad cut just ahead of the staff group, a single
shot rang out, from a regiment that had been holding fire under
old General Trimble's orders. The splendid blue major toppled

from his horse and lay still; the horse trotted smartly off to the rear.

"Oh, too bad!" Selby hardly realized he had spoken. He gazed intently at the still blue stain on the earth, as if he saw his own hope and innocence lying there. "Too bad!"

"No, Captain." A soft, rather high-pitched voice spoke from just behind him. Ol Jack sat his horse not three feet away, looking too at the fallen major. "We must kill the brave ones. They lead on the others."

As if to prove the point, Trimble's men made short work of the fallen major's regiment, and it soon trotted away to cover. So Selby asked himself, too, as he rode alone to the far right of Jackson's line *am I not to be one of the brave ones that lead on the others?* He would never before have dreamed of the question, much less worried about the answer. Now he felt himself ever so subtly tightening the reins on Jeff D., the dream of the night before insistent in his consciousness; could that wild, remembered gallop, taking him ever more swiftly toward nothingness, have been an omen for the day?

But when Selby, peering through the dust from a hidden hillside perch, got a good look at the battle flags and regimental colors crowding along the pike from Gainesville, self-doubt and apprehension vanished. He lingered only long enough to be certain, then wheeled Jeff D. and gave him his lead—realizing in the horse's great speed, and in the exhilaration of what he had to report, that the dream of the night before was coming true in a way that mocked his forebodings.

He was just within earshot of Starke's lines when he waved his hat and began to shout:

"It's Longstreet . . . Longstreet's here!"

And even before he had the last words out, the troops on that end of the line had taken up the news, and the word rolled down Starke's front from company to company, regiment to regiment, like summer rain moving steadily over a parched field:

It's Longstreet . . . Longstreet's come Longstreet's here!

Chapter Eight

∞∞∞∞∞∞∞∞∞∞

August 29—Midday

WHEN PETTIGREW TAPPED at the door, Amy and Bess were work-ing together in a large ground-floor room—once the Judge's, then the General's office—recently fitted out as a "sewing factory."

Pettigrew's tap was not at all apologetic, either for the smells that clung to him or for his interruption of their work.

"Yes, Pettigrew."

"Needs to speak wif Bess." Typically, Pettigrew did not call Amy "Mistis," as most of them did, or anything at all.

"Go ahead, then."

Amy spoke civilly but she was annoyed at the interruption. Owing to the tightening Federal blockade, the pinch of inadequate supplies was beginning to be felt all through the South that sum-mer. Everywhere in the Confederacy, plantations were becoming food rather than cotton or tobacco producers, as well as manu-factories for items no longer available from Europe or the North—clothing, for example, particularly for the Africans, and leather, salt, soap, coffee, tea, dyes.

Before the war, the spinning wheel and the loom had long been out of use at Sycamore. But the blockade had forced the redis-covery of these implements, since custom and necessity required both a spring and a fall issue of clothing for the people in the yard. A number of the older black women remembered well enough how to spin, and they could teach others. Looms required more expertise and muscle, so some of the men helped with the weaving. Traditional folk craft produced dyes from roots and barks, elder-berries and walnut hulls.

Amy, closely assisted by Bess, personally supervised the cutting and the sewing of the resulting homespun and home-dyed cloth—tasks that called for the highest skill and which caused the most waste if botched. In the airy sewing factory at the rear of the house, the two women were preparing that August for the fall issue of heavy clothing. When the job reached its peak, they would have perhaps a dozen of the women from the yard engaged with needle and thread; but Amy and Bess did most of the cutting themselves—a matter of efficiency, but also, Amy had realized, a sensible means of keeping control of the three pairs of scissors she had available. Scissors could be weapons.

When Pettigrew came in from the makeshift tannery about noon, Amy and Bess were cutting from patterns for children's jackets. They knew the driver had come from the tannery because he smelled of it.

After it became clear that store-bought shoes were not going to be available for the people that winter, Amy had sought out detailed instructions for home tanning in *Southern Field and Fireside* magazine. Then she copied out the instructions and read them to Pettigrew, pretending they had come in a letter from the General.

Pettigrew had sniffed and sneered a little but with his usual diligence and competence organized the work at once. It turned out to be a malodorous business—particularly making bate from hen dung. But there was no help for it; bate was needed to wash off the lime used to remove hair from the hides.

Now, smelling strongly of lye and bate and the hides themselves, Pettigrew stood silently and—Amy thought—sullenly in the doorway.

"Well, go on. Speak to her then."

"Inna yard."

Amy hoped neither of them had heard her indrawn breath. She straightened, feeling the strain of the morning's work in her back. Why did he need Bess in the yard? The tall mulatto woman, seated nearby, did not look at Pettigrew, or up from her work.

"You won't speak in front of me? Is that it?"

"Nuffin fret you wid."

"Then it's nothing I can't hear."

Amy knew the argument was futile; he would say nothing if she forced Bess to stay with her. Anyway, he probably only wanted Bess to straighten out one of the younger girls; Pettigrew frequently used Bess as a sort of deputy for such delicate purposes—thereby, of course, keeping whatever the problem was a secret from Amy.

Amy often thought that it was too bad that Pettigrew and Bess had not married—each other, she meant. Pettigrew had a skinny caramel-colored wife who crept about the yard in the shadow of his eminence, as if she were a hound dog kicked once too often by an overbearing master. Amy conceded that it would not be easy to be married to Pettigrew; and, of course, he'd got four children from Reba already.

But Bess! Tough-minded and independent as she was, Bess could have handled even Pettigrew. But Bess had never taken a husband—"Em nigguhs aint wuff killin!" she'd say, when asked about it—and neither the General nor Amy had tried to push her into marriage. The General, Amy was sure (though, of course, they never discussed such matters) did not—as some plantation owners did—regard African women as mere brood mares. Of course, they were all immoral that way, and no doubt Bess with her statuesque body was no better with men than she should be on Saturday nights and holidays. But she could have been a perfect wife for Pettigrew, as even he tacitly recognized by so often using her to help him manage the people. Or maybe that was why he hadn't married Bess; he'd known he couldn't dominate her as he did Reba.

As things were, Pettigrew was unhampered in his reign. But this time, Amy thought, his request and manner were brazen enough, even for him, to force her to protest little, and unusual enough so that she could not help wondering if maybe he had heard something of Jason.

Pettigrew waited stubbornly in the doorway. Bess snip-snipped at homespun, still not looking up. Amy felt her helplessness against their stolid insistence. She leaned forward an inch or two so that the revolver suspended beneath her skirts pressed against the edge of the big table on which she was working. The touch of the metal against her leg gave her resolution.

"Don't be gone long then, Bess. You don't want children to be cold this winter."

Bess put down her scissors and followed Pettigrew down the hall toward the rear of the house, moving almost soundlessly on the wide hardwood flooring the Judge's father had fitted himself.

Amy sat down, wrinkling her nose against the lingering odor of bate. No real reason, of course, to think it was about Jason. But since the sheriff's visit, anything out of the ordinary—an unaccustomed noise in the house, the least hint of a knowing look on a black face, a silence longer than usual where they were working, an unexpected footfall—set her to thinking of Jason; or rather to thinking of him more directly; since he was seldom out of her consciousness at all. She stayed out of the kitchen as much as possible, to avoid Easter's red-rimmed eyes and doleful manner.

If they'd caught him, Sheriff Maxton surely would have sent word. Even more certainly, the Africans in their inexplicable way would have heard the news and given some sign, probably sooner than the sheriff. Amy was not sure whether such a sign would have been of sorrow or of satisfaction. But she was sure that Jason was still at large. And he was *was* married to Easter, which was why Sycamore had been the first place Maxton and his hounds had come looking for him.

"Some nigguh hidin dis place I gone know fo him take two brefs," Pettigrew had said. "Aint need no dawgs yolpin round scarin folks." Could that be why he'd called Bess into the yard?

When Amy sat down, the pistol dangling on its ribbon had slipped between her legs. The General had explained to her that as long as the hammer was down on an empty chamber the gun could not go off accidentally. It would have to be cocked before it could be fired. At first she had worried, anyway, at having the thing hanging under her skirts; she feared shooting off a toe or a kneecap. But she had become used to the weight and touch of the metal on her skin, and every time she thought of Jason she was glad the pistol was there.

Amy closed her thighs on it as she worked, feeling the ribbed ivory of the butt, the slight protuberance of the cylinder as comforting reminders—not just of the weapon but of the General. He was braving death every day, maybe right that moment, in Virginia; surely she could hold herself together, look after little Luke, until they caught that murderer. The General already was proud of her and the way she managed Sycamore with Pettigrew's help. He'd be even prouder, when he learned of it, if she kept up her nerve until they caught Jason.

She worked steadily at the patterns and the homespun, every so often squeezing the warm metal, the rough ivory between her thighs. If they caught him anytime soon, she wouldn't even mind so much being in a condition again—if she really was. No nausea yesterday or today but no sign of her monthlies either. Wonderful if a false alarm. And the next time the General came home, he'd have to control himself, after the scare she'd had and the angry letter she'd written. He'd *have* to, if she proved to be really in a delicate condition.

She squeezed the pistol again, not moving her knees, only the muscles in her thighs. Maybe separate bedrooms. Racy little Jane Moring, visiting from Raleigh, had whispered that that was the way for a woman to send her husband to the yard; but the General would *never* do that and the things Jane said were a scandal anyway. Comforting and warm to sleep next to the man you loved, of course, but it did seem to . . . inflame him. Especially mornings.

In the warm room and the afternoon sunshine coming through the open window, Amy was beginning to be drowsy. She put down the scissors and leaned back in the chair, flexing her thighs rhythmically against the comforting pistol, thinking of the General, wondering where he was, why men were so intent on *that*. Maybe because only women had to suffer the consequences. Maybe because men were so . . . she groped sleepily for a word to express her idea. So prominent. Being made the way they were kept *that* on their minds.

In the warmth and the familiar sounds coming through the open window from the yard—voices, old Marcus's dog barking, the chatter of blue jays, somewhere the sound of a hammer—Amy was almost asleep. In another moment she drifted into a dream of the General, magnificent in dress uniform, with an enormous pistol strapped to his waist. She saw him stride high-booted through the lower hallway of Sycamore, up the stairs his grandfather had built, and into their bedroom; she watched him enter from where she was lying in the big four-poster with its down mattress and the quilts that had been her mother's. He strode to the bed, pulled the pistol from his belt and placed it on her legs. Except that it was not a pistol prominent on the quilt but his . . .

Bess's chair scraped on the floor and Amy awoke with a start, feeling herself flushed. She was embarrassed by her dream and the pistol clenched clammily between her perspiring legs. Bess was picking up her scissors.

"Oh . . . Bess . . . I must of dozed off."

"Why'nt you go up'n take a nap, Mistis?"

"No . . . no . . ." Amy sat straighter, annoyed now by the heavy gun under her skirts. She did not want *that* kind of dream again. "Too much to do."

Then she remembered Pettigrew. She tried to keep her voice light and indifferent. "What secrets you'n Pettigrew keepin?"

Bess sniffed. "Em nigguh gals more'n he kin handle."

"Penny, I bet."

"Aint no need you frettin, Mistis."

Was there something tight, apprehensive, about Bess? As if she might be listening for something? She gave no outward sign; the hand holding the scissors was steady. But Amy knew Bess well, had known her for years. She had come back with a tension in her manner, not quite visible on her face, that had not been there before Pettigrew tapped at the door.

"Was it about Jason?"

"Wha-a-t?" Bess's feigned surprise—the lifted brows, the open mouth—was almost convincing.

"You were talkin about Jason, weren't you?"

"JAY-son! Why, Mistis, aint nobody studyin Jason round-yere."

That was merely evasive. "Easter's studyin'im, all right."

"Oh, yassum, Easter . . . Easter's 'is *woman*." Bess's tone of finality dismissed the idea that Jason's woman could have a serious view of the matter.

"Now, Bess . . . I want the truth. What did Pettigrew tell you about Jason just now?" Under the table, through her skirts, she moved the pistol to rest flatly on top of her right thigh.

Bess snipped cloth. "Pe'grew aint seen hide ner hair-a no Jason."

"He didn't call you out in the yard to tell you *that*." Amy was more determined than usual to get the truth out of one of them; this time, it *mattered*.

"Nome. Say I gotta take a-holt at Penny."

Amy sighed, and cut homespun sleeves. Logical enough, since Penny's mother had died two years earlier, trying to give one more birth than any woman ought. And Penny with her saucy bottom was clearly on the road to perdition.

But Amy was convinced there was news of Jason; she had been so certain for so long that something had to happen that she almost willed it to have happened. Anything better than waiting. But if they wouldn't tell her, it couldn't be good news. Maybe he'd been in touch somehow with Easter. The Africans had their ways about things like that.

Maybe they were even hiding him somewhere on the place. They all stuck together and it would be easy to do, if the dogs didn't come back. Amy was still uncomfortable about Bess sleeping in her room. Every night, now, she woke and listened for Bess's breathing, to make sure of the slow, rhythmic exhalations of a true sleeper. She decided to keep pressing Bess—although she was fearful, too, of what she might learn.

"Does Easter know where Jason is?"

Bess turned her chin up sharply, proudly. "Easter so scairt she aint known funt fum back." The hint of disdain was unmistakable—and the first acknowledgment between them, subtle as it was, of the reality of Jason.

The hint more than the words emboldened Amy to say what she had been thinking since the night Sheriff Maxton had ridden away with the dogs. The General wouldn't like it, if he ever found out. But the General was in Virginia, fighting *his* fight, and hers was here and now. She, not the General, had to deal with Jason.

"Bess . . . if Easter wants to go . . . to Jason, I mean . . ."

The scissors in Bess's hands stopped snipping. She looked at Amy with still, impenetrable eyes.

"*I* wouldn't have to know . . . until too late to stop her."

Bess did not blink or move. Of course she knew what Amy was getting at; they always knew. If Easter went to Jason, Jason would have no reason to come to Sycamore. And no matter what the General might say, that seemed to Amy the surest way to protect little Luke and the Judge, not to mention herself. If Jason had no reason to come.

"Will you tell Easter that?"

"Nome." Bess picked up a piece of blue-dyed homespun and started cutting.

For a moment of flashing anger Amy wanted to slap her insufferable yellow face, knock that maddening secret look out of her nigger eyes. But that moment passed, as it always did, and she took up her own scissors again.

"Then I will."

They worked on in silence. Just as it began to dawn on Amy that the familiar yard sounds—children's laughter, dogs snapping at each other—were no longer coming from the window, Bess spoke without looking up.

"Pe'grew aint lowin none-a de Gin'al's folks run off."

Amy had not thought of that but of course Bess was right. Pettigrew regarded himself as the General's trustee. Pettigrew would know and be after Easter the minute she left.

"Speshly Easter."

While Amy was digesting that, not sure of what it meant, she was uneasily aware of the continuing silence of the yard in the midday heat. Unnatural. Her fears came rushing from deep within her, and she was reaching for the comfort of the pistol on her leg when she heard the first scream. Her hand closed tightly on the gun beneath her skirt and she stood up so quickly her chair went over backward.

"Bess! What . . ."

But Bess was already running to the window. Another scream. Another. Amy thought she recognized Easter's voice. Bound to be Easter's. *Bound to be Jason.* Amy stood paralyzed by the work table, the pistol in its wrapping of skirts and petticoats clutched in her hand.

"O my Jesus," Bess moaned at the window. "Jesus save."

But as coldly as fear had stabbed her at the first scream, Amy knew then that no one was there to save her, *save Luke*—no Jesus, no General—no one but Amy Singleton Arnall. She turned from the work table and ran to the window, holding the scissors in one hand and the gun in the other so it did not slap against her legs. Rudely she pushed against Bess, so that the two of them stood pressing against each other to look into the yard.

By the carriage house a group of Africans, mostly men, were huddled. Nearer, beside the kitchen connected by covered walkway to the house, Easter was down on her knees, screaming, her white apron caught up in her hands, which clutched it to her neck, giving her the appearance of a huge mushroom sprung from the grass. Above the kitchen a pall of smoke rose blackly against a sky unblemished as a china plate. Between Easter and the huddle of Africans at the carriage house, Pettigrew crouched like a man about to dive into a pond, his arms and legs spread, his back to Amy and Bess at the window. Ten feet beyond, circling catlike to Pettigrew's left, Jason held above his head the axe from the kitchen woodpile. Sun glinted from its blade.

"Pe'grew." Bess's murmur at Amy's elbow was barely audible. "Jesus save my Pe'grew."

Pettigrew, Amy saw with horrifying clarity, was not yielding an inch to the threatening axe. Just then Easter quit screaming and went down with her forehead against the grass, the white apron still clutched to her neck. As if the sudden silence were a signal, Jason leaped forward, the axe swinging down in a glittering arc; but Pettigrew leaped away to his right, unscathed, and seized in almost the same motion a stick of split pinewood from the kitchen pile.

Jason recovered quickly and the two men began circling again. Jason's shirt had been ripped half off, and the sun glistened on his deep black chest. Pettigrew was slightly built by comparison, though taller, and wirily powerful. Once Amy had seen him helping some of his men lift the trunk of a tree toppled by lightning into the truck garden, and she had marveled at the rippling muscles and the strength of his slender body. But Jason was built like a bull, thick in the chest and shoulders, his head like a bludgeon on his short neck. And Jason had the axe.

Amy pulled her skirts and petticoats waist high, ignoring for once Bess's presence and her own dread of self-exposure; but Bess never took her eyes from the yard as Amy seized the pistol's ivory butt and quickly snipped the ribbon tied to it. Just as she dropped her skirts and covered her legs again, Jason sprang. This time he swung the axe in a wide horizontal circle. Pettigrew stepped back nimbly as the blade slashed past his stomach, missing by what Amy thought must have been no more than inches; he swung the chunk of wood powerfully at Jason's head. Ducking, Jason took the blow *whupp!* more nearly on his arm and shoulder; all the way to the window, Amy could hear him grunt in pain.

But Jason was quick, too. He swung the axe backhanded at Pettigrew, in an upward arc; the blunt edge of the blade struck the chunk of wood in Pettigrew's hand and sent it sailing out of reach.

With his other hand, Pettigrew caught the axe handle just below the blade. He tried for a moment to wrestle the axe from Jason's grip but succeeded only in swinging the squat black man stumbling to his knees. Briefly they struggled in a panting tug of war, gripping the axe handle between them, Jason glaring up fiercely at Pettigrew still on his feet. Then Jason, twisting his powerful body, pulled Pettigrew to the turf and the two men rolled over, still grappling for the axe.

Amy felt nauseated—not so much from fear as from the raw violence of the two creatures on the ground, savagely beating each other, their grunts and exclamations and panting breaths coming up clearly to the window. Like animals. Amy realized she had never witnessed violence before. She thought she had never seen anything so ugly, so nauseating.

Just then, Pettigrew let go of the axe and sprang away, landing on all fours near Easter's huddled form, alert as a hunting dog, his face contorted, his head weaving from side to side. Six feet away, Jason's powerful body rose to its knees, still holding the axe. Amy could not see his face but his broad shining back—his shirt was by then completely ripped away—loomed up hugely, as if just outside the window, as if she could put the muzzle of the pistol against it.

She raised her arm and saw the weapon shaking in her nervous hand. She tried to point it between Jason's massive shoulders, but she could not bring it to bear. She dropped the scissors from her

left hand and with it seized her right wrist, steadying the pistol.
She tried to pull back the hammer with her right thumb, as the
General had taught her, but it was stiffer than she remembered
from his drill; and just as the hammer reached full cock, it slipped
from her thumb, slammed down, and the pistol went off, bucking
up in her hand as if struck from beneath by Jason's axe. She
staggered a step backward in the deafening roar that filled the
workroom. The scream this time came from Bess, piercing, echoing with the gunshot.

By the carriage house, the watching Africans scattered like
ground squirrels. Jason whirled about on catlike feet, and his black
sweating face glared up at her, his lips pulled back and his eyes
wide, hot, mad, the axe still gripped in one hand. Behind him,
Pettigrew came up on his toes, his body coiling at the opportunity
to spring on Jason from behind. Amy saw his head lash forward
as he leaped. But he did not crash into Jason's stumplike body as
she expected; instead, he sprawled flat on the trampled grass, at
Jason's feet. Jason whirled again; swinging the axe with one arm,
he crunched the blade down on Pettigrew's back.

At the sound—like that of a ripe watermelon dropped and
split—more than at the sight—obscured by Jason's broad shoulders—Amy momentarily covered her eyes with her free hand.
Bess did not scream again; she moaned, a long, shuddering sound
that seemed torn from her. And from the yard Amy could plainly
hear Jason's great panting exhausted breath.

She still was more nauseated by the violence than afraid of
Jason. His real presence had in some brute way dispelled her dark,
ineffable fear of his coming and replaced it with the simple need
to act. The pistol was still in her hand, still loaded. The act of
firing, badly as she'd botched it, seemed to her dissociated from
the animal-like struggle in the yard. The pistol was a mere instrument, impersonal, mechanical, even in its way scientific.
Nothing to do with brute strength, the savagery of bodily clash.

Bess wailed as if in agony and Amy uncovered her eyes, lifting
the pistol. Jason was bending over Pettigrew, his back an easy
target again. Then Amy saw Easter lying on the grass beyond
him, clutching Pettigrew's ankles, as she must have done at the
moment he started to leap on Jason's back. *Jason's woman.*

Amy's hand was still shaking. Before she could steady it and
cock back the hammer again, Jason sprang across Pettigrew, seized
Easter by the arm and ran toward the carriage house, half dragging
Easter along. The few Africans who had drifted back following

Amy's shot scattered again. A good marksman might still have picked Jason off before he disappeared beyond the carriage house, but Amy did not even try.

She stood transfixed at the window, dumb, holding barely to her consciousness, staring at Pettigrew's sprawled, still body with the axe blade buried between its shoulders. The handle pointed steadily up at the window, at Amy; and from the floor, at her feet, Bess's wails rose sorrowful as the kitchen smoke against the impervious sky.

Longstreet was not the only new arrival on the plains of Manassas that morning. Well before noon, both Kearny's and Hooker's Federal divisions—more than 10,000 Peninsula veterans Pope had ordered to Centreville the night before—were moving west on the pike, over the Stone Bridge toward Groveton. Phil Kearny, one-armed, short, and belligerent, arrived first and conferred immediately with Sigel, whose Germans—mostly of Schurz's Division—had borne the brunt of the morning's battle.

Sigel advised Kearny to take his troops north toward Sudley Church, moving for concealment on the east side of the Sudley Springs Road. At some point in that direction, he could come in on the Rebs' left flank. Scouts reported the brigades on Jackson's left strongly posted to defend in front—as Schurz could attest—but perhaps vulnerable on the flank.

Kearny saw the usefulness of extending the Federal line to the right as suggested, and soon had his troops moving north between the road and Bull Run. Sigel held Hooker for the moment in reserve. In the midday heat, the sun relentless in a porcelain sky, silence fell briefly over the fields and woods where the two armies crouched, eyeing one another.

Hoke Arnall's men, coming sullenly back through the woods to his position within the railway cut, were ordered to strip usable ammunition from the dead and wounded over which they passed. Lige Flournoy and Josh did not content themselves with cartridges but rifled pockets and knapsacks, too. Few of the dead Yanks had carried anything valuable into the attack; but Lige struck it lucky. From one knapsack he pulled a shirt with cuffs and collar, a pair of opera glasses, a small sack of coffee, and some dried apple slices hung on a string and tied in a circle. Lige stuck the coffee in his pocket, hung the apples around his neck, and threw the shirt to Josh.

"Bet you aint ever wore a boil shirt, Meat."

While Lige peered through the opera glasses at the woods, still thick with battle smoke, through which they'd fought, Josh unfolded the shirt, stared at it, and dropped it on the dead Yank's chest.

"Wear that, I gotta git some lace on my draws."

South of the pike, Major Jesse Thomas was overseeing Longstreet's divisions as they filed into line roughly perpendicular to the road. God help the Yanks that charge *this* line, he thought. When completed, the front would run along a high ridge that dominated the rolling Manassas plain before it; the approach to the ridge was wooded and Longstreet's orders were to site the brigades on the reverse slope, just below the crest and screened by it and the woods from Federal eyes. Ol Pete knew ground like nobody else.

Miss Letty's handkerchief was carefully tucked inside his jacket. It probably meant nothing, of course. But funny how wanting something to be so sometimes could make it be. For instance, the way he'd wanted some kind of exchange with Miss Letty, if no more than a word. And then the old monkey bringing the handkerchief into camp that night. Lawrence, the mother called'im.

She would be trouble, the mother. A real Virginia snob. If, of course, he ever got back to the Williams house, or survived the war. And if only he'd had a decent gift to send back with Lawrence to Miss Letty! One of his uniform buttons had had to do.

But the morning's crowded tasks left Major Thomas little time for thinking of Miss Letty, whose snow-white bust he'd dreamed of repeatedly in the two nights following the dinner at her house. He ranged up and down the line, making sure Longstreet's orders were being carried out. Hood's Texans, first to arrive, took position from just south of the pike and across it, facing east toward Groveton. D. R. Jones's Division turned south behind Hood and marched along a country lane until the troops crossed the Manassas Gap Railroad; then Jones dug in near Dawkins Branch, on what would be the extreme right of the developing Confederate line. James Kemper's Division moved in between Hood and Jones, and Wilcox's Division was held in reserve near Gainesville. Longstreet's fifth division, under Dick Anderson, was coming on behind, having acted as rear guard during the march through the Gap.

The line Longstreet thus drew south of the pike approached Jackson's, just north of it, in a wide angle. About 150 degrees, Thomas estimated—like the extended jaws of a hungry animal. The two jaws of the army, from Hill's Division on the left to Jones's on the right, stretched for nearly five miles through the woods and fields on either side of the pike.

As Longstreet's men began taking position, Jackson had pulled out the two brigades, Early's and Forno's, that had formed an early-morning blocking force across the pike. These troops moving off to rejoin Jackson's main line momentarily worried Thomas; they left a gap of a quarter mile or so north of the pike, between Jackson's right and Longstreet's left.

Cantering into that gap, however, Thomas saw that the two gaping jaws were hinged by a strong artillery force sited on a ridge between them—eighteen of Jackson's guns lined up almost wheel to wheel.

Thomas rode along the line and pulled up in front of a battery of six-pounders. The gunners eyed him with curiosity, as if he were from another world, not merely from Longstreet's wing of the army.

"Whose battery is this?"

"Cap'n Overholt's, sir. Jackson's old division."

"Had a hard time of it?"

"Give as good's we got."

Alf Gurganous had to admit he was glad to see Longstreet's men arrive. On the other hand, it was high time. Alf was heart and soul a part of what he still thought of as the Valley Army—one of Ol Jack's boys.

"Seem like we-uns alluz doin the heft-a the fightin," he had often said to Jeff Jernigan. But that morning, Alf was in a generous mood. He was reveling in a new pair of Yank underbritches he had finally foraged at Manassas. Not a grayback in 'em. Yit.

"Pope showin some fight?" Jesse Thomas saw things the other way around. It seemed to him that Ol Pete was pulling Jackson's chestnuts out of the fire again, as on the Peninsula.

"Much as Yanks ever do." Jeff Jernigan in his new black hat—the only decent headgear Thomas could see in the whole battery—had come up beside Private Gurganous.

All of Lee's army, after more than a year and a half of war, was ragged and lean and a lot of it barefoot; but it seemed to

Thomas that the men of Overholt's Battery were little more than scarecrows—gaunt-cheeked and hollow eyed, their shirts hanging in tatters, hats shapeless, trousers out at the knees. Unkempt beards and hair made Jackson's men look more like pirates than soldiers. But Overholt's pieces gleamed with loving care. He'd give'em that.

"Gunners over ther we-uns could use rightchere," Alf said, thinking of the twelve-pound Napoleons that had given them fits the evening before. He was giving them the highest compliment he knew how to pay.

Thomas turned his horse's head toward the pike. "Reck'n fore long we'll get a look at'em ourselves."

He waved a casual salute to Overholt's boys and trotted off. A shame to trust the army to scarecrows like that. But Ol Pete had brought in the *real* army in time to save the day.

In the drastically thinned ranks of the Stonewall Brigade, a few hundred yards from Overholt's Battery, Privates Sowell and Stone lay at ease just behind the railroad cut. They had brought in Lott McGrath's piece for old times' sake, and stacked it with the rest of the company's arms. Like the troops around them, they were ready to rush into the cut at the first sign of Yank movement.

"But they aint comin." Gilly had hacked open a tin of potted ham, a prize from Manassas, and was smearing the meat with his pocket knife on a piece of Yank hardtack remarkably free of weevils. "Em sons got a bellyfull yistiddy."

Sowell was not so sure. "This the twenny ninth, aint it? Day Lott seen the sign of."

"He could of read it wrong. Maybe yistiddy wa'nt the wrong day atall."

Sowell gazed at him with contempt. "How come'is luck run out, then, he read the sign wrong? Ask me, we gone ketch it today, sure'n shit."

Gilly ate potted ham and generously offered some to Sowell, who declined. Sowell liked to say he would be beholden to no man; besides, he had filched his own potted ham.

"Right down *queer*," Gilly said. "Him not bein ther."

"Whole durn war's queer. Like last winter I-uz goin down to sign up with Stonewall? Well, I come on down-a road to Sinjun's Run, nearby Hampshire Crossin. Up in the Valley ther?" Stone was a Valley man, too, and nodded recognition. "So durn cold a man's piss'd freeze fore it hit the ground. So I seen this bunch on guard ther at the Run. Some sittin'n some lyin'n some standin. Give'em a holler'n not a man of'em move ner sid a word."

"Ol Jack knew, he'd of had 'em shot. Sleepin on picket."

"Well, I come on crosst the Run. It-uz froze solid. An'em pickets aint sleepin, they's froze. I mean *hard* froze. Eye-sickles hangin off ther hands'n close'n noses. Two of 'em standin up holdin pieces hard-froze as a monu-ment. Still standin guard in heaven, I reck'n, lessen th'other place melt 'em down."

"Wha'd you do?" Gilly licked his knife blade.

"Do? Hightail outten ther fore I froze, too."

Gilly pondered Sowell's story at some length. "But that-uz natchral. Freezin, I mean. Git cold enuf, man gone freeze. Ain't *natchral* Lott not lyin ther wher I seen 'im hit. My own *eyes.*"

Applejack, the company booze-maker, was just then walking past, scratching the redbugs that had infested his belly when he had slept face down the night before, too tired to spread his blankets.

"Lookin fer Lott McGrath?"

Gilly owed Applejack four bits for a half canteen of popskull. He answered cautiously, not knowing what deal Applejack might be working, and spoke in churchly tones:

"Kilt yistiddy, Jack."

"Kilt, my ass. I seen'im ten minutes ago."

Sowell sat up. "You seen Lott?"

"Big's life'n twicet as dirty. Goin toward-a woods." Applejack swept his arm in a vague circle to the north.

Sowell looked at Gilly. "Shore it uz him?"

"Bastard owe me fo bits." Applejack looked narrowly at Gilly. "Too. Aint likely I'd mistake'im."

Sowell got to his feet. "Say he's goin at way?"

"Lookin like he don't know me. But I knowed *him.*" Applejack moved on with dignity befitting a man of business, a creditor at that.

"Le's go, Gilly. Lott's in 'em woods someres."

"Mebbe so." Gilly folded his knife and carefully folded the half-empty tin into his blanket roll. "Mebbe not. But iffen he *is,* that aint natchral neither."

Sowell was impatient. "Must be wounded. Wandrin round needin' help."

"Not with the hole I seen in 'is skull."

"Well, I aim to find 'im." Sowell hitched up the trousers bagging down from his skinny hips and started toward the rear.

"Hey, Sowbelly!" Gilly was on his feet, too. "Sposen he's dead?"

"But Applejack jus seen 'im."

Gilly was profoundly conscious of the importance of what he said next, again in his best church voice:

"I mean sposen he's dead anyhow?"

Sowell stared at him open-mouthed. "War aint *that* queer."

He made for the rear again. Gilly hesitated, then hurried after his friend. They were almost out of the lines when Buzzard Billings, the sergeant commanding the company that morning for lack of officers, shouted:

"Wher'n hell you webfoots think you goin?"

"See the chaplain." Sowell walked on.

Not a bad idee. Gilly shivered even in the heat. Bein at hole'n Lott's head nearbout big enough to stick a Bible in.

The sergeant shouted at them again but was too shorthanded to do anything; and he knew them well enough to think they would be back when needed. As the brief noonday lull ended and the sounds of battle began to reverberate again on Hill's front, Sowell and Gilly disappeared into the forests of Sudley Mountain.

Carl Schurz was a proud man, politically important, who frequently wrote to President Lincoln to advise him on the conduct of the war. When Sigel notified him that Kearny was bypassing him on the right in an effort to turn Jackson's left, the offended Schurz promptly reformed his tired brigades and sent Schimmelfennig and Krzyzanowski back through the woods where the morning's bloody tides had surged. But this time Schimmelfennig's Ohio, Pennsylvania, and West Virginia boys cannily held their fire until they neared the Reb lines.

Word of Longstreet's opportune arrival had not made its way, officially or by grapevine, that far to Jackson's left. But Hoke Arnall, his ranks depleted by the forenoon carnage, had picketed his front rather sparsely and not too far into the woods ahead. He believed the Yanks had had enough of his fiercely defended front and next would try Jackson somewhere else, if at all.

His regiments, too, were worn out from the woods fighting and from five consecutive days of hard marching and sleeping on their arms. Though supposedly on the alert, most of the troops were sprawled and taking what rest they could when at about

12:30 p.m. the Yanks came bursting from the woods, firing as they came.

Foxy Bradshaw had been explaining to Lige, as they lay side by side in the cut:

"Damdest thing y'ever seen. Comin back threw them woods with bluebellies runnin up our tails. So I far'd at one'n slip behind a tree'n reload. Still got my rod inna barl, this big Yank come jumpin round my tree'n pins me up agin it with'is piece. Stuck it right'n my chest.

"'Reb!' he yells. 'You jus kilt my brother'n now I aim to kill you.' Christ, I thought I uz a deader. But when he drawed trigger, y'know what?"

"Misfar'd, I reck'n." Foxy's tales no longer interested Lige.

"Naw." Foxy's voice was triumphant. "*He* uz the deader. Goin over backwards soons he got the words outten'is mouth. Somebody's bullet'n'is head. At-er piece a-hissen goes up'n fars right'n my face but the goddam ball, it goes whooshin up pass my nose so close I kin feel the breeze."

Lige eyed Foxy skeptically. "Thought yuh said y'uz wounded."

"*Hurt*, I said. That muzzle blast right'n my face, I jerk my head backwards, it bang agin-a tree trunk so hard I fell out colder'n a stone."

"Whut happen to the tree?"

Foxy did not choose to answer, or perhaps to hear, and anyway, at that moment, the Yanks ripped out of the woods and poured in their first volley. Lige grabbed his piece and got off a quick shot; Foxy slumped face down and threw his arms over his head.

This time the weight of shock was with Schimmelfennig. Before Dixon's Rifles, manning the front line in the railroad cut, could get off more than a ragged return fire, the blueclads swarmed into the cut and over it, surging through Dixon, through McCrary's second line and up the knoll that anchored Jackson's flank.

Teddy Redmund, still observing from the ridge above, immediately turned his glasses away from the brutish hand-to-hand fighting that resulted to peer at Jackson's threatened left. On that part of the chessboard in his mind, Kearny's approaching blues were screened by woods; but Redmund had been aware for some time of dust rising in that direction, along Bull Run. Bound to be blues, feeling for Jackson's farthest flank. And soon enough the butternut batteries had shifted their attention to the left.

The moment the blues carried Brigadier Arnold's knoll, Redmund realized that if a simultaneous attack came over the open field on Arnold's left, Jackson's flank would be turned and his line rolled up. But as Schimmelfennig's new attack broke over the railroad cut, the Reb batteries opened thunderous fire over the open field across which the flank attack would have to come, and on the woods beyond it, where the blues would have to form for such a charge.

Redmund had no sooner swung his glasses to the left than he concluded that no such attack was coming. Blues over there, no doubt of that, but there'd be no attack for the bloody good reason that amateur troops like these would never charge through the artillery fire that Hill's gunners could lay on the field and the woods.

Sam Stowe had been incensed that Hill had called back Arnall's second counterattack just when his and Thomas's fresh regiments could have chased the Yanks into Bull Run. His fighting instincts, once aroused, still churned in him. Peering over the rail fence at the iron wall of shot and shell Hill's guns were erecting across the field in front of him, Stowe realized as quickly as Redmund that no one was likely to attack through it. Without waiting for orders from Arnall, he about-faced his regiment and charged his South Carolinians into the melee that had erupted behind Arnall's front line.

When the attack hit, Larkin Folsom had been boiling a pot of coffee for the General, although his mind actually had been upon the sonnet he had started composing the day before on the road from Centreville. Corporal Gilmore had seemed to like what he'd heard of it, and that gave Folsom confidence, pride in his work.

The orderly had settled upon a rhyme scheme—*aba, aba*—and finished off the first six lines in his head. Now he was trying out an opening for another six lines of *aba, aba*:

If, too, thy smile were but a candle's ray

which maybe seemed a little obvious but fit the rhyme scheme nicely and also the larger idea:

that flickers golden till the night is done
and dies when dawn refuses to delay . . .

The shattering Yank volley jerked Folsom out of this pleasant preoccupation. Nevertheless, he stayed confidently by the coffeepot until shocked to see Yanks pouring over the knoll. The orderly stared at this blue apparition for no more than a second; then a Minié went past his ear *wheat!* and another dashed the coffeepot off the fire and sent it rolling down the slope, spewing its hot liquid in all directions.

Folsom ran then. He was fast on his feet as a colt, and fright almost literally gave him wings. He was not afraid of the Yanks, but he didn't want them to grab the General's horse. Gin'al have my hide for *sure*, that happen.

Folsom sprinted for the little gully in which he'd tethered Rambler, slid into it feet first, grabbed the musket he'd left there, and rolled over in the dirt. He lay prone with the rifle poised, ready to defend his charge, although he had never fired the musket in anger. Corporal Gilmore had cleaned it for him just that morning.

By then, on the reverse slope of the knoll, Sparks's Tar Heels and Stowe's South Carolinians were locked in a mass struggle with Schimmelfennig's Yanks. Some of Arnall's front- and second-line troops also had drifted back into the fight. Blue and butternut alike had lost rank and order; the men of both armies mingled and surged like a racetrack crowd in panic, many of them falling to be trampled in the dust and broomsedge. Bayonets flashed in the sun; the high-pitched yelping of the butternuts, the hoarser shouts of the Yanks, the screams of the wounded, blended into a hellish chorus. The crack and clatter of small arms rang above the artillery thundering from the ridge, although Folsom wondered how anyone could tell who to shoot at.

Peering over the rim of the gully, the orderly saw Corporal Gilmore swinging his musket by the barrel like a baseball bat, clearing a circle around himself. When a Yank came charging at him from behind, Gilmore twisted about just in time, sidestepped and speared the Yank in the belly with a hand-held bayonet; the Yank stumbled on toward Folsom, a look of incredulity on his face, pitched to his knees clutching his belly, then folded himself carefully to the ground on his side and drew himself into a fetus-like ball.

Gilmore was trying to get through the mob to General Arnall. When the Yanks had come pounding and shooting across the knoll, Arnall had been behind the lines with Sparks's Tar Heels, checking the regiment's casualties and ammunition. Gilmore had been sprawled under a tree where he could watch Folsom's lithe young body moving around and the way the boy's pants stretched over his butt when he bent to the General's coffeepot.

As soon as the first bluecoat topped the knoll, the corporal sprang to his feet and seized his musket. He ran for Arnall's side but before he could get there Yanks were all around, thicker'n flies in a barnyard. The last he had seen of the General, Arnall had had a saber in one hand and his pistol in the other, the latter aimed squarely in the face of a big Yank.

Hoke Arnall had never been in hand-to-hand combat, not even with the Old Army in Indian country. Dispatching the big Yank had been his most immediate personal contribution to the war. But as Gilmore fought to reach him, the General felt himself suddenly and strangely free, bursting with energy, as if the pistol shot had set off an electric charge in his veins—as if the violence exploding around him, in him, had blown away the life he had led and all it had seemed to have made of him. Suddenly, he forgot his arrest, forgot Amy, forgot his ambitions, angers, frustrations, and all the entanglements of duty and morality and religion.

His body responded to the instinct of survival as if it had merely been waiting for brute strength to assume its rightful primacy. In a convulsion of self-preservation—the only realities his saber slashing flesh and bone, the power of the pistol kicking and blasting in his other hand, the sense of invincibility they sent flashing like blood to his brain—he did not *think* at all. The sound of his grunting breath as he maimed and killed echoed an animal response to mortal threat; and the wholeness of that response was joyful as salvation.

Then the moment passed, as joy does. A big and powerful man unrestrained, Arnall cut his way like a scythe through the encircling Yanks. In a few bloody moments he was out of the mob and had to take command again—of himself first.

Organize . . . Jackson's flank . . . clear these people out . . .

He looked around for some sign of military order—a regiment, a company. Any rock to build upon.

But nothing. *Chaos.* Arnall had the vague impression that somewhere in the struggling mass he had seen a planter's hat trampled in the broomsedge. He ran for the knoll.

Can't have chaos. Maybe an organized line still in the cut. *Rally'em. Clear these people out.*

But before he could do anything, a long and menacing line of butternut troops came rolling over a rise of ground to the rear of his position. Arnall felt a surge of immense relief. *Hill. Reinforcements.*

The butternut line trotted forward, yelling, fearsome. Branch's Brigade. Identification turned relief to irritation, doubt. Branch's Brigade saving Hoke Arnall's bacon. Hill had had to send Branch. On top of the arrest.

But Arnall was a professional. The sight of the oncoming line was the rock he needed. He lifted his saber high and waved on Branch's men.

"This way, boys!" His battle voice, he knew, would somehow reach them. "Drive 'em, boys! Give it to'em!"

Even as he yelled, the first bluecoats broke before the new onslaught and began to run back over the knoll. A Yank rifleman, his hat gone, his weapon lost somewhere in the struggle, his mouth hanging open and his eyes rolling in the idiocy of fear, trotted over the knoll toward the cut and the safety of the woods. Arnall shot him in the face with the last charge in the pistol.

It occurred to the General then that there had been no need to call upon God for deliverance. No need at all. God had come to his aid unasked.

Captain Micah G. Duryea was torn between apprehension and disgust as he rode along the flanks of Fitz-John Porter's divisions, marching in brilliant midday sun on the road from Manassas Junction to Gainesville. Duryea was by then certain that General Pope either had lost his grip on the situation or was laboring under a stubborn delusion. If that was the choice, disaster was bound to lie ahead.

Colonel Russell, at least, had appeared impressed with Duryea's appraisal that Jackson was not retreating. But Pope obviously had not been, despite the plain evidence of battle noise and smoke. Then, when Russell called Duryea aside for further orders, even the colonel had disputed the meaning of the dust cloud above the road from Thoroughfare Gap.

"Buford's cavalry's out that way, Duryea. General Pope says that smoke's bound to be him pitching into Stuart."

Duryea had tried to point out that the low gray cloud over the Thoroughfare road was red-tinted dust, not battle smoke. Trained eyes were not required to tell the difference.

But before he could drive home the argument, Russell had

rather impatiently silenced him and sent him off with a letter for
Porter and McDowell. The latter general, Russell told him, was
reported to be with Porter, although in the confusion of the field
no one could be sure. Duryea was to look for him with Porter's
headquarters group.

That was typical of this whole mismanaged collision of the
armies, Duryea thought. Pope could not even be sure where to
find his second-ranking officer, the commander of his largest corps!
But even that, in Duryea's view, was understandable by comparison to the commanding general's inexplicable conviction that
Jackson was trying to get away to rejoin the main southern army
beyond the mountains. Hardheaded analysis of the situation suggested, instead, that the rest of Lee's army was coming over the
mountains to join Jackson.

But orders were orders and Duryea had had no choice but to
ride to Porter with Pope's letter. He found Porter's column, with
King's Division of McDowell's Corps bringing up its rear, strung
out for miles on the narrow road from Manassas to Gainesville.
He guessed the trailing regiments probably had not left Manassas
by the time he caught up to Porter riding at its head. That would
have taken longer had the column not been halted for the last few
minutes of Duryea's ride. When he did reach Porter, the general
was quietly watching skirmishers being deployed across Dawkins
Branch ahead of him.

Duryea had never seen Fitz-John Porter before, although he
knew his fighting reputation from the Peninsula. Porter had a high
forehead, a fine strong nose, and a neatly trimmed beard; he was
a man of erect and soldierly appearance, quite in contrast to portly
Irvin McDowell, who was indeed riding beside him. Duryea handed
Pope's letter to McDowell, the senior of the two generals.

Watching Porter as McDowell read, Duryea's appraising eye
noticed an air of indifference, almost listlessness, about the newcomer from McClellan's army, as if nothing could concern him
less than what his new commanding general might have to say.
Duryea put this down as the sort of air some men assume in times
of danger and decision, as they try to convey to others how cool
and collected they are.

"Strange." McDowell handed the letter to Porter. "Pope seems
to think Longstreet can't get here at least until tomorrow night or
next day."

Across the branch, dust was visible beyond a ridge rising less
than a mile farther ahead. Open fields lay between branch and

ridge. Blueclad skirmishers were zigging and zagging across the fields, low to the ground; an occasional crack of a musket from the woods that covered the ridge slowed and scattered them.

Porter quickly read Pope's letter, frowned, and shook his head. "I can't make out what he wants, General. First he says go on to Gainesville and get in communication with his left wing. But not a word about whether to attack or not. And what's this mean?"

He handed the letter back to McDowell, pointing to a sentence. The senior general read aloud in a slow and emphatic voice:

" 'If any considerable advantages are to be gained by departing from this order, it will not be strictly obeyed.' I guess that's to give us some discretion."

Duryea, listening more to the hoarse roar of the battle to the northeast, decided from its rising volume that Pope must have thrown in more troops in support of Sigel.

"I hope that's what it means anyway," McDowell went on in more normal tones. "Because if we go on to Gainesville the way he wants, it looks to me like we might run right up on Longstreet's corps. If Buford's information is correct."

The reference to "Buford's information" caught Duryea's attention. He had considerable respect for Pope's cavalry commander. Maybe Pope would listen to John Buford if *he* said Longstreet was about to join Jackson and reunite the Rebel army.

"Then how do we get in communication with Pope's left?" Porter asked.

McDowell shook his head and turned to gaze over the wooded terrain in that direction. "I can tell you that's rough country in there . . ." He pointed. "To march troops through. Thick woods, underbrush, a lot of little creeks. Couldn't keep a brigade together, much less this corps." He sighed and spoke matter-of-factly. "Ought to know. I was lost in there all last night."

Duryea barely contained an exclamation thoroughly unsuitable to his sense of the fitness of things. The fate of the army, maybe even the nation, at stake, and Pope's senior corps commander, a former commanding general of the whole army, couldn't find his way out of the woods on a dark night!

No wonder, Duryea thought, the damned slavers were winning the war, overrunning the country with their bullwhips and black concubines and dog killers. With such generals as these, God help the poor old Union!

". . . too far out to fight a battle here, Porter."

Duryea listened in sullen anger as the two generals blathered on—he thought—about how to follow Pope's apparently puzzling order. He could not fully understand their concern, because he did not know that the note from John Buford, casually mentioned by General McDowell, had reported what Duryea would have realized was the most important information of the campaign— that at 8:45 a.m. Buford had counted seventeen butternut regiments, one battery, and 500 cavalry moving from Thoroughfare Gap through Gainesville. Longstreet was already on the field.

Micah G. Duryea believed in lines of responsibility, orderly procedure, rational decision. In his scheme of things, such information would have been passed along immediately to the commanding general, particularly by such a meticulous officer as Irvin McDowell; and Pope would have been persuaded immediately of the true situation by Buford's observation.

Less rigidly disciplined men—Colonel Russell, say, or Colonel Channing—were more used than Duryea to human fallibility, and all too well aware that war was the least certain of human undertakings. They had seen the most careful plans break down, the tightest organization fail. In the terror and confusions of war, they knew, the most elementary necessities could be overlooked even by experienced commanders—just as, that hot day on the road from Manassas to Gainesville, General McDowell had inexplicably failed to pass on Buford's note to John Pope.

The dust Duryea had seen rising beyond Dawkins Branch was not being raised, however, by Longstreet's oncoming divisions. A single company of Jeb Stuart's cavalry, under the temporary supervision of a staff officer, Captain Fargo Hart, was indulging Stuart's talent for ingenuity and theatrics.

After his conference with General Lee near Hay Market, Stuart and his escort had galloped south of the pike, where one of Stuart's brigadiers, Beverley Robertson, already was taking position to guard the approaching Longstreet's right flank.

Stuart had ordered his headquarters set up on a hill that commanded a view over the Manassas plain all the way east to Centreville. From its peak, the smoke of battle near Bull Run was plainly visible, as were the Yanks still creeping in masses westward along the pike to the Stone Bridge.

"These Yankees move slower'n corn growin," Colonel Snowden remarked.

But before Longstreet's line was completely in place or its right flank anchored, the approach of a different force of blue troops, this one along the road from Manassas, had been reported. Another general might have hastened off word to Longstreet either to pull back or to push more quickly into position. Either course might have put Longstreet at a disadvantage against a force of unknown size and mission; either would have been a tacit shifting of responsibility to Longstreet himself. Stuart, more ebullient than ever now that the dangerous division of Lee's forces was near an end, never considered such a message.

"Here's what I aim to do . . ." Cackling with laughter and slapping his thigh, Stuart confided his plan for holding off the unidentified body of Yanks marching up the road from Manassas.

The general sat his horse as easily, Fargo Hart thought, as if he were on a country picnic; and he discussed his plans with Snowden and other staff officers as unconcernedly as if weighing the merits of coon dogs or carriage horses. Hart had often heard Stuart elaborate at the mess table and around the camp fire on the virtues of speed, surprise, audacity; no wonder he had donned his cavalry command like a comfortable suit of clothes, or that Jackson valued him so highly. The two generals believed in action above all.

"But these Yankees take care," Hart had heard Stuart say. "Not a surprise'n Mcclellan's whole army that I ever saw on the Peninsula. I reck'n Pope's crowd'll be about the same."

Now, having outlined his plan, Stuart winked ostentatiously at Hart. "Think you can handle it, Cap'n? Aint it a good un?"

"Sure is, sir." Stuart was not a man of small appetite, for praise or anything else.

"Stop'em in their tracks." Stuart cackled again. "Wait'n see if it don't."

Hart quickly trotted off to find a proper locale. A country lane leading east from the Manassas–Gainesville Road and running through old fields grown up in the underbrush proved suitable. Feeling rather like Joshua marching around Jericho, Hart put the troopers to cutting pine boughs. Then they tied them to their halter straps and dragged them back and forth along the lane, much amused at the wafts of dust thus sent into the air in fine imitation of that raised by marching troops.

"Reck'n this'll really fool'em?" Lieutenant Calloway, in command of the company, peered anxiously toward the rival dust cloud, which they knew to be caused by the real thing, over the Manassas Road.

"Won't have to for long."

The question had aroused Hart from a reverie in which he had been wondering if he could get free to spirit Missy away from Brace's ramshackle house. Longstreet's front was going to be too close to it for safety. Summoned by the lieutenant back to the business at hand, Hart was irritated with himself. What foolishness, that a skinny child could so easily have taken his mind off his duty, so many times, during so active a day! And, of course, it was old Brace's duty, not Hart's, to see to his family's safety.

Durward P. Brace was at that moment not far away, lying flat in underbrush near the top of the wooded ridge toward which Duryea had seen the blue skirmishers advancing north of Dawkins Branch. Henry lay at Brace's side, and one of General Robertson's officers—an engineer captain that Brace had muttered to Henry "wouldn't go knee-high on a piss-ant"—lay just beyond Henry.

The piss-ant captain turned a pair of high-powered glasses on the Yanks beyond the branch and studied them for a long time; then he rolled on his side and put the glasses into their case with conclusive movements, as if weighty matters had been settled.

"Whole corps over ther. Prob'ly Porter. Damn near ruint us at Gaines's Mill."

Brace did not know how big a corps was, nor who Porter might be, and he had never heard of any miller named Gaines in Prince William County. But he knew, as he watched the Yank skirmishers crossing the field, some of them getting close to the woods, exactly what he was going to do. If the piss-ant captain gave him room enough.

"He start crost the crick with that whole corps, he'll run right up Longstreet's shirtfront. Got to git some guns on this ridge."

The captain spoke as confidently as Brace supposed General Lee might have. Then he said exactly what Brace wanted to hear: "You'n your darky stay here." Naturally, he spoke directly to the white man, as if Henry were no more than the barebacked mule he had tethered back over the top of the ridge. "They start to put any force at all over the crick, I mean like a coupla hunnert men or more, or any big guns at all, leave the darky to watch'n hightail it back up the road to warn Gin'al Robertson."

"How bout em boys down'er?" Brace pointed at the blue skirmishers trotting low across the field.

"Enough of our'n here to keep'em busy." The piss-ant captain began crawling back through the underbrush. "Look sharp now!"

Brace felt no fear of the distant Yanks. They scarcely seemed real, that far off, and it had not occurred to him, anyway, that somebody might shoot at him. He did not feel that he was a real part of the army, so why would anybody shoot at him? Besides, his thoughts had been preoccupied with Henry and what he was going to do once Henry was out of the way. At one point, lying there in the sun, he had raised himself a hard-on, remembering Sajie baretitted. The way'er ass felt upside of a hard dick.

Abruptly, Brace crawled after the piss-ant captain getting back over the ridge just as the captain was hoisting himself aboard a horse three times too big for him.

"Wait up there!"

The captain gazed at him severely as Brace rose to his feet and stumbled through the underbrush.

"I uz thinkin . . . you reck'n, all'em Yanks out-er . . . reck'n maybe we oughtta have us a far-arm?"

"Sure God oughtta. Too bad you aint."

"You got two ther."

The captain had a captured Yank carbine in a saddle holster and wore a pistol strapped to his belt.

"Keepin'em both, too. Git on back-er like I told you'n keep'n eye out."

Brace watched him ride off. He had not really expected the piss-ant to part with one of the weapons; and anyway, Brace didn't want to *shoot* Henry. He was no murderer.

He slipped down in the underbrush again and crawled snakelike back over the ridge to Henry's side. The African, lying there solid as a tree trunk, dwarfed him; but Brace suddenly felt himself more powerful, commanding, than just being white had ever meant to him.

"New orders." He did not look at Henry as he whispered. "Cap'n sez he wants you down ther't edge-a the woods."

Henry did not seem to move but Brace felt his eyes sideways on him. Brace stared straight ahead. Some of the Yanks had reached the woods and the cracking of musketry was increasing. All to the good.

"How come he say?"

"Sojers don't ask no questions. Git on down at hill."

Henry didn't move. Brace knew, of course, that in the end he would go. Nigguhs did what white men told'em. That was the law of life. Henry only needed a little pushing.

"Wants a closer look at'em Yanks comin crost there'n sez safer to send you cause Yanks aint gone shoot nobody cullud. They's ab'lishionist."

Still Henry did not move and Brace became impatient. Prob'ly not much time fore the piss-ant come back or sent for'em."

"But em Virginia boys shore-God will. Nigguh don't do what they say do."

Brace gave that a few seconds to sink in. When it did, Henry said nothing still but began to crawl away through the underbrush. Brace thought with satisfaction that he had never seen a nigguh who'd stand up to a white man.

"Alla way down!" Brace's loud whisper was just to make sure. "Edge-at-field!"

Henry crawled on, not so quietly or with as little disturbance of the underbrush as Brace with his thin body would have managed. Henry was a big'un; Brace could follow his progress right down the hill by the rippling motion in the weeds and scrub—like a groundhog tunneling, Brace thought. He did not take his eyes off the telltale passage.

Henry's progress was slow but steady. Brace was satisfied that it also was noisy and visible enough that someone besides himself was bound to spot it—whether one of the Virginia boys concealed in the woods or one of the Yanks in the field or now edging into the woods, he did not care. Brace knew little of war but he had the sure instinct that boys shooting at each other would be nervous. Either side would be likely to shoot anything moving; see what it was later.

Time passed. Nothing happened. Henry crawled on. Brace felt his nerves drawing taut. Confoun fools blind or deef, can't see'n elephant pass.

The sun beat down from the glassy sky. Still nothing happened. But Brace knew it would. He felt his senses rising to an irresistible rush.

The moving underbrush that marked Henry's passage had reached to within a rod, by Brace's estimate, of the indistinct line where woods gave way to field. Suddenly, a Yank skirmisher—looking not unlike a jack-in-the-box Brace once had seen a drummer demonstrate in the store at Gainesville—straightened from his crouch, leaped in a half-turn to his right, brought his musket to his shoulder, and aimed at the trail of movement in the underbrush.

Brace felt the immense surge of satisfaction that had been

gathering in him. *I knowed it knowed it'd work.* He saw the white spurt of smoke from the musket, and did not realize that in his excitement he was clutching his hard penis in his right hand, through his thin trousers.

Just as the flat, amazingly distant smack of the musket reached him from the field, the underbrush above Henry's creeping passage erupted, as if thrown back by sweeping arms and Henry rose into view—at first majestically, a huge imposing figure like a bear leaping from hiding toward its prey; then, in midair, collapsing as if punctured, so that air and substance and life rushed out as one, and Henry's body, limp and grotesque as the hide of a skinned grizzly, disappeared back into the underbrush.

Brace had to squeeze down hard to keep from coming. But his ecstasy was charged with pride. Not since the old skinflint left Kate the farm and the Africans, after all those years of treating Brace like a hired hand, had he felt so much in charge of himself, so in control of his destiny, so sure of his ability to manage. Brace felt like a man, lying there in the brush and the heat and the echoes of musketry, holding himself, knowing he'd done what he'd set out to do. Pulled it off slicker'n a goat's butt, I-God!

He did not understand why the success of his scheme had affected him down there, but he hardly cared because he knew that as soon as he could get to Sajie, he was going to have the real thing. Brace did not think beyond what he aimed to do as soon as he could get to Sajie.

Duryea sat his horse in the cover of trees for several minutes before he ventured briefly into the open to cross the Manassas Gap Railroad line, which had been mostly in disuse since the opening months of the war. Finally, satisfied that no Reb scouts or pickets waited on the other side, he touched spurs to his horse and trotted over the tracks rusted from long disuse and the ties rotting and overgrown with grass. Within seconds he was covered again by woods on the east side of the right-of-way.

Duryea was returning to Pope's headquarters with word that McDowell and Porter had decided to divide their forces. McDowell was to take his own two divisions, King's and Ricketts's, across a narrow road leading from Bethlehem Church, on the Manassas Road, to the wider Sudley Springs Road, which ran north to the pike and beyond that to Sudley Springs and Sudley Church. Porter brought forward his guns to bear on the ridge beyond Dawkins

Branch; behind the guns he held his own troops in readiness on the Manassas–Gainesville Road.

As far as Duryea could tell, McDowell's intention was to bring his own division roundabout to the left of the line Pope already had established from Groveton to Sudley Springs. When he had thus extended the line toward Porter's stalled advance, it would become possible, the two generals hoped, for Porter to push ahead and join his right to McDowell's left. That would stretch Pope's entire front on a northeast-southwest line from the Manassas Gap Railroad near Dawkins Branch to Sudley Springs.

"You put your force in here," Duryea heard McDowell say to Porter, "and I'll take mine up the Sudley Springs Road."

On McDowell's instruction, Duryea was taking this information to Pope. Acting on his own, he had abandoned the roads to check out McDowell's contention that the country lying between Porter's Corps and Groveton was too wooded and broken to move troops through.

Duryea dismounted and led his horse away from the railroad tracks, angling straight north, guiding himself toward Groveton as much by his natural instincts and memory for maps as by the sun. In the thick woods all was still, quiet, except the insects buzzing in his ears; the distant boom and rattle of battle came dulled through the tangled growth. The early afternoon heat was stifling.

He had been prepared to believe that McDowell's description of the rigors of the terrain had been one more fancy of imaginative generals; but he soon discovered that Porter's Corps would have blundered about all day in the brambles and gullies, the boggy little swamps, the thick scrub timber and dangling vines. Even Duryea alone could make better time on foot until he reached cleared ground.

As he made his way, Duryea's anger had turned to depression. He had been too long in the field with Pope to have an up-to-date knowledge of the war situation, but he did know that McClellan had been pulled off the Peninsula; now here was Pope's campaign already lost—Duryea feared—owing to that otherwise insignificant notch in the Bull Run Mountains that Pope had failed to block. Much as he hated retreat, Duryea now believed that Pope should get behind Bull Run and wait on the Centreville heights for reinforcements from McClellan. To fight Lee's reunited army with scattered divisions, tired men, and short supplies was to court disaster.

They'd never win the war that way. Never win without a general who wanted to fight and who knew *how* to fight. But McClellan didn't want to, and it looked as if Pope didn't know how. And even with a general who could win, the troops would have to have something to fight for, the way the secesh fought to hang on to their field hands and concubines.

A New England abolitionist to the bone, Duryea had always favored emancipation immediate and total. He had been virtually born to that view, because his mother had kept a Vermont station on the Underground Railroad to Canada. That August afternoon, as he pushed on through the breathless southern woods, he was ready to believe the war could not be won militarily—not with such pudd'n-head generals anyway—unless it was first won politically by hitting the slavers where they'd be hurt the most.

Free their miserable human property to turn on them. Take their black women away from them. Give our boys a cause to fight for. And show the world what a degenerate dog-killing society it was that had abandoned the old flag to defend its "rights." Some rights! Traffic in flesh. Immoral old men selling girls into a life of degeneracy.

Duryea was not too preoccupied with these thoughts to stop instantly and stand motionless as the dead tree on his left when something off-key pierced his consciousness. He was not sure what had done it—a sound, or the absence of sound, a movement, an odor, some indefinable sense of something suddenly out of kilter. Slowly he moved his hand to his horse's muzzle to prevent any sounds of greeting or alarm. His only other movement was the steady, even turning of his head from left to right as with green, feline eyes he searched the wood for movement, color—anything not there by natural cause.

He heard and saw nothing, but his warning instinct was strong. He stood for three minutes, nothing moving but his head and the horse's tail switching flies. Then, with infinite caution, he moved ahead, careful where he put his feet, and to move branches and rattle the brush as little as possible, no more than a dog trotting through might have, or a wild turkey. As if sensing the necessity, his horse stepped along nearly as silently and just as slowly. After five minutes of this pace, Duryea stood three feet from the edge of the wood bordering the old Warrenton–Alexandria Road. A field of corn was on the other side of the rough dirt track, long since relegated to local use by the wider, straighter Warrenton Pike, a mile to the north.

Duryea's map sense and instinct told him where he was, within half a mile. If he moved left along the old road, within a few hundred yards the path called Lewis Lane would bear off right—north—to Groveton and the left wing of Pope's line. Or, if he went right maybe a mile or more, he'd come to the Sudley Springs Road at New Market. Longstreet should be sending patrols along the old road, to find out what was on the Federal left.

Undoubtedly, that was what had disturbed his sense of things—Reb scouts moving on the old road, making some noise. Duryea squinted at the sun. Plenty of time to reach Pope, long before McDowell could march around by Bethlehem Church. Duryea suddenly was tired of carrying messages, scouting ground, bringing back reports too often ignored or disbelieved. Duryea wanted to put a mark on the slavers—*his* mark. He thought of his faithful dog Garrison wantonly killed, and made up his mind.

The chances were at least even, maybe better, that Longstreet's scouts had been moving *out*, away from the Reb lines, to Duryea's right. If he sat tight, waited a while, they'd maybe come back along the same road. And maybe with the patrol almost over they'd be not quite as alert as they ought to be.

He moved twenty yards back into the woods, tethered his horse behind a tree, then took his Sharps carbine from the saddle holster. Duryea had long ago equipped himself with this cavalry weapon, seventeen inches shorter than the infantry musket, weighing only eight pounds, breech-loading and thus quick-firing. The Sharps lacked accuracy much beyond 150 yards, but Duryea liked to work close in anyway. He checked the linen cartridge in the chamber, moved back to within ten yards of the roadside, and went to ground behind the thick trunk of an oak tree in such a way as to leave a line of fire open to the road.

Duryea had to wait five minutes before he sensed the patrol coming back. Within seconds after he heard their footsteps, he calculated that there were five of them. One was walking just within the woods, another a few rows into the cornfield, three in the road itself. Duryea knew before he could see them that they would be alert, with muskets at the half-cock and carried at the ready. But he was willing to gamble that they were just relaxed enough, as they neared their own lines, to give him his chance.

He let the man in the woods go past by a yard or two. Then he stood the carbine against the tree, rose and slipped swiftly forward, silent as a squirrel on a limb, clasped his hand over the mouth to stifle a scream, and cut the scout's throat. Duryea lowered the body silently, retrieved the carbine from behind the tree, and crept to the edge of the road. The three scouts in the road were by then about twenty-five yards beyond him, one on each side, one ahead and in the middle, their heads moving slowly from side to side.

The Sharps .52-caliber bullet took the man on the near side of the road in the back of the head. While the echo rang, Duryea dived to the ground behind a tree, rolled on his back, pulled down on the trigger guard to expose the still-smoking chamber, inserted another cartridge, and snapped the breechblock closed. Confident that no one looking the other way could have seen the flash of his muzzle and so have pinpointed his location, he rolled over on his stomach, out from behind the tree trunk, and caught a glimpse of a running man only one step from the thin cover of the cornfield.

Duryea's snap shot struck home, he thought, under the left shoulder blade. The Reb pitched forward like a diver into the gray earth of the cornfield and lay still. The bottoms of his bare feet stuck out of the corn rows.

Three out of five, Garrison. Good enough. Duryea could hear the other two Rebs thrashing rapidly through the cornstalks but he tried never to overplay his hand. *Do what you can do,* he liked to remind himself. And be *in omnia paratus*.

Feeling better, much better, remembering suddenly and for no clear reason the apprehensive black faces with their wide eyes that, years ago, he had seen huddled in his mother's root cellar, Duryea looked with satisfaction at the body of the Reb scout lying in the road. Scrawny devil. Dog killer.

Then he mounted and trotted east on the rutted old road, away from the running men. He was certain that within a half mile he would be able to turn and strike for Groveton on another country track he remembered from the maps. He'd be reporting to Pope within the hour, not that *that* would do anybody much good.

Fargo Hart's road-dragging operation had been quickly succeeded by the real thing. Jones's Division of Longstreet was moving guns to bear on Dawkins Branch from the ridge where Brace and Henry had watched the skirmishers coming across the field; and Jones's brigades were posted to cover both the railroad and the wagon road. The rest of Longstreet's troops had got themselves solidly into position from that flank to the Warrenton Pike.

So when Major Jesse Thomas saw the Old Man trotting on his gray horse to Longstreet's headquarters south of the pike, Thomas could guess what was coming. Lee, it had become clear that summer, was no Joe Johnston, retreating, then retreating again, in hopes of finding the perfect defensive position, which of course never appeared. Careful above all to preserve his army, Johnston was. But Lee attacked. Give him half an opening, even the glimmer of a chance, and he'd spill what blood he had to take advantage of it.

Thomas admired that. But he also was impressed with Longstreet's theory of the "aggressive defensive." Maneuver yourself, Longstreet preached, into a good defensive position where the enemy *had* to attack you, but at a disadvantage. Particularly if the enemy had the advantage in numbers, he'd have to waste it slaughtering his men against a dug-in defense. Thus, an outmanned army like Lee's should take the strategic offensive in order to be able to fight advantageously on the tactical defensive.

Watching from the tree against which he was lounging, Thomas could see Lee pointing east along the turnpike. Typical. The battle was that way and the Old Man wanted to get into it. Take the pressure off Jackson's left. But within the hour Thomas himself had delivered to Ol Pete scouting reports that said the Federals on the left of Pope's line—Reynolds's small Pennsylvania division—had pulled back from the pike into a strong defensive position on a ridge confronting Longstreet's front less than a mile away.

Longstreet himself had ridden out near enough Reynolds's new position to gauge its strength. So Thomas was not surprised to see Longstreet shaking his head vigorously, although Lee seemed to be persisting in urging attack. The major knew that a frontal assault on Reynolds would stand Longstreet's "aggressive defensive" theory on its head.

Worse, some kind of Yank force was confronting Jones's guns on Longstreet's right flank, out there on the Manassas Road. Porter's Corps, the first reports had it. And, anyway, as Ol Pete had pointed out to his staff, forcing Reynolds back from the pike and into a defensive position already had lifted his pressure from Jackson's right; so Longstreet's mere presence on the field had afforded Jackson some relief.

"Look like Ol Pete's got his muleskin on." A young captain who had ridden in with Lee's escort group had drifted near Thomas's tree, holding a tin cup of coffee from the headquarters pot. Thomas recognized him as the staff captain, Franklin, who had had the good fortune to sit by Miss Letty at Dabney Williams's dinner table.

"Oh, well." Thomas still envied Franklin that seat—envied, too, his easy Virginia grace and his two good hands. Strange to think it was to him, one-handed Jesse Thomas, not to this handsome young aristocrat, that Miss Letty had sent Lawrence with her handkerchief. "I reck'n Gin'al Lee's kind of strong-natured himself."

"Sure is." Franklin sipped coffee and made a face. "He aims to hit those people. You fellows boil up ol' brogans over here, or what?"

"Horseshit, mostly." Let'im choke on that, Thomas thought. Fop if I ever seen one.

"What *we* do . . . ," Franklin's voice was serious, "is mix it half horseshit'n half gunpowder. Gives it body."

Thomas grinned, only a little grudgingly. "Ol Pete still shakin'is head, Cap'n. He looked over that ground out there in front of us himself. Didn't much like it."

Franklin glanced over his shoulder at the two generals, Lee austere, gray with dust and reserve; Longstreet heavy, dark, immovable. "Then the Ol Man won't *order* it. But he sure wants to give Jackson a hand."

Thomas could not be sure, as he watched Longstreet shake his head again, whether young Franklin had subtly stressed the "he" in that last sentence. Likely he had, and Thomas resented it. But he knew, anyway, what some would surely think if Longstreet did not attack that afternoon.

A mile and a half southeast, just behind the ridge from which Jones's guns now pointed at Dawkins Branch and Porter's quiescent Federal corps, Jeb Stuart and his staff were riding out to the south. They were well beyond both the railroad and the wagon road from Manassas to Gainesville, as they looked for General Beverley Robertson on the extreme right flank of the Confederate line.

Robertson had the reputation of being an excellent drillmaster who tended to lose his composure in battle. Jackson and Stuart were known—that is, they were rumored over the camp fire—to have little use for him; but Lee, whose judgment mattered most, was thought to have refused to relieve him. With Porter's Corps now reported at Dawkins Branch, clearly menacing Longstreet's flank, Stuart obviously was checking up on Robertson's cavalry dispositions.

But the bald and mustachioed Robertson had his pickets well out, his patrols active, and his troopers in hand; not even the demanding Stuart could find fault with anything Robertson had done. During the conference between the two young generals—the precocious Stuart not yet 30, Robertson a comparatively ripe 36—Hart, the Reverend Major Allen, and Coke Mowbray spurred to the crest of the ridge for a look at the Yanks.

Beyond Dawkins Branch, stretching as far as the eye could see along the road to Manassas, blue troops stood in seemingly endless ranks, regiment upon regiment, brigade following brigade. Three quarters of a mile distant, over the east bank of the branch—a substantial stream at that point—Porter's guns glistened in the sun, a menacing line of batteries on either side of the wagon road.

"Christ-amighty," Mowbray said. "Look at..."

"Watch your blasphemous tongue!"

"Yeah, sorry, Rev'rend. Meant to say...uh, Great Scott, they's a lot of 'em, aint they?"

"May God smite 'em hip and thigh!"

The Reverend Major's God, Hart thought again, was not one whose attentions he particularly craved. And suddenly, as if aroused by Allen's booming voice, one of the Federal pieces across the branch emitted a cotton-boll puff of white smoke; a shell screamed toward the spot on the ridge where they sat their horses. The flat *brrumpp* of the cannon rolled across the open ground behind the shell, which rattled harmlessly through the treetops above them.

"Yanks can't hit..." Mowbray was saying gaily, when a heavily falling branch cracked the Reverend Major's horse squarely across its muzzle.

The animal shied, then reared in fright and pain; and the corpulent Reverend Major, never more than an adequate horseman, tumbled backwards from the saddle. Just as he went off, the horse's forelegs came down and the beast bolted forward. The jangling spur on the Reverend's right boot caught in a tangle of leather straps, saddlebag, and canteen hanging below the rolled buffalo robe behind the saddle.

Hart had been leaning nonchalantly on Mercury's neck; but in the instant that he saw Allen's horse drag the Reverend's heavy, dangling body forward, Hart came alive in the saddle, his fingers transmitted instinctive orders through the reins, his spurs touched the black flank so lightly that Mercury could barely have felt the prick. The horse leaped after Allen's mount and the struggling body being dragged head down through the underbrush.

The Yank cannon puffed again; another shell screamed overhead. Hart scarcely noticed as he stood in his stirrups and leaned out to his right, his lithe body stretched to its utmost reach. Above the beat of hooves, he could hear the Reverend Major's head and shoulders bumping over the rough ground like a caisson with a broken wheel, and his grunts and wheezes of pain and exertion.

Then Hart's grasping fingers closed on the bolting horse's halter strap, and within a few yards he had tugged it to a trembling stop. The Federal cannon threw a third shell screaming at them, and this one chewed into the ground and showered dirt and litter all around.

Coke Mowbray, only a length behind Hart, had leaped from his saddle the moment Hart got his hand on the runaway. Swiftly, he disengaged Allen's spur and pulled the Reverend away from his frightened horse's hooves.

"Major . . . y'all right?"

Hart was dismounting as he heard the hoarse whisper from the ground:

" . . . Lord be praised . . . Our Father . . . hath spared His servant."

Hart promptly swung back into the saddle.

"That bein the case . . ." He watched Mowbray fingering the Reverend's bruised and bleeding head. "Whyn't we just let the Lord haul His servant's ass out of here?"

Sam Stowe, bleeding from a cut on the cheekbone where some Yank's lashing rifle barrel had given him a glancing blow, plumped out his crushed hat as best he could and stuck it defiantly back on his head. Stowe had been in the thick of the struggle after the Yanks swarmed over Hoke Arnall's line. He had had no experience of hand-to-hand fighting either, but it had by no means so exhilarated him as it had his brigadier. Stabbing and clubbing was not Colonel Stowe's idea of war; and while he was confident that he had done his share of damage with the saber that had been his only weapon, he had found the business distasteful in the extreme, as he would have a tavern brawl. Nothing about it of courage or skill or science; a brute struggle for survival. Stowe wanted to *lead* men, not join them in braining each other.

But Arnall! Stowe had caught sight of the General cutting his way out of the mob, Colt in one hand and saber in the other, terrifying in his strength and fury, some sixth sense seeming to give him warning of any attacker from whatever quarter, magically conferring on him immunity from blasting muzzles and thrusting bayonets. In that glimpse Stowe had realized that beneath his stiff military posture Hoke Arnall was a man of passion and animality, born to war in its most elementary form—man against man.

Now that Branch's rescuing regiments had helped drive the Yanks back over the railroad cut, Arnall—not pausing for a moment—had reverted to the trained military officer, busily restoring his front. Even under continuing battle pressure, with the Yanks keeping up heavy musket fire on the railroad cut, the General had swiftly re-formed his regiments, got runners on the way for ammunition and the wounded moving back to Sudley Church; now he was striding along the lip of the cut, stiffening his troops with his words and presence.

From the rail fence where his regiment had once again taken post, Colonel Stowe watched Arnall in admiration newly edged with apprehension. The energy, the command in his voice, the decision in his manner—no question but the man was a leader. But Stowe's glimpse of the brawling fighter underneath had been unsettling, as if he had seen a splendid hound suddenly turned mad dog.

Stowe particularly wished Arnall hadn't been so quick to send Branch's regiments back to reserve. The Yanks would be coming again, and sooner or later over the field beyond the fence. He gazed up at the sun. Seem like it hadn't moved since the last time he checked, an hour ago, maybe two. Stowe had never known time to pass so slowly.

But to Hoke Arnall the day had seemed more nearly the tick of a clock, events moving as swiftly as troops charging, and as blurred in his mind as glimpses of the field through smoke drifts. Everything seemed speeded up and heightened in intensity. His long stride seemed to carry him everywhere swiftly, without effort.

"Hold fire, men!" he shouted above the infernal clatter of Yank muskets from the woods. "Don't waste your shot . . . don't shoot unless you can look down their throats!" He was seriously worried about ammunition, half a day's nearly ceaseless firing having all but emptied his men's cartridge boxes. "A Yank for a bullet, boys . . . one Yank, one bullet!"

But the one fact that dominated Arnall's hyperactive con-

sciousness was that the Yanks had broken his line. *That* would
go in Hill's report, too. Branch had had to restore his line, ex-
punging the memory of the morning's counterattack and the clearing of the Federals from the woods. The enemy had broken his
line, and Arnall burned with unholy zeal to remove that blemish,
redeem his record—with faith that God's instrument could not
fail.

"Folsom!"

Even as he called for the orderly, his ear picked up a faint
diminution in the volume of fire from the woods.

"Rightchere, Gin'al!"

"Folsom . . . need cottridges. For the Colt. Get a move on!"

Were the Yanks pulling back? Or had some of them, maybe a
regiment, for some reason ceased fire?

Corporal Gilmore watched as Folsom dashed off toward the
General's saddlebags. He had been pleased all morning to see that
even such a poet-type seemed to have a good head and steady
nerves. In the mob struggle with the Yanks, Gilmore had had no
time or chance to look out for him; but after Branch had run off
the Yanks and Gilmore found time to check, there the boy was,
cool as a cucumber, right where he was supposed to be. Guardin
Ironass's horse.

Gilmore moved along at a discreet distance behind the General,
who'd hardly stood still all morning. Like Stowe, Gilmore admired
Arnall the soldier, if not always the man. And today, the corporal
thought, he'd been at his best. Not a brigade in the Army could
have taken such a pounding and stood in the same tracks it had
been in at dawn.

Every webfoot'n at line, he thought, know he gone feel a
boot'n'is rear, he start givin ground on Ironass.

Suddenly, six feet in front of him, Gilmore saw General Arnall
stop and his body go rigid in attention. Then his saber swept above
his head and his hoarse roar rose above the continuing Yank
musketry:

"In the cut! Yanks in the cut!"

Arnall began to run. "By the right flank, boys . . . fire! By the
right flank . . . fire!"

Teddy Redmund, noting that it was half past one, wondered why
the blues had taken so long to exploit that gaping hundred-yard
interval between Arnold's shaken and shrunken brigade and the

next one to his right. The Federals had been keeping up a steady small-arms fire on both brigades, and on still another just to the right of them. But all day the gap in the line had waited there, like a missing tooth.

Redmund watched from his perch behind Hill's line as at least two regiments of blues poured out of the woods directly in front of the gap and charged into the railway cut. *Yes* Redmund thought *bloody yes* moving blue pieces on Sertorius's chessboard. If the blue generals had them lined up in the woods to keep coming through that gap and into the cut, Arnold was done for, cut off, and isolated for the kill. And Jackson's left was decisively turned.

The same thoughts flashed through Hoke Arnall's head as he saw the first Yank rifleman charging into the cut. Instinctively, he had ordered the nearest troops to face right and fire at them, but he knew that men surprised on the flank were at a disadvantage; even if not demoralized, they could bring only a few muskets to bear at one end of their line. Besides, the Yanks seemed at first glance numberless. Might be coming in on his front again, too. Or across the field on Stowe. Maybe both.

"Gilmer!"

"Yessuh!"

"Bring Sparks . . . quick! While they're still in the cut!"

Arnall did not even look around to see if the corporal understood. He knew his men and that even before he'd got the words out of his mouth Gilmore was running. Nor had he needed to give detailed orders for Sparks; Sparks knew how to send a regiment into a fight. Hoke Arnall had taught him, and God would be at his side.

"Give it to'em!" Arnall shouted at the front-line riflemen, squared around now toward the Yanks in the cut to their right. "Pour it in!"

He ran along the line, toward the blue mass up ahead. *Bayonet. Give'em the bayonet if they come on . . .*

Behind him, toward what was now the rear of Dixon's Rifles, Foxy Bradshaw had faced right with the rest of the regiment but was too paralyzed with fear to do more. Foxy had clenched himself facedown against the bank of the cut throughout the fight behind the knoll and now was completely unnerved by the flank attack. Beside him some yelling butternut fired; the flash singed Foxy's neck and he fell away against the bank just as Josh Beasly stepped out of the line. Josh took two or three steps into the clear and went down on one knee, sighting his rifled musket along the line of the cut. Foxy almost forgot his fear, in the instinct that, this time, Josh was not drawing down on no Yank.

Sonomabitch. Josh saw he had an absolutely clear shot. Ironass reared up over everbody else. Like he think bullets don't hit gin'als.

Arnall was running away from Josh, but in a straight line toward the Yanks. Josh could hit a running rabbit with a rifled ball at better than 200 yards, if he could see the rabbit. He made the range on Ironass just above fifty yards but opening fast.

Sonamabitch buck me the la-a-ast time. Josh's finger tightened on the trigger.

Something light but forceful fetched him a hard blow in his back, with just enough impact to tip a kneeling man off balance. Josh lurched forward and to his right, as the hammer fell on the fulminate cap. As he had planned, the sound of the shot was absorbed in the battle noise; but the barrel of his piece rose as he fell, and the ball flew harmlessly into the trees above the Yanks.

Josh broke his fall with his elbow. He thought at first he must have been hit by a spent Yank bullet. His brain focused slowly and he realized that whatever had happened had ruined his bead on Ironass. *Never got a chancet like at again.*

Josh stood up. He hadn't been hit after all. He was angry at the ruined shot but still it had not occurred to him that *somebody* had ruined it, because he had no idea that anyone would have wanted to. Nobody he knew gave a shit for Ironass. He looked around to see what had hit him.

"He done it! Snotnose done it!" Josh's eyes followed Foxy's pointing finger.

Larkin Folsom, trotting back with a linen bag of cartridges from General Arnall's saddlebags, had seen Arnall running toward the right. The orderly could see that the Yanks had cracked the line again and in the confusion of events this development meant to him only that the General needed his cartridges more than ever. Folsom quickly started after him—a dutiful young man not at all oblivious to whizzing bullets or to the dead and wounded around him, but one who, had he had time to analyze his actions, would have feared injury less than failing his obligations. He was, moreover, so young and full of life that he was unable to realize or even imagine the arrant vulnerability of man to man, and man to chance.

He ran on with the bag of cartridges in his hand, coming up

behind Josh Beasly just as Josh knelt and leveled his sights on Arnall. Folsom froze in his tracks. He knew the common gossip that certain hated officers like Arnall had been "spotted." He could tell that the kneeling man was taking careful aim at somebody, not merely firing at the mass of bluecoats in the cut. He saw Arnall's back as clear and exposed as the killing sun overhead. Reflexively, as he would have tried to ward off a blow, Folsom threw the sack of cartridges as hard as he could at the kneeling man's back.

Only when the man stood up and his yellow-edged eyes, following someone's pointing finger, finally fixed on him did Larkin Folsom understand what he had done with such absence of calculation. He stood staring into those eyes no more than a moment; then, fearful as he had never been made by war, he began to step backward, not looking away from the big man drawing the bayonet from his belt.

Cut'is goddam heart out. Josh felt the razor-like steel in his hand and was glad he'd kept it sharp. He was not concerned with who might be watching. He gave no thought to consequences; he never did. Josh was a simple man, direct as a hammer. Ruint my shot. Cut'is heart out.

Folsom knew he could outrun the man with the yellow eyes, or anybody. He took another step backward, just before breaking into a run, and tripped over Lige Flournoy's outstretched leg. Folsom went down thrashing his arms, falling heavily *whuff!* on his back and shoulders.

Josh jumped forward, but not as Lige expected. He went down face first in the dirt, just short of Lige's boot, the back of his head suddenly a red and spurting mess. Lige could not have distinguished any one shot in the thousands popping all around him in harsh continuous detonation. But he knew what a .58-caliber ball did to the back of a man's head.

With the string of dried apples still around his neck, Lige looked beyond Josh's body and saw Corporal Amon Gilmore, his musket still smoking, staring back at him. Across fifty yards of ground, the two big men gazed steadily at one another.

Several men in Dixon's Rifles, probably some of McCrary's South Carolinians, had seen what Josh Beasly had been about to do. Nobody but Folsom had tried to stop him. Some had wished Arnall dead, too. Others had not cared, or feared Josh, or were immobilized by the continuing battle, or did not wish to be involved. Most had seen Josh fall and some understood that Corporal

Gilmore, not some Yank, had put the bullet in Josh's head.

But all of them, Gilmore and Lige included, knew that nothing would be done about any of it. Troops were not going to inform on one another when the surfeit of death made one more, and the manner of its coming, seem inconsequential. Nobody would be charged, nobody punished—unless one of the two men staring at one another across the littered ground behind Arnall's front took action against the other. Arnall himself was cheering Spark's counterattacking Tar Heels into the cut.

Neither Lige nor Gilmore feared the other, or anyone, and least of all the army. But they were different men. Amos Gilmore wanted to look out for the boy; but Lige Flournoy did not give a hoot in hell whether Josh or any of the meat in the regiment lived or died, or how. He had only tripped up the snotnose to keep the fun going a little longer.

To hell with it, Lige thought, turning his attention back to the fight. In a war, a man fought because it was there to be done, and everybody sooner or later got to be a deader. So what difference it made how you got snuffed, or when, Lige failed to see.

As he started to move forward to get his crack at the Yanks in the cut, he saw Foxy Bradshaw headed for the rear, limping as if he had a leg wound. Lige laughed soundlessly at the notion.

Nothin ther to hit, he thought. Bullet'd sail right thew at sack-a shit.

Teddy Redmund cursed steadily as he watched the blue attack from the cut being pinched between a regiment thrown in on one side by Arnold and another pushed in from the butternut brigade on Arnold's right.

Not that Redmund cared whether blue or butternut brought the game to check; but it grieved him professionally to see such an opportunity wasted. The blues—given their daylong ineptitude—predictably had had nothing in reserve to exploit their sudden possession of the cut, just as all morning they had sent in one attack after another, one assault wave here, one there, yet had never coordinated the weight of their forces, never hit the out-manned butternuts a killing blow after first having knocked them off balance. And over there on the left, toward Bull Run, masses of blues in the woods and beyond were letting themselves be stalled by Hill's guns instead of coming on in concert with the blue brigades in the woods in front of Arnold.

• • •

As the last of the Federal troops—New Yorkers and Pennsylvanians from Krzyzanowski's Brigade— were struggling out of the cut and into the relative safety of the bullet-riddled woods, Major General John Pope, U.S.A., and his staff rode up Buck's Hill, just behind the Stone House at the intersection of the Warrenton Pike and the Manassas–Sudley Road.

Over Buck's Hill, a year earlier, green Reb troops had hastened from positions around the Stone Bridge to a new line on Matthews Hill, confronting McDowell's attempted flanking movement of equally green Yanks. But no one with Pope, that early afternoon of August 29, 1862, either knew that history or would have cared much about it if he had.

Instead, the general and his staff gathered around a solitary pine tree on the crest of Buck's Hill, from which they could gaze west and north over the whole line of battle, even obscured as the view was by smoke and dust. Many of the officers flinched as the pounding of artillery, the ceaseless crash of musketry, rolled over the fields in tangible waves, percussion as well as sound.

Immediately to the front, on Matthews Hill, more than thirty Federal cannon leaped and roared continuously—blazing like furnaces, Cass Fielding thought. A blue brigade rested on its arms behind the line of guns. Hooker's Division stretched endlessly off to the right toward Sudley Springs, in battle line; beyond it, somebody told Fielding, Kearny's Division was reaching around Jackson's left.

To the left of the guns, Sigel's infantry was milling about, many of its men trickling back wounded or exhausted from the woods between them and the Reb line, which was marked only by white smoke rising above Sudley Mountain. Beyond Sigel, on the south side of the pike, blue troops not actively engaged appeared to Fielding to be resting on a hillside. Here and there, in the open fields, the dry broomsedge had caught fire and burned uncertainly in the breezeless heat, sending a thinner smoke than that of gunpowder into the hard blue sky. Reynolds's Division of Pennsylvanians, on the left of Pope's line south of the pike, faced west behind a slight ridge topped with trees. At the east foot of that ridge, just below Reynolds's line, a meandering track led north to Groveton. So well-placed a vantage point was Buck's Hill that Fielding, had he been using field glasses, could have seen Captain Micah G. Duryea riding along that track on his way to report to Pope.

But Fielding could not appreciate the magnificent spectacle of fire and destruction, much less notice small details, because of the Reb shells shrieking over the hill or ploughing into its gravelly surface with a rasping, gouging sound that made his flesh creep. Ducking away from one such shell bursting twenty feet to his left, he saw another strike the span between two battery horses and explode, carrying away a foreleg of one and a hind leg of the other.

The maimed and screaming horses hopped and leaped for a moment in a circle, like dancers waltzing drunkenly. They circled each other several times in ghastly ritual, before one went down spouting blood, dragging the other with him. But each lurched erect again for one more wheel around the other. Then, still harnessed, the horses fell, convulsed, quivered, and lay still.

Fielding could not think what this hideous death duet called to mind. Something.

Chapter Nine

～～～～～～～～～

August 29—Evening

ALBERT STEVENS HALE came out of the White House, and stood for a moment under the north portico wondering whether to cross the lawn to the War Department to call on Assistant Secretary Watson. Then he decided that first he had to think through the startling information President Lincoln himself had just confided.

Hale set off quickly for his office on Twelfth Street. Even in the tropical heat of a Washington afternoon, his step was brisk and he was dressed in a heavy, rather formal suit. His tall black hat could not counter the fact that he was a small man. The President, escorting him to the door of his office, could almost have held an arm straight out over Hale's thinning hair.

Lucky thing he had sent in his card at just the right moment, Hale thought. He hadn't expected to see Lincoln, had merely scribbled on the card: "News from Pope?"

Most times the President replied to journalists who presented him such questions by jotting what he chose to answer on the back of the card; occasionally, however, he called the questioner in for a chat.

"You newspapermen are so often behind the scenes at the front," he'd told Williams of *The Times*, "I frequently get ideas from you that no one else can give."

Hearing that, Forney of the *Washington Chronicle* had complained, "When *I* go to see him, he asks me what's the last good joke I heard."

Hale's own experience suggested that the President's favorite question was, "What news have you?" He often felt more interviewed than informed after a talk with the genial, humorous man who bore the weight of the war on his bony shoulders. Hale was a Republican and an abolitionist who had slowly come to respect the President; but he was Washington bureau chief for a New York newspaper that was making no bones about its impatience at the slow progress of the war. And Hale shared his employer's view that Lincoln was remiss in not proclaiming freedom for southern slaves.

Wasn't that really what the struggle was about? Saying so plainly would transform a civil war into what was needed—a moral crusade. But Lincoln appeared not to grasp the overwhelming sentiment of the country for emancipation. Everybody knew that he'd told Senator Charles Sumner that a decree freeing the slaves would be "too big a lick."

To which the caustic Secretary Stanton was known to have replied—though not to the President's face—that the country "wanted big licks now."

As Hale hurried through the midafternoon heat and the stench of the sewage canal that ran below the White House and near the stump of the unfinished monument to Washington, he was more than usually anxious to get at his daily confidential report to New York. A nervous, bespectacled man, nearsighted and constantly worrying about his health, Hale was, for all that, an incessant worker. He organized and coordinated, as well as anyone could, the work of his paper's correspondents in the field; and one of his worries at the moment was that young Charlie Keach had disappeared. When the other correspondents had been forced by Halleck's order to separate themselves from Pope's Army of Virginia, Keach simply had not returned with them, nor had he been heard from since.

The bureau chief also cultivated some of the most important news sources in Washington—Secretary of State Seward, Secretary of the Treasury Chase, Assistant War Secretary Watson (Hale detested Stanton and sought out his deputy instead), Speaker Colfax, Representatives Covode and Washburne, Senator Sumner, General Wadsworth, and not infrequently the President himself. All contributed, more than they knew, not only to Hale's long and informed dispatches about the government and the conduct of the war, but also to his nightly private report to his editor, Stanley Glenn, in New York.

Just a few nights before, Hale had been able to write Glenn

privately—though carefully masking his source, Secretary of the
Navy Welles—that Lincoln had completed the draft of an Emancipation Proclamation three weeks before. He could not tell Glenn
why its issuance had been delayed, and he had been considerably
embarrassed the next day, when Lincoln's reply to Greeley's "Prayer
of Twenty Million" had been printed in the *New York Tribune*:

> I would save the Union. If there be those who would not
> save the Union, unless they could at the same time save
> slavery, I do not agree with them. If there be those who
> would not save the Union, unless they could at the same
> time destroy slavery, I do not agree with them. My para-
> mount object in this struggle is to save the Union and is not
> either to save or destroy slavery. If I could save the Union
> without freeing any slave, I would do it, and if I could save
> the Union by freeing some and leaving others alone, I would
> also do that . . .

Hale had perfect confidence in his impressive source, who
assured him the Proclamation was indeed down on paper in Lincoln's own hand—the product of a summer's secret work in the
Telegraph Office. But that was not the same as having emancipation proclaimed to the world, and Hale feared Lincoln's letter
to Greeley had damaged his—Hale's—standing with Stanley
Glenn.

So when the President, instead of sending back Hale's card
with a line or two in response, had invited him in for a talk,
Hale had quickly decided to press the emancipation question.
But he never got the chance; for the first time in Hale's experience, Lincoln was in a wrathful mood. Hardly offering civil
welcome, he held up a telegram from General McClellan and
began to excoriate the general for dragging his feet in sending
reinforcements out to Pope.

"He's acted badly toward Pope." Lincoln draped one of his
long legs over the arm of his chair. "He really *wanted* him to fail."

Lincoln had stopped short of showing McClellan's telegram to
Hale; apparently just received, it seemed to have set off the President's tirade. But he did read aloud the operative sentence, in-
flecting his high-pitched voice sarcastically:

"I am clear that one of two courses should be adopted: first,
to concentrate all our available forces to open communications
with Pope; second, to leave Pope to get out of his scrape, and

at once to use all our means to make the capital perfectly safe."

Leave Pope to get out of his scrape! Hale would have found the phrase shocking even had he not already come to regard George B. McClellan as a general moved more by personal ambition than by patriotism. His telegram amounted to a proposal to leave a Federal army to fend for itself against forces of unknown size and disposition.

Even without these indiscretions, the telegram—as Hale pieced together the story from Lincoln's remarks—was an act of insubordination. In it McClellan appeared to have gone over Halleck's head to Lincoln in an effort to hold back some troops the general in chief had ordered out to Pope.

"I tell you, Hale, there's been a design, a *purpose*, in breaking down Pope without regard to the consequences to the country." Lincoln smacked his open palm on his desk. "That's atrocious. It's shocking—but there's no remedy at present. McClellan has the army with him."

Hale had never had such a story; but all correspondents understood that private conversations with Lincoln were never to be attributed to him. And he certainly couldn't publish without documentation what the President had seemed plainly to be suggesting—that Major General George B. McClellan and his toady generals had acted to cause Major General John Pope to be defeated by the Rebels—at the least had declined to assist him.

As Hale crossed Fourteenth Street, he was calculating how best to use this startling information. In the nightly letter to Glenn, of course—though he'd have to ponder whether or not to disclose even confidentially that the news was directly from Lincoln himself. Then, tomorrow, he'd get busy with War Department officials to see if he could use his information to drag the story out of them in publishable form. Maybe Watson would open up.

Of course, he had to allow for the fact that Lincoln was being driven to distraction by the lack of news from Pope. There had been no word for four days. The President could be seizing on McClellan as a scapegoat—which put Hale in mind of his own frustration.

"Where the devil's that Keach?" he muttered, causing an old gentleman passing by to stare at him suspiciously.

But Hale was too single-minded to notice or to give further thought to Keach; he hurried on, anxious to put everything down in his nightly letter.

• • •

At first, Privates Sowell and Stone thought Lott McGrath was dead after all. In the thinning woods near the top of Sudley Mountain, he lay nearly prone under a pine tree, hatless, his eyes closed and his face pale above his familiar red-checked shirt. Gilly was awed at the sight.

"Don't go no closer, Sowbelly. Aint natchral, no dead body gittin itself way up here."

"He aint dead, dammit. Can't be." But Sowell, too, was for a moment reluctant to go nearer Lott's sprawled form. "Lessen maybe he got up yere'n *then* croaked."

Just then Lott opened his eyes and stared at them. Gilly started to back away.

"Didn't I tell you?" Sowell grabbed Gilly's arm. "Thachew, Lott?"

McGrath lay still, looking at them, no sign of recognition on his face. Sowell stepped forward, pulling the reluctant Gilly along.

"Lookin fer y'all day, Lott. How come yuh way up-yere?"

Lott's dull eyes watched their creeping approach.

"Yeah." Gilly was emboldened, the closer they got. "Thought y'uz snuffed till Applejack said he seen yuh."

Lott's eyes did not move, nor did he blink as they approached. Then Gilly and Sowell saw the bullet hole, black as a piece of coal, at Lott's hairline just to the left of his left eye.

"Sho-God tuck a good un, Lott. Inch to the right, you-uz a gone goose."

Sowell knelt by Lott's left side and examined the wound. He could see that the slug had gone all the way through Lott's head, leaving another neat hole behind his ear; but it appeared just barely to have burrowed under the skin before emerging again.

"Didn't I say he uz lucky?" Gilly sounded almost aggrieved. "Gone git'im a leave outten it."

Sowell touched the side of Lott's head between the bullet holes, to see if Lott would flinch. He didn't move or make a sound. No blood either.

"Dawg if I *ever* seen the beat." Sowell stood up. Lott lay still as a stone. "Le's git'im to the bonecrackers."

"Carry'im?"

"He walk *up* yere, he kin walk down. Git a holt of 'is arm ther."

Lott, obedient as a child, rose to his feet with their help. He stared into the blue distance, seeming to notice neither of them.

"Kin yuh walk if we lend a hand?"

Sowell gently urged Lott down the ridge. Lott began to walk, steadily enough, with their hands guiding him along over the pine needles thick on the hillside; but after a rod or two, Sowell stopped.

"Gilly, you got a feelin he'd walk smack into a tree lessen we steered'im round it?"

Lott was staring straight ahead, his eyes and face as blank as the bottom of a cook pot.

Gilly waved his hand in front of Lott's eyes. "Hell, I believe he's dead'n don't know it yit."

"Shit," Sowell said. "Le's git'im on down to the docs."

"Gimme a funny feelin." But Gilly took the other arm, and Lott walked on obediently between them.

Miraculously, Phil Keefe's leg had not had to be amputated. The round, soft lead ball that had struck Keefe had lost its shape on impact, expanded, tumbled, and carried rags of his trousers into his body. The low-velocity ball, instead of piercing cleanly, mangled his flesh, tore up the big muscles in the back of his calf, and cost him huge amounts of blood and pain.

Still, the ball's lacerating track had not shattered a long bone; it had not exploded bone splinters and shards randomly around the wound in numbers impossible to remove, each one a probable source of infection. With his leg bones intact, Keefe might make it without resort to the saw—or so the tired surgeon who had examined him concluded.

Any other medical officer in Hooker's hospital might have had the leg off as quickly as he could have said "chloroform." That was easier than treating the wound, and the surgeons were busy and exhausted; after a year of war, many were cynical about arms and legs. But young Jude Israel, a doctor who treated Keefe, was a newcomer to war and his profession, and still idealistic. He believed, moreover, in innovative techniques, practicing them when he could. He owned one of the few clinical thermometers in the whole Union medical corps. And before repairing, closing, and dressing the terrible rent in Keefe's leg, Captain Israel had given him an injection of morphine, using the only hypodermic syringe in the field hospital—the young surgeon's own property. The needle was considered too newfangled by most of his colleagues,

who preferred to dust morphine into an open wound, or to use
opium pills to relieve pain.

But slowly the morphine had worn off. Keefe came to nightmare consciousness while bouncing along a rutted road in a two-
wheeled ambulance. The canvas-topped vehicle was arranged for
four stretcher cases, two on its bed and two overhead in racks,
one of whom was Phil Keefe. Both front and rear flaps were down
and little air could penetrate, so the baleful Virginia sun turned
the ambulance into a furnace for its passengers.

Keefe had no notion where he was or even that he was in an
ambulance, since nothing that rocked and swayed and bounced so
much could have been thought to have been intended for succor.
In fact, the army had adopted the two-wheeled ambulance only
because it was light enough to be drawn by one horse. And horses
were too sorely needed by the cavalry, the artillery, and the quartermasters for many to be spared to the wounded.

At first Keefe thought he might be dead and in Hell, so fierce
was the heat and so noxious the smells of that canvas inferno; and
he could think of no other explanation for the torturous jolting
and jostling and the searing pain spreading from his leg through
his body. But Phil Keefe was a regular churchgoer who had tried
all his life to abide by the Ten Commandments, and it seemed
monstrously unfair that he should have gone to hell. Besides, he
finally recognized through his sweating agony that the familiar
rhythmic sound punctuating the horrid groans around him—some
of them his own—was that of a trotting horse. Keefe knew no
horse would ever be sent to hell.

Then he realized the horse was pulling the torture chamber in
which he was riding. His consciousness, after that, consisted of
pain and the knowledge that he was alive and going somewhere.
As had the sense of being on the road the night before, that
knowledge sustained him. If he was still alive, Phil Keefe told
himself, he could manage to stay alive; if he was going someplace,
it had to be better than where he was.

Actually, the hospital depot to which Keefe was being transported, though scarcely a spa, consisted of a decent village of tent
flies pitched in and near a cool grove on a hillside just east of
Bull Run, not far from Blackburn's Ford. Trees gave some shelter
from the sun and pine straw provided an aromatic ground cover.

This was the Army of Virginia's central hospital on August
29, 1862. That afternoon it was not yet quite swamped with wounded
because many of those who had gone down in Brawner's pasture

the night before were in the hands of the Rebs, and most of those injured in the morning's attacks on Jackson's left had not yet been moved back from the regimental surgeries. But the depot's surgeons, nurses, and orderlies knew they were facing a long night; to brace themselves, some freely sampled from bottles of medicinal spirits. Already the sights and sounds of the place were fearful.

The bravest of the wounded clenched their teeth and smothered their own groans, making a more terrible sound than those of the less stoical. Some laughed the harsh, mirthless rasp of the hopeless. Stretchers and ambulances were beginning to come in bloody procession across Bull Run, and the surgeons with their dripping hands and gory aprons were turning out row upon row of tormented men, some mutilated as much by medical tools as by shot or shell.

Chaplain E. P. Hornby, who had lain all night by the side of the Warrenton Pike in immediate danger of being crushed by any passing wagon or caisson, had been found just after dawn by men of Reynolds's Division. Owing to his chaplain's insignia, the Pennsylvanians had given him preferred treatment; their surgeon dressed his wounds, set his broken leg, and dosed him liberally with opium pills. Although no one knew where Hatch's Brigade or the Twenty-fourth New York might be, Chaplain Hornby had been carried about noon into the hospital depot near Blackburn's Ford and made as comfortable as possible.

By midafternoon he was coming fitfully awake from the opium. He drifted in and out of sleep in sudden steep rushes; sometimes colors swirled vividly in his head or caught him up like the waters of a polychrome sea. In moments of wakefulness, he was acutely conscious of the groans and cries around him, and sometimes these carried over into the smoky world of dreams into which he repeatedly floated.

Hornby had never been under opiate before, or even the influence of alcohol, which was forbidden by his calling. Possibly the drug unhinged his brain temporarily. Possibly it pried under his prim habits of thought and deed. Possibly opium and the pain it only partially dulled unveiled the faint shapes of visions that had been suppressed in religious sentiment, or rejected by the high moral character upon which he had always congratulated himself.

In any case, sometime in the afternoon, while Phil Keefe's stretcher was being placed on the pine straw not far away, Chaplain Hornby emerged from an opium-tinted dreamworld with a rending groan, a welling cry of despair, as if—instead of his being physically injured—that immortal soul upon which rested his life and understanding might have been torn out of him by Lucifer's own hand. A passing surgeon hurried to the chaplain's side; and Private Keefe, whose own tortured body was by then almost clear of morphine, pitied with all his youthful heart the torment of a man who could utter such a sound.

But the concerned surgeon could find no cause for alarm, save perhaps the copious perspiration in which Chaplain Hornby was bathed. The broken leg was properly splinted; water was dripping as it should upon the dressing of the arm wound. The chaplain's look of haunted fear was common enough in the eyes of men mangled in battle. And since it was natural that the thoughts of those in anguish should turn to their loved ones the surgeon saw nothing strange in Hornby's murmuring, through clenched jaws, again and again:

"Sally . . . Sally . . ."

And once:

"Sally . . . not what you thought!"

"Sponge off his forehead," the surgeon said to his orderly, "and give'im two opium pills."

Few men could recall a sun so hot, or so slow to slide across the blued-steel sky. In its relentless rays, on and on through the creeping afternoon, Pope's blue waves dashed intermittently against Ol Jack's thinning lines on the left and center.

Even after Arnall and Thomas forced Krzyzanowski's men from their threatening position in the railroad cut, no letup came. Hooker's and Reno's divisions of Peninsula veterans immediately relieved Sigel's used-up corps, which since dawn had been throwing itself on Jackson in brave but disjointed attacks.

Reno struck at about 2 p.m. A brigade of New Hampshire, Pennsylvania, and Maryland regiments attacked just west of the road from Sudley Springs to Groveton crossroads, near where the old railroad right-of-way crossed that road. These fresh troops crashed into the Reb line and got over the embankment—two to three feet high and heavily defended at the point of attack. But Ewell's Division, under Lawton, rallied quickly and the Federal commander, Colonel James Nagel, finding himself overexposed and unsupported, withdrew with a loss of 531 men killed, wounded, or missing.

A. P. Hill, meanwhile, having perceived at last the danger of the gap between Arnall and Thomas, had sent Pender's Brigade to fill it. Then the combative Hill—sparing Arnall's hard-hit ranks on the left—threw Thomas and Pender against Hooker's newly formed battle line. The unexpected Reb attack hit Colonel Joseph B. Carr's New York and New Jersey Brigade so hard that its repulse also carried back Colonel Nelson Taylor's Brigade. Pender and Thomas then returned to their stronghold in the railroad cut, leaving a thicker carpet of bodies on its blood-slicked approaches.

But Joe Hooker was a fighter. At 3 p.m. he ordered a New England brigade under Brigadier General Cuvier Grover to attack not far from where Nagel's troops had briefly spilled over the embankment. Grover was ordered to carry the embankment and hold a position in the woods beyond it.

The guns of both armies had been roaring for hours, making the earth shake and the air shimmer with percussion. The crash of small arms rolled over the woods and fields, the meandering lanes, the dreary farm houses. Muskets often grew so hot in the barrel that men dropped them, picked up those of the dead, and fought on. At the slightest pause, butternut scarecrows hopped like carrion birds from Jackson's lines to scavenge the cartridges of the fallen, friend and enemy alike.

As the day wore endlessly on, men on both sides dropped from heat exhaustion and lay as useless as the riddled bodies around them. Dry lips sucked canteens empty; the acrid smoke, the churning dust streaked live faces as black as those of the sun-bloated dead in Brawner's field. Before the old railway, blue bodies lay thick as wildflowers; behind it, butternut corpses lined the bottom of the cut like sandbags supporting a levee. Attackers coming forward, defenders retreating before them, had no choice but to trample the living and the dead underfoot.

Colonel David Channing, who had ranged from one end of the line to the other several times that day, hoped fervently that Hill's slashing counterattack had wound things up. If Pope hadn't had enough of Ol Jack by now, he surely knew that at any minute Longstreet would come crashing down on his left flank.

The colonel watched Captain Thad Selby ride up and offer a creditable salute. But Channing was more gratified to see that Selby's new uniform had been reduced by sweat, smoke, brambles, and dirt into proper Rebel attire. Channing took off his own

droopy hat and wiped his forehead with his jacket sleeve, in lieu
of a return salute.

"Colonel, sir . . . Gin'al Jackson needs to know if Early'n Forno
still in reserve behind Lawton?"

"Tell Gin'al Jackson they right where he put'em. An
Selby . . . better tell'im ol Jube's so hot to fight he's like to swal-
ler'is chaw."

Selby hesitated, then asked:

"They gone come again, Colonel?"

Channing shrugged. "Lots of daylight left."

"Looks like Longstreet could hit'em." Selby's tone was aggrieved. "Seem like our boys doin all the fightin."

Channing felt exactly that way himself. To his knowledge,
Longstreet had been in position at least since noon. All at time,
Yanks givin us hell. And not so much as a one of Pete's brigades
movin over there.

But such things could not be said to a junior officer. "Takes
Longstreet awhile to git set, Cap'n. But when he hits, he hits like
thunder."

Selby rode away, not appearing cheered. And the more Channing
himself thought about Longstreet's inactivity, the more annoyed
he became. He thought bitterly of Jackson, badly as he had needed
sleep, riding out the night before to put his ear to the ground,
listening for help on the way. What the hell was the use in Longstreet being there, if he aimed to do nothing but sit still and rest
up from the march?

Channing rode on along the line, noticing that the musket fire
had slackened. Maybe, just maybe, Pope had decided he'd had
enough; maybe just knowing Longstreet was on the field was
enough to hold Pope back.

At the Groveton–Sudley Springs Road, Channing checked the
sun against his sense of time. Christ! How the hours dragged.
How much more could troops stand, if Pope came on again?

As if to emphasize the question, from straight ahead and nearby,
a tremendous volley of musket fire—like an avenging crack of
lightning—caused Channing's horse to shy and rear, almost un-
seating him.

But the colonel recovered quickly and spurred across the road.
Damn bastard coming again, right over his own dead. As if he
hadn't already paid a big enough butcher's bill.

Scarcely fifty yards past the road, Channing saw ahead and to his left a blue battle line double-timing forward; about two hundred yards behind, a second wave followed. At a glance he estimated two regiments in each line, with a fifth broken out into flanking companies.

Hooker and Grover, learning from Nagel's earlier effort, had chosen an excellent point of attack on Lawton's front, where the low railway embankment faced an open field that sloped *up* to the woods in which Grover's troops had formed and fixed bayonets. Grover ordered his men to dash down the slope without firing until the enemy musketry could be felt, then to charge rapidly on the embankment, firing one volley on command.

When Channing reached the scene, Grover's first wave already was swarming onto the embankment. The advantage of sloping ground; the murderous effect of the one concerted blast of musketry; the demoralizing sight of the advancing bayonets; above all, the New Englanders' relative freshness—for all those reasons, Grover's men hit the tired butternuts harder than had any previous attackers. Fighting over the embankment with bayonets and clubbed muskets, the first Yank line pressed rapidly into Lawton's rear, while the second, cheering, surged toward the embankment at the double-quick.

My God, Channing thought. They've broken us.

Channing was stunned at the suddenness of the disaster, the change in the battle tide. Then he wheeled his horse and galloped for Ol Jack.

Higher up the ridge, Selby already had found the commanding general sitting against the wheel of a caisson, writing a note. The sight bewildered Selby. What could he be writing in the midst of chaos? Smoke swirled around them and a shell burst nearby; it scattered dirt and debris over Jackson and the bit of paper on his booted knee, reminding the young captain of the famous story about a Napoleonic general in much the same situation who said he had "needed no sand to dry his ink."

Jackson himself seemed to pay no attention to the shell burst. Selby saluted and delivered his report, listening nervously to the shriek of another shell coming in. The general thanked him just as the second shell burst, nearer than the first. Then Jackson went on writing.

"Gin'al . . . sir!"

Selby was profoundly impressed with his commander's iron nerves; he himself had had to muster a supreme effort not to throw himself to the ground when he had heard the rising whine of that shell on the way. And because he had not broken, he was strangely prouder of himself than if he had not been afraid. But Jackson, Selby thought, was taking intolerable chances.

"This is a very hot spot, Gin'al!"

Jackson looked up with what Selby thought was genuine puzzlement.

"Why, Cap'n, I believe we've been in hotter places before."

He was about to resume writing when the sound of a massive volley rang back from the line. Jackson stood up quickly, staring toward the sound. It was followed by a throaty cheer from hundreds of voices—a Union sound, Selby knew by then, nothing like the high-pitched, coon-hunter's yelping from Reb throats.

Selby was transfixed, from fear of what might be happening and in fascination at the sight of the great Stonewall peering through the smoke, his whole body seeming to quiver with the effort to penetrate the fogs and distances of war. Selby had not realized how little even a commanding general, even one so renowned as Ol Jack, could know of the actual unfolding of a battle. No general could be everywhere at once. By the time he reached any one point, the situation there might be changed and some other place could demand his presence. What generals needed above all, Selby thought, were eyes that could penetrate smoke, forests, obscuring ground.

Jackson signaled to an orderly to bring his horse and Selby mounted Jeff D. But just as Jackson swung himself into his saddle, a courier came galloping up the ridge. He shouted the news of the Yank attack before his wild-eyed horse had been slowed to a stop.

Jackson seized Selby's bicep in a powerful grip; his pale blue eyes glittered under the forage cap.

"Go to Gin'al Early . . ." The voice was barely audible but the words were rapid, positive. "Tell him to reinforce Gin'al Lawton at once!"

Selby rode as hard as he could, the sounds of battle rising to a crescendo off to his right. He no longer tried to convince himself that he was unafraid; he only forced himself to conceal his fear in self-control. Dodging tree limbs and keeping low against stray bullets, he had little chance, anyway, to think of anything but finding Early. But he knew from Jackson's eyes and the force of his voice that he was carrying the most important message he ever had.

Jeff D. covered the few hundred yards of rough, wooded ground in what seemed no more than seconds. But as Selby pulled to a halt beside General Jubal A. Early, he was surprised to see Forno's Brigade already double-timing in battle line toward the breach in front. Saluting, he rapidly delivered Jackson's message.

Early, who was renowned for his dyspeptic temperament, shifted a wad of tobacco from one bearded cheek to the other, then spat past Selby's boot. His high voice easily penetrated the battle din: "He think I'd just sitchere'n let'em stomp us under?"

Forno's Louisianians, held in reserve all day, went in with "a hoop'n a holler" and a withering blast of lead. Their charge brought Grover's attack to a halt, its second wave piling up behind the first. The New Englanders had penetrated so deeply that had their attack been properly supported, Jackson's army would have been cut in two. But once again Teddy Redmund could only shake his head and stamp his expensive English boot as the chance for a decisive blue move was squandered.

With the rest of Company B, Thirteen Georgia, Private Ambrose Riggin had been pressed back by the first Yank onslaught, but he had not panicked or run or thrown down his piece. He went back with his face to the blue attackers, loading and firing, loading and firing, as methodically as he had forced himself to do on the slope at Brawner's farm the night before, thinking of nothing but loading and firing. As long as he could do that mechanically and ritually, he did not see the faces of the deserters every time he sighted along his hot barrel.

Hill's battered brigades rallied on the left, Lawton sent in a counterattack from the right, and Forno's Louisianians pressed on. Between them, in twenty minutes of the hardest close-quarter fighting most of the men had ever seen, they broke the attack and ripped the New England regiments apart.

Private Riggin, moving back toward the railway embankment in Lawton's counterattack, kept on loading and firing, loading and firing, seeing nothing but smoke and the flash of muzzles and an occasional running blue figure—until, stumbling over a body in his path, he emerged for a second from the haze of battle into air that seemed suddenly to have been washed clean. Only a few yards ahead, a Yank lieutenant waved a pistol and called after his retreating troops to stand and fight.

No one listened, or perhaps even heard. Private Riggin leveled his piece at the lieutenant and began to squeeze the trigger. But before he could get off a shot, the officer looked behind him, his features contorted in disbelief and anger at the quick turn of fate. For a split second, for long enough, that agonized human face was in Private Riggin's gunsight; and he thought of the deserters. Then he saw his own face beyond the sight, and his finger relaxed on the trigger.

The lieutenant jerked up his arm and fired at him; the slug from his pistol burned over Private Riggin's head, so close that he felt a brazen twitch at his cap. Then the smoke closed down and the Yank officer was gone.

Without support, their momentum broken, Grover's men— those who could—pulled sullenly back across the embankment and into the woods. They went slowly and in good order and took their toll of Rebs as they went; Colonel Forno himself was hit by a sharpshooter and had to be carried from the field. But the damage the retreating Yanks inflicted was minor compared to the price they had paid. From the first volley to the final repair of the butternut front, Grover's Brigade lost 41 dead, 327 wounded, and 118 missing or captured—486 altogether, nearly a third of the 1,500 men who had swarmed down the open slope into Ol Jack's line.

It was then about 4 p.m. Four blue divisions in a long day of determined attacks had failed to dislodge the butternuts from the railway line. A fifth, Reynolds's, had also been desultorily engaged on Jackson's right. But all along Jackson's left and center, exhausted men could scarcely lift their heads or sight a musket. Cartridge boxes were empty or nearly so. On Arnall's front, men were piling up rocks against the next assault—which, with soldiers' fatalism, they had no doubt was coming.

Sam Stowe, the only one of Arnall's regimental commanders alive and unwounded, gazed over the open field on the brigade's left, beyond which thick lines of Yanks were barely held at bay by the guns on the heights above him. Only place they aint tried, Stowe thought.

Thad Selby, glancing through the drifting smoke at the great red sun blazing and motionless, wondered if this day would ever end. It seemed to him that nearly all his life had been passed in its smoke and flame and intolerable heat. He recalled then the old biblical story from his youth, how Joshua spake to the Lord on the way that went up to Bethoron saying *Sun, stand thou still upon Gibeon and thou, Moon, in the valley of Ajalon*. And the Lord harkened, so that in the midst of heaven the sun hastened not to go down until the children of Israel had destroyed the armies of the five kings.

Surely Ol Jack was Joshua incarnate, mighty and merciless in the cause of an invincible God. But Selby was shocked to find himself longing faithlessly for Joshua's sun to haste in its setting, to draw the shroud of night even over slaughter sent from heaven.

Afternoon shadows were slanting across the yard at Sycamore when Amy Arnall came down the back stoop with the pistol in her hand. Some of the people had taken Pettigrew's body away. Where it had lain, the grass showed a slight indentation, but in no recognizable shape. Amy was relieved that there was no real reminder to upset Bess again.

As the long afternoon had dragged by, Amy had known, without really letting herself think about it, that sooner or later she would have to visit the cabins, check the barns—make sure that Jason was gone. Somehow, she had not let herself worry about his coming into the house. Not even his crimes were likely to embolden him to that, she told herself. He knew she had the pistol, and he had every reason to be gone with Easter as soon as possible.

Little Luke, awakening from his afternoon nap, had played peacefully in the nursery, apparently unaware of anything amiss even when Bess's haunting cries had echoed through the old house. Incredibly, Judge Arnall had dozed on the verandah, in alcoholic torpor, throughout the commotion in the yard.

"Lot of good *he* is," Amy had complained to an uncomprehending Willis, as he hovered over the Judge.

That was unfair, she knew. What *could* a drunken old man do? But it also seemed bitterly unfair that all the males in her life, even little Luke, were unable to help her when she needed them, when she had been trained to depend on male competence, courage, gallantry. And she was almost sure, in the heat of the day, that the General's seed was again growing within her.

"Jedge, he gone be powful upsot." Willis inclined his head knowingly, as if he had set her straight.

"Yes . . . after it's all over."

The biggest surprise to Amy had been the depth of Bess's grief, which seemed little less than hysterical—so loud and prolonged that it had brought old Willis to the workroom with wringing hands and frightened eyes. Willis usually was good for little other than to dress and undress the Judge, but at least he had been able to go for cloth and a basin of cool water. And he had given Amy the first suggestion of what had so affected Bess.

"She's usually so strong, Willis. I've never *seen* her like this."

"He uz Bess's man."

As he spoke, Willis was creeping off to the verandah to attend the Judge; and despite her repeated calls, he neither came back nor said more—whether because of real deafness or the kind they could so easily feign, Amy could not be sure.

Which he? Hardly Jason. But Pettigrew? Bess had suggested little interest in the curt driver—although Amy recalled that Bess had made an occasional cutting remark about "at skin'n bones wife-a hissen." Reba, Amy had heard Bess mutter, "don't even thow no shadduh." But she had put such talk down to Bess's general attitude of contempt for "em nigguhs."

And if Pettigrew really had been Bess's "man," why hadn't he married her? But Amy could think of no reason for Bess to take on so, except an intensely personal grief for Pettigrew. And only at the sight of her in unquenchable tears did Amy realize how much she had come to rely on Bess for good sense and emotional calm.

At first she herself would resolutely not think about how Pettigrew had died or what she'd do without him. But she conceded that she'd wronged him in suspecting that he might not be willing to turn Jason in. Bess's grief also made clear that neither had *she* connived to protect Jason; otherwise, Amy thought, she'd have been celebrating Jason's escape.

If he and Easter *had* left. But of course they had, as fast as they could get off the place.

Amy held the cold cloth to Bess's face and tried to comfort her. As soon as she'd forced herself from the window and the dreadful pointing axe handle, she knew she had to notify the sheriff. But quieting Bess had been the more immediate task, and anyway she *wanted* to give Jason time to get away, as far away as possible. Because when the sheriff caught him, there'd be more violence; and Sycamore had seen enough violence that day to haunt it forever.

"Bess, Bess," she murmured, rubbing the woman's powerful wrists. "You've got to help me, Bess." She could face almost anything if she could just get Bess back to her calm, competent self.

Who should she send to notify Sheriff Maxton? Pettigrew would have known, but Amy realized that she knew none of the Africans well enough to trust them with such a mission. Maybe Bess, if she ever got herself under control. Not that they'd all necessarily want to help Jason; but all would be afraid of him, and of other bad niggers who might make them pay for tattling to the whites.

"Bess! Stop it now!"

Maybe Willis. Surely not even the worst African in the yard, not even Jason, would touch such an old man, one of their own. But Willis would never leave the Judge, and what would she do with the Judge if he did?

Neither the cool cloth nor kind words or rubbing Bess's wrists seemed to calm the woman. Amy had smelling salts in her dressing room but she feared to leave Bess long enough to go for them; in her hysteria, there was no telling what Bess might do.

"Willis!"

The old man still did not answer. And Amy realized, with a cold touch of fear, that the other servants had run from the house. It felt empty, deserted—a sense all the more chilling in contrast to the usual bustle about its hallways.

"Bess . . . please!"

But Bess only wailed again. Half in an effort to shock her into calm, but half, too, in suddenly erupting exasperation, Amy slapped Bess, hard. She had never struck an African before, or anyone. She had been reared to consider it particularly bad form to hit a servant—not only was it physical contact beneath her station; it was an act of cruelty to the defenseless.

For a moment Amy was aghast, even though she had acted partly to shake Bess from hysteria and could see that indeed the woman's sobs had been momentarily silenced. But a part of her had not only wanted to hit Bess, punish one of *them* for this ordeal and for her own ineffectuality; she had rather enjoyed the sting of it on her hand and the sense it gave her of regaining command rightfully hers.

"Now then, Bess . . . are you all right?"

But Bess was already beginning to wail again. In for a penny, in for a pound. Amy hit her harder, the second slap rocking Bess's head to one side and echoing through the empty house like a firecracker.

Not, Amy thought, at all like the deeper report of the pistol.

No doubt this time that she'd *wanted* to strike. Amy was ashamed but unrepentant. She felt her power. She rose from Bess's side, went to the work table, and picked up the heavy gun. It made her think of the General.

If he were here . . . but he isn't. No good to wish for what isn't.

The sheriff had to be notified. The place had to be checked. To make sure Jason . . . but of course he was gone. Pettigrew . . . had to be seen to. No time for niceties.

Behind her, Bess seemed quiet at last. Holding the pistol, Amy turned and found the woman staring at her wide-eyed, her strong fingers stroking her cheek where Amy had struck it.

"I couldn't get you to stop cryin any other way, Bess."

Bess nodded, tears streaming down her cheeks. Her eyes were fixed on the pistol, as if she had never seen such a thing before. But Amy suspected it really was *she* whom Bess was seeing for the first time—actually seeing. Well, a lot of people at Sycamore were seeing each other clear at last.

Floorboards creaked in the front hall. Amy whirled but realized from the slow steps that Willis and the Judge were only shuffling toward the stairs. She concealed the pistol in her skirtfolds until she could hear them going up. Turning back to Bess, who was wiping her face on her apron, Amy put the pistol down and leaned back against the work table.

"Willis says . . . he says Pettigrew's *your* man." *Was*.

Bess stared at her over the apron.

"You never let on, Bess."

"Nuffin to let on." Bess's voice was quiet, dull. "Nuffin to *do*."

"Why on earth didn't you marry 'im?"

Bess dropped her apron and shook her head. "I wa'nt his woman. An now . . ." She did not have to finish the sentence. *I never will be*.

"But no man'd choose Reba over you."

Bess snuffled. "Aint choose nobody. Onlies reason he marry Reba, Easter won't have 'im."

Amy remembered suddenly the day the sheriff came, how Pettigrew had soothed Easter when she had been screaming and swearing her innocence of any knowledge of Jason. Pettigrew had been so . . . loving, though Amy had not recognized it at the time, had not even connected such a word to the driver and the cook.

"You mean Pettigrew loved Easter?"

Bess seemed limp as a rag doll as she sat against the wall beside the window. Her words were listless, her eyes dull.

"Nobody else . . . evuh."

In her mind's eye, and in horrid detail, Amy saw again Pettigrew poised to leap on Jason's back, saw him sprawled at Jason's feet, Easter's hands clutched around his ankles. *Jason's woman,* Amy had thought then. Jason's woman indeed.

"An she kilt'im." Bess's low voice suddenly was venomous. "Nevuh no woman he care bout but her. An she kilt'im."

"She chose." Amy was stunned at all she had not known, or even conceived, about the people in her yard. "One or the other, and she chose Jason."

What, she could not help but wonder, might *she* have done? What would it be like to have two men in love with you? She had never really known, she realized, any man but the General. It angered her obscurely that such a remarkable thing should have come to an African, a whoring black . . .

"Kilt'im!" Bess seemed to be gathering strength from hatred of Easter. "Good's if she swung at axe herself."

Slowly, in bits and piece, the story came out, Amy's questions pulling some of it from Bess, the rest coming in a monotone so low that even in the quiet house Amy had to strain to hear. And as the afternoon wore on, Amy realized that she was glimpsing, finally, what a lifetime had not until then taught her—that a life of rich complexity existed in the yard, a life of joy and sorrow, passion, expectation, dashed hopes, love fulfilled, love spurned, all inextricably entwined in the workings of chance.

Until she heard Bess's story, Amy simply had not understood that the people in the yard *were people*. She had regarded them as servants, Africans, a different breed, and their life in the yard as having no more complicated humanity than the stereographic pictures the General liked to collect.

Bess, it seemed, long before Pettigrew became the General's driver, had set out to win him—"Onlies man I'd tetch wid a fishin pole"—only to run into the solid wall of his determination to get Easter somehow away from Jason.

"Pe'grew knowed Jason a ba-a-d nigguh. Bound to be trouble . . . trouble."

But Easter, in the infinite perversity of love, wished for nothing but Jason's embrace. Jason once a week—for an hour snatched from the kitchen—was all Easter wanted or thought about. Amy was embarrassed by Bess's blunt judgment:

"At slut got'er legs spread fore Jason cross de fence."

Reba, of course, understood the situation—"Aint a nigguh dis place aint knowed it." Reba had been no more to Pettigrew, as Bess told it, than the completion of his driver's role. That he should have a wife, family, someone to wash his clothes and cook his meals was merely necessary.

"But not dis yere nigguh. Come round me wid at talk, I tole'im I eats de whole apple er none."

But Reba and his children had made no difference in Pettigrew's dogged determination that Easter—"his Easter," Bess called her, with the bitterest inflection Amy had ever heard—should not throw herself finally away on a ba-a-d nigguh.

"But she done it. She *would*."

Bess had only one consolation. As the years had dragged along, Pettigrew often had had to turn to her for help with the problems of the yard, tacitly acknowledging that, wherever his affection lay, Bess had his respect.

"Ceptin at aint done me no good nights when de bed uz cold."

Amy was uncomfortable again at the frankness of the words. But for all her ingrained reticence Amy understood the remark. The sense of being with someone, needing someone, being needed, was never so strong as in the warmth of bed. If only the General could leave it at that!

Then—Bess related—the news from Lakeview had come over the grapevine, implicating Jason long before the sheriff had come to Sycamore with official word.

"How come Jason done it, Miss Tippy she let'er nigguhs run round at place like dey own it. But dis summer she tole'em at son-a hers comin home to run it, she-uz gettin so old. Jason he knowed at son. Knowed at meant whuppins'n hard work. So he gone take Easter'n run off. But Miss Tippy, she keep money'n a bag unner her mattress. Dey all knowed it. So Jason gone grab at money fore he light out."

Amy clapped her hand over her mouth. She felt genuine horror at the idea of one of these lustful African men with their huge . . . one of them creeping into her bedroom at night. Even if just to steal. Her newfound sense of humanity in the yard was not strong enough to overcome her revulsion.

"Jason a ba-a-d nigguh." Bess's tone of voice suggested that this explained much. "But I aint used-a think he really *bad*. I speck he aint meant nothin but grab at money. Den Miss Tippy, she woke up'n start in a-hollerin. Fore he knowed it, he shuttin'er up wid de pilluh."

Amy thought how she had slapped Bess to shut *her* up. Before Amy had known she was going to do it.

"Den Jason so scairt, he try'n fix it so she look like she jes die'n'er sleep."

"But not scared enough to forget about the money?" The memory of the axe handle pointing at the window from Pettigrew's back was too stark for Amy to see anything redeeming in Jason's deeds.

"Nome. Soon's dey burr Miss Tippy'n nobody speck nuffin, Jason he gone run off wid Easter like he plan." Bess sighed heavily. "If some nigguh at Lakeview aint tell on'im, cuz he so scairt dey all git blame, Jason'n Easter be long gone. Instid . . ." Her voice trailed away.

"But how did Jason get away? When they found out?"

"He knowed dey gone put dawgs on'im. Conjur man he put grave-dirt on Jason's feet. Aint no dawgs kin sniff a track thew grave-dirt."

Amy wanted to throw up her hands in bewilderment. Just as it had dawned on her that the Africans were human beings, after all, not that different from their white masters, here was the story of Jason's bestial crime against a kindly old white woman; here was Bess expressing the most ignorant superstition. As if grave-dirt or any other kind of voodoo could help Jason escape the hounds yelping in Sheriff Maxton's pack!

But another implication in Bess's story disturbed her more.

"You *knew* all that? When the sheriff was here?"

"Nome. Pe'grew told me mostly jes today, after Jason come dis mornin. Cose some nigguh tole Pe'grew right off." Pride was husky in her voice. "Em nigguhs tell Pe'grew evuhthing. But Pe'grew, he aint think-a nuffin cept Easter. At slut set on leavin wid'er man." Now contempt made Bess shrill; her hands clenched as if on Easter's throat. "Some man. Smuvocatin at ol lady nevuh raise'er hand at nobody. But Pe'grew knowed right off he got to find Jason, he aim to keep Easter fum runnin off wid'im."

But if Bess had known even part of the story, obviously some of the others had, too, and all had failed to inform the sheriff. Much less Amy herself. Which showed not only how little you could trust them, but again how little whites really knew about the yard, about these people they liked to think were their charges.

Amy could hardly imagine the good-natured cook she had known for years—whose matchless Christmas fruit cakes were known throughout Duplin County—making such a desperate cast at fortune as to stand by a man like Jason. Of course African men were known to be rutting animals, but Amy found it hard to imagine any woman, black or white, who would stay with such a man for that kind of reason. Besides, Easter apparently could have had the superior Pettigrew. What kind of woman could she be, to have set two such different men so aflame with . . . could it be called love? . . . that they had literally fought to the death for her?

"Why didn't Pettigrew or somebody *tell* me, Bess? Or the sheriff?"

Bess's eyes and face were opaque. "Aint know wher at nigguh hidin. Not twill he come dis mornin."

But that was merely the truth, not the reason, and they both knew it. If Bess or Pettigrew *had* known where to find Jason, neither would have told her. If Pettigrew had been fighting for his woman—not for the General's house and family or for the law that subjugated him—perhaps he could hardly be blamed. And Bess at least had tried to ease Amy's fears by moving into her room. It wasn't her fault that Amy had only been alarmed the more.

And why should Bess have helped the whites to catch and hang one of her own, even a criminal like Jason? Even the boy at Lakeview who had informed on Jason had had to be frightened into it. Who, after all, could blame them for standing together in a world in which they were *bound* together? But if that was the case, there could be no ultimate trust between master and slave; and the pretensions of masters that the Africans willingly accepted their lot were lies or self-delusions or both.

"Sides," Bess said, her voice suddenly ringing passionately in the room. "I *want* 'im to git away. Take at slut wid'im. So my man nevuh lay eyes on'er agin."

Silence fell. Bess stared at Amy for a moment, defiantly, then looked into the space beyond Amy's shoulder, opaque again, yielding herself no more.

How different things were going to be from now on! Amy knew she'd never again be able to look at the people in the yard as so many shadows, having no substance. Or as passive recipients of their lot. And without Pettigrew . . . how could she possibly manage Sycamore without Pettigrew? With the General at war?

They were silent for a long time, Bess on the floor against the wall, Amy leaning on the work table, before Amy remembered little Luke. The sheriff to be notified. Almost at once it came to her what to do.

"Bess, pull yourself together and run up to see about Luke. Get him dressed, please. I'm going to have Ned hitch up the buggy." If I can find him. If they haven't all run for the woods. "I'll want you to go with us."

Bess had got up, looking a bit wobbly. "Go wher?"

"Why, to the sheriff, of course."

If she could be sure of no one else carrying the message, she'd go herself, taking Luke and Bess. Willis would look after the Judge, get him some supper if he needed it. That was the only sure way to get the news to the sheriff. And if she took Luke and left, she would not have to make sure Jason had gone, although of course he had. The sheriff would do that.

But Amy saw that Bess was hesitating. After all that had happened, could the woman still be reluctant to inform on Jason? Amy was exasperated again.

"Now Bess . . . you don't *have* to go. But somebody's got to report *Pettigrew's* death. You could look after Luke for me while I drive."

Bess closed her eyes, her oaken-colored face impassive as the wall paneling. Amy tried to imagine the struggle behind that blank wall turned to a white world—the conflict between primitive tribal allegiance, reinforced by the common plight of bondage, and the ordinary human instinct to curb the outlaw and restore the order on which survival depends. In Bess's case, too, the desire to see justice imposed on the murderer of her hopes.

Bess opened her eyes. "Jason a *mean* nigguh, Mistis. I git de baby ready."

Amy listened to the stairs creak as Bess hurried up to Luke. Then she picked up the pistol, held it loosely by her side where her skirts mostly concealed it, and went into the hall. Only as she neared the back door did it seriously occur to her that Jason might be waiting outside. But of course he'd be halfway out of Duplin County by now.

Besides, it was still good daylight. And as she came out on the stoop, forcing herself to look at the spot where Pettigrew had fallen, the yard was quiet, deserted. Nothing moved. No sound but late-day insect noises, bullbats and crickets.

Amy had all she could do not to rush back into the house and bolt all doors and windows. Silly. She started across the grass toward the carriage house. If Ned had made himself scarce, she could hitch up herself. She could do what she had to do, show the General she could manage.

But suppose Jason was waiting there, knowing sooner or later she'd . . . nonsense! Jason and Easter were an hour, nearly two, on their way.

Amy took a deep breath, her heavy breasts rising, and walked on. Still no sound but her own soft footfalls. Then, from the direction of the kitchen on her right, the corner of her eye caught a flicker of movement. Or did it?

Amy fought down the impulse to run back to the house, the urge to scream. She turned slowly toward the kitchen, the ivory pistol butt in her hand as solid and reassuring as the General's broad shoulders would have been. She put her thumb on the hammer.

"Mistis!"

The whisper, in the silence of the yard, was just loud enough to reach Amy's ears. A girl's sibilant whisper. Around the end of the privet hedge, for no more than a second, a dark face under a red kerchief peered out, then disappeared.

Amy stood stock still, her knees so weak she could not take a step. *Oh my God it's Easter. Easter wants me to get her away.* But surely the face had been too thin, too dark to be Easter's.

With an effort of will almost as great as that with which she had pointed the pistol at Jason, Amy forced one step after another, across the grass, over the very spot where . . . she fancied she could smell bate and lye again.

"Mistis! He aint gone!"

Amy almost cried with relief to see Penny's childish face behind the hedge. Then the words sunk in. *Aint gone.* She felt them like blows from the axe.

I can't can't face can't do don't know. But as it had before, her training as a lady, her place as mistress of Sycamore, saved her from abjection. She had to control herself in the presence of a servant; that was the most inflexible, the most tyrannical of the rules by which she lived.

But she could do little more than stammer. "N . . . not gone?"

"At Easter's house. His arm broke."

Amy remembered Pettigrew smashing the stove wood against Jason's arm and shoulder as Jason ducked. Oh, bad luck! *Rotten* luck! Else he'd be gone. She realized that, all along, she'd known somehow that Jason was still there. Still to be dealt with.

"Mistis . . ."

Why, Amy wondered, was Penny hiding in the hedge?

"Reba say tell you . . ." The whisper squeaked and stopped.

Amy saw by Penny's wide child's eyes that she was in terror. Making two of us.

"Go on, P . . . Penny."

"Reba say Jason got nigguhs watchin at ca'ige house. Drive, too. Say you start to leave dis place, Jason gone . . . Jason . . ." Penny choked, stopped, peered at Amy with wide and unblinking eyes.

"All right." The frantic energy of fear made it easy, this time, to cock the stiff hammer with one thumb. "I understand."

Amy turned toward the house, then stopped, not looking back, the discipline of lifetime surpassing even fear. "Please thank Reba, Penny. Please say I'm sorry about Pettigrew."

She was amazed, as she went across the grass toward the house, at her clarity of mind and self-control, as if the dark fruition of what once had seemed only an absurd fear had at least yielded her the will to cope with malignant reality. Her legs and hands were steady, and she was beginning to think what to do as calmly, it seemed to her, as she might once have planned a dinner— perhaps because she was assuring herself that Jason couldn't hurt anybody much with only one arm.

She was looking sharply, too, for the niggers on watch. Fix *them* when I find out who they are.

Just before she went up the stoop, Amy measured the sun against the horizon. If only it could stand still, like Joshua's in the Bible! If only she need not face the night as well as Jason.

General A. P. Hill, like Sam Stowe, believed the Yanks had had enough of attacking him from the woods. The railway cuts and banks made his front hard to break, and the brigades Jackson had distributed along his compact line could be shifted to shore up any threatened point. If they came again, Hill reasoned, they'd come over the open field on his left, attacking along the cut rather than against it.

That was worrisome. Hoke Arnall's troops had been in the thick of it all day. God knew how many casualties there had been. Not an experienced officer was left save Colonel Stowe.

All of Hill's brigades had been too constantly engaged to be pulled out and sent to the ammunition wagons; and runners had not been able to keep them properly supplied.

Hill's reserves were just about used up, too; most were in the line already. He had none with which to relieve Arnall.

Still . . . a move had to be made. Hill sent a courier urgently to find Hoke Arnall.

The courier located the General, his pistol strapped to his waist in the famous Mexican holster, standing with Colonel Stowe at the rail fence. The firing had lagged from its earlier pitch, but muskets were still popping from the woods. Arnall's line was mostly holding its fire to save bullets.

"Gin'al Arnall, sir!" They exchanged salutes. "Gin'al Hill sends me to ask, sir, can you hold off an attack on your left?"

Arnall had no doubt of the answer. But in the style of Lee's army he deferred to the officer who would have the most direct responsibility.

"Sam . . . what about it?"

Stowe removed his trampled straw hat, smeared the sweat on his forehead with a dirty sleeve, and glared at the motionless sun.

"Dark'd be the best thing, Gin'al. But if they come, I reck'n we'll make it hot for'em."

Arnall had always insisted to his officers that he wanted no romantic nonsense when they gauged the truths of battle. He needed hard facts, considered opinion; so, of course, did Hill. If, however elliptically, Stowe said the position could be held, Stowe believed it. Still, he would have wished more fire in Stowe's answer, to suggest more in his belly.

"Course I'm countin on the guns givin'em a goddam fit." Arnall winced at Stowe's casual blasphemy. "An if they come through the woods at the same time, I hope Gin'al Hill got some reserves in hand."

Arnall reckoned Hill had no real reserves, that late in the day. He or Jackson could strengthen the left only by weakening the line somewhere else. But he was faintly annoyed that Stowe should be thinking such thoughts. The Yanks hadn't, in fact, managed a coordinated attack all day. Every time they'd threatened, somehow the boys had held. And they'd do it again. They'd outfight'em. Hadn't they done it all day? That was just the fact of it, not wishful thinking. Arnall felt a fierce surge of confidence in his troops, his position, his God, himself.

He nodded thanks to Stowe, and turned to the courier. "Tell Gin'al Hill I think we can hold. Tell'im my ammunition's about gone but we still got the bayonet."

A bayonet, of course, was worth nothing like a full cartridge box. But the bayonet could scare the wits out of troops not used to cold steel, as Arnall thought most Yanks weren't, and it was deadly in hand-to-hand fighting. Watching the courier hasten off to Hill, Hoke Arnall found himself almost eagerly looking forward to that—another close-quarter fight, no holds barred.

"We got rocks, too." Stowe put his hat back on. "Me, I'd still rather have at sun go down."

Teddy Redmund, even though he knew nothing of Longstreet's arrival, had nevertheless concluded that the blues would not attack Jackson again. In his professional opinion, they'd strewn enough bodies through the woods and on the edge of the railroad cut— and not a few *in* it—to learn their lesson. Of course, they should have turned the position; anybody could see that.

As he mounted his horse in some irritation at Pope's ineptitude, Redmund saw no reason to suppose the blues would try a turning attack now, since the butternut artillery alone had held them off all afternoon. These Americans didn't have much stomach for shellfire; the musket was their weapon. Probably made them feel like the squirrel and pigeon hunters most of them were.

With his havelock streaming behind him, Redmund rode slowly back toward the center of Jackson's line, wondering if at the end of the day's shooting—desultory and sullen now, as if both armies were played out but neither wanted to be first to quit—he might be able to approach Jackson. The man was said to be mad as a hatter, no way to predict what he'd do.

Redmund was burning to know—and Sertorius would have to explain—why the butternut "genius" had precipitated this unnecessary battle against superior forces that was consuming his army piece by piece. Assuming there *was* a reason.

As Redmund rode along the lower levels of Sudley Mountain, General Hill and several of his entourage passed nearby, also riding toward the center. Redmund followed, at first discreetly, then closer, since no one in the group seemed to be noticing him.

Hill's party rode over a knoll and into a shallow draw. Just then two horsemen entered the draw from the opposite side and Hill threw up his hand for a halt. He saluted the first of the two men—the ungainly rider with a long brown beard and a forage cap pulled low on his forehead that Redmund, the evening before, had surmised was the legendary Stonewall.

Not much of a legend to look at. But Redmund wondered if this might not prove to be his best chance to approach Jackson. He edged his horse nearer, hoping to suggest that he was one of Hill's staff party.

". . . attacked again, of course my division will do its best. But we're so weakened, ammunition and men, that I can't be sure of success."

Redmund could just barely make out Jackson's answer.

"General Hill, your men have done nobly. If you're attacked again, you will beat the enemy back."

The Englishman was amazed at Stonewall's calm. Except for a slight emphasis on the word "will," he had the air of an officer of the day accepting the morning report. But just as he finished speaking, the butternut batteries behind the left boomed, as if in unison. Hill swung his horse sharply to the sound; its echoes had hardly died away before the guns were firing individually, as fast—Redmund judged—as they could be served.

"Here it comes!" Hill did not even bother to salute, as he spurred back toward his command.

This time Jackson's voice rang through the roar of the guns: "I'll expect you to beat them!"

Redmund sensed in those few shouted words a powerful intensity—not "Good luck!" or empty exhortation but a flat statement leaving no room for failure or excuse. Hill would "beat them" because Jackson would accept nothing less.

Redmund was about to swing his horse to follow Hill's galloping party when from under the forage cap pale eyes flashed and Jackson's long arm suddenly pointed at him. In a voice that was no longer clear or ringing, he seemed to be saying something to the other rider—a colonel in an abominable jacket and a worse-looking slouch hat. Quickly the colonel moved up beside Redmund, seized his horse's halter strap, and bared yellowing teeth in what no doubt he considered a grin. Foul tobacco breath made Redmund pull his head back in distaste.

"Who might you be, Mister?"

In the thunder of the guns, the question was not so much audible as deduced from the colonel's moving lips. Feeling it hopeless to explain, Redmund began to fish in his pockets for his papers. He saw, beyond the colonel, Jackson turn his horse's head and trot from the draw.

Redmund's searching fingers found the wallet in which he stored his *bona fides;* but just then the colonel, still grinning, put his whiskered face unpleasantly close and shouted:

"Ol Jack thinks you a spy, Mister! So you must *be* a spy!"

• • •

Hill's instinct had been sound. As Hoke Arnall and Sam Stowe gazed over the rail fence, they saw blue ranks unmistakably forming battle lines in the woods beyond the open field. The gunners higher on the ridge saw them, too, and opened up immediately. But this time, despite the heavy cannonading into the woods and the fiery barrier of shell bursts across the ground before them, a brigade of Yanks moved out boldly and in well-spaced waves toward the rail fence.

At 5:30 p.m. General Philip Kearny had received orders from Pope to attack on the far left flank of the Rebel line. Kearny, who wore his empty uniform sleeve pinned across his chest, was known as a fighting terrier of a general. But even he had been reluctant throughout the long afternoon to attack on his own discretion into heavy artillery fire from Sudley Mountain—an advantageous artillery position from which massed Federal batteries had been unable to drive the Rebel guns.

Kearny had no choice but to obey Pope's order. He sent forward General John C. Robinson's Brigade of Pennsylvania and Indiana veterans, who promptly emerged from the woods and moved in good order over the open field toward the rail fence. Shellfire opened gaps in their ranks but Hoke Arnall, sensing within moments of the Yanks' appearance that the shelling was not going to stop them, shifted as many men as he could from the railway cut to the fence.

Hours before, he had given up the effort to maintain a brigade reserve; having lost, by his best estimate, more than a third of his men in ten hours' fighting, he had all he could do to defend his perimeter. Sparks and Dixon were wounded and out of it, McCrary was dead, and Arnall had no proper regimental structure, save for Stowe's South Carolinians. What he had instead was a clutch of skeleton companies, some with no more than sergeants in charge, and all with virtually empty cartridge boxes. They wouldn't average three rounds a musket.

The General stared across the fence, through the drifting smoke, at the oncoming Federals, fresh troops with plenty of ammunition, bent low now, as if against a strong wind, but moving inexorably forward. Come on, Arnall thought. Something in him welcomed their approach. *Keep comin. Just keep comin.*

Stowe touched his arm and put his lips to Arnall's ear: "Hoke . . . whatever happens . . . we gave'em a hell of a fight!"

As if from a great distance, Arnall looked at the colonel in his crushed, ridiculous hat; he felt his lips draw back from his teeth.

A hell of a fight? Whatever happened? The tone of resignation was unmistakable. He sensed himself at that moment, in that world—and what other mattered?—the better man, unshaken, indomitable.

"Whip'em!"

The words snarled from his throat, through his clenched jaw, up from the depths of a warrior's spirit.

"Whip the bastards, Stowe . . . whip'em!"

Skirmishers' bullets began to whine over the fence in multiplying numbers *wheat-wheat-wheat!* Arnall's brain began clinically to record events before him—a blue body thrown backward by shell percussion, a color bearer going down, another Yank seizing the standard before it hit the ground, a geyser of dirt going up from a shell that ploughed along like a massive auger just beneath the earth's surface.

By then, battle was a terrible familiarity. And Hoke Arnall was a different man from the one who had ceremoniously and conspicuously pulled on, so many bloody hours before, the Mexican holster. Then he had been concerned mostly to seize upon his crucial position to make the reputation he coveted, wipe the stain of his arrest from Jackson's consciousness. He had wanted mostly to win approval.

But as the sun had inched in its interminable wheel across the sky, as he had watched his tattered ranks thinning like a cornfield before foragers, as the Yank waves had beat against his position—*his* ground—and fallen back whipped, outfought every time, Hoke Arnall had discovered the terrible freedom, the redeeming joy of violence. When the Yanks had got into the cut between his position and Thomas's, Arnall felt himself aflame with rage—*his* ground trespassed!—but more than that. He had flung himself into the new round of man-to-man fighting with the same ferocity unleashed in him earlier that morning—the more abandoned because Arnall was convinced, by then, that the power of a vengeful God had strengthened his muscles. He had been rewarded at last for the fidelity of his belief and made terrible by His power.

Arnall's pistol had become not just something to wear in a showy holster but an extension of God's merciless strength. When his cartridges were gone—young fool Folsom failing to reach him in time with more—he had used the heavy metal like a club, smashing it repeatedly into Yank faces, over Yank heads, wrists, necks. His saber rose and fell with Jove-like force; once he severed a blue arm as cleanly at the bicep as if with a surgical saw.

Again he seemed immune to danger—God's shadow his shield—though he had saber cuts on both hands, powder burns on his neck and face, the track of a grazing bullet burning on his thigh, a massive lump on the side of his head from a Yank musket butt swung not quite hard enough. As the hours passed and the ground was held, Hoke Arnall never doubted that God had guided his life to this moment, this ground to be held, beneath the unforgiving sun. His judgment would have to be faced if Arnall's ground should be lost.

But Arnall did not aim to lose. Generals were not supposed to be in ranks, fighting hand to hand, clubbing their pistols, but God had His purposes, not to be questioned. Arnall's men had held the ground because God had sent His instrument to show them God's power.

Late in the day Arnall had even stacked up rocks with one of Dixon's bled-out companies, side by side with a barrel-chested private he did not recognize as one of those he had routed the day before from a fenced yard in Centreville. To Arnall, a warrior in the grip of God's awful passion, the men had become nameless, faceless, all as one, in the simple necessity to outfight the Yanks and hold the ground. Life had narrowed to a single proposition. *Whip' em. Whip the bastards.* Nothing mattered here, now, but to win.

He heard Stowe shouting, saw the men at the fence leveling their muskets, new ranks of blue invaders coming on, steadily, confidently, the range closing, smoke and dust hazing over the savage beauty of life and death at the uttermost, at the edge of human capacity, where only God's will determined. He screamed his affirmation—defiance, faith, *victory*—into the crash of Stowe's muskets.

Lige Flournoy put down his piece as soon as it had bucked against his shoulder. He had fired off his last cartridge, careful to draw down on a feisty little blue piece of meat, zigging and zagging across the field as if a man could dance with death and never hear the tune. But the Yanks were not close enough yet for the defenders to club their muskets or use the bayonet; and anyway Lige had a weapon at hand that promised quicker results.

Without looking down, he picked up in his right hand a rock from the pile at his side. He had exercised much care in choosing rocks about the size of a baseball. Lige loved baseball and had been considered to have the strongest throwing arm in Cumberland County. He felt the cool surface between his fingers and waited for a proper target.

A Yank trotting forward dropped to one knee, aimed his piece, then shook it in exasperation. Misfire. As the Yank was capping again, Lige flung the rock at a distance of about home to first base. Even at that range, it caught the Yank high in the chest and knocked him over backward. Not snuffed, but good-feelin as a wing shot on a dove.

Lige had no time for another such long hit. As the Yanks swarmed in through lukewarm fire, he got off two more baseball-sized rocks at close range, one grazing but not stopping a color-bearer, the other doubling over a bluebelly smashed in the belt buckle. With both hands, Lige then smashed a bigger stone into a clutch of Yanks about to jump the fence.

He seized his musket by the barrel and swung it hard against the head of a Yank who was astride the top rail. Lige stepped back, ready to swing again, much preferring to club his musket rather than fix his bayonet. But all around him butternuts who had run out of cartridges were giving the attackers cold steel. Fierce resistance, with musket fire, bayonets, rocks, clubs, even bare fists, held up the first blue ranks at the fence. Others began to pile up behind them.

"Hold'em!" Hoke Arnall roared in his hoarse battle voice. "Hit'em, boys . . . whip'em!"

His pistol blazing and effective at short range, Arnall believed wildly for a moment that the fence might be held by sheer brute strength. But just then, with a smashing volley and a rousing cheer, a second Yank attack broke from the woods, this time against the railroad cut, where only the exhausted remnants of McCrary's South Carolinians waited—mostly with piles of rocks, bayonets, and no more than a round or two per man.

Arnall was too professional, even in his exalted condition, not to realize immediately that the Yanks were sending a coordinated attack at last. And though he could not know it, the double punch Pope had delivered was commanded by two of the hardest fighters in the Federal army—Kearny, under whom in years past Arnall had served in the West, and Major General Isaac Stevens, who had hit him with the brigade attacking the railroad cut.

Arnall saw at once that he could not hold his precious ground, but he did not for a moment consider it lost. He knew—he *believed*—his men would not break. He would lead them with God-given strength so they could *not* break. Like that big one there, swinging a musket like an executioner's axe. Such men would never break if their leader didn't. They'd fight, as he would, with rocks, clubs, hands, teeth—fight any way they could, fight on and on, never quit, never give up, until God sent help in His own good time, and the ground would be recovered.

"Keep your lines, men! Fall back slowly and keep your lines!"

Arnall had no idea how far he could be heard in the deafening collision of blue and butternut across the fence. But his men were well-trained; the officers and noncoms still in action knew what to do; and he saw with satisfaction that the lines were holding their coherence even as the troops grudgingly gave ground.

"Show'em steel, boys! Give it to'em!"

A few regimental colors still straggled over the line as it moved glacially back from the fence and the cut. The Federal momentum was inexorable but Arnall saw that the ground being yielded was covered with blue, so solidly that he thought he might have walked on Yank bodies back to Stowe's original position. The sight filled him with elation, renewed his faith.

"Hold'em, boys! Give'em steel!"

Larkin Folsom, the General's horse in his charge, led the animal to a reasonably safe spot, tethered him, then took up his musket. He had given most of his cartridges to Corporal Gilmore but on the corporal's instructions had saved three rounds "for emergencies."

This Yank attack looked like an emergency to Folsom. He leaned against a tree and carefully capped his already-loaded musket. Then, with the tree to help him steady it, he sighted toward the struggling mass of men near the fence, blues almost indistinguishable from butternuts in the dust that lay alike on all. He waited, quite calmly, for a clear Yank target.

Folsom had never shot anyone. He had often wondered if he could do it since, ordinarily, he would not even shoot a rabbit or a squirrel. But plainly every man, every shot, counted; survival was at stake, the brigade's, his own, Corporal Gilmore's. A Yank staggered or was thrust for a moment clear of the pack of cursing and shouting men up ahead; Folsom put a .69-caliber ball into his chest, seeing dust puff from it like tobacco smoke. He quickly reloaded.

Think about it later, he told himself.

• • •

Slowly, powerfully, Kearny's and Stevens's fighters closed in.
The attack had drawn in Thomas from Arnall's right. And Branch's
depleted regiments, which had been so close behind Arnall and
Thomas as virtually to form a part of the front line, moved up to
join the defense. Still the attackers, fresh and determined, pushed
on, although heavy casualties were wearing down their momentum.

The defenders had fallen far back from the railroad cut that
had halted Yankee attacks so often that day. It was choked, by
then, with dead, wounded, skulkers feigning injury, and the forlorn
litter of battle—strewn muskets, caps, canteens, cartridge boxes,
a half-empty tin of potted ham foraged from Manassas on a happier
day.

Step by step, yard by yard, the butternut troops yielded the
ground they had defended so long. The fight began to lose dis-
cernible shape; only the barest semblance of two lines could be
maintained. Men struggled singly and for life, seldom farther than
a musket length or two apart. Coming on with a whoop behind
Robinson's shock waves, Birney's Brigade of Kearny's Division
swarmed easily over the fence and around it and piled into the
fight, redoubling the pressure on the dwindling band of defenders.

Amos Gilmore, his bayonet slick with gore, had one last charge
in his musket. He had a vague notion, which there was no time
to form into an idea, that just before they snuffed him, he'd take
some blue-bellied son to hell with him. Meantime, the bayonet
would do; and if not that, then the butt end.

Just a little to his left, he saw a Yank drawing down on a barrel-
chested butternut who was cleaning out whole circles of bluecoats
with a piece he was swinging like a windmill. Then Gilmore
realized he knew the rifle swinger, had seen him earlier across
the sprawled body of the man who had drawn his bayonet on the
boy. Without further thought, Gilmore snapped off his last round
into the aiming Yank's blue torso.

Charlie Keach clung to the branches of a pine tree he had shinnied
up in the woods where Robinson had formed his battle line. Keach's
perch afforded an excellent view over the open field and the rail

fence to the titanic struggle beyond, and he wished he were over there in the midst of it. But Kearny's front was always tightly disciplined, and if he ventured out there without weapons or insignia he'd risk arrest. It did not even occur to Keach that he would have. risked death, too, or dismemberment.

But arrest would have been ruinous. Hale would never forgive him for that. Here he was, the only correspondent—so far as he knew—on what had turned out to be one of the biggest battlefields of the war. And now, at the end of the day, almost too late, Pope was breaking Jackson; Pope had in his hand the most important Union victory of the war. And only Charlie Keach would have the eyewitness story.

A cheer went up beneath him, as another blue regiment charged from the woods and across the field. Kearny putting in the clincher! Keach began to climb down from his tree. He'd seen enough. Jackson would have to run for Thoroughfare Gap or Aldie or be crushed. Time to find Pope and get a victory claim.

The three Reb brigades giving ground—not quite breaking—were being swung back on Jackson's line like a gate hinged on the line's left center. Before long, the gate was perpendicular to the line itself. Knowing his left had to swing back even farther or break entirely, A. P. Hill just then made his last move. He pulled Field's worn-out brigade from the railway cut, risking a dangerous gap from its old position to the center of Jackson's line. Hill thought he had to take the risk; he threw Field against the left flank of the Kearny–Stevens attack.

It was then just after 6 p.m. Hoke Arnall did not realize, as he tried to keep something like a line wedged across the path of the swarming federals, that his voice no longer made a sound. He had shouted so much that day, the dust and the smoke had so coated even his larynx, that scarcely a rasp emerged. But even if he had understood that, it would have made little difference to him; he believed he led mostly with his commanding figure, his sheer determination, the immunity God seemed to have granted him.

Sam Stowe, twenty yards away, raised his saber and cheered forward three butternuts with fixed bayonets whose minicharge threw back a segment of Yanks who had stopped to load.

"Hit'em!" Stowe yelled. "Go it, men!"

But even as he shouted, he saw that any respite would be

momentary. The Yanks just kept coming on. So many of 'em. Finished, Stowe thought. *Done for*. It was all he could do not to turn and run; and he might have, except he knew that if he did, so would every butternut in sight of his planter's hat.

Besides, Arnall probably would shoot him on the spot. Stowe swung the hat above his head and raised his bloody sword into the last rays of the sun:

"Let's die here, men! Hold here and die!"

If Lige Flournoy had heard this—and hardly anyone did—he would have considered it officer shit. Sam Stowe, in his patriotism, his honor, his sense of what became a man, perhaps even in his fear of Arnall, regarded dying as the ultimate gift, the greatest sacrifice to a cause he believed in—or rather, to a way of living he preferred.

Lige had no cause. Lige was not a patriot. The politics of secession and war were mysteries that did not interest him. He would not have shed a drop of blood for Stowe's niggers. He had gone to war because Colonel Dixon—a captain then—told him the Yanks had come down looking for a fight. Lige fought now because it was there to be done, and because he sensed what he could not have articulated—that in a life likely to be short and hard, he would not again find anything he could do so well, from which he could take more satisfaction. As for dying, everyone did; if that was a gift or a sacrifice, it was in common coin.

The two lines became so closely locked that musket fire lost effectiveness; no one had much chance to take aim even at a prominent target like Lige, while those within range of his clubbed musket usually found themselves overpowered. He had broken three pieces already, picking up a replacement each time. His list of minor injuries was appalling—a spent Minié come to rest in the outer flesh of his left thigh, numerous bayonet cuts, a broken nose, half an ear shot off at range so close his hair had been singed by the muzzle blast. He could no longer hear from that ear but Lige fought on, mercilessly, brutally, not with a passion like Arnall's but knowing that he was doing what no one else could do better.

Field's men had faced left and swarmed down on the Yank left, between the railroad cut and Thomas's struggling brigade. These reinforcements were as tired as the other butternuts, worn by battle, heat, exhaustion, and fear, and short of ammunition, too. But the desperation of the moment added to the force of their charge; and the blue brigades, at the same time, had surged about as far as their first momentum could carry them.

So Field's men, while too few and too weak to turn the tide, were able to stop it momentarily. The struggle on the left, and therefore the whole day, then hung in the balance, like the blood-red ball of the sun lingering over the mountain ridges to the west.

Captain Thad Selby at last had ditched the ornate sword with which he had gone off to war. After two days of battle, he had not lifted it once in martial purpose; the sword had merely hung on him like the weight of his father's expectations. It was a hindrance getting on and off Jeff D.; and the more action he saw, the more he realized the thing was an affectation anyway. This was not a swordsman's war.

Getting rid of it, like the ruination of his uniform, was a comfort. Selby was beginning to get the welcome feeling of being at home among people and processes once alien. Gin'al Jackson knew his name; Colonel Channing poured on him the same caustic humor he loosed on everyone but Ol Jack himself; and had it not been for his deep-going fear, which he could not dismiss and only barely repressed, Selby would have considered himself a veteran.

But he would not delude himself. Riding hard on his second mission to irascible Jubal Early, Selby knew he lacked both the experience and the courage of a real veteran. He was rapidly acquiring the former and he had so far concealed the absence of the latter. But he was dogged by an unshakable sense of foreboding, a dread of the moment when he would have to face the test, when only courage would suffice, when its lack would be fatal. Or worse, obvious.

When he found Early, the general—his chaw bulging in his cheek—had again anticipated Ol Jack's orders. With the last butternut brigade available on that part of the field, he was already moving to the point of danger. Lawton, also responding to the emergency, was sending the Thirteenth Georgia. Early took along also the Eighth Louisiana of Forno's Brigade, which was just back from a trip to the ammunition wagons.

Impulsively, Selby trotted along on Jeff D., rationalizing that he might be needed to carry a message back to Jackson. As Early's force came out of the woods that had sheltered them into the more open ground behind what had been Jackson's left—in peaceful days, the ploughed field and meadows of a farmer named Sam Moss—Selby caught his breath. He was astonished at the mass hand-to-hand struggle visible across the field and appalled at the distance Hill's brigades had been driven.

The attacks of Kearny and Stevens had finally been halted by the addition of Field to the shaky line of Arnall–Branch–Thomas, but only after the loss—Selby estimated—of three hundred yards at least. The line had been briefly stabilized, moreover, only on a rise of ground past which—even Selby's inexperienced eye could see—if the butternuts were driven they would be doubled all the way back on Ol Jack's center. The whole line then would have to give way unless Longstreet, still strangely quiescent on the right, could be goaded into acting.

Early sent his fresh regiments, flanked on either side by the Louisianians and Georgians, charging forward at once. His own men were tough and experienced Virginians, whom darkness and confusion had kept out of action at Brawner's farm, and of whom little had been demanded that day. They crashed down on the blue coats with full cartridge boxes, terrifying yells, and the rare zeal of troops keyed up for a fight; and the vigor of their attack communicated itself to the Georgia and Louisiana regiments on their flanks.

Hoke Arnall saw these reinforcements coming without surprise. In the smoke and dust and the blurred vision of his heightened nervous energy, he could not at first identify the units. But he knew that the infallible hand of God had delivered at last the stroke that would regain his ground—His ground. Hoke Arnall had been worthy, judged so by Him in whom Arnall had placed all trust, to whom he had prayed so often for favor, but whom he had not even had to ask for deliverance.

Early's men came on rapidly; and as the Federals began to shift to meet them, Arnall ran along what was left of his own line, screaming to his men to lie down. He still did not know that his voice was gone but his gestures and their veterans' common sense made the point. They dropped flat, so that Early's bullets, and soon his ranks, could pass over them.

Arnall saw Stowe still in his mangled hat and tried to shout to him his intention. If the reinforcements failed and the Yanks attacked again, he croaked, "Wait till they're near, then give 'em the bayonet again. Hold here . . . no goin back anymore . . . hold here!"

Stowe could not make out a word; but in Arnall's glaring eyes and flushed face, in his hoarse rasps and rigid intensity, his message was plain. He was still ready to fight. Even eager.

Just then, Arnall realized his voice was gone, and his orders could not be heard. He looked around, bent, and seized a musket from a dead butternut. A bloodied bayonet was fixed to its muzzle; and as the last rank of Early's attackers swept past, Arnall turned and lunged, thrusting the bayonet viciously toward the Yanks.

Mistaking this for a sign-language order to their exhausted troops to get up and charge along with their rescuers, Stowe stumbled back a step or two, as if confronting a wild animal. For the truth of war was in that mad pantomime—the warrior spirit in its illimitable energy, its boundless urge to dominate and destroy, its visceral savagery.

Stowe was in no condition to understand that. But he backed away instinctively, refusing the crazed order, knowing to do so was mutiny, thinking he could always plead a failure to understand. Stowe was a civilized man, not a warrior.

On the right of Early's attack, in Lawton's regiment of Georgians, the New Man trotted along as near as he could stay to Sergeant Owen L. Cade. These-yer Yanks not so tough as em black hats fightin us yistiddy, he thought. But not givin much neither.

The New Man was glad Cady was in charge of the company. Dang Cady's good's any gin'al. The New Man was proud of him. Cady proved what nothing else in a mean life had ever even suggested to him—that a plain old sandhills dirtdobber with no more learnin than a yard dog was as good's any man.

This was the nearest thing to an idea or an inspiration ever to touch the New Man. It opened unexpected worlds to him and it was embodied in the splendid figure of Sergeant Owen L. Cade leading the company across the field as the New Man thought he must have been born to do.

The New Man was not brave or strong but following Cady braced him. He fired, loaded, ran on, fired again in a rhythm set by Cady; he ran, as Cady did, bent and veering, with the Yanks giving ground almost back to the railroad cut. When Cady went to one knee, the New Man and the whole company knelt down;

when Cady waved them on, they went forward with a shout.

So it was natural that when Cady suddenly stopped, then plunged heavily to his knees, the New Man and most of the company paused too. But when Cady's musket slipped from his hands and he toppled on his side, slowly as a pine cut from a Georgia forest, only the New Man ran to his aid.

That was strictly against orders. Nobody in that army was to fall out of ranks to help the wounded. Some said Ol Jack'd shoot the man that done it. And within seconds, most of the company, responding to its companions on either side, jumped up and ran on, leaving Cady and the New Man behind.

"Cady . . . y'all right? Cady?"

Cady did not answer but began to curl up, his hands and arms clutched around his body. The New Man let his piece fall in the dirt and leaned over Cady's writhing body, looking for the wound. He was not yet alarmed. He had too much confidence in Cady.

"Lemme help, huh? Cady . . . wher yuh hit?"

He was leaning close enough to the one side of Cady's contorted face that he could see, to hear the words chewed through Cady's grinding teeth:

"Git . . . back'n ranks . . . goddamyuh . . ."

Beyond them, across the desolation of the sunbaked field with its strewn bodies, Early's and Lawton's men cleared the last Yanks beyond Arnall's old defense line along the ruined rail fence. The New Man was so reassured to see that Cady retained his manner of command, and so respectful of it, that he grabbed his piece and stood up, jumping as always to obey Cady. Then he saw, from that higher perspective, blood and the white curl of innards trickling between Cady's fingers, where his hands were clutched against his stomach.

Gutshot. A shock of despair struck the New Man with the force of a Minié ball. He lifted his head from the sight, and howled his anguish like a dog into the great red crescent of sun still balanced uncaring on the western ridge.

Andrew Peterson had hauled Joe Nathan's truncated body in the Whatsit Wagon west along the Warrenton Pike, past Longstreet's forming lines, through Gainesville, out of the battle zone and into peaceful country near Buckland Mills. On a hillside looking south, and from which no evidences of the battle near Groveton could be seen, Peterson scratched a grave from the rocky soil.

He pinned a clean handkerchief across the top of the broad shoulders and wrapped the body in his linen duster. Not much of a shroud but better than nothing. Then he carried Joe Nathan from the wagon to the grave and covered him gently, while Positive and Negative whuffed and tramped sorrowfully—so, at least, it seemed to Andrew Peterson.

He erected a small cross of dogwood above the grave, mindful of his childhood belief that the tree's notched spring blossoms replicated Christ's stigmata, since men had crucified Him upon a cross of dogwood.

Peterson had been fond of Joe Nathan, whose death was the first in the war that had immediately touched him. Peterson had no close family—parents dead, no children, wife run off four years since with a drummer who had sold Peterson chemicals that were never delivered. He mourned Joe Nathan honestly, trying not to think of the manner of his death. Joe Nathan had lived so little and now lay in a hillside grave. Peterson grieved for himself, too, alone as his servant's senseless death had made him realize he was. Nothing left now but the Whatsit Wagon and the graphic truth he coveted as some men sought love or wealth.

"O God," he said to the emptiness around him, against the far-off murmur of war, "accept thy servant Joe Nathan." He hesitated only a moment, then added the only family name that seemed appropriate. "Thy son . . . Joe Nathan Peterson. A good man. True to his trust. Killed this day . . ." He did not know the date. "Serving the cause of truth here on earth. Be merciful, Lord. Let that cause and his soul be Thine."

But he did not want to turn a prayer for Joe Nathan into one for himself. Standing hatless over the grave he had mounded with the harsh orange rock of northern Virginia, he recited from memory as best he could:

"God is our refuge and strength . . . very present help in trouble.

"Therefore will not we fear, though the earth be moved . . . removed, and though the mountains be carried into the midst of the sea.

"Yea . . . though the waters thereof roar and be troubled, though the mountains shake with the swelling thereof . . ."

There his memory failed him. He thought hard and recalled one more verse. With irony rich on his tongue, he spoke aloud again:

"He madeth wars to cease unto the end of the earth; he breaketh the bow, and cutteth the spear asunder; he burneth chariots in the fire . . ."

But that was all he could call to mind. What did it matter to Joe Nathan anyway? Bible verses were for the living.

"Amen."

The word rang harshly across the hillside. Then there was nothing to do but go back, ready himself for another ghoulish prowl over the fields of war with their harvests of waste and destruction. How manlike! he thought, as the mules ambled down the hill in the drowsy afternoon, how like the sons of Adam to string the dead in putrefying rows over earth cleared to yield the corn and wheat and fodder upon which life depended. But maybe *that* ironic truth was in one of his pictures, or would be before he and the war were done. Maybe that kind of irony, or the metaphor of harvest, something he hadn't planned or even seen himself, would leap someday from one of his coated plates and . . . and what? Change the world?

"Not likely." Peterson spoke aloud, and the mules tossed their heads a little at the sound. Joe Nathan had always talked to them lovingly on the road. "Truth don't change the world." Peterson fancied the mules nodded in agreement. "But the world don't change the truth, either."

Up ahead, a Negro came out of the woods that flanked the road—a big man, tattered as most of them were, barefoot, his broad face expressionless. A common sight. Contrabands everywhere these days; turned loose on the country by the war. A farm burned, a master killed. Or just running off to freedom.

He pulled up the mules. "Need a ride?"

The black man peered suspiciously at the Whatsit Wagon and the horse tethered behind it. Custom would call for him to ride in the back of an ordinary open wagon, if the white man was driving. But the bed of the Whatsit was covered with Peterson's makeshift darkroom and storehouse.

"I'm not patter-roll. Come on if you want a ride." The black man came and stood by the front wheel, looking up at Peterson with red-rimmed eyes.

"Gotta git thew em sojers."

"Can you drive?"

The black man looked at the mules, then back at Peterson, and nodded.

"Get on up here, then. I'd just as soon doze a little."

He watched the African step lightly up into the wagon, belying the heavy look of his body. His big hands took up the reins tenderly as ribbons, and the mules moved smoothly into the traces.

"Got a name?"

"Henry." And a second or two later: "Massa."

"I'm Diogenes," Peterson said, wryly amused at the notion. "Call me Mister Dodge."

Charlie Keach found Pope on Buck's Hill, obviously in a sputtering rage. Standing quietly off to the side of the headquarters camp, the reporter could see the general stamping about, swinging his arms and shouting at subordinates. But as he could not make out the words, in the roar of nearby batteries still pounding Jackson's line, Keach stood alone in the gathering dusk, waiting his chance.

Colonel Russell, however, was in no doubt about the source of Pope's anger, nor was anyone else in the general's official family.

"I tell you," Russell insisted, *"Duryea* took that order to General Porter. Most reliable man we've got. He left here at half-past four sharp and I aint seen the order yet Duryea didn't deliver on time."

Pope threw up his plump hands. "Then it's insubordination!" He turned away, suddenly swung back and put his head near Russell's, his stage whisper sibilant against the blasting guns: "Maybe it's worse, Russell. Worse!"

Lieutenant Fielding, having written out the order in question, knew it had instructed Fitz-John Porter to push forward from his position on the Manassas–Gainesville Road "into action at once on the enemy's flank and, if possible, on his rear."

That language—"at once"—scarcely permitted interpretation; and Fielding had understood that Pope was ordering Porter to attack Jackson's right simultaneously with the attack he had ordered Kearny and Stevens to open on Stonewall's battered left. But in more than an hour since Kearny had struck so hard, no sound of battle had come rumbling across the fields from Porter's position to the west.

So Fitz-John Porter, Fielding gathered, was in a fair way to get himself court-martialed. Particularly since a lot of talk going around the staff had it that McClellan and the Army of the Potomac crowd Porter prominent among them—would not be unhappy to see John Pope fail and McClellan restored to the full command he once had held. That kind of talk would not have failed to reach Pope's sensitive ears.

As Keach waited, he saw General Irvin McDowell ride up Buck's Hill. McDowell had marched his corps up the Sudley Springs Road and left it waiting for further orders near the pike. McDowell and Pope immediately conferred, while Russell listened. McDowell reported that Porter believed Longstreet was on the field and in his front, preventing his advance.

That Duryea! Colonel Russell, his teeth aching, remembered the captain's insistence on the dust cloud toward Thoroughfare Gap. Duryea's eyes were strange and he made Russell nervous; but the fellow's information was just about always right.

Trouble was, as Russell was all too well aware, John Pope had a way of disbelieving or even dismissing information that didn't fit his own ideas; and colonels who wanted to keep high positions on his staff did well not to argue too strongly that a dust cloud was a dust cloud if Pope said it was battle smoke.

And with my teeth, Russell thought, where could I get a better assignment?

Right at that moment, Pope was arguing that if Longstreet *was* up, which Pope didn't for a moment believe, it couldn't have been for long or in full-enough force to hold back Porter's whole corps. Porter could have done *something,* certainly earlier in the day.

"And even now!" Pope took the cigar from his mouth and flung it away. "If he'd attacked an hour ago, as ordered. Or right this minute! That much pressure on Jackson's right could be just enough to crack'im!"

Fortunately for all, Phil Kearny just then appeared. He was, as usual, the model of a fighting general, wearing a regulation forage cap and an old saber in a ragged leather scabbard. His colorless eyes glared from a thin face, he held himself stiffly erect, and his empty sleeve was pinned as always across his bulging chest. Even his voice, Russell thought, was throaty as a gamecock's crow:

"General, I've carried the enemy's position on his left. It was well defended and my loss has been awful, but that of the enemy must be three to one of mine. The ground we occupy and that in front of us is literally covered with their dead bodies."

Even such news could not deflect Pope's anger. Quite the

opposite. "You see?" He pointed dramatically west. "You see, McDowell? Suppose we'd had ten thousand fresh troops striking his right at the same time?"

As Kearny's dramatic news spread through Pope's camp, Charlie Keach had no difficulty picking it up. But it only confirmed his own observation from the pine tree, and made him the more eager to be off. Hale would be proud of him, maybe increase his pay. But the sun was sinking fast. He finally caught Pope's eye, beckoned with his head, and strolled a rod or two down the hill. In three minutes he heard trampling footsteps in the broomsedge.

"Still here, eh, Keach? Never got those orders, eh?"

He nudged Keach with an elbow and both men laughed.

"But I aim to clear out tonight if this is what I think it is."

"What's that?" The rich aroma of Pope's cigar made Keach eager for one of his own. It had been a long day, a long campaign.

"Victory."

"Success." Pope took the cigar out of his mouth and studied the ash minutely. "I'd say success, Keach. We occupy the field on our right. We still hold the ground on our left that we held this morning."

"But surely then . . . Jackson'll have to retreat?"

"Indicated, Keach. That's indicated." Pope hesitated, putting the cigar back in his mouth. "Since you're leaving . . . I can tell you that I've given orders for an attack down the pike with King's Division. Just came up with McDowell."

"This late in the day?"

"Never too late, Keach, if you've got'em on the run. Jackson's left's rolled up. Now King'll hit'em on the right."

Orderlies were beginning to build a headquarters camp fire as Cass Fielding stood in a group of officers around the newly arrived McDowell. Suddenly that general pointed to the western sky.

"Look there!"

A cloud of battle smoke was rising darkly against the setting sun; its red rays streamed brilliantly through the drifts, casting an eerie shifting light over the battlefield.

"What a dramatic and magnificent picture!" McDowell proclaimed in his schoolmarmish manner. "How tame are all Vernet's boasted battle pieces, in comparison with such a scene as this! Indeed, if an artist could successfully represent that effect, it would be criticized as unreal and extravagant."

Fielding, sharing Pope's anger at failed expectations, thought McDowell's burst of lyricism was asinine. He doubted that Stonewall Jackson had time to watch the sunset, or the eye to admire it. Pope had on his hands a war to be fought, not a canvas to be admired; what he needed was more men like Kearny, who fought—not art critics touched more by beauty than by the spirit of war.

Major Jesse Thomas had been worried throughout the afternoon. A day that had begun so auspiciously for his chief, with the quick passage of Thoroughfare Gap, was turning sour. Twice already, Longstreet had resisted Lee's suggestions that he attack Pope's left and relieve the pressure on Jackson—pressure visible in the smoke rising off toward Sudley Springs and audible in the near continuous sounds of battle rolling over the low hills. Now the question of an attack had come up a third time.

Jesse Thomas had total confidence in both generals, but he had more immediate personal relations with, and a professional stake in, James Longstreet. So he shared his chief's view that a forward move by his line into hard defensive ground would expose his right flank to the force on the Manassas Road across Dawkins Branch—a force now positively identified as Porter's formidable corps of ten to twelve thousand Peninsula veterans.

On the other hand, Major Thomas found it hard to argue with Lee's desire for an attack to relieve the day-long pressure on Jackson's line. And Thomas knew all too well that if no attack was made many would say that Longstreet hadn't *wanted* to make it—that he resented Jackson's undeserved fame, was too mule-headed to yield his own opinion even to Lee, didn't want to sacrifice his own troops to help those he considered inferior—even that he held back to avenge Jackson's poor showing around Richmond. A dozen reasons would be advanced for Ol Pete to have sat still while Jackson suffered. None of them would flatter Longstreet.

Never mind that none of those reasons—Thomas was confident—had substance. Longstreet was stubborn, all right, but only when he was convinced he was right. He had reservations about Jackson, of course; but that was not to say he'd sacrifice Jackson, or the army, out of jealousy.

Thus, as the sun dipped lower and lower behind them, the long day approaching its end, Thomas watched anxiously as Lee and Longstreet conferred again. At least now the Old Man conceded that Porter *was* out there beyond Dawkins Branch, a menace on Longstreet's flank.

As the conference broke up, Thomas thought he detected an air of sharpening activity around Longstreet. Lee, gray and impressive as a monument, rode away with his trailing staff, and Jesse Thomas hurried to find out what was happening.

John Bell Hood, the blond young Texan known as Sam who commanded Longstreet's most famous division, was just then mounting his horse. Tall, thin, shy, with a vast dark beard and a long flaring nose, Hood was Thomas's ideal of a field commander. Once he had carried orders through lethal fire to the Texan and found him on the most exposed part of the field, leading his men by example. The fierce light in Hood's blue eyes, under his broad forehead and sagging, sad eyebrows, had made an indelible impression on Jesse Thomas, who thought sometimes that he too might have been such a leader but for the crippling wound taken at Blackburn's Ford the year before.

"No general attack until morning." Hood was an easy man to approach and, at 31 years of age, not much older than Thomas. Differences in rank seemed to mean nothing to the westerner. "Maybe not then, dependin on what happens. For now, I'm to make a reconnaissance in force along the pike." He grinned down at Thomas in the fading light. "See if we can find us some Yanks."

Thomas hastened to Longstreet's side as Hood spurred away. A good solution, he thought. It would keep Kemper and Jones between Porter and Hood's flank, give some relief to Jackson, and develop Pope's position on the pike.

Best of all, he thought, Hood's "reconnaissance" would draw the fangs of vipers like Captain Franklin, eager as they would be to sink them in Ol Pete's mule-like hide. Major Thomas could imagine Franklin, after the war, regaling Miss Letty with tales of the iniquities of Longstreet and his staff.

Fargo Hart, meanwhile, had made up his mind. And once what he had to do was clear to him, he went straight to Stuart. If there was any one thing Jeb Stuart couldn't resist, other than a fine uniform, it was the notion of a lady in distress.

"I b'lieve a distant cousin of mine." Hart with some difficulty managed a straight face at this description of a girl his mother would not have permitted in the house. "I hope maybe I can put'er with a family I know in Gainesville until we clear Pope out of here."

Stuart's face was bright with interest. "By all means, Hart, by all means. Likely to be fightin all up'n down that pike tomorrow. Better get the lady out of there at once."

"Knew you'd understand." Hart saluted and was turning away, not at all ashamed of his duplicity, when Stuart caught his arm.

"*Very* distant cousin, I spect. Right, Hart? *Very* distant."

"Wellsir... not'n the immediate fam'ly, that's true."

Stuart laughed his high-pitched laugh. "Just be back by sunup, Hart. A busy day tomorrow!"

Hart hastened to Mercury. Even the great black horse, he thought, was bound to be getting tired—though a better horse for such service he'd never seen. Hart wondered again where Robaire and his other mounts might be. Trains were strung out behind them half the way to Gordonsville.

As he was about to swing into the saddle, the Reverend Major Allen hastened up in the fading light. The sun would soon be gone behind the mountain ridges, and the afterlight would be short.

"No broken parts, Major?"

"Oh, no... bonecrackers say I'm good as ever, praise be to God. *And* to you."

"Couldn't of done a thing without His help, Major." Hart was impatient to be gone and his distaste for the godly Allen was not diminished by the sight of the buffalo robe folded under the major's arm. "I reck'n God would of found some way to spare *you* without me buttin in."

This irony did not reach the major, who nodded solemnly. "But Hart... we know that God moves in mysterious ways, His wonders to perform. Not for us mortals to question why He chose *you* to save *me*."

Hart was not sure he cared for this distinction. But he only said, "Reck'n not," and lifted himself easily to Mercury's back.

"So I wanted you to have this." Major Allen held up the buffalo robe. "Just as... to show... uh... thanks for what you did today."

Hart was touched, in spite of his dislike for the major and his knowledge of how he'd come by the robe. And he had not been reared to spurn gifts so earnestly offered.

"Why... Major, that aint necessary."

"Maybe not. But I'd feel better. I just feel like maybe God intended *you* to have it."

"Well . . . in that case . . ." Hart took the robe, its fur rich and luxurious in his hands. "Who am I to say no?"

Chapter Ten

❧❧❧❧❧❧❧❧❧❧❧❧

August 29—Night

BY THE TIME he reached his home place, Durward P. Brace long since had had to admit that Henry had been right about one thing: the confoun mare was in no shape to be ridden. Most of the time since he had clambered back up the hill to where the mare and the mule had been left, Brace walked, leading the animals along dusty lanes and through the woods. He had no intention of giving them up to marauding soldiers, certainly not Yanks; so he had spent more time hiding in thickets and gullies and creek bottoms than in making his way across two miles of the roughest country in Prince William County. The few troops he did meet fortunately were Virginians, and they sent him on with instructions to look sharp for Yanks and keep out of the line of fire. Even so, the roundabout, zigzag course he'd had to follow, dodging troops as often as he could, had caused him to walk nigh-on four miles to make two.

Brace was therefore in a thoroughly sour mood—hot, tired, thirsty, hungry—when he finally reached the edge of trees and underbrush bordering his own fields. He also had started to have second thoughts about what he'd done, and why; but these he neither understood nor allowed himself to ponder. His mind was too direct for reflection; he only knew he had done what he wanted and needed to do, so he was able to put aside doubt as often as it returned.

He peered across the field at his silent house, looking deserted in the late-day light. Whole family in the cellar, most likely. Sajie, too.

Thinking of Sajie and what he aimed to do was all that had got him through the fearful afternoon. But in Sajie's case, too, he was irritated by stirrings of what he scarcely recognized as doubt. Not that he was less determined to show her what a white man could do; but the nearer he got to it, the problem seemed more complicated than it had in his moment of high confidence, watching Henry's flopping body on the hillside.

Brace moved slowly along the edge of the woods, not showing himself. Troops might be about, even Yanks. Which was why he'd tethered the mare and the mule a half mile back in a brushy hollow. At least now he had a musket, taken from a dead butternut.

He had been moving cautiously along the old Warrenton Road toward Lewis Lane when he heard the two shots up ahead, a few seconds apart. He hid for five minutes by the side of the road, the animals' nostrils pinched in his hands, until a mounted Yank officer, clean-shaven and straight up as a gun barrel, trotted past to the east. Just up the rutted old road, Brace found a dead Virginia boy, shot in the back of the head; then another with his bare feet sticking out of a cornfield.

Brace took a musket from one, a bayonet in a sling from the other, and all the cartridges and caps from both. But nothing in the dead men's pockets or knapsacks had been worth taking.

The weight of the musket dragged him down, but still he felt better having it. A man needed to be armed, with soldiers swarming about like bees. His property *was* within Virginia lines; but with Sajie practically in reach, he was taking no chances.

As he lingered out of sight, watching his house, he heard a horse on the road, hoofbeats sharp against the dying rumble of guns off toward Sudley Springs. Brace went quickly to one knee behind a tree and some underbrush. He was scarcely down, sweating profusely in the baking heat, when a man on a big black horse leaped the fence and crossed the yard toward the house.

Tarnation! Brace at once recognized the young captain who'd led him and Henry that morning to General Stuart. Nosy bastard'd want to know right off why he was back home, and what had happened to Henry. Brace crouched lower as the captain dismounted by the slanting cellar doors.

"Missy!"

I-God! Brace thought. *Iffen at pup's tumblin my girl, I'm-a blow is damn head off. See'f I don't.*

"Missy! It's me . . . Cap'n Hart!"

The boom of his knuckles on the cellar door drifted across the yard like the distant artillery Brace had been hearing all afternoon. As rapidly as it had come, his anger vanished and he was filled with despair.

What could a man do? Blow an officer's head off, and there'd be all kinds of trouble he couldn't avoid. And probably no Sajie— not anytime soon anyway. If he just ran the pup off, he'd start asking questions about that scouting job and about Henry. No Sajie that way either.

"Come out, Missy!"

Brace watched the cellar doors opening uncertainly, sweeping back in a shaky half arc, until Missy's head and shoulders appeared, her pigtail falling forward over one shoulder. Rage swept him again.

Half a mind let the sumbitch have it anyway. Messin round a decent girl. Sweet talkin God knows what'n'er silly head.

The captain took Missy's hand and she came on up the cellar steps; the doors slapped to behind her. Brace could hear the murmur of their voices but not their words. He watched in consternation as the captain led her to the horse, then lifted her sideways into the saddle. Brace actually raised his musket as he saw the captain leap lightly up behind the saddle.

But Brace knew he could not shoot without maybe hitting Missy. Losing Sajie. As the captain turned the black horse's head toward the road, Wash stuck his head up between the cellar doors and bawled:

"Missy! Maw sez git on back down-yer!"

The horse broke into a trot. Neither the captain nor Missy looked back.

"Missy! God damn you, Maw sez you come back!"

The last words rose to a shriek and Wash bounded up the steps, throwing back the cellar doors with a crack; he ran a few steps across the yard after the horse.

"Stinkin slut!" he screamed. "Come back-ere, slut!"

But by then the horse was trotting toward Gainesville. Wash stopped halfway across the yard, leaping up and down in frustration and screaming curses after his sister. Brace felt much the same way. He beat his fist on his knee, muttering to himself:

"Man gotta confoun thing'n this world, somebody come'n take it. God*dam*'is fancy talk!"

Sajie came up the steps just then and called something to Wash.

I-God! Not Sajie. No black hussy gone run off on *me!*

This resolution stirred Brace. He stood up and started across the yard and Wash turned, still yelling curses, toward Sajie and the cellar doors. The boy saw Brace coming and ran toward him.

"Paw! Missy done run off agin!"

Past Wash, in the last rays of the edge of sun that remained above the ridge, Brace saw Sajie going back into the cellar.

"Run off wid a sojer! She-uz huggin'im, at bitch-uz . . ."

Brace had had enough. He slapped Wash hard across his dirty face, then seized his thin shirt, pulling the boy nearly off his feet.

"Close at fat trap, boy! Or I'll snatch at dirty tongue right outten yuh head! Hear me?"

Wash began to cry, going abruptly from screams of rage to great shuddering, choking sobs that shook him all over. Brace flung his son away in disgust and tramped on toward the cellar.

Not bad nuff Missy done run off on me, I got to have a damn runny-nose yellin'is head off. Orta fetched'im one upside'is head a long time ago.

Brace's eyes took a moment to adjust to the dimness of the cellar. Kate lay on the pallet more or less where he'd left her twelve hours earlier—a great heaving mass of fat he hardly even wanted to look at anymore. But her tear-streaked face, like a moon on a foggy night, rose toward him through the half-light.

"Kin you . . . Missy . . . you gittin Missy back?"

"Back?" Brace stood the musket against one of the posts underpinning the house. "How'm I gone git at slut back?"

The moon sank miserably to the pallet. In the far corner, Brace could just make out Sajie's blue-striped dress, as if a mattress tick had been thrown there.

"Jus a baby, Paw . . . want my baby back!"

"Gone be a baby *in*'er, you git'er back." Brace made a fat belly with his hands. He was just beginning to realize the finality of his loss. He had always thought Missy would somehow change his luck, bring in something worth having. Now . . .

"Look like a man leave home a single confoun day, everthing go to hell."

The cellar smelled of stale air, old potatoes, Kate's fat body, the damp rags of his hopes.

"Sajie!"

". . . a *good* baby . . . my good little . . . baby's gone . . ."

"Yessuh?"

"Git on up-er'n fix me some vittles. I got to git on back . . ."

Kate wailed, and the moon face rose again. "Git on back wher?"

"Gin'al Stuart. Countin on me to scout for'is sojers. I got . . ."

"But...wh-what bout usuns...who's gone look out for ususnes?"

Brace barely restrained himself from kicking in her fat face. Man kin only just take so much in this confoun world.

"Sajie...git on like I tolt you. Wash!"

Kate subsided, moaning, and Sajie went silently past and up the steps. Brace watched her haunches twist under the mattress-ticking dress.

"Wash!" The boy came cautiously to the cellar door, peering down at Brace from the fading light of the yard. "Git down-yer'n look out f'yuh Maw."

"I on'y wanted Missy to come back." Wash was still snuffling.

"Well, she aint. Not in no shape we'd want'er, no-way. Come on down-yer'n quit at whinin."

Wash crept down the steps, as if testing his weight on each.

"Gin'al Stuart's waitin on me." The boy's eyes widened and he came down the last two steps swiftly. "So whilst I'm gone, you stay rightchere'n look out fuh Maw."

"Waitin on you fuh whut?"

"Scoutin."

Wash's face lit up and he grabbed his father's arm. "Lemme go, too. I could..."

"Goddammit, you got to look out fuh Maw. At's *your* job." Brace shook himself loose and went to the steps, thinking of Sajie's haunches, her powerful legs. He picked up his plundered musket, went up one step and looked back. "Kate...Wash'll look out f'yuh now. Won't be long."

Kate moaned unintelligibly and Brace went up the steps into the afterlight, letting the cellar doors slam after him. In the near-darkness of the cellar, Wash felt doubly abandoned.

"Shi-yit!" He kicked at the hard earth floor with his bare foot.

"Wash!"

Maw's whisper was fierce in the warm, still air. Wash glared at her defiantly, expecting to be bawled out and prayed over for saying "shit." He decided to say it again. Maw would never hit him like Paw done. No matter what he did.

"Shit on everything!"

"Wash...come-ere!"

In the gloom he could barely see her beckoning. He moved closer to the pallet and bent down to hear.

"Slip up-er'n see what they doin."

"Whut who's doin?"

"Sajie'n Paw. Don't let'em ketch yuh!"

Wash stared in consternation. "You mean . . . you think . . ." He knew what grown folks did because he'd spied on Henry and Sajie. But he'd never thought of . . .

"Just see what he's doin with at black whoor up'er." Maw clutched Wash's wrist in her moist hand; her whispered words were sharp as needles. "Then come tell yuh Maw."

Wash's cheek still burned from Brace's hard slap. He'd only wanted to get Missy back. Besides if Paw *was* doing what Henry did with Sajie, Wash wanted to see *that*. Feel that funny way it made him feel, watching Henry do it to Sajie.

"Come tell me, now!"

Wash turned and darted for the steps. But before he reached them, a voice somewhere above began shouting military commands. Wash stopped and looked at his mother's terrified moon-like face; she wailed again. The voice shouted more orders; others shouted back. Wash—curiosity overcoming fear—ran halfway up the steps, cautiously lifted one door, and stuck his head barely into the open.

He just had time to see a long line of soldiers kneeling at the edge of the woods. Then he realized that every last single one seemed to be pointing their guns straight at him.

Wash jerked his head down out of sight, the door falling after him, its clatter lost in the crash of the guns firing—first one deafening volley, like the earth itself cracking open, that sent Wash scurrying down the steps to sprawl headlong on the floor with his arms over his head; then the steadily rising *crack–cra-ack–crack!* of hundreds of men firing at will. It sounded to Wash like the old house breaking to pieces and falling around him.

To the disappointment of Major Reverdy Dowd, the Sixth Wisconsin and the rest of Gibbon's Brigade had been held out of the sunset attack of King's Division westward down the Warrenton Pike. Instead, the brigade was marched north of the pike, along the Sudley Springs Road, to the support of artillery batteries still blazing away at what someone said was Jackson's left.

The word was all through the ranks that Stonewall was falling back, and that made Dowd puff out his chest. He himself had heard General McDowell, sitting his horse beside the Sudley Springs Road, call out to King's passing troops:

"We've been driving the enemy all day!"

Then, lifting the odd-shaped cap he always affected—to Dowd's irreverent westerners it looked more like a berry-picking basket— the stout general shouted:

"Give'im a good poke, boys! He's getting sick!"

But Gibbon's Brigade was out of it. A few artillery rounds whistling over the Sixth were not to be compared to the face-to-face encounter with Jackson on the hillside the night before. Major Dowd, while not anxious for another such battle, had been ready for it—not least to test again the newfound satisfactions of command. It was as if he had suddenly mastered the skills of a trade or the intricacies of a foreign language and feared they might become rusty or lost in disuse.

This time, Private Hugh Williams did not fret because Gibbon's Brigade was not going into action. He thought he and his comrades had proved themselves the best in the division and ought to be used as such. But he was more philosophical about inaction than he had been the day before. Now Private Williams felt that he, at least, had nothing to prove—either to himself or to his God. He would fight again, when commanded to, and fight hard; but he knew he would never again be eager to do so or be disappointed if not ordered to the field.

As the first sounds of a new outburst of battle echoed along the pike, just as the sun was sinking at last below the mountain ridge, he realized he was profoundly grateful to his Heavenly Father because he was alive—alive and *well*, not torn to pieces like Cappy Swartz. *I thank thee, Father*. And he knew he would be ready, and just as grateful, when the Lord finally disclosed what it was He'd saved Hugh Williams to do, or be.

Private Fritz Schiml, though he was still determined never to go into battle again, was rather miffed because Gibbon's Brigade had been held in reserve. In the clear hindsight that had succeeded his horrifying experiences in battle and on the long night march to Manassas, Private Schiml had realized that he was in the grip of a malevolent conspiracy. Since the moment of seeming insanity when Lieutenant Gregson's flailing sword had whipped his shoulder blades, Schiml had come to understand that there was nothing mad about it at all; rather, he and the fools marching with him had been duped. *They* might be too stupid to know it, but not

Fritz Schiml. Back in Wisconsin, people said you had to get up early in the morning to get ahead of the Schiml boys.

The fact was that nobody had told any of them, when they had been deceived into signing on for the army, that they would have no more chance than hogs being fattened for the kill—which was about what Colonel Bullock's men really had been, as they were conditioned in camp to march obediently to the slaughter. Nobody had told them their function was to be thrown into the meat grinder of battle the way their fathers ground up hog flesh for sausage. Nobody had told them that on the battlefield the difference in life and death would be the merest chance, or that coming out whole or with a leg gone or an arm missing or a face mutilated beyond recognition was a matter of pure happenstance—certainly not that if a man's luck enabled him to escape once, the odds were only that much shorter the next time around.

Oh no! They'd talked about patriotism and honor and the Union. But Fritz Schiml had a head on his shoulders and eyes to see with, even if the rest of the fattened hogs around him couldn't recognize sausage meat when they saw it. So what he wanted now was opportunity.

At first, he'd planned simply to melt into the night on the march to Manassas; then he realized he might get lost and be picked up at daylight. In the day's hot and thirsty march back to the pike, the officers and noncoms, all part of the conspiracy, had been diligent against straggling. Besides, deserting was a fool's game; they could shoot him for that and no doubt would, if they caught him and realized he was on to them.

No, he'd have to outsmart them, which would be easier in the confusions of battle than in the relative calm behind the lines. He'd have to be quick, sharp, keep his eyes open for a real opportunity, if he wanted to come out alive and turn the tables, tell the world, expose them all. They weren't going to ship Fritz Schiml home in a sausage casing.

The other three brigades of King's Division—owing to King's ill health, it was now commanded by his senior brigadier, General John P. Hatch—advanced through the woods and fields on the south side of the pike in two lines of battle, Doubleday's and Hatch's brigades out front and Patrick's in reserve. Some of the most observant among them realized that in marching west they were exactly reversing the division's direction of the evening before, when Jackson had so unexpectedly fallen on Gibbon's flank.

This time, confident in expectation that the Rebel force was retreating, Hatch's blueclads ran head-on into Longstreet's evening reconnaissance-in-force, mounted by John Bell Hood's Division—Hood's own Texas Brigade, advancing east on the south side of the pike, and Evander Law's Brigade moving north of it.

Thus, as blue and butternut closed on one another in the dusk, with Brace's farmhouse and fields the exact point of the skirmishers' first collision, Hatch had three brigades against Hood's two. But Hatch's men had marched over thirty-eight miles in about thirty-six hours, with little sleep and only hardtack for rations; and Doubleday's Brigade had been hit hard in the murderous hillside clash with Jackson the night before. Hood's troops had been resting in line most of the day, listening to Jackson's battle and itching to show Ol Jack how Longstreet's men—real soldiers—could fight. And unlike the Federals, they were under no illusion that they were pursuing a beaten enemy.

So after the opposing skirmishers stumbled into one another across Brace's fields and around his house, Hood's Brigade went forward with a rush and a bloodcurdling yell that caused Kate Brace to heave her fat body all the way over, so she could put her face down against the cellar floor. In a half-hour's hard fighting, terminated by darkness falling mercifully across the blood-soaked hills and fields of Prince William County, Hood's and Law's fresh fighters forced Hatch's Brigades back along the pike more than half a mile, to just west of Groveton crossroads.

But the Yanks fought hard and gave ground grudgingly, until the blackness of the night stilled the rifles of both sides. Hatch's men gave such a good account of themselves that Hood later reported to Lee and Longstreet that the ground held by these tough Federal troops was strong, and would be dangerous to attack the next day, against such stout defenders. This was the primary information the southern generals obtained from Hood's reconnaissance.

The evening battle also had effectively blocked the pike from the west. Entering the dusty hamlet of Gainesville near sundown, Andrew Peterson and Henry had found the Whatsit Wagon blocked not only by a tangle of troops, wagon trains, artillery caissons and limbers, but by a determined Provost Marshal's patrol.

"Hell to pay down thataway soon." The lieutenant in charge

looked experienced beyond his years, as to Peterson's eye most of these warlike boys did. "Can't let nobody thew."

"Well, if I could just get closer I could be ready at sunup to . . ."

"Orders is orders, Cap'n."

No words, Peterson knew, were more final than those, when pronounced by an underling. He could have tried his impressively signed and sealed pass but that might have caused the lieutenant to call in his superiors for advice; and the more attention they called to themselves, the more likely Henry was to be picked up as contraband. At his direction, Henry pulled the Whatsit into a dusty lot the butternuts were also using for a wagon park.

"What we better do, Henry, is bed down here for the night and get movin first thing in the mornin."

Henry shook his head. "Got to git thew."

Henry had no doubt that Brace had tried to kill him; in fact, he had understood Brace's purpose as soon as Brace had ordered him down the hill. He had gone only because at that moment he had made up his mind to be shut of Brace. *Git Sajie and light out.*

Once out of Brace's direct sight, Henry had paused long enough to grab a dead limb about four feet long. With this stick probing in front of him, Henry had made it appear by the moving underbrush that he was maybe five feet ahead of where he actually was crawling along the hillside.

When the expected happened and the shot came, throwing up dirt and leaves just in front of him, Henry was ready. Lying beside Brace and the short-legged captain, he had seen one of the blue soldiers in the field get shot and go backwards and down like somebody had fetched him a lick with a wagon tongue. Henry reasoned from this that any shot body would be thrown about like a play doll; hence his apparently convulsive leap into the air. He knew Brace would never risk gunfire to make sure he was dead, but Henry wanted to leave him in no doubt about it.

He lay in the underbrush for a half hour, muskets popping from the hill around him, less often from the field out front. Then, for whatever unfathomable reason, the blue soldiers went back across the field and the hot afternoon fell silent except for the ceaseless battle sounds off toward Sudley Springs, and the insect noises in the woods.

Henry assumed that Brace, the mare, and the mule would be long gone. But he crept back up the hill to see for himself. *Sho nuff.* Henry then worked his way on down the other side of the hill, careful not to be seen. The soldiers now were Virginias, mostly horse soldiers.

Henry thought about Brace. The only reason Brace would want to kill him was Sajie. He'd had his eye on Sajie a long time. But Henry was sure that Sajie could take care of herself, Brace come sniffin round. Sajie could handle a no-count like Brace; still, he wanted to get her away as quickly as he could.

Henry knew that part of Prince William County as well as he knew Brace's farm. Moving through overgrown fields, along obscure paths, occasionally in woodland, he circled west of D. R. Jones's guns, struck north by the sun, high and scorching in the August sky, and got over the Manassas Gap Railroad at the west foot of the commanding hill on which Jeb Stuart had set up cavalry headquarters. Henry didn't know about the headquarters—only that he had to be quick to remain unseen in all the coming and going and hoo-hawing the Virginias were doing.

By the time he got around to the east side of the hill—tough going in the thickets on its slopes—he saw that he was not going to be able to get back to Brace's house by that route. Soldiers were thick as fleas on a yard dog clear over the pike. Henry didn't need to be told that no black man could walk through white armies unchallenged.

Retracing his steps to the railroad, he dodged through the trees flanking it, heading for Gainesville and planning to get to the other side of the pike, then circle east to the vicinity of Brace's farm. But that route proved to be blocked, too, by Virginias dug in across the tracks.

So he moved west again, away from his ultimate goal, clumping along purposefully through the skinny pines and scrub oak, in the blistering heat; then he angled north and came out on the pike just west of Gainesville. The only reason he had not stayed under cover until the Whatsit Wagon passed was that the white man driving it plainly was not a soldier, therefore might offer Henry a direct means of passing through Virginia lines unchallenged. The risk was worth taking because he could always duck back into the woods and run from a single white man.

"But why go tonight, Henry?"

"Jes got to git thew." To tell the truth would have been to challenge any white man's tolerance, which Henry had learned never to do.

"They'll pick you up. Troops out there thicker'n broomsedge." Which probably was true; but Peterson conceded to himself that he really wanted Henry to stay because he needed somebody to replace Joe Nathan. And this somber, bull-like African impressed him—not just with his obvious skill at the reins, but with his quiet solidity. Even his stubborn determination to "git thew" bespoke character.

"Reck'n I go try."

Peterson gave up. "Well, come back if you can't make it. Be glad to have you."

Henry climbed down from the wagon. "Look affer em mules fust."

Peterson lit a small fire while Henry unharnessed and tethered Positive and Negative, then fed and watered them, murmuring all the while into their long, sensitive ears. Peterson was acutely reminded of Joe Nathan and his way with animals.

"Some mules." There might have been a faint tone of approval in Henry's voice. "Tuck good keer of."

"Have some coffee fore you go."

"Got to git thew." Henry faded silently from the firelight, then returned. "Thankee, Mist Dodge."

Sally Sutherland Crowell was just about to drop into sound sleep, since the noise of battle over Bull Run had faded into night stillness. She was grateful that there'd been no recurrence, since early morning, of her trouble—although the roar of guns and the parade of horses, wagons, and men through Centreville had been ceaseless. She and Anna had worked all day making bandages from all the old cloth they could find.

Even when Anna had broached her scheme—suddenly pouring out the words like water from a pitcher—Sally had resolutely kept her mind from wandering back to Lawrence's house and his mother's harpsichord.

"They'd let us help, I know they would! All those poor hurt boys! They'd *have* to let us help."

"Don't be too sure." Sally remembered the way the Yankee surgeons had reacted to her efforts to be of use to them. In her own house.

"Besides . . . there's bound to be some of *our* boys there that the Yankees picked up wounded. We could say we wanted to help *them!* And we do, don't we?"

"They'd think we were spies, Anna. And even if they didn't, they don't want women around. They . . ."

"But to *help*'em! There's bound to be so many of'em shot, and it's just right down the ford road . . . we could *walk* that far."

Sally suddenly felt herself the wiser and older woman—although, in fact, she definitely was not the latter. But the day of the battle around Lawrence's house—Anna had not been through that, or its aftermath.

"It's not just gettin there." From childhood, Sally remembered every twist and turn of the road down to the dark, quiet waters of Blackburn's Ford over Bull Run. "It's what we'd be able to *do* when we got there. Or not do, more likely."

Still, as Anna rattled on about her daring plan—they *had* to try it, Anna declared; she'd never forgive herself if *she* didn't—Sally wondered: was she really just being practical, calling on her great experience? Or was she shrinking from any reminder of that *other* day, pulling back from any possibility that its horror might be repeated?

Because of course it would be, in a hospital depot after a great battle—bigger even than the one three weeks ago, if she could judge by the noise and the time it had lasted. But maybe if she *did* go with Anna . . . The thought frightened Sally, yet it held out, too, a certain promise: maybe if she did face up to it again she'd find out something about her trouble, maybe even learn how to deal with it.

". . . just so much nonsense," Anna was saying, "that women are too *delicate* and too *weak* to do anything useful. Such fiddlesticks! It just makes me so *mad* . . ."

At bedtime nothing had been decided. But as Sally pinched out her candle she was encouraged that the thought of going to the hospital . . . maybe seeing *that* again . . . had not set off her trouble. Maybe the thing to do really was to face up. Maybe only that could make the trouble go away.

General Jubal Early, after his and Lawton's regiments pushed the last of Kearny's Yanks beyond the remains of the rail fence and the railroad cut, had quickly pulled his rescuing butternuts back to the cut—but not without searing the smoke-filled air with profanity. By then the darkness was all but complete, and Early—shifting his plug of tobacco from cheek to cheek, as he always did when angry—had discovered that too many Yanks were in front of him for the attack to continue.

The exhausted remnants of Powell Hill's brigades also dragged themselves back into the line. Most fell asleep on their arms, too tired to prepare rations or even think of hunger. Sprawled on the warm ground, they were indistinguishable from the dead at their sides. The guns had muttered into silence, but the groans of the wounded on both sides of the line turned the night hideous. Fireflies came out across the dark landscape, eerily imitating miniature muzzle flashes.

General Arnall sat against a tree by the small fire Larkin Folsom had kindled behind the knoll. The General's exhilaration had long since faded. He was no longer concerned about his arrest, or his career, or the long-ago morning when Branch had had to come to his aid. He knew only that his ground had been held. The line was intact. God had favored him. He had no sense of things other than those. He was tired, empty, a warrior drained of his lust.

Sam Stowe stumbled out of the darkness and sat down—or rather dropped—by the General's fire.

"My God, Hoke . . . I'm bout all you got left." Stowe's hoarse voice barely rose above the crackle of the fire. "Ernie McCrary's dead. Sparks lost 'is arm, might not live. Shell burst tore Dixon to pieces."

Something unintelligible forced itself through Arnall's throat. Stowe took it to be a murmur of shock.

"Ten officers killed altogether, lot more wounded. About half the men down, one way or nother. I . . . my God, Hoke . . . brigade's just damn well shot to hell."

Another croak. Stowe accepted a tin cup of coffee from Arnall's young orderly.

"Shot plumb to hell."

Hoke Arnall raised his head and another rasp came from the dark gash of mouth Stowe could see in the firelight. This time the colonel managed to grasp the last of the General's words:

". . . whipped 'em!"

Stowe sipped hot coffee, scarcely noticing its thick, burned taste from sitting too long on the fire. *Whipped' em!* All it meant to him. Regimental commanders down, brigade shot to hell. Not a thought for any of *that*.

"Yeah." That iron's not just in his ass, Stowe thought. "We whipped 'em, all right."

He sat on for a while, silent by the fire, the groaning night heavy and dark around them. The orderly stepped across the fire and took the cup out of Hoke Arnall's fingers.

"Gin'al's gone to sleep, sir."

Stowe flicked the rest of his coffee into the fire and went stumbling off to his own blankets. Folsom spread Arnall's blanket over the General's lap and shoulders, removed his hat and placed it on the ground beside him. Corporal Gilmore came into the firelight and stared down at the sleeping Arnall.

"You saved 'is life, y'know."

"And you saved mine."

Gilmore ached all over with exhaustion; his body was cut and bruised with petty wounds. He was tired, hungry, and the thirst from the long day's smoke and dust coated his throat like bitter plaster. After any other such ordeal, he would have dropped to the ground and slept where he lay. Tonight, he wanted to look after the boy, be with him; and he was glad to have given them both the gift of Folsom's life.

By common instinct, they moved out of the firelight. Folsom took Gilmore's huge, rough hand and held the back of it against his cheek.

"Thanks, Mister Gilmer."

Gilmore stroked the boy's head. "I . . . ah . . . I found us . . . found a place over ther." He nodded into the darkness, wondering how his rough life could have come, on such a day, to the overpowering gentleness he felt.

"Gin'al's asleep." Folsom really was grateful to Gilmore. But there was more to it than that. He was not sure what, except that he knew this coarse and untutored man would never laugh at his verses. "We can go anywhere you want."

A mile away, in a clearing on the lower slope of Sudley Mountain, Stonewall Jackson sat on a log, sucking a lemon and listening to Colonel Channing's account of the day's carnage. Not far away, slumped irritably against a tree, Theodore Alford St. John Redmund strained to overhear. The unbelievably crude Colonel Channing had accepted his credentials but Jackson's arrest order stood, and Teddy Redmund had learned that there was nothing he could do about it. Nothing *at the moment*, he thought grimly, shuddering at the vile Confederate coffee that was the only ration he'd been offered.

Channing was not just then much concerned about his English charge. His report to Jackson was too depressing. Old Trimble, trumpeting like a bull elephant, had been carried off the field with a bad wound. Added to yesterday's loss of Ewell and Taliaferro, this made losses among senior generals serious. As for the other brigade commanders, Forno in Lawton's Division and Field in Hill's had been wounded and incapacitated. Pender had been knocked down by a shell exploding nearby but had stayed in the field. Archer's horse had been shot from under him. Younger officers, regimental commanders especially, had been decimated.

"Gin'al?"

Jackson sat silent, as if to avoid hearing more.

"You know young Giles?"

Channing knew he did. Giles was the 18-year-old son of one of the general's oldest friends, serving temporarily with Jackson's command before joining a company in which he was to be commissioned.

Stonewall recoiled slightly and stared at Channing, his eyes suddenly flaring in the firelight.

"I'm . . . ah . . . afraid . . . Major Worsham says he won't live the night, Gin'al. Hit too bad to save."

Jackson stood up, glaring at the colonel. His powerful hand gripped Channing's shoulders; and the voice that was ordinarily soft, even hard to hear, demanded savagely, threateningly:

"Is Worsham with him? Can't he . . ."

Then, abruptly, Jackson strode off into the darkness. Channing could hear his tramping feet behind him in dirgelike rhythm. But as abruptly as he had left, the general came back and sat again on the log. Channing had given him the worst news; but after long silence, the colonel spoke again:

"A high price, Gin'al. This day's been won by nothin but the hardest kind of fightin."

"No, no." Ol Jack's voice this time was soft as usual, and he spoke reflectively, almost wonderingly. "It's been won by the blessing and protection of Almighty God."

Even as Mercury trotted out of Brace's yard, Fargo Hart knew Hood's skirmishers were closing in. Missy rode wordlessly before him, her small body warm against his chest. The boy's shrill curses rang in his ears.

"Ought to go back'n scrub'is mouth out."

"Won't do no good. He's got used to tastin soap."

Hart considered the problem of getting through the oncoming skirmishers. They were likely to shoot first and ask questions later; and even if they didn't, he had no great wish to ride through an advancing division with a girl in his arms. He'd never live it down.

So as soon as he was out of sight of Brace's house, Hart dismounted, threw down the rails on the north side of the pike, and led Mercury and Missy into the open fields beyond. Then he leaped up behind the saddle again and trotted rapidly northwest. Missy's head sank against his shoulder; it felt natural there.

"Told you I'd come back, didn't I?"

He felt her squirming in the saddle, closer to him. "I-uz waitin."

A rise of ground to the west concealed them as Mercury moved smoothly through the waving broomsedge. Their course was slightly uphill, around the western slope of Sudley Mountain. Just as the last red edge of the sun slipped below the horizon, Hart edged Mercury into the shelter of a small stand of pines. They stopped and he turned the horse back the way they had come, watching quietly. A minute or two passed. Then the first of Law's skirmishers trotted in a long jagged line over the rise of ground beneath which Hart and Missy had just ridden.

The men were barely visible in the afterlight, and their bodies above the broomsedge appeared to be legless. At that distance they made no sound. Hart did not wait for the main body of Law's force to appear; he turned Mercury's head again and rode northwest in the thickening darkness.

"Got any relatives herebouts?" He could feel her head shaking against his shoulder. "Any friends'd take you in?"

"I'm-a stay with you."

Hart rode on for a minute or two without replying. He had had it in mind all along that they would stay together. But her frankness shocked him; it seemed necessary suddenly to pretend, at least, to observation of the forms.

"How can you stay with me? You can't stay in camp. You . . ."

Her hands closed on the one of his that was clasped around her waist, and moved it to cup her breast. In the last light she looked over her shoulder at him solemnly.

"I'll show you wher."

Before he could answer, the crash of Hood's first volley echoed across the hills and the fields of broomsedge. Turning his head to the sound and to the answering rattle of musketry, Hart estimated that butternuts had run up on Yanks right about at Brace's house. He felt a flash of guilt that he'd left Missy's mother and the unspeakable boy to their fate; then he realized he was really concerned that perhaps Missy, feeling guilty too, would want to turn back. But she made no sound, no movement, as they rode on in the night, and the fitful glare of battle flashed behind them in the starless sky.

When the first volley swept the house, Ol Brace's words were still echoing in Sajie's head like stones rattling in a gourd:
Henry's dead.
Henry. Dead? The two words seemed to have no connection. Sajie could not associate the idea of the one with the meaning of the other to make any sense of them together.

She'd been exploring the safe, looking for vittles for Ol Brace, when she'd heard him come into the kitchen. Out of the corner of her eye, sensing what he had on his mind—after her own foolishness in the field—Sajie saw him stand the gun against the wall, rasp a hand across his stubbled chin, and shove his sweat-stained hat back on his head.
"Henry's dead."
Coming without warning or preamble, the words were loud in the late-day silence. But at first they meant no more to Sajie than the grainy feel of ham against her hands. Even when she finally took their meaning, the words gave off no sense of reality, no more than if Ol Brace had said, "Henry's turnt white" or "bees don't sting." Sajie straightened slowly, hearing through the echoes *Henry's dead Henry's dead dead* the harsh voice speaking again:
"Yanks shot . . ."
But someone shouting outside the house stopped Brace's voice before it could displace the words *Henry's dead* already rattling around in her head and then an explosion of shots outside shook the whole house. A hot wind rattled the door in its frame.
Gone burn now fuh shore.
Brace's next thought was to get Kate out of the cellar before the house turned into a fiery furnace. He watched Sajie whirl away from the safe and back flat against the wall, eyes gone wide with shock. The echoes of the volley reverberated in the room and the vicious popping of muskets suddenly seemed to be coming from all sides. Then Brace could hear again the *wheat–wheat–wheat!* of flying bullets he remembered so well from the hill above Dawkins Branch.
Can't git back at cellar now.
The eerie sounds of the bullets took him back to the sight of Henry's flopping body and actually reminded him of what he

aimed to do. He did not think again of Kate or even that he stood
at last to gain something from the war, if they burned his house.
No goddam sojers cheatin me outten it now.

Brace sprang across the room, kicking aside a straight-backed
chair, seized Sajie, and threw her roughly to the floor. He dived
after her and pulled them both along the pine flooring, until they
were under the heavy old kitchen table. He heard Sajie mumbling
some kind of Jesus talk as he pulled himself on top of her. But
she did not struggle and he lay still, covering her, as the muskets
crashed and the bullets whined past the house, some thudding into
its thin old walls with the sound of outsize hailstones.

Brace had no sense of how long it took the battle to surge on
past his house to the east, toward Groveton. While it roared around
him he felt little fear, except that Sajie might be hit and he be
cheated. The hellish burst of gunfire, his own decisiveness in
pulling her down under him, swept away his self-doubts; and as
he began to realize that the fight was moving away and bullets
were no longer slashing past the house, he became aware mostly
of the warm flesh beneath him in the darkness, moving ever so
slightly with Sajie's breathing, and the hot, forbidden smell of
her.

He felt Sajie beginning to twist and turn underneath him, and
he put the soldiers out of his mind. He moved his own hips,
feeling himself grow hard against her. Black slut wanted it, all
right. Like bitches in heat, all of 'em.

Wash turned back one of the cellar doors and emerged into full
darkness. He no longer had much hope of catching Paw and Sajie.
Couldn't of been goin at it with all at gunfar blazin round. But
he half-expected to find them dead, and that was enough to bring
him eagerly out of the cellar the first minute he thought it safe.

As he crept away from the steps toward the back of the house,
Maw snufflin behind him like a hog in slops, Wash took care to
make no noise himself. Mought still be Yanks around.

Just past the corner, he stumbled and went down heavily, managing to break his fall with his hands. He scrambled away from
whatever it was, then froze as somewhere nearby someone groaned
and coughed. Wash held still what seemed a long time to him,
until his eyes got used to the night. Then he could barely see that
he had stumbled over a man's body.

Looking around, he could just make out a few other forms

scattered in the yard, one or two thrashing around a little. Wash's heart was pumping hard. He had never expected such luck, the war coming right to his own house. *Dead men a-lyin rightchere in m'own yard*.

He crawled on all fours to the corpse he had fallen over, feeling bold as a cat at a mousehole. If it had been laid out in a coffin, he'd have been afraid of it; or maybe if he had had to look at the face. But on a *battlefield*, even if between the house and the barn where he'd roamed all his life, he didn't have to be afraid of death or dead men. *Nothin scary bout folks at's on'y shot*.

He fumbled about the body in the dark, not knowing what he'd do if he stuck his hand in the blood; but he didn't, and in a minute he found what he was looking for. He stood up, holding a heavy musket that towered a good head over his own. He felt with his thumb that the hammer was down and guessed the gun had been fired and the soldier killed before he'd loaded up again.

It was too dark to find the cap box and shot pouch, but the gun was the main thing anyway; the rest could wait for the daylight. Wash turned toward the back steps, thinking Paw and Sajie maybe really *were* dead, since he hadn't heard a croak out of 'em.

"Aint gone miss'im a bit." Ol Brace was breathing heavily in her ear. "Aint gone miss'im *none*, you see what I got for you."

Sajie knew what he had for her; he was jabbing it at her thighs as he lay on top of her beneath the kitchen table. But she hardly noticed. The fear that had seized her when the explosion of the guns seemed to fling her bodily against the wall had passed almost as soon as Ol Brace had thrown her to the floor and crawled up on her. And as the battle had crashed and echoed around the house, the bullets buzzing like monster horseflies, the words *Henry's dead* still tumbling in her head, she knew that it was true. *Henry's dead*.

It had to be true. Not just because Ol Brace finally was trying to get what she'd known for years he craved, although always before he'd been too afraid of Henry to try. But the main thing was the sound of the guns and the words *Yanks shot* that Brace had just got out before the guns went off.

Yanks shot Henry he'd started to say, plain as the nose on his face, and the guns were bound to be the Lord's way of telling her to believe it. *Goin off right then. Em guns uz my good Lawd sayin Henry's dead. Knowin I never gone b'lieve Ol Brace*.

So she had no doubt of it. *Henry's dead* drummed in Sajie's head with the finality of a hammer on coffin lumber. Grief wracked her. In the moment of knowing he was gone, she sensed too, as never before, how much her being had been bound to his. She did not miss *him*—his silences, his sometimes lumpish ways, the unquestioned power he exercised over her—so much as she missed *her* life, felt torn from a frame of existence that had become, to her, the necessary outlines of herself.

Henry's dead. Sajie felt cold, remote, abandoned, almost angry at him. Nothing now to guide her, nothing to limit her or call her to account. She grieved in those first moments of knowing *Henry's dead dead* mostly for the comfort of the known, the warmth of the familiar. She was alone, and alone was a strange and forbidding place, where nothing seemed right and surely no one could *belong*.

"Sajie . . . lemme git it . . . Sajie . . . help me . . ."

Ol Brace had it out of his pants by then, and her skirts up, and she could feel it between her thighs, long and skinny and slick as a tallow candle. Not thick or hotly alive like Henry. Henry never needed help—certainly not for *that*. Sajie moved and evaded Brace again but she did not really care what he or anyone did since she knew *Henry's dead dead dead* . . .

Then she realized that whether *she* cared or not, Henry would have—Henry, who had held Brace in such contempt, and valued himself so highly in comparison. And hadn't it been Brace who'd led Henry off to be shot, who'd come back like a fox to the henhouse to tell her *Henry's dead?* Then thowed'er onna floor fust thing.

"Git off me, ol man!"

Sajie's whisper struck Brace like a knife in the ear. And the sudden lunge and twist of her body had nearly thrown him off, when he was just before getting it in. But he still had tight hold of her wrists and he quickly got one leg over one of hers so that he was half astride.

"Goddam . . . Sajie . . . you want it, too!"

But Sajie was bucking under him like a mule with a wasp on its nose. She was big and strong, tall as Brace and weighing almost as much; he remembered those powerful legs and haunches as he clung to her. Then she arched her back and sprung herself upward from the floor, banging the back of his head against the underside of the table.

"Git off . . . git away now!"

But Brace had made up his mind. He was not going to be

cheated again. *Tooken ever confoun thing*. But not this. He released Sajie's left wrist and smashed his right hand across her
face, knocking her head back against the floor. Then he backhanded the other side of her face and clamped his legs around her
hips and thighs.

"Gone git it." He would not be cheated this time. Show her
some muscle of his own. "Gone git it no matter!"

Her body had ceased thrashing and he knew she was at least
momentarily stunned; so Brace hit her again, with his fist this
time, and felt her go limp beneath him. Then he *knew* he was
going to get it, knew everything would be the way he'd planned—
Henry, Sajie, ever last thing. Durward P. Brace finally would
show the stuff he was made out of.

Sajie's skirts were still up around her hips, where he'd pulled
them before she began to fight. In a second he clawed away her
coarse underpants and spread her massive legs. He was still just
hard enough, after struggling with the bitch, to get the head of it
in.

"Ahh . . . h . . . h . . . God!"

He shoved it in to the hilt. Again. *Gah-ahd*. Again. Every time
he shoved it in, he smashed Henry's face. Every time he shoved
it in *Ahh Gah-ahd* he clubbed Henry between the eyes *Ahh . . . Gah-
ahd . . .*

Brace was huge now, huge with power, bigger and stronger
than Henry, or anybody. Nothing he couldn't do. Nothing Henry
could stop him. Nothing Henry could scare. Smashing Henry's
face *Ahh Gahd* crushing Henry's skull *Ahh Gahd* Henry's face a
pulp *Ahh Gahd . . .*

Wash lay on his side on the porch, hearing Paw grunt, seeing the
vague shapes heaving under the table. He'd come creeping up just
in time to hear the crack of Paw's hand against Sajie's face and
the thump of her head against the floor, but he'd had no idea what
the sounds meant. They'd only caused him to lie down quickly,
almost stop breathing, and peer around the doorjamb with eyes
already used to the dark.

Down the road toward Groveton the troops were still firing.
But Wash paid no attention; he'd even forgotten the dead man's
gun lying by his side on the porch. Paw's grunts, the heaving
shapes—Wash quickly understood what was going on under the
table, though he could see little. But from his spying, he knew

the way Sajie looked with her legs up over Henry's black butt.

Wash guessed Paw was doin it to Sajie down-er, same way Henry did. And Sajie'd be lyin back with'er eyes closed'n'er mouth open . . . Oh, he knew exactly what they were doing there on the floor, and he could hardly lie still; Wash wished *he* was doing it to Missy, every time Paw heaved himself down on Sajie. Wash felt the way he felt when he played with his peter or peeped at Missy's titties in the tub.

Like I'm gone bust. So good inside I'm gone bust'n git the good feelin out.

Wash felt just that way, so good that he began to rub himself through his pants. Then somethin struck him wrong about Paw doing it to Sajie. *Seem like on'y a nigger orta do it to a nigger.* But he kept right on rubbing himself.

Brace's bony fist had blacked Sajie out for a few seconds, just long enough so that he was rutting deep into her by the time her head cleared. Discovering that, Sajie thought two things, one right after the other:

Stronger'n he look.

Spoilt.

So without thinking further she lay still and limp. She did not so much *endure* his savage thrusting and his sour grunting breath and the slimy tallow feel of him; rather, she scarcely noticed. What Ol Brace was doing was nothing; what he had done, by his strength, was everything.

Spoilt. For Henry. For good. And even if she could manage to reach the kitchen knife she'd dropped on the table and cut Ol Brace's throat with it, the spoil would still be on her, in her.

Brace hardly even realized when he came. *Ahh Gah-ahd God* down he went into Henry's pulpy face crushed skull smashed eyes down down *Ahh God* until he lay still and moaning on top of Sajie.

On the porch, bewildered, clutching himself, bursting at last, Wash came too, for the first time in his life, not knowing what was happening to his body, the good feeling overpowering, reminding him of Missy. He lay exhausted as Brace himself, sticky, scared, worried, the good feeling soon gone.

He decided he would not tell that part of it to Maw. How the good feelin busted out.

Amy Arnall, trying to think what to do, sat for a long time at the work table where, only a few hours before, she and Bess had been peacefully cutting material for jackets. Little Luke was brought down to be fed, and to his mother for a good-night kiss; Willis was dispatched to the Judge's room with a cold supper. The house was still, quiet as Amy had never known it. Doors were tightly latched. Darkness came down, but long before it was full Amy lit candles on the work table. For awhile she listened for the miraculous coming of the sheriff's—anyone's—carriage wheels or hoofbeats. But, of course, none came, or would.

She was afraid, but not as before. Now, at least, she knew what she had to deal with. She had managed to ease down the hammer without firing the pistol, and it lay solid and comforting in the candlelight glinting off its barrel.

Jason, she calculated, would stay on the place at least until dawn. He'd want rest, a night's sleep, a full belly, probably his brutish pleasures from Easter, before they fled. He wouldn't be afraid of anyone's being summoned to Amy's help—not with his African friends watching the carriage house and the drive.

As she sat thinking about Jason, Pettigrew, her virtual captivity, the General's absence, Amy occasionally touched the pistol. Rage began slowly to rise in her—not least at herself. She had been a fool not to have gone on to the carriage house after Penny's warning. She should have hitched up and left right then, defying Jason and his black toadies, shooting her way out of the yard if she had to, as the General would have done.

But *of course* the General was not there. All very well that *he* would not have missed Jason with that single shot that had so nearly saved Pettigrew and solved the problem. No doubt the General would not even have let this mess come about. Certainly he'd never have sat like a prisoner in his own house, while his black ape of a captor caroused and rutted in the cabins. The General was not a helpless woman, to be pinned in place by a few African monkeys watching the carriage house and drive. But then again, the General was not *there*.

Amy picked up the gun. Well, neither would *she* be a helpless woman any longer, just because . . . and then what had been running through her head unrealized forced itself into her consciousness. Penny had said Jason's African friends—someday she'd see to it that the General sold *them* to the meanest whip-wielding master in Mississippi—were *watching the carriage house and drive*. Plenty of other ways to get away from Sycamore for anyone on foot. Anyone who knew the place, who'd spent a lifetime there. Like Bess.

With the pistol in one hand, a candle in another, Amy walked quickly over creaking floorboards to a writing desk pushed into a corner, out of the way of the big sewing and cutting table Pettigrew had erected in the center of the room. The General's heavy iron safe, containing only a few documents, sat by the writing desk. Amy put down the gun and candle, found paper and pen, and wrote quickly.

> Pass Bess of Sycamore Plntn. on the way to Shf. Maxton and come quick to Sycamore. Miss Tippy's Jason hiding here.

She hesitated a moment, wondering whether to invoke the General's name for greater authority, then signed herself boldly: *Amy Singleton Arnall*. She dated the note "29th inst." and carried it with the gun and the candle into the hall, calling softly for Bess. When she heard the woman coming, she went back to the work table and laid the gun plainly in the light of the candle.

"Bess, I want you to go for the sheriff. Tell'im Jason killed Pettigrew and's still here."

Bess looked stricken, then eyed the gun. Amy placed her hand on it decisively, possessively.

"Get that white apron off, and that headband. Take the black velvet cape out of my closet and wrap it around you."

"Aint Penny said dey's watchin?"

"Just the carriage house and the drive. You can slip out the side door and get away in a minute. Through the woods to Rockfish Road." She handed Bess the note. "Show this to the first white person you meet. Then go on to the sheriff, fast as you can."

"Aint know wher to find no shurf."

Bess's face was sullen in the candlelight. Amy picked up the gun and tapped the barrel twice on the table, then spoke rapidly, as if to brook no argument:

"Take Rockfish Road to Island Creek Store. You've been there with me. If you can rouse anybody there, show'em the note. Then take the left-hand crossroad and follow it till . . ."

She made the directions to Kenansville plain enough for a child to understand, although she suspected Bess knew the way well enough; then she sent her for the cape with a menacing wave of the pistol.

Rage, by then, was positively seething in Amy. To be threatened and terrorized by some black buck in her own house! To be left alone to face such dangers in the middle of an African village! Abandoned among murderers and concubines hardly a generation out of the jungle! And not a useful white hand—let alone a husband's—to be lifted in her defense.

But Amy Singleton Arnall was not going to be treated that way without fighting back. Even a woman, she told herself bitterly, would fight back at last.

She snuffed the candles and carried the pistol and the chair to the window from which she and Bess had watched Jason and Pettigrew battle to the death. The yard was pitch dark. She could see nothing but the dimmest outline of the kitchen roof, a shade darker than the night sky.

"Ready, Mistis."

Bess's voice, from the doorway, now seemed more apprehensive than sullen.

"Quickly, Bess! But be as quiet as you can."

She could neither see nor hear Bess leave, but Amy knew when the woman was gone; she could sense the greater emptiness of the house. She listened for the betraying sound of the side door but heard nothing. Creeping through the house by touch, she locked the door behind Bess and returned to the window.

If they caught Bess, would they hold back from hurting another nigger? Or would it go harder on Bess for being one of them. Amy hoped they wouldn't . . . she had never even let herself think the word, but in her simmering rage at her plight, at Jason, the Africans, the General, his seed in her belly, the world that had given her woman's unequal lot, she faced it. She hoped they wouldn't rape Bess if they caught her carrying a white's message to catch Jason.

She was immediately sorry for letting herself think such a thing. If they would rape Bess, one of their own, how much more likely that they would . . . well, everybody knew what some black men would do to a white woman if they ever got the chance. Amy shuddered, thinking of bull-like Jason; maybe a good thing, after all, that he had Easter to satisfy his carnal desires. Surely that slut could do it.

As her eyes had adjusted to a night without moon or starlight, the shape of the kitchen building had become clearer against the sky. Soon, through the window, she could make out the expanse of lawn where they'd fought, lying between house and kitchen like the still surface of a millpond. Amy took off her shoes because they hurt her feet and in order to move about the house quietly if she had to. Then she settled back in her chair, the pistol heavy in her lap. No sleep tonight for Amy Singleton Arnall.

Of course, Bess might for some reason just hide out in the woods until Jason left, or the sheriff came, or she thought she was safe. Even if she went for help as ordered, she might not find anyone for hours, on lonely roads in the dark of night. And anyone she did meet, or rouse from sleep at some farmhouse, might be too old or scared or indifferent to come. Or might be just some other woman, who would, of course, be as useless as Amy herself had been.

All in all, the best chance was that Bess might reach the sheriff—supposing she found him at all—by dawn. That would mean, at best, that he, on horseback, and his dogs might reach Sycamore by early morning. Until then, *if* then, she could count on no one and nothing but herself and the pistol.

So even if she was only a woman, she told herself, her eyes fixed on the dark stretch of lawn across which Jason would have to come, she and the pistol would have to be enough.

The sunset collision between Hood and Hatch had sputtered finally into silence, save for the occasional popping of a nervous picket's musket and the groaning undertone of shattered men left on the field. Camp fires flickered in the pastures and on the hillsides—at busy headquarters camps, or where company and regimental officers gathered to boast of or decry the day's events, or where the few butternuts with strength enough boiled coffee. Ambulance teams stumbled about in thick darkness.

Most of the men of the two armies, gratefully quit of the sun that had assaulted them through twelve hours of virtually unbroken fighting, lay asleep—some fitfully, some soundly, some forever, many on the exact ground where they had faced the enemy all that blazing day.

General Arnall slept by his guttering camp fire in exhaustion too deep, for once, to produce his torturing nightly dreams of Amy's enveloping breasts and thighs. On Buck's Hill, General Pope and Colonel Russell pumped field officers for any news they could glean of the progress of Jackson's withdrawal. A. P. Hill's Division surgery, set up around Sudley Church, had become a torch-lit charnel house of mutilated bodies, groaning men, and bloodsoaked surgeons.

Near the Reb center, just south of the pike, Major Jesse Thomas sat quietly in the firelight of Longstreet's headquarters, listening to the military chatter around him while he fingered Miss Letty's handkerchief and remembered again the flash of her eyes and the lilt of her laughing Virginian voice. At the foot of Sudley Mountain, Privates Sowell and Stone, having led Lott McGrath about all day like a trained pony, were wrapped in their blankets among their mates of the Stonewall Brigade. Lott himself sat bolt upright and wide awake against a tree, peering into the darkness deeper than the night.

Lige Flournoy, having gouged the Minié ball out of his thigh with the tip of his bayonet, built a small fire. In his tin cup he boiled cloudy water from his canteen with some of the coffee plundered that morning from the dead Yank. Then he ate all the slices of dried apple from the string that had remained around his neck throughout the afternoon's fight. Lige had some difficulty breathing through his broken nose, and he still had no hearing in the ear half shot off and wrapped with a strip torn from his shirt. But he was feeling good.

"Hey, Meat." He nudged the shoulder of a man lying next to him on the slope of the railroad cut. "See me knock off at Yank with at rock?"

The man slept on, unmoving.

"Good hunnert feet. Went down like a pine tree."

But the other man never moved. Lige grunted in disgust. In spite of himself, he wished Josh was still around. Been right smart hep in a fight like at-un today. Probably would of seen me chunk at rock, too. And Ironass still struttin round bigger'n life.

Lige gave no thought to the missing Foxy Bradshaw, who—curled into the fetal position—was then sleeping in the woods on Sudley Mountain, well back from the line. Foxy's hands were clutched between his legs guarding his peter. He aimed to light out West but he had been too scared of blundering into Yanks or—worse—other butternuts in the darkness.

Sides, he told himself, I aint earnt a little rest, dang'f I know who has.

Private Ambrose Riggin was exhausted, too, but lay sleepless in the woods that sheltered Lawton's Division, some distance back

from the railway embankment. He was not a man of education or
intellectual curiosity; his life, before the army, had been entirely
spent in the hard red hills of Georgia, where he worried more
about the essentials—weather and crops—than about the complexities of life. But Private Riggin had been forced by his failure—rather, his refusal—to shoot the Yank lieutenant to try to
figure something out for himself.

If you killed a deserter before a firing squad, he had been told,
you did it so your own men would draw the lesson and keep on
killing. But if you killed an enemy soldier on the line, you obviously did it so he wouldn't kill you or someone else in your
company. In the one case, you killed men to make men keep on
killing. In the other, you killed men to stop men from killing.

But that don't square. Tried it every which of a way but it just
don't square.

It bothered Private Riggin, too, now that he thought about it,
that both cases ran against the plain commandment of the Lord:
Thou shalt not kill. Maggie set a lot of store by the Ten Commandments. But Ambrose Riggin had supposed that in the case
of a war, the army was allowed to set that one aside—although
they didn't let up on *Thou shalt not steal*. Not that he could see.
Or *covet thy neighbor's wife*.

The deserters' faces beyond his rifle sight had put *Thou shalt
not kill* powerfully back into Ambrose Riggin's mind. But most
immediately, Private Riggin was troubled by the knowledge that
after sparing the Yank lieutenant, he had not fired again that day,
despite opportunities aplenty—*duty*, as he'd always understood
it. Not after seeing his own face in the sight, as in his dream. So
hadn't that made him a kind of deserter himself, that he had not
fired at the enemy when obliged to?

I aint goin to no more, neither.

This decision came to him clear, like a man might make up
his mind on what he wanted for supper; not reasoned out, or the
product of understanding, the resolution was nevertheless certain
in his head, and calmed him.

He wished he could talk it over with Maggie, who had a good
head on her shoulders for a woman. But Maggie was in Georgia;
in her absence, just before he slept, he vowed again:

No more. I aint shootin no more.

• • •

At the Army of Virginia's hospital depot east of Bull Run, Phil Keefe slept comfortably, although the ghastly cries of those more recently wounded rang ceaselessly through the pine grove and the tent village. Keefe had no reason to know it, but the expert attention of Surgeon Israel, who had first attended him that morning at Manassas, had saved his life as well as his leg. The opium pills he had later been given for sleep were not as effective as the morning's hypodermic injection, but his improved condition and the pills together enabled him to fall into healing slumber.

Not so Chaplain E. P. Hornby, who was lying nearby. Like Keefe, he was not considered seriously enough wounded to rate more intensive care within the tents—a fortunate circumstance, since it was cooler outside on the pine-straw beds, the air less offensive and the groans a little less terrible.

But Hornby's opium-induced sleep was scarcely more restful than his frequent waking spells; his tossings and turnings and mutterings seemed to increase, as if in dreams he found more pain than in reality—or as if, perhaps, the harsher reality lay in his dreams. From one such contorted fit of sleep, he woke with a shout:

"No . . . no! I didn't . . ."

He sat as nearly straight up as was possible with a splinted leg, looking walleyed and shocked in the flicker of a torch nearby. A passing orderly knelt by his side.

"Now just lay back'n take'er easy, Parson."

The feverish chaplain was one of the few patients who had acquired among the medical personnel an identity beyond his wounds.

"But you don't understand." Chaplain Horny slumped back to the blanket covering his pine straw. "It's not what you think at all. I only meant . . ." His voice trailed away.

The orderly produced a damp cloth from somewhere and started to touch it to the chaplain's forehead. But at the sight of it, the wounded man sat up again, his eyes wide and fearful.

"No! I tell you, I didn't mean . . . Sally . . . listen to me, Sally!"

Then, to the orderly's consternation, Chaplain Hornby slumped back and began to weep loudly. The behavior of wounded men had long since ceased to mystify or even arouse the wonder of the orderly; but he had never before seen a chaplain who'd been shot, and it seemed to him that the man might take a leaf out of the Good Book and lift up his eyes to the hills from whence came— the orderly privately believed—better help than any of these medical butcher boys could give.

*   *   *

After loosening the cinch on Mercury's new Yank saddle and leaving the black to graze nearby, Fargo Hart spread the buffalo robe in a grove of trees on the floor of which pine straw lay pungent as resin. A swift little run, from which Mercury could refresh himself, trickled musically nearby. The captain's heart was beating fast; it had been a long time since France, since the pleasures first discovered there.

"Prettiest place in Prince William County," Missy had said. "I come up yere a lot."

But when he had finished gathering the thick layer of aromatic pine needles and spread the buffalo robe on top of it, the bulky Le Mat and the silver turnip watch tucked under one corner, he found himself alone. He could hear Mercury's hooves shuffling at the other side of the grove but even in the thick darkness he knew Missy was no longer near.

"Missy?"

He did not call loudly; the habits of wartime were too fixed in him. When there was no answer, he felt his way deeper into the grove, got behind a substantial tree, and urinated against its thick trunk, careful to make no embarrassing sound. Then he strolled back to the pine-straw bed. Still no Missy.

Surely she hadn't run off. He walked toward the swift little run, thinking perhaps she had gone to fill the canteen, or to splash her face. But when he reached the bank, she was not there either.

"Missy?"

His voice barely carried above the splashing of water over rocks. The run was not much more than ten feet wide.

"Over here."

Her voice seemed to come from upstream and he stumbled that way, the darkness like a wall in front of him. A bush brushed stiffly against his leg; he put out his hand to hold it back and felt her clothes spread on it.

"In here."

He barely made out the white blur of her face against the water, perhaps three feet away from his boots.

"Deep here. Kind of a pool."

"You . . . what're you doin in *there?*"

He felt, as he spoke, how foolish the question, how foolish he must look, standing there with his mouth open—if she could see that much of him in the infernal darkness.

"Gittin clean."

Cleanliness, in Fargo Hart's experience of farmgirls, was not high among their concerns. The Italian wench who'd taught him to make love upside down had smelled like goat cheese. He had thought the night before that this girl carried with her the odors of earth, nature, animals. But now . . .

Above the ripple of the water past downstream rocks, she laughed lightly. He had never heard her laugh, and he thought inadequately of bells, a shepherd's pipe once heard in Tuscany, the cheerful whistle of the *patissier* beneath his Paris window.

"Use to come up-ere'n wash to keep Wash from peepin at me."

This confused Hart until he remembered that the deplorable younger brother was named Wash.

"But even up-ere, Wash cotch me one day. Henry aint come'n drug'im away, I'd of never got out. Aintchuh comin in?"

"Well . . . uh . . . sure."

He took off his hat and hung it on a bush, realizing with a certain baffled amusement that *she* was leading *him*—the man Stuart's staff believed a cynical rake returned from Paris. He should have been as anxious as a bull, pawing up the earth to get at his natural business with her; but this stunning little pigtailed child seemed to know better than he did what to do, and to do it more naturally. He unbuttoned his jacket, astounded to be suddenly so embarrassed.

Durward P. Brace heaved himself off Sajie and out from under the kitchen table. The house was dark, silent; Sajie's breathing was loud and regular as a sleeper's. Giv'er a good un all right. Be beggin for more fore breakfus.

He pulled his trousers up from his ankles, the heavy bayonet in its sling banging against his hip, and stumbled out to the gallery at the rear of the house where the air was a mite cooler. So it was done. I-God! Just like I plan, too. Durward P. Brace done showed who's who round-yere.

But he was too tired to feel much of anything except a craving for sleep. Long hot day. Plum wore out. He tried to think how good it had felt, up on Sajie. But he could not remember if dark meat was everything they said it was. He was too tuckered.

Brace went down the steps and around the corner of the house, stumbling over the dead man Wash had robbed of his gun. Too wore out to bother bout corpses. Time enough come day to think

•

what they's left to do. Henry gone and Sajie put by.

He opened one of the cellar doors and went down the steps far enough to close it over his head. The cellar was pitch dark, hot and odorous. Brace was too tired to care. He crawled across the dirt floor, the bayonet dragging at his side, until he felt the great soft mass of Kate's belly. He put his head down on it and slept.

The New Man leaned back against a headstone in the small burying ground of Sudley Church. He was relieved to have made sure that he was not sitting on the grave itself. On such a dark night he had not at first been certain, and he could feel with his fingertips that lettering was carved on both sides of the stone. Then it had come to him that if he leaned against the narrow edge rather than either flat side he could hardly be sitting on the grave; and though it caused Cady considerable pain to be moved, the New Man thought it better for both of them to show no possible disrespect for the dead.

Besides, he was by then getting the hang of hefting Cady around, even though the sergeant was by far the bigger of the two. When he'd tried to lift Cady up just after he'd been hit, Cady had been too heavy and had screamed in mortal anguish. The New Man knew how proud Cady was; if he could be brung to yell like at, he was awful bad hurt.

So he had crouched by the wounded man—who made no further sound—for what he made out was maybe an hour, occasionally touching Cady's shoulder and muttering something soothing, until the sun had dropped behind the ridge and the relative cool of night touched his forehead like the moist side of a dipper.

Then the ambulance men, the bandsmen, and others detailed to help the wounded came onto the field with their lanterns and candles sparkling—like angels, the New Man thought, like the angels he'd once seen in a traveling preacher's Bible, with circles of light spread around their heads.

"Gone get you fixed up now." He fanned Cady with the wide-brimmed hat the sergeant had always worn rakishly cocked to the side.

"Bullshit." Cady's voice was still strong. "Goner."

"See bout *that* pretty soon. When we git to the bonecrackers."

One of the circles of light finally came to the New Man's side and was held low over Cady. A hand came into the light and with difficulty unclasped Cady's fingers from the wound.

"Got to git'im sewed back up, huh?"

"What for?" The circle of light rose again to head height. "Tore to pieces down ther."

"See bout *that*." What did an amblance man know? "Lemme hep you tote'im."

The circle of light moved toward the New Man's face. "Wher you hit?"

"Oh, I aint . . ." But he remembered in time that Ol Jack would have him shot for leaving ranks. ". . . hit bad. Scratch onna hand."

The circle of light dipped again; the candle was stuck into the ground. The dark shape that had been carrying it knelt and none too gently, ignoring Cady's groan, wrestled Cady's blanket roll off his shoulders. The ambulance man folded the blanket expertly into a stretcher while the New Man surreptitiously ripped off one of his rotting shirt-sleeves and wrapped it around his trigger hand. Then they eased Cady onto his blanket; another groan burst from his tight lips.

The ambulance man pulled a bottle from his waistband, uncorked it, and took a long pull.

"Here now." Grice's mouth watered at the sight, but he still thought it was not fittin. "Ain't that stuff for the wounded?"

"This un's gutshot. Hit'd pour right thew'im." He did not offer the bottle to Grice.

Carrying the inert sergeant across the field to Sudley Church was a nightmare the New Man doubted he'd forget. The heavy weight in the blanket bent their backs. They had to step their way among the dead and wounded as if crossing a creek on slick rocks sticking out of the water. Where the New Man did put down his bare feet, the footing was sometimes swampy with blood, guts, and bowels gone loose in death and agony. The groans of violated men rose around them, and the circles of light put the New Man in mind of lives barely flickering, rather than of angels.

The grounds of Sudley Church were flaringly lit by pine-knot torches. They found a spot for Cady under a trestle table at which in better times folks stood to eat ham and chicken at reunions and church feasts. The ambulance man trudged back to the field without a word, pulling his candle from his hip pocket.

The New Man went to the church itself, seeking a surgeon. Inside, on planks laid over the backs of pews the bonecrackers were hard at work. Men lay on the uncovered pews, under them, in the aisle, behind the pulpit. The atmosphere was smoky from the flares that supplemented the church candles, and what the New Man now recognized as the stink of blood and torn flesh mingled with sharp whiffs of chloroform, the stale smell of sweating bodies, and the odors of rot and filth. Orderlies hurried about with buckets of water to swab down the bloody planks and the surgeons' gory tools.

The New Man took only one quick look inside. Never get no bonecracker ther. He went back across the churchyard, through its covering of writhing bodies, to the trestle table. Nare thing to do but wait. He crawled under the table and took Cady's head in his lap.

"Back in ranks." Cady struggled to raise his head.

"Hesh, now. Gone be all right soon's a bonecracker come."

"Grice! Orders is . . . ord . . . ord . . ." Cady's head fell back.

Orders mought be orders but hell with 'em. The New Man aimed to look out for Cady, orders or no orders, hell or high water.

He sat holding Cady's head, occasionally wiping the sergeant's brow with the hand wrapped in torn shirt-sleeve, for perhaps another hour, trying not to hear the groans and shrieks echoing around him and from the old church lopsided on its hillside site. More bodies came in, whether dead or alive the New Man could not always tell. More surgeons, too, probably from some part of the line where they'd had it easy.

Soon he noticed men moving purposefully among the wounded in the churchyard and a major came to examine someone lying on the trestle table above Cady and the New Man.

"Hellfire." The major's voice was sharp with anger. "Scratch like that'n you lyin here makin a fuss?"

The man on the table groaned energetically, and the New Man watched the major's boots shift as he turned to an orderly.

"Take this-un over there with those others aint hurt bad enough to fool with."

As the orderly helped the loudly groaning man off the table, the New Man plucked at the major's trousers with his unbandaged hand. The major went down on one knee and held a candle under the table; in its light the New Man could make out long mustaches under a plowshare of a nose.

"Sarge needs sewin back up, Doc."

Major Douglas Worsham, who had brought in a group of surgeons from the other divisions to help out Hill's overworked medical teams, handed the candle to the New Man. Then he pulled Cady's hands from their clasp across his stomach. He peered closely at the wound and at Cady's face, and lifted one of his eyelids. He carefully peeled back the folds of Cady's shirt to study the wound more thoroughly. He probed with one finger and a burst of pain exploded from Cady's throat like no sound the New Man had ever heard.

"Done for." Major Worsham pulled the shirt back over the wound and lightly placed Cady's hands over it again. "Too many we can save to waste time on goners."

"Goners? But this-yer's Cady, he aint..."

"If he was Gin'al Lee and I was ordered to, I might sew 'im up. But he'd still be a goner. Le's see that hand."

The New Man was too stunned by the major's dismissal of Cady to resist as his hand was unwrapped. Even after seeing the hole in Cady's belly and the guts plopping out of it like bloody dumplings, he'd been sure that somehow Cady would survive. How could Cady be whupped by anything?

"Listen..." Probably the major was just too busy. "Cady gone pull thew if you hep 'im. Sew 'im back up'n see if Cady don't..."

"Oughta have you shot for a deserter." Major Worsham threw the New Man's uninjured hand away from him as if it had been chopped off at the wrist. "Skulkin back here with a fake wound."

But the New Man had made up his mind hours before. "I aint skulkin." He knew where a man's duty lay as well as he knew Ol Jack's orders. "I'm lookin out for Cady."

"Back...in ranks." Cady's voice was just audible above the mournful groans in the churchyard.

Major Worsham looked at Cady again, then stared angrily into the New Man's eyes.

"I swear, Doc, you sew ol Cady back up 'n he'll..."

"Say you lookin out for 'im, eh?"

"Yeah'n if you'll sew'im..."

"Look here, soldier. That-un I just sent off..." The major jerked his head up toward the table above them. "We got lots like him could go back in the line at daybreak. In yonder..." He pointed at the church. "Most are bad hit but just might live if we can get to'em all soon enough. The sergeant here..." He shook his head. "Got lots like him, too. Start trying to save the goners, we won't have time enough for the one's at'll live."

The New Man understood, then. The bonecracker's words fit his experience: *Somebody always bein held out fuh better'n somebody else.*

"So y'aint even gone sew Cady back up?"

"Won't stop 'im from dyin if I do."

The New Man understood that, too: *Who's on top always say no way to hep who's on bottom.*

"I had my piece handy, Doc, I'd blow a hole thew yuh goddamn gut."

Major Worsham nodded, his mustaches drooping in the candlelight.

"Reck'n you would. But come daylight, Ol Jack'll have marshals in here roundin up skulkers and walkin wounded. Y'aim to look out for the sergeant here, better get 'im over with those other goners. Maybe they won't come lookin too close over ther."

So with the help of an orderly, the New Man had moved Cady to the side of the churchyard where they were laying out the goners and stacking up the dead. It signified nothing to Grice that this area included the Sudley Church burying ground. He had too little imagination to conceive of ghosts or the dead walking, even on a pitch-black night; he was merely concerned not to step on graves and show disrespect, and pleased to see that the burying ground was in a grove of big old trees. They would at least shade Cady from the sun that would all too soon rise beyond Bull Run.

"Back . . . in . . . ranks." Cady's voice by then was little more than a whisper.

"See bout *that*," the New Man said.

Colonel Channing returned to the log by the headquarters fire, having seen to the dispatch of the last of the general's orders for the coming day. He was pleased to see that Jackson had rolled into his blankets and was sound asleep, though sitting erect against the remains of an old haystack. Ol Jack could sleep through a tornado.

It was good to have such a day over and done, Channing thought. And maybe tomorrow would be better, with Longstreet on hand. Not that he pulled trigger to help us out today. But maybe Pope'll go for *him* next time. Or pull back across Bull Run to wait for reinforcements.

Someone moved into the firelight and sat down on the other end of the log. Channing sighed; he was ready for the blankets himself, but he turned politely enough and asked:

"They give you some rations?"

"Cup of coffee and two apples."

Channing grinned at the fire. "Roast beef kind of skimpy round here."

"That I don't mind. In the field, one understands that sort of thing." Though no British general of regulars, Teddy Redmund thought, would be so poorly organized or careless of impressions as to lose touch even for a day with his batman and mess chest. "I must say, however, I *don't* understand . . ."

"Sorry, Duke, Gin'al don't even tell *me* what he's up to most times. You shouldn't wonder he's touchy bout spies."

Redmund barely controlled his annoyance. "I am *not* a duke."

"Sure act like one."

Redmund was in as sour a mood as he'd known during this backwoods war. Not only had he had to endure these farmers treating him as a prisoner, a spy! He had also had to admit to himself, as the roar of battle on Jackson's left had mounted again, that he'd guessed wrong in leaving that sector. He could speculate that the blues—as Sertorius had expected all day—finally had come across the cornfield on Brigadier Arnold's left. But neither the battle sounds nor these unmannerly Rebels had given him the details of the struggle. He could only speculate from Jackson's untroubled headquarters that the attack had at least been contained.

"But I *am* one of the Queen's officers and my papers are perfectly in order. You know I'm not a spy."

"Gin'al's peculiar, aint he? Quick to judge, you mought say."

Redmund threw up his hands in exasperation. "Why don't he have me shot, then?"

"Oh, I reck'n he'll leave that to Gin'al Lee."

Lee? The reference puzzled Redmund. Did this bumpkin mean Jackson actually intended to ship him off south of the Rappahannock to Rebel Army headquarters? Violation, that, of all rules of civilized warfare. Or could it be possible . . . Redmund decided to feel his way.

"Does the general expect . . . ah . . . more fighting tomorrow?"

"If he does or he don't, he aint told me."

"But he's not withdrawing. Obviously."

"Not Ol Jack."

Redmund tried to think how to proceed. Only the hiss and crackle of the fire and Virginia's infernal insect noises broke the silence.

"I'd think there's no reason for Pope to pull out either."

"Maybe not. Then again maybe there is."

He could have just said no, or nothing. But what reason could Pope have for backing away from the battle, outnumbering Jackson the way he obviously did, with victory all but in his grasp? No reason, unless . . . Redmund's facile mind raced with possibilities.

"I shall demand to be taken to General Lee in the morning."

"Demand what you please, Duke."

This time, Teddy was too excited even to notice the insolent appellation. If Lee and Longstreet were where Redmund had thought, somewhere south of the Rappahannock, surely this Colonel Hayseed would have made some derisive response to the idea of seeing the commanding general *in the morning*. But he hadn't, and Redmund was suddenly as sure as he was of his own good breeding that Lee and the rest of his army had joined Jackson.

The idea stunned him. If he was right, the whole situation was changed, and dramatically. Pope, rather than Jackson, would have his head in the jaws of the lion. And if that was the case . . .

"Good God!"

Redmund's voice was startling in the quiet camp. If that *was* the case, then Sertorius could explain after all why the inscrutable Jackson, betraying his safe haven above the pike, had attacked that innocently passing division of blues the evening before.

Colonel Channing stared, as the Englishman's voice echoed in the stillness around the fire. A strange bird. Not really a spy, of course, but too pushy with his questions.

"Apples give you the heartburn?"

Redmund shook his head impatiently. "Colonel . . . if there *is* fighting tomorrow, will I be permitted to observe?"

Channing stood up abruptly. He was suddenly tired of conversation, tired of the English bird who never removed his hat. Better things to do, he thought, than parley with a foreigner who thinks he's smarter than anybody else.

"Y'aint in irons, and we got your parole. I don't reck'n the gin'al aims to blindfold a duke."

"Talk about your general, my dear fellow! I must say you aren't terribly informative yourself."

The amused English voice annoyed Channing further.

"Around Ol Jack," he said, "a tight lip's ketchin."

Just over ten crow's-flight miles to the southeast, after two hours of maddeningly difficult riding through strange country on a nearly impenetrable night, Charlie Keach pounded on the deckhouse door of a small steamer. It was moored to a rickety wharf jutting a few feet into Pohick Bay, an arm of the Potomac River.

"Who's it?" The voice from inside was an irritable mutter.

"Keach. Your charter."

Water lapped at the steamer's hull. Keach turned toward shore, barely able in the darkness to make out the old man holding the horses.

"He's here, Lundy! You can take the horses on back. And thanks!"

The old man muttered something peevish; he and the horses rapidly faded into the night, the sound of the hoofbeats coming back for a long time over the flat Virginia landscape. The old man had been a good guide, Keach thought, even though grumbling at much of a night's sleep lost. Worth every dollar I paid'im.

The deckhouse door opened a crack.

"Get up steam," Keach said. "I got to move."

At the kind of expense that only Keach's paper was prepared to meet—or so Hale liked to boast at the Ebbit House bar—Keach had had the chartered steamer standing by since he had come out from Washington. Hale's political pull at the War Department had kept it from being commandeered by the military.

"We...uh...we could wait'll daylight'n make..."

"Now! Let's go!"

Keach could hardly contain his impatience as the seedy captain reluctantly fired up the boiler. On the Peninsula he had painfully learned the most fundamental fact of journalism—that no story was any better than his ability to get it into his paper. Before attaching himself to John Pope's Army of Virginia, he had impressed upon Hale his resolve not to be thwarted again, whatever the expense of getting his story through.

"I got to be in Washington in two hours, Captain. No excuses if we don't make it...now make that boiler sing!"

His foresight was about to pay off. In fact, it already had, in the fresh horse he'd kept stabled at Lundy's farm, and in the old man's surefooted guidance along a maze of country roads on a Stygian night. Via the steamer, he'd have a fighting chance to catch a train in Washington that would connect him to an express out of Baltimore, which would put him into Jersey City early in the morning. Keach didn't have to be told that it was safer to deliver his story personally, rather than expose it to the crudities of Secretary Stanton's telegraph censors. Hale's connections could do him no good with *them*.

And what a story he had! Nothing less than a victory for John

Pope over the fabled Stonewall . . . *Exclusive to Our Readers!*

"Can't we get a move on?" Keach stomped his boot impatiently on the deck. "Let's go, Captain . . . let's go!"

His story, of course, was of more than immediate importance. With McClellan out of favor after his failure on the Peninsula, Pope's victory would not only make him preeminent in the army; what had happened on the banks of Bull Run—Keach noted the felicitous phrase for later use—also was bound to have favorable impact for Lincoln and his party in the November elections, and to brace up the whole North for a stronger effort to prosecute the war.

No one had had such a story since the war began. Keach savored the thought of other correspondents reading it, knowing it was his. Hale would be impressed. As the steamer edged away from the dock and its nose began to swing toward the Potomac, he started phrasing his lead in his head. *Victory has come at last to the Union* . . . maybe something like that. Or *As night fell across the banks of Bull Run, the Union stood at last triumphant* . . .

But there was no doubt about the most important line: *Eyewitness Account by Our Own Correspondent.*

Cipher Operator James F. Grady, who had been feeling all day a vague sense of unease, was about to jump out of his chair with excitement. The message he was putting into plain language would have the same effect, he believed, on General Halleck and President Lincoln, to whom it was jointly addressed by good old Colonel Haupt.

Grady's assignment to the Telegraph Office, literally next door to the Secretary of War, with the general in chief close at hand and the President himself frequently dropping in, gave the young man a strong feeling of identification with these great figures; and Grady's work, dealing with the flow of information to and from the armies, placed him, in his estimation, at the nerve center of the war.

Besides, Grady's affection and respect for the President and his devotion to the Union were the feelings of a generous and believing nature. He had not yet been battered by experience into the guarded skepticism that passes, with most men, for maturity. Nor had he mellowed with age into a forgiving sense of the fallibility shared even by the greatest mortals. Grady had faith in his expectations.

So he suffered as he had no doubt Mr. Lincoln suffered when

there was bad news or—sometimes worse—no news. Grady rejoiced, too, when the clicking instruments of his craft drew from the long wires he imagined humming musically across the continent the kind of news that would lighten Mr. Lincoln's terrible burdens or bolster his public support—weak enough, that summer, to infuriate Cipher Operator Grady. In fact, Grady felt himself as mysteriously but profoundly connected to Mr. Lincoln as his telegraph key was to the vast forces moving in Virginia, in Kentucky, down the Mississippi, and on all the far coasts. In both cases, the essential link was the news pumping like heartbeats on the murmurous wires.

Earlier that night, as Grady had pored over the file of messages that had moved since his previous shift, his unease had deepened into the same anxiety and concern that must have borne down Mr. Lincoln as he pondered the fate of Pope's army out there in the Virginia hills. At 2:30 p.m. the President, picking up a tantalizing hint in a dispatch from Burnside at Falmouth, had inquired directly:

> Any further news? Does Colonel Deven mean that sound of firing was heard in direction of Warrenton, as stated, or in direction of Warrenton Junction?
>
> A. Lincoln

And a telegram from Halleck to Burnside laconically suggested the high-level fears that Grady shared with all his passionate heart:

> I have heard nothing from Pope for four days, except through you. He seems to have permitted a part of the enemy's force to march around him.

Four days! during which the only word from a great army in the field, fighting before the capital city itself, had been either secondhand or thirdhand rumors or, if official, so delayed on the roundabout route through Falmouth as to give no indication whether or not the situation had changed in the ten or twelve hours or a day since it had been sent. General Halleck and Mr. Lincoln—as well as their ardent young shadow in the Telegraph Office—were like grown men playing pin-the-tail-on-the-donkey with the elusive suggestions and pieces of gossip and detail floating along the wires.

So it was with initial relief that Grady had read a later telegram from Halleck:

Major General Pope:

Trains will be started immediately to reconstruct bridges
and carry out supplies. Yours of yesterday, 10 p.m., is the
first I have received from you for four days. Live on the
country as much as possible till we can supply you. Push
the enemy as much as possible, but be sure to keep your
connection with Alexandria.

H. W. Halleck
General in Chief

But elation turned to disappointment when Grady could find
no indication in the file of *what* Halleck finally had heard from
Pope. The cipher operator was scarcely more chagrined to be shut
out of this vital information than to realize that the message must
have been courier-delivered—to Grady a virtual insult to the wiz-
ardry he could command with his fingertips, which could link
most parts of the country with the flick of a hand.

As he reread Halleck's message, moreover, he realized that it
meant little more than that Pope had opened a "connection" to
Alexandria. Whatever news he'd sent along "yesterday, 10 p.m."
had been nearly twenty-four hours out of date by the time Halleck
replied. In twenty-four hours, armies could be destroyed.

Even so, Grady would have been delighted had he known the
contents of the letter Cass Fielding had copied from Pope's original, after the general and his staff had watched from the Centreville heights as Jackson's attack on Gibbon's Brigade lit up the
night skies over Brawner's farm. But Pope's letter had been delayed by an unusually dark night, by the courier's cautious concern
for roving Confederate cavalry, by the confusions of a war theater
and frequent guardpoint challenges—all compounded by the army's usual sloth and indifference, once the courier had entrusted
his missive to official channels at Alexandria. So it had not been
placed before Halleck until 6:45 p.m., twenty-one hours after
Lieutenant Fielding had scratched it out for Pope's flourishing
signature.

Young Grady would have exulted, as Halleck undoubtedly
did—since neither knew anything of the sanguinary events that
had unfolded during those twenty-one hours—to learn from Pope's
letter that on the afternoon of the 27th Joe Hooker had encountered
Stonewall Jackson's men along Kettle Run, between Bristoe Station and Manassas Junction, and "routed them completely." Grady

would have clapped his hands to read that, on the 28th, in the night battle at Brawner's farm, the Rebs had been "driven back at all points, and thus the affair rests."

Possibly it would have meant little to young Grady, but it surely had gratified Henry Halleck's strategic sense (he was known in the army, if not for a fighter, as "Old Brains") to know that Longstreet had been driven back through Thoroughfare Gap by hard-hitting Irvin McDowell. Old Brains would have grasped in an instant that this meant Jackson was isolated and at Pope's mercy, while the rest of Lee's divided army was walled off from him by the Bull Run Mountains.

But since Grady actually had none of the reassuring information in Pope's letter, he was only faintly encouraged by Halleck's acknowledgment of it. So, at 11 p.m., when Colonel Haupt's message began clacking and stuttering from the key, and as Grady worked to decipher it, his excitement and relief were as sharp as he confidently expected Mr. Lincoln's to be.

President Lincoln and General Halleck:

General Pope was at Centreville this morning at 6 o'clock. Seemed to be in good spirits. Hooker is driving enemy before him; McDowell and Sigel cutting off his retreat. Army out of forage and subsistence. Force of enemy 60,000. This is the substance of information communicated by two ambulance drivers, who came in from Centreville, and who also gave many particulars confirming previous statements.

H. Haupt

Well! Sixty thousand was a passel of Rebs, but with all of McClellan's troops going out to him, Pope would have enough to handle 'em. And Colonel Haupt could be counted on, if anyone could, to push through supply trains. Thus, the important thing— what would give Mr. Lincoln, for once, a good night's sleep— was the news that Hooker was driving the great Stonewall, while McDowell and the Germans were cutting off his retreat.

Grady quickly got copies moving to Mr. Lincoln and the general in chief, then sat back in satisfaction. Nothing pleased him more than to please the man he admired above all others; and he felt almost as useful, in having so efficiently hurried on the news, as he would have had he been the victorious Pope himself. Just then he sensed someone behind him, and a hand touched his shoulder.

"What's all those feathers round your mouth, Grady?"

Stoddert, one of the President's clerks, stood over him, grinning. He and Grady were rather good friends, although the telegrapher privately deplored Stoddert's tendency to practical jokes. He suspected that Mr. Lincoln's fondness for storytelling had wrongly encouraged the clerk to act as if he, too, were a humorist. Bad judgment.

"Feathers?" Even as he spoke, Grady knew he was falling into one of Stoddert's traps.

"Well, aint you a cat that's swallowed a canary? You look like it."

A poor imitation, indeed, of Mr. Lincoln's real gift for homely illustration. Once in Grady's hearing the President had said of a general assigned to important but noncombat duty, "If he can't skin, he can hold a leg." Another time, he'd lamented to Superintendent Eckert that sending reinforcements to McClellan on the Peninsula was "like shoveling flies across a barnyard." Grady also had heard the President introduce a visitor to Secretary Stanton as "a gentleman who knows all about the South and can tell us how high that raccoon can spring."

Stoddert's cat–canary remark was weak stuff by comparison. But except for such lapses, he was a decent fellow and had promised to introduce Grady to a sister whose likeness showed her to be a real beauty. Besides, he shared Grady's reverence for Mr. Lincoln, and anyone who worked directly for the President was worth giving a little leeway. So Grady handed Stoddert a copy of Haupt's telegram.

"There's my canary."

Stoddert read the message eagerly, glanced at Grady with lifted brows, and read it again.

"Jehosophat! Grady . . . know what this means?"

"That's not hard to figure out."

"No, no, I don't mean just chasing off old Stonewall. That's great but . . ." Stoddert gazed rather conspiratorially around the Telegraph Office. But none of the other operators was paying attention to them; the big room was quiet, the instruments still. No breeze stirred at the open windows, beyond which the heat and darkness lay thickly on the city.

"Listen, Grady . . . *he's* been waiting for the right moment, don't you see?"

"Anytime one of our generals can beat Stonewall Jackson, I'd say *that's* the right moment."

"But I reckon you don't know what's in that desk over there, do you?" Stoddert jerked his head toward Eckert's big oaken desk by the window.

Grady was both excited and annoyed. He'd been curious most of the summer about the document on which Mr. Lincoln had so often worked, and which he knew was locked in Eckert's desk. But it irritated him to be in the position of knowing less than Stoddert. Usually, because of Grady's prior access to the message file, it was the other way around.

"I know it must be something important, as hard as he's worked on it." Such a lame response fed his irritation.

"I'll say it's important." Stoddert looked around again, then put his lips close to Grady's ear. "The Africans!"

"What?" But Grady's irritation vanished in excitement.

Stoddert tapped Grady's shoulder with a clenched fist. "Slavers want a war down there, they'll *get* a war!"

Grady stared at him, scarcely able to take in such news—the last he had expected to hear. The issue had been discussed so often and so angrily and for so long that it amazed him to think of even Mr. Lincoln deciding such a matter once and for all. Besides, Grady had always supposed that the war would have to be won before the President or anyone could free the slaves.

Of course, it was the *right* thing to do, no doubt about that. In Grady's opinion, the slaves were the real reason the war was worth fighting—so the Union could be free everywhere and for everybody.

"That's why he's been waiting for the right moment, Grady—for a *victory.* A thing like this, you don't want it to be like the Pope's bull against the comet, you know. You want everybody to know you can do what you say you'll do."

Grady suspected Stoddert had swiped the Pope's bull analogy; it sounded more like Mr. Lincoln than his clerk. But the point was nevertheless clear: with McClellan abandoning the Peninsula, a decree freeing the slaves would have looked like an empty, desperate gesture. But with Federal armies driving Stonewall Jackson, nobody would doubt Mr. Lincoln's power to do just what he said he'd do.

"England'll never come in against us after that." Stoddert nodded wisely at his own words. "And our boys'll have something they can *really* fight for."

Grady figured he was hearing Mr. Lincoln's own reasoning, probably at third hand, as Stoddert would more likely have got it from somebody closer to the President, maybe his secretary, Mr.

John Hay. Still, what Stoddert had said sounded right—particularly since Grady assumed that all Union soldiers despised slavery as he did.

"Besides, the whole Reb shebang's in for it now." Stoddert peered again at Haupt's telegram. "Not just Stonewall."

Grady, too, believed that freeing the slaves would cause them to rise up against their former masters—most of whom, presumably, would be off somewhere in the secesh armies. They'd have to rush home or risk their families' being massacred.

"Serve 'em right." Grady was not a hard man—not yet; but he believed as the Bible taught: woe to him from whom offenses come.

"I ought not to of told you. But this news just sort of knocked it right out of me."

Grady's annoyance returned. "Look here, Stoddert. I keep secrets all the time."

But never one like this, he conceded to himself. Oh, Mr. Lincoln was readying a master stroke, all right; maybe the war'd even be over before the November elections. And to think that he, James F. Grady, had been the bearer of the tidings that would bring about such a great event! That was almost enough to cause him to forgive Stoddert for his prior knowledge.

"After this . . ." Stoddert handed the Haupt telegram back to Grady. "I wouldn't be surprised if he went ahead and did it tomorrow."

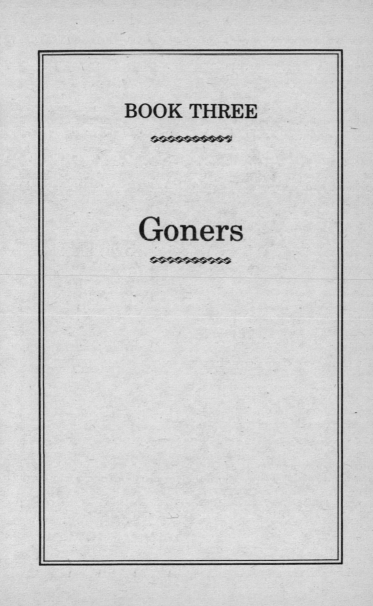

BOOK THREE

Goners

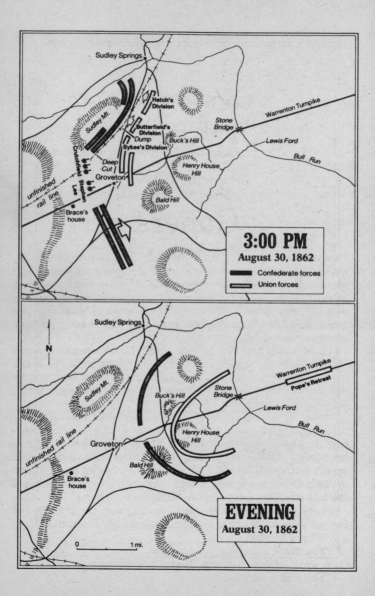

3:00 PM
August 30, 1862

Confederate forces
Union forces

EVENING
August 30, 1862

N

Sudley Springs

Hatch's Division

Butterfield's Division

Sykes's Division

Dump

Buck's Hill

Stone Bridge

Warrenton Turnpike

Lewis Ford

Bull Run

Sudley Mt.

Deep Cut

Groveton

Henry House Hill

Bald Hill

unfinished rail line

Stephen Lee

Brace's house

Sudley Springs

Sudley Mt.

Buck's Hill

Stone Bridge

Warrenton Turnpike

Pope's Retreat

Lewis Ford

Bull Run

unfinished rail line

Groveton

Henry House Hill

Bald Hill

Brace's house

0   1 mi.

Chapter Eleven

❧❧❧❧❧❧❧❧❧❧❧❧❧❧

August 30—
Midnight to Dawn

FARGO HART AWOKE to the sound of crickets and the brook running, and Missy's breath, light as a moth, in his ear. In the darkness of the night and the warm folds of the buffalo robe he felt himself hidden, secure; in the warmth of Missy's body bare against his own, he knew himself replete. He had no sense of foreboding, no doubts about her, no skepticism about love. So he knew this was a moment that might never come again.

He moved farther into the robe, against Missy, her breasts soft against his back, her legs entwined with his, one of her hands between his arm and ribs. Desire hardened him at once and he put his hand on her thigh. Then her breath in his ear became a whisper:

"Love..."

Something *European* about her. That was what he'd been sensing. He stroked the trim flesh of her thigh where it rounded into her buttock. European. An odd thing to think about a girl whose speech was appalling and who had never even been out of Prince William County; at least she didn't *think* so, since she confessed she had no clear idea where its boundaries might be.

Hart chuckled, a small deep sound against the crickets but enough to make her head rise alertly above his shoulder.

"What's funny?"

"You are."

A small, shocked silence. Hart chuckled again.

"You aint American."

Missy was faintly defiant. "I'm Virginia."

"Not exactly that either."

Hart turned slightly toward her, feeling his shoulder slip deliciously between her breasts. That too was European, he thought. French, anyway. Big soft bosom but slender as a flower stem everywhere else. Most American women looked like hourglasses—thick in the hips and bottom, thick through the chest.

"I mean you're kind of European. In a way."

He struggled farther over on his back, the pine needles under the robe helping to cushion his hip bone against the hard earth, and got his left arm under and around her so that he could hold her left breast in his hand.

"You like that?"

He squeezed gently. "Sure do."

"I mean me bein kindly European."

He turned his head and took her nipple in his mouth. It grew hard and sharp, and he squeezed her other nipple between his thumb and forefinger, feeling it expanding, too. Missy sighed and put her leg between his. With her right hand, she held herself up to his avid mouth.

He looked up at her. *"That's* what I mean. You..."

Missy thrust her nipple to his lips again. "Don't stop."

He sucked for a long time, deeply at peace.

"Like a baby." Her hand found him.

He lay back, luxuriating in the soft pull of her fingers.

"Some baby."

"My baby."

Of course, he had known—since awakening with his head in her lap under the sycamore tree, since she'd first flown into his arms like a wild thing, her tears streaking his face—he'd known he could do with her as he would. But he'd sensed, too, that a quick tumble in the nearest haystack would not be enough. Even so, he had not been prepared for this... wonder.

He certainly had not expected that it would have to be she who took charge as he'd fumbled with his clothes, earlier that night on the bank of the run. As if she'd understood his sudden embarrassment, Missy had started to chatter as he undressed; her voice was soft as the summer air, in tune with the rushing water and the crickets' whir:

"Water's kindly cold. But don't take long to git use to it. Gits lots colder'n this in spring. First time I come up-ere uz April. Sun

shinin, redbud's out, dogwood bloomin everwher. April beats all
in Prince William. So I just skip in-ere like it-uz a tub at home.
My stars! I like to *froze* for I-uz up to my knees. But if you git
in all ovuh, it gits kindly nice pretty quick . . . water sort of whirls
all ovuh yuh."

Hart stepped hastily into the stream, which was almost knee-
deep at the bank. The water was cold indeed, as it ran pell-mell
down from the mountains, but he sat abruptly, wanting cravenly
to cover himself as soon as possible. The creek bottom was pebbly,
but the water was too soothing against his tired body for him to
notice that; and suddenly her white floating face was only a foot
from his own.

"See? Aint so cold, now, is it?"

Hart began to relax. In the army, a man could forget what a
bath felt like. Not to mention how a woman felt.

"Sort of my secret place. Grove'n this pool. Evuh since I-uz
a little girl."

As if she were much more than that now. Hart let his legs
stretch out before him, the cold water floating him up a little from
the scratchy creek bed.

"I'd just lay up unner em pines 'n smell pine needles 'n watch
clouds go ovuh makin shadduhs onna grass." She laughed again,
the shepherd's pipe trilling with the water. "Sometimes I'd run
along inside the shadduhs. Like they could take me with'm. Wherever they's goin. Maw used-a say little girls all dream they's
somewher they aint. Maw used-a be . . ."

Her voice trailed away in the rush of the water, and Hart
watched her face tip back a little as if she were trying to remember
something, or make out where the clouds used to be. Then, abruptly:

"Bet *you* had a secret place, too."

"A tree. Big ol oak in our yard. I'd get up high's I could. Sit
for hours on this one branch where they couldn't see me from the
ground."

"Way up ther alone." Missy's voice was admiring.

"Thinkin and dreamin. Playin these funny games in my head
I was some kind of great man. Doin great things."

"A sojer?"

"Never a soldier."

"Wash, he wants to go be a sojer so bad I speck he gone run
off any day."

"He does, they'll use'im. No, I had in mind to be maybe a

painter. Or a sculptor. Cept I couldn't draw an apple so's you'd know it. Then a writer. I'd still like to be a writer someday, if this war's ever over."

"A writer bout what?"

Funny kind of talk to be having with a naked girl in the dark of night, neck-deep in a creek not more than a few miles from the war. But Hart felt himself opening to Missy and their explorations the way his body was opening to the smooth flow of the water. He had been cooped up inside himself so long, in an army alien to his sense of himself, in a war he hated—then, suddenly, his outburst to Peterson, the enigmatic photographer. Now here he was rambling on about youthful dreams with a white face floating a few inches from his in the ceaseless stream of memory.

"Oh . . . history. Great men. How things used to be. Ought to be."

"Like fairy tales?"

"Something like that."

"I-uz goin to school over to Groveton a while. Aint had no teacher sincet-a war, though. We read some fairy tales."

"You liked 'em?"

"I loved it *all*."

In the eagerness of her words, Hart could sense the intensity she would have brought to learning—what decent schooling might have meant to her in other circumstances, another world.

"At girl with-a long hair?" Missy went on. "Let it down from a tower so's'er hero could climb up'n rescue'er?"

"Rapunzel."

"I'd-a let *my* hair grow like at, I'd-a thought *you'd* come rescue me."

"Didn't have to. I rescued you anyway. Twice."

The water caressed Hart's body like a mother's hands; it was cool between his legs, on his back turned to the current, under his arms as he leaned back on his elbows. In the darkness he could not see the white shade of his body floating out before him, although he knew he was covered by only a few inches of water. He was easy in his mind by then, the sensuality of the water and the flow of talk having overcome embarrassment and uncertainty. Daringly, he thought of arching his hips, floating himself on the surface like some nibbling fish eager to feed.

Then Missy stood up in a sudden whirl of water, a slender white pillar rising suddenly above him, water flicking off her body and sprinkling down in his face. In the dark, he could make out little more than her slimness and whiteness; but he did see the perfect, heartbreaking feminine ease with which one leg bent ever so slightly at the knee, and turned inward in a movement of such timeless beauty that he thought in one instant of Venus rising from the sea, and in the next noticed only that that one impeccable movement, as if practiced by all women through all the centuries, so that now it was no longer effort or effect but instinct with all of them—that one flawless inward turning had effectively hidden what otherwise would have been the single dark patch breaking the whiteness rising above him.

"Clean now . . ."

A splash or two in the water, the apparition fading, a sigh, the whisk of leaves. Darkness. She was gone.

Hart arched his hips and tried to see his penis above the water. In the darkness, still flaccid, it moved with the current, sensual as a massage. But he was in no hurry, though she had been naked and within arms' reach; in the night and the stream their nearness and openness had seemed childlike, not lustful.

Hart felt pure. *Clean now.* He sensed the meaning of the words, though he doubted if in her starved life she had had the experience to understand it herself. Pure. Cleansed. He could go to her now, in two minutes, anytime, rise from the purifying stream as she had risen, unburdened, unstained, absolved, not so much of sin— for whatever his, surely *she* had none, had never had the opportunity to take corruption like fruit in her mouth—but of preoccupation with self, restraint, caution, custom. So purified, in their Eden, they could be as children without care, and taste of one another, and shrink from nothing, and never think of dawn.

"Behold . . . thou art fair, my beloved." Hart's murmur was no louder than the water licking at the line of his jaw. "Yea, pleasant . . . and our bed is green."

He could not have told where the words came from, but he knew they were biblical in cadence and he knew how deeply the old teachings burrowed, how easily they came to the tongue, or spoke to the ear, when the heart gave reason.

He rose to his feet and stood a moment, up to his knees in the water, the warm night air moving on a faint breeze from the west. As it touched his buttocks, between his thighs, along his back and on the damp hair at the nape of his neck, drying him with faintly lascivious fingers, he felt himself thickening, rising, and put his hand down to feel the inexplicable—love and wanting made flesh.

He reached the bank in two strides, turned to face the breeze, and stood a moment longer, holding himself—male now, swaggering his shoulders and chest in his maleness, savoring it, proud, aggressive, wanting. Then he left his clothes where they lay in the broomsedge and found Missy waiting on the pine-straw bed, a fold of the buffalo robe concealing all but her face, floating against the darkness of the grove as it had against the waters of the run.

He was not conscious of his nakedness as he lay beside her. She carried the fold of the robe over him, too, and they lay close, her arm touching his, breathing in time, the crickets loud in the lightless night, Mercury huffing occasionally at the edge of the grove.

"If some cloud'd carry me off now, I wouldn't go."

"And if I could be the greatest writer in the world, I'd rather be here with you."

He was not sure how to begin but he was comfortable lying there beside her. So again it was she who moved first, running the tips of her fingers lightly along his jaw and over his lips. The wraith-like touch set him afire and he turned to take her in his arms, crushing her against his chest, his hardness against her thighs. Their mouths met fiercely, for a long time. When he ran his tongue between her lips and teeth, as Janelle had first shown him how, she accepted it as naturally as she'd let him sweep her onto his horse the night before. Her fingers moved on his back.

Hart took his mouth away. "I don't mean to . . . rush."

"Why not?"

He put his forehead against her, hoping she could see his smile. "You want me to rush? And do what?"

"What Sajie'n Henry do. An Dogan's bull with Paw's cows."

He moved against her thighs. "You know what *that* is?"

"I give Wash baths, he-uz little. Put Paw to bed drunk. I *ought* to know."

Sorry lout ought to be horsewhipped. But Hart was by then too excited to care. Like Dogan's bull, he thought.

"You're not afraid?"

"Just inna hurry."

Missy said the last word against his mouth, this time putting her tongue between his lips. He sucked it hungrily, groping for the softness of her. She moved back a little to open her breasts to him, and he took his mouth away from hers and kissed her nipples, then licked a circle around each with his tongue.

"Just know everthing, donchuh? Everthing they is to do..."

But in her naturalness, he thought, she was the one who *knew*. He took her breasts in both hands and put his face in the sweet vale between them. He wished briefly for light, to see her, to get a visual sense of her body to go with the exotic feel of it, the pounding desire it drove in his veins. Then he did not think anymore, or wish for anything.

"Oh, love," Missy said when he entered her. "Love."

Then silence, except for their gasping breaths and the night noises and a groan he muffled against her shoulder. Until, as his self burst into hers, she whispered again:

"Love...love..."

How long they had slept afterwards, Hart did not know, except that he believed she had waked before he did. Lying back while she handled him with gentle fingers, he knew that nothing he had experienced before had had meaning; he had learned movements, like soldiers at drill, with no sense of what they could signify, what they might convey.

"You *like* bein this way. With me, I mean."

"I like you. I *love* you."

"But you know something, Missy? You've never once called me by my name."

She kissed him. "Love's your name."

More like hers, he thought. He took both her hands and held them against his face. "Say my real name. Hart. Fargo Hart."

"Sound like love to me."

"No...it's spelled *H-a-r-t.*"

"Still sound like love."

Hart laughed, realizing she had little notion of spelling. "I guess you know. I guess you know more about love than anybody I ever met."

"More'n your wife?"

He raised himself on an elbow and stared down in consternation, at the blur of her face. "You think I'm *married?* And still you're...here?"

"If you-uz marr'd to *six* women. Still be rightchere."

"I don't even have *one* wife. You really think I'm such a rascal I'd be with you like this if I did?" European, he thought, knowing what she'd say, feeling her fingers stroking him again. Downright European.

"We b'long together. Nuthin else matters."

He was reminded then of how young she was. Only the young could be so sure. But *European*. Despite her naiveté, her farmgirl ignorance.

"Thing is . . . little girl like you . . . reason I say you're European . . ." Difficult to concentrate with her hand moving so deliciously on him. "You *know* so much. Not ashamed of knowin it."

Her fingers slipped lower and cupped him.

"Not so much's you think. Whut's these-yer for?"

"Just go with the other."

"Dont see no use in'em. Funny . . . it so hard'n'em so little'n soft."

"Sajie'd tell you to watch out for the hard one."

They laughed like children with a secret.

"Figgered *that* for m'self."

Well, she was a miracle. Janelle had been as straightforward but Janelle would not have known love from a bottle of champagne; Janelle thought love was an expensive present or a fancy compliment.

"Know what Sajie *did* tell me?"

And what did *he* think? What was love to Fargo Hart? Resolutely and at once he turned his thoughts away from what he knew immediately would be a burden on the moment, one that had no place with them this night.

Oh, he'd have to come to it soon enough, face up to what this meant to him, what *she* meant, where she could fit in the great pigeonhole desk. He would have to face the idea of love itself, measure its power to cope with the world's expectations—even his own.

But he would not think about that, or about anything that would stain the purity of the moment. They were as if in a sanctuary— away from the war, the world, the past, the future. Maybe that was the only purity.

He kissed her lightly. "What did Sajie tell you, Missy Know-it-all?"

She put her face on his chest and began to lick it. He felt her mouth moving down his stomach, heard her voice muffled under the buffalo robe:

"Her secret."

Janelle, he thought. Janelle would do that. "Ah, Missy . . . no . . . you don't . . ."

But her tongue stroked drily down his belly, down the inside of one thigh, up the other. He grasped for her shoulders to pull her head up, moving so that for the first time he felt the hard, reminding bulk of the Le Mat under the robe. She was too young, too naive, too trusting; she could not know, would never believe he might have to go away. He could not take so much from her.

"Don't . . . you don't have to . . ."

But her warm tongue turned his words into a helpless groan; and in the last of reason he knew it was too late, the purity was tarnished—not by the beauty of her loving, but by the intrusion, grim as the Le Mat's touch, of fear—*his* fear that he could never give her enough of himself to be worthy. He tried again to speak, to keep things equal; but he could only writhe instead in the idiot throes of ecstasy.

Less than two beeline miles away, Larkin Folsom lay awake, leaning on one elbow and looking down with gratification at the dark sleeping form of Amos Gilmore. The corporal stirred in his sleep and muttered something profane, his powerful legs thrashing suddenly, giving Folsom a painful kick. The boy put his hand soothingly on Gilmore's shoulder.

Exhausted, he thought. But bad dreams anyway. Kind of fight we had today who wouldn't have bad dreams?

All around them, the dark night was troubled with the screams and pleas of the wounded, the fearful mutterings of bloody dreams; over his shoulder Folsom could see the dull orange glow above the groaning yard of Sudley Church. Folsom thought the fires of Hell might cast a light like that of the surgery torches.

By the nature of his job, the orderly had not been much involved in the grisly hand-to-hand struggle that had left most survivors of Arnall's Brigade either shattered and bleeding or—like Gilmore and the General himself—in a stupor of fatigue. Even looking back on the one Yank he'd shot, the man had been so distant, the shot had seemed so impersonal, the impact of the bullet so unimaginable, that Folsom hardly felt he'd done it.

He'd slept briefly, then been awakened by Gilmore's heavy body turning partially over on him in their blankets. He lay like that for awhile, enjoying even in the hellish resonances of the night the feel of the corporal's body against his. When he finally freed himself from its warm weight, his brain was too active for sleep, and he found himself pondering his strange new friendship, as he still thought of it.

Folsom was not merely grateful to Corporal Gilmore for saving his life; that was the least of it. He had discovered that this ostensibly rough and threatening man could recognize the worth—and the recognition was unique in the orderly's brief experience—of the gentleness at the core of Larkin Folsom's nature. Astoundingly, something in Gilmore's own violent being had responded to that gentleness, even in a way matched it—a response Folsom never doubted that only he had ever seen.

He was proud of that. He, Larkin Folsom, had evoked a generosity, a largeness of spirit, that had only been waiting in Amos Gilmore for discovery and nourishment. So he thought the two of them knew each other's secret selves as no one else ever had bothered to do. They had *shared* themselves.

Having no scientific or religious explanation for such things, the orderly also believed that the intense pleasure of their strokings, the warmth with which he and Corporal Gilmore held each other close, were natural expressions of that secret sharing—and therefore beautiful. But he knew from painful experience what the world could and would make of any kind of unusual behavior—writing poetry, say, when college mates were out drinking and carousing and contesting to see who could fart the loudest or piss the farthest.

So Folsom supposed his and the corporal's friendship was somehow against someone's rules; things he cherished usually were. No doubt General Arnall would send him packing if he knew.

But to Folsom that only represented the same standard, the same insensitivity that had classified Amos Gilmore irrevocably as a brute. That was just the world outside their blankets. It was only in that outside world, Folsom believed, that two people sharing themselves could be called a sin. Or gentleness derided. Or caring.

Anyway, what he felt with Corporal Gilmore was just like the viscerally remembered touch of his mother's hands—the first conscious feelings of physical pleasure that he could recall. Only his mother and the corporal had ever touched him down there. Folsom told himself these experiences therefore were bound to be akin. But he was under no illusion that his mother would accept *that*.

I don't care, Folsom thought, feeling suddenly free of his mother's clear intent—clear in hindsight, anyway—to keep him as closely tied to her, as dependent upon her, as she often tearfully claimed to be upon him. His joining the army, she'd said, had been like cutting a bond of flesh between them—which, he suddenly admitted to himself, was exactly why he'd done it, against all his other instincts.

Corporal Gilmore sat straight up in his blankets and looked around madly, one of his eyes reflecting a tiny spot of light from a far-off torch in Sudley churchyard.

"Yanks in the cut! Yanks in the cut!"

Gilmore's hoarse shout was loud enough to wake—Folsom stopped himself before he reached the old cliché, incongruous as it would have been on that field of corpses. He pressed the corporal back to the hard earth.

"Gin'al sez hit'em . . ." Gilmore's voice trailed off into a low mutter, then rose slightly. "Hit the bas'ards . . ."

Folsom smoothed the blanket over the massive body beside him until Gilmore slept again. The orderly resented the outburst—not just that in his dreams the corporal had reverted to his rough old self, but that Folsom knew it was bound to be so, that the brute world of violence and blood and death had staked too large a claim on Amos Gilmore. He could never escape it—General Arnall would never let him—for more than a stolen moment or two in that quiet other world, in the blankets he and Folsom could share so fleetingly and might at any moment lose forever.

Folsom put his lips against the corporal's jawbone, feeling the power of it, the rough scratch of beard stubble. The resentment fled, then, and lines flashed in his head as clearly as if whispered passionately in his ear:

> Still I'd persist in offering to pay
> Love's homage, love, to beauty and to . . .

To what? In the reverberant night he could not even think where the lines would fit in his sonnet, or if they would at all, much less what words should come next.

With the pistol heavy and comforting in her lap, Amy Arnall stayed awake—she knew from the old clock that chimed through the silent house—until well past midnight. She did not realize even then that she was sleepy, so determined was she that when Jason came she would deal with him not as a mere woman but as an armed guardian of her household.

The rage that had boiled in her had long since evaporated. She knew, within half an hour of Bess's departure, that the woman must either have reached the Rockfish Road safely or gone into hiding in the woods. If they'd caught her, Amy was sure, she'd have heard some kind of commotion. So Bess would either bring Sheriff Maxton or she wouldn't. Amy could do nothing further about that.

But if that bitch—Amy was surprised how easily the distasteful word rose to her mind—if that bitch quit on me, I'll take it out of her black hide later on.

If there *were* a later on. For in the dark night, as Amy sat tensely by the window, her eyes never leaving the barely visible stretch of lawn across which Jason would have to come from the cabins, the conviction grew in her that he *would* come.

"He'll come," she said aloud, when she was sure. The quiet words were like a shriek in the darkness.

After that, every so often, as if to remind herself she would say it again: "He'll come." Or maybe just "Yes, he will." And once:

"Got to come for it."

She was not sure if she spoke to keep herself awake, to give herself false courage, or just to break the silence that lay so tangibly around her that she fancied her words bounced off it, as they would have from the sounding boards in the choir loft of the Mount Zion M. E. Church. Nor was she sure how she had reached the conclusion that Jason would certainly come. It had seemed more likely that he would spend the night resting, eating, and rutting, then be gone with Easter at daylight. Besides, what could he do with one arm, probably in pain, maybe with nothing but ridiculous jungle remedies to ease him?

But then why, she had asked herself—suddenly, for no reason of which she was conscious—had he stayed at all, even with a broken arm? He could have taken Easter and food with him, and surely a night's rest was worth less than a night's head start on Sheriff Maxton's dogs.

So Jason had a *reason* to stay, to take such a chance. No other explanation. She puzzled for a while over what could possibly have caused him so greatly to increase his risk of being captured. Then she realized—almost with shame for her own stupidity— that the reason had been right in front of her all along.

Found the purse'n money hid up under'is bed the sheriff had said. Miss Tippy's purse. Jason's bed.

Of course, that was it. Jason wanted money. He'd murdered Miss Tippy for money, murdered Pettigrew trying to escape, and still he had no money to show for any of it.

At first Amy tried to think whether there was money in the house. Real money. She could wake Willis, send money out to Jason . . . but of course she wouldn't find more than a few dollars, no matter where she looked. Not even in the General's old safe. Sycamore didn't run on cash.

Knowing there wasn't any money, that she couldn't buy Jason off, stiffened her again. *Even if I had it I wouldn't give it to that black ape.*

Oh, that would have been the womanish way—fearful, cringing—exactly the way Amy had decided she'd no longer be. She touched the pistol in her lap, knowing then for sure that Jason would come. *He* would not know there was no money; he would assume there *had* to be money in the big house, the master's house.

"So he's got to come for it."

The words came back at her from the dark rooms, mocking her resolution. She wished she hadn't sent Bess away. Bess was big and strong; she could have been a help when Jason came.

When he finds out there's no money.

What would he do then, angry and frustrated there in that house of masters—a black man alone with a white woman? Amy knew exactly what Jason would do, and she stood up, for the first time since she'd taken her place by the window, and went two steps toward the hall door, wanting to run, to fly right through the walls, hide in the woods, go anywhere Jason couldn't catch her. Then she remembered his broken arm, felt the grim metal of the pistol in her hand, and her panic stilled again. She went back to her chair, peering over the lawn toward the cabins.

So it had come down to this. Her life, the customs that had controlled her, the rules she'd followed so religiously—in the end they'd only brought her here, alone, with a gun in her hand, waiting for Jason. No protection in the customs, no deliverance in the rules. She put the revolver in her lap, feeling it heavy, intrusive; it reminded her of the General, the child she guarded, the one she probably carried within her. And suddenly Amy was eager for Jason to come. *That* would be reality, after a lifetime of deception.

But the moment of eagerness passed as quickly as it had come, leaving Amy thankful to Pettigrew for breaking Jason's arm. Because he can't, she thought. Even Jason can't throw me down and do it to me with only one arm.

That was the last thought that went through Amy's head before her eyes closed.

Charlie Keach had had no time, on his breakneck dash through Washington, to get in touch with Hale. Keach was nervous about that; Hale might never forgive him for bypassing his bureau chief on the best story of the war. On the other hand, Hale lived for their newspaper. Surley he'd realize, when Keach had a chance to explain, that getting on to New York with the copy was the important thing.

When the steamer had docked, there'd been barely enough time to catch the Baltimore train—and at that, Keach, unable to find a hack, had had to run most of the way across Washington to the station. Well, he'd just have to hope the nigger boy he'd hired had been honest enough to deliver his note to Hale, because Hale could make or break his correspondents.

Keach knew he should be exhausted—up most of the night before, on the field all day, often under fire; then the wearying ride to Pohick and the steam trip up the Potomac, the race across Washington, the rattling ride to Baltimore that had put him on the New York express with just under five minutes to spare. In fact, he was fired up like the huffing locomotive up front; the long ride ahead of him seemed too short for the work he had to do—the story that would cheer up the nation and make him famous.

Keach had taken a window seat and was annoyed when at the last minute, as the express began to pull out of the Baltimore station, the aisle seat next to him was occupied by a portly man in a checked suit who pulled an apple from his pocket, and began to eat it with loud cracking noises. Soon, most of the few other passengers in the swaying car were asleep or nodding.

"Don't know about you, friend." The checked suit dropped the apple core into a spittoon. "But come November, I'm going Democrat."

"Ummm."

In the dim light from the overhead lanterns, Keach was forcing himself to review the notes he'd managed to take, scribble off recollections he'd had no time to write down earlier, and organize his thoughts and impressions. The wheels clicked steadily over the rails. He really wanted to get right at the story itself, but Hale had taught him that proper preparation was essential.

Not enough just to give the news of victory; in a story of such importance, he had to convey *how* it had happened, how it had looked and sounded. Hale said a good reporter never forgot that nothing happened in an empty room. The reader wanted to know the circumstances, the surroundings, the weather, every detail that could help him see as well as understand.

Up ahead, the locomotive sounded its whistle mournfully. Keach tried to remember Pope's precise words in their last conversation. *We occupy the field on our right. We still hold . . .*

"That Linkum, he aint fit to drive a two-mule team, much less run no war. Oh, I'm going Democrat, all right."

Had Pope said *the ground* or *the position on our left that we held this morning?*

"Not that I aint patriotic as the next man. But what I say, friend, you gonna fight a war, you ought to fight to win it. Right?"

"I'm sorry," Keach said. "I'm trying to work."

"Oh, say, I'd never interfere a man's work. You just go right ahead, don't pay no mind to me."

The only question was how successful King's twilight attack down the pike might have been. Keach knew he'd had to leave when he did, or he wouldn't be speeding through the night on the New York express, bound for fame. Still, if King had hit Jackson as hard on the right as Kearny had hit him on the left . . .

"I always say a man's got to work, he's just got to work. Got to put bread on the table and clothes on the little woman's back."

Keach was about ready to start writing. He was not sure whether his first impulse—to start right off with victory in the first line—was correct. Hale said that sometimes you should back into it, building up a little atmosphere and suspense.

But Keach's major problems at the moment were a surface to write on, and paper. He'd had no time to get hold of paper even if there'd been a place to buy it in the middle of the night. Of course, Hale would have thought to have paper stored away somewhere, no matter how long he'd been in the field.

"Linkum's got trouble that way, so they say. His old woman can't stay outten the dress shops."

Keach had a few blank pages in his pocket notebook and an old letter from his father fortunately written on only one side of each of three sheets. He had snatched two train-schedule flyers from a Baltimore station bulletin board and could write on their blank sides. That would have to do, although he knew he could write forever, just go on and on, about what he'd decided to call "Pope's master stroke at Manassas."

"Say, friend . . ." The man in the checked suit leaned close and lowered his voice to a rasp: "You ever heard Linkum got a little touch-a the tarbrush?"

Keach stood up, stuffing his notes and paper into his pockets. "Friend," he said, "whyn't you shut your goddamn dirty mouth?"

He pushed past the checkered trousers and went along the aisle, between sleeping passengers, toward the potbellied stove at the rear end of the car.

"Whatsa matter . . ." The rasp followed him relentlessly. "You a damn Republican?"

Balancing himself against the rocking of the car, Keach walked on to the stove, which was cold in August. Its flat top was dirty but would have to do for a desk; he liked to write standing up anyway. Opening the notebook to the first clean page, he thought a minute, tonguing his pencil, trying to look at things with Hale's eyes. Then he made up his mind.

He began to write his lead just as he had first planned it on the deck of the little steamer struggling up the Potomac:

As darkness closed a sanguinary day on the banks of Bull Run and the trampled fields that flank it, Mars quenched at last the Union's thirst for victory . . .

The night wore on, hideous with screams, and the orange torch-glow fell over the Sudley churchyard as it had on the camp meetings recalled from youth. But Sergeant Owen L. Cade, Company D, Thirteenth Georgia, would not let himself lose consciousness.

He knew he was a goner. He'd seen enough Miniés in the gut to know how they tore up everything in there. No point thinkin bout it.

He set his mind, instead, upon one objective as grimly as if he were again leading the Company across the field toward the rail fence and the swarming Yanks. He made up his mind that he would see the sun rise one more time.

Hardly count the times I seen it a-ready. Not just in Ol Jack's army, where a man who woke up with the sun in his eyes risked hard duty and short rations. On the farm, too—all those years of sunup to sundown. Man wants to scratch a livin outten land what'll go back to brush while he takes a nap, he got to look sharp.

So he'd seen sunup . . . oh, how many times? In his pain and determination, not letting himself think of anything else, Cady calculated intently.

Twenty-four year old, nearbout. Say inna field age six to twenny-two. Fourteen year. No . . . sixteen. April into fall'n then some. Make it six month time sixteen.

Cady's schooling had stopped at the tenth table and he was not up to the sum. But he could figure that ten years times six months was sixty and six more years was thirty-six more months, so he rounded off at one hundred months of thirty days each. Making either three hundred or three thousand sunrises. Minus Sundays.

Too much trouble to tell which, with a hole clear thew my gut. Don't make no nevermind noway. More sunups'n a man got'ny use fer. Plus Ol Jack fer nigh two more year callin it dawn anytime past midnight.

So why, then, on his last legs, dumped in a graveyard with the other goners, would a body with that kind of practice make a fuss even to himself about one more sun?

Ought to be gittin right with the Good Lord instead. Makin a will, was they aught to leave. Or anybody savin Paw to leave it to. An Paw no better'n a goner hisself. His age'n broke by the plow.

Still, Cady swore that he *would* see one more sunup. It was one thing to be a goner. But it was another just to lie down and die. Even gutshot.

See at sunrise cause I set my *mind* to see it.

And Grice. Cady had no clear sense that he was lying with his head in the New Man's lap. But he knew that come sunup, Grice would have to be dealt with. Walkin off ranks. Thing like at git started, won't be no ranks. Ruin the Compny. Don't watch out, Ol Jack'll round'im up'n shoot'im fer a deserter.

Cady did not aim to let that happen, but not because Grice had misguidedly tried to help him. Cady had too much respect for orders and discipline to take such a sentimental view. Speshly since at damn fool ought to see I-uz a goner soon's I-uz hit.

But even more than order and discipline — except that he knew they were of a piece, inseparable — Cady loved and respected Company D, Thirteenth Georgia. The Compny had given him what even in the flickering torchglow he felt to have been greater

riches than he had ever had a right to hope for, back-er on Paw's
ol piece of a farm.

Oh, Paw'd done'is best. And he'd taught Cady always to do
the same, no matter how hopeless things looked. But the Compny
had given Cady a place, a purpose, pride in both, the respect of
men; far different, what the Compny gave, than anything a man
could scratch out of Georgia dirt, sunup to sundown.

Way the Compny followed *me,* Owen L. Cade, what never
saw the inside of a officer's uniform—now that-uz a thing to
remember. Compny knew a man to follow, they got a look at'im.
Couldn't fool the Compny, I-God!

Even with his guts in his hands, Cady felt again the mastery
of those moments crossing the field in the dying light of the sun.
The Compny had made up for all that Georgia dirt. The Compny
was Cady's life, that was the long and short of it; and in the
graveyard among the goners, holding out for the sun to rise, he
thanked his lucky stars that the Compny had given him that life,
even at the price of death.

And Grice was part of the Compny, pore excuse that he was.
So Grice had to be looked out for, even if he had gone against
orders. Cady did not intend that any man of the Compny—*his*
Compny, I-God!—should be shot for a deserter or held up as a
disgrace to Ol Jack. Not even one as sorry as the New Man.

In the torchglow he could just see Grice's face above him.
Asleep with his mouth open. Damn fool, Cady thought, as the
stabs of pain in his vitals, recurrent as breath, searing as claws,
convulsed him again around the spilling core of his life. Damn
fool could of been back witha Company by now, nobody knowin
the better. He did not realize that he had groaned aloud, a sound
as tortured as if his soul were being drawn out of the hole in his
stomach.

Well, come sunup. Deal with Grice. Come sunup. Deal with
everdam thing.

"Cady?" The New Man leaned over him anxiously. "Y'all
right? Want'ny thing?"

"Sunup," Cady said.

Sometime after that, Chaplain Hornby lay wide awake at last,
hurting from his broken leg and the wound in his arm, but in
agony from the fear in his heart. The effect of the opium pills had

worn off. He wished for more to ease his physical pain, but he dared not risk again opium's spoiled harvest of dreams—if, real as these nightmares seemed, they were dreams, not some sort of horrid unrealized truth.

Waking or sleeping, he saw her tiny fine-boned features floating near him, like the face of a drowned person drifting just beneath the water—haunting him, wracking him with what he dared not think might be his own innate desires; surely they were instead opium's evil distortions. Horrible, inexplicable, that in his drugged delirium he had seen her actually naked (when in conscious life he had never so much as glimpsed a woman's limbs above the ankle, let alone the unimaginable rest of one), writhing on a bed of scarlet like some diminutive demon of allure; worse, he had seen himself yielding, their bodies entwining. He could not bear to recall how eagerly he had indulged, in the devilish glow of opium, a carnality he could not believe lurked so near the surface of a believing Christian's life. Was he not of God's work a witness, of God's law an officer?

In his despair the chaplain even wished for pain from his arm and leg to overwhelm these tormenting memories—no, no, dreams! Nightmares! For memory registered nothing like these drug-born orgies. He had only tried to protect her; and she had seemed scarcely more than a child in need of manly aid...

Chaplain Hornby had been looking that day for his brother (of the Ninety-seventh New York). The chaplain thought himself well in the rear of the Federal lines when the battle he had stumbled into—later called Slaughter's Mountain—began to surge in the Rebels' favor. Hornby supposed so, at least, for the blueclad groups of men streaming past him to the rear were bigger, more numerous; and a group of Federal surgeons and their orderlies hurriedly began leaving a white frame house, surrounded by open fields in which the two armies had clashed. The house obviously had been made into a field hospital.

Hornby, seeing he had got too near the lines of battle, was about to make his own retreat when he caught sight of a figure sprawled on the porch of the frame house, one of dozens of men lying there or on the trampled lawn. Something in this particular form so resembled Hornby's inner impression of his brother that, for a moment forgetting danger, he dismounted and ran to the house. But when he knelt by the wounded man, he saw immediately that it was not his brother—a good thing, because the man had had his jaw blown away and stared up at the chaplain with puzzled, furious, dying eyes.

As Hornby backed hastily away—the funerals he had preached had been over closed coffins; death, to him, had not been associated with the human form—he came abreast of a window opening on the porch and was amazed to see a woman staring out at him from only a few feet away. He had not seen a woman so close at hand in months and he had no idea how this lady—he could tell she was one from her bearing and the modish dress fringed with lace at collar and cuffs—came to be there in the midst of carnage. In his hazy view through drifting smoke and the faintly distorting glass, he thought for a moment she might be a vision.

The chaplain stepped quickly to the door; but as soon as he entered a hallway littered with more dead and wounded, the stench of blood, death, excretion, and chloroform made him gag and stop. Steadying himself, he strode on over the smashed men on the floor, into the room where he had seen the woman.

She stood unmoving, her hands clasped before her, staring out the window; small, he saw, boned as delicately as a wren, with a face of ineffable sorrow.

"Ma'am? May I be of help?"

She took no notice of his appearance or words.

"Ohhh . . . *God* . . . it hurts . . . God!"

The chaplain paid no attention to the blasphemy of the wounded—could not let himself think of them, for whom he could do so little, when this birdlike rigid creature, obviously lost amid the horrors underfoot, seemed so in need of help he might actually be able to give.

"Chaplain Hornby." He took a step forward, extending his arm toward her. "Twenty-fourth New York. I . . ."

Then he saw the pile of arms and legs under the harpsichord behind her, and stopped speaking, stunned and sickened. Trickles of darkening blood spilled drying from the human refuse, and Hornby thought weirdly for a moment of his mother's compost pile behind the house in Elmira. On it she had thrown the table scraps, chicken bones, coffee grounds, stale bread, and kitchen garbage that would decompose into fertilizer for her truck garden. But what foul crop could spring from the compost under the harpsichord? The chaplain hastily averted his eyes and stepped closer to the woman's side.

"Got to come away from here, ma'am. You can't stay in this charnel house!"

Still she did not move, nor did her sorrowing face lighten at the sound of his voice. Hornby thought she probably had not heard—perhaps because of the musketry crackling ever closer, more likely because she was far off, mad perhaps, driven from sanity by sights Hornby believed no woman and few men should see or could stand.

"Ma'am . . . are you all *right?* Can . . ."

Through the window just then he caught sight of Rebs running past the house, pausing to fire, running on—lean, bearded men, frightening in their nondescript tatters, looking more like bandits than soldiers. Panic rose in Hornby; he had never seen Rebs before, or heard muskets fired in anger. He looked wildly around, saw through the open door to the hall the first steps of a carpeted staircase.

Hide upstairs. But she . . . can't just leave her . . .

Not thinking, fear urging him, he swept the woman into his arms, her slightness hardly a burden, and ran from the room, nearly tripping over the extended leg of a corspe with a fixed derisive grin above its gaping neck. The woman made no effort to resist but held herself rigidly as a doll in his arms.

Hornby took the curving flight of stairs two at a time, then ran heavily along a hallway—no bodies, Thanks Be for no bodies in the hall—with two doors on each side. He kicked open the rear door on the left and entered a large bedroom with a canopied four-poster against one wall.

The chaplain nudged the door closed behind him and carefully placed the woman, as if she might break, on the spacious bed. As he did so, he saw ornate letters engraved on a silver watch pinned to her slight bosom: a large C in the center, entwined by two smaller S's. She stared at him calmly, seeing nothing, her mournful face unchanged.

Mad, he thought. Driven mad. Such a beautiful creature. Like Dresden.

He was still frightened by the battle surging around the house but he edged to the side of the room's only window and looked toward where the main battle seemed to have been fought. Fierce-looking Rebs were still running past, though the sounds of battle had moved farther on. For the first time it occurred to him that he might be captured. He had only thought before of being hit, reduced to the kind of hulk he had seen littered on the floor below.

Hornby shrank away from the window, pondering his predicament. Maybe if the Rebs kept moving, he could hide out here till dark, then get away if necessary on foot. He shouldn't have left his horse. Maybe if they caught him, they'd give a chaplain special treatment, even if they did look like a band of marauders. Rebs were said to be God-fearing, in their own way.

He saw that the room was warm, sunny, neat. The kind of room, he thought, you'd expect for a delicate person like the exquisite little being on the bed. The room's dominant color was a soft blue, and there were touches everywhere—an embroidered cushion, lace on the arms of a chair, a ruffle on the four-poster— that Hornby thought of as feminine. Even with war's explosions just outside and its bloody residue scattered below, the room maintained a certain tranquillity that the chaplain, brought up in a family without sisters, associated with the women he had known before the war, at prayer meetings or over teacups.

He opened a heavy Bible, prominent on a writing table, to the family page and ran a finger down the inked entries until he came to the one he wanted:

Lawrence Morton Crowell m Sally Dean Sutherland At Centreville, Va. 5th October 1860. Till death do them part.

SSC. Sally Sutherland Crowell. Hornby was surprised. More like a child than a married woman.

But there was one more entry:

Lt. Lawrence Morton Crowell, 1st Va. Cavalry. Of blessed memory. Died near Stone Bridge, 21 July 1861, serving God and Country.

A widow. This child! Couldn't even be eighteen years old. No wonder she had lost her reason. Married less than a year before the first battle of the war had widowed her. And now that dreadful mess under her harpsichord.

She was as still on the bed as the pillows cushioning her. Chaplain Hornby tiptoed nearer; but he no longer sought to speak to her, in fact almost feared to arouse her. Knowing what she'd endured, he now thought she might be truly mad, and he did not want a lunatic on his hands, with the whole Confederate army running by outside.

Then he saw with revulsion that the delicate white boot on her left foot was darkly smeared, over the instep and up to the point at which he had seen to it that her long skirt covered her ankles. He tiptoed to the bedside and leaned closer. Blood, of course. All over the boot.

Hornby found this sight inexpressibly shocking, as if he had witnessed the desecration of something sacred. In his sermons, he did not dwell on the Virgin Mary. All that, he believed, could be left to the Romans, with their curious need for lurid paintings, crucifixes, saints' finger bones, and other images and symbols of religion made flesh. As a Methodist, the Reverend E. P. Hornby preached instead on the Word and the Trinity, although he sometimes thought approvingly to himself of the Immaculate Conception.

As he stared down at the little bloodstained boot that marred the white wraithlike form on the bed, confused impressions raced across his frightened mind—the Virgin Mother, bleeding feet of Christ on the Cross, flesh under the harpsichord, sacrifice of a virginal child to blood gods . . .

Chaplain Hornby could not bear, finally, the sight of that white boot darkened by corruption. With trembling hands, one under the heel, the other on the laces, he lifted the boot from the bed and began to remove it from her foot. But as his fingers fumbled at the laces, he saw that the hem on her skirt, too, was rimmed with drying blood. Instinctively, he snatched at the stained hem to prevent any touch of it against innocent flesh.

As befitted his calling and his sensibility, E. P. Hornby was proudly chaste; he would have averted his eyes from the least glimpse of a woman's limbs until that moment when in shock and horror he lifted Sally Sutherland Crowell's skirt. Oddly, her ankle appeared to him then as a calming vision; he thought he had never seen a form so beautiful, so nearly perfect in line and curve, so moving in its vulnerability to the obscene smear on boot and hem. Sally's ankle, like Sally herself, was lovely, and suggestive of sorrow beyond measure.

Just then her boot came away in his hand and her tiny foot dropped to the coverlet. Perhaps the movement somehow penetrated the comatose state in which Hornby had found her; perhaps some fierce crash from beyond the house, not even noticed by the chaplain in his fixation upon her ankle, pierced her suspended consciousness. Or perhaps not. But as Hornby's tender fingers just touched her, Sally began to scream.

"No!" the chaplain cried. "Please . . . no! Oh, don't . . . please
don't . . ."

"Goddammit." A medical orderly who had been sneaking a
drink of surgical brandy behind some nearby bushes handed the
bottle to a friend. "Crazy parson's yelling again. If he don't beat
all."

Not far from the hospital depot, at General Pope's headquarters
camp, Captain Micah G. Duryea was just then awakened in pitch
darkness by an impatient hand on his shoulder.

"Work for you." Colonel Russell's voice identified the shape
kneeling beside Duryea's blankets. "Hurry it up now."

Duryea quickly pulled on his boots and joined the colonel by
the low flicker of a camp fire.

"Pickets just sent back word they're hearing sounds over there
like Hood's maybe pulling back west."

"From where?"

"From where Hatch run into'im on the pike at sundown. Right
about Groveton."

"Hood's with Longstreet, isn't he?"

"One of the best he's got."

"So . . ." Duryea could not resist the moment. "Longstreet *is*
up."

"Well . . . Hood is, anyway. We know that much." Russell chose
his words so carefully that Duryea assumed the colonel spoke
someone else's thoughts. "General Pope doubts they could've got
Longstreet's whole crowd here yet. Nobody saw anything of 'em
until sundown and then just Hood."

Duryea hoped his silence was eloquent enough to convey his
contempt for this reasoning.

"Now pickets telling us Hood sounds like he's pulling back.
Hatch hit'im pretty hard tonight but he was outgunned. And it got
dark fore we could reinforce'im."

Unusually garrulous, Duryea thought. Though Russell had never
been tight-lipped. Might have had a few drinks—for his bad teeth,
of course.

"I don't want to wake Pope up unless I'm sure the pickets are
right. Don't get enough sleep as it is. So slip down the pike aways
and see if Hood's moving or if the pickets just got jumpy nerves."

"He could just be pulling back from an exposed position. Back
to the rest of Longstreet's line."

"If Longstreet's got a line. Which the general don't think he has."

Duryea tried hard to keep the impatience out of his voice, yet to speak with the urgency he felt. "Colonel . . . Longstreet's out there in front of Porter. Come daylight, I can take you over there and show you his battle flags. Lee's got his whole army in front of you."

Russell sighed. The fire popped and hissed. Not far away, men were snoring and sighing in the sleep of exhaustion. The predawn darkness was so thick the colonel was only a vague form against the fire.

"I wouldn't be surprised, Duryea. But Pope . . . he feels like he whipped'em yesterday. He thinks they'll be running for the mountains today."

Duryea judged from the resigned, almost relieved, tone of Russell's words that he did not believe them either—that he might even have tried, himself, to convince Pope of the truth.

"Never saw a man so full of himself." Russell nudged a log with the toe of his boot; a tongue of fire flared above the embers, and died. "Kicking Tom Jackson's tail like that."

Duryea suddenly knew that he could stand no more. *Ex nihilo nihil fit!* He remembered almost wistfully the satisfying moment by the old Warrenton road when he had acted on his own, done what needed to be done without dither or remorse, if they were ever to whip the slavers.

"I'll go see about Hood, Colonel."

The captain faded into the darkness. Russell stretched out full-length by the fire, his head on his saddle, and gazed up into the void where the heavens should have been.

No more sleep tonight. Not with my teeth. And so much on my mind. Besides, Duryea was probably right. As usual.

Colonel Russell hoped Duryea would report back that the pickets were wrong, that Hood was still across the pike, right where he'd stopped after driving Hatch back at sundown. Because if Hood *was* pulling back, the way the pickets claimed, that would be one more bit of evidence to feed John Pope's feverish conviction that the Rebs were on the run—that he'd whipped'em, by God, and was on the verge of the biggest victory of the war.

Well, maybe so. Maybe Pope's got better instincts than any of us. Why he's in command and we ain't.

Pope was a fighter, you had to give him that; and Colonel Russell had seen enough of war to know that a fighter's hunches could be his most important weapons. Then again, not always. But you had to allow a fighter his hunches anyway. Lee would certainly let Stonewall have his.

Tom Jackson. Who'd ever thought, back at the Point, that Tom Jackson would turn into the famous Stonewall? With his crazy diet and looking on horseback like a crow about to fly.

Colonel Russell sat up, hoping the change of position might ease his aching teeth. But it didn't.

Trouble with Pope's hunch was, if Duryea proved as right as he usually did and Lee's whole army was out there ready to fight, the "pursuit" Pope planned would be like sticking your head down a cannon's mouth while looking for the shot. Especially since Pope, raging at Fitz-John Porter's failure to attack on the left that afternoon, had ordered Porter peremptorily to march his corps to the field of battle—Pope's field, of course, where Sigel and Hooker and Kearny had fought their all-day battle with Stonewall.

Because if Duryea *was* right, what Pope had done with that order was to pull Porter off Longstreet's flank, where he'd have been in position to keep that wing of the Reb army on the defensive. Take Porter off Longstreet's flank and there'd be nothing to stop Lee from sending Jackson *and* Longstreet over to the offensive. In which case, who would turn out to be pursuing whom?

Russell sighed again, feeling his teeth and his years, knowing it was easy for him to question Pope's decisions since he himself had to make none of such consequence. He was glad of that, and a little ashamed to be glad—not what they'd taught him at the Point. But Pope was like a sea captain in a fog; if he read the signals wrong, he'd go down with his ship. Who'd want to be in such a position?

Still, Russell knew what he'd do if he were in command. And he thought he just might be hearing the foghorns and warning bells more clearly than John Pope. And as for mighty Stonewall Jackson . . . well . . . Delancy Russell just happened to have finished higher in *his* class than Tom Jackson had in his. And that was in the records for anyone who wanted to see.

He heard heavy footsteps behind him and turned to see a bulky form, preceded by the glowing tip of a cigar, emerge from the darkness.

"That you, Russell?" General Pope sounded surprised to find anyone before him at the fire. "Heard anything from that damned Porter?"

The snake was black, glistening; it writhed across the grass in lazy S's longer than those of the entwined serpents on a doctor's staff. In no hurry, the snake came on steadily, its diamond eyes and flicking tongue searching ahead. It crossed the spot where Pettigrew's body had lain, then coiled on toward the house, the faint trail it left in the grass erasing itself almost as soon as the thick body passed.

Amy watched as if in a trance the snake's sinuous approach She was afraid of snakes. Practically everybody was, of course, but Amy's fear was particular; she'd got it from her mother, who would turn pale and fainting at the mere thought of what she always referred to only as "things"—as if the word "snake" itself could strike.

Amy's greatest secret horror was of waking to find a snake in her bed, as the General had told her sometimes happened to soldiers rolled in their blankets in the western desert; and she was not quick to dismiss the Africans' tales of coach-whip, which could lash a human to death with its powerful tail, or the hoopsnake, which took its tail in its mouth and rolled like a wheel, faster than anyone could run, until it overtook its prey.

But this snake was no such mythical creature. This was the real thing, exotic only in its glistening blackness and its insinuating undulant evil. Despite her fear, or perhaps because of it, Amy could not take her eyes from it; and as it neared, the tongue flashed farther and faster, red against the black, and the sensuous body grew thicker and longer, until—as its tail was just gliding across the place where Pettigrew had fallen—the head with its brilliant eyes began to rise wickedly before the window.

The snake coiling in the grass made a dry, rasping sound. Amy was transfixed in horror. The long red tongue lashed suddenly against the window pane with a sharp crack . . .

Startled from sleep, Amy woke with sweat moist on her forehead, under her arms, between her breasts. The window was before her, clear, untouched, and beyond it the lawn she had watched all night; as her eyes adjusted to wakefulness, she saw that the lawn, too, was as it had been—empty, dark, menacing. The gun lay heavily on her clenched thighs.

Then she heard again the rasp of the snake on the grass; but instead of the crack of the red omnivorous tongue against the

window, a faint loose rattle of wood echoed through the dark
house. Amy recognized this time the sound of the parlor window
closing—the one that opened into the house from the verandah.
Its sash was loose in the frame and always rattled that way; so
she knew Jason was in the house, had crept across the lawn while
she dreamed the snake's approach.

But she felt no panic. As she eased back the hammer of the
General's pistol, in fact, Amy was even relieved by the reality of
what she had fancied from the beginning, that she would come
face to face with Jason—no more hiding within voluminous skirts,
hemmed in by rigid rules of conduct. The gun, not a woman's
implement, was solid in her hand; its butt was clammy with her
sweat—sweat a lady was no more supposed to possess than she
was a gun. She was ready, against all expectations, in the darkness
that equalized all.

She stood up and in her stocking feet moved soundlessly across
the office floor, past the big table of the sewing factory, and to
the door that led into the wide-paneled hall. She realized she
actually had advantages other than the pistol; she knew every
corner of the house, even which steps and which floorboards
creaked. Jason didn't. And he had a broken arm.

The hall was opaque. Nothing seemed to be moving. But Jason
was inside the house. Amy could tell his presence, tangible to her
as the cold porcelain of the doorknob in her free hand. She understood then how it would be to wake with a snake in her bed; she
would not have to see it or hear it to know its malign presence.

She stepped into the hall, over the board that quacked like a
duck when anyone stepped on it, and went quickly across to the
staircase. Between railings of the banister she could look through
an open double doorway into the parlor.

Amy *knew* that from knowing the old house, its every angle
and space; actually she could *see* nothing but a faintly lighter
rectangle against the darkness—the parlor window. The crack
when he forced it must have awakened her; then the rasp and rattle
of its closing behind him had signaled his entry.

Almost without thinking Amy had taken post by the staircase;
but she realized her instinct had been sound. For the steps led not
just to Luke but to her bed. And though she knew Jason had come
for money, she feared that he also meant to have her white body
for his black pleasure. She tightened her grip on the pistol butt,
her heartbeat quickening.

If Jason came out of the parlor into the hall, he'd be outlined momentarily against the lighter space of the window. She aimed through the railings at the vague rectangle, holding the pistol in both hands, resting them on a step at chest height.

Then she heard . . . something. But the sound was not from the parlor, or of someone moving. It was farther back in the house, in the dining room that was linked to the parlor by another set of double doors

The sound came again—clinking, rather musical. Then again. She listened carefully, every sense strained, until she felt no doubt. Jason was removing the table silver from the old sideboard in the dining room.

Amy felt terror returning, her knees weakening. She squeezed them together, clenching her muscles, rigid all over, until she was in control again, until she thought how to handle this new situation. Quietly, with infinite care, she pulled the pistol from between the railings of the banister and slipped back across the hall to the office, careful not to make the duck board quack.

Jason had known exactly which window was loose and accessible. He'd been able in pitch darkness to find the sideboard in the dining room. Someone, Easter probably, had coached him. Someone who knew the house well enough to know that there was a safe in the General's old office. Someone who would *not* know there was no money in the safe—only the General's old army commission and records, their marriage certificate, some ledgers reflecting the farm operations of Sycamore, the deed to some worthless, rattlesnake-infested land he'd bought in Texas.

First the silver. Then Jason would have a try at the safe, looking for the money he needed—the money he coveted enough to have got himself into his desperate predicament. Too nigger ignorant to know he couldn't open a safe without a keg of gunpowder to blow the door off. And when he found *that* out . . . he'd surely think he needed Amy to open it for him. *Before* he did the other.

So they'd settle it, at last, in the old office, now the sewing factory, where the safe was. Amy left the hall door widely ajar, then stationed herself against the wall behind it, retaining an angle of vision across the sewing-factory table toward the window before which she had sat for most of the night, against which the nightmare snake had lashed its searching tongue. The pistol was still cocked but now she held it pointing at the floor, as if its weight dragged down her weak woman's arms.

Amy listened to the eerie clink of silver. Strange ghostly music of entrance and violation! Its dissonance and irregularity were as intrusive upon the stillness of the house as Jason himself. But when the sound faded into silence, with a last, louder ring—a serving spoon, perhaps, dropped among the heavy old A-mono-grammed knives and forks that had come down to Amy from some forgotten Arnall wife (the General believed perhaps his great-grandmother)—when the sound was gone, she wished she could hear it again. It placed Jason.

But Amy had stopped running, as she knew she had run all her woman's life. She was at bay, without men or the rules they set or their wealth to shelter her; and Jason was coming snakelike out of the night. Amy had no choice but to confront him; and in the terrible equality of the darkness, she told herself she was capable of anything.

The duck board quacked in the hall. Amy raised the gun, pointing it at the window, sensing the springed resistance of the trigger. Squeeze it, the General had said. Squeeze it—don't jerk. Just the way he'd taught her to handle his other thing. She braced herself, as he'd told her to, against the weapon's upward thrust, the crashing concussion from its muzzle.

A shadow intruded on the gray rectangle of the window. Calmly, Amy moved the pistol two inches left to bear on the center of the shadow. No choice now. She tightened her finger on the trigger. Squeeze. Don't jerk. Squeeze . . .

Then the roar of the gun, unbelievably louder in the closed room than she had expected, the powerful upward kick, the powder flash lurid as lightning, the echoes crashing from the walls. When her eyes cleared from the muzzle flare and her ears stopped ringing, Amy saw the lighter rectangle unmarred by shadow; and heard from beyond the sewing table something scraping and gasping on the floor, with the horrid sibilance of a gigantic snake coiling and uncoiling in the night.

Sergeant Amos Gilmore, despite his exhaustion, woke with the first dull light of the new day and was immediately conscious of the boy sleeping beside him. Restraining his own movements so he would not wake him, the sergeant lifted his head and shoulders and peered around to make sure no one was about. Couldn't be too careful.

But no one was visible from the little gully where they'd spread their blankets. Gilmore lay back and cocked an eye at the eastern sky. He gave himself a few minutes to stay warm in his blankets, savor the good night's sleep he'd had, and feel the long leanness of the boy against his side.

Miracle just to be alive after the fight they'd had yesterday. And a double miracle to wake up with the boy and know there was still a little time.

Gilmore cared little for God; if there was one, he reasoned, He'd be for officers. Certainly He'd have no time for a Carolina woodsman who offered the world little but a hard dick and a marksman's eye—nothing God needed. Still, Gilmore had an odd, inexplicable feeling about the business with the boy—as if maybe God, having no other use for the likes of Amos Gilmore, had meddled a little here and cleared the way there so as to hand the boy over to him on purpose.

"Gilmor," he could believe God just might have said, looking of course to His own purposes, "Gilmer, you personly aint shit But see if for once in at no-count life-a yourn yuh can make y'self useful. Take care-a this-yer poet-type that can't likely do it for hisself."

Which Amos Gilmore aimed to do even if God hadn't said any such thing, which He probly hadn't, being an officer's God for sure. As for what he and the boy did in their blankets, that was no business even of God's, let alone any earthly creature, for the simple and sound reason—as the sergeant saw it—that they wa'n't hurtin a soul.

Course Ironass wouldn't see it that way. Might come huntin'is orderly any minute, too.

Gilmore groped carefully under the blankets and took hold of Folsom. He put his lips against the boy's ear and whispered:

"Gittin light."

Folsom sighed and stirred; Gilmore could feel the boy's flesh rising in his hand, warm as a cat. He stroked a little and the boy moaned, turned his head and kissed the sergeant, just as a distant shout from Ironass blasted the morning silence:

"Folsom! You Folsom! Get up here'n get some fire goin!"

Missy also had awakened with the dawn. In the warmth of the buffalo robe, his muscular body half-turned against her and his breathing regular and deep in her ear, she thought the first moment of consciousness might have been her finest ever—finer even than all the fine moments of the night before, because then she'd been half out of her mind, carried away by her body and his, hardly thinking, just *being*.

But this morning she not only had it all to recall, every second of it, every touch, every feeling, every word and sigh and response, so that it was almost as if it were all happening again; she could *think* about it, too, about the things he'd said and she'd said, and what it all might mean. She could not only feel his mouth on her titties again and all of him inside her; she could know quite certainly that the way it had happened for her was better than it had ever happened for any other woman, any time, anywhere in the whole world. She'd never dreamed how it would be. And Sajie hadn't even told her the half of it—since neither Sajie nor any other woman ever would know, could know, what becoming a woman had been like for Missy Brace.

I am going to have this all of my life, Missy thought. This to remember, whatever else happens to me, ever.

She looked down at his head on her shoulder, the line of his jaw. She still did not even like to think his name; a name limited him, made him something shaped other than by *her* sense of him, in which he had no name but love. So she thought only, in the spreading light, how beautiful he was, with his curly hair and strong face and the touch of sadness in the corners of his mouth.

Missy thought she knew why he was sad. It made her sad, too; but she didn't have to think about it just yet, any more than she had the night before. Time enough for sadness when it couldn't be avoided. Time now only for...

His breathing changed, the arm flung across her shoulders moved a bit, and she knew he was awake. Turning her head to kiss his damp forehead, she drew her fingertips lightly down his spine to the rise of his buttocks until he stirred and whimpered.

She could see the barrel of his pistol sticking out from under the robe, an ugly reminder of the world they had so briefly escaped. Manlike, of course, he'd want to be off to his war, now that day had come. Missy understood that, had seen it even in her father— that men thought it was more important than anything to be up and about. But Missy believed she knew, too, better than any woman in the world would have, just how to keep him a little longer.

She was proud of what she knew—so much more than he'd had any idea she could know. Like taking him in her mouth that way. Sajie hadn't told her that—a thing no woman would talk about. But the one time she'd peeped with Wash, she'd seen Sajie do it with Henry. And now she could be glad even of something she was ashamed of, spying on Sajie and Henry. Because it had taught her what to do for him.

She brushed his spine with her fingertips again, moved her leg between his just so, and touched the lobe of his ear with her tongue. Time enough for war, too. But not now.

"Ummm . . . mmm."

He lifted his head and looked down at her with sleep-filled eyes, only half knowing where he was. Or who I am, she thought, understanding that, too. Then she saw in his face things coming clear; and thought his eyes lit with pleasure, and her heart jumped at the sight, she thought she saw, too, the sadness deepen in the downturn of his mouth.

"So . . . you weren't a dream, then?" He touched both of her eyes with his lips.

"Maybe I am. Maybe you're a dream, too."

Watching his mouth, she was certain of the sadness. But she would not give him time for that. Missy knew what she wanted— not just because she'd loved making love with him, more than she'd believed possible, and not even because, that morning, she loved *him* as soaringly as if, all her life, she'd been putting him together in her heart, so that he stood for everything she'd ever hoped or dreamed, everything she'd ever wished. She wanted also to take no chances; she wanted to make sure, before his maleness surrendered again to the war and the world, that she'd have him inescapably, the dream made part of her flesh.

So she moved and touched and kissed and whispered quite deliberately, with the confident newfound expertise of love's first joy; and before long she saw with satisfaction the sadness go out of his mouth and the war out of his mind, and at just the right moment, which she felt proudly she'd been born to recognize, she rolled on top of him. Because, as she had not failed to note in the night, he liked to squeeze her breasts as he entered her, just as she liked to have him do it.

And though their bodies strained together more passionately than before, their frenzy mounted more quickly, wildly, yet she managed to keep one corner of her mind clear and determined, self-possessed; so that before his warm inevitable flooding she rolled again, bringing him expertly above, believing that only in that way could her belly surely retain his bursting love. Only when she was certain, only when she knew herself full of him, she let her body race out of control in answer to his.

"My love," Missy murmured after a while, into the damp ringlets above his ear, in the momentary limitless sincerity of love. "My heart."

He lay on her for a long time, warm and unmoving. She felt him shrinking inside of her, but that was all right because she had him by then. Even when he went away, she would have him.

He moved onto his back beside her, and she felt the first faint tug of her own sadness and pushed it away, not so easily as before.

"First time." His hand groped for hers and held it tightly.

"For what?"

"You called my name."

Missy did not remember doing so but let it pass. Whatever made him happy would hold him longer.

"Listen . . . Missy . . . you know I got to go."

"To the war."

"Maybe it'll be over soon. Maybe after today."

She could tell by his tone that he was joking. She wouldn't have believed it anyway. Missy knew little about the war, but she had a strong sense that things never worked out like that—wars or anything else ending or beginning just when somebody wanted them to.

She thought of her Paw the way Maw talked of him as a young man, lean and tough, making Maw's suspicious old devil of a father accept him; and the way life and care and worn-out fields and a wife gone to fat and fear had ruined Paw, left him nothing but the bottle and the kind of false pride that expressed itself in petty tyranny over Henry and Sajie.

Missy was clear that Paw was common; he was what most of the time you had to expect, even if he was her Paw. *This* beautiful man with his ringlets and his words and the way he had of making you feel lifted out of the way things were—this man was a dream. But a person would always wake up from a dream.

Love is generous, love is understanding, and Missy was both, but more. She was pitiless, too, womanly, and her sadness was beginning to choke her.

"Aint gone be over today."

"But surely soon."

"War aint all you goin back to, anyway."

"Right now it is."

"But iffen it's over soon, way you say?"

"Oh," he said. "Well."

The light was full by then, the first edge of the sun climbing into the sky over Bull Run. Missy listened to birdcalls and felt for the first time the weight of the buffalo robe growing oppressive. She touched the hair over his ear, smoothing it back.

"S'all right."

Suddenly he was holding her fiercely. "No, it's *not* all right." His face was buried in her shoulder and his voice was muffled. "But I need you, Missy. God, how I need you."

"S'why it's all right."

She knew, as if he had said it, that he meant he needed her *now,* and she stroked the smooth skin of his shoulder again—not in order to arouse him, but soothingly, as if he were a hurt child. The stubble of his beard rasped the soft flesh of her arm as he moved his head to make his voice clearer, and his arms relaxed around her:

"See . . . I'm not part of this war. At least I don't want to be. I have to be *in* it . . . but . . . what I mean . . . most of the time I don't feel *part* of it. I'm like a man watchin a play on the stage knowin that sooner or later I have to get up there, too, and play a part. And when that time comes, I do it. Sometimes good, sometimes bad. But I'm just playin, just recitin lines. Not a real part of it."

"Like Wash play-likin he's a sojer?"

"Except that he really is playin like. I *am* a soldier, Missy, I *am* in the war. An sometimes . . ."

She sensed him groping for words, more than words, and could only stroke his shoulder.

"Sometimes . . . sometimes when I start out playin my part, I get . . . caught up. Carried away. Then I'm not playin anymore. Then I'm really part of the war, a killer, as bloodthirsty as anybody else." He lifted and turned his head to peer at her. "Make any sense?"

Missy understood only that he was trying to explain why he needed her *now,* when both of them knew he wouldn't anymore, when the war was over and the armies were gone. She pressed his head back down, welcoming the beard stubble live and immediate against her shoulder.

"But then I'm myself again . . . just lookin, just watchin the play. And I never feel so bad . . . Missy, I never feel so much like a . . . *Judas,* as I do then. After those times when I let myself be a part of the war. A killer."

Missy tried to imagine killing and war. The nearest she could come to it were the candlelit faces of all those shot boys, mangled and groaning in Brawner's field. But she could not imagine *him*—with his soft eyes and his sad mouth—having any more to do with that than sweeping her up on his black horse to carry her away from it.

"Is at why you need me?"

She loved the beard scratching her as he nodded yes.

"To be in another world. Not to be a killer."

As far as Missy understood him, this only confirmed what she had felt instinctively—that now, for her, was everything. Would have to be. Because when the war was over, he would be in another world *all the time,* safe from whatever scared him in the war. A world in which there would be no need for Isabella Brace.

"Gittin good light." She had not stopped stroking his shoulder.

"Got to go then."

She nodded, blinking back tears, though he could see neither movement. Her sadness was coming strong now, with a rush, as if all the blood in her body was moving at once to her chest; sadness was filling her, making her ache.

He sat up, looking businesslike.

"Shall I take you home?"

The thought of returning to Paw's house had not occurred to Missy. She knew Paw too well; and besides she had not looked back at all, or wanted to.

"Paw won't have me back."

He looked stern. "I'd have something to say about that. But could still be some fightin round here today."

"I'm-a stay here." Maybe never leave. Just stay right here till the snow comes and cover me up.

"Will you be all right?" Suddenly he seemed hesitant.

"Don't see why not. Aint no ways to walk, I want-a go home."

He was still hesitating and then she knew why. Their clothes were still on the bank of the run. For the first time since he'd ridden into Paw's yard, the day the Yanks came, she was irritated with him; her sadness dissolved momentarily in anger, at him, at men, life, the war, the unfairness of things.

Missy threw back the buffalo robe and got to her knees, deliberately swinging her titties in his face. She stood up and walked toward the run, swaying her hips and behind the way Maw said not to. Let'im git a good look. Let'im remember.

But a quick, cold splash in the run dashed her anger, and she was ashamed—not of displaying herself but because he'd think she was trying to hold him that way, when he had no real choice but to go. She would not have wanted him to stay anyway, unless he wanted to be with her. She dressed quickly, fighting the return of sadness, and carried his clothes to him.

He was still covered to the waist with the buffalo robe. "European." He smiled a bit sheepishly. "Positively European."

"You best hurry." Missy busied herself, folding the robe, turning her back while he pulled on his trousers.

"Keep that here, why don't you? Maybe . . ." He turned her to him with his hands on her arms. "Maybe we can meet here again tonight."

"Iffen the war aint over, you mean?"

He smiled at her and picked up his shirt. She thought she'd never seen anything as beautiful as the muscles rippling in his chest; impulsively, she put her mouth on one of his titties, as he had on hers. But he stiffened and pulled away; he was smiling but she saw that he was strangely embarrassed.

"I won't let it end. I'll make sure it lasts at least one more day."

She held out the robe. "Need it fer the war."

"But I want you to have it. If anything happens to me, I'd . . ."

He stopped, and she thought her stricken feeling must have reflected itself in her face and eyes. That he might be killed or torn up like the boys in Brawner's field had not until then occurred to her. She had been too preoccupied with her own loss, the sadness she had been fighting down like nausea. She was ashamed to have been so selfish, and pressed the buffalo robe into his arms.

"I be all right."

He did not protest further and in a few minutes was ready to go, the robe strapped behind the saddle, black Mercury looking huge and eager in the morning light.

"Tonight, then?"

Missy stroked the horse's muzzle.

"*I* be here."

"Then so will I, if I . . . if all goes well."

The sadness was so huge and heavy in her chest that she felt she would burst, and the sadness come pouring from her like water. She would not see him again, she was sure, so she tried her best to hold in her memory every detail of him—the kind brown eyes crinkled at the corners, the mustache, the ringlets, the way his ears showed through the dark hair, the chest she had tried to kiss, the sad little way his mouth turned down. She remembered how his hands touched her, and his lips, and the fullness of him within her; and she was sure, too, that she held him in her belly, alive and growing and not to be taken from her by the war or its end. But still she was sad, because she knew nothing in her life could ever take her again to the heights she had climbed already.

He swung up into his saddle, graceful as a deer on the run.

"You know, Missy . . . I don't reckon I'll ever be happier . . . than I was last night, I mean. With my European girl."

She nodded dumbly, feeling tears hot and irrepressible, believing that it might be true: even after the war, in his other world, he might not again reach such heights, either. But that only made the sadness less bearable, because she knew it didn't even matter. That wasn't his choice to make.

Missy wrapped her arms around his boots and wept openly, deep sobs racking her whole body. But she didn't care anymore; she had tried long enough to bear the sadness. In a moment she felt his hands under her arms, felt herself lifted again as easily as if she had been a flower plucked from the earth. He held her tightly against him, smothering her sobs with kisses; and her tears flowed on his cheeks, too.

"Missy . . . I love you . . . I'll love you as long as I live."

She did not try to answer or cling to him when he set her down, nor did she look after him as he rode away. That was not the way she wanted to remember him, riding off; and long after he was out of sight, she was still looking the other way, as if even the dust from Mercury's hooves might suggest a curtain falling, or a ghost, or the mist into which dreams fade.

Chapter Twelve

August 30—Morning

GENERAL HOKE ARNALL strode out of the morning mist as Sam Stowe pulled on his boots.

"Mornin, Sam." The General's voice was hoarse and rasping still, but strong again. "Need a head count soon's you can get it."

"Won't take long today, Gin'al."

Colonel Stowe had awakened with an indefinable feeling of loss. Sitting up and gazing about in the misty gray just before sunrise, he knew he was not just feeling the death of many comrades. He had become too accustomed to death for even the butchery of Arnall's Brigade and his own regiment to have induced such a profound depression. Replacements were a fact of life in the army anyway, except that there were never enough of them. A man went down and another replaced him until he went down, too; and Stowe had had to teach himself not to grieve too much over replaceable people.

He stood up and put on his straw hat, or what was left of it. Arnall grinned at him, thinly, mirthlessly.

"That's your fightin hat, aint it, Sam? Likely you'll need it again today."

In the words and the grin, Stowe sensed—he could not quite realize—what he had lost. He had thought the war an honorable enterprise; he had thought death, destruction, torn bodies, men in agony were worthwhile sacrifices for the cause, and he had been ready enough to make his own. But Sam Stowe was haunted, in

503

that bitter gray dawn, by the memory of Hoke Arnall signaling with a bloody bayonet for the slaughter to go on forever; and the grief he could not define was for his faith in the honor of the enterprise, the primacy of the cause.

"I'll be ready, Hoke. But we could sure use some more ammunition.

The General nodded. "Couldn't scare up more'n a round per man." He grinned his mirthless grin again. "Plenty of rocks on hand though."

Stowe was not a man who could face truth with unblinking eyes; he was a man of belief; and he could not push himself past even a shaken faith to the question actually troubling him: whether men fought for a cause, or for something both less and larger— not the victory but the winning of it, the mythic realization of it, the savage joy of mastery. He could not accept the knowledge that he had seen the warrior spirit wearing the mask of the cause.

"Hoke, you ever think whether . . ."

He paused, wondering how to ask what he told himself he wanted to know—whether slaughter was less justifiable because you could see a man's eyes roll and smell his bowels loosen when you stuck your bayonet in his gut?

But before he could frame the question less offensively, a messenger arrived from division headquarters. The colonel watched Arnall read the note.

"Pullin us out of the line right now, Sam. Get your men movin to the rear to cook breakfast and fill cartridge boxes."

Welcoming this news, Stowe decided not to press his question. He was not sure it was valid anyway. Was he, Sam Stowe, ready to defend his way of living, his property and heritage and family, at musket range but not at arm's length? Where blood was invisible but not where it spattered on his boots?

"Don't forget the head count, Sam."

"I'd sooner. But I won't."

He touched his hat brim and watched Arnall stride away. He knew he would have to put yesterday's mad scenes out of his mind. In a war, questions wouldn't do; questions got in the way of the business at hand.

Jubal Early's Brigade, which had come up in the nick of time the night before, had been ordered into the railroad cut on Arnall's right and now was designated to hold the left flank until Arnall's men could return. So before Private Larkin Folsom could boil General Arnall's morning coffee, he had to stamp out his fire and join the movement out of the line. In the absence of explanation, Folsom assumed that Hill's Division and probably the army were retreating. High time, he thought, grabbing up his few cooking utensils.

"Lemme give yuh a hand ther." Sergeant Gilmore picked up General Arnall's small wooden mess chest as lightly as if it had been an abandoned canteen.

"Glad we're gettin out of here." Folsom gazed in distaste at the unburied Yanks still littering the rocky ground.

"Reck'n we be back." Gilmore squinted over his shoulder at Early's men, on alert in the railroad cut. "Ol Jack, he aint givin up no ground he aint druv off of."

Colonel Channing, who was already circulating General Jackson's orders for the day, would have made the same point in somewhat more proper military terminology. He knew Jackson was preparing for another fight—counts the day lost without one, Channing thought—and had no intention of giving up the cuts and embankments that had proved such a formidable defense line.

Instead, the orders for the day divided Jackson's force into two lines. A thin front was to be maintained along the old railroad, but most of the brigades were pulled back about 200 yards, up the wooded ridge behind, where they could rest, feed themselves, and replenish their ammunition—and where, not least, they were hidden from Federal field glasses.

Jackson, as usual, had kept his own counsel, but Channing assumed these dispositions were designed to lure Pope into renewed attack. Privately, the colonel doubted the ruse would fool a wet-eared plebe; but Channing had learned not to question Ol Jack's plans, let alone his instincts.

"You think they comin again?" Captain Thad Selby was riding with Channing toward the right flank to see what signs of Yank activity might be visible from there.

"With Longstreet up and us still here . . ." Channing drew rein to pick a handful of blackberries the troops had somehow overlooked. "Was I Pope, I'd git Bull Run twixt him'n us. But I aint, and he mought not."

"Seem like he took enough of a lickin yesterday."

"Probly thinks the same bout us. Have some blackberries."

"I better not, Colonel. My belly's like it's on fire."

They rode on along the line. "Don't worry bout it, son." Boy's got a case of nerves, Channing thought. Better git'im busy. "Any man's belly can stand a war, sump'm's *really* wrong with'im."

When they reached the far right flank, Colonel Channing and Captain Selby paused to observe the artillery linking Jackson's wing to Longstreet's. In a broken line running down toward the Warrenton Pike, four batteries deploying eighteen of Jackson's pieces, their tubes shining with lethal promise, were ready for action.

"Now that..." A touch of awe deepened Channing's voice. *"That* is a position, son."

He was not an artilleryman, but men who followed Ol Jack came to know ground; and Channing saw at once that these guns formed a powerful hinge between Jackson's and Longstreet's infantry lines, where they met in a slightly open angle. All were pointing east—roughly parallel to the Warrenton Pike—and had a clear field of fire over undulating pastures and orchards spanned by several rail fences. Even in the early-morning light and the peace of a new day the colonel could imagine the shattering of their muzzles erupting as one. Murder, he thought.

"Looks like they could whip Pope by themself." Selby almost forgot his stomach at the sight of the guns.

Shouting voices drifted up the slope. Some of Jackson's gunners seemed to be running about and playing games in the broomsedge.

"Boys in good spirits, looks like."

Channing pushed back his slouch hat; already the day was hot enough for sweat to pop on his forehead. He touched his horse's flanks and ambled along the ridge for a closer look, Selby following.

The gunners had discovered that the woods and fields abounded with rabbits; but they had been kept too closely on the alert the day before to take advantage of the sport and provender thus offered. Some, filling their pockets and hats with rocks, had seized the opportunity a quiet morning afforded. They formed lines and moved over the field, somewhat too noisily for good results.

But one of the gunners finally flushed a rabbit and chased it toward his battery mates. As the terrified animal bounded toward them, they converged on it with low whoops. One let fly a rock at the rabbit's head but missed by a yard. As other rocks pelted around it, the rabbit veered right, straight toward a stocky young private who slammed a rock into the ground a foot ahead of its nose. Leaping to its left, the rabbit broke through the closing circle of gunners. They gave laughing chase, straight toward Channing and Selby.

The two officers pulled up to stay out of the way, just as the stocky private threw his last rock. It caught the rabbit in the back and knocked it flat. The gunners closed in. More rocks flew, smashing the rabbit's head and one of its legs and part of its ribcage. Then the stocky private leaned down and seized the rabbit by the ears and held it up, bleeding and jerking, while his companions applauded.

"Run like Yanks from Ol Jack!" Private Alf Gurganous of Overholt's Battery called to Colonel Channing. "But a damn sight harder to hit!"

Colonel Channing threw back his head and laughed out loud. But Thad Selby was revolted by the quivering rabbit and the blood dripping from its mouth and eyes. The smashed animal brought back in all their sickening detail the sights he had been trying for two days to shut out of his mind: a man's torso severed from its legs...blood pumping from a rifleman's chest as if his heart refused to stop its work...the long red gash across General Taliaferro's neck...a single shot toppling a splendid blue major from his horse.

"We must kill the brave ones," Ol Jack had said, watching the major fall. *But the rabbits too* Selby thought *the rabbits die, too.*

"Hope the huntin's as good the rest of the day!"

Channing waved his hat to the gunners and turned his horse away, just as a sudden crackle of musket fire, far toward the other end of Jackson's line, broke the morning stillness. Channing reined in again.

"Skirmishers. Sound like Pope aint had enough after all."

Captain Selby, one hand on his stomach, hunched a little in his saddle, trying not to think of the bleeding rabbit. You *can't* be sick, he told himself. Even if they're coming again. You *can't.*

He straightened, the pain like hot coals under his belt, and said to Channing:

"Then we'll just have to lick'em again, sir!"

Private Ambrose Riggin was an honorable man. So when he heard the firing break out, he knew at once what he had to do. He had awakened as determined as he had been the night before that he was through shooting; the early-morning skirmishing meant to him that he had no grace period. He had to face up.

Private Riggin went immediately to his corporal, who took him to his sergeant.

"The shit you aint," the sergeant said, and took him to Lieutenant Ransom B. Varnum, the sole surviving commissioned officer of Company B, Thirteenth Georgia.

Lieutenant Varnum had taken a bullet crease across the side of his neck the day before, leaving him an ugly red scar and a heightened sense of mortality. He had had nothing but an apple to eat that morning, his coffee had tasted like boiled bootsole, and graybacks in his crotch were driving him crazy.

"What'n hell you talkin bout, soldier?"

Private Riggin held his ground. "Made up my mind last night, sir. I aint no deserter. But I come to it clear. I just aint shootin no more."

Lieutenant Varnum scratched his crotch fervently. "Not a deserter. But not shootin no more. What'n tarnation you talkin bout?"

"I kin work with-a surgeons. Drive a team. Whatevuh you want. But I aint shootin no more."

"What I call *that*, soldier, is a coward. Aint that bout right?"

Ambrose Riggin had known Ranse Varnum before the war. Not personally—Varnums too high'n mighty for that—but as a hell-raiser around Colquitt county. Maggie had always said no good would come of Ranse Varnum's being an officer.

"I-uz on the Peninsula. Up to here, I fought good's any man inna Thirteenth Georgia. I just aint shootin no more, is all."

"Well, why aint that cowardice? Desertin, too?"

"You read Duterrominy." Ambrose Riggin believed he was delivering the clinching argument. "See what at Sixth Commandment says."

"On'y commandment counts round here is Ol Jack's." Lieutenant Varnum scratched his crotch again. "Arrest'im, Sarge. Turn'im over to reg'ment'n haul ass back here quick's you can."

The skirmishers' firing woke up the New Man for good. All night, trying to keep an eye out for Cady, he had dozed fitfully against the tombstone; he had fallen into good sound sleep only just before dawn. But when the skirmishers came in on Jackson's left, they ran into resistance in the woods only a few hundred yards from where the New Man held Cady's head in his lap in Sudley Church graveyard.

Grice was enough of a veteran to tell, before long, that the firing didn't amount to much. He put his ear down anxiously to Cady's face. Cady's breathing was weak and irregular.

"Wha's at far'n?"

The New Man nodded admiringly. Even gutshot, Cady was all sojer.

"Yank skirmishers, sound like."

"Grice?"

"Yeah?"

"I aint see'n so good. At sun up yit?"

"Naw. Aint much more'n just dawn."

"You tell me, then."

"Tell yuh whut?"

"When at sun come up."

"Right." Grice was happy to take orders from Cady again. "Sound like you feelin better."

"Shit," Cady said.

The firing was dropping off a little. The New Man was not sure what to do next. He was hungry as a working mule but he knew Cady could not eat or drink anything with a hole in his gut. And he did not want to leave the sergeant, though he still found it difficult to believe that Cady could die.

"Got ny water ther?"

Grice picked up his canteen and poured some water in his hand, then dribbled it over Cady's lips, the way he'd learned during the night. That way the sergeant could get his mouth and throat a little wet without taking anything down into his open belly.

"S'good. How's at sun comin?"

Grice looked over his shoulder to the east. "Won't be long now."

"Bend down-yere a little."

Grice was stiff from sitting all night in one position, and his legs were cramped from the weight of Cady's head and shoulders, but he obediently put his ear close to Cady's lips.

"Compny aint had a single deserter."

"Reck'n not. S'your Compny."

"Till you."

Grice was indignant. "I aint desertin."

"Left ranks."

"Lookin after you is why. I aint . . ."

"At sun come up, you hightail back to the Compny. You hear?"

Grice straightened up, thinking. His wakeful night had been filled with confusion and resentment. Since the bonecracker had refused to sew up Cady, the New Man had been thinking how often things were like that—some folks took care of, some not. Some gittin a chancet, some not. And a hell of a lot more of the last kind. Which meant that the *most* got the least while the *least* got the most, even though more folks by a long shot was like Cady than like at goddam bonecracker called'im a goner.

But not until Cady ordered him to return to the Company did Grice realize that he had no intention of going back.

"You hear, Grice?"

"Yeah. Sunup, you said."

"Orta go right now. Cept I need yuh . . . tell me when it's up."

Grice could not at once link his decision not to go back with his resentment of the treatment given Cady. He only knew he was determined, and couldn't let the sergeant know it.

"Cady? Kin I tell you sump'm?"

"Long's you aint desertin the Compny."

"You leadin us yistiddy. I-uz proud-a that."

"Done . . . my best."

"Never been proud of a forn thing my whole life till then."

Cady's eyes, rolling up to look at the New Man bending over him, seemed to clear a little.

"The Compny. S'what makes you proud."

"Naw it aint. Seein whut a man kin do." Grice had it then, but he hesitated a little to say it. "Man like you." He hesitated again, then came out with it. "Maybe even me, I had the chancet."

"Stick with . . . with-a Compny. You'll see."

But Grice knew that that was the one thing he was not going to do. And somehow, once realized, it seemed as inevitable as the sun coming up—as inevitable, he conceded finally, as the death of a man with his gut shot out. But no need to rile up Cady now.

"Oh, I will."

Tears were suddenly salt and hot on the New Man's dirty cheeks, for the merciful deathbed lie seemed like dropping clods on Cady's coffin. Grice put his hand on Cady's cheek and stroked it gently, feeling the strong jawline, the dark insistent beard stubble. He wished he could lie down beside Cady and hold him in his arms. Wet his lips and ease his pain. He wished he could die and Cady live.

Cady was just then wracked with pain so terrible that he thought
it must be God's way of making him welcome death. Having all
he could do not to scream or to pull the bayonet from his belt and
cut out his own stomach to end the pain, he did not notice the
New Man shaking with sobs. If he had, he would have been
amazed. Owen L. Cade had never in his life cried for another
human being, not even for his mother. Her death had seemed a
mercy, as his own would be.

"Howzat . . . sun?"

Cady hardly knew if he'd actually spoken, or only tried to.
Wouldn't be long now. Shaddas comin down. Way they did when
you'd know it'uz bout time to quit the field, git on home to cold
supper with Paw. Funny to keep thinkin-a Paw.

"Comin up, Cady . . . coming up."

Paw'd done best a man could, raisin a young'un by hisself.
Never whop me even when he should of. Been proud-a me yistiddy, Paw would. Leadin-a Compny.

In the shadows falling on him, the chill now as deep as the
pain, Cady felt a sudden small touch of warmth.

"Kin see the top edge now, Cady. Sun comin up."

Cady was trying to turn his head to make sure, when he remembered Grice saying he'd been proud, too. But Paw had
raised'im. Paw was the only people he had. Grice was just the
New Man in the Compny.

"Grice?"

"Yup?"

"S'up, ain't it?" He'd made the both of'em proud. Sump'm in
at . . . but Cady couldn't quite lay hold of it.

"Yup."

"Kin . . . feel it."

Even if he couldn't see it. Even if the shadows were deep and
the feel of the sun no more than a splinter burning against the cold
in his bones. Even if the thing with Paw'n Grice was kind of
comin clear. The sun was up. Cady could feel it. That was all
he'd promised himself.

"Paw," Cady said, or thought he did, and knew he should name
Grice, too, among his people.

He tried.

Wash woke up thinking about Paw and Sajie, his pants leg stiff
with what had come pumping out of him while Paw was doing it

to her. That worried Wash a little. He had known the man put it in the woman down there, the way Dogan's bull put it in the cows, but he had not known about the sticky stuff that came out of the man, or if it was supposed to. He wondered if it was like bleeding, or the white stuff that came out of the boil he'd once had on his backside.

Wash stopped worrying when he remembered how good it had felt coming out. And before that, when he could hear Paw doing it to Sajie. He felt himself with satisfaction. Hard as a poker, like last night.

Morning light was seeping around the cellar door, and through the cracks in its boards; but in the dimness, Wash could barely make out his mother's massive shapeless bulk. Paw slept by her, sprawled facedown on the dirt floor. Wash could see nothing of Sajie.

Maybe run off. But no place much to go, without Henry. Wash wondered vaguely what had become of Henry. But his thoughts kept returning to Sajie and Paw puttin it in'er. Prob'ly still up-er inna kitchen. Fraid to face Maw.

Maw and Paw were unmoving. Maw's regular sighing breath deep and peaceful. Wash crept across the floor to the steps, climbed them on all fours, careful to make no sound, and took a long time easing up the left-hand door, the one that didn't squeak on its hinges, just enough to slip outside. He let the door down quietly then stood up. Somewhere in the distance, he could hear a rattle of gunfire; he blinked in the beginning light, then stared.

Thinking so much about Paw doing it to Sajie, Wash had forgotten the night battle and the bodies in the yard, even the musket he'd taken and left in the cellar. The corpse at the corner of the house was grinning widely at the sky, its mouth pulled back in a gaping O from yellow teeth. Wash walked over and inspected this sight avidly, then gazed at the wound below the man's belt. Hole at big, could of been hit by a cannon ball, look like.

Other bodies lay in the yard; one, near the well, was groaning and coughing and calling for his mother. Wash went to the well, pulled up the bucket, and held out a dipperful to the wounded man. His eyes bugged and his head lolled at the sight of the water but he was not able to reach for the dipper. Wash carefully poured water over his face and thought the man got a little of it in his mouth. More'd choke'im.

Probably more wounded around. Wash thought briefly of finding and helping them. But that could come later. He still was thinking mostly of Sajie.

Wash put the dipper back in the bucket and hurried across the yard, his bare feet making no sound. He tiptoed across the back gallery, knowing well how squeaky its uncertain flooring was. The gunfire in the distance had slackened.

Something was strange; something was missing from the morning. Wash looked around nervously. The bodies were still there; otherwise the yard was empty, silent in the rising sun. The old barn's broad, open entrance gaped at him. The chicken yard . . . that was it! None of the usual morning cluckings and cackle. The chickens were gone. Em sojers back'n forth round-yere last night must of stole'em ever one.

Sajie was in the kitchen, on her back under the table, one arm flung over her face, skirts up high enough to show her thick dark legs sprawling. Wash thought maybe at first she was dead. Maybe Paw done it too hard.

Then he heard her breathing. He lay down and snaked across the floor until he could look up between her legs and see the dark place up in-er where Paw'n Henry put it in'er.

He was hard again and he unbuttoned his pants and jerked his peter with one hand while with the other he reached slowly up between Sajie's legs. He remembered once almost touching Missy up in there—fore she woke up'n hit me cross the face with a fly switch.

Sajie dreamed bleakly of Ol Brace holding a tallow candle in his hand and grinning down at her, while something spoiled and stinking dripped from the candle on her bare body. She shrank from the drippings and curled her body and turned on her side.

"Sajie! Lemme do it, too!" The whisper pierced her dream like foul hot drippings. "Sajie . . . lemme!"

She woke with Wash's hand fumbling between her legs. Sajie hit him so hard with the back of her hand she thought she felt the knuckle bones crack. The blow caught Wash across the jaw and threw him backward, against a wooden chair that clattered down on top of him.

He lay looking at her with wide dazed eyes; she saw his pants unbuttoned and remembered everything. Anger filled her, the hottest she'd ever known. She'd soon grieve for Henry; oh she'd cry out her soul for Henry, but first Ol Brace had to be dealt with . . . Ol Brace who'd spoilt her.

Sajie lunged from under the table like a catamount and seized Brace's whelp's thin arm above the elbow. She lifted him from under the chair with a powerful jerk, scarcely knowing her own strength, and slung him under her other arm as if he were a sack of cornmeal, his head hanging, his feet kicking.

But Wash was strangely silent, still dazed from her blow. She strode out of the kitchen and across the gallery. She hoped she'd busted his jaw so he'd be a long time op'nin at filthy mouth-a hissen again.

Sajie's outrage was so great, lent such energy to her body and such single-mindedness to her purpose, that she stepped right over the corpse at the corner of the house and strode on toward the cellar door. Wash's dangling head almost dragged across the dead grinning face.

Sajie threw back the wooden doors with a startling clatter and clumped down the steps, careless of Wash's hanging head, and flung the boy to the dirt floor, against Ol Brace. Kate Brace's great white moony face rose beyond her husband's sprawled form.

"Whut . . . whut . . . Sajie? Wash? They fightin again?"

"I be's jes a nigguh." Sajie felt herself powerful, relentless. "Jes a nigguh. But I aint gone have these-yer nocount menfolk-a your'n crawling on me no more. You hear, white woman?"

Kate's mouth fell open soundlessly. She stared at Sajie with round terrified eyes, as if she had never seen her before, or anything so frightening. Ol Brace didn't even move or make a sound. Sajie in her rage and power had just begun to wonder why, when Wash screamed. He screamed over and over, rolling away from his father across the dirt floor.

Jaw aint busted after all, Sajie thought.

Then, at each turn of Wash's body, she saw that his shirt and face were darkly smeared. He rolled all the way to the wall and tried to hide himself against it, still screaming. Kate Brace screamed, too; and only when Sajie looked from Wash's huddled form back to his mother's pallet did she notice at last the pool of blood that had seeped from under Ol Brace's thin body, and congealed on the dirt floor like blackberry jam.

Headquarters of Battle
Near Groveton, Va.
August 30, 1862—5 a.m.

Major-General Halleck, General-in-Chief:

We fought a terrific battle here yesterday with the combined forces of the enemy, which lasted with continuous fury from daylight until dark, by which time the enemy was driven from the field, which we now occupy. Our troops are too much exhausted yet to push matters, but I shall do so in the course of the morning, as soon as Fitz John Porter's Corps comes up from Manassas. The enemy is still in our front, but badly used up. We have lost not less than 8,000 men killed and wounded, but from the appearance of the field the enemy lost at least two to one. He stood strictly on the defensive, and every assault was made by ourselves. Our troops behaved splendidly. The battle was fought on the identical battlefield of Bull Run, which greatly increased the enthusiasm of our men. The news just reaches me from the front that the enemy is retreating toward the mountains. I go forward at once to see. We have made great captures, but I am not able yet to form an idea of their extent.

JNO. POPE
Major-General

At Pope's headquarters camp east of Bull Run, Lieutenant Cass Fielding was in a fever of anticipation. As he finished a meager breakfast of hardtack and coffee and got ready for the day's business, even Fielding's poor military ear could detect that skirmishers evidently had clashed somewhere on the right of the Federal battle line.

But morning skirmishes were commonplace. Fielding was far more interested in General Pope himself. The lieutenant had never seen his commander in such a state—excited one minute about the thumping he'd given Stonewall the day before, blackly angry the next at General Fitz-John Porter's failure to follow his orders and pitch into Jackson's right.

"*Dammit*, Russell!" Fielding had overheard the general say. "I'll have Porter court-martialed, I tell you! We could have *destroyed* Jackson, we'd . . ."

The general was striding away and Fielding did not catch the rest. But he knew what was coming because he'd copied Pope's final angry order to Porter the night before: Major General Fitz-John Porter, upon its receipt, was to march his corps to "the field of battle" and report *in person* to the commanding general as soon as possible. Fielding relished the thought of the confrontation that was bound to result. So he applied himself with unusual diligence to clerkly duties that kept him near Pope's tent.

Pope, Fielding knew, had more than one cause for the anger that rumbled periodically from his barrel chest. At daybreak, a note from Major General William B. Franklin, one of McClellan's corps commanders, had arrived by courier—to Fielding's knowledge, the first direct message in days from the Union forces around Washington. He watched Pope snatch the message, eagerly read it, raise his eyes to heaven as if in disbelief, read it again, then crumble it and fling it at Colonel Russell's boots.

"*Now* you'll believe me, Russell! Read *that* . . . just see what McClellan's crowd'll do for us!"

Russell spread the note flat and read it, shaking his head, while Pope stamped off into the morning mist like a goaded bull. Later, Fielding carefully filed the courier's neatly penned message:

August 29, 1862—8 p.m.

To the Commanding Officer,
Centreville, Va.

I have been instructed by General McClellan to inform you that he will have all available wagons at Alexandria loaded with rations for your troops, and all of the cars also, as soon as you will send in a cavalry escort to Alexandria as a guard to the trains.

Respectfully,

W. B. Franklin
Major General
Commanding Sixth Corps

No wonder Pope had been enraged! Franklin hadn't even done him the courtesy of using his name. And even the unmilitary Fielding knew—as Franklin surely should have—that the Army of Virginia's cavalry was poor at best, and worn out after weeks of maneuvering. Even if it had been fresh, what commander in the field could spare cavalry for a sixty-mile round trip to and from his home base? And Alexandria was bound to be swarming with troops McClellan could easily have spared for escort duty.

"Hey, Duryea." Fielding considered the captain a surly eccentric, but he knew Russell respected the man's knowledge. "What good are cavalry for guarding railway trains?"

"None." Duryea, who sat against a tree studying a map, did not even look up.

Fitz-John Porter arrived early, dust-covered, looking stern and reserved—too much so, Fielding thought. Bound to know he was about to catch hell, and from an officer McClellan's crowd held in contempt. But Colonel Russell greeted Porter cordially enough and nodded in approval as the stern-looking corps commander reported that his two divisions were moving up the Sudley Road to its junction with the Warrenton Pike.

"General Pope's in here."

Russell indicated the tent, and Fielding thought he saw Porter square his shoulders. No wonder; that last order he'd received would have peeled the paint off a barn.

As the two officers entered Pope's tent, Fielding strode purposefully toward it and seated himself at a camp desk he had placed nearby, when Russell was not looking. Fielding spread some papers—mostly copies of yesterday's orders—and ostentatiously began looking through them.

". . . whole force in front of me, General. And between my command and Jackson. I . . ."

"Couldn't be!" Pope's deep voice almost boomed through the tent wall. "Longstreet couldn't have got up that soon."

"Well, sir . . . of course, that *was* Hood that Hatch ran into last night on the pike."

Russell's voice was tentative; Fielding could not help grinning at the colonel's plight. Not easy to cool down John Pope when he had up a head of steam.

"That's only one division, Russell. And pickets heard *it* pull back during the night."

"Sir, I sent a scout out to check. Duryea. He's sure Hood just moved back along the pike a ways to straighten out Longstreet's line."

"Exactly what Hood would do." Fitz-John Porter's voice was crisp with assurance. Don't scare easy, Fielding thought. "Longstreet's in line from the pike all the way to Dawkins Branch, General. He's . . ."

"Oh, yes . . . certainly." Pope's sarcasm was heavy, contemptuous. "That's why you couldn't obey my orders to attack yesterday. That's what you said already."

"General Morell and General Sykes can confirm what I say. I believe General McDowell will, too. He . . ."

Fielding was all ears as the debate went on within the tent. He did not notice the slowing of the skirmishers' fire. The lieutenant was sure Porter was making no headway at all with Pope, and Fielding thought he knew why. He himself had copied Pope's letter to Halleck the night before last, in which Pope had stated flatly that Longstreet had been turned back at Thoroughfare Gap. That couldn't be, if Porter was right; which had to be why Pope so adamantly refused to believe Porter.

"...but, General," Russell was saying, in his carefully tentative way, "even if *you're* not convinced Longstreet's up yet ...well, sir, seems to me...all due respect...maybe we'd do well to fall the army back on Centreville. Get behind Bull Run and hold the crossings. Occupy the Centreville fortifications and wait for reinforcements from McClellan. That way..."

"Ha!" Pope's snort of disgust silenced Russell in mid-sentence. "Reinforcements from McClellan, you say? Didn't you see that note from Franklin? D'you really still believe there'll *be* any more reinforcements from McClellan?"

"Well, sir, we'd surely be better off, waiting to find out, if we had Bull Run between us and Stonewall. Especially if General Porter here turns out to be..."

"Aint General Porter one of McClellan's friends?"

Great God! Who'd of believed it? This kind of thing going on in the middle of a war. If folks back home *knew*, Fielding thought, they'd be hell to pay.

"...I tell you, the shape we're in for food and forage, not to mention the shape the men are in, and no help coming from Washington...I knew *that* the minute I saw Franklin's message...we finish off Jackson *today*, Russell, or never. *Then* we'll get behind Bull Run..."

The talk rumbled on, sometimes inaudibly. Fielding was listening so avidly that he forgot to shuffle the papers before him and was startled when someone touched his shoulder. He looked up at Colonel Russell's angry face.

"Hearing everything all right, Fielding?"

"Why...uh...sir...just going over these papers here. I thought..."

"Get your fat butt up and go find Duryea. Send'im to me and thank your stars I don't put you under arrest."

Fielding hurried away, less fearful than indignant. He'd done nothing to be arrested for. Russell just didn't like him; Russell didn't like anybody smarter than he was. Besides, hearing what he'd heard had been worth the colonel's anger; and anyway Russell knew too well who Cass Fielding's father was to be serious about arrest.

Fielding wondered briefly whether maybe he should write his father, tell him about the true state of things in the army. His father could see to it that Mr. Lincoln saw the letter. But would that be the making of a young officer? Or the breaking? The army had ways to punish anybody who caused trouble, even for good patriotic reasons. Rock the boat, you could find yourself in the front line, exposed to fire.

Lieutenant Fielding had not decided what to do by the time he found Duryea.

"Colonel Russell wants you in General Pope's tent."

Duryea, who had been gazing intently in the direction from which the skirmishing had been heard, turned away immediately. Snotty bastard, Fielding thought. He trotted to keep up.

"Having a hell of a fight in there. With Porter."

Duryea strode toward the tent, still saying nothing.

"Porter's trying to tell'im Longstreet's whole army's on the field. Aint that a good un?"

"None of *your* business, is it?"

Duryea's cold eyes not only stilled Fielding's answer but stopped him in his tracks. Thinks he's somebody, Fielding thought, thinks he knows something. But who could *he* write to about what's going on in this army? If he even knew.

Duryea had not needed to be told that Fitz-John Porter had failed in the effort to convince John Pope of the danger before him. That was foreordained. Pope was enraged that Porter had not attacked as ordered the evening before; Pope thought Porter was only making an excuse for that failure when Porter claimed that Longstreet had been in his front. So, to keep on believing that Porter had failed in his duty and kept Pope from the victory he'd thought in his grasp, Pope had to keep on believing, too, that Longstreet was still on the other side of Thoroughfare Gap and the mountains blue in the distance. And vice versa.

But Pope was in command; there was nothing to be done but follow his orders and hope for the best. What a sorry way to fight a war against the damned slavers!

Fitz-John Porter had returned to his troops by the time Duryea entered General Pope's tent and saluted Colonel Russell. Pope, busy writing at a camp desk, did not look up.

"Oh, yes . . . Duryea." Russell's eyes were evasive but he spoke with exaggerated authority. "General Pope has determined that the enemy is in retreat toward the mountains. He intends to pursue. Please take the general's compliments to General McDowell and ask him to come to General Pope's headquarters tent as soon as possible."

Duryea saluted, thinking quickly: he didn't have to tell me why they want McDowell. He's inviting me to speak up. As if I could change Pope's mind when he and Porter couldn't.

But he was nevertheless ordering his thoughts and gathering his nerve to question the general's intention when a sudden commotion outside the tent caught Pope'e ear. He turned from the desk and looked up as a dusty courier, a young lieutenant Duryea had never seen, entered the tent and saluted.

"Compliments of General Reno, sir. Instructs me, sir, to report that Hill's Division appears to be pulling back on Jackson's left flank."

Pope put a cigar in his mouth and clenched it at a jaunty angle. "And how does General Reno know that?"

"Sent in skirmishers to feel out the Reb line, sir. Found out the brigade on Hill's left pulled back just after dawn. Skirmishers hit the next brigade in line, felt 'em out, and withdrew."

Porter took the cigar out of his mouth. "Thank you, Lieutenant. Get yourself some coffee." The lieutenant went out and Pope winked heavily at Russell. "That's the clincher, ain't it, Russell?"

"Captain . . ." Russell touched Duryea's elbow. "Better bring General McDowell at once."

Private Hugh Williams of the Sixth Wisconsin had awakened that morning to clear skies and a rising sun that put him momentarily in mind of old days in his father's wheatfields. But then he heard again the cries of the wounded from a nearby stone house that had been taken over as a surgery. All night the groans and screams from that house had troubled his sleep, and not even dawn could dispel his eerie sense that the sounds were less those of wounded men than of souls unready to meet their Maker.

Private Williams had pulled his bedroll together, drunk his morning coffee, and fallen in with his company. After that, as usual, there was nothing to do but stand at ease in ranks and wait for whatever the day would bring. When he heard the skirmish firing not far off to the northeast, on the right of Pope's line, he was interested but not alarmed; battle held no further fears for him. He pulled a well-thumbed copy of the Cromwell Scholar's Pocket Bible from his haversack and opened it at random; for on every page, he knew, there were words to comfort and strengthen a man.

"Way I hear it," somebody down the rank grumbled, "they grab off enough our supplies at Manassas Junction to win the damfool war with."

"And just how you think it got left there for 'em to grab so easy?" Private Fritz Schiml's penetrating voice left the company in no doubt. "On purpose, that's how. Like everything else keeping this war going. On purpose."

Well, he'd had enough of it. They weren't going to use Fritz Schiml for target practice anymore. Not a day longer. Not a minute longer than it would take him to do what he'd woke up knowing he was going to do. Oh, they thought they had you coming and going—cannon fodder if you took their orders, a deserter if you didn't. Shot dead either way.

But even *they* had to get up early in the morning to get ahead of the Schiml boys. Everybody said that back home. And the one thing *they* hadn't thought of was that in all that smoke and noise and madness—for one moment Schiml almost screamed at the recollection of those terrible endless minutes of insanity and despair on the slope above the pike—in all that crazy shooting and killing, a man who kept his wits could outsmart the bastards and no one the wiser. And this time, Fritz Schiml aimed to do it.

"Feller tole me while ago them Rebs pulling out west." Another voice from the ranks was more hopeful than confident.

"Ho, ho, ho," Schiml said. "If wishin made it so, I'd be crost the O-hi-o."

The Swede, who spoke so little English that he understood almost nothing of what was said in the company—save the most obvious orders—was deeply troubled that morning. Not so much by the gunfire, which he could tell was not serious—not compared to the battle the Sixth had fought the day before yesterday. What bothered the Swede was the evil omen he'd stumbled across.

Helping the evening before to scratch out a shallow latrine, he had been at one end of a line of shovelers. Working methodically, he had dug up what at first he took to be a whitish rock, long and thin. But in the gathering darkness, as he looked more closely, he had seen that the object in his shovel was the skeleton of a human hand.

"They retreating so fast . . ." Fritz Schiml's harsh voice, speaking unintelligible words, barely registered on the Swede. "How come we aint taking out after 'em?"

The Swede vaguely understood that the war was being fought to hold the country together. That seemed worth doing to him, though he knew nothing of the country beyond Wisconsin, where he arrived with his parents barely a year before he'd signed up with the other boys from his home county, and Virginia, where they'd been soldiering ever since. But owing to his inability to speak or understand English, he had no idea that the war's first big battle had been fought a year earlier over the very fields and thickets where Pope's army was now engaged. So it did not occur to him that they were digging their latrine on the site of one of the mass graves where the dead of that first battle had been unceremoniously dumped.

"Hey, Schiml! Whyn't you help Gin'ral Pope run this army sted of all at farting through your mouth?"

The Swede had hastily tossed the terrible object in his shovel back into the hole he had dug; then he threw dirt over it and moved from that end to the middle of the line of digging men.

He did not for a moment suppose that covering the thing up could remove its evil power. Unquestionably a harbinger of death, bony and pointing. What the Swede could not figure out—what troubled him still, as the Sixth waited in formation in the morning sun—was whether the omen pointed only to him, or to the company, or even maybe to the whole Sixth Wisconsin. But he did not have the words to ask more knowledgeable comrades.

"Maybe he don't need *my* help." Fritz Schiml was taking no lip from anybody. "But he sure-God needs *some*body's."

Gibbon's Brigade had bivouacked for the night on a hill rising just northwest of the intersection of the pike and the Sudley Springs Road. Hooker's and Kearny's divisions, which had borne much of the previous day's fighting, stretched away to the north in a formidable battle line. Across the pike to the south, Union forces were massed in open fields, under clouds of dust and cooking smoke; and to the west, more blue troops were moving into the angle between the pike and the narrow road that led from Groveton to Sudley Church. These arriving troops were Fitz-John Porter's, completing their early morning march from Dawkins Branch.

Major Reverdy Dowd was deeply impressed by the Federal army spread all around him. He had seldom seen so many brigades at once, certainly not in so small an area, and he was both reassured and stirred by the sight. What Reb army could conceivably stand before such a mighty array? Particularly when right happened also to be on the side of might—indeed, when all this might had been gathered for no other purpose than to serve the right and save the Union.

Nevertheless, Major Dowd—chafing under a premonition of another day's inactivity, after the Sixth had been held out of the twilight battle the night before—watched rather sourly as Porter's Corps moved in between Gibbon's Brigade and the secesh line, hidden by rolling ground and stands of timber.

Dowd still nourished an angry memory from the morning before at Manassas, when the battered Sixth had just roused itself from brief sleep after its hillside battle with Jackson and its nightmare retreat. Porter's Corps had been tramping past, up the road to Gainesville, down which the Sixth Wisconsin and the rest of King's Division had struggled the night before. Porter's men, looking fresh and well-fed, marched with the rapid stride of the Peninsula veterans they were.

"You fellers Pope's army?" someone shouted from their well-dressed ranks.

One of Dowd's black-hatted riflemen looked up from boiling coffee. "What's it to you?"

"Aim to show you strawfeet how to fight!"

Major Dowd had been glad to see that this evoked loud whistles and catcalls from his tired ranks.

"Wait'll you git where we been!" the man boiling coffee yelled above the din. "Take the slack outen your britches!"

Still, the moment rankled. Dowd was well aware that however manfully the Sixth had stood up to Stonewall Jackson, they ultimately had had to leave the field to the Rebs. Old King's damnfool orders, of course, but that didn't take the sting out of it. Nor did it help much that the army was buzzing about Porter's failure—for all the brag of his troops—to get into the battle the day before.

"I got it straight . . ." Captain Black spoke in his best confidential voice, "from the horse's mouth. Pope's itching to put Porter under summary arrest."

"But that don't make sense, Blackie. Anybody'll tell you Porter's Corps made just about the hardest fighters McClellan had on the Peninsula."

"Ah, yes." Blackie looked mysterious. "*McClellan's* army. That don't do Pope much good, way he sees it."

"Well . . . now they're here and ready-looking."

Dowd could not bring himself to accept Black's obvious implication—that McClellan men would not fight for John Pope, even though they supposedly raised the same flag. Dowd was a patriot; he had his loyalties, as any soldier did, particularly to the Sixth Wisconsin; but above all he'd signed on to fight for his country and he found it hard to believe that anyone under the flag wouldn't feel the same way.

"Bet you can guess who'll be out front *today*." Black winked knowingly. "If Porter aint, you can bet your bottom dollar Pope'll have'im up on charges before sundown."

This brought little comfort to Reverdy Dowd. In the first place, among Captain Black's usual collection of facts, opinions, and rumors was a report that the Rebs were retreating—although Dowd himself could see no sign of it, and in fact had chatted over the camp fire the night before with a courier who said that even Kearny had had to fall back from his hard-won ground on Pope's right, so tenaciously were Stonewall's men holding on. But if the Rebs *were* pulling out—which was maybe plausible, given the size of Pope's force—then serious fighting was unlikely that day.

"You hear bout Dexter Henry? Over'n the Second Wisconsin?"

In the second place, if they did have a fight, Blackie obviously was right: after his mysterious failure of the day before, Porter would surely be given the heft of the work to do.

"That night Stonewall jumped us there, down the pike aways? Dexter, he couldn't get his horse to face front. Kind of a nervous bay. He'd pull'im around, Dexter, facing the Rebs; but as soon's they'd let off a volley, that horse'd spin around'n give'em his rump again."

Dowd grunted, in no mood for one of Blackie's yarns. Gibbon's Brigade and the Sixth Wisconsin wouldn't have much chance to pull trigger, he was thinking, especially if Stonewall did retreat.

This depressed Dowd more than anything else; he wanted his black hats to have a chance to show Porter's Corps a thing or two. Strawfeet, indeed! Reverdy Dowd's men were as good as the army had to offer. And anybody who led men like them could hope to go far, if the war lasted. Maybe right up to a general's stars.

"So Colonel Bisbee watches old Dex awhile, trying to get that jumpy bay to hold steady while the Rebs are blazing away. Then Bisbee rides up to Dex, says 'Captain,' Bisbee says, 'By God, sir, you can't make that horse do right, then sit'im backwards so's at least one of you's facing the enemy!'"

Captain Black's laugh exploded over the ranks of the Sixth Wisconsin. Hearing it, Fritz Schiml was disgusted that anyone could find anything to laugh at before the coming slaughter. Hugh Williams, absorbed in the Book of Isaiah, did not notice the laugh at all. The Swede thought it ominous; a sort of jeering death cackle. Major Dowd, chuckling politely, felt that he was himself rather like the unfortunate Dexter Henry. He wanted to fight but the army, General King, fate—something—kept pointing him the other way.

When Sajie forced herself to bend over Durward P. Brace and edge one of his bony shoulders off the floor, she could see that the blackening pool of blood had spilled from his gaping throat. Then she realized that Wash was still screaming but Mistis had stopped.

Sajie looked up just in time to leap back from the slashing arc of the long smeared knife in Kate Brace's hands.

"Black slut! Messin round a white man . . . gone cut you open! Strip at black hide offen yuh fat carcass . . ."

Again she slashed the air with the long knife, but Sajie jumped well out of reach. She was not afraid; Mistis was too fat to get up without help, or to get close enough to cut her. But Sajie stared in horror at the long dark blade.

Cut Ol Brace's throat. *Like a hog-killin.* Then laid ther all night beside'im. Holdin at knife.

"Whoor!" Kate Brace swung the blade again, weakly this time, as though she knew it was hopeless. Her strident voice rang off the cellar walls. "Teach you! Mess with a white man."

The knife point ripped feebly across Durward P. Brace's back, pulling half of his faded shirt away from his body.

"Nigguh!" Kate spat across him toward Sajie but her spittle, like the knife, fell short. "Bitch!"

Which was maybe, Sajie thought wearily, feeling sick to her stomach, what she deserved for that one time lettin Ol Brace touch her. But surely he hadn't told his wife what he'd done on the kitchen floor.

"Cut your slutty heart out . . ." Mistis was half moaning, half sobbing, clutching the knife handle to her vast bosom as if it were a treasured keepsake. "Swear I will . . . swear I'll . . ."

As if jerked by a string, Wash leaped up from his huddle against the wall and whirled toward his mother.

"Didn have to *kill* Paw . . . didn say you'd *kill* 'im!"

Mistis slumped on her pallet, her white moon face going down beyond Ol Brace's ripped shirt.

"Tole me they-uz doin it . . . you *said* they was!"

"But I didn aim for you to *kill*'im!"

So the dirty-mouth done it. Sajie was not surprised. She and Henry had known Wash spied on them ever chancet he got, like a varmint in the walls. So he'd spied on'is Paw'n tattled to'is Maw. Now they both laid ther onna floor, the one with'is thoat cut'n th'other too fat to git up.

Let'em lie, Sajie thought. Let'em lie longside one-nother, wher they b'long.

"Paw." Wash looked down at Brace's slack body. "Paw?"

"She done kilt'im." Sajie wanted to go up the stairs and out into the light and breathe clean air.

"Count of you!" The moon face rose a moment above Brace's shoulder, glared at Sajie, and sank back.

"Aint no need you killin Paw." Wash was still staring at Ol Brace. He moved his foot as if to nudge the body, then pulled it back. "Even if they-uz doin it."

Raped me Sajie started to say. But having to explain—thinking she had to explain—seemed to her the hardest injustice of all. She had no need to explain anything to anyone but Henry, and Henry was *dead dead dead*. She could never make the only explanation that mattered.

Wash turned and went across the cellar to the far wall, to his own pallet.

"You come-ere, Wash Brace! Come-ere'n hep yuh Maw up!"

Wash picked up something lying beside his pallet and came back across the cellar. Sajie's heart almost stopped. Wash was carrying a gun taller than he was. For a moment—the hard look on his face, the way he hunched up like a cat about to jump—Sajie was sure he'd shoot them both, her first, then his Maw. Didn't even look like a boy no more, carryin at gun.

"Wash! You hear me?"

But Wash paid no attention to either of them. He walked past Sajie, and she saw then that he didn't look like a man either—trying to hold back tears, and look mean, and like he didn't care, all at the same time.

"Wash! Come back-ere now! Wash!"

Sajie watched Wash carry the gun up the cellar steps and disappear into the light—sunlight now, not just the gray shadows of dawn. First Missy runnin off with-a first sojer that took'er eye.

Then Ol Brace's thoat cut by his fat sow wife. Now Wash gone off with'is gun. Henry dead . . . *dead dead*. Shot by Yankees.

"White woman," Sajie said. "You'n me aint got shit." She felt again the vast empty aloneness in which Henry had left her.

"Tha's right."

Mistis did not lift the white moon face, her voice floated over Brace's body as if from far off, like the whistle of the trains Sajie could remember passing on the line down from the mountains, in the quiet time before the white folks' war:

"Tha's right. I *am* white. You are *exactly* right about that. We was *always* white'n this fam'ly. My Paw said they wa'nt a drop-a black blood in our vangs. Paw-uz a proud man that way. How come he-uz hard on Brace."

The moon face rose briefly, staring at Sajie solemnly.

"Said Brace *might* of had some. Said couldn't never tell bout po whites." Kate sank back to the pallet. "Cose I knowed better. Said to Paw, I said, he's white's you'n me, Brace is. Cause if he wa'nt, I could *tell*."

Crazy, Sajie thought. Right-down crazy.

Mistis waved the knife in the air in bloody good-bye to something. "So Paw come round. But he never stop worryin till Missy come. Scairt maybe sump'm gone show on'er. But Missy come'n nuthin showed'n Paw finely quit worryin. He up'n pass away the next week, cause they aint nuthin left to worry'im."

Sajie remembered the old man—scrawny, mean, grudging Henry so much as a piece of fatback for his greens. But kept the place a sight better'n Ol Brace ever done. Henry had hated and respected the old man.

Kate's voice sharpened a little. "S'why I worry bout at nigguh whoor shakin'er fat bottom round Brace. Since I been sick. At slut know a man's weakness. Don't she ever! But I aint gone have Brace mixin this fam'ly up with no black blood."

A shadow seemed to Sajie to fall across the cellar.

"So when Wash tole me Brace-uz doin it with at nigguh bitch inna kitchen . . ." The white moon face rose again over Brace's sprawled body and Mistis spoke pleadingly, as if to a judge: "Why, they wa'nt but one thing to *do*. So I done it. Way Paw would of . . ."

"Sajie?"

The deep voice from the top of the cellar steps sounded like Henry's—so much so that Sajie turned in consternation, wondering whose voice could be that much like his. A huge square shape, as big as Henry's would have been, stood at the top of the steps, black against the sunlight, menacing as death.

Sajie's knees buckled. She had not been afraid of Mistis's knife, and only for a moment of Wash's gun, but she knew Henry was dead and that this looming visitor who sounded like Henry and looked like Henry and was even as big as Henry could only have come from the unfathomable darkness that no one living had entered, or could. Maybe even Henry himself risen from the grave. Such things could be. Henry himself had told her so. The darkness had powers. Sajie went down in a heap on the floor, her head in her hands.

"Sajie!"

The deep voice again. Clomping footsteps on the cellar floor. A halfhearted scream from Mistis. A powerful hand seized Sajie's hair.

"Git up, woman!"

The hand jerked her head back, pulled her to her feet by her hair. Sajie thought her scalp was being peeled back. But that didn't matter, in the terror of the voice and the knowledge of the darkness.

"Say de trufe?" Henry glared down in her face. "At woman?"

Sajie could not stand on her sagging legs. She was terrified of the living dark. She was astounded that Henry was alive. And she was nearly hysterical, not knowing which was true. She swung by the hair from Henry's hand, unable to steady herself on the earth.

"Done it with Brace," Mistis said. "Onna kitchen floor. Wash seen'em."

Holding Sajie up by the hair with his right hand, Henry slapped her hard with his left palm, then the back of his hand. Then he flung her like a dead cat across the cellar. She lay on her side staring back at his glaring eyes, the white teeth between his drawn-back lips. *Aint dead* she knew then *Henry aint dead* and realized she might as well be.

He stared at her, across the dim cellar. A strange odor was in her nostrils. Then Sajie understood that she had been thrown down on a pallet, and the smell was the varmint smell of Wash.

Henry went down on one knee beside Brace and lifted the slack torso long enough to see the slashed throat.

"Rape me," Sajie said.

"You kill'im?"

"*I* kilt'im."

Kate Brace flicked the knife weakly at Henry. He drew his

head back from its arc, seized her wrist, and took away the knife as easily as he might have swatted a fly. Holding her wrist, he stared at Sajie.

"He rape you but *she* kilt'im?"

No use saying anything. He would never believe her, or take her back if he did. Not Henry.

But Sajie was just glad that Henry was alive. As long as she was alive and Henry was alive she would not be alone. She need not feel the unbearable aloneness she had known the night before when Brace said Henry was dead; and again when she had realized that nothing was left of the only life she knew except Mistis's mad, bereft moanings.

Henry stood up, looked at Sajie again, took the knife by its smeared tip, and flung it at the dirt floor near Sajie. It stuck upright, burying itself in the earth by an inch or two; she watched the handle quiver and still.

"Whoor." Henry went up the steps and into the light, not looking back.

Sajie listened to his heavy footfalls as long as she could hear them. She was strangely pleased. She had always counted on Henry; and as always, he had done exactly what she had expected him to do.

What, after all, had been his choice? She'd known it as soon as she'd felt Ol Brace's skinny ol tallow-feeling dick up inside of her.

Spoilt.

She couldn't fault Henry for smelling the spoil on her. She wouldn't fault Henry for anything, as long as she knew he was alive, so that she was not alone.

Headquarters
Department of Northern Virginia
Near Groveton, Virginia
August 30, 1862

Mr. President:

My despatches will have informed you of the march of this portion of the army. Its progress has been necessarily slow, having a large and superior force on its flank, narrow & rough roads to travel, and the difficulties of obtaining forage & provisions to contend with. It has so far advanced in safety and has succeeded in deceiving the enemy as to its object. The movement has, as far as I am able to judge, drawn the enemy from the Rappahannock frontier and caused him to concentrate his troops between Manassas and Centreville. My desire has been to avoid a general engagement, being the weaker force, & by maneuvering to relieve the portion of the country referred to. I think if not overpowered we shall be able to relieve other portions of the country, as it seems to be the purpose of the enemy to collect his strength here.

I have the honor to be with high respect, your obt. servant

R. E. Lee
Genl.

About 8 a.m., Yank batteries began a slow fire from near Groveton. But Major Jesse Thomas, listening closely, could tell at once that the gunners were not preparing the way for an attack; they were maybe hoping to draw fire and thus waste some of Lee's ammunition—which Thomas knew to be in short supply.

Major Thomas was disappointed that morning. After Longstreet's apparent inaction of the day before, he was anxious for his chief to vindicate himself, and he had thought the opportunity at hand. Reports had come in before dawn that the heavy Federal force—probably Fitz-John Porter's Fifth Corps—had pulled back from Dawkins Branch along the road to Manassas.

"So there's nothing on our right flank anymore."

Thomas had carried the news to Longstreet's tent and pointed out the Federal movement on the general's map.

"Pope's had enough." Longstreet spoke with only a moment's reflection but the kind of finality that, Thomas had learned, represented stubborn conviction. "He'll get over Bull Run today or tonight and fall back on the Washington defenses."

To Thomas's surprise, Longstreet made no effort to prepare an attack or to prevent the Federal retreat he had predicted.

"But General . . . if he really is pulling back across Bull Run, wouldn't that be a good time to hit him?" The enemy was out there within rifle shot and Jesse Thomas wanted to go for him.

"Hood reports Pope's defenses strong along the pike, Thomas. And he'd hold the Bull Run crossings like a tiger."

When Major Thomas later rode with Longstreet to Lee's headquarters, on a low hill south of the pike, he was even more surprised to learn from Colonel Tatum that the aggressive commanding general apparently did not propose to attack either.

"Look at it this way." As they sprawled under a shade tree, the colonel's tone was fatherly. A little condescending too. But maybe that was what you had to expect from a man who knew what was being said in Lee's tent. "We know from Hood's reconnaissance that an attack along the pike would mean a hard fight for maybe not much gain."

"But Pope'll get away over Bull Run if we don't attack. He's already got Porter movin'."

Colonel Tatum leaned forward. His whisper was heavily confidential. "If Pope pulls out, we can move around his right again. Push Jackson over Bull Run at Sudley Ford to parallel 'im on the Little River Turnpike."

Thomas listened glumly. The flank movement Tatum described might, of course, allow Lee's army to interpose between Pope and Washington. Generals were supposed to obey orders. But it seemed a long way around the barn to Jesse Thomas, and it would put Jackson in the lead again. Thomas was tired of bringing up the rear.

"That would move the theater of war farther away from Richmond," Tatum said importantly. "Throw a scare into Washington." He looked around conspiratorially. "Even threaten Maryland." He clapped Thomas's shoulder, stood up, and hurried away.

Maryland! The word eased Thomas's disappointment. Could even R. E. Lee, that ice-blooded gambler, actually be planning to carry the war north of the Potomac?

The major surreptitiously took Miss Letty's handkerchief from his pocket, folded it in his hand, and sniffed it; only the faintest scent of perfume remained, but enough to remind him of her sparkling eyes and white bosom. Maryland! What a thing it would be to send Miss Letty a letter from Maryland.

This was not precisely the effect Colonel Tatum had wanted, but close enough. The colonel had been alarmed and angered by Longstreet's successful resistance to General Lee's plain desire for an attack to relieve Jackson the day before. Longstreet's solid, rocklike self-assurance had prevailed over Lee's better judgment. It did not matter to Colonel Tatum that, on the evidence of Hood's reconnaissance in force, Longstreet might on this occasion have been right; what the colonel feared was that the phlegmatic Georgian might have been encouraged to stand fast again, the next time he happened to disagree with the commanding general, and with worse results. Because Lee might again be too much the Virginia gentleman to give peremptory orders to a valued but assertive subordinate.

A decision to cross the Potomac with a hungry, barefoot army and nearly empty ammunition trains could be just the thing to evoke Longstreet's stubborn opposition again, since the man had no glimmer of Lee's strategic daring and little comprehension of the political factors that influenced the commanding general as strongly as the military situation. Colonel Tatum wanted every possible influence working on Longstreet to approve the move into Maryland, if it became possible; and young Thomas with his fiery eyes would want to be the first to splash across the Potomac, unless Tatum missed his guess.

Foxy Bradshaw's luck was just then running out. He had slept later than he intended, exhausted as he was from his exertions the day before, and the fear that continually wracked him. Even in sleep, he could not escape it; he'd dreamed he put his hands between his legs and found nothing there, nothing at all—just a smooth hairless crotch where his legs and his belly and his ass came together. His stones were gone, his asshole, his peter, and he'd awakened sweating, groping to reassure himself. Then he'd dreamed of Josh—drawing down on Ironass one minute, snuffed the next. That was the way it happened, out of the blue. Foxy had had enough.

Hungry, skittish, never thinking of going back, he'd tried to circle well behind the army so he could head west on the road they'd marched when they came down from the mountains four or five days, maybe a week before. Foxy wasn't sure. If he could just get over the mountains, he could make tracks west a lot faster than the army could catch up. *Sposin it-uz comin thataway too.*

Maybe he was in too big a hurry. Maybe in his fear his normal craftiness deserted him. Or maybe he thought too often of Josh's head, opened up in back. *Like Josh tooken a lick from an axe.* In any case, Foxy didn't hear the hoofbeats soon enough, or pay attention to them if he did.

When he finally realized that horsemen were coming over a rise in the Hay Market Road just ahead of him, he scuttled like a rabbit for cover in the roadside brush, flung himself face down, tried to scrunch down into the earth, feeling suddenly as huge and conspicuous as Lige Flournoy.

Too late! He heard the horses halt, jingle of spurs and metal, running footsteps; but he knew he could not run fast enough or far enough, so with his face and hands and feet he burrowed into broomsedge and dirt until rough hands seized him and jerked him to his feet.

"Grab up'is piece ther, Kenny."

A sergeant wearing the yellow armband of a provost marshal flung Foxy toward a small, ragged band of men standing slumped and weary in the road. They were guarded by two armbanded men on horseback, holding carbines. Two other horses—evidently those of Kenny and the sergeant—cropped peacefully at the brush that had failed to hide Foxy Bradshaw.

"I-uz goin back," he bleated. "I aint desertin, I-uz just . . ."

"Goin back wher?" The sergeant, striding toward his horse, shoved Foxy to his knees among the other captives. "You headed fuh the Dump with 'em other boys."

At Lee's headquarters, Major Thomas was still holding Miss Letty's handkerchief hidden in his hand when a mighty clatter of horses and clink of metal announced the arrival of General J. E. B. Stuart and staff, in Stuart's usual cloud of dust.

Thomas watched this showy descent a little warily; he knew Stuart was an outstanding officer but he found it hard to take seriously a general who liked to wear feathers in his hat, sing at the top of his voice, and keep a banjo player on his staff. Besides, Stuart and staff habitually stirred up more dust than a division on the march.

Nevertheless, General Lee and General Longstreet gave Stuart a hearty welcome and drew him immediately into their conference. Longstreet, despite his own calm ways, set a lot of store by the information Stuart brought in—though Thomas suspected that Longstreet was secretly amused by Stuart's peacock strut.

The staff officers of all these generals were laughing and talking near Lee's headquarters tent and Thomas rather tentatively joined them. He always had the feeling that Captain Franklin or someone would question the date of his commission. But Coke Mowbray, one of Stuart's officers with whom Thomas had developed a friendship, clapped him cheerfully on the back.

"Ol Pete gone hit'em today, Jess?"

"Not the way they talkin now."

"Maybe best." Mowbray nodded wisely. "From our camp you kin see nigh to Bull Run. Must be a million bluecoats out ther."

"Fear them not!" a voice boomed in Thomas's ear. "For I have delivered them into thine hand. There shall not a man of them stand before thee!"

A burly major with a dark scab on his face shook his fist in the general direction of Pope's army, then glared about as if daring dissent.

"Maybe half a million anyway." Another of Stuart's officers, whom Thomas did not know, moved into the group. He wore captain's insignia and a clipped mustache; his eyes were calm, brown, almost disinterested—another damn snotty Virginian, Thomas thought.

"More Yanks than *I* ever seen, anyway. You fellows know Jess Thomas? Ol Pete's right-hand man."

Thomas grinned and held up his neatly pinned right sleeve. "Not so's you'd notice."

"Oh, hell—. ." Mowbray looked stricken. "I didn't mean . . ."

"Don't matter."

Thomas started to put out his left hand to the brown-eyed captain, then realized he still was clutching Miss Letty's handkerchief. He stuffed it hastily into his jacket.

"Praise be!" The Bible-quoting major stared with reverence at Thomas's empty sleeve. "In the Lord's service, Brother Thomas. Aint His judgments true and righteous altogether?"

Fargo Hart thought that the black scab down the middle of Major Allen's face was a stigmatic marking, a badge of war, in which the Reverend Major sometimes seemed to find more meaning and comfort than he did in his religion—if a man who considered war God's work could even make a distinction between them.

"Tell you what," Thomas said evenly. "I'll trade you His judgment on me for at good right hand of yours."

Hart could not help laughing out loud. "There's a deal for you, Reverend."

Major Allen gazed at him severely. "Too much serious work to be done this day, Brother Hart, for levity." He shook a long, admonitory finger. "'Pursue after your enemies and smite the hindmost of 'em!'"

He strode away with elephantine dignity, spurs clinking. Thomas stared after him.

"I think you winged 'im, Major."

The lacy handkerchief Thomas had stuffed into his jacket had caught Hart's eye and imagination. A wife's or a sweetheart's? Sent on by mail or bestowed in some sentimental personal exchange? Having come so recently from Missy's arms, feeling himself suddenly the possessor of a sweet, secret life, Hart was acutely sensitive to another man's inner world of love or sorrow, joy or fear.

"Never had much use for chaplains." Thomas spoke a little defiantly, as if he expected disapproval of such heresy. "Not since I heard bout the one at Fair Oaks. Just fore the shootin started there. 'Remember, boys!' he tells'is brigade. 'He who's killed today will sup tonight in Paradise!' So this one webfoot ups and says to'im, says, 'Come on, then, Parson . . . take supper with us!'

"Bout then, the Yanks open up. That chaplain puts spurs to'is horse'n lights out for the rear.

"'Hey, boys!' the webfoot yells. 'Parson aint hungry!'"

Hart found this standard army yarn good for a laugh, coming as it did from a man with the right to tell it—especially one who had put the Reverend Major so firmly in his place.

"Cept the maje aint no chaplain." Mowbray, grinning, looked after the retreating Allen. "Say this for'im, too: he'd as lief kill Yanks as quote Scripture. How's a man get a cuppa coffee round-yere?"

Hart watched Mowbray and Thomas make their way toward the headquarters coffee pot. He thought again about the handkerchief tucked into the major's jacket. All war's ferocity could not dim the importance of such small things. The memory of Missy's hair, or her lips on his—only such symbols of humanity's enduring emotions could survive the inhumanity of war. It was well known in the army, in fact, that even Ol Jack cherished letters from his wife, and wrote frequently to her, as if to remain somehow in touch not just with a woman he loved but with a world that war denied.

The spirit that goeth upward. Surely that was what he and Missy had shared—what must infuse the letters Ol Jack sent and read. Love lifted man out of himself, out of the dark passages of ordinary life as well as the violent eruptions of war. Love and love's fruit—compassion, concern, pity, generosity—could no more be vanquished in war than subdued in the daily trials of existence. Maybe finding Missy vivid as Queen Anne's lace in the dust and blood of the battlefield was a truth as hardy as life itself.

Why then—Hart had been asking himself all that morning, with the sense of Missy still in his arms, the way men like Thomas were said to feel for months, even years, the presence of their missing hands or arms or legs—why then *the spirit that goeth downward?*

Why the mindless slaughter of men, most of whom could not have said why they fought, or what the war was about, or what would be accomplished that could validate its vast impersonal grinding?

Hart had found no answer, either in his experience or in the studies that now seemed so far behind him, in another world. No answer except that love and savagery abide, share the same body, tug at the same spirit. And no comfort except that even on Ol Jack's field, a man might find Missy, and another would always carry a lover's handkerchief in his jacket.

Someone put a heavy arm across his shoulders. "How'd you leave your *cousin,* Hart? Your *distant* cousin, I mean."

Hart looked around into Colonel Snowden's leering face. "Not so distant, Colonel."

"A little parly-view, huh? Sang-fraud?" Snowden screwed up the right side of his face in an elaborate wink.

If you only knew, Hart thought, feeling suddenly rich in his secret love, his mellow sense of the world. *If you had any idea.* But then he thought that perhaps the colonel did. Who was Fargo Hart to assume himself wiser, deeper in experience, than any other man?

"Actually," he said, "the lady don't speak French, Colonel." He screwed up his own face in a wink as exaggerated as Snowden's. "But we communicated in the . . . ah . . . universal language. *N'est-ce pas?*"

On the other side of the pike, in the pine woods a hundred yards back from the railroad embankment, Privates Gillum Stone and James F. Sowell were making a breakfast of slosh for themselves and Private Lott McGrath. Lott took no interest in this, or in anything else, remaining indifferent to everything around him. The black hole in his temple made Gilly nervous, as did Lott's blank face.

Sowell mixed their small supply of flour with water, while Stone fried the single hunk of bacon they had left from the rich haul at Manassas. Their twig fire produced a flame not much larger than a candle's.

"Don't b'long yere, Sowbelly. Shape he's in."

"Keep thinkin he'll come outten it. Aint natchral, way he just set there'n stare."

"Make a man's skin crawl, don't it?"

"Bacon fried out yit?"

"I reck'n."

Gilly speared the bacon with his bayonet and put it on a piece of pine bark. He watched glumly as Sowell poured the flour-and-water paste from his tin cup into the hot grease.

"I say soon's we eat, we turn'im over't the bonecrackers."

"On'y thing is, aint nuthin *wrong* with'im. Walk good's you'n me. Ceptin at hole, look just as good, too. Em docs got no time, man don't have'is arm or leg shot off."

"Alla same . . ." Gilly gave the slosh a stir with his bayonet. "Sposin they's a fight. What we gone do with'im then?"

"Could be jus the thing. I mean, Yanks come, ol Lott jus mought grab up'is piece'n let fly like he useter."

"But iffen he just set ther like now, somebody got to look out fer'im."

They divided the bacon and slosh meticulously into three equal portions, but Lott ignored his.

"Don't blame'im," Gilly said.

As they ate their own breakfasts, Sowell and Stone decided to walk McGrath to the regimental surgery and see if the bonecrackers would help. After dividing Lott's uneaten food and cleaning their few utensils, they set out for the rear. Lott in his red-checked shirt walked along obediently, carrying his piece on his shoulder.

"You'd-a tole me I'd ever see Lott McGrath go a whole day'n never say a *word*, Gilly, I'd-a said you'uz the crazy one."

"Think he's crazy?"

Sowbelly looked at him incredulously. "You think he *aint?*"

"Hey, you two! Wher you goin?"

Four mounted men approached, wearing yellow armbands. They pulled up and a lean corporal dismounted. A livid scar ran from his ear across his left cheek to the corner of his mouth.

"Takin McGrath here to surg'ry."

"What's wrong with'im?"

"Hole in'is head." Sowell turned Lott so the corporal could see the wound. "Messed'im up so's he aint said nare word since."

"Look able-body to me." The scarred corporal scarcely bothered to inspect Lott's wound, as if his own demeaned any other.

Gilly made a circling motion with his finger pointed at his ear. "Jus aint right. Gotta see a sawbones."

"What good's that gone do if he's..." The corporal repeated Gilly's circling motion. "We'll take'im."

"But he aint done nuthin cept tooken at slug th'other night."

The corporal shrugged. "Got my orders. We'll take'im." He seized Lott's arm and Lott turned obediently toward him.

"Now *wait* a minute here, he's hurt, he aint..."

"You wanta come, too?" The corporal glared at Sowell and shoved Lott toward the other marshals. "Need all the bodies we kin find."

"But y'aint spose to grab up no *wounded.*"

The corporal put his scarred face close to Sowell's. "Gimme some more at shit. Tell me what I aint spose to do."

"But lissen..." Sowell felt Gilly's nervous fingers pulling at his arm. "We-uz jus takin'im to surg'ry. We aint..."

"Takin'im nowhers. One more word, *y'all* goin with us."

Private James F. Sowell was a temperate man. He was also a veteran. he knew the army had no more to do with justice than did war itself. But he and Gilly and Lott had been together a long time. Up and down the Valley and on the Peninsula with Ol Jack. They had looked out for each other. Now he and Gilly had found Lott with a hole by his eye and a blank in his head. Sowell's view was uncomplicated; he believed it still was up to them to look out for Lott, as he had no doubt Lott would have done for either of them. Justice had nothing to do with it and loyalty was a big word; but they had to look out for each other. No one else would.

Sowell did not even need to think such things. They were too clear to him to require thought. So he put the muzzle of his piece up under the corporal's chin.

"You aint takin nobody nowhers, Scrapeface."

Past the corporal's upreared startled face and mouth suddenly displaying horseshoes of yellow teeth, Sowell could see the three mounted marshals stiffen and reach for sidearms.

"Draw'n I'll blow'is damn head off, boys. She's cocked."

Sowell knew just what he meant to do. They'd walk Scrapeface with them to the surgery and let the docs take Lott, if they would. After that, Sowell was willing to accept whatever Scrapeface could do about it. After looking out for Lott.

Private Gillum Stone might well have been willing to follow

the same plan, had he understood it. But he didn't. He saw nothing but madness in Sowell's action; and while he, too, was loyal to Lott and mindful of Lott's plight, Gilly was not one to look for trouble. He knew the ordinarily restrained Sowell was capable of violent rage at real or fancied affront. Gilly's instinct was to get them all out of a mess Sowell was taking them into.

"Wait a *minute*, ther . . . Sowbelly! . . . we can't . . ."

His fingers closed on Sowell's arm; with an instinctive jerk, he half-turned him away from Scrapeface— just long enough for the corporal to knock Sowell's rifle barrel aside, duck, and drive his shoulder into Sowell's ribs.

"Dammit! Gilly . . ."

But Sowell's shout was cut short by Scrapeface's flailing fist. For a moment the two men struggled in a swarm of arms and legs. Realizing too late what he'd done, Gilly looked on helplessly. Beside him Lott McGrath stared at the struggling men with still, inscrutable eyes.

"Hold it right ther!"

A mounted marshal was aiming a pistol at the men on the ground. The other two, dismounted, ran to help Scrapeface.

Gilly wanted to pitch into them, undo what he'd done, save Sowbelly. But he saw no way to do it. He couldn't fight them all. If Sowell only hadn't gone off half-cocked . . .

"Break it up! Goddamyuh! Break it up!"

One of the marshals knelt and shoved his pistol barrel against Sowell's ear; with his other hand, he seized Sowell's hair and jerked his head back, hard. Gilly watched Scrapeface rise slowly to his feet, gasping for breath.

"Damn you . . . Gilly . . ." Sowell's voice was choked, raging. "You aint got *shit* for brains . . . you . . ."

Scrapeface kicked him on the hip. "More brains than you." He dismissed Gilly with a jerk of his head. "Git on back t'yuh compny, sojer."

"But whut about . . . lissen . . . they aint . . ." Gilly was at once relieved to be out of it and ashamed for Sowbelly's trouble.

"Two for the Dump," Scrapeface said. "Git this'un's ass up'n git him'n the loony moving." He glared at Gilly. "Didn't I tell you to git back t'yuh compny."

"You shit, Gilly," Sowell said. "Stinkin polecat pile-a ratshit."

"But I didn mean . . . Sowbelly, I on'y tried . . ."

"Gitchuh ass movin quick," Scrapeface said. "Don't, we kin use you at the Dump, too."

• • •

For more than two hours after Cady died, the New Man sat against the headstone, holding the sergeant's body. He had known the exact moment of death, not by any sign from Cady or anything visible, but by the sudden slack feel of him. One moment he had held an unmistakably vital thing against his chest, a being with its own impulses, however faint. Then Cady had said, quite calmly, "Aw"—or maybe "Paul," except that Grice didn't know anybody named Paul in the Compny. The next moment there was an inert mass in the New Man's arms.

He had thought immediately of something barely recalled from brief childhood exposure to the Bible, something about *the quick and the dead*. He understood the words precisely. He had felt Cady quick in his arms; and then Cady was dead.

By the time it had happened—Cady suddenly not Cady or anything anymore—Grice was almost ready for it. Not entirely. He wept briefly, as much for his own emptiness as for the end that had come to Cady. Then he wondered whether that really *was* an end.

Preachers claimed there was a life after death, but to the extent the New Man had ever considered the matter, that seemed out of kilter with what he knew of things. Seemed too easy. Like bragging on a fish you'd caught when nobody'd seen the fish but you, or ever would. Seemed queer, too, that life before death was so hard and life after death was supposed to be milk and honey.

Nor had it escaped Grice that the one was here and now, something he *knew*, and the other was only promised, something nobody had ever seen or reported on firsthand. Just promised, at that, only by preachers who had no other stock in trade but the notion that things would get better for you if you did thus and so and believed this and that. In Grice's experience, no matter what you did, things got worse.

Like Cady dead with his belly blown open. Which was so bad that the New Man had to wonder anew about life after death. Beyond all reason that a man like Cady, just coming into his prime—Ol jack would have made Cady an officer; Grice had always believed in both too much to doubt it for a moment— beyond reason a man so valuable could just be snuffed into whatever there was if there wasn't no life after death.

Grice realized then that he couldn't imagine, had not even the faintest hint of an idea, what there *could* be after death if not another life. He was too ignorant to conceive of nothingness, the most difficult idea for anyone to grasp. He was too practical to think that he, or certainly a man like Cady, might not *be*—not just be *alive* but be *anything* or *anywhere*. So Cady's death forced him to the conclusion, after all, that there must be a life after death, simply because there was no alternative he could even think of, much less credit, worthy of Cady.

That was one thing he decided in the grim morning hours after Cady ceased to be quick, with the sun rising ugly and blistering into the eastern sky and the bodies still being hauled wholesale into Sudley churchyard to the bloodsoaked surgeons. All around him the dead and the goners lay among the graves, but for a while Grice felt at home. Cady belonged with the dead, and Grice felt that he belonged with Cady for a while longer.

But gradually, sweating under the relentless sun and with the weight of Cady sagging on him like responsibility, Grice also decided that he had to light out. Marshals would be coming to pick up stragglers. He had to light out because he was *not* going back to the Compny. Too much to do, to make Cady's life and death mean something. And they wouldn't unless . . . unless what, the New Man was not sure. But he knew people like Cady somehow deserved better than they got. And he believed that in his deathbed lie to Cady, his decision not to go back, he had accepted an obligation to them.

He took a long time getting out from under Cady's body, so that it would lie back undisturbed against the side of the tombstone. He made sure Cady's hands still were clasped over the wound in his belly, partially concealing its indignity. He found Cady's slouch hat and put it on his head, tipping it down to shade the closed eyes; and he braced Cady's chin against his chest so he would not be found with flies crawling in his open mouth. If Grice had known how to write, he would have left a note in the pocket of Cady's worn shirt: Sergeant Owen L. Cade, Company D, Thirteenth Georgia.

But he could only hope Cady had identification on him somewhere. Already, the sergeant was beginning not to look like himself—smaller, Grice thought, than he'd been in life. His cheeks were sunken and the wrists protruding from his ragged sleeves looked scrawny as birdlegs. Grice remembered Cady's prediction that Reb deaders, filled with food stolen from Manassas, would puff up in the sun like toad-frogs, same as Yanks did. Cady knew about such things so it might happen yet, as the sun rose; but there was nothing Grice could do to stop it.

The New Man had not until then studied the dead carefully,

although he had seen many. Deaders had seemed unreal to him, more like scarecrows tipped over than remnants of real persons. But as he took his last intent look at what seemed a shrunken Cady, a new thought occurred to him: maybe a man's soul had size and shape inside of him; maybe when it flew off to life after death it was like meal had been poured out of a sack. And what else was the sack for, except to hold the meal?

Grice turned his back resolutely, and started to walk away. He had a sense of starting over. Thanks to Cady, he knew something at last. He did not know what he was going to do but he knew something—that things were going to be different for him.

"Hey, Johnny . . . aint you spose to be somewhere else?"

In his concern with Cady, Grice had not seen the provost-marshal squad enter the churchyard, wearing their yellow armbands. Two of them confronted him at the edge of the graveyard.

"Lookin out for my sarge."

"Trouble with at," one of the marshals said, "Ol Jack don't low no nursemaidin round-yere."

"Sergeant Cade." Grice tried to speak as if this would settle the matter in his favor, but he was not practiced at sounding confident. "They'd of sewed'im up, he mought of made it."

"Cashed in?" The marshal sounded friendly.

"Bout sunup."

"Trouble with at," the marshal said, "you should of hightailed it bout then, too. *You* mought of made it."

Well, it was time, Grice thought. Time to git started on whatever his new life was to be. Because whatever else he did from here on out, he aimed to stand up.

"I aint goin back, boys." He squared his shoulders as he imagined Cady might have done, and thrust out his jaw.

The marshal looked surprised. "Cose not," he said. "Orders is, deserters to the Dump."

Chapter Thirteen

August 30—Forenoon

AMY ARNALL WAS lying wide awake in her bed when she heard the rapid clopping of hooves and the yelping of Sheriff Maxton's dogs coming up the lane to Sycamore.

Now he comes, she thought bitterly, illogically. Only a few hours too late.

Perversely, she made no move to get up or freshen her clothes and appearance. Let him find out what he could from Judge Arnall first; Amy Singleton Arnall would not go rushing down like a schoolgirl squealing the news. The Judge would still be sober and happy to chatter on for awhile.

Odd how quickly everything had fallen back into routine. Willis wheeling the Judge out to the verandah as if nothing had happened. Little Luke playing happily in the nursery under Reba's watchful eye. Already not a trace left in the sewing factory of what had happened.

"Except *every*thing's changed now."

Her own voice startled Amy; she had not realized that she had spoken aloud. Suddenly, listening to the commotion of horses and dogs in the yard, she wanted to lock her door, pull the covers over her head, and stay forever hidden and alone. *Eep, ipe, eat a piece of pipe . . . jump in the bed, cover up your head . . .* the childhood nonsense rhyme leaped to her mind but disappeared instantly. The mere thought of covering up her head had sent quivering through her an echoing sense of the sewing factory, and the dark, and the silence.

While the blast of the gun had still reverberated in her head like a drumroll, Amy's back had slipped down the wall behind the open door. Her knees had not buckled; she hadn't collapsed. But the strength of her legs drained slowly away, like snow melting, and gradually she sank toward the floor. At one point, when the echoes of the shot had almost died, her legs and body seemed to have reached a kind of equilibrium, and she found herself in a rigid seated position, her back flat against the wall, her thighs perpendicular to her torso, her calves and ankles perpendicular to her thighs, her feet flat on the floor. But there was no chair beneath her, and even in ordinary circumstances her legs would not have been strong enough to sustain this position.

Gradually, Amy slipped on down until she sat on the floor, still against the wall, her knees hunched up in front of her face, the pistol in her hand on the floor beside her. As the last echo of the shot faded from the room—though not from her head—she let go of the ivory butt, clasped both arms around her legs, and put her face tightly against her knees.

It's done I did it.

She told herself again and again *it's done I did it it's done I did it* rhythmically, rapidly *it's done I did it* an incantation against thought, a ritual as relieving as laudanum *it's done I did it . . .*

But even sedatives wear off. Before long she was forcing the litany, losing its deadening effect. After its soothing rhythm had stopped entirely, however, Amy kept her face pressed to her knees and her back to the wall.

The rattle and scrape of the thing on the floor had long since ceased. She had no need to look at it; Amy *knew* what she would find. She had killed. She . . . a *lady*.

Of course, it had had to be done. Jason would have tried to open the safe. In his rage when he found he couldn't, he'd have thrown her on the floor, ripped off her clothes, and raped her. Her screams would have awakened little Luke, even the Judge. Then Jason would have had to kill them all. Eventually, he'd have killed them all. So she'd had to do it. No doubt about that. Anybody would say she'd had to do it.

But I'm a lady.

The story would spread like poison ivy. Everybody would hear it. The General. What would the General think about his wife shooting a nigger? A wife supposed to be a lady. He wouldn't *know* how it had been. Or, if he did, he'd probably think she just panicked like a woman.

His career. Everybody would hear the story. General Lee would

hear it. What would happen to the General's career when everybody knew he had a wife that shot a nigger who was trying to
rape her? Amy had no illusions about the relative value to the
General of his career and his wife. He could get another wife.

Some people, of course, would think Jason *had* raped her.
Always be somebody to think that. Jane Moring, for one. And
even those who didn't would *wonder*. People would wonder for
the rest of her life. Pressing her face against her knees, alone in
the dark, envisioning the future, Amy knew that quite certainly.

Not just wonder if Jason really had done it to her. But wonder
how a *lady* could have killed somebody, even a nigger. And since
the killing was a fact, there'd be those who'd say she wasn't a
lady. Couldn't be. Not anymore, anyway.

That seemed to Amy the one thing she could not face. Being
a lady was her life, like being the General was his. Being a lady
enabled her to cope with being a woman. If people—men, the
Africans, tradespeople, other ladies—thought you were a lady
and you conducted yourself as if you were, they acted as if you
were. But if they came to think Amy Singleton Arnall was *not* a
lady, they would act as if she were not.

Jason might as well have done it to her, Amy thought bitterly.
All she'd done was try to protect herself and her child and the
General's house. And she would probably never live it down
because nobody else would know how it had been. How she'd
had to do it to Jason.

Jason. After all these hours and days of fear, of not letting
herself think about what he would do to her, suddenly she felt no
longer alone. She seemed to share an eerie intimacy with Jason—
just as they had shared the darkness that made them equal, that
made everything so easy for both of them. Easy for her to squeeze
not jerk the trigger. And the scraping and gagging had really not
lasted long. Even in the echoes of the shot, she'd been able to
tell that. So if it had hurt him, it hadn't hurt for long.

She could not feel horror—as she had at the fight between
Jason and Pettigrew—because she did not feel as if she had done
a violent thing. *Just squeeze not jerk.* Nothing like Jason standing
over Miss Tippy with the pillow. Or the quilt. Whichever. Not
like slamming the axe into Pettigrew. Jason had surely hurt Pettigrew. And if Miss Tippy hadn't been hurt exactly, what would
have been worse were the last moments of darkness with the pillow
coming down. Or the quilt. And Miss Tippy not able to breathe
or scream, there under the darkness and the smothering weight,
maybe just barely able to clutch Jason's apish wrists in her tiny

old ladylike hands. Had Miss Tippy then felt the same strange intimacy with him that Amy felt now? The participation?

Amy shuddered, her whole body quivering against the wall, her forehead aching with the pressure of her knees. Jason had deserved what he got. She'd had to do it. But . . . they'd *shared* so much.

A light tap at her bedroom door roused Amy from memory. "What is it?"

"Shurf, Mistis. Spectfully say kin he speak wid you?"

"Say I'll be down, then."

In my own good time, she thought, listening to light footsteps trot away along the hall. Took *his* getting here.

Which was, of course, not fair. Undoubtedly the man had come as soon as Bess had found him. But why should she be fair to him? Who had been fair to her? What was fair about anything that had happened, none of which she'd asked for?

Amy was not clear how long she had huddled herself in a fetal position against the wall, behind the door she had left ajar for Jason. She might have dozed a little, come awake, dozed again. She didn't even think about time, any more than she thought about silence. She *did* think about darkness; for it seemed fitting that she and Jason should still be alone there in the equalizing night.

She became aware of the silence only when it was broken, softly and shapelessly; simultaneously she wondered what time it was. The sounds that aroused her were not definite or alarming. Not like the clink of silver or the rattle of death. Nor did they seem to be in the house. More like a breeze moving, or leaves being raked in the fall; maybe the people moving in the yard on a slow summer day . . .

People *were* in the yard. As Amy realized that, separated at least one of the sounds into an indistinct mutter of voices, she lifted her head at last—careful to look well to her left, at the back of the door rather than at the center of the room. Dull pre-sunrise light was drifting like mist in the sewing factory. The night was over, its brief equality banished; and Amy felt suddenly an alien, all intimacy destroyed by gray light in that room of death. She began to rise to her feet, her muscles stiff and balky, the pistol abandoned on the floor. Someone rapped at the back door.

Time suddenly took meaning; Amy wished the night could have gone on sheltering her, concealing what she had done to Jason. But as she stood up, peering steadfastly at the back of the door, she was relieved, too. The intimacy of the night now seemed horrid, perverse; she was glad it was done.

Jerkily, like a marionette, she forced her stiff body to move out of the sewing factory—still not looking at what she had caused, lying heaped in the middle of the floor—and went slowly along the hall to the rear door. The rapping came again, more sharply.

Amy took a long time unlatching the door. Then she took a deep breath before opening it. Pulling it back, looking out into the world would be the beginning of a different life. It was not a start she could lightly make; but after awhile, the porcelain knob chilly in her hand, Amy opened the door.

Reba stood on the stoop, a look of fear only barely held in check on her thin yellow face.

"Ohh . . . Mistis . . . we aint . . ."

Tears suddenly sprang in Reba's eyes, and her voice choked. Amy did not notice. Nor did she see any of the other Africans— two men, three women—standing silently in the yard.

She saw no one but Jason. He stood just below Reba on the stoop, his arm in a crude sling; he was shorter than she remembered, or maybe just a little bent over, blacker, not so powerful looking, or so menacing. Jason looked tired.

Amy felt betrayed. *Didn't come wasn't going to . . .*

She had no time to think more than that before Jason pushed past Reba, stepped around Amy, and ran along the hall. Amy heard the duck board quack again, as it had in the night; then a moment of silence hung in the hall like the second between lightning and thunderclap; and she heard in her heart, before it rang in her ears, Jason's cry of mortal anguish— more nearly a howl, she realized later, as if one of the sheriff's hounds might have bayed the faraway moon.

The sound seemed to release her from paralysis of the brain, just as she felt her body release at last the telltale flow that for weeks it had so inexplicably stanched; and she thought desolately, in the gray light of dawn *deceived everything deceives.*

Amy swung her legs to the floor and sat on the edge of the bed, feeling unjustly soured and spoiled. She was angrier at the General now for her false concern than she had been when she thought it justified; and she had never hated Jason as much, when she feared him, as she did now in the knowledge of his treachery.

Footsteps came along the hall; someone tapped again at the door.

"I'm comin. Tell'im I'll be down in a minute."

"Yessum."

Amy plodded across the room and peered at herself in the mirror, without much interest, uncomfortable with cramps. She looked as if she needed sleep and to wash her hair—otherwise, no different. Nothing showing. A little powder on her face, a quick brush, and she could get by for now. She would not look like a woman who had killed.

Amazing that that had not been her first thought *I killed* while the echoes still rang through the sewing factory. Astonishing how adeptly the mind could avoid for awhile *took life* what was finally inescapable. Pathetic the way the human sensibility tried to submerge the truth *thou shall not* clothe it, as she concealed her body in petticoats, in layer upon layer of rationalization and justification. Reprehensible the false concerns consciousness could rear in the way of realization.

Sinned against God.

Amy went into her small dressing room, opened her Bible to Revelations, and found the key to her secret drawer, where once the pistol had seemed so incongruous. She picked up first the bottle of laudanum, fingered it briefly, longingly, and put it back. Laudanum later.

Then she took out the little pot of rouge. For it seemed fitting that a woman of shame should go down with a painted face to explain to Sheriff Maxton how she had shot Easter dead on the sewing factory floor.

When they put the fair-haired boy on the bloody altar table, he was singing the chorus from "Faith of our Fathers." The thin young voice reminded Major Worsham of the wheezy pump organ in the Methodist Church, back home in Rockbridge County.

. . . we will be true . . . to thee-e till death.

"What's your name, boy?" Major Worsham had already started cutting away the bloodstained shirt. It was so worn, anyway, that it almost came apart in his hands.

"Muh . . . Muh-gee, sir."

"Sounds Irish, McGee."

The fair-haired boy's eyes flashed in his pain-wracked face. "Not me!"

"Too bad." The major bent nearer the wound. A Minié appeared to have penetrated clean through the elbow. "Always say you can't hardly kill an Irishman."

Major Worsham had had a long, hard night in Sudley Church. Since the Stonewall Brigade had seen little action the day before, he'd been helping out the surgeons of Hill's Division, who had more to do than they could handle. They still did.

"I aint no Roman," the boy said.

"Oh, it aint religion that saves the Irish. All at whiskey they guzzle." Tired as he was, Worsham still tried to keep up a sort of reassuring chatter with the torn and bloodied scarecrows who followed in quick succession to his operating table.

"Aint no drunkard, neither."

"Fulla piss'n vinegar though. One of Ol Jack's boys, aint you?"

Near a joint, the ends of bones were more resilient, like hard rubber; farther along the shaft, a bone struck even by a round ball would splinter like kindling. So when a conical Minié came tumbling through rent flesh to strike bone, you'd get the worst kind of comminution. Major Worsham, like every battle surgeon, had concluded that when a long bone in arm or leg took such a shattering hit, the only thing to do was to amputate as soon as possible. But this reedy-voiced young'un—Worsham made him out to be no more than eighteen or nineteen—had taken the ball through the joint instead. The long bones were intact and the arm looked salvageable.

Faith of our fa-athers . . . li-iving still . . .

A real believer. Well, who wouldn't be, with his arm drilled open? Who wouldn't call for some kind of help?

Worsham finished his inspection and made up his mind. If only he weren't so damn tired, up all night cutting and sawing like a butcher in a packinghouse, the sickening stench of gore so familiar that he could even control his nausea . . . anyway, if he were coming to it fresh he had no doubt he could keep this psalm-singer whole. Badly damaged, but whole.

"All right, McGee, hush up now'n listen. I can do one of two things with at arm. Cut it off across here . . ." Major Worsham drew a line with his finger across the boy's skinny bicep, white below his pecan-colored face and neck. "When'd you git hit?"

The boy's eyes, under his fair hair, bulged with fear. His voice choked. "Jes . . . 'fore sundown."

"Fourteen . . . maybe fifteen hours ago. I cut it off, I'd give you at least eight chances out of ten you'll live a long life'n learn to write love letters left-handed."

Worsham had studied, in the few quiet days after the Peninsula fighting, a report from the bloody field of Shiloh, in the west, that documented what he and other surgeons had observed: primary amputations, performed within twenty-four hours of a wound, were far more successful—in elementary terms of living and dying—than secondary operations done later. At Shiloh, eight out of ten wounded men requiring amputation but failing to get surgery within twenty-four hours had died.

A better statistical history from the Crimean War made the same point. Worsham's private estimate after the Peninsula was that at least twice as many immediate deaths followed secondary amputations as primary—although he had no way of knowing how many men died long after from the effects of either.

But the boy on the table was gulping and writhing, his eyes still bulging, and Major Worsham tensed to jump out of the way. Some'd throw up all over you. Prob'ly more at the news than from the wound.

"On the other hand, so to speak, that Yankee lead sort of slid through your elbow without smashing up too much in there. So I could try a resection."

"That's better, aint it, sir?"

Graspin at straws. Wouldn't know a resection from a ligature.

"Depends, McGee. You'd keep your arm if it worked. But not what's in your elbow that hooks up this part of it . . ." He touched the boy's forearm. "To up here. You'd keep the arm'n look more or less like anybody else. But that arm'd be the same as tits on a boy. No real use to anybody. Just hangin there."

"That's better, though." The boy was listening intently. "Lots better, sir."

"Cept I do that, I'm not givin you eight chances out of ten. Even if I do my job right . . ." Worsham held up his hands and stared at them critically. *Steady still.* "Which I reckn you can trust me for that. But the danger of infection goes way up, with at hole still in your arm and you laid up longer. We know how to cut off'n arm a lot better'n we know how to save one."

Worsham knew, however, that troops had their own way of looking at things. The fear of the quick knife was so great in the army that men who were in agony and bleeding to death had been known to refuse to seek medical attention. Nor were they entirely wrong, Worsham conceded; the proven need for early surgery made too many bonecrackers *too* eager to amputate—not wanting, at best, to take chances; not bothering, at worst, with any but the quickest and easiest step. Some would resort to the knife for a compound fracture, as if a man could grow back a leg or an arm the way a lizard reproduced its tail.

"I b'leeve on the Lord Jesus Christ. He leadeth me."

"That heps you maybe. Don't hep me a bit what *you* believe."

"A good shepherd," the boy said. "Giveth his life for'is sheep."

"Want me to leave it on, then?"

"One fold . . . one shepherd." And the reedy voice rose again: "Faith of our fa-athers . . ."

The resection was what Worsham wanted to do anyway, as much to prove his skill as from conviction that it was better for the boy; so he took Christian affirmation for medical consent and told his one-eyed orderly to start the chloroform. Ordinarily, he might have done that himself, but under the pressure of all the work they'd been doing the orderly had learned the procedure well. Might make a surgeon himself some day, was he crazy enough to want such a life.

The major took advantage of his first respite in hours, and stepped outside the reeking church. But outside was little better than in. The putrid smell of blood, death, and feces hovered in the air. The dead and wounded lay everywhere in the grove and the graveyard, their groans and ravings a steady maniacal chorus. Somewhere in the distance guns rumbled, a prelude to more cutting and sawing and stanching and sewing.

Worsham badly wanted a good long swig from one of the bottles of medical spirits beside his altar-operating table. But that was an impulse to which he never yielded—not till he could find a long-enough lull in the fighting to get himself blind drunk without consequence to others. And well away from Ol Jack's abstemious eye.

They *knew* so little. So he and his colleagues did their jobs inadequately—were bound to. Yet Ol Jack needed every fighting man he had. If the damned abolitionist invaders ever were going to be thrown out of Virginia and taught their lesson, he needed every wounded man patched up quickly and sent back to ranks. And the Surgeons' Corps just wasn't up to the job, as hard as its members tried.

That was what bedeviled Major Worsham, night and day. That and the mangled bodies he didn't know how to heal. A terrible thing to have to offer that boy in there a choice like that—no arm, or a useless arm.

Lately, Worsham had felt as if he were in a vast unlit room with only the tiniest of guttering candles to guide him; and the more experience taught him of the darkness, the more he realized its opacity. The more he knew he did *not* know. And nobody did. If you learned through hard reality that for some wounds only amputation could avoid fatal infection, that still didn't tell you what you really needed to know—what caused the infection, and how to prevent or cure it.

Worsham had seen them all—tetanus, erysipelas, pyemia. He had been one of the first to notice, after Jackson's victory at Port Republic earlier that summer, a form of infection that was progressively becoming more of a menace. Everybody had his theory about what caused hospital gangrene, as they were calling it—fatigue, depression, bad food, dysentery, something in the atmosphere of crowded camps and hospitals. Numerous remedies had been tried—sesquichloride of iron, quinine dissolved in alcohol, local applications of turpentine, tincture of iron, Darby's Fluid. Some of these treatments worked, sometimes.

Worsham personally refused to apply nitric acid to burn out gangrenous tissue, as some surgeons did; he could not believe that anything causing such intense pain—even with chloroform for the patient—for so little provable result could be good medicine. But the gangrene cases kept piling up; and the only thing he felt reasonably sure about was that the farther from the actual field of battle, the more gangrene he saw. So it was caused by something *they*—not Yankee bullets—were doing. Or not doing.

A surgeon named Bankhead from Pender's Brigade came out of the church and lit up a cigar. Worsham knew him only vaguely in the normal sense; but he had seen the man working as steadily and bloodily through the night as he had. That was something more than a mere acquaintance.

Bankhead came over and offered a cigar.

"Thanks . . . not a smoker."

"Me neither. But mought be good to smell tobacco smoke. Stead of . . . all this."

"Burn a whole field of it, if it is."

They stood a moment in tired silence. Then Bankhead took the cigar out of his mouth and crushed it under his boot.

"Don't hep. You hear bout Gin'al Ewell?"

"Heard he got hit th'other night."

"Lost'is leg."

Well, the Minié was no respecter of rank. "Gone live?"

"Hard to tell. Took it off to the hip."

"Christ."

In the Crimea, the Limeys had lost nearly two thirds of thigh amputees. Worsham doubted he and his colleagues were doing much better.

"Major Daniel took it off. So I hear."

"Good man." But the truth of it was that none of them was good enough. Or knew enough. God help Ewell, for Ol Jack needed him more than most.

Bankhead took a piece of tarnished metal from one pocket and a pair of pliers from another. With the pliers he began twisting and bending one prong of what Worsham saw was a cheap table fork. Worsham watched curiously.

"I'm-a break this prong off, then bend the other'n into a hook. It'll do me for a tenaculum."

Every surgeon Worsham knew—every one who cared about his work—had become an innovator. They'd found that the juice of green persimmons would stop bleeding if no other styptic was at hand. The simplest penknife would do for a scalpel in a pinch. A carpenter's saw had had to rasp through many a long bone. Worsham had learned to boil horsehairs to make them pliant and soft enough to do for sutures. He knew surgeons who claimed to have observed that maggoty wounds healed better, because the maggots consumed infected tissue.

"Back to work." Worsham gestured at the men lying in the churchyard. "Got to send some-a these sons back to kill Yanks."

"Prob'ly more to come." Bankhead snapped off the prong triumphantly and gestured with the fork toward the sound of the guns. "Ol Jack aint finished yet."

But as Worsham went up the church steps the guns in the distance didn't sound to him as if more were happening. He stepped gingerly along the body-cluttered center aisle toward his altar-operating table, under which his orderly was adjusting the position of the wooden tub that would catch the fair-haired boy's blood. Worsham saw that the boy's face was calm now, childlike and a bit slack in the repose of chloroform.

"Good'n limber." The orderly flexed the boy's unhurt arm to demonstrate. "Went off like a baby."

Worsham checked over his instruments. "Good for him. I aint in the mood for more damn hymns."

At Jackson's headquarters near the center of the line, but in the pine woods behind it, Teddy Redmund was in better spirits. Jackson's staff had seen to it that he breakfasted almost decently on powerful coffee, stony biscuits, and leathery bacon. *They*, at least, didn't seem to credit the notion that an English officer and a gentleman might be a spy, but chatted amiably—if not informatively—about the war, inquiring with interest about his experience in the Crimea. They did not seem to share, however, his respect for General McClellan. Young Captain Selby offered the most succinct judgment on the matter:

"Couldn't carry Jackson's saddlebags."

Redmund thought it expedient not to mention what he knew from diligent research—that as a matter of direct comparison, Thomas J. Jackson had stood only seventeenth of fifty-nine in the West Point class of 1846. George B. McClellan had been second in the same class.

But it was Colonel Channing—somewhat friendlier than he had seemed the night before—who seemed most anxious to convince Redmund of Jackson's excellence:

"Most determined man I ever saw." In the rising heat of the morning, Channing unbuttoned the deplorable jacket that was too tight across his bony chest. "Don't let a thing stand in'is way just cause it's *there*. Gin'al Wilcox, over with Longstreet, he was in the same class at the Point. Wilcox says Jackson use to keep a notebook full of rules for himself. Very first one was, 'You may be whatever you resolve to be.'"

Had there been, at the mention of Longstreet, the merest bob of Channing's head off to the right, as if to suggest Longstreet's actual presence? Redmund thought so, but could not be sure.

"You know, Duke, Stonewall got'is nickname fightin on a Sunday, right down the road ther. But he won't read a letter, not even from'is wife, or mail one on a Sunday, kin he avoid it. Or march troops. More prayin and thankin Providence than a Methody preacher. But then you see'im inna fight, you mought think you-uz seein Joshuway himself. Cept *he* was a Jew. Like as if it-uz Ol Jack, not Joshuway, that the Lord told to stretch out the spear in thy hand, and I will deliver thine enemies. Cause when Ol Jack fights, the Lord usely does."

Redmund, who had fled the church at an early age, found disconcerting the tendency of Americans, particularly these southern rustics, to quote the Bible. As if they all knew it by heart and took it literally! Better some of these officers should be quoting Jomini than Scripture.

"Major Worsham's talking with'im one night after a hard day's fight. He's right familiar with Jackson. So Jackson turns to'im like he's just discovered something, says: 'How horrible is war!'

"But this Worsham's a fire-eater. 'Yes,' he says, 'but what can we do? They invaded *us*.'

"Jackson looks at Worsham like he's crazy. 'Do? Kill'em, sir! Kill evry man!' Fights like he aims to do it, too."

To Redmund, Channing actually was making Jackson seem crazier even than he'd supposed—an Old Testament warrior of fire and sword, transplanted to the modern nineteenth century.

Still, if Lee and Longstreet actually *had* come on to join him—
and that seemed more and more likely, with Jackson obviously
staying in his lines despite Pope's gathering strength—Sertorius
in his report would not be able to avoid the conclusion that there
was more to the secretive Stonewall than the ram's horn and the
spear that had prevailed for Joshua.

"Troops, they don't mind if he's strange in'is ways." Channing's long beard moved with his emphatically nodding head.
"They forgive'im if he's got their tongues hangin out with fast
marchin in all directions. Troops've learnt he'll bring'em out where
Yanks aint lookin for'em. Troops know they'll take some casualties, cause Ol Jack fights. But they'd follow'im blindfold, cause
he wins."

"Very hard pressed here, though." Redmund chose his words
as tactfully as he could. "If Pope attacks again." Unless Longstreet
really has come up, he thought.

"Pope." Channing spat amber into the pine straw. "I wouldn't
hit a hog'n the ass with John Pope."

Of this crude reference, Redmund understood only that it was
contemptuous. "But Channing . . . whatever you think of him, Pope's
too strong for Jackson to attack alone, or even hold off much
longer. What's he going to do?"

Channing leered knowingly. But before he could offer an answer, General Jackson himself appeared among his staff and beckoned to Channing. They conferred in low tones. Redmund rose
from the stump on which he'd been sitting, wishing he were in
somewhat better fig—not good for one of the Queen's officers to
lower himself to the deplorable level of dress and manner he saw
in Jackson's staff—and drifted nearer. He was determined to press
his case directly to Jackson. Spy indeed!

". . . looks as if there will be no fight today," Jackson was
saying. "But have the men kept in line and ready for action."

Before Redmund could get closer, Jackson turned and went to
his horse; Channing followed. The two officers mounted and started
out of the headquarters camp at a walk. He'd seldom seen two
more awkward-looking riders, Redmund thought. But might they
be going to confer with Longstreet? Even Lee himself?

Abruptly, Jackson turned his horse's head and came toward
him. He pulled the sorrel to a halt.

"Colonel Channing tells me you are English, sir." The voice
was soft, nearly inaudible.

Redmund considered this at least tacit acceptance of his *bona
fides*. He thought it proper therefore to give Jackson a smart salute.

"Late of Her Majesty's Fourth Hussars, General!"

Jackson touched the brim of his cap.

"I've visited your beautiful country, sir, and shall never forget what I saw there."

In spite of himself, Redmund was impressed by the steadiness of the pale eyes, the bearing of the man. Beneath the beard he thought he perceived the outlines of an iron jaw.

"And in London, General, yours is a famous name."

This judicious flattery produced not so much as the blink of an eye. "Such things are earthly and transitory, sir. Tell me . . . are you familiar with the chapels and cloisters of Oxford?"

Redmund was not sure whether he was being tested or whether Jackson really wanted to discuss the glories of Her Majesty's realm. Unfortunately, he had never paid the slightest attention to chapels and cloisters; so he decided to take the initiative.

"Magnificent, General. If I could show you my credentials, sir, I believe . . ."

"In all my travels . . ." Jackson's voice was still soft, but it nevertheless silenced Redmund. "I think I have seen nothing so beautiful as the lancet windows in York Minster Cathedral. Good day, sir."

He put his fingers to his cap brim and rode on, ignoring Redmund's proffered papers. Channing, following, looked down sadly at the Englishman.

"Give a lot to see'em cathedrals myself, Duke."

"That's the worst piece of copy I *ever* saw."

Charlie Keach stared at Clyde Sharpe, the chief compositor, in consternation. He thought for a second of rising to snatch his story from the man's pudgy hands.

"You can't set it, find somebody that will."

He heard his voice as if from another room, and knew the fatigue he had held off by force of will was about to overcome him.

Sharpe, a paunchy man with an ink-stained apron over his trousers, looked at Keach calmly, through spectacles that seemed to hang on the tip of his nose.

"Correspondents."

In the single word, Keach thought, Sharpe managed to express all the disdain of every working man for those who did inexplicable things with their brains instead of obvious things with their hands. As if the "worst piece of copy" Sharpe had ever seen was not also the biggest story of the war! Bigger even than the *Herald*'s great exclusive account of Shiloh.

"Mister Sharpe...ah...you can hardly expect...ah... copperplate." Stanley Glenn, the managing editor, had read Keach's story the moment Keach had staggered into the building. "Mister Keach here wrote it...ah...standing up. On the night train from Baltimore."

Sharpe was unimpressed. "Thing is, Mister Glenn, I got compositors in the shop got to read this mess fore they can set it." He peered over his spectacles at Keach. "Could of at least wrote it on clean paper."

"I didn't have any." *Wipe your ass on it for all I care,* Keach thought.

And he really didn't care anymore, he told himself. Ordeal he'd had, getting here at all. Then to have some inky little bastard act like he'd handed him garbage instead of a masterpiece of reporting and writing. For that matter, Glenn himself had been none too effusive. But Hale said that was always Glenn's way.

"Come on, Mister Sharpe." Glenn's voice was patient but urgent, too. "Your men're paid...ah...to read copy as well as set it. I...ah...want it ready for a special...ah...soon as possible."

Special edition! That was something *like*, Keach thought. Hours on that swaying, half-lit train, trying to get the story written on top of a dirty old iron stove. Hours going by without a moment of sleep or a bite to eat. And all that on top of days in the field.

When the express from Baltimore had pulled into Jersey City, Keach had had only the last few paragraphs to write; he finished them on the Hudson River ferry, then grabbed the Manhattan crosstown omnibus to Nassau Street. Having been hired by Hale in Washington, Keach had never set foot in the home office or met his editors. But as he expected, Glenn was already at his desk; Hale had told him that Glenn as good as lived at his office, particularly when big war news might be expected.

"Keach, eh? Hale's been...ah...worried about you, Keach."

Hale had warned Keach that Glenn could be a terror when aroused. Keach decided the best defense was a good offense. He pulled the battered sheaf of copy from his jacket pocket and laid it in front of Glenn. Then he slumped into a chair, feeling sleep gain on him, as Glenn read without a word. Trying to keep awake, Keach picked up a copy of the previous day's issue; even the headlines seemed a blur before his tired eyes.

But one item startled him. Generals Burnside and Pope, it

reported, had fought their way through Rebel forces and effected a junction with McClellan's army near Centreville.

Where did those deskbound idiots in Washington come up with such junk? How could Hale let a story like that go in the paper, when whoever wrote it clearly hadn't been farther out into Virginia than Alexandria or Fairfax?

News of the Rebel raid on Catlett's Station was just finding its way into print, too. A week after it happened. That was why Charlie Keach had forced himself to travel all night; the war was moving too fast for week-old news to do anyone much good.

Glenn stood up, still without a word, and left his office. Keach kept trying to read the news. Officers of the Pacific Mail Steamship Company had been notified of the "total loss of the *Golden Gate*, by fire" on the 27th, fifteen minutes westward of Manzanillo.

But Keach was only interested in his own story; impatiently, he cast the paper aside. If Stanley Glenn had nothing to say about such a story, then Charlie Keach was in the wrong business. Or maybe Stanley Glenn was. Except that Hale said Glenn was as tight with praise as a Scotchman's purse.

Glenn came back and sat down behind his desk. "I've . . . ah . . . sent for the printers. To come in early."

Keach was not too tired to deduce what *that* meant. He began to wonder how big his pay raise might be. But Glenn still seemed strangely unexcited.

"Since you've been to such trouble, I . . . ah . . . I presume it's . . . ah . . . exclusive."

"No other correspondents with Pope, sir."

"Hale told me about Halleck's orders. How'd you . . . ah . . . manage to stay?"

Keach told him, happy to get his licks in with the managing editor before he had to explain himself to Hale. He could not help embellishing a little his last hurried conversation with Pope.

"Puts his hand on my arm, sir, and says, 'Keach,' he says, 'don't fail to get through. Don't fail the country, Keach.' Well, of course, after that, I *had* to get here, sir." Glenn nodded almost imperceptibly. "But I didn't think it was right to note *that* in my story, of course. Too personal."

"Ummm. Ummm. Ah." Glenn drummed his fingers on his desk. "Ah, I suppose not. Pretty rough out there, Keach?"

Rough? As if Glenn would have any idea, Keach thought. Sitting here in an office with plush chairs and a fireplace. As if he'd know how rough it is to wear one shirt and one pair of drawers for weeks at a time. Sleep on a pile of rails, if not the ground.

Jackknife for spoon, knife, fork, toothpick, and weapon. Stealing corn for your horse when you're hungry enough to eat raw meat yourself. Not to mention that if you really wanted a story, you had to go under fire like a soldier. Oftener than some.

"Rough, Mister Glenn? I wouldn't say too rough. Anyway . . . I . . . ah . . . managed."

"I . . . ah . . . I meant . . . rough for the troops?"

Too late, Keach remembered Hale's advice: Stanley Glenn was not interested in a reporter's problems in getting a story; Glenn was only interested in the story itself. Well, to hell with it. Keach was too tired to care.

"A hell of a lot of deaders, Mister Glenn."

Glenn's eyes widened at the slang. A lot any of *them* knew, Keach thought. Sitting in front of their fireplaces.

"But the deaders," Keach said, "are better off than . . . ah . . . what's left of some of the living."

By the time Clyde Sharpe had arrived with his spectacles precariously—and contemptuously, Keach thought—on his nose, an uncomfortable silence had fallen over Stanley Glenn's office. As worn out as he was, Keach was glad enough of that; but he did wish the managing editor could have found a word or two of praise for his efforts. Only one thing was for sure: he'd gotten the story, gotten it here, and they couldn't take that away from him.

"I got six men waiting." Sharpe shuffled Keach's copy grudgingly. "I'll parcel it out to'em best I can."

"Then get'em cracking, Mister Sharpe."

Again, urgency sharpened Glenn's mild voice. And as the compositor reached the door of the office, Glenn called after him:

"Slug that story, 'Victory,' Mister Sharpe. And mark it: 'By Our Own Correspondent.'"

Charlie Keach remembered, then, that Stanley Glenn had not made so much as a pencil mark on his copy, or questioned a word of it. Let Hale put *that* in his pipe and smoke it!

In his office at Alexandria, across the Potomac River from Washington, Colonel Herman Haupt was composing a telegram to the Assistant Secretary of War:

August 30, 1862

P.H. Watson:

I have just had a conversation with M. P. Wood, Master

Machinist, who has had charge of the machine shop in Fredericksburg. He says that after having used the forges two days, it was discovered that a loaded shell had been placed in each. I think the proprietor, John Scott, now under arrest, should not be released. His is an aggravated case.

H. Haupt

Secesh sympathizers everywhere. Haupt handed his telegram to a waiting clerk, then studied Moore's telegram again. Moore was a good man, entirely trustworthy, and his message puzzled the colonel.

Manassas
August 30, 1862

Colonel Haupt:

I left force to work at Bull Run, and walked to Bristoe Station. Churchill and the force of contrabands finished Kettle Run bridge last night, and will be working at Broad Run this afternoon. The track stringers are destroyed and most of the posts cut off. Will do the best to repair it until we get lumber. I return to Bull Run bridge this evening. I can hear nothing of the construction corps.

J. J. Moore

Early that morning, Haupt had sent out four trains—one to clear wreckage from the track, followed by a construction train to repair bridges, then one train of forage for Pope's animals and another of bread and meat for his troops. The supply trains were to go only to Sangster's Station, four miles east of Centreville, but the construction train was to push on to Bull Run, with a force of 200 riflemen on top of the cars for protection.

An engineer and a trainman to the bone, Haupt was determined to repair the burned Bull Run bridge as soon as possible. He was angered every time he thought of headstrong General Taylor disobeying his clear orders and crossing over to pick a fight with Stonewall Jackson; if the man had only guarded the bridge as he'd been instructed, it might still be standing and supplies could be carried all the way to Manassas.

So the construction crew Haupt had sent out that morning had been well-manned and equipped, and under J. J. Moore's able direction. To power its train, Haupt had chosen good old *Vulcan* and Engineer D. D. Morgan, who had proved his nerve in escaping the raid on Catlett's Station. Unlike some other available engineers, Morgan was a veteran of enemy fire. His propensity for nipping the bottle could be tolerated, in view of this experience.

Haupt pulled his railroad watch from his vest pocket. Morgan would have delivered the construction crew to Bull Run sometime ago, unless they'd run into trouble. But that wasn't likely, since Moore said he'd "left force to work at Bull Run."

So what did he mean that he could "hear nothing" of the construction corps? Maybe it was good news. Maybe he meant he could "hear nothing" of the crews at Bull Run being fired upon. But why hadn't he made that clear? Haupt feared Moore meant that no information from Bull Run was coming through to him at Bristoc. Of course, *that* could mean that nothing worth reporting had happened. Or it could mean the construction crew had been attacked, or even captured.

Not for the first time, Herman Haupt reflected on the difficulty of finding out even the simplest facts about what was going on just a few miles away. The famous "fog of war" sometimes was more like an impenetrable night; even commanders in the thick of battle could not always follow what was happening to their brigades—sometimes to whole divisions or corps. So much less could those waiting anxiously in the rear.

The telegraph had helped immeasurably in this war, no doubt of it. But wires could be cut, operators captured or killed. Worse, through design or ignorance, those sending messages did not necessarily send truth, at least the whole truth. Often they simply didn't know what they were talking about. Or, if they did, their "knowledge" had been made inaccurate or irrelevant by events. Sometimes they simply didn't express themselves clearly. And Haupt knew enough about human nature to know that the telegraph had provided an instrument for concealing or distorting facts, as well as reporting them accurately. The wires could transmit rapidly and efficiently—but only the information that fallible, often bewildered, sometimes disreputable people provided.

Haupt shuffled through his morning's telegrams to find the one that he could not much longer delay answering.

August 30, 1862
9 a.m.

Colonel Haupt:

What news?

A. Lincoln

Haupt sighed and picked up his pencil. The President's hunger for information was insatiable. And no matter how hard Haupt tried to be careful in feeding it, he could never be sure enough. He was already dubious, that morning, of the report he'd passed along the evening before of a force of 60,000 Rebs being driven by Pope. The more he thought about it, the more unlikely it seemed that Stonewall could have got in Pope's rear with that many troops; or that if he *had,* Pope's army had whipped and "driven" him anyway.

But he had to tell the President something. So Haupt informed him first about his train movements and the riflemen sent to protect them; that much he could be sure of. Then he added what little other information he had—"news," he feared, about as reliable as what Mr. Lincoln could read in the newspapers.

The intelligence last evening was that Hooker and Pope were pushing the enemy towards the Gaps in the mountains through which they had advanced, and that McDowell and Sigel were heading them off. This morning the direction of the firing seemed to be changing, and it is not impossible that the enemy's forces may be changing direction and trying to escape towards Fredericksburg. In this case my trains will be in great danger. I await intelligence with some anxiety, and will communicate anything of importance that I hear.

H. Haupt

Across the river in his office on Twelfth Street, Albert Stevens Hale was just then receiving a telegram of his own:

Hale:

Missing person here. Bishop knocks down fence. Herald in dark.

Glenn

The managing editor, whose nature was secretive anyway, had a penchant for amateur codes and paraphrases, particularly in messages to Washington. He envisioned the capital city, not without reason, as a warming nest of spies for the Confederacy and—worse!—the archrival *Herald*. But Hale had no trouble translating Glenn's message.

He had already known from Charlie Keach's midnight note

that his presumptuous young correspondent, after so many days
of silence, had bypassed him on his way to New York, leaving
not a hint about the content of his story. Except, of course, that
it was earthshaking—in Keach's view, anyway. Now he obviously
had arrived in New York with his exclusive story—which to
Stanley Glenn, would mean one that the *Herald* did not have.

Bishop knocks down fence. Glenn's idea of deception was simple as a child's. Anybody in Washington, Hale thought, including
telegraph operators and *Herald* informants, would read that as
"Pope defeats Stonewall"—which *was* reasonably close to earth-
shaking news, if true. Politically as well as militarily important.

But Hale was worried less about the transparence of the managing editor's telegram than about Glenn's relative lack of knowledge of the war, and his hunger to beat the *Herald*.

Stanley Glenn in his years as managing editor—Hale was the
first to admit—had made their staid old publication a real newspaper. Still too heavy, perhaps, on the editorial side and, for Hale's
taste, preoccupied with too many "leadership" crusades—for
emancipation just then, and against McClellan. Hale shared these
views, but he thought a newspaper should print the news first,
and editorials in whatever space might be left.

So did Glenn. As managing editor, he even had started earlier
that year to publish news stories on the front page—an innovation
the *Herald* and the *Times* had adopted before the war. And it was
Glenn who had sent Hale to Washington to catch up on the big
lead established by the *Herald* in war coverage. It was Glenn who
had given Hale money and license to hire the best correspondents
he could find, as many as he needed to beat the *Herald*.

When the news of Shiloh up to then the biggest of the war—
had nevertheless broken first in the *Herald*, Glenn had been infuriated. Hale knew he was lucky to have survived that crisis,
although Shiloh was in Tennessee, well out of his Washington
jurisdiction, and the *Herald* exclusive had been something of a
fluke. Its correspondent's story had been dispatched form Pitts-
burgh Landing by riverboat no sooner than that of any other cor
respondent; but it had been telegraphed first from Fort Henry—
whether by favor or by chance Hale was not sure.

Glenn, of course, thought bribery, and argued that the only
thing that mattered was who printed the news first. He had been
not the least impressed by Whitelaw Reid's far more comprehen-
sive and accurate—but unquestionably later—account of Shiloh
in the Cincinnati *Gazette*.

So Glenn burned with passion to beat the *Herald* as badly as he thought he'd been whipped on the Shiloh story. And that was why his telegram caused Hale misgivings. *Herald in dark.* If Glenn thought he had the *Herald* beaten on major news, he would not for a second stop to question the correspondent or the story that did the job.

Bishop knocks down fence.

Glenn knew politics; he'd know that story could save the November election for the Republicans, therefore maybe the war for the Union. But Glenn did not really know much about the war itself. He was only an editor; which was why Hale worked so hard every night in his long private letters to educate him. Correspondents in the field, Hale knew, could be no better than the way their stories were handled and presented by deskbound editors.

He picked up the note the nigger boy had delivered in the middle of the night:

Mr. Hale:

Running for Balto train & NY express. Story too big to risk this note. Sorry no time inform. Return soonest.

Keach

Hale could applaud Keach's initiative. He'd tried to instill such a sense of urgency in all his correspondents, the most traditional of whom understood neither the entirely new pace demanded of war reporters nor Glenn's zeal to be first with the news. But he wished profoundly that he could have put his own pencil to Keach's story, checking it against his own sources.

When he'd stopped in on Assistant Secretary Watson's chief clerk early that morning—part of Hale's daily ritual—he'd been shown a telegram from Haupt in Alexandria to the President and Halleck. Haupt reported Pope's army driving the enemy.

"But you'll notice, Hale, the whole thing's based on what two ambulance drivers think they saw. Or what somebody told'em they may have seen."

"You don't believe it?"

"The cables I've read, if John Pope came in that door yonder and laid Stonewall's head on the floor, I'd advise Watson to convene a court of inquiry to prove it was him."

Hale had his own more personal doubts about what was happening. He'd never known his sources to be so jumpy—some so outright pessimistic. Heavily on his mind was what the President had told him about McClellan's recalcitrance in reinforcing Pope.

A gloomy pall seemed to lie over Washington, tangible as the stench from the canal; Hale had a sense of things coming apart, dissolution, disaster. The night before, he'd written Glenn:

> For the first time, I believe it distinctly possible that Washington may be taken. In the absence of instructions, and being accredited to the government, I take my duty to be that I stay while it stays, and leave when it leaves . . .

But Glenn would not yet have received that letter and Hale was troubled by more than the lack of corroboration for the startling Bishop–fence story. He told himself he had no pride of rank about it; if the story turned out to be true, the credit *should* go to Keach, although his bureau chief had trusted him with the Virginia assignment and laid out a lot of hard cash for his horses and the hired steamer.

Hale had realized that morning, however, that he had some reservations about Keach's judgment. Oh, the man was resourceful, that was why he'd hired him. And he was brave, which was one reason he'd been given the risky assignment to Pope's army. But Hale feared Keach might be *too* brave and resourceful. He'd insist on getting as close to the action as possible; Keach would go in with skirmishers if they'd let him.

But that was no way to cover a battle. Up front, Hale had learned under fire at Bull Run, a man might not see the forest for the trees. It would be easy to mistake a tactical gain for an overall victory, if you knew what was happening on only one part of the field.

Hale had noticed, moreover, in Keach's early dispatches a certain tone of flattery in references to John Pope. Hale was an old hand; he did not doubt that the flattery had something to do with Keach's ability to defy Halleck's orders and stay with Pope, when all other correspondents were sent back to Washington. And Pope just might have been slick enough to keep ambitious Charlie Keach around for his own purposes. *Bishop knocks down fence.*

Well, too late to do anything about it now. Glenn would have Keach's story on the streets as soon as he could. And he was the managing editor; he'd have to take the responsibility, since Keach had bypassed his Washington chief and gone straight to New York.

Abruptly, Hale stood up and took a turn around his roomy office, along the walls of which piles of his own and rival newspapers were stacked. The room was stifling from the morning sun but he wore his usual heavy coat and vest. He looked out the open window for a moment at busy Twelfth Street, without really noticing the passing wagons and pedestrians; then he sat down at his desk again, took paper from a drawer, and in his precise script began to compose a telegram:

Glenn, M. E.

Urge close questions missing person. If fence down, unconfirmed here.

Hale, WB

A responsible bureau chief could do no less, although Hale knew the second sentence might merely spur Glenn on to his exclusive. And if Hale's message also happened to make the record absolutely clear... well so be it.

Because it had occurred to Albert Stevens Hale that if Keach's story failed to prove out, the paper might well need a new managing editor, one with no responsibility for having published it.

Andrew Peterson, lamenting the loss of Joe Nathan more and more, had spent a morning of frustration. He had been stirring since shortly past sunup to take advantage of the early light; but by the time he got coffee boiled, the mules hitched, and the Whatsit Wagon out of the crowded lot at Gainesville, the provost marshal's men in their yellow armbands had blocked the roads toward the battle lines.

Peterson first tried the Warrenton Pike east, which would lead most directly to the scene of yesterday's fighting.

"Cap'n, this-yere'll git you most anywhere you wanta go." A beardless young marshal handed him back the pass signed by Jefferson Davis. "Cept thew Gin'al Longstreet's line ther. Fore long, they gone be cannon balls flyin down at road thicker'n hailstones."

On the Thoroughfare Road, which would connect him to a route circling behind Jackson's lines, Peterson had no better luck.

"Nawsuh, I just can't." This marshal had a cud bulging in his jaw. "They's trains parked back-yere most as far's the Gap. You couldn't get thew nohow."

Even the route to Manassas, which was well out of Peterson's way, was directly blocked by the ranks of R. H. Anderson's Confederate Division, which had come in early in the morning and was being held in reserve behind Longstreet. Peterson reluctantly returned to the Gainesville lot.

There he brought out his heavy camera and moved about, recording scenes of rear-echelon life—a couple of teamsters willing to halt their wagons long enough to be photographed as they gazed stiff-necked and embarrassed into the lens; a portable army smithy in operation with a clang of iron and a hiss of bellows; an abandoned wagon with one wheel off, spilling boxes of supplies into a ditch—tame stuff by comparison to the battlefield itself. After each exposure Peterson had to run back to the Whatsit Wagon to treat the plate.

He gave up well before noon and carried the camera back to the wagon. Henry was rubbing down the mules.

"Well! I thought you must of got where you were goin when you didn't come back last night."

Henry nodded, and went on with his work. Peterson stowed away the camera, sat down in the shade of the wagon, and lit a cigar. Maybe it would be possible to take the pike west toward Warrenton, turn right on the road he'd found four days before from Buckland to Hay Market, and get behind the marshals that way.

Contemplating this idea, he watched Henry handling the mules like favored children.

"You got folks round here, Henry?"

"Nawsuh, Mist Dodge."

Of course the man was contraband. If he'd been manumitted, he'd have said so and shown papers.

"Where'd you try to get through to?"

Henry brushed down Positive's off foreleg before answering. "Had folks down de pike. Not no mo."

"They gone, you mean?" Not surprising, with two armies crunching over the countryside.

"Yassuh."

Peterson decided to accept the story. In the chaos of war, it could even be true.

"Want a job then?"

"Dese-yere's good mules, Mist Dodge. You want I look after'em?"

"Can't pay you much. Guarantee you'll eat when I do, though. Might even teach you the trade."

Henry stopped brushing and looked suspiciously at the Whatsit Wagon. "I just look affer dese mules."

All he really wanted was to get as far out of Prince William County as he could. Ol Brace dead'n'is woman crazy. Too many folks round-yer knowin me. Got to git gone.

Driving Mist Dodge's wagon was what he'd hoped for when he decided to come back. Henry was not trying to get far away from Sajie, or reminders of her. He was not thinking about Sajie at all, much less grieving her loss. Going up Ol Brace's cellar steps for the last time, he'd had a moment of regret—for the way Sajie cooked greens, the feel of her under the quilts on a cold night, how she could take his whole hard dick inside and squeeze it all over with what felt like hidden fingers up in there. But then Henry thought of Sajie and Brace on the kitchen floor and put her out of his mind forever.

"Hitch'em up, then, Henry." Mist Dodge stood up, the half-smoked cigar clenched in his teeth. "Aim to get this outfit on the road, one way or another."

Missy awakened when the sun, moving nearly overhead, struck her in the eyes. Sleeping with her back to a tree, she'd been dreaming—not of Hart, as she'd hoped, but of the shot boys in Brawner's field. Not a scary dream so much as a sad one; all the boys with their broken bodies and bleeding mouths and staring eyes had kept trying to call out to her. But none of them could make a sound; and she'd been floating above their silent pain, helpless to know what they wanted to say. In some ways it seemed worse than the groans and screams she'd actually heard that night, before Hart carried her off.

Missy had never understood why the Yankees had come to Virginia and started the war; and once she'd seen the boys in Brawner's field, she'd lost whatever notions she'd had that war was a matter of handsome men and fine uniforms and prancing horses. Since then, though mostly preoccupied with thoughts of Hart, she'd studied some about those wounded and dead boys.

She couldn't figure out what was to be gained by men tearing each other to pieces like that, or by so much pain and killing. As far as she was concerned, if the Yankees wanted Prince William County, or even Sajie and Henry the way Paw said, they could have them. Nothing was worth what she'd seen at Brawner's. Or something bad happening to Hart.

He'd raised that possibility, then tried to play like he hadn't. Worrying what she'd think. She had a swift, horrid vision of him on the ground, mangled and dying like the boys at Brawner's, his mouth bleeding under his mustache; and she felt a stab at her breast, whether of pain or of fear she could hardly say.

"Hart," she murmured out loud, to the crickets and the soft sigh of the pines. "My Hart." A blue jay answered angrily.

She would not let herself think of him again like that—on the ground at Brawner's. She tried to figure out, instead, what he'd meant about not being a part of the war. She could tell he felt bad about that, but it made no sense to her; if he had to ride off and leave her, that seemed all too much like being part of the war. Especially—she had to face it—since he was not likely coming back.

Maybe we can meet here again tonight he'd said.

I be here.

Then so will I. If all goes well.

But just feel in my bones he aint comin. So what would she do if he didn't? Paw would not take her back, even if she wanted to go. She'd heard Paw say too often how he aimed to marry his daughter to advantage, maybe to get more niggers. Even if he mostly said things like that when he was drunk, Missy believed *that* was when he came out with what he really thought, deep down.

Now Paw'd just think she was damaged goods. She'd have to tell him she was sure she carried Hart's child.

No. On'y way Paw'd have me back was iffen I'uz Hart's wife.

Missy did not delude herself about *that*. So she could not go back home. Now she had time to think about it, that made her kind of sad. Home was all she knew. Cept Hart. She thought about Maw and Sajie. Henry. For a moment, she even missed Wash. Cept first time he tried to feel of me again, I'd whop'im a good'un.

She decided not to worry about the future. She could clean and scrub, cook a little. Once the armies were out of Prince William, she'd find somebody to take her in. And after Hart's child came—she calculated on her fingers; be spring then—they'd go West. Start a new life, with Hart's child. Paw said out West-uz places you would pick up gold offen-a ground.

Paw'd mostly been good to her. Paw wa'nt mean. Jus kind of wore out an bad to drink.

Missy remembered, then, that Hart had said they'd be fighting round the house today. She jumped up quickly. She could scout round home some anyway. See if Paw'uz ther. If he'd gone off again, like yistiddy, Maw'd be skeert to death. And Wash on'y good for plaguin'er.

Missy looked at the bed of pine straw on which Hart had spread the buffalo robe the night before. She'd put more straw on it, before her nap, to make it softer. *Case he come back.*

Missy was sure he wouldn't. But after she ran home to see if Maw was all right, she'd be back in time if he did. *Be rightchere ever night till no hope left.*

"Y'all home in ther?"

Corporal Odie Ray Short of Robertson's Cavalry, designated that day for duty with Longstreet's provost marshal, leaned far down from his horse and rapped with his knuckles on the front stoop.

He straightened, listening for an answer. But none came back from the unpainted old frame house with the sycamore in the yard.

"Sound like they skedaddle, Gummer."

Trooper Junius B. Hearn, who was riding with Short that morning to warn civilians out of the way of the army, had lost most of his teeth when a Yank smashed him across the mouth with a rifle butt near Cross Keys.

"They'uz smart, they did."

Trooper Hearn perked up his ears for the sound of chickens. Never could tell what some folks'd leave behind, they got skeert bad nuff.

"Gone take a quick look." Corporal Short dismounted and winked at Trooper Hearn. "Mought of left some vittles in ther."

Short knew the house was empty as soon as his spurs echoed in the hallway. Felt deserted. Even a little cold, despite the hot morning. He went down the hall, looked out on the back gallery, then entered the kitchen that opened off it. *Sho nuff.* The butt of a ham and a slice off it lay on a table, crawling with flies. The safe stood open, too, and in it Short found some sugar and coffee.

Whisking off flies, the corporal quickly sliced the rest of the ham, most of which was fat and gristle, bundled it in a dirty cloth he found hanging from a peg, and stuffed the package inside his shirt. Gummer couldn't eat ham noway. Too tough. But Short decided to share the sugar and coffee as a matter of equity. When he went out, he seized an army musket that was leaning against the wall, wondering briefly what it was doing there.

Sajie listened nervously as the corporal's boots stamped about overhead. The cellar was hot and airless, and a strange smell was beginning to rise from the blood pooled thickly around Ol Brace's body. The smell reminded Sajie of chicken feathers, wet down in boiling water for plucking. She had always hated that smell, and plucking chicken feathers.

Her hand was clasped over fat Kate's blubbery mouth. Not that Kate was trying to call out to whoever was stomping round the house; now that she no longer had the knife, she was easy to handle. But she kept up a flow of muttering chat to herself *plum outten'er mind* that Sajie feared might be just loud enough to give them away.

"Hey, Gummer." The boots went back along the hall to the front stoop, and the voice carried dully into the cellar. "We gone wash down at slosh wid real coffee tonight."

Sajie had eaten nothing that morning; nor was she hungry there in Ol Brace's inert presence and the smell of his blood. But they had to do something, get out of there, sooner or later; they'd have to eat, get started—get started on *what*, without Henry or Ol Brace around, or Wash and Missy, Sajie realized she didn't know. But something.

The house was quiet above; in a moment Sajie could hear horses leaving the yard at a trot. She took her hand off Mistis's mouth.

"...used-a go to Sudley Church ever Sunday..." The woman's voice just continued, as if all the while she'd been talking into Sajie's palm. "Wore a white dress pink pipin onna waist Paw he'd take my hand goin uppa steps be so proud he'd show'is girl off ever chancet he got he'd..."

Sajie stopped listening and tried to think. The voice murmured in the cellar like the sound of bumblebees, or a conversation from another room, closed and private. Sajie suddenly knew the first thing to do; it had been evident in the sounds of horses in the yard and the rap on the stoop, and the way she'd instinctively cut off Mistis's mouth with her hand.

"Got to beh'y Ol Brace," Sajie said.

But Mistis went rambling on about white dresses and the way Paw he'd seen to it she'd got a new one when she growed to need it. *No hep ther.*

But if they found Ol Brace with his throat cut like a hog's— Sajie had no clear notion who "they" were, except that of course they'd be white—they'd think *she'd* done it. White folks would not believe for a moment that a white woman had killed her own husband, not when they'd have a nigger to blame it on. *An nobody to say diffrunt, Wash gone.*

"I got to beh'y Ol Brace."

This time, Mistis stopped talking and laughed gaily, but only for a moment. Then she went on:

"Brace he tole Paw he gone marry me or bust a gut say he don't care how long it take gone show Paw he aint white trash he kin take care-a Paw's girl good's Paw kin'n you kin bank on at . . . Brace he had curly hair'n em days he . . ."

An sposin Missy come back. Sajie was not much surprised that Missy had run off with a soldier, because lately Missy had taken to asking Sajie what most young girls asked their mothers. And some things most wouldn't. Thinkin too much what she got twixter legs. But Missy had been friendly and nice. For white folks anyway. Not devilish like Wash. So it wouldn't be right if she came back and found out her Maw had killed her Paw. Sides, can't leave no dead body outten-a ground. Not even Ol Brace.

Anyway Sajie looked at it, the first thing to do was to bury him. And the right place to do it was under the dirt floor of the cellar, where nobody would see her digging. Where nobody would ever think to look for Brace's body.

Sajie got laboriously to her feet and went across the cellar to the knife still sticking upright from the dirt. She had never seen a bayonet before, but recognized it then as the long blade Ol Brace had had buckled around his waist the night before. Not what she needed to bury him with.

Mistis too fat to git outten-a cellar by herself. So Sajie heaved herself up the steps, feeling a hundred years old. Sore, too. Her head ached, and her jaw was bruised, tender to the touch. Cautiously, she lifted one of the cellar doors. Quiet outside; hot sun baking down.

She let the door down silently behind her, shutting out at last the bumblebee sound of Mistis's muttering. This time, Sajie noticed the corpses in the yard right away. One at the corner of the house. Another by the well. Two farther away. The one at the corner was beginning to swell in the sun, face turning purplish. Sajie hurried past; flies rose at her passage, then swarmed down again.

In the dim cool of the barn she found a hoe and a pickaxe. Reluctantly she went back out into the fierce sunlight, among dead men, and crossed the yard toward the old house. Off to her left, peaceful looking and dreamlike, she could see the cabin where she and Henry had lived, and the front stoop on which he always took his evening pipe.

But she'd never see Henry there again, waiting for her to cook his greens the way he liked. Big tears welled in her eyes and rolled down her cheeks. The pickaxe was heavy across her shoulder, and the hoe in her hand. *No Henry to hep beh'y Ol Brace. No Henry atall. No more.*

She circled widely around the body at the corner of Ol Brace's house. Tears streaked her dark cheeks still, and her shoulders sagged. But she did not look back again at the cabin and Henry's stoop. She had to get on.

Sheriff Maxton opened the door of Easter's cabin without knocking. At least a dozen, maybe more, niggers were crowded into the small room with its fireplace at one side. A small table had been pushed against a wall. Sunlight streamed in from two windows and the door the sheriff left open behind him.

"Come for Jason."

He flicked his crop lightly against his boots. Uncertainty wouldn't do in front of slaves.

Black faces looked at him without expression. Nobody said anything. For a moment, Maxton thought there might be trouble; maybe they'd crowd together into a wall of bodies to protect Jason.

But nobody moved. The sheriff tapped his boot again.

"Jason here?"

He made his voice a shade more imperative. Even the boldest African was too accustomed to obey authority to defy for long a commanding manner.

"I's Jason."

The voice—a little higher pitched than Maxton had expected, from the picture in his mind of a slave murderer—came from somewhere in the silent group in the cabin. At the sound, although hardly anyone seemed to move, something of a lane opened; through it, the sheriff saw a thick-set African with a head like a cannonball set on a short, muscular neck. Jason's shoulders were slumped and his face looked drawn and a little befuddled. He sat on the edge of a low bed built into a corner; his arm was in a sling that might have been torn from someone's homespun shirt, or a woman's underclothes.

So he was right where Miz Arnall had said he'd be. *Didn't take no dogs to find'im.*

"Jason . . . I arrest you . . ."

Except for the crop, Maxton was unarmed because using weapons to manage Africans undermined the natural moral authority of a white man. But as he took a step forward, he was glad his deputies, waiting outside, were carrying sidearms and shotguns.

"I arrest you for the murder by smotheration of Miz Theodora Poteat of Lakeview, night of August twenny-third, eighteen an sixty-two."

Nobody moved or spoke. Maxton took two more steps forward. They were all around him by then, could swarm all over him before the deputies outside could move in. But they wouldn't. Not if he knew niggers. Not if he moved right on and showed'em who was in charge.

"Also murder of the slave Pettigrew of Sycamore, propitty Gin'al Arnall, August twenny-nine, eighteen an sixty-two."

The sheriff thought Jason nodded minutely, but still no one said anything. Maxton took a last step forward and put his hand on Jason's good shoulder.

"Come peaceful, Jason."

Beside the squat African, he saw Easter laid out on the bed in a clean blue dress, barefoot, her hands folded on her stomach. A dark cloth was draped over the head, most of the left half of which Miz Arnall said had been blown away by the shot. *Can't see no way how a woman handle at big of a sidearm.*

"Yassuh." Jason looked up at him with red eyes trembling with tears. "Ain't make no trouble."

"Praise-a Good Lawd," somebody mumbled. A few scattered "Amens" responded.

"Do right, Jason!" a woman's voice sang out.

"Ony-est thang . . ." Jason's eyes spilled tears on his cheeks. Not such big stuff now, the sheriff thought. "Gone beh'y Eas'er tomarr."

"Can't wait for no fun'ral, Jason. Law don't work at way."

"Kin I stay fuh de beh'in, y'all kin hang me soon's she . . ." Jason looked then at Easter and his voice broke. ". . . she in de ground."

"Nobody gone hang you thout a trial, Jason. Law don't work at way, neither."

"But whut . . . whut bout de beh'in?"

"Got no reg'lar preachuh nohow." An older man, with grizzled hair and gray stubble on his gaunt face pushed through to stand beside the sheriff. "Aint gone be no proper beh'in till he come round. Not fuh Pe'grew neither."

Jason looked as if he had been struck with Maxton's crop.

"Den whutchuh gone *do?*"

"Beh'y'em tomarr. Primus he say services bes he kin. Den, reg'lar preachuh come read it proper, we gone fun'alize Eas'er. Pe'grew, too."

"Tha's it," a man said.

"Tha's exactly *right.*"

"You *right,* Frank."

"No preachuh tomarr?" Jason sounded more like a puzzled child than the double murderer the sheriff had come to seize.

"Aint comin till next week," Frank said.

Jason's red-rimmed eyes turned to the sheriff. "Dey fun'alize Eas'er next week, I come back?"

Maxton saw his opening. "Might manage it someway." His grip on Jason's shoulder tightened.

"You g'won den," Frank said. "Be's nuff trouble, Jason."

The sheriff could feel Jason's indecision through his grip on the African's shoulder. Then he felt the shoulder muscles tensing and he braced himself; but Jason only stretched out his hand, square, blunt-fingered, huge, and laid it over both of Easter's, folded on the blue burial dress.

"Comin back. See my Eas'er beh'd right. Donchuh take on bout dat, my chile."

"Eas'er aint takin on." Frank's gentle voice fell into a kind of singsong. "Eas'er gone to de good Lawd's throne. Eas'er safe wid de good Lawd's flock. Aint taking on at de good Lawd's feet."

"Eas'er eatin de milk'n honey," Jason said.

"That's *right*...cert'ny is...bless my Lawd," voices answered. "Done cross ovuh Jerd'n...res'n in de Promise Land."

Jason stood up then, and Maxton took his hand off the broad shoulder and took hold of Jason's bicep. It was solid as a brick.

"See my Eas'er at de Golden Throne."

"Oh, yes, you will...you will on de *Judg*ment Day!"

Sheriff Maxton doubted seriously if anybody hanged for two murders would ever get near the Golden Throne, or that Jason would much like what happened to *him* on Judgment Day. Or Easter either, the way Miz Arnall told the story.

But Jason left Easter's cabin peacefully, to the accompaniment of much weeping, wailing, and clapping of hands. Gray-headed old Frank came out behind them into the brilliant sunlight, blinking after the dimness of the cabin. He looked expectantly at the sheriff. Maxton handed Jason over to a deputy and went back to the old man.

"Much oblige yuh hep, Uncle."

"Nuff trouble," Frank said. "Shurf, Pe'grew start at fight wid Jason."

"Tryin-a capture a fugitive. At's still a murder charge on Jason."

"Cept Pe'grew, he wants Jason's woman, too."

The sheriff was not surprised. *Darkies got their dicks out half the time.* And he doubted a jury would care much, one way or another, why a runaway nigger had killed a valuable propitty like Pettigrew.

"We'll look into it, Uncle."

He turned back to his deputies. Some of the Africans inside Easter's cabin had started singing:

I met my soul at de bar of God,
I heard a mighty lumber . . .

"Want we should tie'im up, Shurf?"

Maxton kicked away a hound sniffing at Jason's legs.

"Not'll we git'im outta sight."

Hit was my sin fell down to Hell
Jes like a clap of thunder.

"Gone bring me back, time at preachuh come?" Jason stumbled off in front of the mounted deputies.

"Told you we'd see bout it." *Cold day in Georgia, we do.* Maxton lifted his bulk into the buggy in which he'd driven the big nigger gal back to Sycamore.

Mary she come runnin by,
Tell how she weep'n wonder . . .

As the horses moved slowly toward the main house, the dogs set up their own yelping music. The singing went on from Easter's cabin:

Mary washin up Jesus feet,
Angel walkin up de golden street . . .

About the peculiarest situation he'd ever run into, the sheriff thought. Walking in there and finding him like that. No fight left in him at all. *Funny Miz Arnall knew it'd be that way.*

Run home, believer, run home.

The sheriff actually felt somewhat foolish. He'd had himself all worked up to a Jason eight feet tall with fire coming out of his eyes and iron claws for hands. And it turned out that a woman had dealt with this murderous Jason all by herself.

Some woman, though. Cool as well water. She could hardly be blamed for the mixup, when she'd only been guarding her own house and child. And how could she know if maybe Jason didn't aim to attack *her*? A white woman alone out here.

"You dawgs . . . hesh at fuss!"

The hounds paid no more attention than he'd expected. But the sheriff wanted to distress Miz Arnall as little as possible.

Fine-looking lady, he thought. Pink-cheek as a girl. Some heft to'er, too.

Sheriff Maxton liked a full-bodied woman. He reflected sourly on his own wife. Gaunt as a rail fence. But a man could git hisself warm nights upside a scrumptious female like Miz Arnall.

The sheriff allowed himself a moment of envy toward General Hoke Arnall, whom he'd never liked. Not even before he got to be a general. The old Judge was a fine man sober, but his son had mighty tall ways. *Like he walk by, everbody spose to fall in ranks.*

Still, Maxton respected quality and the Arnalls were not only quality; they married quality. So he had never presumed to think about Amy Arnall as a desirable woman . . . not before that morning.

"Gone stop atta house, Shurf?"

"A minute. Y'all go on."

As Maxton had always seen it, a man could mess with whores and nigger gals if he wanted, but he ought not to even *think* about quality ladies that way. Even if his own wife had no more meat on her bones than a fresh-hatched quail.

He got down from the buggy, grunting a little, and went up the steps to the verandah, tipping his hat to the Judge.

Amy had been wandering through the house, avoiding the sewing factory, while the sheriff went for Jason. She tried to think about choosing another cook. She checked twice on little Luke, who was playing happily. Then she went out to the verandah to speak to the Judge, who seemed unaware that anything much had happened.

"Fine man," the Judge had said. "Shurf Max'on, I mean."

Nothing hindered the Judge's consumption of toddies.

"Is he?"

Amy turned back into the house. Fine, indeed. Looking me over like a mare at auction. Well, that would be something she'd have to get used to.

Hey boys! Here comes at woman whut kill at nigguh gal!

But if she was lucky, at least they'd hang Jason before she ever had to look at *him* again; Maxton had said that if Jason confessed to killing Pettigrew, she wouldn't even have to testify. And, of course, Jason would confess.

Amy was sure of that, just as she had no doubt the porcine Maxton would find Jason at Easter's bier, causing no trouble. Because when she'd gone running back to the sewing factory that morning, after Jason's single piercing howl of grief, and found him sprawled facedown over Easter's body, appearing at first glance as lifeless as she, the truth was at once as plain to Amy as Easter's blood on the floor, or the brown outflung hand just beyond which the silver spilling from a flour sack sparkled in the morning sun.

Jason would confess because love for Easter had driven his every act; with Easter dead nothing drove him anymore. Oh, he'd confess, all right, how he'd smothered Miss Tippy for money to get Easter away from Sycamore, how he'd killed Pettigrew to get Easter away, how he'd sent Easter to the house for silver and money to get them both away. He'd confess, because without his passion to take Easter away with him, Jason was nothing but the anxious stooped darky near exhaustion she'd seen past Reba's yellow face at dawn on the stoop.

Bess was waiting in the dim cool hall, wearing a fresh dress and headcloth.

"You must be tired, Bess. Up all night'n that long walk to town."

"Aint all at far, Mistis."

"I appreciate what you did. I . . . I don't know what I'd have done without you." Amy remembered with shame some of her bitter, panicky thoughts about Bess.

"All ovuh now."

"Not for me."

She knew she would hear the echoes of the pistol shot all of her life. See Easter on the floor every waking morning.

Bess's face was inscrutable as usual. But Amy had had a brief glimpse of the woman behind that mask. And she had no one else to whom she could turn.

"Are the . . . you think the people will hate me now?"

Bess made a sour face. "Count of Easter?"

"Because I . . . because of what happened."

"Em nigguhs," Bess said contemptuously. "Whut dey know?"

Bess was well aware that she had put Mistis in her debt by going off in the middle of the night to fetch the sheriff. *Same time, he nigguhs dis place turn up dey nose, me heppin Mistis catch Jason.*

All the way back to Sycamore in the sheriff's buggy—*him tryin-a rub' is fat leg upside-a mine*—she'd thought what to do. And the more she thought, the more it was clear to Bess that if she could make Mistis even *more* grateful to her—dependent on her—she'd have the power to handle anybody on the place. *Way Pe' grew done.*

"Whut dey know?" Bess said. "I aint hate you, Mistis."

Amy was not surprised, knowing how Bess had felt about Easter, and why, and that Easter's terrible choice was at least half responsible for Pettigrew's death. Still, Amy was encouraged. She put her hand on Bess's arm. She wanted to say more. She wanted to tell Bess how she had felt, waiting alone in the darkness of the sewing factory. She wanted to confess her sin. But her life was too much for Amy still; she had been too well trained to maintain the appearance of things.

"Thank you, Bess."

Reluctantly, not knowing from her life's shaping what else to say, Amy turned away and started upstairs, feeling alone again. But in a moment she heard Bess coming up behind her.

"Mistis . . ." Bess's voice was soft, little more than a murmur. "Aint nuthin you could of hep." Amy turned to look down into her face. *Cept iffen you hit Jason fust time you far at gun aint none-a dis happen. Pe' grew be still here.*

But Bess had known for years that she was never going to get Pettigrew. She grieved him, truly did—would cry in the night for sweet Pettigrew; but she'd been doing *that* all along. He was not much more lost to her dead than he'd been alive. And what she'd figured out in the sheriff's buggy was how to take his place, as near as a woman or anybody could.

"Nobody got no right to blame you, Mistis."

Amy was still looking into Bess's strong close face. Intimate, she thought. *Bess and me*. She hardly heard Bess's words for the importance of the moment. Because in the cool old house, silent except for Bess's voice murmurous in the stairwell, Amy Singleton Arnall sensed herself emerging mothlike, tentative but compelled, from the cocoon of custom and contrivance that for so many years had contained and sheltered her life. She spoke her true feelings at last, in a rush:

"Bess . . . I *wanted* to kill Jason. That's why Easter's dead."

"Aint yo fault he sent at slut to tief yo . . ."

Amy stopped her with a raised finger. "They could have had the silver. I thought he was going to *rape* me." She had never before said the word aloud. "I was so sure of it, I . . . I . . ." She struggled for words to express what she *knew*—that Easter coming in Jason's expected place had confounded her life's understanding of things.

Bess first felt surprise that Mistis would talk so, as shy as she was about her own naked body. Not even letting on she knew how her baby got inside her. But Bess sensed that white ladies made more out of bodies and babies and how the one begot the other than they ever let on. And she wondered if maybe under all their powder and all their layers of clothes and all their fancy ways . . . if maybe white ladies thought black men *wanted* them. As if they were so white and pretty that no ugly black man could keep his hands off of them. *Be jes like' em think that. Think they so much cause they white.*

But Jason had only wanted Easter. Bess doubted Jason had ever even thought about Mistis as a woman. But she sensed further opportunity.

"Jason'a bad nigguh, Mistis. He mought of . . ."

"But he didn't, Bess! He didn't even come!"

Suddenly Amy seized Bess's shoulders and shook her, once, hard, as if to vent her own rage and regret.

"I hope they hang'im, Bess!"

Deceived, betrayed! Amy hated herself as a willing victim, hated Jason more for having failed her conception of the way things were.

"Higher than a pine tree!"

Bess looked bewildered. Oh, how can I make her *see?* Amy thought. Because he wanted to rape me, I wanted to kill him . . . so if he'd only come and I'd killed *him,* that would have been . . . confirmation. Of the woman I thought I was. Had to be. Can't be anymore. Of everything I knew.

"Don't you see, Bess? How wrong I was?"

Unmoving on the stairs the Judge's father had built in the time of Jefferson, in a world they had inherited, the two women stared for a long time into each other's eyes.

Wrong Amy thought—wrong to be so sure he was like that. Men were. Everything was.

Wrong Bess repeated to herself. Chile bout outten'er mind jes fuh killin at black slut.

And because I was sure about him, about myself . . . everything . . . I killed *her*. To have been sure, Amy thought, was her real sin.

Bess felt genuine sympathy for Amy's distress. She saw clearly, too, her next move. She took Amy in her arms.

"Nuthin you could of hep, Mistis."

Strong, enfolding, protective. Even forgiving, Amy thought. But that doesn't change anything. *Because Jason didn't come, and now I'm not sure of anything. Except I killed Easter.*

Just then she heard the sheriff's heavy tread on the verandah, his peremptory rap. She pulled back a little and looked again into Bess's eyes.

"I'll have to count on you now, Bess. With Pettigrew gone."

"Kin manage, Mistis."

With an effort, Bess kept her face expressionless. She wished Pettigrew were alive to see her take his place. And Easter dead.

When Amy came out on the verandah, she could just see mounted deputies and yelping dogs far down the lane. But not Jason.

"Jes like you said, ma'am." Maxton took off his hat and mopped his brow with his red handkerchief.

So Jason really was caught at last. Amy let out a long breath she had not even known she was holding. At that moment, breathing rapidly, she realized—as if charged by fresh air to her lungs— that she had survived. Not just her duel with the Jason of her certaintics, but the old unquestioned life that had formed them in her; she had survived both. Suddenly, she knew she was strong, whatever else; as she had been ready to face the imagined Jason, she could face, too, the loss of old, unfounded surety. She could face anything.

"I'm glad, Sheriff." Amy took another deep breath, ready now to deal with him.

Look at em beauties rise'n fall, Maxton thought. Looking, he pointed vaguely after his deputies.

"Goin peaceful's you please."

"That's good." Good to have Jason off the place. *So I can begin again.*

"They's one thing, ma'am."

Amy frowned at him. She wanted him off the place, too, with his intrusive eyes and noisy dogs and villainous-looking deputies. She wanted as few reminders as possible. She wanted to look ahead. She and Bess could manage.

"Get'im to come peaceable, I sort of let'em think I'd bring'im back when they git a preacher for Easter'n Pettigrew."

"But of course you won't."

Maxton knew this was not a question. "No'm. But some-a the Gin'al's people mought be a little upset when I don't."

He watched as Miz Arnall seemed to draw herself taller. *Woman like at'd fuck a man to death.* The sheriff was amazed, then ashamed of this novel notion about a lady. Then he thought *well goddammit why not? Kilt at nigguh gal didn't she? Cool as a cucumber.*

"I'll handle my people, Sheriff."

Beyond her, in the dim hall, he caught a glimpse of the darky gal who'd awakened him that morning and ridden back in the buggy with him. *Shinin up to me a little.*

"Need the least bit-a hep with'em, ma'am, ner anythin else, you just send word, you hear?"

"Thank you, Sheriff."

He put his hat on, fitting it to the red crease in his forehead, and went down the steps, thinking again about how it'd be with such a woman. But as the buggy sagged under his weight, he remembered what he had in mind for his son Benjy, home from the war with three fingers missing from his right hand. *Prob'ly blowed'em off hisself.* Sweating hard in the midday sun, the sheriff looked back at Miz Arnall, standing there ripe as an August melon.

"Aint you gone need a man to hep outchere, ma'am? Who's gone run this place now?"

"I am," Amy said. "Good day, Sheriff."

Chapter Fourteen

~~~~~~~~~~~~~~~~~~~~~~~~~~~~~~~~~~~~

August 30—Midday

<div align="right">

Headquarters near Groveton
August 30, 1862—12 m.

</div>

The following forces will be immediately thrown forward in pursuit of the enemy and press him vigorously during the whole day. Major-General McDowell is assigned to the command of the pursuit.

Major-General Porter's corps will push forward on the Warrenton turnpike, followed by the divisions of the Brigadier-Generals King and Reynolds. The division of Brigadier-General Ricketts will pursue the Hay Market Road followed by the corps of Major-General Heintzelman. The necessary cavalry will be assigned to these columns by Major-General McDowell, to whom regular and frequent reports will be made. The general headquarters will be somewhere on the Warrenton turnpike.

<div align="right">

By Command of General Pope

</div>

Before signing these special orders, Colonel Russell reviewed them with some misgivings. The insistence of Duryea and Porter that Longstreet was on the field had made a strong impression on him, if not on Pope; but Russell knew that the commanding general's mind was made up. And in the end a commander had to command and a soldier had to obey.

But Russell could not help thinking *glad it's not me glad it's Pope that takes the responsibility.*

Scarcely two miles to the west, Major Jesse Thomas was marveling that the long, hot morning had worn on so quietly. Had to be upwards of 150,000 men (if Pope had what they thought he had) huddled ready for battle within perhaps ten square miles on the relatively open plains of Manassas. Yet only skirmishers' muskets and an occasional rumble of guns—both just threatening enough to keep Longstreet's headquarters alert—had broken the calm of the morning.

"You mought even think," Coke Mowbray had said as he and Thomas drank piercing headquarters coffee, "they don't aim to rile us up over here."

"Or us them."

Thomas still feared that the generals' decision not to attack Pope would let the Yankees get away intact. This troubled him because as he recalled from Colonel Tatum's loose dinner-table talk at Miss Letty's house, the idea of the campaign was to destroy Pope before he and McClellan could join forces. Especially, it seemed to Thomas, if Lee really was thinking about going into Maryland. He did not mention this possibility to Mowbray, of course. Probably just more of Tatum's gossip anyway; but if it wasn't, the fewer who knew of it the better.

The main event of the morning had been Thomas's first really good look at the famous Stonewall. Everybody knew Jackson was not much for show; neither was Longstreet, for that matter. Lee was usually somewhat more formally attired, and Stuart was a real bird of plumage.

But at close range, Thomas thought Jackson nearly disreputable in his worn, homespun suit, more nearly brown than gray, displaying no signs of rank or distinction. Ol Jack looked less like a famous general—though he was easily the most renowned of the four who had conferred that morning—than a none-too-prosperous farmer.

"*We* know who he is and what he's done," Thomas conceded to Mowbray. "But if you didn't, would you pick *him* out for Jackson?"

"Lord, no. Stuart sort of look like he ought to be Stonewall, don't he?"

Thomas wondered if Jackson's appearance had anything to do with Longstreet's reserved opinion of him. Pete had never known Jackson in the Old Army or even met him before Lee summoned the Valley forces down to Richmond in June. The fighting after that had not been Jackson's finest hour, and he was obviously a man who made no effort to impress anybody.

Before long, Stonewall and the even seedier colonel accompanying him rode off down the hill toward the pike. On horseback, Thomas noted, Jackson with his short stirrups and flaring elbows looked less than ever like a soldier. But his seat was firm and steady.

The brown-eyed captain named Hart joined Thomas and Mowbray as they watched Stonewall ride away. Suddenly, Jackson raised his left arm above his head; he rode on that way, as if ready to signal an attack.

"Ther he goes," Mowbray said. "Rev'rend Major says Ol Jack's prayin, he holds up'is arm like at."

"Not what I heard." Thomas explained that *he* had been told on good authority that Jackson—who was known to be a health crank—believed his left arm was heavier than his right; so he sometimes held the left up in the air to drain blood back into his body and lighten the arm.

"Jackson's not *that* crazy." Captain Hart looked amused. "I hate to disillusion you boys but the surgeon of the Stonewall Brigade told *me* . . ." He gave them Major Worsham's explanation, that Jackson held the arm aloft to ease the pain of his old hand wound.

"I like the Rev'rend Major's way best," Mowbray said. "I aint above a little prayin myself, I hear'em Miniés wheeze."

That was how legends started, Hart thought. But of course an army needed legends. Soldiers needed something larger than themselves, not just to believe in but to give themselves hope or courage or amusement, the capacity to endure, to do more than they'd thought they could. Jackson was a warrior who gave the army vital legends—above all, in the nickname "Stonewall," the legend of its invincibility. And that was one legend Lee's ragged, hungry ranks could not do without.

August 29, 1862
Near Groveton, Va.

By Our Own Correspondent

As darkness closed a sanguinary day on the banks of

Bull Run and the trampled fields that flank it, Mars quenched at last the Union's thirst for victory and shattered the myth of Southern invincibility.

As if in Divine redemption of the ground upon which he received his famed sobriquet a year ago, it was upon the fabled "Stonewall" that the Union blows fell, powerfully and repeatedly, until Jackson's secessionist legions gave grudging way before General John Pope's relentless Army of Virginia. . . .

Charlie Keach, sitting quietly in a corner of Stanley Glenn's office, wondered if maybe now, at last, he could close his eyes and get some sleep.

He'd done it. The ink smearing his fingers, the bold headlines, the commotion in the building as the special edition began moving toward the streets—it was all as he'd expected it would be. So everything had been worthwhile, the long, exhausting summer, the toadying to Pope, the dangers of battle, the endless night of travel by horseback, steamer, train, and ferry. His career was made, no matter what Hale thought. The country was maybe even saved.

Keach could hardly take his eyes, tired as they were, from the inky evidence of his achievement:

The doughty Stonewall had destroyed Pope's depot with one of his patented lightning strikes, at Manassas Junction on the Orange & Alexandria Railroad. But as the Rebel captain sought escape westward on the evening of the 28th, he stumbled against the untried but stalwart blueclads of King's Division: more particularly, a brigade of fierce midwestern fighters under General Gibbon, wearing black hats and already being called, as a result of their valiant stand, "the Iron Brigade". . . .

Private Larkin Folsom had some doubts about his sonnet. He had written fourteen lines in an unusual but—he thought—effective rhyme scheme of *aba aba aba aba ab;* and technically speaking, Folsom thought the lines passable. But what bothered him was not technical.

Folsom had started writing about an imagined woman, since he didn't know any real women for whom he could write verses;

and his theme was the contrast between the ephemerality of physical beauty and the steadfastness of love, about at least the latter
of which, he now realized, he had known little. And his friendship—as Folsom still overtly thought of it—with Corporal Gilmore had caused the orderly to *sense* enough about real-life emotions
to make his verses seem a little contrived and sentimental.

Nevertheless, the lines that had come to him in the night:

> *Still, I'd persist in offering to pay*
> *Love's homage, love . . .*

had helped him finish it, and their origin had lent the whole thing
a more genuine feel. As he seized the quiet morning's opportunity
to make a fair copy on a blank page torn from the diary of a dead
Yankee, Folsom was not sure whether or not to read the completed
sonnet to Corporal Gilmore.

No hurry to decide. The corporal was out on another scout for
General Arnall. Folsom had no idea what Gilmore did on such
missions; and he had been too unnerved at stealing paper from
the corpse (though he'd hastily put the rest of the diary back in
the dead man's pocket) to try to imagine Gilmore's activities. He
didn't much want to know, anyway. Gilmore the scout was another
man—not Folsom's friend of the blankets.

The orderly finished the fair copy and signed it with a flourish:
Larkin Folsom, August 30, 1862—near Sudley Springs, Va. He
thought a minute, wet the pencil with his tongue, and scratched
out his original title, "I'd Love No Less." He wrote in its place:
"To a Friend."

Folsom folded the diary page, put it in the breast pocket of
his shirt, and settled back to enjoy the moment—the General
resting, the Yanks quiet, Corporal Gilmore soon to return. With
luck, some were saying, there'd be no fight today. Pope, they
thought, had had his fill of Ol Jack and would tuck tail behind
Bull Run.

Colonel Sam Stowe was not one of those who thought so. He
regarded Jackson's intact lines as a near miracle, considering Pope's
sustained attacks of the day before and the obviously greater Union
strength. And this close to Washington, Pope surely would have
been reinforced during the night. Stowe would just as soon have
seen the army on its way to Thoroughfare Gap.

"What's your name, soldier?"

"Private Barton, sir!"

"Not you. The big one there."

Lige Flourney was sleeping peacefully in the railroad cut, with his hat pulled over his eyes. Knowing his man, Private Barton gingerly touched Lige's shoulder.

"Cut the shit, Meat."

One I'm after all right, Stowe thought.

"Colonel's talkin to yuh."

The big man tipped up his hat and looked at Stowe.

"Yessuh?"

"What's your name?"

Lige was still half asleep and mumbled only his first name.

"That fight last night. Didn't I see you cleanin out plenny-a Yanks with a musket butt?"

"See me snuff at'un chargin-a fence? With a rock this big?" Lige curved a huge hand around an imaginary stone.

Stowe hadn't, but didn't doubt the story. Anything could have happened in *that* fight. But this was undoubtedly the man he wanted.

"Special detail, Clyde. Gin'al Jackson wants the toughest men we got for a hot job. You just volunteered."

One fight was like another to Lige; if anything he was pleased to have been recognized for what he knew he was, even if the colonel had his name wrong.

"What'd I volunteer fer?"

"Place down the line aways, where they planned to build a bridge. Dumped rocks on either side of a crick to carry the line up to it, but they never built the bridge itself. Leaves a hell of a hole in our line."

"Which I done volunteered to plug?"

"Way I hear it, Ol Jack doubled the provost marshal's men this morning. They're roundin up ever straggler'n deserter anywhere around. Gonna send ever last one of'em to plug it up."

Listening, Lige had hefted his bruised and aching body erect and stood as nearly at attention as he thought the colonel expected in such circumstances. He had no particular feeling about deserters—might have been one himself if he had had anything better to do than fight. But he still didn't understand just what he'd "volunteered" to do.

"They'll stack deserters in that gap like sandbags," Stowe said. "Sandbags with guns. Orders is, you volunteers'll be right behind 'em and shoot anybody that tries to run. Ol Jack aims to hold this line."

Dumping deserters into the gap seemed sensible enough to Lige. "But we gone shoot Yanks, too, aint we?"

"Lessen you too busy shootin deserters."

Hoke Arnall also had seized on the midday lull for a nap. One night of sleep had hardly refreshed him from the physical and emotional strain of the previous day's fighting; and he had spent a busy morning getting his men to the ammunition wagons and back, dispersing their reduced numbers to cover his flanking position as effectively as possible, and seeing to it that surviving officers and noncoms had taken command wherever necessary.

These new dispositions had been discouraging. Hasty head counts disclosed that of the more than 1,500 men Hoke Arnall had led into battle the day before, above 700 were now out of action—exactly how many killed, how many wounded or missing had not been determined. But half of Arnall's Brigade was gone. Eight of eleven field officers were dead or wounded too seriously to keep the field; half the company officers had been swept away in Pope's day-long assault on Jackson's left.

But Arnall took grim satisfaction in the knowledge that daylight had confirmed—Arnall's Brigade had exacted a terrible price from its attackers. Blue bodies were strewn everywhere on the ground that neither Sigel nor Hooker nor Kearny had been able to seize and hold. These bodies had been taken, early that morning, beyond the railway cut and left for the Yankees to pick up. Arnall's own dead had been carried off to mass graves in the rear.

Now, propped against a pine tree, its shade falling coolly around him, its needles softening the earth beneath, the General fell quickly into a dream of Amy. She stood beyond a rail fence in a cool meadow, wearing a white dress above which her black hair fell about her shoulders in a startling contrast.

But General Arnall could not easily reach her because he had first to fight his way through a swarm of Yankees between him and the fence. But they stood before his sword and pistol no longer than they had the day before, and he soon vaulted the rail fence into the meadow.

Amy had not until then seen him coming, or appeared to notice the battle. When she looked up, terror crossed her face, and her hands flew to the white bodice covering her breasts. Arnall realized that he was grimy with battle smoke and dripping with blood; she couldn't recognize her husband beneath these frightening traces of war and as he ran toward her, her horrified gaze was fixed upon the sword and pistol in his hands. He threw them away, but Amy seemed to be moving backward, floating away as fast as he approached.

The General stirred and muttered against the pine; even in its shade he had broken into a sweat. Stowe, passing nearby, was sure Arnall was reliving in his dreams the fight of the day before.

In fact, he was trying to reach Amy, running faster and faster as she swayed beyond him. Finally, despairingly, he threw out his arms to her; they seemed abnormally long, and he barely caught the folds of the white dress. It tore away, entangled itself around her feet, and she went down in the grass, naked in his arms, white body heaving, round soft hips bucking under him.

He was not surprised that she fought him, powerfully, angrily; Amy seldom yielded easily. The blood soon dripping on her face, her smooth body, fell not from his wounds of battle but from her nails on his throat and chest. But Hoke Arnall was powerful, too, and determined at last to conquer; so with his arms and legs and heavy body he pinned her to the grass of the meadow, buried his face between her breasts, at last sank himself deep within her. Again and again, he plunged desperately, yearning, until just when he thought she would never . . . knew it was hopeless . . . felt within himself the chill of living death, loveless life . . . just then Amy began to stir and surge beneath him, in the blind, helpless, rising flow of . . .

"Gin'al Arnall!"

A hand on his shoulder shook him abruptly awake. He looked in befuddlement into the stubbled face of a young captain. What was *he* doing in the meadow? Where was Amy?

"Cap'n Selby, sir. Sorry to wake you. Messages from Gin'al Jackson."

Arnall's head cleared quickly. He shifted one leg to cover his embarrassment, amazed at the lingering reality of his dream. As if he could actually *feel* Amy in his arms, naked on the grass.

Selby handed him an envelope, formally addressed. "Also sends'is complints'n wanted to know if you can give'im a good idea what the enemy's doin in your front."

The routine message irritated Arnall. Just when she'd been coming around, the way she so seldom did when actually in his arms.

"Beyond the woods, he means."

"Well . . . I've had a scout out, Selby. Le's see if he's come in yet."

Arnall struggled to his feet, still hiding his erection. Deep down inside, he'd always thought that under all the protests Amy liked it more than she'd let on . . . for that matter, more than *he* wanted to admit of a woman he'd married. The dream seemed to confirm his impression; and he was both thrilled and embarrassed at the ardor he'd finally felt in her in that dream moment of surrender.

"Oh, Sam . . . Gilmer back yet?"

"Hasn't reported to me, sir."

"Jackson wants to know what's on our front. I guess right away?" He raised his eyebrows at Selby.

"Think so, Gin'al."

Arnall had himself more or less under control by then, and could concentrate on military matters. He opened the envelope, wondering in irritation where Gilmore was. Which he knew was unfair, since the corporal hadn't been told to report back at any particular time.

"Aint heard so much as a Yank musket," Stowe said. "Not since that little skirmish this mornin."

Arnall took the folded sheet from the envelope, read it, then stared in astonishment and rising anger. Jackson had formally preferred charges. Arnall could scarcely believe it, but there it was in neat script. In the middle of battle with Pope, maybe for survival of his force, Jackson had somehow found time to charge the officer holding his left flank with a petty dereliction of duty!

"What'll I tell Gin'al Jackson, sir?" Selby was polite but insistent.

Arnall controlled his anger with difficulty. Not going to take this lying down, he thought. *Not when he ought to be sending me thanks for saving his neck*. He was about to give a snappish answer when his glance fell on the pine tree against which he'd been napping. It rose tall and straight, higher than any tree around it; and from its top branches someone might be able to see beyond the woods in their front. If troops were formed up over there, they'd be flying battle flags that could be spotted.

He looked around and saw Private Folsom who had just been warned that Ironass was awake. Folsom was hurrying forward for whatever might be needed of him.

The lad was lean and wiry. Tall, too. "Folsom! Get over here!"

Folsom ran to Arnall's side and saluted. Before he got his hand down, Arnall seized his arm. When Hoke Arnall went before a court-martial to demand justice, Stonewall Jackson would have no cause to complain of delay in obtaining information from Arnall's Brigade. And maybe *then* he'd look as crazy as he had to be, persecuting a fighting officer for a minor infraction he hadn't even committed.

"Up that tree over there, Folsom! High's you can climb."

At Longstreet's headquarters, nearly two miles away, an orderly trotted up to Major Thomas.

"Gin'al Longstreet wants you should come quick, sir!"

Thomas hurried to the headquarters tent and found Longstreet alone. Word had come in from enough scouts so that it could no longer be doubted, the general said, that the strong position Hood had encountered along the pike the evening before had been abandoned by Pope's army. Now nothing of importance appeared to be in Longstreet's front; and nothing had been on his right flank since early morning, when Porter had backed away from Dawkins Branch.

"That stump of yours itchin, Thomas?"

"Like chiggers eatin it!"

"Then here's what I want..."

Longstreet and Lee—who had gone out to look at the field himself—had decided to increase the pressure on Pope, who seemed to them to be contracting his lines to cover a retreat east of Bull Run. So Longstreet's whole line would be pivoted forward. With Hood's Division—which would creep forward on the pike to just west of Groveton—as their hinge, Kemper's Division on Hood's right and D. R. Jones's on Kemper's right were to swing like a giant barn door to the northeast.

The wheeling movement would be concealed by masses of woodland and rolling ground; the divisions were to advance about a mile at the outer flank of the movement. R. H. Anderson's newly arrived division would then be moved from reserve on the pike past Kemper's and Jones's divisions, to extend Longstreet's right.

As he ran for his horse to help distribute these orders, Thomas felt better. At least the open jaws of the army were beginning to close a little! Pope might not get away after all.

Private Philip Keefe of the Second Wisconsin, Gibbon's Brigade, was feeling much better. A good night's sleep, marred only by the nightmare screams of some crazy parson—as an orderly had described him—clean bandages on his leg wound, and a soothing salve on his raw hands and knees had made him feel almost human again. The hospital victuals—a bowl of warm broth and a johnny cake—weren't much but Keefe was so glad to be alive and mending that he would happily have subsisted on cool water, of which there was plenty.

He was in pain, of course, more than he'd ever dreamed possible. But what was a little pain, once the surgeons assured him he'd keep his leg? Having already received such a gift, Keefe vowed never again to ask the good Lord for anything. He even waved away an orderly who offered him opium pills.

"Don't need em things."

"Make you float off on a pink cloud." The orderly winked at him.

That was just the trouble, Keefe thought; opium was ungodly. He doubted if his father or his preacher back home would have swallowed anything that floated them off on pink clouds.

Chaplain E. P. Hornby, just down the line of pine-straw pallets in the shady grove where the hospital had been established, also had refused more opium. Not that he was as philosophical as Keefe about the severe pain of his wounds; Chaplain Hornby was sure, rather, that the opium had manufactured his evil dreams of Sally Crowell.

Chinamen smoked the stuff, didn't they, to waft themselves into a dream world of evil and decadence? Chaplain Hornby was loath to believe himself capable of such despicable dreams, even if opium-induced; but he preferred that explanation to viewing carnality and lust as part of his real life.

Scarcely an hour before being hit by the sudden shellfire on the road—how many days before?—the chaplain had selected the text for his next sermon. That had been, he was reasonably sure, on Thursday.

"Orderly, what day is this?"

"Sad'day, Parson. Reckon you won't be preachin this Sunday."

But a minister of the Lord could never be sure. Men in the hospital surely needed spiritual guidance, and their Heavenly Father might conceivably send down the necessary strength so that E. P. Hornby could rise and point the way.

Hornby hoped so. He liked to preach; he felt at his best in the pulpit. So he tried to recall the previously chosen text. If he could concentrate on a sermon, he'd not only be ready if called; he could also keep his mind off Sally Crowell—off those unspeakable dreams.

Private Keefe was dozing in the afternoon heat when a slight commotion in the hospital grove aroused him. He raised his head slightly, then stared in disbelief. Two young ladies—even at a distance, Keefe assumed they were young because they were not fat—were walking down the ranks of pallets in the company of a pair of prancing officers in clean blue uniforms. When the attentions of these dandies allowed, the young ladies were stopping to talk with the wounded men lying on their pallets under the trees.

Keefe was goggle-eyed as the ladies came nearer. Weeks, maybe even months, since he'd seen any females but string-bean farm wives and slovenly fat niggers peering blank-faced at passing troops. But what were ladies doing in a place of such stench and foulness? Keefe thought that he should be offended on their behalf, probably at the dandified officers chattering around them like blue jays. On the other hand, he was delighted, embarrassed, curious. Could they possibly be visiting the wounded just to offer them comfort? Keefe could hardly imagine such angels as that.

The ladies in their beautiful dresses and ribbons and hats stopped at the pallet next to Keefe's, giving him a good look at them while one of the pretty boys explained that the water dripping from a suspended bottle onto the man's bandages would ease his pain and help his wound cicatrize.

"We've had to learn a lot—and fast—about treating wounds, ma'am," one of the dandies said importantly.

"Just *amazin* what medicine can do."

The taller of the ladies looked at the officer with too much admiration for Keefe's taste. From the look of the man's clean uniform and shaved face, he'd had more experience impressing females than dressing wounds.

Keefe liked the look of the other lady better, anyway. Slight, pale, she seemed little more than a child; yet she held herself with a quiet dignity that reminded Phil Keefe somehow of his mother. As the sleek escort officers chattered on with the other, talkier one—her animated voice joining theirs—the pale lady came to Keefe's pallet and leaned over him.

"I'm Sally Crowell . . . hope you're not real bad hurt."

Keefe was stupefied. She was a *Rebel* lady; he could tell by her accent. He'd never expected to meet a Rebel lady, let alone one with such a kindly voice and sweet face; which was maybe why he'd paid no mind to the talky one's accent.

"Were you wounded in battle, sir?"

"Ma'am . . ."

Keefe tried hard to think of something interesting to say, how to say it. But he could barely manage to answer her question.

"In the leg, ma'am."

Beyond her, one of the fancy uniforms went past Keefe's pallet with the other lady, both talking a blue streak.

"Will you . . . will it . . . be all right?"

The second dandy peered over her shoulder at Keefe, without much interest.

"Yes, ma'am . . . I . . . I . . . think so."

"Oh, we get'em up'n out of here pretty fast." The officer puffed himself up toadlike, but Keefe paid him no attention.

"Ma'am?"

She leaned down to hear him better. He wished he dared stroke her pale cheek. And he saw something mournful, infinitely sad in her face. Suddenly he was conscious of his naked, bandaged body under the thin hospital sheet.

"This aint no place for a lady like you."

Faint color tinged her cheeks—though not, as Keefe naturally supposed, the blush of innocence. Sally's own sense of his naked body under the sheet had brought Lawrence powerfully back to her, in a way she had hardly thought of him since his death—as he and she had been in the hot delirious nights of a marriage that had first frightened, then astonished, then delighted them with its forbidden sensuality. Remembering Lawrence that way suddenly made him real again, made Sally strangely, poignantly happy—and hotly aware of this Yankee boy's barely concealed maleness.

"That's what everybody warned us." She spoke as primly as she could manage. "But we only thought . . . we . . . maybe we could cheer some of you up."

At first, of course, the officer in command wouldn't hear of their actually going among the wounded; he'd said orderlies would distribute the buttermilk and biscuits they'd brought. But Anna had kept after him, the way she could, and in the end the two officers from the administrative staff had volunteered to protect them from the worst sights. At that, the officer in command gave up—probably, Sally suspected, to get Anna out of his tent.

"But you're a *Rebel* lady."

The Yankee boy looked so amazed that Sally smiled at him. Even in the presence of so much suffering, she now believed that coming to the hospital might have been a good start on getting over her own trouble. At least, she knew now, she had not been made merely fearful by the terrible pile of human leavings under the harpsichord in Lawrence's house. And suddenly Lawrence was back with her, a remembered joy driving out sorrow.

"But even if I *am* a Rebel, this isn't a battlefield. And I don't hate anybody anyway. Do you?"

Phil Keefe was already powerfully in love with this slight angel with her mourning face and skin so fair it put him in mind of fresh milk. And to think she'd come to this place of horrors only to try to make things easier, more cheerful for her homefolks' enemies.

"No *ma'am* . . . speshly not you."

"Better be moving on."

Keefe wanted to get up and hit the fluttering fop. But Sally Crowell stretched out her tiny hand and he took it instead, feeling the warmth of her palm through her white glove.

"I hope you'll be all right . . . I hope you'll be goin home soon."

Watching her move on down the line of pallets, Keefe hoped he might never have to go home, or anywhere else except where that pale angel might be waiting for him. Would she come back tomorrow? If she'd visit every day, he'd be content to stay in the hospital forever. He put the palm of his hand, where she'd touched it, to his lips.

Chaplain Hornby, meanwhile, had remembered his text:

Except a corn of wheat fall into the ground and die, it abideth alone: but if it die it bringeth forth much fruit.

"John twelve: twenty-four," he murmured.

The possibilities arising from this teaching, Hornby thought, had great relevance for troops going into battle, if he could make them see "much fruit" being brought forth from the laying down of their lives. He was sure he would be able to show them how those lives were but as corns of wheat abiding alone unless they were *willing* to lay them down for the Lord in His righteous cause.

"Well . . ." A bright chattering voice broke his concentration. *"You* don't look too badly hurt!"

Hornby had been pondering his prospective sermon too deeply to have noticed the two unusual visitors and their escorts, or the stir thus created among the nearby pallets. When Anna Sutherland spoke to him, he was startled and confused to see a woman leaning over him. He noticed at once, moreover, Anna's southern accent. She must therefore be an owner of slaves and for that reason ought probably to be treated with reserve.

But she was pretty and animated, too, altogether an apparition Hornby had not expected to see among the wounded and dying. So he put aside his principles; and his natural sophistication and expertise in dealing with members of congregations enabled him quickly to recover his poise. Just the right lines rose to his lips, as artfully as a proper text for a sermon:

• • •

"'. . . O Welcome, pure-eyed Faith, white-handed Hope, Thou hovering angel girt with golden wings . . .'"

"Why sir! that's mighty pretty from a wounded man."

"Not so wounded, ma'am, as to misperceive what even blind Milton must have seen, were he on this poor bed instead of me."

Anna had never read Milton, or much of anything else, and this speech would have puzzled her except that she heard in it the reassuring tone of flirtatious raillery that had characterized most of her conversations with young men. Yankees were not so different after all, she thought.

Her coxcomb escort tried to speak solemnly. "This gentleman is a chaplain, Mrs. Sutherland. Major Hornby. In this cruel war, not even the Lord's servants can always be spared."

No, just the headquarters wimps, Anna thought. She was not as empty-headed as she sometimes liked to appear, and her husband Roger was off somewhere with Fitz Lee's cavalry—in the thick of the fighting, if she knew Roger. Anna had not failed to notice the accompanying officers' clean uniforms, well-combed appearance, and soft hands—hardly those of fighters or even working surgeons.

"Ah, sir, the church militant . . ." Between thoughts of his sermon and the appearance of this pretty young Rebel, Hornby's spirits had risen rapidly. "Why *should* she be spared?"

Anna looked over her shoulder for Sally, who was interested in poetry and religion, and saw her sister-in-law about to pass on to the next pallet.

"Stop here a minute," Anna called. "A chaplain."

Hornby had not until then seen Anna's companion. As she turned and came toward his pallet, with her small white face beginning to break into a smile, Hornby's first thought—he knew his Milton—was that the vision he'd already cited was now complete:

And thou unblemished form of Chastity!

When Sally reached Anna's side and looked down at the wounded man, she felt her foot go instantly cold as ice. The sensation was so painful she nearly cried out.

A chaplain Anna had said.

Sally felt the nausea and the nameless dread again, and as if someone had lit a lantern in a dark closet, she saw the Yankee chaplain standing by her bed . . .

"Sally . . ." Anna's chirrupy voice barely pierced Sally's shocked recall. "This is Chaplain Hornby, he's . . ."

Sally! Hornby saw then—instead of a pale young woman *unblemished form of chastity* staring down at him—the naked writhing body with which in his nightmare he had entwined himself on a bed of scarlet. He saw again the perfect form, the fragile curves of ankle and calf, felt again the softness and roundness of her thigh . . .

". . . not hurt too bad to recite you a pretty verse."

The words pulled Hornby back from his nightmare. He saw Sally's pale face tightening, her mouth beginning to open just as it had that day in her bedroom with battle sounds crashing outside the window.

"No!" the chaplain cried. "Please . . . no!"

That goddam crazy parson, a nearby orderly said to himself.

Sally might have been able to retain control if Chaplain Hornby had not cried out. But at his first word *no!* she knew that that was the voice *please no!* this was the man, and she saw him again in the twilight of her room *oh don't!* in the clatter and crash of the battle outside *please don't* holding in his hands as if for her inspection one of the bloody severed feet from the trash heap beneath the harpsichord.

So she screamed again, as she remembered screaming then. She screamed over and over, as she had done that day, remembering it all at last, his thick fumbling fingers on her, the bloody foot in his hand, the horror and the night closing down, a sort of death from which she had not awakened until neighbors came the next day and aroused her to the real, deceptive world.

At the first sound of Sally's piercing screams, Phil Keefe sat straight up, despite the excruciating agony that seared through his wounded leg. He had been about to doze off again, in the stifling heat, this time with shimmering visions in his young head of her mourning face and gentle eyes and the little smile that transfigured them.

No place for her Keefe thought, as Sally screamed and ran toward him along the line of pallets. Torn inside of himself—as fearfully as the Minié had torn his leg—by that soft voice suddenly agonized and in terror, Keefe stumbled up from his pine straw. Blinded by love and pity for his mourning angel, made oblivious to pain by his pasion to protect and comfort her, he lurched into her path with outstretched arms.

"Not what she thought!" Chaplain Hornby cried into Anna's amazed, unbelieving face.

But he knew his nightmare had been real. In that moment when he had lifted Sally's blood-corrupted hem to protect the purity of her flesh, when he had seen the beauty of her ankle—so unsuspected, so perfect that it actually had calmed his horror of the blood, and drawn him as powerfully as his love of the true God . . .

"Parson . . ." The orderly brushed past Anna and the dandy surgeon who was trying to pull her away. "I knowed you should of took em pills."

In that moment of revelation, Chaplain Hornby had stroked with one hand her beautiful limb as he might have touched a stone bust of Venus, with awe and reverence; her bloody boot had come off in his other hand; and she had started to scream. Hornby had run then, down the stairs, out of her house, into the gathering night, run as far as he could, crying to himself *not what she thought not what she thought* running from himself until he could believe it *not what she thought*. He had willed himself to keep on believing it, until he heard her scream again above his pallet.

Sally never saw Phil Keefe. As she ran past the end of his pallet, her shoulder struck one of his outstretched arms, and spun him half around. Keefe was falling anyway, his wounded leg giving way under his compulsive leap to his feet.

He went down heavily, as Sally ran on, out of the grove, out of his life as suddenly as she had entered it, her screams echoing and fading among the startled wounded, one of the dandies pounding after her. Keefe's neatly dressed wound, suddenly spurting blood, raked across the top of a bucket of dirty water in which an orderly had just washed off the suppurating arm stump of the man on the next pallet. The bucket turned over, spilling the water over Phil Keefe's leg and soaking his bandage.

Keefe lay on the ground moaning, not so much from the great grinding pain that surged up through his body as for the mourning angel flown, the sweet chance lost forever.

Larkin Folsom would have thought General Arnall was joking if he had not known so well that the General never joked.

"Tree, sir?"

"That one." Unsmiling, General Arnall pointed out the one he meant. "Up you go, lad."

"Hoke . . . I doubt he can see much, even from up there." Colonel Stowe knew. Yankee sharpshooters were in the woods beyond the railroad. But the General already was leading Folsom by the arm to the tree.

"Must of climb many a tree when you were a tyke back home. Just shinny up there the same way'n call back down what you see."

"Yessir."

Folsom had never climbed a tree in his life, except a clumpy dogwood in his mother's yard, into the low, spreading branches of which he had sometimes ventured—never more than five or six feet off the ground. Folsom had done his daydreaming not in the tops of trees but in a hammock his mother had had slung for him between two hickories. But he was a soldier. If Gin'al Arnall wanted him up there, he had no choice but to start climbing. Folsom put a tentative hand on the rough bark.

"Git those boots off, lad," Colonel Stowe had followed them with the messenger captain. "Better grip barefoot."

"But hurry!" Arnall gestured at the captain. "Selby here don't want to keep Stonewall waitin."

Private Folsom had often found it onerous having always to be ready to jump when the General sneezed; but he had been too glad to get out of the infantry line to complain. Now, as he sat down and tugged off his boots, Folsom would have given a year's sugar ration to be over in the railroad cut with the butternuts.

"Hop to it, boy!"

Disinterested, impersonal, Arnall stared at him as if at a piece of equipment. Perhaps useful, but a piece that could be replaced.

The orderly took hold of the tree trunk—resinous in the midday sun—placed one foot on it, and heaved himself up a few feet. His other foot quickly propped him there, like a squirrel.

"Right on up, Folsom . . . keep goin."

Folsom's arms were aching already. He looked up at the trunk rising into the clouds—as it suddenly seemed—and tried to put one foot higher on the trunk. But he feared that the movement, putting more weight on his arms, would cause him to fall.

Suddenly, two strong hands under his rump gave him a powerful upward shove, high enough up the rough, sticky trunk that he could seize a branch thick enough to take some of his weight. He caught a quick glimpse of the messenger captain looking up.

"You'll be all right now," the captain called to him.

But looking down had increased Folsom's sense of height and isolation. He managed to haul himself up to stand on the branch he'd first caught, relieved to be no longer dependent on his aching arms. He peered uncertainly toward where he supposed the Yanks might be.

"The other way, Folsom!" Arnall's voice seemed to sear the bottom of his feet.

Resin was sticky under Folsom's hands. Pine needles pricked his face and neck. He peered into the heat-shimmering distance.

"Can't see a thing, sir!"

"Then keep goin till you can!"

Folsom climbed farther into thinning branches that felt weak as reeds beneath his feet. Desperately, he clasped the trunk with knees and arms. The heavy pine smell and the hot sun were overpowering and he still could see nothing but the woods. He felt alone, exposed.

"Still nothin, sir!"

Something clipped a branch near Larkin Folsom's left foot and he hugged the tree in panic. Not alone after all; the shot made him feel naked as well as exposed.

"Where'd that come from, Folsom?"

"Don't know, sir!"

"Keep your eyes open, dammit! Get on!"

Another shot. This time Folsom saw a bluish-white puff of smoke drift from a patch of trees up ahead, as a bullet thwacked solidly into the tree trunk beneath his knees.

"Up there!" He felt his life staked on his ability to point out the sharpshooter. "Patch of woods!"

"Which way, idiot?"

Folsom pointed. As his hand, sticky with resin, left the tree trunk, another shot, another puff of smoke, caused him to jerk it back as if he had touched flame. Before he could open his mouth two more shots cracked the silence; in the pine needles around him bullets hissed and rattled like snakes.

"Piney woods!" Folsom dug his forehead hard into the scaly bark. "Up left near a dead tree!"

A bullet thudded into the trunk; another scattered bark and needles on the top of Folsom's head.

"What else you see?" The General seemed less interested in sharpshooters than Larkin Folsom was. "Any guns? Cavalry?"

"Nosir!"

"Then on up higher, boy! What's other side-a those woods?"

"Hoke." Colonel Stowe suddenly saw again a crazed figure lunging out of battlesmoke, thrusting a bayonet after the enemy. "I don't think he'll git high enough to see 'nything."

"Le's just find out, Sam."

"When your scout comes in . . ." Captain Selby's words were

tentative, as befitted a junior officer. *"He* could report to Gin'al Jackson. That'd..."

"You think Jackson wants to wait for an answer, Cap'n, you don't know'im like I do. Keep goin, Folsom!"

Stonewall was not going to get Gilmore away from him, either. *Best scout I ever had. And I found'im.* Arnall was sure that if Jackson got a look at the corporal and heard one of his detailed reports, he'd never send him back to Arnall's Brigade. Besides, if Folsom could get the information now, the sooner it'd be on its way to Jackson and the less chance he could make a case against Hoke Arnall for any kind of dereliction.

"Folsom...what you see now?"

Folsom saw nothing but green trees, puffs of smoke coming from them all too often. He thought suddenly of Corporal Gilmore over there beyond the trees somewhere.

"Still nothin, sir!"

Corporal Gilmore would know what to do. Corporal Gilmore would get him out of this fix.

"Get higher then!"

Folsom was so nearly paralyzed by fear of the snickering bullets that he could hardly even have climbed *down,* if ordered to. He wanted only to flatten himself into the tree trunk, even though it was too narrow to cover all of him. The thought of going even higher—he could feel a slight sway of the thinning trunk—nauseated him. But it did not occur to him to defy or disobey Gin'al Arnall.

"I'll try, sir!"

He got his right foot on a higher branch that felt scarcely able to share his weight. Folsom desperately did not want to risk hoisting his body on it. But he believed he had no real choice. He could do his duty and meet his obligations, as the General demanded; or he could go back down the tree a coward and a failure, to meet Ironass's certain retribution.

So with his arms and his right leg he levered himself higher, the bark of the tree scraping painfully on his forehead; but the branch held. Folsom quickly drew up his left foot to rest on another limb.

Two more shots. A bullet cut a twig by his ear. Another burned hotly across his exposed hip; it tore through his trousers, opened a gouge in his flesh an eighth of an inch deep and two inches long, and passed on—*wheat!*—through the pine boughs.

The searing pain caused him to clutch the tree trunk convulsively; but the movement pulled his head up. Beyond the woods that sheltered the sharpshooters, he saw a stretch of open, partly level ground and on it a far blue mass of men.

General Jackson and Colonel Channing, returning from the conference at Lee's headquarters, were just about then pausing in front of Starke's lines—Jackson's old division—too look over the field. All seemed quiet, peaceful, even languorous in the midday heat. Insects buzzed. Behind Jackson's batteries, some of the gunners threw a ball around. A few carrion birds wheeled patiently overhead, black against the soft clouds drifting in the diamond-hard sky. To the south, a sullen afternoon sun burned low over Manassas Junction.

Jackson pointed at something beyond the pike. Channing, following the direction of the general's long arm, just made out the tubes of four Federal guns sited beyond the crest of a slight ridge. Their carriages were invisible.

The general's voice was soft but carrying. "Let's get those guns off there, Colonel."

Channing trotted over to the nearest battery. Young Captain Overholt walked out to meet him.

Channing pointed. "Gin'al Jackson wants em guns offen at ridge."

Overholt squinted in the brilliant sun, then saluted. "Sharp eyes, Colonel. They wa'n't ther a half hour ago."

Channing and Jackson watched as the ball game broke up, horses were quickly brought forward and harnessed, and Overholt's Battery trotted out in a cloud of dust, a rumble of wheels, a clinking of trace chains, the hoarse shouts of drivers:

"Hum-up ther, blast you! Hahhh! Hahhh!"

Overholt, trotting on a glistening bay across the sloping broomsedge field, directed his four six-pounders to a roll of ground halfway to the pike. Their brass tubes flashed in the sun; Queen Anne's lace swathed their wheels in white.

"Good boys." Channing admired the speed with which Overholt's batterymen unlimbered, moved horses to the rear, and began sighting on the Federal guns. He guessed the range at 1,200 yards. "Overholt keeps 'em jumpin."

Jackson, still as a statue on his sorrel, said nothing. An artilleryman himself, he always took sharp interest in the work of his guns.

Private Alf Gurganous was glad to have a job to do after the long morning of waiting; besides, he was always proud of the precision and speed with which Overholt's Battery did its work. Especially in the open as they were now, they needed to fire first, if possible.

Working No. 1 as usual, with reliable Jeff Jernigan loading in the No. 2 position, Alf rammed home the first solid shot within seconds of the order to load.

"Trail right!" Sergeant Jocko Payne sang out as he sighted Matthew.

The No. 3 man, Private Harry Moore, stepped to the handspike and hefted the trail, moving the tube slightly left. Private Bubba Carpenter, assigned No. 4, hooked the lanyard to the primer and deftly placed the primer in the vent. He and Moore moved outside the wheels.

"Fire!"

Overholt's voice rang across the field, and Matthew, Mark, Luke, and John roared in unison. Before the echoes died, Alf saw smoke puff from the tubes of the Federal guns, too. Twelvepounders. Seem like Yanks alluz had the weight of shell.

Even so, Yank gunners had to go some to get the beat of Overholt's Battery. Even while sponging Matthew for the second round, Alf could see one of the enemy guns sag to the axle.

Wheel smashed. But the four Yankee rounds fell harmlessly short, kicking up thick spumes of dust; one bounced like a rubber ball between Matthew and Mark.

"Can't hit shit!" Jeff Jernigan yelled as he put in the second shot.

Alf rammed it home and stepped back. Jocko had the piece laid right as usual and needed little adjustment. Overholt's four guns, firing at will, began laying a relentless barrage on the Federal position.

"Gettin ther money's worth," Channing shouted. "Em Yanks're gettin ther money's worth!" Old Jack sat still, watching.

Alf saw right away that these Yank gunners were by no means the match of those they'd met the evening of the fight with the black hats. These seemed little better than beginners, getting off maybe only two rounds to three or four they took, aiming mostly long, after their first rounds fell short.

Still, the Yanks did some damage. Alf saw Hank Gooding, who was down on his knees holding horses, thrown straight up in the air by a shell burst right in front of him. Another shell, coming in on top of that one, decapitated a horse that had reared in fright. A shell fragment struck Captain Overholt's fine bay just in front of the saddle; blood spurted from the wound in a stream thicker than Alf's wrist, but Overholt leaped off unhurt before the animal sank rolling and screaming to the ground. Overholt quickly put a pistol shot in its head.

But the outcome was in little doubt after the first exchange. Overholt's pieces poured solid shot into the Federal battery in a continuous stream, as if four giant battering rams were pounding away. The fight was over quickly—two Yank guns hit, the other two pulled back out of sight.

"Good . . . good." Ol Jack's voice was deeper, harsher, Colonel Channing thought.

Hank Gooding had the wind knocked out and a headache good for three or four days; but except for Overholt's bay and the beheaded battery horse, the worst they'd been hurt was when Private Jimmy Lee Pruitte, working No. 3 on Luke, tripped and fell just before his No. 4 pulled the lanyard. On recoil, Luke's iron-rimmed wheel came down on Jimmy Lee's foot and ankle carrying the weight of 1,784 pounds of brass tube and wooden carriage.

Jeff Jernigan went to look, after the firing stopped. On the way back to their original position near Starke's Division, Jeff reported to Alf:

"Had to scrape Jimmy Lee's foot outten-a dirt. Bonecrackers aint hardly even got to cut it off. Jes kind of wring it a little, like a chicken neck."

Captain Overholt, deprived of his mount, rode back as driver on the lead pair of the team hauling Matthew. Colonel Channing and General Jackson trotted out to meet him. Overholt pulled the team to a halt and saluted.

"That was handsomely done, Captain," Alf Gurganous heard Stonewall say. "Very handsomely done."

Colonel Channing reckoned that that was as near to a speech of praise as he'd ever heard form Ol Jack. Overholt, he thought, had a yarn he could carry to the grave. Tell his grandchildren, he lived to have any.

"Troops, sir!" Larkin Folsom almost forgot the pain in his hip in the excitement of his discovery. "Troops in ranks!"

"What troops, man? Cavalry?"

"Infantry, sir! Oceans of 'em!"

"Flags?"

"Lots of flags!"

"Count 'em, man . . . count flags out loud, Folsom!"

"One . . . two . . ."

"Louder!"

Selby watched the traces of sharpshooter bullets all around the boy in the tree as the shouted count came down. Crazy, the captain thought. Why not a quick estimate of the number of flags to report to Arnall on the ground?

"Four, five . . ." More rifle shots drowned the boy's voice.

"Keep countin . . . louder!" Hoke Arnall was jubilant; his instinct had told him something could be seen from that tree, if Folsom just got up high enough.

"Seven . . . eight . . ."

Eight regiments! Pope's coming, Stowe thought. No reason to line up that many troops unless he's coming again.

"Nine . . . nine I can see, sir!"

"Any guns?"

As he concentrated on the flags, Folsom had lost the sharpest edge of his fear. He boldly stuck his head around the tree again to look for guns. but he could see only the blue mass, and the flags above it.

"None in sight, sir!"

"Massin'is guns somewhere else."

Selby thought Arnall spoke with the same impressive calm he had observed in General Jackson. Nine Yank regiments over there within eyesight and Arnall acted as if they were maybe on parade.

"All right, Folsom . . . come on down!"

Bullets were still whining through the tree, but fewer now, as if the sharpshooters had lost their enthusiasm. Folsom congratulated himself on having stuck it out. But the scratch on his hip was fiery, and he was still a bit nauseated from the faint sway of the tree. He needed no urging to stretch his bare left foot down toward a branch beneath him. As he did so, nearly his full weight remained on his right foot, braced on one of the last small branches he had reached near the top of the tree. The branch cracked.

Folsom's whole body lurched to the right; for a moment only his arms clutched around the tree trunk kept him from falling. He kicked in panic to get his left leg around the trunk and felt his heel strike hard against the bark.

Thus struggling, Folsom did not hear the next shot, or the bullet that struck and broke his right shoulder; he only felt as if he had been smashed with a sledgehammer. The impact thrust his body back, away from the tree trunk, and broke the hold of his right arm on it, only his left arm and hand retaining a grip. They could not halt his fall. Folsom felt himself going, his right shoulder on fire and crunched at the same time, his left foot scraping the bark, his left arm slipping.

"Oh my God!" Captain Selby stared up at the orderly's body sprawling downward through the branches.

Folsom closed his eyes when his left hand lost its clasp on the trunk. Then he fell backward. The back of his head struck something, hard; fire flashed in his head, joined the flame in his shoulder.

"Son of a bitch," Sam Stowe said.

Half conscious, Folsom nevertheless kept kicking and stretching for the tree trunk. Around his feet somewhere. He felt himself bouncing among the branches, scraping bark; he smelled turpentine, burned like a torch, caught a glimpse of sky. He was going down so slowly through the retarding branches of the tree, thrashing like a treed coon shaken down for the hounds, that it seemed to him entirely possible he would catch on to something and halt his fall.

"Grab at branch, Folsom!"

Again, he did his best to obey the General's shouted command. But he could get a hold on nothing. Where was Corporal Gilmore? Nothing to hold on to.

"Son of a goddam bitch." Sam Stowe put his hand over his eyes and turned away.

But Captain Selby was transfixed. He saw Folsom's left foot catch in the crotch of a small branch springing from the main trunk. It held, and the orderly's body swung on down in a long thrashing arc, bounced heavily off the trunk, and hung a moment, head down.

"Grab it!" Arnall yelled. "The trunk, man, the trunk!"

Folsom had felt his left ankle break off sharply, an even fiercer pain. *Breakin to pieces.* But his thrashing left arm and right leg found no grip. He dangled upside down by his left leg caught in the single branch, until the branch broke.

Another smaller limb falling from the tree cracked across Thad Selby's forehead. He hardly noticed it, did not know he shouted again:

"Oh, my God!"

Yes my God, Folsom falling head down had time to think. *Yes my God falling, burning Mother flailing Corp . . .*

But Corporal Gilmore trotted across the trampled cornfield and vaulted what was left of the rail fence only in time to see the boy hit the ground headfirst at General Arnall's booted feet.

• • •

Major Reverdy Dowd of the Sixth Wisconsin had been premature in supposing that if any fighting was to be done that day, King's Division (now commanded by Brigadier General J. P. Hatch) would be out of it. As the main body of the division moved north of the Warrenton Pike and was rejoined by Gibbon's Brigade, Dowd saw that it was forming up on Porter's right flank, just as if it were a part of Porter's Corps.

At brigade headquarters, General Gibbon himself outlined Pope's Special Order to his regimental commanders.

"Pursuit?" Dowd said. "General, is Jackson sposed to be retreating?"

"That's what General Pope believes." Gibbon, Dowd suspected at once, was not so sure. "Anyway, General Hatch tells me that in the . . . uh . . . pursuit, Porter will command our division as part of his attack force. We'll move out on the right, with Butterfield's Division of Porter on our left, in Porter's center. Porter's other division—Sykes's—will be on the left flank, with *his* left on the turnpike. Reynolds's Division and Sigel's whole corps in reserve."

A hell of an attack force, Dowd thought. A three-division front. Even if Pope did prove wrong about Stonewall retreating, he'd allocated plenty of power to the "pursuit."

"Now listen closely, gentlemen. General Hatch wants our division deployed in column of brigades, each brigade in two lines of battle. Hatch's own brigade first; Colonel Sullivan's taking command of it. Then Patrick. We'll be the third brigade in column . . ."

Dowd calculated rapidly that with each brigade in two lines, Gibbon's Brigade would make up only the fifth and six lines of the division deployment. But at least they'd be part of the attack with Porter's arrogant Peninsula veterans.

". . . Doubleday next. Now for the two lines in *our* brigade, I want the Sixth and Seventh Wisconsin abreast, Seventh on the left, Sixth on the right, about fifty yards behind Patrick's second line. Fifty yards behind that, Second Wisconsin on the left, Nineteenth Indiana on the right. That clear?"

Captain Black took Dowd aside, after the brigade council was concluded.

"Something funny going on, Rev."

"That's what I think. If Stonewall's retreating, I'll eat your hat, braid and all."

"No bet. But what I mean . . . they say over't Hatch's H.Q. that fight they had on the pike last night was with Longstreet."

This puzzled rather than surprised Dowd. He had supposed only Jackson was in their front and he knew so little of the Confederate Army organization that the significance of Longstreet's presence escaped him. But Captain Black took his lack of comprehension for doubt.

"Hatch took prisoners from Hood's Texas Brigade, man. That's Longstreet."

"Well, what's Longstreet got? A division or something?"

"A corps, Rev. Rebs call it a wing but it's a *corps*."

Dowd understood *that*. "And his whole corps's..." He gestured vaguely west. "Out there?"

Captain Black assumed his favorite air of superior knowledge. "Stands to reason. Hood aint here all by himself. Hood's here, Hatch says, Longstreet's here." He leaned close to Dowd's ear to deliver his most interesting news. "Only what I hear... Pope don't believe it."

Not far from the Stone House at the intersection of the pike and the Manassas–Sudley Road, Captain Micah G. Duryea was reporting Longstreet's forward wheel to Major General Irvin McDowell.

"Not guesswork, General. Longstreet's got three divisions in line southeast from the pike, from just west of Groveton corners to the vicinity of..." He put a finger on McDowell's outspread map. "A farmhouse here. And I'm pretty sure another division's getting ready to extend the line farther to Longstreet's right."

Duryea had roamed the country south of the pike for most of the morning. Surely, he thought, the experienced McDowell would grasp the meaning of his report. The great "pursuit" Pope had ordered, that Porter was readying under cover of the woods and rolling ground north of the pike, would march under the swinging hammer of Longstreet, which would crush Porter's divisions against the anvil of Jackson.

In his schoolmasterly manner, General McDowell gazed at Duryea as calmly as if the captain had brought him a report on forage available for battery horses. McDowell sat on an upended box behind a camp desk under an oak tree. Colonel Russell stood at his side, having just come from Pope for a report on preparations for the pursuit.

"You've verified these movements yourself, Captain?"

"I have, General."

"If a division were available, do you have in mind a sound defensive position for it south of the pike?"

Duryea had studied the ground with just that in mind.

"Bald Hill, sir, just west of the Sudley Road."

And just south, he realized as he put his finger on the map again, of the point of farthest advance of McDowell's own army the year before, in the war's opening battle, when people thought it would all be over quickly. But McDowell probably would not wish to be reminded of *that*.

"Then go to General Reynolds of the Pennsylvania Division. Give him my compliments, Captain, and my orders to take up a defensive position on Bald Hill, and guide him there."

"But, sir..." Colonel Russell's voice showed his concern. "Won't that weaken Porter's attack?"

"He should be strong enough. Withdrawing Reynolds still leaves him three divisions and Sigel's Corps in reserve."

"But General Pope wants Porter to have the strongest possible force. He..."

"*I* command the pursuit, Colonel. And Porter *does* have the strongest force possible...since Duryea reports Longstreet on Porter's left."

Duryea was relieved not to have encountered the kind of blank resistance Pope had offered to any mention of Longstreet's possible presence. Still...he was a patriot before he was a soldier. *Meo periculo,* he thought. He could always go back to Vermont and train dogs.

"Do you think, sir, that one division will be enough to guard Porter's left flank?"

He would not have asked so impertinent a question in less pressing circumstances. Hearing it, McDowell raised donnish eyebrows. Even sitting on a flimsy crate, Duryea thought, the general looked not unlike a high-ranking War Department clerk.

"General Porter's attack...you know General Pope has great expectations for it." Duryea detected a faint nod of McDowell's head toward Russell. "So taking even one division from General Porter's attack force is...ah...difficult."

And more, Duryea understood, would be impossible. Well, so be it. He saluted and hurried to his horse. Colonel Russell followed and put a hand on his shoulder. He looked harried, exhausted; Duryea remembered that his teeth probably hurt.

"You see a real danger on the left, Duryea?"

"Colonel...begging your pardon and with all due respect . . . from what I've seen south of the pike, General Porter's attack may not be . . . ah . . . wise."

Colonel Russell stared at him in consternation. "But it's *ordered*, Duryea."

"Couldn't it be stopped?"

Russell turned away and leaned against a tree, looking off toward Buck's Hill and Pope's headquarters.

"A man commanding an army, Captain . . ." He broke off for a moment. "A man commanding an army in the field has to act on what he . . ." Russell hesitated again, then chose his word. "What he perceives. History shows he'll be wrong maybe half the time. Maybe more. But he has to act, Duryea. It's his responsibility. I wouldn't interfere with that if I could."

Duryea saluted again. *Jure divino*, he thought. For the army, anyway. "Then I'll go to General Reynolds, sir . . . as ordered."

He had protested as far as he could. Perhaps Russell had too. Now . . . soldiers had to be soldiers. Their responsibility was to do what had to be done, as best they could.

He swung up into the saddle. Colonel Russell looked up at him with drawn face and tired eyes.

"Too late to call off the attack anyway. Even if Pope decided to do it, he couldn't get the orders out in time."

Russell's saggin figure showed, Duryea thought, the terrible weight of responsibility in war, even though Russell's was only at second or third remove. Russell probably "perceived," unlike his commander, that Jackson was not retreating, that Longstreet was on the field, that the slavers were not beaten. If so, even second or thirdhand responsibility would be a heavy burden. Duryea felt an unaccustomed sympathy. But that was something he did not know how to express and doubted a senior officer would welcome from a junior.

"I have to ride to General Reynolds, Colonel."

"Come back to McDowell here as soon's you can." Russell's voice was not quite apologetic. "We may be able to find some more strength to send to Porter's left flank . . . ah . . . after General Pope hears about our report."

Andrew Peterson and Henry, following the roundabout route through Buckland, had managed to get the Whatsit Wagon across thick wagon traffic on the Thoroughfare–Gainesville Road without being challenged. In the glare of the afternoon sun they headed

east on the Hay Market Road. Just as Peterson had hoped, once
away from the road intersections around Gainesville, the provost
marshals were not often to be seen. Military traffic was heavy on
the Hay Market, but no one tried to stop them.

"Trouble is . . ." Peterson had lit a self-congratulatory cigar,
once they were safely on the road east. "I guess they could start
fightin again any minute, anywhere round here." He had a brief,
horrid vision of Joe Nathan's headless shoulders, the porthole in
the tree.

But no turning back. Positive and Negative were drawing them
steadily nearer the scene of yesterday's heavy fighting. He had
enough plates for one more day's good work, one more recording
of the bitter truths his camera documented better than any historian.
Then back to Richmond to refit as best he could in a blockaded
city.

After that . . . who knew? How much more war did he or anyone
need, how much was required to expose its depravity, its criminal
waste of lives and energy, the perils to a people's soul in achieving
even useful ends by so much violence and destruction?

"Humm-on, mules."

Henry had no idea where Mist Dodge thought he was going.
He only knew that if they followed it far enough, the Hay Market
Road would carry them to Sudley Ford over Bull Run, out of
Prince William County. Henry knew that was in the direction of
Washington, the Potomac . . . *Nawth. Freedom! Gone-a cross Jer-
dan, ol folks say*.

"Hahh, mules!"

The reins were easy in his hands, keeping just the right tension
on Positive and Negative. As if aware of Henry's destination, they
had settled well into the traces and plodded steadily on at his soft
urgings, their hooves rhythmic on the road, small plops of dust
rising at each step.

Missy reached the rail fence beside the pike just after Hood's
Division had moved cautiously past, as Longstreet wheeled his
whole line forward. The old house where she'd lived all her life
stood empty-looking and silent. The front door was half open
above the shaky stoop neither Paw nor Henry had ever got around
to fixing.

As she was gathering her nerve to step from behind the cedar
and sumac that shrouded the fence along the pike, the cellar door
creaked open. Sajie came out with a bucket and started toward

the back of the house. Emboldened, Missy flitted across the pike and ran after her—until stopped abruptly by the bloated corpse at the rear corner of the house. Its huge face was blackening in the sun.

Paw got to clean up this yard Missy thought foolishly. She circled far around the ugliness on the ground.

"Sajie!"

In the quiet of the yard, her whisper carried like a rifle shot. Sajie spun around, raising the bucket like a shield. Missy came running, light as a squirrel in a tree, then stopped again, staring at another body near the wall.

"What . . . who're *they?*"

"Sojers. Fightin all round-yere last night after you run off."

In the heat of the afternoon and the airless cellar, Ol Brace's body and the black jellied blood had started to bother Sajie's stomach. But at least Mistis had fallen asleep and her babbling had ceased. And in another hour or less Sajie would have Ol Brace in the ground and covered over. Then they could get out of the cellar—sposin she could git Mistis up em steps—and get on with things.

But Sajie was dirty from digging, parched with thirst and still sore from Ol Brace's manhandling. *Head achin wuss'n ever.* She took the empty water bucket and went out to the well, as tired and dispirited as she'd ever been. Missy's sudden appearance vaguely angered her. *Now she show up. She been here last night, maybe . . .*

"Is . . . is everybody all right, Sajie?"

Sajie had thought through her story. "Yuh Maw is. Yuh Paw he gone scoutin. Tooken Wash. At sojer boy done run off on you, aint he?"

Missy drew herself up. "Cose not. Comin back tonight."

"How come? Ainchuh done give'im all he wants?"

"He aint like at. He be back."

Sajie doubted it. But she was glad if Missy believed it.

"Y'aint home fuh good, den?"

Missy suddenly felt lonely. She felt lost. But she stuck out her chin.

"Jus come see how y'all gittin on."

Sajie's brief anger had faded. *Chile stay off one mo night she aint never gone know whut'er Maw done. Whut happen to'er Paw. Lessen she b'lieve'er Maw's crazy talk.*

"Wher's Maw? Inna cellar still?"

"Say she aint comin out twill em sojers gone fum yere."

"Go speak to'er then." Missy started to turn away.

"Naw'm," Sajie said. "Y'aint comin home fuh good, I-uz you, I jes let'er alone. She tuck on sump'm awful you run off at sojer boy."

"Aint no sojer boy. He's a *cap'n*."

"Yessum. But you go down-er now'n den leave again, Mistis gone start in hollerin'n cryin all ovuh."

Missy was pleased to have been so missed; at the same time, she regretted having upset her mother. And she could see the good sense in what Sajie said.

"Mought be back tomarr then. Iffen he got to go off with at ol army. Is Paw turble mad?"

"Not no mo."

"Donchuh tell'im I-uz here'n didn stay."

Sajie had given her a ray of hope that maybe Paw'd take her back after all. When Hart had to go on. Missy turned, trotted lightly across the yard in her bare feet, then stopped and looked back at Sajie still standing at the well near the dead men.

"Kainchuh git Henry t'carry off em-er?" She pointed.

"Not right now."

Just like white folks, Sajie thought, picking up the full bucket as Missy ran on around the house toward the road. *Nare word bout Henry cept kin he do sump'm they could do theyself.*

General Arnall readily, almost eagerly, had given Corporal Gilmore the necessary permission. So, cradling the boy's head against his chest to keep it from bobbling around on his broken neck, Gilmore carried the slight young boy through the afternoon quiet to Sudley Church. The right arm and the left foot hung at awkward angles.

Gilmore had known the moment he reached the boy's side that the bonecrackers could do nothing for him. And Gilmore had no religion save self-sufficiency—at least he'd had none until a few days before, and he had not yet had time to sort out what might have happened since then. So Gilmore took the boy to the church graveyard neither for medical nor religious reasons, and not even to bury him. But there would be shade trees there, and the peace of the dead, and he could hold the boy in his arms awhile, away from those who'd killed him. There would be shade in the graveyard for them both.

Colonel Stowe had hastily printed an identification in large, block letters on a piece of paper torn from a letter. LARKIN

FOLSOM, Hq. Co., Arnall's Brig. Gilmore could not read the lettering but as he walked along toward the church he thought the boy's name, over and over. Larkin Folsom. Larkin Folsom.

"Larkin Folsom," he said out loud.

Sounded like a poet. Sounded like what Amos Gilmore could put no words to—that which he and the boy had known in the few stolen moments alone in their blankets, alone in the world, as Gilmore had once, in another life, valued above all being alone in the woods with the sun coming through the trees, the smell of pine needles thick in the air, and no one to plague him.

"Larkin Folsom."

This time, his voice saying the boy's name was bitter in his throat. But when Gilmore reached the churchyard and sat for awhile under a horse chestnut tree with the boy in his arms, he put out of his mind what he was going to do, blanked out everything but memory—not so much the memory of the way they'd touched and held each other, as the way they'd briefly talked, the sense Gilmore had had of the boy's gentleness, and the rare knowledge that something in *him*, in Amos Gilmore, the woodsman who had valued himself at no more than big fists and a hard dick— something in *him* had appealed miraculously to that gentleness, that sweet nature of the poet.

"Well," Gilmore said to a God he'd never really believed in— or, rather, had never thought could or would believe in *him:* "I reckon I didn't do so good. But I tried to look out for'im like yuh tole me."

He thought he knew God's reply all too well:

"Jus like I made out'n-a first place, Gilmer. You aint shit'n nare will be. All I ast was could you keep one-a my poet types alive'n you mess at up like everthing else you ever done cept shoot Yanks."

I'd-a got back one minute sooner, Gilmore thought, *just one minute* sooner, I could-a tole Arnall myself what-uz out ther. Just one minute sooner, the boy'd be alive.

Gilmore would have cried if he could; but he didn't know how. He was not much shocked, however; somehow he'd known the thing wouldn't last, anymore than those old-time moments in the woods could last. Nor did he sit long cradling the body in his arms, because he knew anger and hatred would inevitably consume him, and he did not want to grieve Larkin Folsom, who'd never known either, with such things in his heart. He stood up, the lean young form still tight against his chest, went to his knees, and laid the boy out under the horse chestnut, propping the fine head against a root so that the face looked to the sky, as Gilmore thought a poet's should.

The corporal tucked the identification into the boy's shirt pocket, and found another piece of paper there. Gilmore pulled it out and saw it was covered with the boy's fine-educated hand. Even though he could not read lettering, he put the paper in his own pocket. Then he kissed the boy's forehead and touched each of his eyes with a thick thumb, wanting to make sure he would not be lying there with open eyes for anyone to look into, because not everyone would have seen that they were the eyes of a poet.

Gilmore did not look back as he walked away. He went to the church, stepping carefully among the numerous wounded and dead men still lying about. Major Worsham, nearly out on his feet after all night and the heft of the day at the operating table, had just come out to sit on the top step and try to convince himself he'd done all any man could.

With dull eyes he watched the big, mean-looking corporal come up the steps and stop in front of him.

"You bout the first whole man I seen since yesterday, Corp'ral."

"Yessir. Beggin your pardon, Major . . . you mind readin this-yere for me?"

For Christ sake, Worsham thought. Can't even see straight and he wants me to read 'is letter. But when he took the piece of paper, he saw right away that it was not a letter.

"To a Friend." He looked up at the corporal standing patiently in front of him. "Where'd you get this?"

"Found it on . . . a dead man I knew."

"Must of been a poet."

"Yessir."

"It's a love poem. Funny he called 'is sweetheart 'a friend,' though."

Worsham was too tired to declaim, so he read slowly, quietly, without emphasis:

> "If all thy beauty were a summer's day
> That blossomed sweetly . . ."

That's it, Gilmore thought. The one he said some of to me.

> "... from the fertile sun
> And lay on earth as soft as new-mown hay,
> And I recalled that yonder autumn lay,

Its yellow leaves a costume merely spun
To fall, and be by winter swept away . . ."

The major looked up. "Is there somebody this ought to go to,
Corp'ral? Somebody that'd want it to remember 'im by?"
"Yessir. Is they more?"

"If, too, thy smile were but a candle's ray
That flickers golden till the night is done,
Then dims when dawn refuses to delay;
Still, I'd persist in offering to pay
Love's homage, love . . .

"Love's homage. I like that, Corp'ral, don't you?"
Corporal Gilmore did not know what the word "homage" meant;
he had never heard it before. But he liked the sound of it, as he
liked the sound of the boy's name. Larkin Folsom.
"Yessir. Like it fine."

" . . . love's homage, love, to beauty and to one
Whose grace no age could dull, nor season gray.
If all thy beauty were a summer's day,
I'd love no less because it could not stay."

" 'Larkin Folsom,' Say, he wrote this today, Corp'ral. It's dated
just today."
The big man took the paper abruptly out of Worsham's hand.
Tears were streaming down his saddle-colored face.
"Been workin . . ." The corporal choked, and wiped his cheeks
with a huge dirty hand, smearing them like a child's. "He'd been
writin on it . . . these last few days."

Not long after 3 p.m., Colonel Russell was satisfied that Fitz-John
Porter's attack was ready. By then, the attack front ran about a
mile and a quarter, from Porter's left flank on the Warrenton Pike
due north to the right flank of Hatch's Division. Along that front,
or in attack columns behind it, Porter had massed three divisions,
thirty-seven regiments altogether.
"Better'n twelve thousand men." General Pope, at his Buck's
Hill headquarters, had listened to Russell's report with apparent
satisfaction, a cigar jutting from his plump jaw. "Most powerful

attack I know of in this war, Russell." He was obviously pleased
with the distinction, despite his anger at Porter.

But Cass Fielding, listening carefully, thought he heard a tone
of uneasiness in Russell's reply:

"Ought to be strong enough, sir. It ought to be."

Porter's troops, well sheltered by woods and by four low north–
south rolls of ground, were packed like salt cod in a barrel—so
it seemed to Major Reverdy Dowd—into the triangle formed by
the pike, the Groveton–Sudley Springs Road and the Manassas–
Sudley Road. Sigel's Corps and the divisions of Reno, Stevens,
and Hooker were in reserve in the same triangle, behind Porter's
first lines of attack. Twenty-eight batteries of artillery would support Porter's assault.

But Major Dowd, anxiously riding along his lines on patient
Rosie, was worried about his right flank. With Hatch's Division
deployed on the right of Porter's striking force, and Dowd's Sixth
Wisconsin on Hatch's right, he felt naked on that flank. He had
put his best companies there. Still . . .

"Orders as plain as day," Captain Black had assured him in
the afternoon. "Ricketts's Division's out on your right. You'll be
covered like a whore on Saturday night."

But I wish I could *see* Ricketts out there, Dowd thought, gazing
into the timber that supposedly sheltered the flanking division.
Nothing could be seen except underbrush and tree trunks. He
turned Rosie's head and moved slowly along the line in the other
direction.

In fact, Ricketts's Division *was* on Dowd's right, though a bit
separated. Beyond Ricketts was the battle line of Kearny's Division (some of whose regimental flags had been spotted from the
treetop by Larkin Folsom). But Dowd would have been dismayed
to know that on the advice of Colonel Russell and General
McDowell, acting on Captain Duryea's reports, Pope had reluctantly permitted two of Ricketts's four brigades to be withdrawn.

McDowell had sent these brigades to strengthen the Federal
left, south of the pike, along with Reynolds's Pennsylvanians and
two other brigades he had wrested from Sigel's Corps. Captain
Duryea had helped place these forces along a ridge running roughly
northwest from Bald Hill toward Groveton.

Duryea had been surprised, while so engaged, to find that the small New York brigade of Colonel Gouverneur K. Warren also had moved south of the pike and into a defensive position.

"By whose order?" Duryea inquired of one of Warren's regimental commanders.

"Damn if I know. We saw Reynolds's Division pull out of this area. Next thing I know, Warren moves us in."

Warren's two regiments could hardly fill the gap left by a division; but if, as it appeared to Duryea, Warren had moved on his own initiative to help protect Porter's left, Pope's army could use more of that kind of gumption.

By the time Major Jesse Thomas reported to Longstreet in mid-afternoon that his forward wheel had been completed, R. E. Lee's Army of Northern Virginia was deployed along a five-mile crescent. From its extreme left at Sudley Church, Lee's line ran along the old railroad right-of-way held by Jackson's three divisions to a point slightly north and east of Brawner's abandoned farmhouse; there it curved south through Jackson's batteries to the turnpike. Four divisions under Longstreet—those of Wilcox, Hood, Kemper, and Jones—extended the long curve southeastward across ridges, runs, and fields; when R. H. Anderson came up on the far right, the line would far overlap Pope's concentrations.

Thomas still worried that Pope's retreating army might pull back safely over Bull Run. But had the dispositions of both sides been mapped for Teddy Redmund, or if he could have had a bird's-eye view from the observation balloon Professor Lowe had employed for McClellan on the Peninsula, the experienced eye of Sertorius would have seen instantly that Lee's crescent enclosed Pope's army—much of the latter massed by Fitz-John Porter within the wooded, ridged triangle north of the pike.

Having spent most of the day packed in among Porter's waiting ranks, Private Fritz Schiml had reached a peak of simmering rage.

"You really think *that*'ll save your skin?"

In file behind Private Hugh Williams, Schiml had been irritated all the long day by Williams's constant Bible reading.

But Hugh Williams did not trouble himself about anyone else's attitude toward his religion. When he took his vows, he'd try to save some souls. Until then, he'd mind his own.

"No . . . that's not what the Bible's for."

"Because if you *do,* you got a sprise coming, Preacher. *Noth-*ing'll keep any of us cannon fodder alive lessen the Rebs run out of gunpowder."

But despite his gripes, Fritz Schiml had no intention of dying. And he knew just what he was going to do to save himself—had spent the hot, crawling hours figuring it out so they couldn't stop him. He aimed to fall down as if hit. Then, when the Rebs whipped them as they always did, he'd leave his piece and go hands-up into their lines. Prisoner of war. No disgrace in that—and no way *they* could ever prove anything else on him.

From Professor Lowe's balloon, Sertorius also might have recognized that the Sixth Wisconsin and the rest of Porter's striking force faced a certain disadvantage. The front lines of Sykes, Butterfield, and Hatch faced *due west* from the Groveton–Sudley Road; but Jackson's defensive line along the old railway ran roughly *northeast–southwest*—diagonally to the Federal front. Thus, when Porter's massed divisions moved out, Sykes and Butterfield on the left and in the center would have to right-oblique their men across open ground—a difficult maneuver under fire—to confront the Confederate line straight on. But Hatch, on the right, would quickly find his right flank—including the Sixth Wisconsin—in collision with Jackson.

About a quarter mile west of the Sixth Wisconsin, beyond the gap between the two armies, Lige Flournoy had about decided that if the Yankees had taken all day to get ready, they probably were not coming. Lige had no formal knowledge of military science, but experience had given him a practical lesson in one of war's cardinal facts—that the more time an attacker took to prepare, the more time he gave the defender to prepare.

Lige had hoped for an attack on the Dump because he was looking forward to seeing how the deserters stood up. He didn't particularly want to shoot any of them; but he figured that men who'd lit out once were likely to do it again, and orders were orders.

"You gone desert'n git caught," he'd told Foxy Bradshaw when he discovered Foxy in line with the others, "you worse off'n before, Meat."

"Lige . . . lissen . . . whyn't me *an* you light outten-ere? We aint . . ."

"Shit, Meat, Ol Jack's *count* in on me. Says I got to shoot you a new asshole, you even *look* the wrong way."

Sertorius, from Professor Lowe's balloon, would hardly have failed to spot another problem for Porter's attack force—the artillery batteries that linked Jackson to Longstreet. These looked out for 2,000 yards or so over the open rolling fields Porter's men would have to cross to reach the old railway line.

Jackson's eighteen guns, under Major Shumaker, had been reinforced by a battalion of reserve artillery—eighteen more guns—commanded by Colonel Stephen D. Lee of South Carolina. Colonel Lee, arriving after an overnight march from Thoroughfare Gap, had deployed his pieces between Jackson's and the pike, on a ridge that gave him a position from which to rake a Federal force coming out of the woods and turning right-oblique toward the railway cut.

General R. E. Lee himself, though he expected no attack that day, had looked over Stephen Lee's position and quietly told the colonel:

"You are just where I wanted you. Stay there."

Private Alf Gurganous, with Overholt's Battery in Major Shumaker's group of eighteen guns at the right front of the Stonewall Division, skinned his rabbit that afternoon in preparation for a royal supper. Alf was not worried; he calculated that the field in front of Jackson's batteries was little better than a target range.

"All our pieces far'n crost-er at oncet . . ." He pointed with his bloody bayonet. "This-yer rabbit couldn't hop over at field alive."

Jeff Jernigan contemplated the disemboweled rabbit with relish. "On'y thing is, mought be some Yanks over ther got onions in ther knapsack. Sure could use onions in at stew."

Unfortunately for Sertorius, Teddy Redmund—chafing in idleness at Jackson's headquarters camp that afternoon—in fact had neither maps nor Professor Lowe's balloon. He had nevertheless convinced himself that Longstreet had to be on the field. He'd heard too many incautious remarks from Jackson's officers, and seen too much coming and going on the right of Jackson's line. No other explanation seemed possible.

Redmund had therefore begun to question his previous opinion of the famous, if obviously eccentric, Stonewall. He knew nothing of the day's troop dispositions on either side, so he had no idea what would happen next. It still seemed likely that these amateur armies were mostly groping and flailing around in a giant game of Blind Man's Buff; but if Lee's whole army was now confronting Pope, Redmund had to admit at least the possibility that this was the stake Jackson had been playing for all along.

"I say, Colonel Channing . . ." Redmund had been doing his best to establish something like a gentlemanly relationship with Jackson's oafish aide. "D'you suppose when this campaign ends General Jackson might be willing to be interviewed?"

Channing looked at him with sunken, red-tinged eyes. "Iffen he was, I know just about what he'd tell you."

"What's that?"

"It uz all the hand of Providence. Whichever way it come out."

Channing was not at all sure which way that would be. He had confidence in the men, and in Ol Jack . . . but the losses they'd taken! Aside from Ewell and Taliaferro and a disastrous list of field officers, morning returns showed the ranks thinned down like a cornfield in a hailstorm. In Jackson's old brigade, the Stonewall, the Fourth Virginia had less than a hundred muskets ready for action; the Twenty-seventh Virginia had only forty-five. Not a regimental officer left in the whole brigade ranking better than captain. Over in Hill's Division, Arnall's Brigade had been cut in two; some of Lawton's units were no better off. Jackson thought there'd be no battle that day, and Channing devoutly hoped not; they needed a day to rest and recover as best they could. Privately, the colonel expected to hear Federal guns any minute.

"Providence," Redmund said, "is something I wouldn't want to depend on in war."

"Oh . . . I wouldn't say Ol Jack *depends* on it, Duke. He just *calls* on it."

Stonewall Jackson sat on a rail fence not far away, seeming oblivious to everything but the lemon he was sucking. As usual, his forage cap was pulled so low that only his beard showed beneath its visor. Captain Thad Selby, who had reported to Jackson the intelligence for which Arnall's orderly had paid with his life, admired the general for his calm.

But Selby's mind was with the orderly in the tree. Arnall's murderous-looking scout had come in with the same information

almost before the body hit the ground, but even before that, before
he understood the futility of the thing, Selby had wondered if *he*
would have been able to climb up there and hang on amid the spit
and slash of the Minié balls. He questioned, too, whether he would
have had—what? the courage? the indifference?—to send the
orderly up into those viperish bullets and keep him there, as Arnall
had done.

Selby had thought Colonel Stowe, too, might be doubtful. But
when he ventured a question, the colonel had spoken sharply,
almost angrily.

"He can get a new orderly, Selby. Anytime."

Selby, still staring at Jackson calmly sucking his lemon, his
left arm now raised above his head, felt a chill even in the afternoon
heat. Ol Jack could get a new captain, too. Anytime.

A half-mile west of Sudley Church, Andrew Peterson and Henry
stopped to rest the mules and bathe their faces in the cool water
of a small run that meandered across the Hay Market Road. Just
beyond it, they could see some of the parked trains of Jackson's
command, many of the teamsters sleeping under their wagons in
the afternoon heat.

"Might just bed down here for the night." Peterson pointed
south. "They were fightin all day yesterday just down the ridge
there."

About five miles due south, Crew Chief J. J. Moore was walking
along the main line of the Orange & Alexandria Railroad between
Bristoe Station and Manassas Junction. Sweating profusely in the
August heat, Moore noticed again how singularly quiet the day
was. Two big armies were somewhere nearby but he'd heard little
more than an occasional brief rumble of cannon.

Moore had left the construction gang at Broad Run—mostly
contrabands—hard at work on the ruined bridge. He was pleased
with the progress he'd already reported to Herman Haupt—the
Kettle Run bridge repairs completed; and he'd be able to add when
he got back to Alexandria that much had been accomplished during
the day at Broad Run, too. And no trouble from the Rebs. Maybe
that meant Pope was keeping them busy, although the day seemed
too quiet for that.

As he neared Manassas Junction, Moore also was hoping to

be able to tell Haupt—a demanding man if ever there was one—that the Bull Run bridge was being quickly rebuilt. A longer span and a tougher job. And if what the construction crews reported was true, the Rebs were maybe near enough to swoop down on it again, any minute.

Moore chuckled, remembering D. D. Morgan's reaction when he heard that news. The engineer of *Vulcan* had spat tobacco juice defiantly toward Bull Run.

"Them bastards tried to take my engine oncet. Try it again, catch hot steam up their ass."

But of course if the Rebs did attack the construction site, Haupt's orders were for Morgan and *Vulcan* to pull the crew and the riflemen guards to safety as fast as possible. Which had Moore a little worried; he hadn't heard anything that sounded like shooting from the direction of Bull Run. But you never could tell. If the work train had had to run for it, he'd either have a long walk to Alexandria or a hard night in the woods.

Moore picked his way carefully through the ruins of the old Manassas Junction supply depot, where the Rebs had torn up track for a mile or two. The destruction and desolation of the place shocked Moore, even though he'd already seen it when walking through the other way that morning. Burned buildings, overturned cars, empty boxes and cartons strewn everywhere, tattered Reb clothing thrown away, debris of every sort littering the ground as far as Moore could see—even the aftermath of a hurricane would not have disclosed so much destruction. Off to the left, two tall brick smoke stacks stood nakedly in the ruins of the shops burned at their feet. The remains of the great pile of burned bacon, the charred buildings, and tons of horse manure everywhere raised a stench of waste and death.

But what shocked J. J. Moore the most were the huge wheel-trucks of burned burden cars scattered about like giant saucers. Moore knew the cars had been legitimate targets of war, but he was a railroad man; it hurt him to see rolling stock treated like so much kindling wood.

His experienced eye nevertheless calculated that repairing the uptorn track would not take long. The Rebs had probably been in too much of a hurry to make a real job of it. Once the bridges were open again, they'd have traffic moving through Manassas in no time. Haupt and his crews had track repair down to a fine art.

Suddenly, as he gauged what had to be done to repair the Rebs' dirty work, it struck J. J. Moore that there were two sides to a war. He was a self-taught man whose builder's hands complemented a hidden appreciation for the shape of an idea as well as the utility of a tool. This new idea excited him.

Take Haupt. The first job he'd done for the government, in the spring of 1862, was the rebuilding of the burned-out Potomac Creek rail bridge—a four-hundred-foot span over a gorge nearly one hundred feet deep. Haupt had done the job in only nine working days, mostly with contraband labor, devising new techniques on the spot and improvising for materials. The result had been a major advance in bridge engineering and a span so spectacular that President Lincoln had come out to see it, remarking later to his Cabinet that "upon my word, gentlemen, there is nothing in it but beanpoles and cornstalks"—which was not so far from the truth.

Now Haupt was having wooden bridge spans of his own design built and sized to be hauled on flat cars; when they began coming out of the shops, Haupt would be reopening bridges as fast as the Rebs could blow or burn them. Already, under the pressures of war, Haupt's crews had learned to lay track and string telegraph wire faster than anyone had thought possible a year earlier.

So the war was bringing on new ideas and developments even as it visited destruction on the land. Ironclad ships. Aerial balloons. Photographers out with the troops. Ships that could go under the water. Haupt was designing a new kind of pontoon to speed the building of temporary foot and wagon bridges.

Moore strode on in the hot afternoon sun, leaving behind the ruins and litter at Manassas. Could it be possible, he wondered, that destruction itself produced a kind of creativity in response— that the energies and force that tore things down, once released, built them right up again, sometimes better than they were to begin with?

Moore determined to talk the matter over with Colonel Haupt. Haupt was learned. Maybe he'd know, Moore thought, moving on toward the cool, dark waters of Bull Run—maybe Haupt would know if the same thing in men that made them destroy made them turn right around and build again.

Charlie Keach woke briefly in late afternoon, not knowing where he was. He sat up in an unfamiliarly soft bed, sweating hard in the August heat. Then his eye fell on the newspaper scattered on the floor by his bed; through an open window he could hear the

noises of a city street. He fell back, relaxed, remembering the
hotel to which Stanley Glenn had directed him. He remembered
Hale's telegram, too, and swore to himself. What right did Hale
have to question his story? Who'd been in the middle of the battle
anyway?

He reached for the paper on the floor and in the dim afternoon
light read his story through again. To hell with Hale; the story
was a masterpiece. Keach savored again, just before returning to
sleep, his peroration:

> With Jackson's left broken at sundown and Pope's victorious
> columns ready to strike the crushing blow at dawn, the
> vanquished Stonewall had little choice but to retreat west-
> ward toward the shelter of the Bull Run Mountains. Whether
> King's bold twilight sally down the Warrenton Pike delayed
> or prevented the escape could not be learned before this
> correspondent departed the front to convey tidings of long-
> awaited victory to an anxious people.
>
> Certain it was, however, that the humiliated Stonewall
> could not keep the field so dearly bought by Union valor,
> and that when day broke once again over Bull Run, the sun
> of victory would smite the backs of Rebels fleeing to the
> west.

In New York and Virginia, it was 4 p.m. All across the plains of
Manassas the afternoon was quiet, tense. Artillery fire had died
out along the pike. Here and there, where patches of dry broomsedge had caught fire from hot shells, trails of smoke ran whitely
into a cerulean sky. The malignant August sun beat without letup
on the troops of both sides; and the brass tubes of Stephen Lee's
pieces, most unfired that day, were nevertheless hot to the touch.
Horses, somnolent in the heat, dropped their heads; along Jackson's line, the calmest of his veterans dozed in the railway cut or
in the woods behind it.

Fargo Hart, riding from Stuart's headquarters with orders for General Beverley Robertson—who was patrolling on the far right flank
of Longstreet—pulled Mercury to a halt in a patch of shade.
Trotting along the old Warrenton–Alexandria Road in the glaring
sunlight, thinking of Missy, of love, of life, he suddenly and

without warning had not known anything—not where he was, or where he was going, even *who* he was, or why; remembered nothing, expected nothing, felt nothing, was lost in glaring nothingness, brilliantly empty as the sky above.

The moment passed in terror, terror for which he was profoundly grateful. A man in terror was at least *not nothing,* at least not *in nothingness.* He was identifiable, a soldier on a mission.

Hart did not, of course, believe in omens. He was an educated, rational man. He thought he had merely suffered some moment of faintness in the sun, or some strange passing mental quirk. Nevertheless, he stopped in the shade, drew a small notebook from his pocket, tore out a leaf, printed his name and rank and STUART'S HQ in large block letters, and stuck the paper in his breast pocket.

Missy . . . I'll come back if I can.

Private Hugh Williams, a minute figure in the ranks of the Sixth Wisconsin, itself a tiny part of Porter's massed divisions, pulled out his Pocket Bible again. He could tell from the activity around him that they were about to march, and something had moved him to one last quest. He opened the book at random.

A verse halfway down the first column on the left seemed to leap to his eye. He knew at once that God had spoken to him directly and personally. He read again to be sure:

Father, save me from this hour: but for this cause came I unto this hour.

"Forrwurrd!" Major Reverdy Dowd shouted to the Sixth Wisconsin. "Guide cen*terrr . . .*"

Chapter Fifteen

PRIVATE GILLUM STONE, lounging with what was left of the Stonewall Brigade in the pine woods behind the railroad cut, heard the boom of a single signal gun. As if its muzzle flare had touched off a giant fuse, Federal cannon roared all across the eastern horizon. Stone fell on his face, his arms over his head. The screaming wind of the shells scorched the air, and their explosions spewed iron fragments hissing and thudding into the earth around him.

But veterans like Gilly had learned that long-range shelling was louder and more frightening than it was effective. At a shouted command, he and the rest of the brigade jumped to their feet and ran through the bursting fire to the old railroad cut. At that point, though broad at the top, its banks had crumbled to little more than a footpath at the bottom.

As the running butternuts lunged into its shelter, those who kept their heads up saw through the smoke and the dust enemy skirmishers pushing out of the woods and into the open, about a thousand yards distant.

"Lord God!" Private Stone thumbed back his musket to full cock. "They's a million of 'em!"

Suddenly he felt defenseless and alone, without Sowbelly and Lott at his side as usual. First fight without 'em, he thought. Kind of lonely.

The blue skirmishers fronted two brigades—Lansing's and Roberts's—of Butterfield's Division, in the center of Fitz-John Porter's three-division front. Butterfield's Division had emerged from the woods first, because on its left Sykes's Division had immediately collided with Rebel skirmishers of Hood's Division; and because on Butterfield's right, Hatch's Division quickly crashed its right flank into Stonewall Jackson's main defense line.

Thus, the divisions on both flanks of the three-division front sagged back from Butterfield's advance in the center. But like the point of an arrow Butterfield's leading regiments burst from the woods and out into rolling fields, level at first, then sloping up for two hundred yards or more to the hundred yards of flat ground immediately in front of the "Deep Cut," a sector where the old railway line had been gouged more than ten feet into the earth.

Private Alf Gurganous could hardly believe his eyes as the blue troops smartly dressed their lines in the field. He slung the skinned rabbit, which he had been about to cut into pieces for stewing, into the shot chest and ran for his No. 1 station beside Matthew. He had never dreamed the Yanks would hand them such a target.

"Goddammit!" Jeff Jernigan ran beside him. "Ther goes supper!"

Captain Overholt yelled for solid shot, his voice barely audible amid the earth-shaking rumble of the Federal artillery. His position was not under shellfire, since the Yankee bombardment was laid on Jackson's infantry line to soften it for the attack. So Overholt's men ran out their pieces, loaded, and were ready to fire in less than a minute.

"Hold fire!"

Major Shumaker, commanding Overholt's and the other three batteries to the right of Jackson's defense line, had sited them so they could be aimed to fire along the front of the railway cut, taking in flank any attackers who might get that far. Now Shumaker ordered his eighteen pieces trained around to pour oblique fire into the front ranks of troops as they charged up the hill. To Shumaker's right, down the slope toward the pike, Colonel Stephen D. Lee's eighteen pieces already were booming away at Butterfield's blue ranks.

But Butterfield's men, all veterans of the Peninsula battles, had rested all the day before on the Manassas–Gainesville Road, across Dawkins Branch from Longstreet; and some, at least, were aware that much of Pope's army believed Porter's Corps had shirked the first day's battle. So they marched in good order out of the woods, quickly dressed their ranks, gave three cheers heard even above the cannon fire, and charged across the fields of the Dogan farm with the pent-up power of water breaking down a dam. And behind Lansing's and Roberts's leading regiments came succeeding waves of cheering blue troops—confident, experienced, ready for a fight.

Major Shumaker gave the signal and Captain Overholt shouted: "Commence firing!"

Matthew, Mark, Luke, and John roared and leaped; down the slope Butterfield's leading ranks splintered. Blue troops went down like wildflowers under foot. Alf Gurganous leaped to the tube with dripping swab, flinching at the thought of the slaughter now begun.

Lansing's assault regiment, on the left, was followed by four succeeding regiments in column, each of which upon emerging from the woods and reaching cleared ground opened like swinging double doors into battle line and moved out after the regiment ahead of it. Roberts's first two regiments had cleared the woods in battle line, one behind the other, and started cheering across the field; his third and fourth regiments came out in column, opened fanlike into battle lines, and followed.

Thus, in Fitz-John Porter's center alone, nine veteran regiments, nearly 3,000 tough and experienced soldiers, rolled out of the woods in successive waves, crossed Dogan's field, leaped a ditch, and breasted the long slope up toward the Deep Cut. Quickstep evolved into double-quick, then the run; and the powerful blue tide rolled up the hill, closing ranks against the toll of Reb muskets and artillery fire.

"Lord God!" Gilly yelled after the first shot. "Look at 'em comin!" He and the Stonewall Brigade manned the line just to the right of the Deep Cut.

"Aim low, men!" Sergeant Buzzard Billings, still in command of the company, bellowed above the battle crash. "Aim low'n keep far'n!"

Just then, with the discipline and precision of veterans, the leading blue regiments paused on command and took aim; their first volley exploded and echoed across the hillside. Powder smoke blossomed acidly from more than 500 rifle barrels at once, and joined the dust of thousands of trampling feet and the smoke drifting from the Reb gun tubes.

The blue regiments charged on up the hill, taking punishing fire from front and flank; but their confidence, momentum, and fighting spirit carried their leading ranks irresistibly to the level stretch of ground on the lip of the railway cut.

"Em Yanks mean business, Alfi!"

Jeff Jernigan was loading and Alf ramming as fast as they could; but after each recoil from solid shot, Matthew had to be aimed again. Just two aimed shots a minute was first-rate gunnery; and they had got off only five rounds before the blue masses were swarming up toward the Deep Cut at such close range that Overholt ordered a switch to canister.

Now we'll see, Alf thought, watching Jernigan rip the paper bag off the sabot of the first canister round, with its load of packed musket balls, chain links, and nail fragments. Canister converted Matthew into an enormous shotgun. And they could get off maybe four rounds a minute, since there was no need to aim.

Just let 'er fly, Alf thought, ramming home the round. Cut 'em down.

Gillum Stone and the rest of Starke's depleted division were pouring a hot fire from the cut into the oncoming blue waves. After their first mighty volley, the Yankees had to pause frequently to load and fire. Slowed by the musketry from the railway, the close-range cannonading and their own firing, the first lines of Butterfield's assault began to be pushed and scrambled by the regiments surging up behind them. Before long, the Yankees on the level ground in front of the Deep Cut looked more like a swarming mob than neatly aligned formations. Still they pushed on, some into the cut itself.

"Fix bayonets!" Sergeant Billings yelled. "Fix . . ." His voice was abruptly silenced by a Minié that smashed his throat.

One attacker leaped right over Gilly's head and sprawled in the cut below him, struggling to raise his piece to a firing angle. Amazed, Gilly bludgeoned the Yank's head with his musket butt, just as another blueclad landed on his shoulders and back with heavy-shod feet. A butternut standing on the floor of the Deep Cut dispatched the second invader with a quick shot, but Gilly feared his back might be broken. And he could not get used to fighting without Sowbelly and Lott at his side.

He fumbled for his bayonet, got it fixed on his musket barrel, and turned to the front in time to see a bareheaded Yank with blood streaming on his forehead leveling his piece a yard from Gilly's face. Gilly slammed his head into the dirt of the cutbank. The Yankee piece crashed in his ears and singed the hair on the back of his head; he felt burning powder grains like wasp stings on his neck, and slapped at them in frenzy. When he looked up, the bloody-faced Yank was either gone or down, and Gilly pushed his own piece over the edge of the cut and fired again into the smoke and dust swirling about the blue mass struggling in front of him.

Lord God. Look like the end o' the world.

To the right of Butterfield's attack on the Deep Cut, Hatch's Division, too, was locked in a fierce struggle. After the division had crossed the Groveton–Sudley Road and moved into the thick timber on the other side, the right flank of its leading brigade— Hatch's own, now commanded by Colonel Sullivan—blundered at an acute angle right into Lawton's Division in the center of Stonewall Jackson's line, sheltered behind the old railway embankment.

Rebel bullets immediately lacerated Sullivan's right flank. Farther back, Major Reverdy Dowd heard the firing in his front and found his worst fears realized. He swore with great feeling.

"Covered like a whore, Blackie said . . . goddamn his eyes!"

Hatch's two leading brigades took terrible punishment from the flank fire coming through the thick woods; they came near breaking. Some men did panic and run back toward the road. Trying to form a line to face the Rebs rather than presenting them his flank, Hatch pivoted Sullivan's Brigade to the right and tried to swing the brigades following him, including Gibbon's, around to Sullivan's left.

Gibbon's Brigade thus floundered through the woods in confusion; the fire from the right was unabated and Confederate shelling raked the woods from Gibbon's left. Blue stragglers from the brigades up front appeared, first in a trickle, then as a broad flow of men running for the rear.

"Sixth Wisconsin!" Dowd shouted. "Lie down! Keep down, men! Don't let these cowards tramp on you!"

He was startled to see General Gibbon himself running through

the woods, toward the front—a trim, athletic figure holding a
huge revolver.

"Dowd! Stop those stragglers . . . make 'em fall in on you!
Shoot them if they don't!"

Without going to that extreme, Gibbon, Dowd, and other brigade officers succeeded in rallying some of the stragglers; others
ran on blindly, madly, oblivious to shouts and threats.

Nothing, Dowd thought, was more demoralizing to troops than
sudden flank fire from an unseen enemy. The thick, resounding
woods, fogged with eerie drifts of smoke, alive with bullets shrill
as enormous mosquitoes, added to the terrifying effect. Even panicked men could hardly know which way to run.

Private Fritz Schiml had not fired a shot, lifted his head from the
pine straw, or opened his eyes since Major Dowd first yelled the
Sixth Wisconsin to earth. Hearing that shout, Schiml had flung
up his arms, let his piece whirl away behind him, screamed like
a tortured child, and fallen as limply as he could. Then he convulsed his body into a sort of fetal knot, as he imagined a mortally
hit man might do, and unfolded into a sprawled posture of death.

Even so, Private Schiml—knowing the madness all around
him, hearing death wheezing past his hips, his head, his feet—
had all he could do to lie still. No sane man could stay in that
insane place. No rational cause for such irrational acts. No need . . . no
sense . . . no *sense*.

Only the knowledge that *they* would be waiting for him if he
ran, that *they* would kill him here or kill him there, so that there
was no other escape than the one he had planned, kept him lying
still, breathless, tense as rigor mortis. After awhile, he pissed in
his pants again and did not even notice.

The Swede, braced on his elbows nearby and firing at nothing he
could see, was not panicked; he simply did not understand what
was happening. The voices shouting mostly gibberish, the shots
coming from nowhere and everywhere, the bullets he was shooting
off into the smoky void up ahead—he could make no sense of
any of them. But he knew with dread certainty what would happen.

He was so sure of it that he was not even surprised when a
Reb bullet the size of a cat's eye tore through the back of his left

hand, shattering its intricate tangle of bones like matchsticks, and gouged out through his palm, opening its flesh into a bloody-petaled flower.

The pain was intense but the Swede was not surprised by that, either. He had been expecting precisely such a wound ever since finding the omen while digging the latrine. He had even predicted which hand it would be—the same as the omen—and he was almost relieved to have it over with. So he threw down his piece and began to walk out of the woods, unworried by the bullets zinging round him. The omen was fulfilled, wasn't it?

The only thing that concerned the Swede, in fact, was whether the surgeons would let him keep his hand after they chopped it off. Maybe in a jar, or some kind of soft wrapping. He did not like to think of his hand buried in a ditch like human waste dropped in a latrine.

The Sixth Wisconsin had stumbled through the timber to a position opposite and somewhat oblique to the segment of the railway embankment that included the Dump. A sort of leper colony in Jackson's lines, the Dump lay between the right flank of Lawton's Division, holding Jackson's center, and the left flank of Starke's Division, holding Jackson's right. The Dump was in fact a gap in the embankment where a railroad bridge had been planned to cross a wet-weather creek, dry in August.

Where the bridge would have stood, the embankment had been built up with stone and earth, sloping up to a height of nearly ten feet on either side. The gap was about twelve feet wide at the top of the embankment; at ground level it was perhaps eight feet wide, with the shallow, dry creekbed running through its middle.

Lige Flournoy and the other men detailed to hold the deserters in line had deployed about a dozen lying down in front of the gap in the embankment; another ten knelt in the gap itself, or just behind it; behind them, still another line stood up to fire over the heads of the deserters ahead.

Private Ambrose Riggin, once of the Thirteenth Georgia, lay on his belly in the front defense line, determined not actually to fire at the Yankees. He could see little ahead of him but underbrush and timber, the occasional flash of a musket, or tree limbs falling from artillery fire. He was methodically tearing cartridges with his teeth and pouring the powder down the barrel of his piece.

But he was then palming the bullet, ramming the powder, capping, and firing blank.

He felt no qualms about the deception, even as the small pile of bullets on the ground beneath him grew. Nor was he particularly afraid of his ruse being discovered. What could they do to him for refusing to kill anymore? Ambrose Riggin felt true to himself, to Maggie.

He had managed, before the fight started, to scrawl on the back of her own last letter a few lines explaining to Maggie that he just couldn't any longer square the Lord's Commandments with this war.

So will have to pray God will look out for me now bring me threw it all a live. Pray for me Maggie. Fare thee well Dear and if forever then forever fare thee well. Goodby Maggie.

A. G. Riggin

"Keep far'n ther, Meat!"

Lige's barrel was hot in his hands as he yelled at the deserters. He had taken station at the end of the embankment on Lawton's side, from which he could shoot Yankees as well as keep a close eye on the sorry likes of Foxy Bradshaw.

"Keep far'n so's Ol Jack'll know you mean it!"

Lige was particularly watching the loony with the hole in his head. He was just naturally curious about a man still alive with a hole in his head. Easy to spot in at red-checked shirt. He and the Meat that'd come with 'im, in Lige's judgment, had no business at the Dump with deserters. Loony b'long to the bonecrackers. Th'other'n just tryin' to look out for'im.

Lige squeezed off a round into the woods. Em marshals grab up everybody they could. Nare thing fair in a war.

Private James F. Sowell, kneeling beside Lott McGrath in the second deserters' line, was as hot with rage as the sun that blazed intermittently through the treetops above him. When he got out of the Dump, he had sworn to himself, first off he'd kill at goddam rotten son-of a-bitch Stone. Then he'd get proper medical attention for Lott. *Then* he was going home, and to hell with any goddam army blind enough to call a man with a hole in his head a deserter. Much less one lookin out for his buddy.

Private Sowell never even thought of being killed himself. The whole thing was too crazy for a man to get killed over. And he was encouraged to see that, whatever else had happened to him, Lott was still a good hand with a piece. Far'n away as if at hole'n 'is head just for show.

Sowell fired into the smoke and underbrush, lowered his musket, and put his lips near Lott's ear.

"Aint seen a single Yank yit! Maybe . . ."

A Minié ball struck him directly in the left ear. Sowell's head exploded inside itself; the bullet came out from behind his other ear, taking with it a piece of his skull the size of a gold dollar. Sowell's body was flung backward like a discarded overcoat, and he never did see a single Yank shooting at the Dump.

But quite a few of them were doing so. After the first impact of the sudden Rebel fire on the flank of Hatch's leading brigade, his other troops stiffened, particularly around the disciplined line established by John Gibbon's black hats. Lying prone or taking refuge behind trees, Gibbon's men had worked themselves around to face Jackson's unseen line, and were sending back rapid musket fire.

That was not good enough for Reverdy Dowd. The woods fighting, against a virtually unseen enemy, did not exhilarate him as had the twilight stand-up fight above the turnpike; or perhaps it was just that no other fight ever was like a man's first. Still, he was looking for a chance to charge the enemy, not lie in the woods like a bump on a log.

He peered around the trunk of a pine tree that sheltered him, saw a thicker oak ten yards ahead, ran for it, and flattened his back against its trunk.

"Major!" someone yelled. "Git away from ther!"

Dowd, only then noticing three blueclad bodies sprawled near the tree, hit the pine straw in a long flat dive. Behind him he heard bullets striking the oak *thock thock . . . thock!* He crawled quickly behind another tree and saw a smeared, dirty face grinning at him.

"Sharpshooters pickin on at oak, Maje."

Private Hugh Williams, firing as rapidly as he could into the gloom and smoke, saw a blue uniform crawling toward him through the underbrush, twenty-five yards ahead. The man lifted his head; blood covered one side of his face like a red bandanna awry. Private Williams distinctly saw the man's mouth form the shrieked word *help!* before his stained head fell back to the pine straw.

Hugh laid down his piece, careful to get no trash in the breech or barrel, and rose to one knee.

For this cause came I unto this hour.

But before he could crawl forward toward the sprawled blue uniform, Corporal Wilhelm Ruckelhaupt leaped past him and ran toward the same man. Bullets cut the air around him but Corporal Ruckelhaupt ran on. He reached the fallen man, knelt, and seized the blue arms. Then the corporal's body pitched forward and fell across the man on the ground. Both lay still, and Hugh Williams could see a red stain rapidly spreading across Billy Ruckelhaupt's back.

"Sharpshooter," Hugh said out loud.

The word was lost in the musketry, the derisive snicker of bullets, the madly yelling voices all around. He and Ruckelhaupt had known each other since earliest school days, and Private Williams was not at all insensitive to his friend's death; still, he knew his own body would be lying there bleeding, had he run to the rescue first. But he had not; and that reinforced his sense of having been chosen, of having some purpose that would disclose itself in this hour.

Hugh picked up his musket, shifted left to get Ruckelhaupt's body out of his field of fire, peered into the smoke, and put a round into a muzzle flash from the Rebel line.

Lord, be kind to Billy.

The right flank of Hatch's Division had become uncovered—as Reverdy Dowd had feared—because Ricketts's Division had been deployed along the Groveton–Sudley Road where it curved northeast. Hatch's Division had been deployed along the road where it ran north–south. Thus, when the two divisions moved across the part of the road in front of each, they were advancing in diverging directions. Hatch's right flank regiments moved west through the woods into Jackson's center; Ricketts's, and Kearny on Ricketts's right flank, slammed northwest into A. P. Hill's Division on Jackson's left. Within a few minutes, Ricketts's left flank was about a quarter mile distant from Hatch's right, through thick timber.

Ricketts's and Kearny's officers were under the impression that Jackson was indeed retreating, as Pope had stated in his special order; they believed their assault would carry them swiftly past the railway line and Sudley Church to the Hay Market Road. Instead, on substantially the same ground Kearny and Hill had contested the day before, Ricketts and Kearny ran head-on into Hill's front line—the brigades of Archer, Thomas, and Arnall—supported by artillery from the ridge behind.

Colonel Sam Stowe, now occupying a segment of the embankment with his shell of a regiment, was not surprised to see the Yanks coming again. But he was dismayed by the force of their attack and painfully aware that Hill's brigades were badly depleted and worn down physically.

"They just keep comin, Hoke, we'll run out of ammunition again."

Arnall, reloading his pistol, did not even look up.

"Gave 'em bayonets once. Give 'em bayonets again."

But the new attack had developed so suddenly that Arnall was not yet in hottest fighting temper; he felt nothing like the God-sent fever in which he'd led the sundown defense the day before. And, oddly, even in the noise of battle he still seemed to hear the hollow *thuh-wump!* of Folsom's head, then his body, hitting the ground, and the distinct crack of his neck breaking, like a pine bough snapped over a man's knee.

Men died in war, of course; that was what soldiers were for. But Hoke Arnall did not look forward to writing young Folsom's mother about this particular death; and he would have felt better if Corporal Gilmore had not brought in, almost before the boy stopped breathing, essentially the same information Folsom had shouted down from the tree.

"Must grow men on trees over ther!" Stowe had been striding up and down behind one of his skeleton companies; he stopped near Arnall and pointed across the embankment. "Thicker'n hick'ry nuts!"

Arnall spun the cylinder of his Colt .44 and stared at Stowe with unblinking eyes. In war, one man's life meant nothing; besides, he told himself, the boy had given him the information he needed. Ol Jack had been waiting; and there had been no way to be sure when Gilmore would come back.

"Then let's pick us some nuts, Sam."

Strange the way Gilmore had seemed affected. Rough brute like that. And Folsom just a moony kid. But Arnall had been glad for the corporal to carry the body off to Sudley Church. Something he could tell the boy's mother.

The Yanks were inching steadily forward, keeping up a tremendous fire. Corporal Amos Gilmore, hovering near Arnall as usual, knew Hill's exhausted brigades could not hold the embankment for long unless reinforcements came.

Fine with me, Gilmore thought. Jus fine.

Since leaving the boy's body in the churchyard, he had had no reason to push back his hate and anger. The boy was in the past, and could no longer be hurt or disappointed by Amos Gilmore. *Done, finished.*

Now Gilmore thought only of Ironass; he had no room in his head for anything *but* Ironass, and hate, and anger. Which was why it was just fine with him if the Yanks forced Arnall to back away from the embankment again, because in the scramble and haste of a brigade being driven, Gilmore could all the more easily spot the murdering son of a bitch. He could all the more easily finish the job the boy himself had prevented Josh Beasly from doing. If only he hadn't!

In the left rear of Arnall's Brigade, near Jackson's parked trains on the Hay Market Road, a Federal shell that had screamed too high over the railway line crashed into an enclosed wagon that had been pulled to the side of the road. The shell was a three-inch rifled Parrott, weighing 9.5 pounds and fitted with an impact fuse. Its nose struck just above the wagon's right front wheel, at a downward angle toward the rear of the wagon bed. The shell exploded instantly, and the combined force of impact and explosion blew the wagon and its contents to pieces.

One wheel was thrown into the branches of a tree, under which Andrew Peterson, hearing the incoming shriek of the shell, had thrown himself face down. The bits and pieces of the Whatsit Wagon, his camera, his plates, his work, his life, pelted down around him; and as he sat up to stare in consternation at where the wagon had been, the wheel slid from the tree, hit on its iron rim beside him, bounced a few inches, and toppled heavily into his lap.

Peterson looked stupidly across the wheel at Henry, who had come up on his knees to survey the damage.

"S'all right, Mist Dodge... aint even tetched 'em mules!"

Theodore Alford St. John Redmund's experienced ear told him that this time Pope had engaged Jackson from one end of Stonewall's line to the other. No piecemeal attacks on shifting points of assault; Pope was finally using his manpower superiority—which Redmund assumed he had to have, owing to his short inner lines to Washington. So Jackson would not be able, in this new attack, to shift his men from one danger point to another.

General R. E. Lee, from his headquarters on a hill south of the pike, also saw the sweep of Pope's attack. As the roar of battle rose in intensity all across Jackson's front, Lee summoned his signal officer, Captain Joseph L. Bartlett. Soon Bartlett's signaler had a flag in motion:

> General Jackson:
>
> What is result of movements on your left?
>
> Lee

Teddy Redmund had been allowed to trail along with Colonel Channing, who was observing for Jackson the action at the Deep Cut. The two men watched wave after wave of blue troops coming up the slope. Quickstepping as regularly as if in drill, they charged into the ever-more confused mass of struggling Yankees before the cut, and the blue carpet of dead and wounded upon which they trod. Sometimes the oncoming waves would falter, break, fall back a little way down the slope; but always they would rally and come on again.

My God, Channing thought, how long can they keep it up? He was not sure if he meant the Yankees or Ol Jack's men—or just the nameless, faceless tangle of humanity killing and dying for the Deep Cut.

The colonel saw a Yankee regimental flag carried within ten feet of the forward lip of the cut; six times he saw the flag go down, only to be raised again in much the same position, before it finally stayed down. Butternuts leveled unceasing musket fire from the cut; the line of guns to the right front swept the Federal waves with canister; and some defenders, short on ammunition, were even hurling rocks out of the cut at the nearest blue troops.

General Lee:

So far, enemy appear to be trying to get possession of a piece of woods to withdraw out of our sight.

Jackson

Colonel Stowe, had he seen and translated that signal, would have thrown up his hands in disbelief. The crushing five-brigade attack on Hill's weary ranks was again pressing back Jackson's left, away from the embankment and into the open fields and broken woods behind. Ammunition was low. The volume of fire from the oncoming blues was punishing. So was the sun, and the dust, the acrid smoke, and the infernal noise of battle.

"The bayonet!" Hoke Arnall yelled. "Give 'em the bayonet, men!"

He knew, as he had known the day before, that God would help his servant hold the ground. But Arnall was a realist, too. He seized Corporal Amos Gilmore by the arm.

"Go to Gin'al Hill . . . tell 'im . . . reinforcements . . . hurry, Gilmer! Hurry!"

In the center, Jackson's troops were under somewhat less pressure than on either flank, owing to the thick fronting woods through which Hatch's troops had found it hard to maneuver, and the awkward angle at which they had first blundered into the embankment. But the inviting gap at the Dump had soon been scouted out and assaulted.

No durn wonder they call it the Dump, the New Man thought. Dumpin us in-yer like garbage.

He was in the front line of deserters, lying prone. A few paces behind, Foxy Bradshaw—kneeling where Lige Flournoy had placed him in the line between the old bridge abutments—fired his last round.

Foxy had had enough anyway. He had been loading and firing

in mounting terror of the whistling Miniés thick as skeeters about
his ears; and he had been held in line only by his equal fear of
Lige shootin 'im a new asshole, as promised. But the last of his
rounds going off gave him hope. Even Lige wouldn't snuff a man
for going to the cottridge box. *An once outten-a line . . .*

"Cottridges!" Foxy shrieked. "Goin fer cottridges!"

As he turned he saw that Lige, up on the embankment, was
not even looking. So he had a chance. His piece in one hand, his
works cupped in the other, Foxy broke for the rear.

"Cottridges! Goin for cottridges!"

But nobody could hear him shout in the crash of gunfire. Sergeant Gilbert W. Posey of the Second Virginia, Stonewall Brigade,
detailed to oversee deserters owing to the misfortune of having
that morning kicked over a hornet's nest, saw through eyes swollen
nearly shut a blurry figure running to the rear. Grabbin'is crotch.
Maybe going to take a piss.

But a man with a dozen hornet stings on his face and neck had
the right to take it out on *somebody*. Sides, the sergeant told
himself, orders is orders.

At range too close to miss, even with puffed-up eyes, Sergeant
Posey brought down the running man with one shot to the head.
Foxy Bradshaw went down plunging, holding his peter safe from
bullets forever.

As discouraging reports came in and the volume of firing swelled
all along the line, Stonewall Jackson returned to the rail fence
without his lemon and beckoned for Captain Thad Selby. Leading
Jeff D., Selby trotted to Jackson's perch. Stonewall leaned down
and spoke in the captain's ear, his soft voice urgent:

"Go to Gin'al Lee at once. Tell him I must have reinforcements
soon as possible. Hurry, Cap'n!"

Fargo Hart, hearing the rising din of the assault on Jackson, half-
regretted being far out on Longstreet's quiet right flank. He did
not wish to be in battle; he did not consider himself a warrior.
But he was young, hungry for life—so he wanted always to be
at the heart of things. As he reported to Brigadier General Beverley
Robertson, he fingered with some embarrassment the identification
paper he had stuck in his shirt pocket after that moment of oblivion
on the old Warrenton road. Melodramatic.

"Gin'al Stuart's orders, sir . . ."

In the event of a successful forward movement by Longstreet, Robertson's cavalry brigade was instructed to push straight for Lewis's and Ball's Fords, get over Bull Run quickly, attack any Federal retreat via Stone Bridge, and cut off traffic on the pike to Centreville.

"I'm to stay with you, sir."

Hart, relaxed in his saddle and leaning back with one hand on the buffalo robe strapped behind him, was unconscious, save for the ordinary courtesies, of the difference in rank between captain and brigadier; in Hart's assured world, such momentary differences were without distinction.

"Case you need liaison with Gin'al Stuart," he explained.

The mustachioed Robertson grunted without enthusiasm. Hart knew, and suspected Robertson did too, that he was really to remain because Stuart mistrusted Robertson's battle composure. Stuart wanted to make sure his orders were carried out.

"Then, sir, be good enough to ride on up ther to Colonel Munford in the advance." Robertson pointed ahead. "Make sure, sir, he understands em orders."

Alf Gurganous, Jeff Jernigan, and the rest of Overholt's gunners were serving their pieces relentlessly. Alf rammed home the loads like a pile driver, his movements always certain, always the same, and Matthew as reliably spewed canister with its scattering balls, its bits of trace chain, its hunks of railroad iron, its clutches of nails.

"Lordy!" Jernigan's voice, croaky from yelling and from bitter inhalation of powder smoke, was barely audible from four feet. "Most rounds we *evuh* got off!"

As Teddy Redmund had expected—given the natural advantages of the defense—frontal musket fire from the Deep Cut and canister from the guns raking the blue left flank had inevitably slowed the attack. The bodies of dead and wounded covered much of the level ground that extended nearly a hundred yards in front of the cut. More blue bodies lay in the cut itself, and hung over its lip, with not a few butternut companions.

As Gillum Stone—his neck still stinging from powder burns, blood flowing warmly down his side from a Minié that had sliced between his arm and ribs, taking skin from both—as Gilly looked over the rim of the cut into the smoke covering much of the field, he suddenly made out that the Yanks were no longer really attacking. They were even pulling back a little, but keeping some semblance of ranks, and still laying hot fire on the men in the cut. Only a few bluebellies were slipping away toward the rear.

Gilly knew those clinging to the hill were not yet beaten. More than ever, he wished for the reassuring presence of Lott and Sowbelly. Lord God, he thought, don't nothin seem right without'em. Don't seem like I even oughtta *be* here.

Hatch's Division, separated by thick woods from the attack on the Deep Cut, scarcely felt the stalemating of Butterfield's troops. Most of Hatch's units already had pulled back from the embankment to the Groveton–Sudley Road. But before the Dump, Gibbon's black hats held steady, though they could gain no ground.

"We have *no* orders to retreat!" General Gibbon yelled at Captain Black, when the latter came crawling through the underbrush with the news that they were isolated. "We stay here till we're *ordered* out. Understand, Black?"

Fifty yards away, in front of the Dump, the man lying next to Grice took a Minié in the neck, rose to his knees with blood pumping from his throat, and dropped down on Grice. The New Man scrambled madly to get out from under the dead man and his spouting blood. Finally, he toppled the body backwards and rolled free. That left Grice lying next to a private who was loading and firing methodically.

"Runnin' outta shot!"

Cady uz here, the New Man was thinking, us-uns clear em Yanks clean outten-ese woods.

"Me, too." But the man beside him handed Grice three paper cartridges.

Lott McGrath also had run out of ammunition. But he knew where to get more. Without leaving his place in the line of kneeling men, he reached behind him and ripped the cartridge box from the belt of the one who had brought him there. Lott could not remember who the man was; but then he couldn't remember who *he* was, either.

* * *

As Gillum Stone had expected, the lull in front of the Deep Cut did not last long. In the fields between the cut and the Groveton–Sudley Road, Butterfield's experienced troops halted, milled about, then formed a rough new alignment and started doggedly back up the slope.

"Fuckers comin agin." Gilly's lips and throat were parched with heat, dust, smoke, and fear.

Applejack, lying next to him below the rim of the cut, cocked his piece. "Must not want-a fuck no more."

Loading again, watching the blue wave come on, Gilly thought *Got to git right with ol Sowbelly.*

Then Shumaker's batteries opened again, spreading canister along the front of the cut and into the new attack. A small length of chain, whirling wild, lashed Stone's right shoulder, laid it bare to the bone, and whirled on. He screamed, toppled backward to the footpath on the floor of the cut, and lay still, his shoulder a bleeding mess. Someone stepped on his belly and moved on, up the bank of the cut.

Gilly stared with bulging eyes at the hot blue sky; from it, the sun beat down on his face like the fire of God, fallen from heaven.

Captain Selby got more speed out of Jeff D. then he ever had, even in his dream, as he made his way over rough ground and through the debris of war. Circling as closely as he could behind Starke's Division, he caught a glimpse of Butterfield's hard-hit brigades, still charging the Deep Cut. Then he raced for the pike behind Shumaker's and Stephen Lee's booming guns, dodged around Wilcox's divisional battle line just north of the pike, and charged Jeff D. up the hill to Lee's headquarters—all in six minutes flat. Colonel Tatum took him immediately to the commanding general.

As they approached, General Lee was staring at some ammunition wagons moving up to Longstreet's line. He turned and spoke to an attentive staff officer:

"I observe that some of those mules are without shoes." His stern voice carried through the roar of the battle across the pike. "I wish you would see to it that all the animals are shod at once."

"Courier from Gin'al Jackson, sir."

Selby had ridden so hard to deliver Jackson's request for reinforcements that he had forgotten his sour stomach and the fear rancid in his throat. Now, confronting R. E. Lee himself, he was so overwhelmed by the general's appearance of icy calm and the dignity with which he carried himself that he could hardly speak. Colonel Tatum touched his elbow reassuringly, as if he had many times seen the same reaction.

Still, for a moment, Selby couldn't get words out; then he saw the burning eyes above Lee's graying beard and patrician nose. Selby had never seen a harder, *fiercer* gaze—direct, aggressive, lit with a consuming fire. Not calm at all, not those eyes—not unlike Ol Jack's eyes, the captain thought.

"Sir! Gin'al Jackson's compliments! Sends me to say, sir, he *must* have reinforcements. Soon's possible, sir!"

The general's warrior eyes did not wink or his face change; his voice was as calm as if he were lecturing students. But his instructions were clear and delivered without hesitation. Selby was to ride to General Longstreet, repeat General Jackson's request, and give General Longstreet the commanding general's wish that he should at once send a division to Jackson's relief. And he must hurry.

"You'll find Longstreet with Hood." Colonel Tatum pointed east as Selby mounted again. "On that high ground yonder left of the pike . . . now ride, man!"

Major Reverdy Dowd, frustrated at being pinned down in the woods with the Sixth Wisconsin, decided to take matters into his own hands. He sent men crawling to his company commanders with instructions; then he sprang to his feet and with a wave of his hat ordered the charge.

"For*ward!*" he bellowed. "Forward Sixth!"

The companies that could see him got up and went forward, firing; some that could see these companies followed; the others stayed put, either not understanding what Dowd wanted or unwilling to challenge the Rebel fire. Hugh Williams went forward boldly, but two fights had taught him something about soldiering. He ran with his nose down low, like a bird dog on a scent; he ducked from tree to tree, firing and loading behind each, then running on to the next. Not that he was much worried about being hit, considering the sign he'd had from his Heavenly Father; but

Hugh Williams wanted to be a good soldier. He always wanted to do things the right and sensible way.

"Give it to 'em, Sixth! Forward!"

Dowd ran on shouting. Had he had enough men, they might conceivably, under his leadership, have charged into the gap at the Dump. Even if he had had only enough men like Hugh Williams, who had learned to fight Indian-style, the Dump might have been carried and Jackson's line broken. But Dowd had neither; before he had advanced his jagged line twenty yards, it was pinned down by musket fire so thick it might as well have been a solid plane of lead extended through the woods about two and a half feet above the ground.

Dowd lay, finally, on his back behind a thick tree trunk. Someone crawled up to his feet. General Gibbon lifted his head above Dowd's boots.

"What do you think you're doing, Major?"

His blood hot with battle, Dowd gave no deference to the general. "Carry that damned position, that's what!"

Gibbon stared at him. "With dead men, sir? That's all you'll have when you get there."

"We can try, General. My boys can . . ."

"I guess you'd better not, Major! You'd better not try it!"

Major Jesse Thomas was at the side of General James Longstreet when the young captain skidded his big gray horse to a halt nearby. Controlling the lathered beast with difficulty, the captain saluted Longstreet and began speaking in an excited voice.

Thomas was not surprised to hear the message. From where Longstreet had been conferring with Hood, they had a full view of the surging battle in front of the Deep Cut. Elsewhere along Jackson's line, rising clouds of smoke and dust, together with the deafening boom and clatter of battle, testified to the powerful assault Pope had mounted. But the scene on Jackson's right was directly in front of them: the great masses of Federals on the slope and before the cut, the dogged resistance of Jackson's line, the artillery blasting at the Yankee flank. Only drifting smoke obscured the chaotic scene.

". . . not sure . . ." Thomas heard Longstreet say. ". . . get there in time . . ."

Christ, Thomas thought. He's *got* to go in now.

As if to make the necessity plain, Sykes's Division—on the left of Fitz-John Porter's attack force—finally began emerging from the woods along the pike, where its ranks had been held up by the stiff resistance of Hood's skirmishers. Sykes deployed two brigades, in columns of regiments in battle line—eleven regiments in all, upwards of 4,000 experienced U.S. regulars, reinforcements more than doubling the number of Federals assaulting the already hard-pressed defenders of the Deep Cut.

Thomas cursed; Sykes had appeared to bolster the attack just when Butterfield's first wave had seemed to be faltering. He watched the solid blocks of regulars dress their lines, oblique right, and quickstep across the level field below the bloody upward slope. Their line of advance would ring them in on the left of Butterfield's now largely disorganized troops in front of the cut.

Too much Thomas thought. *Too many. Swarm right over Jackson.*

Regiment after regiment of the fresh blue division came out of the woods and began following the first lines across the field. Surely Ol Pete would move now. He had no choice but to save Jackson. Save the army.

It was then not quite 4:30 p.m. Captain Selby watched with sinking heart the new Federal forces coming on the field. But suddenly the thunder of battle seemed deeper; Sykes's fresh blue ranks shivered, staggered, almost broke; and through rifts of smoke Selby saw scores of men on the ground, writhing, crawling, some quite still.

Major Thomas, a more experienced soldier, observed the same development and realized at once that the new Federal division, *marching to the left of the first assault wave,* had put itself within deadly range of the butternut batteries commanded by Colonel Stephen D. Lee. And that officer had slightly shifted his pieces so that every step took the Yankees closer, and exposed them more directly to Lee's eighteen blasting muzzles.

Maybe 400 yards' range, Thomas thought. On the flank. Murder.

"Thomas!"

Longstreet's battle voice was clear, deep, steady. In crisis, he seemed to exchange some of his habitual stolidity for a soldier's fire; and his self-confidence seemed to be heightened. Thomas had never known a man more sure of himself, and the hotter the fighting the more so. He spurred to Longstreet's side.

"Troops can't live under fire like that!" The general pointed across the pike. "Bring up any other batteries you can find nearby." The long arm swung to point at an advantageous swell of ground, though not so close to the Federal flank as Stephen Lee's position. "Place 'em there! Hurry!"

Thomas galloped off, feeling relieved and rebuked. Ol Pete always knew what he was doing.

The major also was calculating hard. He knew where Chapman's Battery and Reilly's were, both hitched up and waiting for orders. Some of Kemper's guns might be close at hand, too.

General Longstreet turned to Selby. "Artillery will break that attack in ten minutes, Captain. Long before we could march troops to save Jackson."

Longstreet gazed imperturbably at the blue ranks already reeling under Stephen Lee's flank fire. Selby saluted again, not sure this would satisfy General Jackson—and not much liking the reference to "saving" Jackson. Helping him out would have been more like it.

But Selby only said: "I'll report back, sir," and rode hard for Ol Jack's lines.

Only Jackson's center was then holding strongly. His right was under the new pressure of Sykes's Division; and Arnall's Brigade, together with Archer's and Thomas's, had been so fiercely attacked by Kearney and Ricketts that once again, as late in the day before, Jackson's left was being doubled back toward his center.

Colonel Stowe, cheering on his troops, took a wound in the thigh. "Oh, Goddamn!" he heard himself scream.

But no one seemed to hear or to notice that he had gone down. Nearly panicked by the stunning force of the hit, which had knocked him sprawling, Stowe tore frenziedly at the cloth of his trousers to get a look at the wound. Surely, so paralyzing had been the blow, the bone must have been broken, in which case the leg was a goner.

Stowe just stopped himself from screaming again as the cloth ripped away. But when he saw the neat black-rimmed hole near the outer side of his thigh, and the relatively small flow of blood, he was immensely cheered, despite the chaos around him and the relentless blue attack. He had seen many such minor flesh wounds before.

Stowe managed to get to his feet, his torn trouser leg flapping. He started limping off toward Sudley Church, his thigh aching and burning as if from a branding iron. But he already was thinking about hospital time, leave; maybe home for awhile—though not likely, shape the brigade was in.

Just then Corporal Gilmore came loping along in his woods-man's stride. He didn't notice Stowe's wound; nobody seemed to.

"Sir . . . got to find Gin'al Arnall!"

Stowe pointed vaguely over his shoulder, and Gilmore ran on.

"Tell 'im I'm hit, Gilmer! Leavin the field!" Stowe could not tell if the scout had heard. "Tell 'im I'm *hit*, goddammit!"

Gilmore heard but was not much interested; nor was he thinking about the reinforcements Hill was sending. Gilmore only wanted to get back where he could watch out for the right crack at Arnall— a surefire shot. Gilmore was not in too much of a hurry for that; he did not want to mess the thing up. He had time; there was always time to die—if not in this fight, then the next.

Captain Micah G. Duryea of Pope's staff, riding southeast along McDowell's hastily established defenses guarding the left flank of the army, paused on Bald Hill to see what he could see of Porter's attack. Rolling terrain and lines of timber blocked most of his view; and on the slope rising toward Jackson's position along the old railway, battle smoke drifted heavily, only occa-sionally parting to disclose what looked like a disorganized mass of blue troops pressing forward. The sounds of battle were louder, more continuous than any Duryea had heard the day before.

"Retreating?" he said out loud. "Jackson's retreating, is he?"

But Duryea had little time to survey the spectacle beyond the pike, or to vent his irritation at Pope's mismanagement of what ought to have been his opportunity—one of the most important any Union general had had in the war—to destroy Jackson and all his force. Duryea had to find General John Buford, Pope's reliable cavalry commander. McDowell wanted Buford's horse-men to take station on a hill between Lewis's and Ball's fords

over Bull Run, in the vicinity of a plantation house called Portici.
From that hill, Buford could cover both fords against Reb cavalry
that might try to get over Bull Run.

Which, Duryea thought bitterly, the damned slavers might well
be trying to do, and before long—if *in articulo mortis* Pope's
army had to withdraw by that one narrow road over the Stone
Bridge to Centreville. Serve Pope right; but what good did that
do for the Union cause?

When Captain Black reached Reverdy Dowd with Gibbon's orders—relayed from General Hatch—for the Sixth Wisconsin to
pull out of the woods, Dowd swore loudly. He knew, nonetheless,
that their position was hopeless. Dowd had crawled far enough
forward, under the hail of secesh bullets, to get a glimpse through
underbrush of the formidable earth wall that sheltered the Rebs.
Even the curious gap at the dry creekbed seemed to be stoutly
defended. Worse, with no support on its right flank, the Sixth
Wisconsin was vulnerable to counterattack by Rebs foraying from
behind the embankment.

Gibbon's orders, therefore, found Dowd prepared. He designated one company to form a skirmish line between the regiment
and the Rebs, and to keep up a hot protective fire. The other
companies, still in battle line, were to walk *backward* to the
Groveton–Sudley road, firing if they saw a target, and ready to
fight where they stood if pursued.

"Besides which," Dowd shouted at Captain Black, "I aint aiming to show any goddam Rebs the Sixth Wisconsin's backside!"

The New Man, in the forward defensive line at the Dump, sensed
at once the slackening of fire through the woods, as the mostly
unseen Yanks in their front began to pull back. He was out of
shot anyway.

Gradually, steadily, the musketry diminished. After awhile,
when he felt himself at least momentarily safe, anger surged in
Grice again.

*Tooken me fer a deserter, did they? Gone show 'em a deserter,
goddam 'em.*

He poked his elbow against the arm of the man who had given
him cartridges—assuming *he* really *was* a deserter.

"Much oblige em rounds, Johnny. Le's see kin you'n me haul ass outten-yere."

The deserter did not reply. Grice realized the man's head was down in the dirt and turned away, but couldn't tell if he was dead or not. Then Grice pulled on the man's shoulder, and the way the head flopped answered the question. But before he let the body fall back, he saw a peculiar thing. Beneath the dead man's chest was a scattering of unfired bullets, torn from their paper cartridges.

Well ... see ever damn kind of quar sight they is in a war. Grice let the deserter's body slump back down on the unfired bullets. He was more than ever determined to cut loose from such doins. Show'em they couldn't just throw a man like Cady onna scrapheap. *Or even me.* Aint gone thow me on no more dumps.

Private Fritz Schiml, once he was sure the last retreating riflemen of the Sixth Wisconsin were well behind him, inched his head up from the dead man's pose and saw nothing ahead of him but empty woods. His body felt as stiff as if blood really were no longer pumping through it; but Fritz Schiml knew his moment had come.

Just like folks said back home; you had to get up early in the morning to get ahead of the Schiml boys. Now *they* would never get him back; he would never have to hear another bullet snicker at his plight.

Lige Flournoy had climbed down from the embankment to check up on the loony with the hole in his head. He located him by his red-checked shirt, kneeling patiently in the line between the old abutments, as if the fight were still going on.

"Hey, Meat ..." Lige paid no attention to the nearby corpse of Private James F. Sowell, on whose unscarred face an angry scowl was fixed forever. "Yanks aint snuffed you yit?"

Lott McGrath looked at the big, grinning man with unblinking eyes. Lott had found a certain comfort—a welcome familiarity— in loading and firing the piece. He was not sure why he was doing it or how he had learned, but the rote movements had given him a sense of identity, of *having been* somebody even if he had become nobody—nameless, pastless, pointless, a body with no

being. Except for loading and firing the piece. Then this big man
had appeared where the other one had been.

Fritz Schiml crawled forward for awhile. All was quiet in the
woods that a few moments before had been hellish with battle;
the crash of gunfire off to his left seemed far away. Schiml stood
up, stretched his arms high above his head, and walked toward
the embankment he now saw for the first time.

The other one, the dead one, had shown Lott what to do for awhile.
Lott took the big one's grinning interest to mean that *he* would
now show him what to do.

"Come on, Meat," the big one said. "Got to git us some cottridges."

Lott rose obediently. Sonomabitch if he aint *real* meat, Lige
thought. With a hole'n is head. Jus doin what he's tole.

As he started to lead the way to the rear, Lige caught a glimpse
of something blue moving in the woods. But he had fired his last
round.

Private Schiml, his arms above his head, saw what looked like
a man in a red shirt rising from the underbrush near the embankment.

"Hey, Meat . . . Yank out ther!"

The red shirt seemed strange to Fritz Schiml but he was taking
no chances; he opened his mouth and began to yell:

"Prisoner of . . ."

Lott McGrath, told what to do and happy to feel again the
comforting familiarity of the piece at his shoulder, squeezed off
his shot just before Lige saw that the oncoming bluebelly had his
arms up and was calling out his surrender. So Private Fritz Schiml's
last prediction came true: he never heard another bullet snicker
past his ear.

Lige watched the blueclad body spin, fall into a scrub pine,
and dangle from it by the armpits, while the knees buckled to the
ground. *Shit* Lige thought *could of saved at round.*

But the kick of the piece against his shoulder pleased Lott
McGrath. It was so *familiar*. Which meant that this big one, too,
knew what he was supposed to do. Lott felt greatly relieved; all
he needed, he realized, was someone to tell him what to do.

"Come on, Meat," Lige said. "I aim to keep you round for luck."

General Lawton, in Jackson's center, ordered no pursuit of the retreating Federals in the woods, since none of his men had more than a round or two of ammunition. Meanwhile, General A. P. Hill had sent the brigades of Pender and the wounded Field—the latter now commanded by Colonel Brockenbrough—to the relief of Hoke Arnall and the other hard-pressed brigades on the left. These reserves managed to bring the advance of Kearny and Ricketts to a halt; then Hill's five brigades regrouped and launched a counterattack that in fierce fighting reestablished the morning's lines on Jackson's left. But the assault on his right roared on.

Major Jesse Thomas had managed to collect three batteries, a total of twelve guns. Major B. W. Froebel, Hood's chief artillerist, quickly deployed them on the ground Longstreet had designated. Before Thomas could report this to Longstreet, Froebel had all twelve pieces working.

By then, too, the whole of Sykes's Division of regulars was out of the woods and moving across the fields toward the Deep Cut. Sykes's well-drilled ranks made a frightening show, and both sides knew that if these troops could be joined to Butterfield's men still struggling on the hillside, the doubled surge against the old railway line would be irresistible.

But Froebel's twelve guns were raking Sykes's attack from his left rear while Stephen Lee's eighteen pieces inflicted terrible close-range damage on his left flank. And Major Shumaker now trained Jackson's eighteen guns from the right front of the Deep Cut against Sykes's advance.

"My God!" Alf Gurganous shouted, as Matthew's crew shifted from canister to case. "Tube's so hot it like to far itself!"

Jeff Jernigan dropped in a shell and stepped out of the way. Alf rammed it down to a firm seat on the charge. The gun roared and leaped and Alf imagined, even in the thick smoke, that he could see Yanks going down in heaps from that particular shot.

With Shumaker's change of target, forty-eight Reb guns were playing at relatively short range on the left front, left flank, and left rear of Sykes's advancing formations. Close-range fire of such intensity cut lethal swaths through the blue ranks and exploded over their heads in deadly showers of iron fragments. Marching men entangled themselves on the bodies of those who fell in the ranks ahead. Tough veterans trying to keep tight formation suffered new tunnels of death blasted through them from front, left, rear. Solid shot sometimes bowed down whole files of men in marching order; or a shot might take off one man's arm and disembowel another; and some screamed through milling crowds as if with pitying eyes, touching no one.

Rifled shells, if aimed too low, bored themselves into the ground, exploded deep in the earth, and threw up harmless but frightening geysers of dirt. Round shot from smooth bores like Alf Gurganous's Matthew sometimes bounced like rubber balls, and still smashed men to pieces on the second or third hop. For every few yards of ground quickstepping men could cover, more rounds of iron and fire gouged among them, killing, maiming, wounding, terrifying.

Three blue regiments, moving not so much in coordination but as if each had been goaded unendurably, suddenly swung left and charged angrily on the slight ridge from which Stephen Lee's guns spewed flat streams of death along a path nearly 200 yards wide. Lee's gunners gave the attacking regiments canister at 300 yards and blew them down like cotton stalks plowed under. When the charge broke and the survivors backed away firing, some blue bodies lay within 200 yards of the eighteen still-flaming muzzles.

Captain Bartlett was just then signaling:

General Jackson:

Do you still want reinforcements?

Lee

When Sykes's regiments, or parts of them, began to drift back down the slope, with the rest pinned down by Rebel fire, the men of Butterfield's first wave could not hope to hold their ground before the Deep Cut. Colonel Channing, peering anxiously through the smoke and dust, saw that most of the bluecoats were beginning to fall back, slowly, sullenly, firing as they went. Then others began running down the hillside, throwing away their weapons, breaking the ranks of less demoralized units.

Panic spread slowly, then like fever; and soon the proud regiments Fitz-John Porter had sent across Dogan's pasture and up to the Deep Cut were a running, routed mob, racing for the cover of the woods from where they had marched so boldly.

But whether they moved forward or backward, the terrible fire of Froebel's, Stephen Lee's, and Shumaker's guns rained shot and shell on them like a shower of comets, increasing their confusion and disorder, toppling row upon row of blue amid the white sprinkling of Queen Anne's lace and the yellow patches of goldenrod waving in the field. And a horse would have had to be finicky and quick, Colonel Channing thought, to have got across the twenty yards directly in front of the Deep Cut without stepping on the blue bodies that nearly covered the ground.

General Lee:

No, the enemy are giving way.

Jackson

It was not long before 5 p.m. The sun hung above the western mountains, red as God's sleepless eye, merciless as chance. James Longstreet, calmly sitting his horse on the hill from which he had watched artillery break Porter's attack, realized that the left wing of Pope's reeling army was open to counterattack. R. E. Lee, at at his hilltop headquarters, saw the opportunity, too. On Sudley Mountain, Stonewall Jackson, knowing Pope's right could not hold if his left collapsed, recognized that one of his strongest military principles now applied: press the pursuit of a beaten enemy.

The moment had not been planned or anticipated by any of them. Warriors all, as if connected by invisible sensory links forged in the fires of war, they reached the same judgment at the same time.

Lee dispatched an order to Longstreet. Even before Longstreet received it, his own couriers were galloping along his lines. Jackson's orders were moving, too, to Early's Brigade in reserve, and to Hill on the left. Tattered Reb veterans, having themselves seen the blue ranks breaking, hardly needed to be told what to do.

All along the butternut line, bugles rang in the dying afternoon and red flags of battle rose against the failing light. From Sudley Church at Bull Run, along the old railway line littered with blue and butternut bodies joined in the indissoluble union of death, past the Dump and the Deep Cut, curving south by Stephen Lee's still-booming guns, then southeast through the fresh, linked divisions of Longstreet's Corps, to Robertson's cavalry pawing the earth near New Market—in one great crescent five miles long from end to end and enveloping Pope's battered divisions on three sides, more than forty thousand gaunt, bearded men surged forward, their coon-hunter's yells unearthly against the rumble of guns.

Teddy Redmund, scribbling Sertorius's notes at Colonel Channing's side, saw some of Lee's counterattack. So did Longstreet, and Lee himself, and Jackson; so did Irvin McDowell, even Pope on Buck's Hill.

The Reverend Major Burkeley Allen, who happened to be standing atop Stuart's Hill, with its panoromic view to the east, perhaps saw more of the Rebel surge than anyone—the whole of Longstreet's five divisions going forward side by side, none in less than two forward-curving lines, some in more, gunsmoke puffing above them in blue-white clouds looking, at a distance, like cotton balls suspended above toy soldiers on a child's play table.

Stupefied by the spectacle, the Reverend Major stared from his hilltop with open mouth, the black scab scarlike down the middle of his face. Then the appropriate text came to him, as sooner or later it always would to a battler for the Lord. He threw back his head and spread his arms. His huge body slumped to its knees. Oblivious to the stares of those nearby, he sang mightily into the thunder of war:

"And it came to pass! When the people heard the sound of the trumpet! And the people shouted with a great shout! The wall fell down flat..." He stretched his powerful arms toward the slate-hard sky. "And they burnt the city with fire!"

But no one could see *all* of the counterattack, because of timber patches and the low hills and the thick smoke soon drifting across the plains of Manassas.

Sertorius, the student of war, could see just enough of the field, that hot and dying afternoon, to realize that rarely if ever again would he have such an opportunity—to observe entire armies engaged on a scale so comprehensible that a man on a fast horse might have circled the whole battle in an hour.

Fargo Hart—not too far out on the butternut right to sense the scope of the attack—felt with a history student's sensibility something ancient and unchanged, derived from the roots of man, in the charging clash of warriors he could hear erupting over the rolling fields.

But no one had much time for reflection, as the butternut lines swept on, over the easy rounded ridges running at roughly right angles to the turnpike—artillery dashing to the next ridge, limbering to the front, pouring quick rounds into the retreating Federals, then galloping for the next ridge, infantry following closely. All across the field, Pope's troops were in general retreat; and although most of his units maintained formation and put up substantial resistance, along the pike a host of panicked men were surging madly to the rear.

Lee quickly realized the unified power of the charge, in contrast to the piecemeal, disjointed efforts of his troops against McClellan on the Peninsula. Despite his own inactivity the day before, Longstreet now felt that Jackson's divisions did not respond to the moment with the vigor and spirit of his own. Jackson, though not an ironist, might have thought fleetingly that Lee's ring of fire was closing upon that very hill where, thirteen months before, Barnard Bee had rallied his troops with the urgent shout:

"Look! There stands Jackson like a stone wall!"

Teddy Redmund saw Early's Brigade lash like a snake from Jackson's lines at Porter's defeated troops trying to regroup in the woods near Groveton, and drive them in further confusion. Jesse Thomas watched Featherston's Brigade of Wilcox's Division strike along the pike at the same disorganized units. A. P. Hill, setting the counterattack in motion from Jackson's left, pressed it toward Bull Run—holding back Arnall's exhausted brigade from further action. Lige Flournoy and Lott McGrath went forward with Starke's and Lawton's divisions; but both units were short of ammunition and could advance only briefly anyway, owing to Confederate artillery still sweeping the meadows and woods across Jackson's old front.

General Lee, riding to the front over Longstreet's protests, saw the first rush of Hood's Texans all but wipe out Gouverneur K. Warren's small New York brigade, which Warren had so boldly moved south of the pike to guard Porter's flank. Irvin McDowell, trying to hold a defensive line on the Federal left, watched Kemper's and Jones's divisions, after hard fighting, drive three Union brigades from the positions to which McDowell had shifted them. R. H. Anderson's Division extended the attack of Kemper and

Jones to the right, so that Longstreet's men also drove Reynold's Pennsylvanians from Bald Hill, where Micah J. Duryea had placed them.

But McDowell's hastily constructed defense was by no means routed. Slowly as the butternut advance lengthened—Texans, Georgians, Tar Heels going forward at a run, their wild yells ripping through the deeper roar of battle, their muskets grown hot in their hands—the blue lines contracted, closed in upon themselves, slowed; here and there, they began to stand; and as the butternuts came on relentlessly in the shadows of the summer evening, they found resistance thickening in the ravines and pine groves. Yanks had to be rooted out regiment by regiment, company by company, almost man by man, in vicious close-quarter fighting. Federal artillery posted on its own ridges began tearing gaps in Longstreet's charging lines.

The afternoon passed slowly into twilight, as the defense stiffened and the great counterattack slowed to a walk, then to a creep, in some sectors to a standstill, its precision and power exhausted against the force of natural and human obstacles. Reynolds kept his Pennsylvania brigades intact and got them across the Manassas–Sudley Road at the southeast base of the Henry Hill, saving a main approach to the vital Stone Bridge. Sykes's Division of regulars, so recently driven from the pastures before the Deep Cut, collected itself for an orderly withdrawal and arrived in time to extend Reynolds's new line across the Henry Hill to the left, toward Bull Run. That gave McDowell a stout defensive line to guard the southern approaches to the Stone Bridge.

North of the Warrenton Pike, Sigel's Corps, in reserve all afternoon, clung to a strong blocking position that allowed other troops driven from the Deep Cut and the old railway line to retreat past Sigel in reasonably good order. The Confederates Hood and Wilcox, pursuing with Froebel's three persistent batteries, were fended off by Sigel until they flanked him on the right. Then the German troops fell back and formed a new line near the Stone Bridge.

The Federal divisions of Kearny, Ricketts, and Isaac Stevens, with all of Pope's army to their left in retreat, were forced to fall back before A. P. Hill's counterattack. These Union generals nevertheless established a tenuous line anchored on Bull Run and curving toward the intersection of the pike and the Sudley–Manassas road.

Thus, on both sides of the approach to the Stone Bridge, the beaten Federal troops managed to hold a short defensive arc that gave Pope's Army of Virginia its last chance to retreat east over Bull Run.

The battle rumbled on, in approaching darkness. The fierce beauty of the evening scene—the crescent of ragged men under their red flags, the long lines moving over the broomsedge fields in the exaltation of bugles and power—faded into smoke, and dust, and an overcast sky that veiled at last the bloody prophecy of the setting sun.

Late that afternoon, three rough-looking men walked west along the edge of the pike, partially hiding themselves behind the cedar and sumac lining the rail fence that flanked it. They carried guns on their shoulders and kept a cautious watch all about them; but they did not look like soldiers. They were even more ragged, dirty, and hungry-looking than the Rebel troops fighting just to the east.

The three men stopped across the pike from Brace's house, looking it over carefully. Then all three climbed the fence, slipped swiftly across the road, and went past the loosely swinging gate to the rickety stoop.

They stood silently looking around for a few seconds, until two of the men clumped into the house without bothering to call or knock. The third opened his pants and urinated at length against the sycamore tree. Then he sat on the stoop with his gun across his lap until the other two came out and slammed the door behind them.

"Nare thang worth shit in-er."

"Cept we maybe jus miss sump'm *nice*."

One of the men held up Missy's best blue dress. She had left it spread over the back of a chair after hemming it in hopes she could wear it sometime for Hart. The man held it against himself and switched his hips.

"Whut go inside this-yer just whut a man need, huh, Bobby?"

"How'd jew know?" Bobby said. "Ain't nare use at prick-a your'n cept to piss."

"How bout at time I stuck it uppen y'ol lady's butt?"

Two of the men guffawed, but Bobby spat tobacco juice on the stoop.

"Take two like your'n make my ol lady even notice." Bobby snatched the blue dress roughly away and bundled it against his face. He looked up and spat again.

"Smell the cunny on it."

"Man git plum hard up for some-a that, don't he?" The third man's voice was whiny as a cur dog begging food.

"Tell yuh whut we gone do." Bobby threw the blue dress down on the stoop and spread it out. "Jes cause at bitch didn wait round-yere t'git it tore offen-er."

He took a cartridge from his shot pouch, tore its paper cover, and sprinkled a thin line of black powder on the skirt.

"Hot damn." The whiny voice was excited. "Lemme do it, Bobby, I gotta cap, I . . ."

But Bobby pushed him roughly aside and picked up a small stone, then another.

"Gimme at cap."

The third man handed it over. Bobby knelt on the lowest step, put the cap on one of the stones, held it just over the line of powder, and cracked the cap with the other stone. A spark flashed and the powder flared up. Bobby jumped away as the dress began to burn.

"Teach em sluts to run'n hide."

They watched the dress flare up brightly. The dry old boards of the stoop quickly ignited. Almost before the first smoke had risen above the roofline, the stoop was blazing and flames were creeping toward the unpainted clapboard of the house.

The men watched the rising flames as solemnly as if judging horseflesh. Soon the front of the house was ablaze, the flames crackling hungrily up the dry planks, smoke rising straight into the windless sky. The third man began to caper in the yard like a cat on hot coals.

"Cut at shit," Bobby said abruptly. "Le's haul ass outten-ere fore em damn marshals come."

They went back across the road and walked on, beyond the sumac bushes. The third man reappeared briefly, craning over the fence for a last look at the flames rising, by then, toward the old shake roof.

Sajie had heard the stomping around the house, just as she finished concealing Ol Brace's grave, smoothing it over until she doubted anyone could guess the dirt floor ever had been disturbed. As she listened to the heavy footfalls, she no longer feared that

Mistis might give them away. For when the late afternoon battle
had erupted across the road with a crash and a roar like the end
of the world, Mistis had reared up out of sleep, screamed once,
and fallen back, her eyes rolling in a dead faint.

Terrified herself, Sajie had thrown her arms over her head and
fallen forward to the floor. She expected to hear the house collapsing above her and she held her breath, waiting for the final
darkness. Then she realized it was not the end of the world she
was hearing—only one of the white folks's war battles. She lifted
her head and saw Kate Brace lying still unconscious, her moun-
tainous body flaccid on the pallet.

Sajie returned to work on the grave, resolutely ignoring the
battle noise. Eventually it had faded eastward, down the pike
toward Groveton. So when the men started walking around overhead, Sajie could hear them clearly. She heard the front door slam,
voices laughing and talking in the yard. Then silence. But she
waited a long time before moving or risking a sound, to make
sure they were gone. Mistis snuffled on her pallet.

Now that the grave was concealed, Sajie thought briefly about
running off. But where to? Ol Brace's place wa'nt much but at
least she'd be needed, maybe now more than ever.

Nearest thing they is to home, Sajie thought. And no more
Brace to plague me.

She smelled smoke before she heard fire. Looking up appre-
hensively, she stared in consternation as the first wisps drifted like
blue dust through the ceiling. Set dis house on fire, she thought.
Em sojers did. Like it got no bidness standin inna way.

She crawled across the floor and shook Mistis's fat shoulder,
waggling Mistis's head and making her cheeks wobble like clabber.

"Mistis! Got to git up!"

The open mouth drooled and moaned a little, just as Sajie
recognized through the far-off rumble of battle the dry snap and
pop of fire nearby. Lawd God, she thought. My good Lawd God
above.

Andrew Peterson could save almost nothing worth having from
the disaster. The Whatsit Wagon and his camera were smashed
beyond repair; the few unbroken plates were not among his best;
his chemicals had mostly disappeared. His horse had been killed
by flying debris. A few clothes, packed in a chest, had been spared.

After picking through the wreckage, Peterson shook his head and grinned painfully at Henry.

"Well, I always heard the world can't stand the truth. Now I reckon I believe it."

Henry, not knowing what to look for, had not been much help in the search. In the late sunlight, with the sounds of Lee's great counterattack rumbling across the fields, through the thick woods, he stared at Peterson with his inscrutable eyes. But his voice struck an anxious note.

"Mist Dodge . . . whut you gone do wid'em mules?"

"Damn if I know. I could ride one'n you could ride th'other, but I got no idea where we'd go."

"Was jus thinkin . . "

"More'n I can do right now."

"You aint wantin-a go nawf. I aint wantin-a go souf."

Well, by God, Peterson thought. Of course. The Whatsit gone, the camera, all the work. What little hard money he had was in a belt around his waist. Not much hope of replacing his equipment in the blockaded South.

"Em mules take us long way off fum yere."

"West."

"Anyway but souf."

The gunfire seemed to be rising in volume. Of course, the war would go on to its inevitable end. But Peterson realized that the goal he'd pursued so long and so purposefully—burning war's truth into unchallengeable glass—would have to be reached by someone else, if anyone. The inexplicable chance that had delivered the shell on the Whatsit Wagon had settled that.

Peterson felt oddly relieved at the admission. He felt free. The shell had destroyed more than his work; it had blown away his bondage, as the war would Henry's.

"You want the light-un or the dark-un?"

For the first time since he'd known Henry, Peterson saw something near a smile touch the black man's face, and widen his eyes.

"Take the white one," Peterson said. "Fair play."

Maybe truth was more to be pursued, anyway, than found and preserved, Peterson thought as he tried to make a rope bridle for Negative. Maybe it was only arrogance to have thought that at some point he could catch truth as plain and singular as a man sitting for his portrait. And maybe the worst arrogance was to think that truth would even be comprehensible to a mere man, if he did happen to find it.

In which case, Peterson realized a few minutes later, as he tied a few clothes and a blanket from the chest into a bedroll—in which case, there might well have been more truth in that chance shell than in anything it had destroyed.

Missy saw the black pillar of smoke clearly from the grove where she'd promised to wait for Hart. It was not like the smoke of battle, which floated in clouds and layers and hung low over the far-off thundering guns. This smoke rose straight and high, a thin black column against the evening sky. And as she looked at it, the conviction grew in her that Paw's house was burning.

There was nothing she could do, but Missy jumped up and ran for home anyway, flitting lightly over the hills and fields. As she ran, she told herself that of course Maw'd be all right. Sajie'd see to that. Maybe the sojers had hepped'em. She ran on, faster, her fears multiplying her strength.

Controlling her instinct to run up the steps, get out as fast as she could, Sajie kept trying to rouse Kate Brace. She chafed the woman's limp wrists, lightly slapped her wobbly cheeks—habit was too ingrained for her to hit Mistis hard—and finally dipped water from the bucket and dribbled it over the white moon face. But Mistis just drooled and lay there like a great mound of lard.

By then, Sajie could hear the fire racing, roaring through the old house like an angry wind. The smoke drifting into the cellar was making her eyes burn and her breathing difficult.

"Mistis! Got to get out!"

But Mistis only drooled some more. Sajie could feel the heat like a summer sun on her back. And just as she tried one more time to rouse Mistis with a splash of water on her face, something gave way above and crashed downward. Sajie screamed and fell forward on the fat inert body beneath her, trying to scrabble beneath it, into the earth, anywhere to shield herself from the collapsing house above.

But the cellar held, even as walls and timbers crashed down on it. Sajie quickly recovered from panic; she pushed herself to her knees, realizing anyway that she was wasting time trying to wake up Mistis. Even if she could rouse the woman, she would never be able to get her huge bulk up the steps.

Got to git hep. Sajie got to her feet and hurried to the stairs, took two steps up and pushed with her hands and stout arms. The cellar door wouldn't move.

Didn't seem right to Sajie. *Em doors lighter'n a feather*. She used all her great strength. Still the door wouldn't budge. She tried the other. It wouldn't move an inch.

Sump'n down acrost'em. Heavy.

Sajie was not really worried. She trusted her strength too much. She backed up the steps as far as she could go, and got her powerful shoulders well up under the doors. She heaved up confidently. The doors didn't move.

She relaxed a moment and heaved again. Nothing. She strained a long time, until her eyes were bulging, veins showed in her neck, and sweat streamed between her breasts. Still the doors held firm.

Brace's cellar had filled with smoke. Through it, Sajie could hardly see Mistis on the dirt floor. And when she paused from her exertions, she could hear flames crackling and popping fiercely. Intense heat was circulating down from the burning house; even the doors against her back, Sajie realized, were almost hot to the touch.

By the time Missy reached the fence along the pike, the house was enveloped in flames. The second floor seemed to have collapsed onto the first and the dry old wood blazed so furiously that the heat blasted across the road. Missy flinched back from its searing force, instead of climbing the fence and running into the yard the way she wanted.

"Maw!" she screamed. "Sajie!"

In the crackle of burning wood, the roar of flames, she could hardly hear her own voice.

Down the pike, the unfathomable battle rumbled on. If any of the troops on either side had noticed the house burning, they would have thought little of it. Destruction was the essence of war.

From her desperate effort to open the jammed cellar doors, Sajie fell briefly into resignation. She pondered whether this might be her punishment for what had happened with Ol Brace by the washpot. She could hardly believe she'd done anything for which God would burn her literally on earth before He did so in Hell; but she could see flickers of fire poking insidiously through the ceiling. The heat was becoming intense, roasting, and the smoke made her eyes water and her nostrils smart. Her lungs began to burn with it.

Across the pike, Missy listened in agony for Maw's screams. But there were none. Even as the fire rose higher in the darkening sky, she began to hope again that maybe they were all right. Maybe they'd got out. But where were they? Where could they have gone?

She climbed the fence and sat on the top rail awhile, watching the fire. Then she made out someone coming along the pike carrying a gun. She started to scramble back over the fence and run, until she recognized Wash wandering along, staring at the fire.

He looked stooped, older somehow, though still in his usual tattered clothes and with his usual dirty boy's face. The gun over his shoulder was longer than he was tall.

"Wash? Wher'd you get at thing?"

When he saw his sister sitting on the fence, Wash dropped the gun in the dust. He ran across the pike and clutched her legs.

"Missy . . . yuh come back!"

"Aint been nowhers." She gestured at the burning house. "Wher's Paw'n Maw?"

"Aint seen Maw. Paw's dead." Wash stared up at her with wide, scared eyes. His words, and the fire, were too much for Missy to take in. Speechless, she stared back at him.

"Dead's a mack'rel." Wash took a child's perverse satisfaction in the magnitude of his news. "Maw stab'im." Missy saw then that his shirt was stained with something dark and the side of his face was bruised.

"You the bigges ol liar in Prince William County!"

"Hope my die! He done it to Sajie, so Maw stab'im with a knife."

Missy jumped down from the fence and grabbed his bony shoulders.

"I'm gone slap you silly, Wash, I'm . . ."

"Aint lyin! Paw's *dead*. I aint seen Maw ner Sajie since mornin."

He turned his bruised cheek against her breasts and clutched his arms around her. His thin body began shaking with soundless sobs. Missy knew then, with the terrible clarity of fire, that Wash was telling the truth. She stared across the road at the flames

licking up from what was left of the old house that had sheltered
them all. Wash was telling a truth that, by keeping her out of the
cellar, Sajie had hidden from her that afternoon.

But Paw and Sajie? Hardly seem possible. Maw stab Paw?
Don't seem possible at all. *Cept nothin seem too far-fetch since
the war come.*

The old house was going fast; soon what was left of its gaunt
frame would collapse into the cellar. And everything she'd known
might be going with it— Paw'n Maw, Sajie'n Henry, home, the
way of life they'd shared. The war had come—bringing Hart, she
remembered briefly, gratefully, bringing love—but bringing the
shot boys in Brawner's pasture, too, and the fire, and whatever
lay ahead when the armies went away. The war had come and
nothing would be the same again.

Wash lifted his head and snuffled: "Reck'n they burn to death?"

Just a child, mean as he was. Maybe all she had left. Missy
hugged him closer.

Colonel Thomas T. Munford led the Second Virginia Cavalry
across the open fields of the Matthew Lee farm, between the
Manassas–Sudley Road and Bull Run. To his left, around the
southern foot of the Henry Hill, Jones's and Anderson's butternut
divisions were in a hard fight with Sykes's regulars, lately withdrawn from the Federal attack on the Deep Cut.

"Got to git'em off ther fore we go over the fords." Colonel
Munford pointed toward Bull Run.

Captain Fargo Hart, following Munford's direction, saw what
appeared to be a troop of blueclad cavalry drawn up on the crest
of a rolling hill about 400 yards ahead.

Munford called a halt. His Second Virginia was in the van of
Robertson's cavalry brigade; he and Hart knew, from the sounds
of battle, that Longstreet had rolled forward to the Henry Hill; so
Stuart's orders to get over Bull Run and cut off retreat on the pike
to Centreville had become imperative. Yet progress had been slow
because Buford, the Federal cavalry commander, had been harassing Munford with small unit attacks, quick hit-and-run tactics,
always falling back but contesting the ground tenaciously.

Hart glanced at his father's watch. The sun had set beyond the
mountains, and in the fast-fading twilight the Federal cavalry on
the hill seemed little more than silhouettes.

"Not much daylight left, Colonel."

"So let's get it over with."

Munford rose in his stirrups and gave swift orders. A bugle sounded over the fields and echoed against the slackening roar of the infantry battle around Henry Hill. The bugle sent a squadron of the Second Virginia charging up the hill in a battle line—first at the trot, then quickly into maneuvering gallop, over the last 200 yards at the full gallop, the troopers yelling and firing as they went.

When they were within ten seconds of the hillcrest, the waiting Federal cavalry troop leaped forward to meet them with a rattle of carbine fire. And behind them, coming rapidly over the hill in a hard-riding battle line, a regiment of blueclad horsemen suddenly appeared.

Ambush, Hart thought. But he had to admire Colonel Munford's quick response; without a moment's hesitation, Munford ordered the rest of the Second Virginia into line of battle and forward at the gallop. Before Hart had time to think, he found himself pounding ahead, too, on Mercury's powerful legs, the Le Mat heavy in his hand.

Up ahead, the blue troopers of the First Michigan Cavalry had brushed past Munford's isolated squadron, so that in the twilight the two regiments, each in two lines, closed swiftly on a front of 500 to 600 yards, carbines and pistol fire already lashing across the dusty fields.

A few traditionalists in both forces held drawn sabers, though most cavalrymen preferred pistols or carbines. The raised blades, the crackle of fire, the pounding of thousands of hooves, the cheers of the Federals, the piercing Rebel screams—again, as unaccountably as at Catlett's Station and just as against the reason Hart treasured, the moment of conflict, of ultimate challenge, of life or death, rushed to his veins. The Le Mat bucked in his hand; and from the deepest heart of his maleness, the warrior spirit burned in him like black powder.

So Fargo Hart galloped screaming and firing into the shattering collision of the two charging lines. They met with the impact of locomotives going head on; the shock spilled horses and men to earth, sent others reeling back, while some hurtled like projectiles through the oncoming force. Sabers swinging, pistols at close range, carbines blazing or clubbed, fists, heavy boots, raking spurs, even horses' hooves—they assaulted one another in every way men could.

Hart, with black Mercury shouldering his way through the oncoming blue line, discharged his buckshot barrel at a blurred passing face, ducked under a whistling saber, and wheeled Mercury to reenter the melee. He heard himself screaming, felt his blood running like wine, and spurred hard into the milling mass of men into which the cavalry charge had degenerated. He swung the Le Mat by the barrel against a blue trooper's head, put his booted foot in the chest of another, and shoved him off his horse. Seizing an unpraised arm with one hand, he shoved the pistol into its holster with the other, then wrestled the Yank for his saber. With strength multiplied by excitement, Hart wrenched it away and swung wildly, feeling the blade bite into flesh and bone. He screamed again, in carnal delight.

Two and a half miles away, at the ruined rail bridge over Bull Run, construction superintendent J. J. Moore was just then saying:

"All right, Morgan. Let's get this crew outta here while we got the chance."

D. D. Morgan gazed from the engineer's cab of *Vulcan* toward where the battle had been crashing and roaring in the late afternoon.

"Sound like it's gittin closer. All them riflemen on board back there?"

"Yep. Don't look like they want no part of *that*." Moore jerked his head toward the battle sounds. He could just hear, through the uproar, *Vulcan*'s steamy breath; Morgan's fireman had been stoking the engine ever since the battle started.

"How bout the bridge gang? They all aboard?"

"I'll check one more time to make sure."

Moore trotted along the track toward the bridge. Wouldn't do to leave a good workman behind. But when he reached the stone abutments and the makeshift beginnings of the new wooden span, he found no stragglers.

Not as much progress as he'd hoped to be able to report to Haupt, he thought, staring critically at the day's work; but the colonel would be eager to hear about the huge battle that had so suddenly erupted just over the hills. Colonel Haupt was always eager to know what was going on.

• • •

As the horsemen grappled in the dimming light on the hill between Lewis's and Ball's fords, Buford sent forward two more Federal cavalry regiments and Beverley Robertson came up with the Twelfth Virginia to support Munford. With the other men of the Second, Fargo Hart—still clutching his captured saber— withdrew from the first wild entanglement. Both sides regrouped for new onslaughts.

Robertson, riding up in advance of the Twelfth, quickly surveyed the situation and seized Hart's arm.

"This fight's for the fords, Cap'n! Ride back that way . . ." He pointed toward the Manassas Road. "This side-a the road somewhere you'll find Cap'n Rogers's horse battery. Request some guns up here to help us grab em fords!"

Hart glanced across the field at Buford's men forming for attack in the near darkness.

"You need ev'ry man here, Gin'al, I'd . . ."

"I need support! Ride, Hart . . . now!"

Even in his warrior delirium, Hart was too good a soldier to dispute direct orders. He swung Mercury and galloped for the road.

Micah G. Duryea, who had helped guide Buford in his hit-and-run defense of the fords, had been riding with the First Michigan. Duryea never surrendered to the kind of battle urges that had overcome Fargo Hart; Duryea never even felt them. Duryea was a killer, not a warrior. He operated alone; and he did what he did only when he was sure he could do it.

So when Duryea charged with the First Michigan, it was not in headlong abandon but for opportunity. As always, he held back, a little to the side, judged the situation coolly. As the two galloping lines of horsemen smashed into one another and crumbled into swirling disorder, he leveled his Sharps and picked off three Rebel horsemen from a short distance. And as the first vicious tangle of the lines uncoiled and drew back for the next clash, Duryea saw the slaver on the magnificent black horse, with the buffalo robe strapped behind the saddle.

Duryea did not waste a shot on a bad angle, in the gathering darkness. Instead, he holstered the Sharps immediately, circled off behind the regrouping Federal horsemen, and rode to their right, back toward the Sudley–Manassas Road. He reckoned he had three to five minutes of enough daylight to get off a decent shot at, say, half or less of the Sharps's 150-yard effective range; so if the dog killer Reb would only isolate himself for as much as fifteen seconds, while the two regiments got ready to smash into each other, the whoremonger would never sleep again wrapped in that stolen buffalo robe.

Duryea gambled that no one would pay attention to a lone rider out at the edge of vision, and no one did. Still, he could hardly believe his luck when the great black horse broke from the milling secesh lines and galloped west, angling slightly on a course that would take the dog-killer directly across Duryea's path. Duryea spurred his own horse and watched the angle of interception narrowing, the distance shortening. He pulled the Sharps again from its holster and snapped a .52-caliber linen cartridge into the chamber.

Fargo Hart, still in the flush of battle and resentful of being forced to the rear, *felt* the approach before he saw and heard it; in his exhilaration, his senses were keen-edged as a good razor. Then he saw the dark horseman closing on him.

Without thought or question, he swung Mercury sharply to the right. Saber in hand, choking back a yell of defiance and delight, Hart galloped directly toward the dark horseman coming at him from the murk of evening.

The move startled Duryea—not that he had been seen, but that the slaver had taken aggressive instead of evasive action. Duryea had assumed a dog-killer would be a coward; and he himself rarely challenged anyone head-on. Besides, a closing shot could be trickier than one on the wing.

Hart saw the dark charging horseman level a carbine without even slackening speed. *Dead shot got to be . . .*

Duryea began to squeeze the trigger just as Hart shook his right foot from the stirrup and dropped to the left, most of his weight on his left stirrup, his right leg clinging across the saddle. Hearing the shot, and the bullet *whitt!* above Mercury's head, Hart pulled himself immediately upright.

As he fired, Duryea had seen just enough of Hart's side-slipping motion to know he would miss. By the time Hart sat up in the saddle again, Duryea had the carbine barrel gripped like a club and drawn back for the swing. *Slaver.* The two horses' heads were scarcely five yards apart. *Dog-killer.*

With an all but imperceptible shift of his weight, and with the horseman's instinct that was his father's legacy, Hart turned Mercury a step out to the left. He saw the butt of the carbine swinging at his head; he thrust the captured saber to his right, toward the dark horseman's torso. Even as he lunged right, he jerked his head as far over on his left shoulder as he could.

Because of Mercury's sidestep and the snap of Hart's head, the hardwood butt of Duryea's Sharps—seventeen inches shorter than a musket—swished a half inch past Hart's head. And because Hart's head had jerked left and down, he did not see the saber pierce the dark horseman's body, just below the right breast. Instead, he felt his arm nearly wrenched from its socket before he could let go of the saber hilt; and the momentum of the horseman in the other direction almost pulled Hart off Mercury.

But he clung to the saddle with his legs, his lifelong instinct for horses and riding holding him on Mercury's back when nothing else could have. Quickly he regained a solid seat, pulled Mercury short, and wheeled around in the other direction. In the last faint light of the day, he saw the dark horseman topple and fall, the saber emerging from his body like the handle of the Devil's pitchfork.

Suddenly, Hart was lonely. Just the two of them there in the murderous dusk, just the two of them in those few galloping seconds. He had not even seen the dark horseman's face, or heard his voice, or panting breath. But the horseman's challenge had been his face, his voice, and Hart's response had been his; so the challenge had been *personal* anyway. Hart believed for a moment that they actually had known each other, in the most intense way, to the uttermost limits of being.

Not like war's ritual slaughter of faceless men. *Personal*. Hart's exhilaration, the rush like wine in his veins, the carnal throb of his flesh, were gone with the dark horseman and the captured saber.

Hart was alone with himself, in the dark; and from the southeast, across the plains of Manassas, all the way from the ruined bridge that terminated the O & A at Bull Run, a train whistle blew. Hart felt the first cold drops of rain on his face as he listened once again to *Vulcan* melancholy in the night.

From the lower slopes of the Henry Hill, Major Reverdy Dowd, too, heard the whistle barely piercing the crash of musketry along the Manassas–Sudley Road. But he paid little heed; he was too busy trying to get the Sixth Wisconsin linked with the Federal force on its left before full dark, and he was so angered and dispirited by defeat that he was tempted to grab some dead man's musket and go after the Rebs himself.

The scene on the pike, even more than the Sixth's experience in the woods, had shocked Dowd. He felt shamed by the leaderless, disorganized mass of thousands of blue troops headed for the Stone Bridge over Bull Run as blindly as horses to water. Panicked men had thrown down arms, knapsacks, flags, and honor; gunners had abandoned their pieces; even some officers had so far betrayed their duty as to join the mob—all making for the rear, Washington, safety, shame—anywhere to get away from the oncoming waves of screaming butternuts, the steady pounding of artillery and rifle fire.

But General Gibbon had ordered his black hats, once they were out of the woods, to fall back into the thin Union lines that were shakily holding open the approaches for the Stone Bridge. The Sixth Wisconsin, shaken but intact under Dowd's intimidating eye, had virtually had to cut its way across the stream of humanity floundering east of the pike.

"Damned cowards! Yellowbelly bastards!"

But even as he yelled, Dowd knew it would have been easier to dam Bull Run itself than the flow of demoralized troops heading mindlessly across it.

He was furious to think of even one of *his* brave boys dying to hold open the Stone Bridge for a craven mob running from the enemy. But as a few drops of rain touched his hot cheeks, he was glad that some of the army was still a functioning organization; gladder still that the Sixth was part of that stubborn line holding the bridge for the fleeing mob.

Private Hugh Williams also heard *Vulcan's* plaintive call. Even in the din of battle, even with his musket hot in his hands and his shoulder sore from its repeated kick, he thought that someday he'd get on a train and let it carry him a far piece—to the ocean maybe. West. Of course, trains already had carried him to Virginia, with the rest of the Sixth, but that didn't count; that was east, not west. That was duty. That wasn't the new world a train whistle promised.

The firing slackened when the last light vanished. The Federal troops on the slope above the Manassas–Sudley Road knew then that they had held the Henry Hill, and beyond it the Stone Bridge; so the remains of the army could get over Bull Run, mostly intact and in some kind of order.

But for proud men driven from the field, mere escape provided little satisfaction. Neither did the cooling raindrops that fell in fits and starts. Reverdy Dowd, under cover of night, wept scalding tears. Some men swore and shook their fists at the darkness and the Rebs hidden by it. John Gibbon clinched his jaw in bitter resolve. Here and there, soldiers pressed their foreheads to the hot earth, or said silent prayers of thanks to have been spared.

But Hugh Williams was perplexed. All the signs had seemed so clear, and yet God had called upon him for nothing beyond a soldier's plain duty. He had expected something special, unmistakable, heroic—maybe even the sacrifice of his life. But God had not spoken to him since he had opened the Bible that last time, and found the sign.

Just then a bolt of lightning, lancing down the sky in a brilliant orange arrow, lit the plain in front of Private Williams brighter than the muzzle flashes of a hundred cannon; and he saw a lone rider on a tall horse a hundred yards away, trotting toward the road and the Rebel lines.

Sajie had gone up the cellar steps twice more—the last time near exhaustion from effort and the roasting heat from the house blazing above. She did so less in hope of heaving open the jammed doors than because just to sit in the cellar saying her prayers and letting fiery death come down seemed to her all wrong. Henry would have struggled to the end; would her good Lord God expect less of a woman?

Besides—there was always the possibility that He was only testing her, seeing if she would just roll up in a ball and die like a hawg on a spit, or if she would maybe curse Him who would have willed her fate, or if she would hold steady to the end, believing His judgments righteous in all things but His mercy never failing to those deserving it.

But the doors would not move. The last time she tried, the wood was so hot that Sajie felt her shoulders seared as if with flame itself. That left no doubt in her mind.

Thy will be done.

She went slowly down the steps, her shoulders hot with pain, the heat on her face and bare arms almost as fiery, her lungs

burning. On her pallet, Mistis still lay in dazed, merciful sleep—
or maybe already gone, the thick smoke filling her lungs. The
flames jutted down through the old floorboards in long, vengeful
fingers, wrapping around the beams that still resisted their fatal
clutch.

Seeing them, on last hope occurred to Sajie; maybe she'd be
like old Shadderrack'n em others in de fiery furnace. Maybe count
of her faith, good Lawd God'd give at ol fire no power over *her*
nor let a hair of her head be singed nor smell of fire pass on her.

But when the first beam gave way, she saw, too, that the fire
coming down looked the way the preachers described Hell. And
as the rest of the floor above her began to fall in, Sajie thought
rebelliously:

Henry could of move em doors . . . Henry . . .

Wash and Missy, huddled together across the pike, watched the
blazing old house collapse rumbling and hissing into its cellar.
Sparks had set small, tentative grass fires in the yard where they
had played all their lives. To the east, the sounds of battle had
faded with darkness, and they could hear the harsh crackling of
dry old timbers. As if the cellar were a well-made fireplace with
a good-drawing chimney, flames leaped from it high into the air;
and through their roar Missy plainly heard a single agonized scream,
cut mercifully short.

Wash clutched her more tightly. "Thy-uz in ther."

"No, they warn't."

"I heard a scream."

"No, yuh didn't."

Of course, Maw *was* in there, buried in the flaming rubble.
Sajie, too. Maybe Paw. Her whole life wiped out, gone, as if it
never had been. All but Wash.

But even as tears rose in Missy's eyes, and her throat tightened
and ached, she felt love, too, warm in her belly. She drew Wash
around in front of her and pressed him close, so that perhaps he,
too, might feel it—the love in her, the life in her. She knew,
then, that she could bear it—the collapsing old life, the consuming
fire, even that *he* was never coming back. Love was warm within
her, and she could go on.

"I bet they was." Wash's face was between her breasts. "I bet
they's sizzlin in-er like sidemeat."

Before Missy could shove him away and slap his face, an

orange lash of lightning flared in the eastern sky, more brilliantly than the flames from the furnace-like cellar. It seemed a kind of warning. Missy clutched Wash closer, instead of slapping him; she felt rain on her face, tentative, consoling.

Fargo Hart still was trying to find Captain Rogers's battery, even though in the darkness and the beginning rainfall he doubted the cavalry battle for the fords could continue. The apathy into which he had descended after his duel with the dark horseman was thicker than the night, and he hardly thought where he was going, letting Mercury pick the way.

The lurid flash in the sky caused the horse to shy and start. Instinctively, Hart controlled him; but the lightning seemed to him accusing, like God's pointing finger.

Killer, he thought. *Killer at heart.*

He could still feel in his arm and shoulder the wrench of the saber blade finding its target. But it was not that enforced duel that kept the mournful wail of *Vulcan* sounding in his ear. His throat ached from his own exultant screams as he had spurred Mercury forward with Munford's yelling cavalry, while the wild spirit of battle, challenge, conquest, pounded in his veins, quelling memory and reason, freeing the most profound instincts of his nature. *Spirit that . . .*

Private Hugh Williams knew instantly that the moment had come after all. The Lord's terrible light finally had revealed His purpose. Undoubtedly, the rider on the tall horse was an emissary of the Devil—delivering some message, carrying some intelligence that would aid the secesh and rend the Union. The Lord had pointed him out to Hugh Williams, his chosen instrument at last.

The lightning's glare troubled Private Williams's eyes only for a second. When they readjusted to the night with his customary cat's vision he immediately picked up the rider on the tall horse, still trotting along the road as if oblivious to the armies on either side, the occasional crack of musketry and the deeper *cru-ump* of the few guns still firing.

Private Williams had carefully shielded the breech of his piece from the spitting rain. Grateful for revelation, to know why God had given him his extraordinary ability to see in the dark, he took aim, deciding to go for the body rather than risk a more difficult head-shot. A merciful God's command would not necessarily be to kill— only to bring down the rider before he could complete the Devil's mission.

. . . goeth downward with the beasts.

Which was why, Hart told himself, he was going back to Missy. As soon as he found Rogers's battery. In the aftermath of a great battle, he wouldn't be missed before dawn. He was going back to Missy and somewhere in the great pigeonhole desk they'd . . .

For this cause came I unto this hour.

. . . find a place. And the warrior blood would be stilled forever, *in the spirit that. . .*

A giant fist against Hart's chest hurled him backwards out of the saddle.

. . . goeth upward.

Falling, he heard the crack of a nearby rifle. But the Minié, entering an inch above the silver turnip watch, had drilled his heart. He did not even know it when his body slammed into the earth, becoming a part of it forever.

Mercury reared, dashed ahead a few steps, then calmed and turned back, lowering his muzzle. He sniffed the familiar body motionless in the road, circled it once, sniffed again, snuffling, then backed away a step and stood quietly in the cooling rain, the buffalo robe still buckled behind the empty saddle.

Even Hugh Williams's cat eyes could not see the sprawled body. But he could plainly make out the tall horse empty-saddled above it, and he reloaded his piece with joy surging in his heart.

Thy will be done, on earth as it is in heaven.

At about 8 p.m., General John Pope, commanding the Army of Virginia, sent orders to the generals holding the approaches to the Stone Bridge to "retire to Centreville tonight with your commands." A few minutes after these orders were dispatched, darkness had fallen in a concealing shroud over the plains of Manassas.

"If we could be of any further service I would remain," Pope's usually booming voice sounded eerily soft and calm to Colonel Russell. "But as everything is now arranged, we'll ride back to Centreville."

The battle was over. And as Pope and Russell made their way along the jammed pike east of Bull Run, real—not man-made—thunder and lightning rumbled and glared across the fields, the ridges and runs, speeding into silence their earthly imitators. The tentative rain became a downpour—heavy, steady, the tears of heaven soaking the dead and the quick alike, the blue and the butternut, the bold and the fearful, washing away the blood of all in rivulets on the trampled earth.

Rain stilled the last flares of battle, as the Army of Virginia filed—sullenly, slowly, no longer in panic—east over the Stone Bridge and the swelling fords of Bull Run, and victorious Rebs dropped in their tracks to sleep without cover. Rain eventually quenched the fire in Brace's cellar; but by then Missy and Wash slept clutched together in the barn, so exhausted with shock that Wash did not even feel his sister's body against his own. Rain poured an unseasonable torrent down the creekbed that ran through the Dump, and washed away the letter to Maggie that spilled out of Private Ambrose Riggin's shirt pocket.

Rain drummed on the roof of Sudley Church, in the dim yellow interior of which Major Worsham, going without sleep for the second night, again was piling up arms and legs, fingers and feet, around the foot of the pulpit. On the other side of Bull Run, rain soaked the pallets of the Reverend Major E. P. Hornby, who as if spiritually purged slept deep and dreamless in the grip of opium, and Private Philip Keefe, who lay with his wound putrefying, in agony so terrible that it had taken all his will power and faith in God to continue refusing opium pills.

Rain scarcely touched General Hoke Arnall, whose new orderly had rigged a tent for him out of gum blankets from the bedrolls of dead men, and who dreamed again of Amy naked and unyielding in the meadow; or Corporal Amos Gilmore, wrapped snugly in his own waterproof. Corporal Gilmore had his lurid dream, too—not of the boy, but of the back of General Arnall's head looking like that of Josh Beasly.

Rain cooled the parched lips of Private Gillum Stone, still on his back near the Deep Cut and unable to move because of a heavy Yankee corpse pinning him down, the pain in his mangled shoulder deadened by shock and the deceptive languor of the dying. And rain poured in trickles through the leaky roof of the abandoned pole barn near Aldie Gap where Andrew Peterson and Henry, on their way west, had taken shelter with the mules. For the first time in years, Peterson dreamed of the young wife who had darkened his life in the long ago. Henry slept soundly.

Rain streamed down the windowpanes by Sally Crowell's bed, where she lay awake listening to Federal troops slog along the mud road through Centreville. She had made up her mind to go to Lawrence's people in South Carolina, where the war could never reach. Rain pounded, too, on the roof of the house two doors away, where Pope and McDowell sat quietly discussing the day, and where in a nearby room Lieutenant Cass Fielding was writing a letter to his influential father about the disgraceful behavior of Fitz-John Porter and what Fielding had heard General Pope call "the McClellan crowd."

Rain made it hard to start General R. E. Lee's headquarters camp fire. But eventually enough dry boards were torn from nearby barns and sheds and piled in a great heap that burned from the inside out, lighting dimly a few yards of the open field in which the commanding general's tent had been pitched. Cloaked in a gum coat that fell below his knees, Lee stood near the board fire, water dripping from his hat brim, and read the dispatches coming in from all corners of the field.

Major Jesse Thomas, soaked to the skin but in the exaltation of victory scarcely noticing, rode in with Longstreet. In the flickering light of the fire Thomas watched Lee's usually ascetic face barely containing a smile as he listened to Longstreet's account of the right wing's charge.

He'll do it now, Thomas thought. He'll take us north for sure. Thomas knew just how he would head his first letter to Miss Letty. *With Lee in Maryland*.

Longstreet returned to his own camp, leaving Thomas as liaison. The major watched as Colonel Tatum rode in from a long reconnaissance to report the positions of the lines. Seeming ready to burst with energy, Lee stamped up and down, rain glistening on his gum coat in the dull glow of the fire. He read aloud a dispatch from Jeb Stuart reporting that Beverley Robertson was across Bull Run, harassing the Federal retreat on the road to Centreville.

Presently, General Hood rode up, his long beard soaked on his chest.

"Well, General!" Lee shook his hand heartily. 'What's become of all those people over there?"

"Gone east." Hood swung out of his saddle and the two generals moved to the fire. "Driven over Bull Run to the man. General, I must say . . . I never saw a more beautiful sight than our battle flags chasin theirs this afternoon. Sort of dancin in the air."

Thomas watched Hood's wet uniform begin to steam in the heat of the fire. Something in his words seemed to dampen Lee's ebullience.

"God forbid . . ." The general's tone was brooding but his voice was fervent. "God forbid that I should ever live to see our colors moving in the opposite direction."

The words brought tears to Jesse Thomas's eyes. Such a leader, with such an army, could never be defeated. They could do anything. And at that moment, even in the steadily falling rain and the fatigue of days in the saddle, Jesse Thomas wanted nothing more in life—not even to be with Miss Letty—than to be a part of that army, to follow the colors to victory with R. E. Lee.

Across the pike on the slope of Sudley Ridge, Jackson's headquarters camp fire sputtered and hissed in the rain, giving off more smoke than light or heat. Captain Thad Selby, his once-fine gray uniform soaked and heavy, stood brooding above the fire. His father had not provided a gum blanket for his kit, and Captain Selby had been unable to bring himself to plunder one from a dead man. That, he thought, was only the final ludicrous demonstration of his unfitness for war; cowardly in battle, squeamish in victory. His father would . . . but he did not have to worry about *that*, not yet; for at least he hadn't publicly disgraced himself or his name. *But you will.* Sooner or later, he would break. Sure of it, Selby stared glumly into the fire, flickering as fitfully as his future, and felt the cold rain ominous on his neck.

Theodore Alford St. John Redmund, wrapped in an expensive London waterproof, sat hunched against a tree not far away, his mind alive with inquiry. Surely Lee would see him tomorrow, even if the eccentric Jackson already had declined an interview on any subject other than the Durham Cathedral. Lee was a gentleman. As such, surely he'd be willing to say, soldier to soldier, how much this victory—amazing its magnitude—had resulted from a calculated campaign, how much from the luck of encounter.

A week earlier, the question would not even have entered Redmund's mind. But one had to admit—the Englishman shook his head, the wet cloth of his havelock flapping on his neck—Lee's forces had been brought together at exactly the right time and the right place. One couldn't ascribe *that* to luck alone. And as for Jackson . . . Redmund stared at what he could see of the man in the dim firelight. Jackson was a puzzle.

The general, sitting hunched on an upended ammunition crate under a sheltering tree, had draped a gum blanket over himself like a tent. He held a small guttering candle on one knee and appeared to be writing on a piece of paper spread on the other knee.

Colonel Channing, stamping into the firelight from a visit to the latrine—something had set off his bowels again; but then almost anything would—knew at once what Ol Jack was writing. No question about it. He'd be getting off a letter to his wife before the clock turned Sunday and his religion wouldn't let him.

We were engaged with the enemy at and near Manassas Junction Tuesday and Wednesday, and again near the field of battle of Manassas on Thursday, Friday and Saturday; in all of which God gave us the victory. May He ever be with us, and we ever be His devoted people, is my earnest prayer . . . and I pray that He will make our arms entirely successful, and that all the glory will be given to His holy name, and none of it to man . . .

Channing went to dry himself by the fire. He saw young Selby just turning away, but before he could call to the lad to keep him company, a Negro boy came hesitantly into the firelight, looking wet and miserable.

"Sah?" He spoke apologetically, and his eyes were wide with anxiety.

"Whose boy're you?" Most of the army's body servants had been left far behind on the Rappahannock, in the chase after Pope.

"Sah . . . Ise Roe Bear." Or so it sounded to Colonel Channing. "Cap'n Hart's boy."

His soft voice was almost lost in the sound of the rain. But had the colonel not been so tired and so wet, had he not already started wondering what Ol Jack was likely figuring for their next move, he might have recalled the young captain named Hart on Stuart's staff. Colonel Channing was a generous man to young officers.

"Lookin fuh Cap'n Hart, sah."

"Never heard of 'im." But Channing was generous to servants, too. "Better stand by the fire here, boy, 'n gitchuh feet dry."

Colonel Stowe's Speech

August 29, 1887

CONFEDERATE
HISTORICAL ASSOCIATION PAPERS

Vol. XIV Montgomery, Alabama
March–April 1888

Arnall's Brigade in the Second Battle of Manassas

By SAMUEL H. STOWE, *Colonel, Thirteenth South Carolina Volunteers*

[An address before the survivors of Dixon's Rifle Regiment, North Carolina Volunteers, at Jackson Springs, North Carolina, 29th August 1887.]

By Permission of the Author

The 25th annual reunion of Dixon's Rifle Regiment, North Carolina Volunteers, was held on the morning of Aug. 29, 1887, in the Grand Ballroom of the Jackson Springs Hotel. At 10 a.m., the members of the regiment marched into the hall in a body and took their seats. "The Assembly" was sounded on the bugle and the colors were presented.

Address of the Day
by Colonel Samuel H. Stowe

Comrades of the Old Flag:

I cannot help but recall, as I look over this peaceful gathering and see quiet faces once ablaze with the fires of battle, together with so many maimed and scarred bodies—I cannot help but recall those who are *not* with us, those lost friends who gave their lives in a lost Cause which the buffetings of a quarter century have not taught us was unworthy of them. And I cannot help but notice, too, how few we are, compared to the numbers that would have been drawn, only a few years ago, by any regimental reunion of the bravest and most feared army any nation ever sent to the field! *(Cheers and applause)*

Ah, my friends! How quickly time passes! Does it not seem only yesterday that we crossed the Rappahannock behind the matchless Jackson? And the Potomac in Lee's eager ranks? But now, to the sad lists of those fallen in the Cause, we must add every year the growing numbers of those faithful old soldiers who, having fought the good fight and maintained honor even in a hard and inequitable peace, have gone on to the greater reunion awaiting all who followed the Old Flag.

But the ever-quickening passage of time, my faithful companions in war and peace, perhaps compensates for its ravages in this—that it also dulls the sharpest edges of the past and heals the deepest wounds of sensibility. Thus, to those who knew them, the most rending sights and sounds of battle faded long ago into mellow memories of ennobling Cause, sacred brotherhood in arms, shared sacrifice to demanding duty. How petty the hardships once complained of, in the long perspective of twenty-five years! How ephemeral the horrors of war, in the golden light of steadfast faith and unwavering spirit! And what army of ancient glory ever contributed so much to the song and story by which men will ever gauge the valor and honor of their deeds?

Thus, how appropriate it is that we should meet on the twenty-fifth anniversary of that day when our old brigade fought from sunup to sunset, almost without pause, to hold the left of General Jackson's line against the hardest blows "the miscreant Pope" could deal! Of the four commanders who led their regiments into battle under General Arnall that day, by nightfall, "I only was escaped alone to tell thee" of it; and of the approximately fifteen hundred men we four commanded at dawn that day, official records show that 722 fell on a field of incomparable valor—116 never to look again upon their loved ones.

I had myself the misfortune, next day, to suffer a minor leg wound, too trifling to keep me out of the Maryland campaign. The gallant General Arnall, putting himself as usual in the thick of the fight, went to his bedroll on that memorable twenty-ninth August with almost innumerable wounds, surviving only to suffer the cruel fate that so soon deprived us of his fierce and devoted leadership.

Some there may be, I must tell you, who think this reunion should have been scheduled tomorrow. And indeed the great vic tory of thirtieth August, by our combined forces over those of Pope and a portion of McClellan's, receives the greater plaudits of history. Even at the time, a great New York newspaper went so far as to publish the laughable claim that Pope actually had "vanquished" the great Stonewall on the twenty-ninth. *(Laughter and jeering)* The name of him who perpetrated that farcical foot- note to great events is fortunately lost to history, my friends. But he and his Republican sheet did succeed for a time in confusing the public—not an unusual thing for the press—as to what actually happened during those stirring few days a quarter century ago.

The ultimate victory of Second Manassas was, of course, the most significant and decisive of the war to that point. As to the magnitude of our success, I need merely quote briefly from Gen- eral Lee's report of Federal losses: "Seven thousand prisoners, in addition to 2,000 wounded; thirty pieces of artillery, upward of 20,000 stand of small arms, numerous colors, and a large amount of stores, besides those taken by General Jackson at Manassas Junction." *(Applause and laughter)* And as we shall see, these material fruits of victory were the least of it.

Let me give you another indication of our achievement at Sec- ond Manassas. Captain Emery P. Overholt of Jackson's Division, writing in a letter to me of the artillery fire that broke the Federal attack on thirtieth August, reckons that the four guns of his battery delivered better than eighty rounds each in something more than thirty minutes. At that rate, the four batteries commanded by Major L. M. Shumaker on Jackson's right, of which Overholt's was one, poured upwards of 1,400 rounds into the attacking ranks in the same period. This probably was matched, Captain Overholt writes, by the fire of eighteen guns from the Army Reserve under Colonel Stephen D. Lee, fighting almost wheel-to-wheel with Shumaker's pieces.

Not even at Gettysburg or in any European conflict before or since does history record such volume of artillery fire. Up to that time, indeed, no more overwhelming stroke of coordinated military power had been seen on the North American continent than Lee's devastating counterattack of thirtieth August, 1862, which—none of us is likely to forget—drove Pope in confusion across Bull Run and reeling back to Washington.

But the important preliminaries of the twenty-ninth are too often passed over, owing not just to the triumph of the next day, but also to such ill-informed military judgments as that of the late Board of Officers reviewing the court-martial of General Fitz-John Porter. I quote:

> That battle [of twenty-ninth August] consisted of a number of sharp and gallant combats between small portions of the opposing forces . . . of short duration . . . separated by long intervals of simple skirmishing and artillery duels. Until after six o'clock only a small part of the troops on either side were engaged at any time during the afternoon.

But let us hear what General T. J. Jackson, in his official report, had to say of these events "of short duration":

> Assault after assault was made on the left, exhibiting on the part of the enemy great pertinacity and determination; but every advance was most successfully and gallantly driven back. General Hill reports that six separate and distinct assaults were then met and repulsed by his division . . .

And my own report, made for General Arnall's Brigade before my wound had healed and while memory was fresh, may have some testimonial value:

> We stood and fought, with intervals of cessation, from early in the morning until dark.

So you see, my old comrades, ample evidence establishes what *you* well know—that there *was* a battle of heroic dimension on the left of Jackson's line twenty-five years ago this day. I do not think any of the brave men of Sigel and Schurz and Hooker and Kearny, who confronted us through those hot and interminable hours, would deny it. Many of the scars we proudly bear attest to it as no historian can; and the memory of the fallen demands that we and all survivors of Arnall's proud brigade bear witness to the truth.

Indeed, I do not think it too much to say that Hill's Division— the great old Light Division—with Arnall's Brigade as its cornerstone and linchpin, saved Jackson's Valley Army, Lee's left wing, on twenty-ninth August, 1862. All gathered here this morning played their part, however small, in that signal achievement; and because we fought through that endless day, and refused to break, and held the left—even with ammunition all but gone and nothing between us and annihilation but the bayonet and clubbed muskets and the rocks some of you threw—because of that stand, my gallant comrades, we made possible the rightly renowned victory of the next day.

I have no reluctance to make that claim; and no fear that any man can refute it, owing to the palpable fact that in enabling the immortal Stonewall to hold fast his line along Sudley Mountain, in the cuts and embankments of the old railway line no man among us will ever forget, Arnall's Brigade and Hill's Division provided the time General Lee needed to unite his army for the assault on the braggart but combative Pope.

Even as we made our stubborn fight in the railroad cut and the woods in front of it, we know now—what comfort it would have brought beleaguered men to have known it then!—Longstreet was coming on the field to join Jackson; and as we beat off every assault, restored every break in the line, held fast even against the combined flank attacks of Kearny and Stevens, General Lee was disposing those fresh new troops for the devastating blow to be delivered the next day.

You need not, proud comrades, take the unsupported word of one who, after all, having played his own part in these events, might be thought somewhat expansive in his claims. Here, in my support, is the considered judgment, rendered some years after the war, of the renowned British military historian known as Sertorius, who personally observed the field of Second Manassas from his station as a guest of General Jackson:

On the evening of twenty-eighth August, Stonewall Jackson with his customary acuity did not fail to recognize that Pope was moving his army rapidly east, across the formidable barrier of Bull Run, to a concentration in the fortifications around Centreville. Once safely there, with detachments

holding the fords, and with the road to Washington open
for reinforcements from McClellan, Pope would be safe
from attack even by the combined forces of Longstreet and
Jackson.

Thus it was that Jackson, thinking strategically rather than
tactically, took the apparently foolhardy step of lashing out
from his lair on Sudley Mountain at the peacefully passing
division of the Federal General King. Only those few of us
privy to his devious purpose understood that in striking such
an unnecessary blow, as it then appeared, the wily Jackson
was purposely *making known his whereabouts to Pope*.

For it was the genius of Stonewall Jackson to have judged
Pope precisely; and to have divined that that energetic but
somewhat rash officer, once so alerted, would not resist the
temptation to recall his forces, concentrate them against the
newly discovered Jackson, and attempt to destroy him—at
the least, to "bag the whole crowd," as Pope put it in one
of his less fortunate dispatches.

In doing so, of course, Pope would have to remain with the
bulk of his forces *west of Bull Run* and separated by it from
the Centreville earthworks and from McClellan—precisely
where Lee, hence Jackson, wanted Pope, until Longstreet
should come up to close the baited trap.[1]

That being Jackson's strategic purpose, it could have been
accomplished by holding fast his lines during twenty-ninth August,
until Longstreet was in position for the combined attack. So you
see, my valiant comrades, well may we say without claiming too
much that our ability to hold against all odds Jackson's left flank—
the collapse of which would have left him no alternative but to
withdraw toward the mountains, exposing Longstreet to equal
disaster—our stand on the twenty-ninth was the real key to the
massive combined counterattack that routed Pope on thirtieth
August.

But in war, all events tend to flow together in a greater tide;
and just as our part in the victory of Second Manassas is sometimes
forgotten in celebration of the more spectacular triumph of thirtieth
August, so too Second Manassas itself is sometimes overlooked,
even forgotten, against the panoply of important events that followed.

I do not refer to the fact that Pope, after his boast and brag, was removed from command for his failure; or to the fact that he nevertheless was allowed his scapegoat in the unfortunate person of Fitz-John Porter—a blameless and, on other fields, greatly distinguished officer who, in 1863, was nevertheless court-martialed and cashiered in appeasement of the anger and fear occasioned at the North by Pope's defeat.[2] Nor am I referring to McClellan's reinstatement as commander of the Army of the Potomac—his own force plus Pope's beaten Army of Virginia—despite criticism at Washington that he had failed to provide timely assistance to his rival Pope.

No, my brave comrades, the principal consequence of Second Manassas was this—that Lee was emboldened to take our army north of the Potomac, into Maryland, notwithstanding that army's ragged condition, its severe shortages of supplies, particularly ammunition, and the certainty of its being outnumbered by an enemy operating on interior lines of supply. Most of the men who made that epic journey with us did not even have shoes, a fact as important as the strength of any Federal army they faced during the war.

General Lee's plan, of course, was not just to gather supplies, horses, and new recruits in a region hitherto untouched by war. As he plainly stated:

> The purpose, if discovered, will have the effect of carrying the enemy north of the Potomac, and if prevented, will not result in much evil. The army is not properly equipped for an invasion . . . [s]till we cannot afford to be idle and though weaker than our opponents in men and military equipments, must endeavor to harass, if we cannot destroy them.[3]

In plain words, Lee intended to force the enemy to follow him out of Virginia. What a difference two summer months had made! In June, two great Federal armies deep into Virginia, on the banks of the James and the Rappahannock; in September, both driven back in defeat to Washington and our own forces surging into northern territory. Thus, might it not have been hoped, old comrades of good times and bad, that even partial success might have justified in some way a new nation's aspirations—the fall of Washington, European intervention, the collapse of the will to make war at the North?

And yet... and yet... so much depended, did it not, on so little? Thinking of that immortal army, as it forded the Potomac into Maryland, bands playing and flags flying, at the end of a summer of success and in the brilliant sunshine of hope, I am moved to recall the tribute of a Federal officer who only a little later found himself our prisoner:

> Their artillery horses are poor, starved frames of beasts, tied to their carriages and caissons with odds and ends of rope and strips of rawhide; their supply and ammunition trains look like a congregation of all the crippled California emigrant trains that ever escaped off the desert... The men are ill-dressed, ill-equipped and ill-provided—a set of ragamuffins that a man is ashamed to be seen among, even when he is a prisoner and can't help it. And yet they have beaten us fairly, beaten us all to pieces, beaten us so easily that we are objects of contempt even to their commonest private soldiers with no shirts to hang out the holes of their pantaloons, and cartridge-boxes tied around their waists with strands of rope.

Indeed, we who marched north in the campaign of 1862 will recall that the plains of Manassas, and later the bloody field of Sharpsburg, were strewn with fallen heroes whose bare feet were cut deep by the rocks of the lanes and pikes over which they plodded to their noble destinies.

It was this invasion of the North in 1862, I have always thought and often argued, not the perhaps more storied invasion turned back at Gettysburg in 1863, that denoted the true highwater mark of our Cause. Never again were we to have such prospects as those Lee took north from Second Manassas. For it was after the repulse of seventeen September, 1862, at Sharpsburg, of Lee's doughty troops—starving, bloody-footed, down to their last rounds, outnumbered, outgunned, and even spurned by luck in the matter of the famous "lost order" that revealed Lee's plan of operation to McClellan—it was the repulse at Sharpsburg, I say, and the turning back of that first bold invasion that gave Mr. Lincoln the opportunity and the plausibility to issue the Emancipation Proclamation, so-called.

And though he took care not to apply the provisions of that extraordinary document anywhere that, at the time, his government had the power to enforce it, I believe we can see in the clarifying light of history that here, if only dimly perceived at the time, was a turning point of profound importance. Not, my proud comrades, that "emancipation" in itself was anything more than a gesture founded on an almost total and to some extent *willful* misunderstanding at the North of customs and institutions common at the South, and clearly sanctioned in the compact of the states that formed the Union of the Constitution.

Nay! The real importance of Mr. Lincoln's clever instrument was that thenceforth the possibility of European recognition, even perhaps European assistance, in the struggle for states' rights, true constitutionalism, and southern independence was mooted by the fraudulent conversion at the North of that worthy struggle into one for the "emancipation" of a protected and dependent people; and for their ultimate inclusion not only in the brutalized gangs laboring in the manufactories of the northern "free" states, but also in the voracious ranks of the Radical Republican party.

But let us eschew bitterness, my old comrades, and bootless railing against the malice of Fortune, as becomes brave men, in the sterling example of our greatest leaders in the Cause. Suffice it to say, a quarter century after that Thermopylaean day on which, while the August sun hung in the heavens as if the night might never bring surcease to gallant men—suffice it to say that had not Arnall's Brigade, most of all, and Dixon's Rifles not least, waged their struggle so pertinaciously on Jackson's left flank, the greatest display of effective military power in the short but brilliant life of the Confederate States of America could never have been staged, and that Confederacy's best opportunity for ultimate victory would never have materialized.

But despite the Herculean efforts of devoted men like those I gaze upon so proudly this morning, that opportunity came to grief, perhaps inevitably, at Sharpsburg. Yet those who faced us across Antietam Creek that sanguinary September day surely know how near run the thing was—how close Lee's first invasion of the North came to realizing the opportunity that you, my unyielding comrades, as much as anyone, afforded him and our Cause by your nonpareil efforts of twenty-five years ago today.

Shall we say now, anymore than we did then, that those efforts were in vain and for naught? (*Cries of "No! No!"*) Quite the opposite, I agree; for who knows better than we, in the ashes and dust of brilliant dreams and noble hopes, that defeat is the discipline by which heroic souls fashion their further endeavors? Defeat was the wilderness through which a mighty and demanding

God led his children; and in the welding together of our people in the fiery trials of war, reconstruction, and threatened servile domination, He has made us mighty as a river, yea, more powerful even than when our armies first marched north. And if the government to which we freely give allegiance today is to maintain liberty and protect the Christian moral values of a favored race, it yet must call upon the purified spiritual power of the South to show the way.

Let *that* be our continuing, even our final, campaign, my stalwart friends; pursue it with the spirit and courage that carried us over so many fields of shot and shell. Do not listen to voices that would mar our ancient unity. Disdain, I say, the divisive tirades of Tillman and Polk and Grice, Macune and Watson, who would undermine old and tested values with the poison of radical and insidious economic doctrine. And never forget that what set our armed struggle and our fledgling nation apart, gave them their true purity, strength and endurance, namely their indomitable Christian faith, can infuse us in this further struggle, too, with its illimitable power.

I cannot, of course, discuss the Maryland campaign before survivors of the old brigade without recalling that it was only two days before Sharpsburg that our gallant brigade leader gave up his life, our noble Cause thus losing one of its most able and dedicated leaders—a man who captured the unstinting admiration of all who knew and especially those who followed him, and earned from some of the latter that admiring appellation, "the Iron General."

A personal word: I was at Hoke Arnall's side at the moment of his demise, in Harper's Ferry, Virginia, fifteenth September 1862, about 4 p.m. After the capture of that mountain stronghold by Jackson, Hill's Division had been left behind—you will recall—to parole prisoners and collect supplies, while the rest of Jackson's wing marched to rejoin Lee at Sharpsburg. As we moved about that small, picturesque community, where the ghost of John Brown seemed still to cast a malevolent spell, a sniper not yet flushed from his cowardly nest and never located despite the most diligent search, put a felon's bullet in the back of our leader's head. He died instantly, falling at my feet on the cobblestones, in late afternoon sunshine; and though he was not granted time by an inscrutable God for final words, I can report to you, his followers of old, that only minutes before he expired, he had turned to me and said:

"Colonel Stowe, there was no time on Sunday..." This was

Monday. "No time on Sunday for religious services. See to it that services are provided this evening for those of our men desirous of them."

Only minutes later, that great life was taken from us. And from his loved ones. In his boyhood he had nourished noble ambitions, in his young manhood he had won a fame greater than his modest nature ever dreamed; how tragic that he could not be accorded, on the field of battle where he so excelled, that death counted "sweet and honorable."

But there may be no finer monument to any of the leaders of our great Cause than that last, characteristic wish of Hoke Arnall's—which, needless to relate, I was deeply moved to carry out. Has it occurred to you, as many times it has to me, how like he was to that other peerless Christian warrior, the great Stonewall himself?

Terrible in combat they certainly were, and swift and unerring in their country's service. Yet purer hearts, more devoted Christian souls, never set foot on the field of strife, nor labored so selflessly in a Cause higher than self.

"Duty is ours," said Stonewall. "Consequences are God's." And I never knew Hoke Arnall to deviate from that unswerving and uncomplaining course of duty, anymore than did he who charted it.

The morning wears on, my old companions of march and camp; yet I am loath to close. Here among you, as if in the bosom of family, I feel at home. Here with you, I sense the past in all its valor and nobility, inspiriting as youth, purifying as fire, the stuff of dreams and myth. And we need not regret the war that shaped and still shapes our lives and our nation, nor even its result; for its causes were implanted in the Constitution itself. And how we bore ourselves in a struggle for what we believed, then and now, to be the right, will be a source of pride down to the furthest generations of our cherished race.

And so, my friends, let us go to the feast prepared for us, then forth from this place, in the old Cause and in good heart, in the spirit of those immortal words from the late departed poet who shared our brotherhood:

> *Lies in the dust the shattered staff*
> *That bore aloft on sea and shore*
> *That blazing flag, amid the storm!*
> *And none are now so poor!*

So poor to do it reverence
Now when it flames no more!

Furl the great flag, hide cross and star.
Thrust into darkness star and bar,
But look! Across the ages far
It flames forevermore![4]

[Colonel Stowe was loudly applauded at the close of his address, and cordially congratulated by his old comrades. A vote of thanks was adopted, and a copy of his address solicited for publication.]

[1] *Stonewall Jackson in the Campaign of 1862*, by Sertorius. American Edition, New York: D. Appleton and Co., 1879.
[2] The aforementioned Board of Officers recommended Porter's reinstatement in 1878. Congress took no action but President Arthur remitted his sentence in 1882 and on fifth August 1886, Porter was appointed Colonel, to rank from fourteenth May, 1861, but without back pay. He retired two days later.
[3] Letter to President Jefferson Davis, C.S.A., written at Dranesville, Virginia, third September, 1862.
[4] *The Broken Mug*, by John Esten Cooke, C.S.A.

Author's Postscript

THE IDEA OF writing this novel first occurred to me when, as a young man, I read Douglas Southall Freeman's somewhat romantic account, in *Lee's Lieutenants*, of Stonewall Jackson's epic march around Pope. Years later, as the new owner of a rundown piece of land in Rappahannock County, Virginia, I discovered nearby a state historical marker at a place where Jackson's army had passed on its way to Manassas Junction. I got out of my car and walked a little way along the road, feeling shivery at being in the actual footsteps of history.

Sometime thereafter, flying for the first time on a Boeing 747, I looked nervously out the window as the monster lumbered off from Dulles Airport, not far from Manassas. As we rose, it came to me that I could see almost the whole of the Virginia theater of war, across which the armies ultimately commanded by Lee and Grant had struggled for four of the bloodiest years of American history. I was moved by the realization; and as I peered down with my twentieth-century bird's eye at the rapidly diminishing earth, I tried to imagine through a century of time—more obscuring than the clouds that drifted beneath the 747—the war-torn Virginia of 1862 and the people who fought over its fields and hills.

On that flight to California, I made my first real plans for a novel about the Civil War, building on old memories of Freeman's pages about Jackson's march and the ghostly sensation of walking in the tracks of his men. But the job proved more complicated than this impulsive beginning.

In something like a decade of generalized reading, then in a year or more of specialized research in a wealth of documents and books, and on the battlefields of Manassas—not to mention four years of actual writing and continuing research—I discovered that a single undisputed "history" of an event (especially a battle) seldom exists. Out of all sorts of contradictions and mystifications, he or she has to put together what seems the most plausible version of happenings no one now can certify—perhaps never could—as having occurred in one particular way, or for indisputable reasons. And the munificence of detail available on a well-documented period like that of the Civil War—Little Sorrel, Jackson's horse, was a pacer; General Pope was an early riser; the War Department's Telegraph Office had five windows looking out on Pennsylvania Avenue—unfortunately does not always help to answer the central question: what *really* happened?

Records don't show, for one important example, why General Pope, commanding the Army of Virginia, still refused to believe as late as noon on August 30 that Longstreet had rejoined Jackson on the morning of August 29, so that Pope confronted Lee's whole army on the Plains of Manassas. Twenty years later, writing in *Battles and Leaders of the Civil War,* Pope *still* seemed not to believe it. Finally, I had to accept the inexplicable, uncertainly attributing Pope's myopia to his unwillingness to admit he'd been out-generaled.

I can assure readers, therefore, only that this novel about Jackson's march around Pope and the subsequent battle of Second Manassas is as nearly true to history as diligent research and controlled deduction could make it. It is not a "nonfiction novel" or "faction"; it is first and last a *novel,* although the needs of fiction have been kept as much as possible from intruding upon or distorting what is known about the history it depicts.

The train wrecks at Bristoe Station on August 26 actually happened, for example, though my account of them in Chapter Two is imagined. And skirmishing took place where and when I describe it, in the otherwise fictitious scene in which Brace sends Henry to his fate. A cavalry engagement did take place on the evening of August 30, near Lewis's Ford, just as recounted in Chapter 15; so it was entirely plausible to stage the climactic encounter between Fargo Hart and Micah G. Duryea at that time and place. It is even true that Jackson and Stuart mistrusted General Beverley Robertson in battle; so Stuart might well have sent someone like Hart to make sure his orders were carried out.

The greatest difficulty lay in trying to include historical persons as presences in a work of fiction, with reasonable fidelity to what such persons actually said and thought. Two or more accounts of the same event, for example, may each give a different version of what someone like Jackson or Lee actually said, or may report it only in indirect quotation; and all too often some memoirists plainly have dressed ordinary or perhaps profane comment in the purple robes of oratory. Sometimes there is no record at all of spoken words.

Still, in this novel virtually every remark in direct quotation attributed to a historical person can be reasonably well authenticated in one of three ways: because it was quoted in plausible language by someone who heard it said; because it could be responsibly reconstructed from indirect quotation; or because it could be reasonably inferred from established facts and situation.

As an example of such an inference, in Chapter 12 Generals Pope and Porter have an angry confrontation about Porter's failure to attack on August 29. Such a meeting, in fact, took place when I suggest that it did, and it certainly was heated; but accounts of it are sketchy and mine is mostly invented, necessarily including all the dialogue. But the imaginary scene reflects the battle situation, what is known about the two generals' differing views of the enemy they faced, and Pope's well-recorded fury at Porter (whom he later caused to be court-martialed).

Similarly, the conversation in Chapter Two between Pope and Colonel Russell obviously must be fictitious, since Russell is a fictitious character. But its substance is based on what Pope himself wrote in *Battles and Leaders* that he felt and thought when he learned that Confederate troops had circled into his rear; and so emotional a man almost certainly vented some of his feelings at the time. The text of the telegram that informed him of the danger also is invented, as I could not find the actual text in the *Official Records;* but again, the invented text is based on Pope's and numerous other accounts. All other military telegrams, letters, and dispatches quoted are the actual documents of the time.

Civil War students will quickly recognize that my fictitious General W. F. Hoke Arnall and his fictitious brigade play the parts that, in history, were the lot of the real General Maxcy Gregg and his South Carolina brigade. I have not, however, depicted General Gregg by another name; my General Arnall is entirely invented and is not intended to resemble any historical person. The battle exploits of Arnall's Brigade are modeled, of course, on those of Gregg's Brigade; but all of Arnall's officers and men, like himself, are imaginary.

All other Federal and Confederate units identified in these pages were real, and did in fact what they're described as doing. But Major Reverdy Dowd, who takes command of the Sixth Wisconsin in Chapter Five, is fictitious, as are all the other officers and men of Dowd's Sixth.

I have frequently imagined stories and characters from recorded fact. At the end of Chapter One, for instance, Stonewall Jackson orders one of his generals arrested for having failed to place a picket at a road turning. Captain W. W. Blackford reported this incident in his memoir, *War Years with Jeb Stuart;* but Blackford did not cite the name of the arrested general, so I gave the role to my fictitious General Arnall. And since Blackford did not relate the results of the arrest, I felt free to take the story forward into fiction.

Captain Blackford also told how he was prevented by a guard dog from "capturing" a Federal officer's robe during Stuart's raid on Catlett's Station—a real happening that I expanded into a story line of some importance to my novel. The buttermilk incident, in which Fargo Hart meets Missy, was also adapted from Blackford's anecdote of a similar episode. And it was Blackford, too, who described Jackson's personal reconnaissance of King's passing troops, suggesting the novel's opening pages.

The entire story of Amy Arnall and her trials with Jason is fictitious, but I based it on a few passages in Mary Boykin Chestnut's *Diary from Dixie.* Lest anyone doubt the authenticity of General Arnall's letter to Amy in Chapter Five, with its proposed remedy for her "condition," the letter was adapted from a real one by General Dorsey Pender to his wife, Fannie.

Sometimes I have taken slight liberties with the context of actual events. In Chapter Two, for example, Generals Lee and Longstreet have dinner with a Virginia farm family on the night of August 26, 1862. The fact that, with some of their staff officers, they did dine that night at a country house is amply recorded; but the family that invited them is not identified in any source I could find. So I invented the family, invented the other officers, and placed Lee and Longstreet, with historical accuracy, in a scene that is imaginary in all other respects.

In this scene, General Lee speaks twice—once about Pope, once about his nephew, Louis Marshall, who had scandalized Virginia by serving on Pope's staff. Both quotations are historically recorded; but of course Lee made these remarks on other occasions. I consider it plausible, however, that he *might* have said these same things at that wartime dinner table at which he actually sat.

General Longstreet, on the same occasion, gives his opinions of several of his West Point classmates—including Pope—then serving in the Federal or Confederate armies. These opinions can be found in his article on Second Manassas, written years after the war, for *Battles and Leaders.* I merely transposed them into imaginary wartime conversation, I think not unreasonably.

Hale, in the novel the Washington bureau chief of a New York newspaper, is imaginary; so, therefore, is his interview with President Lincoln in Chapter Nine. But that interview comes about in the way the real reporters of the period often found themselves talking to Lincoln; and the President's critical remarks about General McClellan actually were spoken, as reported by his secretary, John Hay, in his biography of Lincoln. But the real comments were made several days *after* August 29, when the fictitious Hale is presented as interviewing Lincoln. Other records show that Lincoln's attitude toward McClellan had been well formed by August 29.

Some seemingly fantastic events, however, are faithful to recorded fact. The singular fate of Joe Nathan in Chapter Seven, for example, really did befall a Confederate soldier and is described in two separate memoirs, by Colonel W. T. Poague and Private Edward A. Moore, both of the Rockbridge Artillery. (The guns in Poague's Battery, like those of the fictitious Captain Overholt, were called Matthew, Mark, Luke, and John, because they spoke with powerful voices.)

Private James F. Sowell's recollection of the frozen pickets in Chapter Eight is taken from *Company Aych,* by Sam Watkins, a foot soldier's recollections of service with Jackson. So is the anecdote of the chaplain who proclaimed that anyone killed "will sup tonight in Paradise!" and Lott McGrath's story of the private who predicted his own death.

Teddy Redmund and "Sertorius" are imaginary, but British visitors, journalistic and otherwise, were not uncommon in Civil War camps. Charlie Keach's journey to New York, though fictitious, is similar to an epic trip actually made by George Smalley of the *New York Tribune* after the later battle of Sharpsburg. Keach's story suggests some of the pitfalls and vanities of journalism, then and now.

I have used or adapted incidents from history as often as possible. Private Moore described an artillery duel similar to the one that takes place in Chapter Fourteen, including the incidents of the gun caisson crushing a man's foot and the horse wounded in the hip. The "death duet" of the two dying battery horses at the end of Chapter Eight was seen by Colonel Strother of Pope's staff, whose memoir in *Harper's Magazine* for August 1867 was invaluable to me. Strother recorded many details of the Federal command during Second Manassas, including General McDowell's tribute to the beauty of the sunset, repeated in Chapter Nine.

The scenes in the Telegraph Office, though imagined, are derived from *Lincoln in the Telegraph Office*, by David H. Bates, who worked there during the war. Lincoln did write much of the Emancipation Proclamation in that office. And records show that just before Second Manassas, several deserters from Jackson's ranks were executed in the manner that preys, in this novel, on the mind of Private Ambrose Riggin.

The remarkable Herman Haupt left a voluminous record of his deeds, words, and thoughts during the period of Second Manassas. Rufus A. Dawes, an officer in the Sixth Wisconsin, later a brigadier general, set down a detailed account of the battle of Brawner's farm, closely followed here. William C. Oates, who fought in Law's Alabama brigade, also wrote extensively of Second Manassas in his *The War Between the Union and the Confederacy*. Oates told of the use of deserters to defend "The Dump," which is also suggested by a historical marker at the site; but my account of what happened there is entirely fictitious.

The words that open this novel—"The road was blue with them"—are from Oates's eyewitness description of King's Division marching past Brawner's farm on August 28, 1862. And the passage that closes the novel—Colonel Stowe's address—though fictitious, is akin to many resounding speeches made at Confederate veterans' gatherings in the decades after the war and reprinted in the papers of the Southern Historical Society. One such address, by Colonel Edward McCrady, Jr., of Gregg's Brigade, is one of the most valuable documents on the August 29 phase of Second Manassas.

The sloping field from which Oates—and Stonewall Jackson in the opening scene—watched King's passing troops lies along the old Warrenton Pike (now U.S. 211, four lanes wide). Above it, another house rests on the foundation of what was Brawner's farmhouse in 1862. Not far away, in the woods on Sudley Ridge, the cuts and embankments of the unfinished railway line that sheltered Jackson's troops are still to be seen, much as they were in 1862; the Dump and the Deep Cut almost tell their own stories. A single tree still stands atop Buck's Hill, as a tree did when Pope set up headquarters there on August 29; and a newer building, still called Sudley Church, stands on the ground where the New Man watched over Sergeant Cade.

But the growth of timber, the decline of farming in the area, and modern installations like the Stonewall Memory Gardens have changed some aspects of the battlefield, although both it and the battle sites of July 1861 are protected as a national park. I never could determine to my satisfaction the exact ground from which Stephen Lee's guns broke Fitz-John Porter's attack on August 30, or decide just which "rocky knoll" marked the exact position of Gregg's—hence Arnall's—Brigade on August 29 and 30, 1862.

All that ground—over which anyone can walk in a day or less—is fresh in my imagination, as it was in 1862 with the Bull Run Mountains, notched by Thoroughfare Gap, misty in the distance and the dust of troops hanging in the air; to me, the road is always blue with them. But I'm not nostalgic for the "old South" or romantic about a war that destroyed one nation and forged another; how could I be? If the United States in World War II had suffered casualties at the rate the Confederate armies did, six million American men would have died between 1941 and 1945, instead of just over 300,000.

The "ordeal of the Union," terrible as it was, is nevertheless the most dramatic and fascinating story I know. I think it tells much about what we are as a people, and how we came to be that way. In reconstructing an important part of it, by applying my imagination to what I could learn of history, I hoped to make that story live for others as it does for me.

Tom Wicker
Rochester, Vermont
February 25, 1983